THE VENGEANCE OF ROME

Previous books in this sequence

Byzantium Endures
The Laughter of Carthage
Jerusalem Commands

THE VENGEANCE OF ROME

Michael Moorcock

JONATHAN CAPE
LONDON

Published by Jonathan Cape 2006

2 4 6 8 10 9 7 5 3 1

First published in Great Britain in 2006 by
Jonathan Cape
Random House, 20 Vauxhall Bridge Road, London SW1V 2SA

Random House Australia (Pty) Limited
20 Alfred Street, Milsons Point, Sydney,
New South Wales 2061, Australia

Random House New Zealand Limited
18 Poland Road, Glenfield,
Auckland 10, New Zealand

Random House, South Africa (Pty) Limited
Isle of Houghton, Corner of Boundary and Carse O'Gowrie Roads,
Houghton 2198, South Africa

The Random House Group Limited Reg. No. 954009
www.randomhouse.co.uk

A CIP catalogue record for this book
is available from the British Library

ISBN 0–224–03119–8

Papers used by Random House are natural, recyclable products made from
wood grown in sustainable forests. The manufacturing processes conform to
the environmental regulations of the country of origin

Typeset in Bembo by Palimpsest Book Production Limited,
Polmont, Stirlingshire

Printed and bound in Great Britain by
Mackays of Chatham plc, Chatham, Kent

To the memory of John Blackwell

I have at last completed the final volume of Colonel Pyat's memoir. His life began in 1900 and ended in 1977, a few years after he had commissioned me to help him write the book he originally intended to call variously 'The Life of Mrs Cornelius' or 'My Adventures with Mrs Cornelius Between the Wars'. He believed that Mrs Cornelius, a well-known local Notting Hill figure during the 1950s and 60s, was world-famous and that the public would pay him handsomely for his reminiscences. Mrs Cornelius had died a year or two earlier, her career as a minor film actress and entertainer completely forgotten. After publication of the first volume, her children almost immediately began litigation to stop me publishing any further work about her. Only in recent years did we reach an understanding. That is one reason why this volume has taken so long to appear. Another reason was the death of my original editor, the extraordinary John Blackwell, who had helped me considerably, both with translations and interpretations and whose loss has been felt by many other authors and publishers.

When I moved to Texas, and deposited the papers and tapes still in my possession with Texas A&M University, I was able to interview one or two of those friends and acquaintances of Pyat's who were by then living in the USA, among them Colonel H. W. Mix, who saw long service with the CIA before retiring to Florida, and Karl Schnauben, who served a prison sentence for his SS activities but had settled in Wisconsin, where he had family. I also interviewed survivors and relatives of survivors from the 1930s and 40s with whom I could check various accounts of Nazis and ex-Nazis who had known Pyat in Germany, including Kurt Ludecke, Ernst Hanfstaengl, Issolde Krone and the woman who still prefers to be called 'Catherine Oberhauser'.

In England I had been fortunate enough to discover Desmond

Reid, who had acted in films with Pyat in Germany, and Major John Nye, who had served in British Military Intelligence and had been well acquainted with Mrs Cornelius and Colonel Pyat since the 1920s. Over a hundred, Major Nye retired to Wexford in Ireland and in 2001 died in the care of his eldest daughter, Mrs O'Dowd, formerly Lady Begg.

The task of turning Pyat's vast collection of papers and tapes into some kind of coherent narrative has been considerable. Where Colonel Pyat repeated a story, it often varied a little, depending on the context, and I had to choose the account which seemed most credible. Some of the least likely stories, however, have been confirmed by other sources, so I have done my best not to confine his reminiscences only to the mundane. Much material was written in a variety of languages, including a kind of international patois he developed for himself. Chiefly, however, he wrote in English, Russian, French, German, Italian and Yiddish, though here and there I came across pages in Turkish, Spanish, Greek, Arabic and Hebrew. Most of the languages, with the exception of Yiddish and Russian, were rendered inexpertly and even the Yiddish was not always exact. I have attempted to give some of the original material's flavour, with its disgressions and sudden switches into other languages. Almost all the tapes I made, for instance, are in English and these form the basis of the narrative. I have, as usual, limited Colonel Pyat's racialist, homophobic and other diatribes to the minimum, especially in the light of the recent revival of anti-Semitic rhetoric in parts of Europe and America, but his memoir would not be understood, I believe, if I had removed everything I found offensive. This particularly concerns the scenes in which Adolf Hitler appears. That these descriptions and ideas are the antithesis of my own I am sure the reader realises.

I am extremely grateful, too, to my friends Lord David Holland and Professor Richard Meadley, who supplied me with missing information. My wife Linda Moorcock did an heroic job of reading and editing my manuscript. She also did much of the final typing and had to live with Pyat for some twenty-five years. She will be as relieved as I am that I have at last completed the work as I promised. Others to whom I am grateful for their conversation and ideas on the subject include my late guardian Dr Ernst Jellinek, Peter Ackroyd, my first wife Hilary Bailey, Barrington Bayley, the late Angela Carter, Tom Disch, Jean-Luc Fromental, M. John Harrison,

Dr David Harvey, Harvey Jacobs, Richard Klaw, Dr Rafael Medoff, Dr Josef Nesvadba, Stuart Reid, David Shapiro, Iain Sinclair, Lili Stejnes, Emma Tennant, Alan Wall, Claire Walsh, Zoran Zivkovic, my friend and agent Howard Morhaim, my friend and agent Georges Hoffman, and my good friend and father of my god-daughter Oona, Christian, Count von Baudissin, who also looked over the final manuscript and made valuable suggestions, as did Anthony Rudolf, who shares an interest with myself and Sinclair in the Princelet Street synagogue. My other much loved friend who helped me with her insights and encouragement through the whole course of this volume and died too soon to see it completed was Andrea Dworkin to whom I dedicated an earlier volume. She died far too young. She was as close to me as any sister and I miss her terribly.

One last note: I was able to verify much of what Pyat wrote about his time in Italy, Germany and elsewhere by interviewing survivors or reading texts like Ludecke's. It became plain to me in this process, as I searched through hundreds of books, newspapers, magazines and documents, that only those who did not wish to know about the Nazi concentration camps and treatment of Jews from 1933 onwards, did not know, and that the American and British governments of the day by no means did everything they could and, in my view, should have done to resist Hitler and his policies. For further information about this shameful episode in Anglo-American foreign policy, I refer you to the David S. Wyman Institute for Holocaust Studies (of which I am a member) at their website: www.WymanInstitute.org

Michael Moorcock,
The Old Circle Squared,
Port Sabatini, Texas
May 2005

My achievements are a matter of history. A record. I am the voice and the conscience of civilised Europe. I am one of the great inventors of my age. I am a child of the century and as old as the century. Unlike Göring and Goebbels and those lickspittles of the SA and SS, I was never afraid to be judged by my actions. No court in the civilised world would countenance such allegations. They are absolutely insubstantial. Yet still that Turk, whose filthy fried-meat shop remains a nightmare for those of us forced to live in its ambience, insists I am a Jew he knew in Pera! I would have been five years old! What could he remember? I suspect a familiar hand in this but am allowed to say nothing. These days, even a casual mention of Comrade Brodmann means Mrs Cornelius will mock me until we have a row. My heart is not strong enough. I console myself. At my age I fear only God's disapproval and there can be precious little of that in store for one who has devoted so much of his life to the service of Christ!

I was always of an evangelical disposition and had meditated a great deal on matters of religion while in service to El Glaoui, so my conversation more readily turned to spiritual matters which was why Mr Mix sometimes likened me to an Old Testament prophet. We had discovered that our cattle truck was not going directly to Casablanca and my normally genial darkie had grown disconsolate. I reassured him that at least our train was bearing us away from the medieval dangers of Marrakech and the sinister whimsicality of her Caïd, and to pass the time I attempted to instil a sense of our Greek faith into my loyal companion. At length the usually easygoing black insisted that Baptist was good enough for him; he always felt uneasy around incense and chanting. 'That voodoo stuff gives me the willies.' Had I seen *Ben-Hur*? Or was he thinking of *Intolerance*? Confining my answer to the murmured remark that the early Church was

4

scarcely the same as Babylonian paganism, I was content to avoid controversy while we travelled in intimate discomfort and as a result fell into the pleasant habit we had developed in the USA of discussing favourite films. We were both great 'buffs'.

TWO

Oh, the boy. That boy. Her boy. How I loved him. He was going to be my son. I was teaching him everything. At first he listened. Then he became restless. The most important information is that which you don't wish to hear. He lied to me. He lied to me. He was the first one, that erstwhile son of hers! What was I? Some Abraham? Fear thou not Jacob, my servant. Though thou make a nest as high as the eagle and though thou set it among the stars, I will bring thee down from hence. He lied to me. Elijah lied to me. I know. You do not believe it. Nobody can believe it. He lied. He lied. There was no precedent for this. This was the worst of all captivities and it had not been predicted. It taught us that not every lesson is, after all, a big lesson. Big lessons are made up of many small lessons, said the Jew in Arcadia. He wanted me to escape with something. I forget what.

—❧ THREE ❧—

The Jew in Arcadia predicted I would lose what I most valued in the ruins of what I least knew I valued. He called me *meshumad*. They said he was a *tsaddik, eyn maskil*. He thought I was slow. He thought he confused me with his riddles. I was not slow and I was not confused by him. I followed his arguments but I could not agree with them, that was all. He was the slow one. I was too quick for his old-fashioned parlour games. *Mutti! Mutti! Wer ist das?* They believe they are so sophisticated in their provincial professionalism. But it would be rude to challenge them. It would be stupid to make enemies. I can smell the yellow blossoms, the green and yellow stalks in the red mud turned up by the ploughman's skill. The fog rolls across the fields. The smoke drifts through the market. I can smell the market, the *plotki*, the cooking *zrazy*, the tubs of *lokshen*; brass and copper wink among the iron, the enamelled trays, the glittering bowls of dumpling soup. I can smell the golden stones of my old Kiev, the Hero City of the Russ. Oh, Russia, my homeland. Oh, Ukraine, my home. Golden grass blooms in Babi Yar. Golden grass still blooms in my Babi Yar. *Mia madre!* O, Esmé, how we rose towards the stars that day over the old gorge. And what if only these memories remain? Is there any crime forgetting pain? Is a meek man of any more or less worth than a proud man? We are rarely given the example. Our prophet celebrated the meek. Our society continues to celebrate the violent. I know all this. I followed it through the 1950s. They were saying it on the radio and TV. But gradually we forgot. The meek hero disappeared.

City of sleeping cats. City of goats. City of Greeks. We lived in that world, the Jew and I. We lived in the deep history of it, so deep that no enemy could find us. Our only fear was that a friend should betray us. It was the life of a very fortunate intellectual rat but it was life. That's show business, says Brady, the child-killer. Is there some primitive sense they have that by killing us they empower themselves? They eat our brains. There are more terrible ideas than this, I suppose. But they behave like film stars, these secret service interrogators, these prison guards. I read what I could in the camps. For a while they let me use the library, but first all you were allowed was *Mein Kampf* or *Völkischer Beobachter*. They were not exactly designed to stimulate the mind but rather to reduce it. There are teachers who take great joy in passing on wisdom. But we must not forget the other kind of teacher who loves to repress knowledge and leave us more ignorant and brutal than themselves. Believe me, I am not complaining. I had it easy compared to most. But, of course, my imprisonment was completely unjust. I had done nothing to deserve those camps. There were a number of others, like myself. Guilty or not, few deserved to be props for the showmanship of illiterates or sadists. In the camps my old friends turned into terrifying enemies. *Jude, mach Mores! Jude, verrecke! Hep! Hep!* Even in Dachau they had their *Judengasse. Zionismus ist ein überwundener Standpunkt!*

I came out of Egypt. I came out of Libya and Abyssinia. I came out of the land of the Moors and the land of Sefarad, Zarefat and all the lands of Edom or Ishmael. I came out of Zarefat and Rome and Carthage. I came out of Troy and Athens, Constantinople and London. Out of New York and Los Angeles. Captive and conqueror both. I came out of Atlanta and Memphis and Cairo. I will come out of the world. My cities shall fly.

FOUR

1648, you say? As if this somehow makes up for 1492. Everyone is talking in that dingy distance. A no man's land of howls, imploring shrieks. And then they are talking again. And you say there is nothing to fear from the East? I say you are looking in the wrong places. Look to Australia or China or Siam, not to Russia or her empire, who will always be European, for it is Christendom herself she defends. It is her free Cossacks who will ensure Christendom's boundaries. For it is written that the borders were drawn upon the world by God's own finger tracing them as He traced the mosaics of our history.

Abraham, der als erster seiner eigenen Menschlichkeit ein Opfer brachte: Wo traf dein Messer deinen vertrauensvollen Sohn?

Those decent horsemen riding into Ur, their eyes bright with the significance of a new idea. Such expressions were worn by the men who saw the wheel invented and the women who learned to card wool. By Norsemen who carried the banner of Christ. By Easterners who bore their own flags. Sooner or later, as many predicted, East and West would meet, either at war or having learned a way of peace. On one side the gold, white, red, black, green and blue of Christendom. On the other side the dark emerald of Islam, the scarlet crescent and whatever colours of convenience thrown up by criminals, kulaks and cowboys of modern Zion. Who would be a Jew?

FIVE

Days passed. We drank what water we could collect but rarely dared emerge from our truck while the train was standing, in case we should fail to get back on or attract the eye of some zealot in blue and red serge who would make it his mission to place us under arrest. I could not afford to be investigated by the French, especially since their diplomacy at that time favoured my ex-master, El Glaoui. If any description of us had been published I would be instantly recognised. Few Europeans travelled about Morocco wearing native costume, accompanied by a huge American Negro servant. For this reason, even when at night we ventured a few feet from our truck as it rested in a siding, we kept our heads covered with our djellaba hoods.

We had expected to arrive in Casablanca in less than a day. Of course our train, fuelled more by red tape than coal, went everywhere but Casablanca. The military bureaucrats in Paris sent it first to Meknès, then to Rabat, then to Fez, then back to Meknès and from there to Tangier, loading and unloading nothing, but in Rabat adding two private horseboxes, presumably at the request of the Sultan. Our three central cattle cars remained unused at every stage, but the smell of horse manure was added to that of cow dung and the boiled-egg smell of steam. Though tempted by glimpses of towns, we were reluctant to disembark at an inland station, especially since Mr Mix had left Meknès under a cloud and was well known in the area, but early one morning we at last glimpsed the familiar blue waters of the Mediterranean, the green palms, white tenements and pink towers of a seaport which could only be Tangier.

No sooner had we realised our destination than we understood our danger. Our only choice was to disembark. Already the train was shunting along the military quay to the waiting ships. The docks were thick with French soldiers, with Negro Zouaves. Our only hope was that they lacked the sense to recognise us. Mr Mix and I took familiar positions on both sides of the doors, slid them back and prepared to jump. As we had guessed, the soldiers assumed us to be workers. They paid us no attention. I was to go first. The quay moved slowly past. A gap appeared in the Zouave ranks. I threw my carpet bag and sack of films on to a pile of mail and with triumphant elation made to leap after them, but my celebration was short-lived, as at the very moment I began to jump, I found myself staring directly down into the seedy features of that treacherous little turncoat Bolsover, late of the *Hope Dempsey*. By providence or bribery the snivelling cockney hophead had escaped Egyptian justice, weaselled his way into a job with the French as a civilian clerk, and arrived at the free port just in time to recognise me! The worst possible luck!

I had no time to shout a warning to Mr Mix. Like me he was already jumping. Bolsover meanwhile became a maniac, tugging at the sleeves of every uniformed Negro nearby, screaming in English that a dangerous criminal was among us. As Mr Mix began to run, his hood blew back from his head revealing those magnificent, unmistakable features. We had no chance of making a discreet exit or of talking ourselves out of danger. The black had given us away! I saw his huge head snap up as he vaulted a barrier then ran through the yards towards the passenger station, a pair of baffled Zouaves in pursuit. He would have made a magnificent athlete.

Bolsover, a mass of excited duff, had poor success in attracting any further help. All attention was now on the boxes where a French officer, concerned that the animals should not injure themselves, struggled to command his unruly men and calm the horses.

My emotional resources were already very low. Rather than waste time remonstrating, I shouted for Mr Mix to keep running while my own strategy was to point to his fleeing back, crying in Arabic: 'There he goes!' and, with my hood over my head, my sack over my back and my bag in my hand, mingle with the gathering crowd of dock workers attracted by the double commotion. I heard Bolsover's grating French: 'He's a famous Parisian crook! He's wanted for fraud and manslaughter!' The man had developed some bizarre grudge against me. He was obsessed. Who else would give credence to that Parisian airship business? Forced to leave for New York before I could prove my case to the *Sûreté*, which with its usual lazy prejudice had fixed on me as an easy scapegoat, I had been unable to defend myself.

11

By the time it was safe to trudge slowly up to the passenger station I saw that they had caught poor Mr Mix. I think he was wounded, as he shouted at them furiously in Arabic. I could do nothing for him, but I did not believe he was in serious danger. At worst he would be repatriated to his native USA. This could be the making of him, for he had a wonderful career awaiting him in the lucrative field of Race Kinema. If they were to catch me I would be lucky not to be sent to Devil's Island. Nonetheless, I knew a pang of sadness. I was sure it was the last I would ever see of *meyn hertrescher* sidekick but meanwhile I was still at liberty.

Elijah raises his staff against black skies. He points, signalling the end of misery. My cities will fly. My sons will survive. Who will lift this burden from me? Did I not try to help them? But their blood is not mine, neither is it upon me. My flesh is clean and I have cleaned my heart. *Le'shanah haba'ah bi-Jerushalayim.* I know these things. I mourn their dead. Not all are ignorant. I do not lie. *Barach dayan emet.* You think I can accept this *trayf*, I say. *Lashon ha-ra.* They speak nothing but lies. *Brit milah*, indeed! What do they know?

For the next few months I was forced to enter Tangier's notorious shadow world, where Spanish officers and the local *demi-monde* mingled and where, by a variety of undignified means, I was able to sustain myself. My life became almost civilised. I even managed to spend my birthday at the Hotel Cecil in the company of Captain Juan Lopez-Allemany of the Spanish Foreign Legion, the brute who was for a while my friend and patron. I was frequently a guest at the house of Hussein de Fora, one of the best-educated and wealthiest hide-merchants in the city, and I kept a liaison with Madame de Brille, wife of the French concessionaire.

To all these I was known as Gallibasta. In that name, Madame de Brille was kind enough to obtain for me a French diplomatic passport (she had some idea of continuing our liaison when she returned home). I was offered several permanent business opportunities which I was obliged to refuse. My duty I now knew was to get to Rome as soon as possible. Also, the jobs on offer were either unsavoury or liable to place me in peril again. I had had my fill of perils. The secure magnificence of Il Duce's Italy so near at hand was much more attractive. Even this caution was not enough, however. Soon I learned that enquiries were being made about me in the Outer

Market and shortly afterwards I was arrested. Happily it was on a trumped-up vice charge. Even the police thought it ludicrous. They told me they sensed the hand of a jealous woman but I could not help thinking of my old enemy Brodmann. I had nothing to gain by using the French passport. The authorities accepted my Spanish papers, so I was able to pay my way clear only, needless to say, to find myself the subject of extortion. I was rapidly growing reconciled to accepting a previously rejected prospect when one rainy afternoon in the Inner Market, not far from the British Post Office, I recognised two welcome faces.

Only a Russian, especially a South Russian, will understand the joy of meeting fellow countrymen in a world as alien as Tangier's. When one of those countrymen is a relative it is no surprise that your Russian will shout out his pleasure and run, arms wide, to embrace him! The faces belonged to none other than my dear cousin Shura and his elegant boss, the Ukrainian turned Parisian, that famous *éminence grise* of French politics, Monsieur Stavisky, whom I had known when a boy and met later at a party of Mistinguett's in Paris. I had not seen Shura since he had disembarked from our boat at Tripoli, on some business of Stavisky's. Now the two sophisticates strolled through the market as if they took the air along the Arcadian corniche. Ignoring the light rain, they were chatting and enjoying the sights and the warm weather. Their stylish suits, in canary yellow and lavender respectively, with matching spats, drew admiring attention from the ever-present touts and beggars of the Tangier streets. Hugging him I noted that Shura's sleeve, empty since the War, was now filled. I admired his artificial limb. The hand that projected from the crisp linen of his shirt-cuff looked almost real. 'Oh, Shura! Shura!' Shura laughed heartily as he recognised me. Even the cool Stavisky showed pleasure at the coincidence. 'It is a small world, this,' he said. 'Let's have some of that terrible fig brandy they sell here.' He pointed to a café and we soon took our seats at a little outside table. 'What are you calling yourself these days, Dimka? Are you still a film star? Are you on location? Or on the run?' He laughed and clapped me on the shoulder.

My life was suddenly enriched. These true friends understood the necessity and usefulness of a *nom de guerre,* and only needed to learn that I was Señor Juan Miguel Gallibasta, an import/export agent, to accept that I was now, to all intents and purposes, a Spanish national.

The two Ukrainians were in Tangier on business, making their way to keep an appointment at the Banque d'État du Maroc to take care of the paperwork. Shura was delighted to meet me alive in Tangier. Rumour had it, he said, that I had died upriver in Egypt. Before he disappeared into the bank, Stavisky amiably suggested I join him and Shura on his yacht *Les Bon' Temps* that evening. 'We'll have an Odessa reunion,' he said. He was leaving for Casa in the morning but Shura would remain with the boat.

Once again Odessa, the location of my transfiguration, was proving central to my fate. In that city of Odysseus my adventures had begun and my destiny had been determined. There Shura had been my mentor, my alter ego, my hero. There I had discovered all the world's pleasures and not a little of its pain, and there I had met Mrs Cornelius. I have always known that the turning point of my life was in Odessa, but I have never properly been able to understand why. It does me no good to recall those days. Perhaps it was the Jew in Arcadia. But what did he do?

There is a piece of metal in my womb. The Nazi doctor found it. Oh, yes, he said. It is certainly there. It was on the X-ray. In the shape of a Star of David, as you say. He had no reason to humour me.

That is how they did it, I explained. That is how they transformed me. You must tell your superiors immediately. I must be released. I am the victim of a disgusting plot. The Reds are behind it. My father was German. I served the Reich in 1919. I am an engineer. The Führer is a personal friend. I have used my skills in the service of the Fatherland. This is a matter of historical fact.

—My dear chap!

—Those Jews in the *shtetl*. They put it there. They poisoned me.

—My dear chap! Do not cry, he said. —There, there, there. We will soon have you well. But first you must be clean. You must get rid of all this dirty clothing. You must have a shower and a shave and be deloused. The Fatherland has great work for you.

When later I joined him aboard his magnificent yacht and explained my rather difficult position, Stavisky gave me a name and an address where I could obtain an exit visa in my Spanish passport. Within a day my means of escape was accomplished. When the yacht left port Shura insisted that I go with him. He was heading for Europe, he said, to a particularly nice little spot in the Balearics where their organisation did quite a bit of business. The customs boys knew them well and the system was amiable, as in Tangier.

14

The luxury and security of the boat, the polished brass and gleaming oak, the wealth of exquisite cocaine and cognac aboard, the sheer relief of not being hunted or suspected, filled me with a sense of well-being I had not experienced for years and soon we were racing away from the African shore into the relatively tranquil waters of Europe. *Les Bon' Temps* was a steam-yacht. Under another name she had once served the Russian imperial family. She had been seized by the Reds during the Civil War then changed hands several times to be sold eventually by her mutinying crew in Albania, whereupon she came into Stavisky's hands. As a tribute, he told me, to our beloved Tsar he had restored her to her full magnificence. It was a privilege to be permitted to sail in her, I replied. He dismissed my thanks. We 'Moldavians' should stick together. He referred, of course, to the Moldavanka in Odessa where I had lived for so many happy months under the protection of Shura's father, who had been killed by anarchists during one of several occupations of the city.

Early one morning, just as Tangier's cypresses and palms grew black against a powder pink sky and she began to yell her cacophonic dawn chorus, a pale blue Duesenberg tourer pulled up on the quayside. Stavisky stepped elegantly down the gangplank, entered the car and waved farewell to us even as our crew bustled to catch the first tide. Then almost before the Duesenberg was out of sight, swallowed in the surging mass of white cotton and red fezes which swept down to the docks as soon as the prayers were over, we, too, were leaving Morocco. From Spain, Shura assured me, it would be an easy step to Italy. They had no intention of returning to Marseilles or to Cassis for a while. We were bound for the pleasant, unspoiled island of Majorca where many of Spain's wealthiest nobility summered and where, Shura confided with a happy wink, the customs regulations were extremely relaxed. In 1930 Stavisky had many reasons to prefer the less public coves of the Balearics!

In my cabin I was able to check my films and take some sort of inventory of the reels we had rescued from El Glaoui. They had a projector and screen aboard the yacht, and Shura insisted I use all the facilities. Stavisky, he said, was famous for his generosity, especially towards old friends and countrypeople. I asked if he would care to watch the films with me. He declined. Perhaps later. He had a great deal of paperwork to catch up on. After looking into the little theatre to admire the riding of a Masked Buckaroo who, as it happened, was a stand-in, he left with an apology.

15

Thus, in solitude, I communed with my former self.

The experience was a mixed one. As I recalled my salad days in Hollywood, watching, sometimes for the first time, the scratched and jerking evidence of my cinema stardom, I had not expected to be filled with quite such a sense of loss and disappointment.

I had rescued a complete serial, *Buckaroo's Secret*, both reels of *White Aces*, several reels of *Buckaroo Justice*, *Ace Among Aces*, *The Masked Buckaroo and the Devil's Tramway* and *The War Hawks*. I relabelled and rewound them until they were in the finest possible condition. These and the scientific plans I carried in my bag were the best credentials to present to Signor Mussolini when I was finally granted an audience with him.

In common with many other serious people I saw Mussolini as an effective antidote to Stalin. Until his coming, Christendom's leading intellectuals feared we must soon descend into a series of bloody tribal wars, which would mark the end of Western civilisation. The Balkans were to be the powder keg and Mussolini the fireman, forever playing his hose upon that volatile zone and periodically stepping in to stamp out the beginnings of an unmanageable conflagration. I think this view did him insufficient credit as the dreamer and sometimes impractical idealist he really was. The Mussolini I knew was a poet. Since the Second World War it has become fashionable to denigrate the Italian dictator, but in my day men of conscience, who saw the whole of Europe slipping into chaos, admired him.

Entering the Straits I enjoyed the distant view of the Rif Mountains and below them, among cypresses and palms, the little white boxes, tall towers and red clay domes of villages, while on the other side lay the blue outline of the Spanish coast which for a while grew more distinctive and then, too, vanished as in open sea I put Africa behind me for ever. A day later our destination, that much disputed island paradise, rose up over a pale grey horizon, her lower slopes shrouded in bright, silvery mist and white, transparent clouds upon her peaks. Sunlight glinted on her limestone terraces, cast deep shadows into her evergreens and butter-coloured settlements, but for me the next sight was even more inspiring!

If you, too, are a believer you will understand the joy and relief I felt at seeing the cross of Christ lifted everywhere, on steeples, walls and banners. Majorca had defended her Christian honour against the Saracen for a thousand years or more. She had fallen long after the whole of Spain had fallen. Better than most, she knew the meaning and the value of Christ's cross.

Only then did I realise how much I had longed for the security which that cross represented to me. In Majorca I arrived as a respectable Spanish citizen, a Christian gentleman. In Morocco I had been suspected of being a Jew or a French spy, of being all the treacherous, nefarious things a Nazarene can be in the Arab's mind. For years, since setting foot in Egypt, my life had been under constant threat. No surprise, I thought, that the Jews elected to leave their native Palestine for the enlightened and humane Christian lands across the Mediterranean whose laws protected and even facilitated their natural proclivities. Offering a gentle transition from ancient Carthage, the dark heart of Oriental Africa, to modern Rome, the blazing light of European civilisation and justice, Majorca lay on the border between the two spheres.

Our yacht sailed slowly along the island's rocky coast. Very occasionally we sighted a small beach or a cove, but nothing good enough for landing until the boat turned a headland, entering the mouth of a long, narrow bay flanked by carob trees, pines and wild olives clinging to tall cliffs of pink stone. In the wooded hills high above were the roofs and walls of large white houses, their balconies engulfed by bougainvillea and hibiscus, oleanders and geraniums, looking exactly as they might have done in Roman times.

Ahead of us was a little fishing harbour, with brightly painted hulls bobbing at the quayside, their red and yellow sails reefed, their prehistoric eyes winking in the sunlight. I would not have been surprised to see patricians in togas and sandals leaning out to look at the new arrival. Shura came to stand beside me and sniff, as if at the ozone. 'Good, eh, Dimka? That's the smell of money, my dear! We are entering the Port of Andratx. Only the most exclusive people spend their summers here.' The harbour was indeed a mixture of disparate vessels, though workaday fishing ketches predominated, with magnificent private schooners taking second place in the magical tranquillity of the tiny bay.

Shura was pleased with my delight. 'It's like Cassis, only better. Hardly anyone knows about it.'

We anchored offshore at the far western end of the harbour and rowed one of our boats up to the quay, whose cobbles smelled strongly of fish. I slipped in blood and innards as I stepped ashore and was caught from falling by a grinning ape with lively brown eyes who might have been a minor Tuscan deity. He shouted some amiable observation at me in what seemed a barbaric mixture of French, Italian, Spanish, Arabic and Portuguese and laughed enormously when I tried to thank him in Spanish. Shura took my arm and led me over the cobbles to the little road that led up into the town. 'Come and meet some pals of mine. They'll love you. I know you'll take to them.' He nudged me in the ribs. His grin was full of its old charm. I remembered those wonderful first months in Odessa, when he had dragged me all over the Moldava Quarter, introducing me to the best circle of friends I have ever known. Through him I had gained my first sexual experiences, discovering the harsh realities of this world as well as her pleasures. If I had an opportunity to return to an almost perfect point in my past it would be to Odessa before the folly of World War engulfed us in the stink of fear and a taste for gunpowder. With her warm and welcoming streets Odessa was a breathing, brilliant entity. Jews, Moslems and Christians lived in wonderful harmony. Only rarely did the roar of Cossack cavalry echo through the streets. The stories have been much exaggerated. Odessa respected all faiths and all men of faith. She had no fear of the alien. She welcomed him. She had her mighty cathedral, her tolling bells, her confidence in the strength of Christ. She could afford to tolerate and even encourage a diversity of people. She was everything that was best in the Russian heart. The joyous writers came from Odessa. Only when they went to live in Moscow did they grow gloomy. They tell you such lies about places. Odessa was, in comparison to most modern cities, a paradise of peace and cosmopolitanism. They make you think Belfast is nothing but bombs and gunplay, but everyone says it's the boredom that's the worst of it. I am always amused when Americans, who are used to living with thousands upon thousands of murders every year in their own country, become nervous of visiting a place where one or two minor outrages have been reported. If I could relive at this little Balearic port just a fraction of the happiness I had known in Odessa, I would be enduringly grateful both to friends and to God.

And so it was.

Shura's 'pals' included many famous stars of literature and the entertainment business who chose what the natives called Port d'Andratx as the perfect location for their luxury hideaways. The little town built up above the quay was dominated by an eighteenth-century church of local stone, topped by a clock and a conventional angel, doubtless their domestic saint. The perfect whiteness of the houses was broken by oddly fashioned chimney pots and slates, their soft curving lines in gentle contrast to the ultra-modern vivid yellow and blue Egyptianate Hotel Bristol which was patronised chiefly by the yachting crowd. They had colonised the fishing port in recent years, bringing with them a glamorous lifestyle and easy habits of spending and were revered by all but the most committed socialist. On warm nights the Bristol's were usually the only lights still burning at dawn.

Andratx was the haunt of Continental film stars like Rose Blanche and Corinne Sweet, Pola Negri and Elfrieda Juergen, of politicians like Primo de Rivera and magnates like Vickers and Zaharoff, of international writers such as Felix Faust, E. Phillips Oppenheim, Lester Dent, G. H. Teed, W. Somerset Maugham, Dornford Yates, Romain Rolland, Anatole France, Erich Maria Remarque, Howard Marion Crawford and Charles Hamilton, most of whom had their own yachts. In those days the world valued its tale-spinners and rewarded them accordingly. Now, by virtue of a beneficent state rather than any honest work or public acclaim, only fawning lapdogs of the establishment can afford such pleasures. The predictable result of the so-called National Health Service.

We dined every evening in the harbour restaurant next to the Bristol. Shura, the debonair man of affairs, always knew at least half the people at the other tables. He was forever up and shaking hands with some fantastic *prima donna*, some painfully shy *écrivain* or distinguished member of the Fascist Legion who bore Mussolini's greatest honour on a discreet lapel. Spanish officers, mostly of the aristocratic class, were as happy as anyone else to pass the time of day with Shura, introducing him as a close confidant of Stavisky, that 'master rogue' as the papers would call him as soon as he was safely assassinated. They would enquire after Stavisky's business exploits and adventures as if they were following a popular serial.

Clearly Stavisky's power extended further than I had ever guessed. Shura's claims of watertight political connections (which he guaranteed he would employ to correct my record in France as soon as possible) were entirely authenticated. Through Shura I was privileged to join the inner entourage of a post-war prince, who comprised all the traditional virtues of a great Russian *seigneur*, an outlaw lord, a man of substance and influence. Stavisky's empire stretched from the Black Sea to the English Channel and

19

beyond. His decisions determined the fate of small nations and large governments.

Shura was genuinely popular in the port. He never discussed his boss's affairs in front of me. He always took his colleagues aside for any business exchanges. I think he still felt protective and affectionately sheltered me from the sordid world of politics and commerce. For the moment I was content to rest under his brotherly concern and to indulge myself in his circle's singularly fine cocaine. As the Bedouin tribesmen had done in the desert, Shura treated me as a kind of mascot. He admired me as a dreamer and an artist. I am not even sure he really believed my stories of my life since I had last seen him, yet he was surprisingly familiar with my screen work and boasted to acquaintances how I had been a Hollywood star. He was, however, amiably reluctant to watch the films that were proof of this. He said he had enjoyed them when they first came out. In the end I would talk to him as one would talk to a cat, for relief and comfort and to sound out ideas, while he listened to me with abstracted good humour much as if a favourite pet made comforting, uninterpretable noises. Occasionally he grew mysteriously irritable with me.

As a matter of urgency my name had to be cleared in France. I must get to London to pick up the papers and money awaiting me with Mr Green, my Uncle Semyon's agent. Most importantly I must find a way to offer my skills to Mussolini, in whom all my idealism was invested. The newspapers confirmed everything I had guessed. Il Duce brought a dash of romance and tough common sense to politics. Steadfastly he refused to let the forces of international finance and communism dictate his policies as they dictated those of other modern governments. Since my arrival in Tangier, I had read all I could about the great dictator. I had seen him on the newsreels. Enthusiastically I had followed his career, noting how he had healed political divisions in Italy, bringing together a confusion of disparate radical faiths. Socialist, Christian Democrat, nationalist, anarchist, communist, republican and monarchist were united under one coherent Fascist system, tempered in the fires of self-discipline and rigorous military training. What was more, he attracted the most original thinkers and artists of the day. Film-makers, engineers, scientists of every persuasion flocked to Il Duce's court. The *Novecenta* was famous as the mecca of modern art. Italian design and engineering presented a flair even the French could not match.

Miss von Bek had described this to me, of course, while crossing the Sahara. I wondered if she had succeeded in reaching Italy, piloting my 'Bee', taking news of me to her master even before I arrived?

When I spoke of these ambitions and ideals I was humoured by Shura. I began to feel a small frustration, even though I was still content to rest for a while and play the simple soul he wished me to be. Given that I needed to relax and restore myself, there was no better way than in an exclusive Mediterranean resort while Shura's business was conducted. I had the pick of the best Palma whores and was left to make friends of both sexes, indulging every desire.

For all my vast and varied experience, I was still a young man of thirty. Moreover, I had gained easy access to an inner brotherhood of power and lechery, in which the most refined sexual appetites were developed and satisfied. I found it difficult to resist these distractions. Consequently, I became well acquainted with a number of Spanish officers, two or three leading Italian Fascists, French entrepreneurs, American playboys. Among the female adventuresses inevitably attracted to this company was a Romanian woman whose willingness to experiment in every sexual variation became dangerous to us both. When I attempted to break off the relationship, she grew persistent in her demands, and when at last I refused, threatened to blackmail me. I confided my dilemma to my old friend, who told me to ignore the woman. She was no threat, he said. As it happened, a day or two later Shura needed me to go with him to Barcelona and keep an eye on the yacht there while he was ashore. When we got back to Andratx she had grown bored and left, we were told, for Marseilles. Only three weeks later she was found dead 'of heart failure' on the promenade at St Malo, just across from the fortress. She had been attempting to watch the cricket match which the defiant British always played in full view of the French on the Jersey side. They found a telescope in her hand. There was some talk in the press of her being the employee of a foreign power.

What an exciting time in world politics! Shura told me that when people lost faith in their representatives and leaders they turned to the likes of his boss for some sort of certainty. Stavisky could act and not have to produce forty pages of double-talk first. That's what people liked about him, just as they liked Mussolini. He could get things done quickly without excessive publicity. 'When governments need mercenaries to do their work it's clear to me that the world needs new governments,' said Boris our café friend. And Shura had winked at me.

For all his apparent cynicism, Shura was merely realistic. Stavisky was one of those concerned men of power prepared to stand up to the corrupt forces of big business. At the Bristol there was much talk of returning to old values by new, radical methods – of 'thinking the unthinkable' as the phrase went in those days, 'and forgiving the unforgivable'. Everywhere was chaos. Only ruthless, decisive action could restore society and return nations to their former pre-war stability and prosperity.

This heady talk, the intellectual cut and thrust, was a huge treat for me. In recent months, aside from brief meetings with Rosie von Bek, when we had little time for this sort of conversation, I had known only the pronouncements of a pagan prince and the opinions of an intelligent Negro, neither of whom had been exposed to the main streams of European politics.

Rose von Bek, admittedly, had prepared me for some of the ideas I now encountered, but it was elixir to my soul to hear all the details of what Mussolini was doing for Italy. The communists were ruining Germany, civil war in France was almost inevitable, republicanism was destroying Spain, the union-bankrupted British were effectively a spent force, American neutralism was fuelled by their vast domestic problems, and Stalin threatened the very foundations of Christendom. The old political structures were proving useless in the modern world; party divisions were defeating the very democracy they were supposed to defend, creating only misery and uncertainty. The majority of people were not anyway natural democrats. Careless liberalism was the enemy of everyone, even those it pretended to represent.

I began to spend much of my time with a charming young Spanish officer. Lieutenant Jaime Pujol shared many of my frustrations and much of my idealism. He was a gentle soul forever concerned about the pain of the world. How could we eradicate it? 'It is not right that people live in uncertainty and terror. Society has failed them. Even the Church is failing them. The left offered them justice and failed to provide it. The right offers stability but at too high a price. Where can they turn? Fear is becoming a way of life in far too many parts of the world, especially in Europe. The power has been torn from the hands of the men of conscience. Gangsters rule everywhere – in Russia, in Germany, in America, and increasingly in

Spain. Their "revolutions" are meaningless, self-serving and cruel. They have no religion or morality. But we cannot merely replace one tyranny with another. What's the answer, my dear Señor Gallibasta? Not all strong leaders are gangsters, surely?'

He mourned both the fall of the old politicians and the fashion among Europe's crowned heads for abdication. 'They are seized with some kind of collective guilt. They are frightened by what happened to their Tsar. They believe the process towards republicanism is inevitable. Mussolini has proven that idea a lie, yet still they continue as if they are responding to the will of the people rather than the will of a tiny minority of leftist zealots. Believe me, Señor Gallibasta, I have every sympathy with their anger and share their understanding of the world's injustices, but these imbalances must be addressed by men of conscience, not by the politics of envy. How has such a frightful situation come about?'

I was no better equipped than my friend to answer this increasingly familiar question and, like him, could only point to Mussolini. 'The will of a single individual,' I said, 'is what it takes – if his will represents also the will of the nation. Really, it's all fascism offers – security through unity. But it takes a great man to combine the best ideas from a collection of isms, shape them into a coherent whole and create unity. Unity must be more important than our differences. Unity must be desired by the common will. Unity cannot be imposed from above. Only a very great man can express the public will in a broad, far-ranging programme of dramatic, even revolutionary ideas. Mussolini offers our antidote to the lure of Bolshevism. But believe me, Mussolini is modern Italy as Hindenburg can never be modern Germany. Old Hindenburg lacks the common touch. Rhetoric is simply not enough. We need action. Even the best-intentioned professional politicians and soldiers are divorced from those they represent. Today's leaders have to be men of the people who can reach across divisions and shake hands with an experienced ruling class, headed by a modern, socially concerned monarch, and arrive at a compromise which satisfies and benefits all. Italy unites her people in a common purpose to establish the rule of law and appeal to the selfless sense of community which lies within us. And the Church must help.'

Pujol's passionate idealism might seem strange to the contemporary listener, but in those days we were desperately looking for certainties in a dangerously uncertain world. Fascism offered those certainties. The pure form was a response to the soul's yearning and to honest, human needs.

'To fight Stalin,' I suggested, 'we need a champion of the same metal. And with one exception we have only pygmies. The planet is crying out for a paladin, for some new Charlemagne, to drag Christendom from the Dark Ages. Or are we too far degenerated into chaos to be rescued?'

Lieutenant Pujol passionately hoped that this was not the case. It was the duty of men of conscience to discover such leaders and give them the power they needed to restore a new world order.

We talked often of such matters. Many of the Italians in Majorca seemed reluctant to discuss the ideas and ideals of Fascism, except in a very general way. These were the individuals burdened with the task of making the national dream a continuing reality. They were sober about the practicalities of their task. They admitted, however, that Mussolini was a singular force, the driving inspiration behind their movement. Most of the men we met were regional *ras*, or governors, without much direct contact with Rome and unrepresentative of the intellectual wing of their party. They were on vacation from their considerable responsibilities, so we did not press them. For a while they were here to enjoy the simple beauties of the island and escape their cares.

During that season, we made the social rounds of the various yachts. Gradually I became part of a set whose relish for politics was as considerable as its pursuit of pleasure. The nightmares of my life in the Middle East and North Africa were put behind me. My scars might never disappear, but at least my wounds were healing. The atrocities and humiliations I had suffered had tempered me in the fires of experience, given me a subtler understanding of the world and those who suffered in it. Perhaps this is how God chooses to educate those He favours?

My trials had invested me with a kind of clear-sighted innocence which some of my new friends chose to take as simple-mindedness. They did not always treat my contributions to the conversation very seriously, but I was content to be their Simplicissimus while it suited me. The ease of Majorcan life was hugely rejuvenating for one subjected to such horrors and hardships in the past couple of years. I had been forced to live an almost feral existence. Now I had rediscovered the European way of life I had lost and almost forgotten. It was a joy to experience again, although I still felt the occasional pang, missing my Esmé who, in the old days, had shared so much of my social round. To have had a sophisticated woman like Rosie von Bek at my side would have done much to make those occasions perfect.

Of course, we knew who had made money out of the War and who was still making money. We knew that the real villain was international finance which was bent on centralising its operations in New York (or New Jerusalem as we called it), controlling a secret empire more powerful even than Stalin's, with which it had well-defined links. Alone, Mussolini was not strong enough to challenge Stalin, but if Il Duce were to gather some strong European allies to him, we knew that a pre-emptive strike on Moscow would be possible. We needed to pull society's disparate forces together and turn them into one mighty modern social machine which benefited all, not just a few rich businessmen who drained our nations of their wealth and hid it in Swiss banks. We believed education would raise the consciousness of the masses, but we had been wrong. Now people must be disciplined into putting the common interest before their own short-sighted greed.

I was to appreciate later how thoroughly Majorca helped in my restoration. I still revisit my old haunts occasionally. Mrs Cornelius takes the OAP specials to Palma Nova and sometimes I go with her. I would stay in Port d'Andratx if I could, but it is so expensive now. I am forced to rub shoulders with lager-swilling 'tomatoes' as the locals call the English. I, of course, do everything to maintain my standards. I always wear a good linen suit and a panama. When Mrs Cornelius prefers to spend time on the beach or in the pubs, I take cultural bus trips. I called on Graves, last time I was there. I only had about an hour before the bus left Deya, which is nothing but Germans now. Apparently Graves wasn't in. I hear these days he's a slave to marijuana. This has happened to several of the intellectuals who remained. Others left for Ibiza or Formentera. But before its vulgarisation the island was to prove a benign friend to European gentle people.

During the time I was with Lieutenant Pujol, Shura came and went from the harbour. Very infrequently Shura asked me to join him on *Les Bon' Temps* and remain aboard to check periodically with the radio operator while my cousin made a visit ashore. Stavisky kept a permanent hotel suite at the Bristol and while we were in port we used it, transferring from our cabins on the yacht to the suite. We lived like kings. Because of his old wound, Shura was fond of morphine and marijuana as well as cocaine, and he was a great drinker, but I lacked his capacity. Meanwhile, and I do not remember how, I again became known by my Odessa nickname, translated into French as 'the Colonel' or 'the Cossack', and because this gave me a frisson of secure familiarity I did not object, even though it did not go especially well with my new *nom de guerre*. Of course, there were few who believed me a native-born son of Spain. Many accepted me for what I actually was – a Russian aristocrat preferring not to use his title and so reveal his true ancestry. I had many reasons for keeping quiet about such things in those days. I had become used to a certain kind of anonymity.

Imagine, therefore, the considerable shock to me one morning when, having rowed myself from the yacht to the quayside, still a little bleary, I walked up the cobbled lane to the baker's for my usual cup of coffee and croissant and heard, as if from nowhere, someone shout: 'Max! Max Pyatnitski! Still in the airship business?' I detected mockery in the tone.

Had Brodmann found me at last? Feeling sick, I turned, seeking the source of what was surely my nemesis.

SIX

There are patterns to our universe. Patterns so vast and at the same time so minuscule that we rarely detect them. They present a problem of unimaginable scale. If we could detect them they could explain the mysterious movement of all creatures across the face of the planet. I am convinced that physically or spiritually, though quite unconsciously, men and women of a particular disposition travel broadly similar routes. Those of us who move about the world and are active in its business know how coincidences occur in life far more than in fiction. Cautious, incurious people after all rarely travel. As in Malory, when one bumps into a fellow knight errant, another Seeker of the Grail, one might well greet him with joy, but with only a modicum of astonishment.

Thus on that little cobbled street in a Majorcan fishing village I found myself embracing as a brother a friend I had not seen for ten years. 'Fiorello!' – laughing and shaking his hand as heartily as he shook mine. He was older, of course, but retained the long, comical face of a pantomime horse, his enormous lips drawn back from massive yellow teeth, his huge brown eyes sparkling with the flames of his generous, eternally ebullient soul. He still wore the wide-brimmed white hat, the lilac cape and gloves, the patent-leather shoes with their lavender spats, the perfect linen suit, a cream silk shirt and canary cravat. Flourishing his ivory-headed cane, he indicated his companions. Glancing at us with some curiosity, they remained seated demurely outside the bakery.

'My dear fellow! I heard you became an actor and made a name for yourself in American politics? You must tell me everything!'

Remembering his manners, he turned, a graceful grotesque, to introduce us. 'Sweet ladies! My apologies! Bazzanno is an oaf! Ladies, may I introduce my dear friend, my mentor, my inspiration, His Excellency Prince Maxim Arturovitch Pyatnitski, late of the Imperial

Russian Court, a philosopher and engineer of genius – one of the greatest Russians of modern times!'

The two beautiful women were Signora Margherita Sarfatti and Miss Miranda Butter. The first was his mistress. La Sarfatti was a brunette in her mid-forties, of aristocratic felinity and an arrogant, comradely disposition, whom I took to at once. The second woman was a young American redhead with a rather prim nose and lips who had travelled from Paris to see the new Italy with which, she said, she was in love. She loved Spain, too, she added, or at least this island. She was a journalist on the staff of the *Houston Chronicle*; she smiled a little uncertainly at me.

No stranger to genius, as I would discover, Signora Sarfatti had an air of easy power as she lazed across two rattan chairs. Keeping her cool, slitted Atlantic-green gaze on me, she listened with an amused air to the younger woman's gushing praise of the country she thought was my own. Mrs Sarfatti was delighted to make my acquaintance, she said. I removed my hat and bowed. I kissed their hands.

My old friend from Rome, Fiorello da Bazzanno, was now the editor of *Il Gruppo* art magazine, distinguished member of the Italian Academy and a leading figure in Mussolini's court. He and his friends had set off from Naples. On their way to Algiers they had developed engine trouble and put in to Majorca to make repairs. They were enjoying the pleasures of Andratx but had been gone too long already and by the following week must return to Venice where Sarfatti and da Bazzanno were to open an exhibition of new Fascist art.

'That function is the only justification for my enormous salary, dear comrade.' He winked. 'I am rich. But I am no longer my own man!'

'Surely you haven't given up your painting?' I asked him.

He was, he admitted, not painting much these days.

'I always argued how politics was the century's only valid art form and here I am proving it. It's our millennium, dear Max, the triumph of the human imagination over the mundane world! At last the illusion becomes reality! What keeps you up so late?' He assumed that I, like himself and his companions, had not yet gone to bed. When I told him the truth he was enormously amused. As we sat down, he continued to sing my praises to the ladies, telling them how I had been a hero of the Russian Civil War, a daring cavalry officer, a flyer and an inventor whose genius, had it not been for Bolshevik treachery, would have turned the tide in the Whites' favour. 'The perfect hero of the new Renaissance!'

I enjoyed all this, of course, and blossomed under the admiring attentions of the women. It made a pleasant change from Shura's amiable disrespect. I had forgotten how much I relished recognition when it was properly earned. Da Bazzanno asked me what I was doing in Majorca.

Rather than disappoint him, I told him that I had come on Stavisky's yacht and hinted that I was here on special business. He received this with another of his enormous knowing winks. He informed the women that I was in the confidence of more than one national government and we must therefore be discreet. I waved such a suggestion aside. 'It's simply not conversation for the public square.' Recalling his duty to his companions, Fiorello suggested that I dine aboard their vessel that evening. I saw no new boats in the harbour. He explained that they had had to anchor on the other side of the headland.

'She's called *La Farfalla Nera*.' He would send his launch for me to *Les Bon' Temps*. I told him that I was not certain of my movements. I had companions, a cousin. Then naturally I must bring him too, said da Bazzanno. 'But you must warn him that we shall monopolise the conversation. We have years to catch up on, you and I, old comrade!'

He spoke of the dozens of mutual acquaintances from the old Rome days. How was Laura, for instance? I asked. I did not mention that she had been his fiancée. His face clouded and he shrugged. 'Oh, we're no longer in touch. She's so hard-headed. You know what these unregenerate communists are like.' He was clearly unwilling to say more. I accepted this and left with a promise to see him shortly after sunset.

I returned to *Les Bon' Temps* with my good news. Yet even as I rowed the short distance from shore to boat, I began to wonder if my two worlds were wholly compatible. Shura and Stavisky saw me as one of their own, a kind of poor relation of high-class criminals, whereas da Bazzanno, generous as always, had painted me in quite a different light, considerably closer to the truth.

As it happened, Shura had no interest in the artistic small talk he expected to hear at such a gathering, so he declined, energetically encouraging me to go. 'Exactly what you need, dear Dimka,' he assured me. 'You will be able to relax with your own kind. Let your hair down, say what you like without causing offence. Holding back can be a strain no matter how good the company.'

I told him I knew exactly what he meant. That evening I donned my dinner jacket with a clear conscience and a light heart.

I had forgotten how thoroughly happy I had been in Rome. With Esmé at my side I was secure in the company of good friends. I had enjoyed the pleasure of talk for its own sake, the wild eloquence which seemed to come over us all. The best that was ever said in those days was never recorded. In comparison, Mr 'Greene', Mr Hemingway, or Prince Nabokov-Serin and their kind produce gibberish. But these were the years before tape recorders made us all cautious.

Fiorello's launch called for me at seven. With a little too much rouge on lips and cheeks and too much powder on her fresh, oval face, Miranda Butter, her bobbed hair covered by one of her host's lilac scarves, wore a wonderfully fashionable evening dress in green and pink silk. Standing unsteadily beside the seaman at the wheel, she waved to me with an empty martini glass as the other sailor helped me aboard. I had already noted her evident interest in me and hoped she had left behind that irritating habit Americans share with Moslems, of drinking for the illicit thrill of it.

I joined her under the launch's awning. 'I needed a few minutes with you alone,' she said in that direct American manner. To my relief, she seemed perfectly sober. 'Your story sounds so wonderful! I know that a lot of what you do is secret, but I'd guess there's more than enough for an article. Or even a series.'

Assuming she sought a useful rationale for a liaison, I paid little attention to this at first. Since Americans were so ignorant of the realities of Europe and the Middle East, I hinted it might be possible for me to say a few words and illustrate them with an anecdote or two, but I must first consider the wisdom of such a decision.

She interpreted this as cautious acquiescence to her approaches and we were both for the moment satisfied.

The launch rounded the point. Even though I had been prepared for something reflecting Fiorello's demanding modernist taste, I had not expected to see a magnificent long-distance flying boat built on the very latest lines, large enough to accommodate a substantial number of passengers and crew. I was impressed. We drew alongside *La Farfalla Nera*. She was a breathing mass of dark glowing paint and red brass straining at her anchor like a captured bird. She represented the aggressive, arrogant, triumphant spirit of what even the provincial *ras* referred to as *mussolinismo*. Some of these *ras* grumbled that the cult of Il Duce conspired to diminish Fascism, but for most of us Mussolini *was* Fascism, *was* Italy, *was* the living embodiment of our faith in a glorious future. He was the voice, the strength, the will of all those millions of us who had been disinherited in the Great War.

For young people grubbing among the dresses and shawls I sell in Portobello Road, the twenties was a Golden Age of flappers and jazz, but for those of us who lived through them they were an Age of Assassination and Chaos in which year in and year out we heard of the death of this nationalist intellectual or that left-wing premier almost always by pistol, sometimes by bomb, by one rival political group or another. It is fashionable, these days, to blame the fascists for everything. But before them the German parliamentarians were murdering one another willy-nilly and the same was true in France, Greece, Italy and Spain. The Great War had familiarised them with the smell of death. Even in England Winston Churchill called out the troops to fire upon revolutionists. In mainland Europe, our future was non-existent until Mussolini and Hitler came along.

At dinner that evening, surrounded by the elegant appointments of the marvellous flying boat, all ivory and mother-of-pearl inlays and polished chrome, I was the centre of attention. Everyone wanted to know about my experiences in Egypt and North Africa and while I had to dress the facts in a less alarming and even less dramatic way in order to make them convincing, I regaled them with tales of the *Dar-al-Habashiya*, the Thieves' Road across the Sahara, of the powerful Berber kingdoms no outsider had ever penetrated, of the lost oases and the bizarre mirages, the character and disposition of native chieftains, and so on. Their own interest, of course, was in Libya where Italy, some thought, was spending far too much money. 'Those natives live like pampered house pets while Italians at home are having to tighten their belts,' declared Margherita Sarfatti suddenly and then laughed. 'But Il Duce knows best. The investment will benefit us eventually. You said you met some rebel Senussi, Prince Max? They're good-looking savages, I hear.'

That was her description of the great Saharan lawmakers. The Senussi were revered by Arab and Berber alike. While following the caravan to Khufra I had heard them spoken of with hatred, with

31

admiration, but always with respect. I said as much to the other guests. The Senussi leader Omar was known as a scholar and a statesman of impeccable probity. One fellow, a bucolic *ras* from Tuscany with some pretensions as a folk poet, violently objected to my description, insisting the Senussi were ignorant zealots sworn to destroy all Christians and drive our Faith out of Africa, restoring the old Moorish Empire and extending it as far as the Baltic. He had a brother, he said, who was a personal friend of Cesare de Vecchi, Governor of Somalia. De Vecchi had earned the Moslems' respect by riding his horse into their mosques and pissing on their shrines. It was only 'What they would do to us if they could. Raw power is what they respect. The Senussi were a spent force the moment we hanged that monster Omar.'

With my usual social graces, I was able to turn the conversation to less controversial subjects, such as the success of the Nazi Party and its chances of bringing Germany under the fascist umbrella. Could fascism create the united Europe of which Mussolini would be both the chief architect and first premier? Ultimately it would take more than one member of a select company to shoulder the responsibilities of leadership. I told my fellow guests of my dream – to see a company of Carolingian knights – a court, attracting the paladins of the Christian nations – ruling Europe and perhaps America. A great wall of Western chivalry against the Eastern barbarian, ensuring that Constantinople would never fall again. But in those days it was unfashionable to speak positively of Christianity. Many of the best fascists felt the role of the Church to be over in modern life. Consequently, I clothed my remarks in the most general language.

'I'd agree we need good men for the job.' Margherita Sarfatti held a long cigarette holder of polished marble and smoked foul-smelling Turkish ovals. As she drank, she seemed to become a little more angry, a little more cutting, a little more bored. She found most of the company irritating and it was clear she did not much care for da Bazzanno's diplomatic invitation to the gentleman from Tuscany who was now repeating some gossip he swore he had from the lips of Il Duce himself, to the effect that the German National Socialists were 'a bunch of limp-wristed interior decorators and ballet-masters to a creature!' which, presumably, was how he would also have dismissed the Spartan Hundred. This bumpkin asserted with hearty prurience that the would-be German Duce actually wore rouge in public. The only gentleman among them, the only heterosexual with any kind of war record, was the ex-flyer Hermann Göring, who was a great fan of Mussolini's and who got on famously with him.

'His are the kind who should lead the new Germany,' said the *ras*'s cow-faced wife, continuing the speech for him while he took a breath, 'people of the old stock but with new ideas. Hitler and the others are illiterate, mannerless dullards. Not one knows a fork from a dinner knife or a dinner knife from a dagger. They are typical lower-class Huns. They have no style. The Germans could never take such people seriously. They worship the Old Prussian order. They want the Kaiser back. They certainly don't want to be represented by the worst examples of their own kind!'

'Which is why Prince August, the Kaiser's son, is now a Nazi, perhaps,' I said. 'Who better to lead them?'

Whereupon the folk poet, revived by wine and a puff on his cigar, ignored my pointed remark and continued his lecture on the fundamental discipline of the Germans and how they loved a leader, on the arrogant insouciance of the British and how they believed themselves and their nation unquestionably superior to all others, merely because of the voracious greed and cunning cupidity of those who had almost accidentally acquired their empire. This was, he supposed, the source of their strength and why they had no nationalist party and why they were so decadent. On almost every issue I found myself in irritable disagreement with that provincial bigwig. Most Italians were pro-British and dismissive of the Germans, who they feared would threaten Italy from Austria if they had the chance. They did not wish to fight another war.

The *ras* seemed utterly unworthy of his leader's trust or of the honour bestowed upon him. His manners and opinions would have shocked a Chicago gangster. I began to make this comparison when da Bazzanno, perhaps conscious of his duties towards the rest of us, gracefully changed the subject and suggested that we all go to the observation deck on the roof of the aircraft. A full moon had risen over the bay and would be worth seeing. Miranda Butter took my arm as we went up. On three sides were steep wooded limestone terraces sharply defined by the light of a large yellow moon which made a silvery causeway across the lapping water to the dark, glinting metal of our little observation deck, bathing us all in its cold light.

Though I had grown used to women again, Miranda Butter's healthy young American body stirred a certain memory in my blood.

I was reminded a little of Rosie von Bek. Even her perfume lacked ambiguity. She radiated energy and enthusiasm, frequently absent in modern European women. Most women I had met in those days preferred the languid life of a pampered *poule du chambre* to any active engagement in the world's affairs.

Ideally one should have two women: a comrade to stand side by side with you in the struggle against Chaos and a compliant sexual partner, always eager to serve your needs. My inability to choose between these equally attractive types has left me the companionless old man I am today, though Mrs Cornelius was of course a considerable comfort. When she died, there was no one.

Miranda Butter had the same frank sexuality. Like Mrs Cornelius she was largely unconscious of it. Though she was only twenty-two years old, her naivety and directness had evidently opened doors for her in Europe, giving unusual access to the famous people she interviewed for her paper. Another advantage was the sheer romanticism of her origins. Everyone had heard of Texas. Everyone felt a certain romantic yearning for the land of Zane Grey and Karl May whose worlds had been brought to life in thousands of picture-plays, even before the drawling accents of their cowboy heroes were heard and imitated anywhere that a projector could be linked to sound. By addressing Texans through her pages, Europeans knew they were reaching the 'true' Americans – the great, open-hearted, idealistic frontiers-men and -women who typified all that was bravest and best in the old race, yet was untainted by Yankee-dollar madness or Albany politics. I often yearned for that American vivacity during my years abroad. The chance to experience it again was a marvellous treat.

I remember my magical evening aboard *La Farfalla Nera* with great nostalgia. I did not return to *Les Bon' Temps* but, at her request, accompanied Miranda Butter to her cabin to discuss a series of interviews in which I would give Houston's readers the benefit of my predictions about the Future of Europe.

This first act of our charade opened on the settee of her little cabin. We would begin, she said, with some background. She opened her reporter's notebook and brandished a pencil. Her readers would want to know if I was married.

Sadly, I told her, I am a widower.

At this she became deliciously sympathetic. A small tear brightened her eye as she told me she understood that I must find the subject too painful to discuss. Of course, I was still technically married

34

to Mrs Cornelius, but I returned to Esmé. Indeed, the circumstances of our parting, the cruelty of her ultimate betrayal, were things I am still reluctant to discuss. Sometimes I am too much of a gentleman for my own good. When it became clear to Miranda that I had lost my wife at the hands of a Bolshevist gang I did not elaborate. After all, I had lost my original Esmé in this way and no doubt by now she was dead in some anarchist trench. 'Maddy' asked why I had left Russia. I told her my departure had not been voluntary. The Reds were the reason I had left. They had stolen everything.

Estates? she wanted to know.

'Property is nothing,' I told her. 'They stole my future. I share that view, at least, with the great Tolstoy and with Prince Kropotkin. My patents and prototypes.'

Priceless?

She possessed an uncanny understanding of my situation and my values. Such delicious, eager approval from so voluptuous an acolyte was irresistible. Before I embraced her, she was talking of telegraphing her paper to see if they would run a feature in their Sunday section. I saw this as useful publicity should I ever wish to return to my twin careers as actor and engineer in the US. And while I had never made any reference to my aristocratic blood, it seemed no harm would be done if she chose to refer to me, even in the first hours of our lovemaking, as Prince Max. I told her I preferred to be known as simple Max Peters or, in Spain, as Señor Gallibasta, but as Prince Max I was best recognised thereafter in Italy. She asked me if I knew how much I resembled Rudolph Valentino. I told her delicately that I had never considered the comparison flattering.

She added gracefully that my looks were, of course, a far more refined version of his. And she believed there were better actors than Valentino.

'You must judge for yourself,' I said. I promised her that I would take her over to *Les Bon' Temps* the next day and show her some of the films I rescued from Morocco.

In the morning she paid me the supreme compliment: only Benito Mussolini had a personality as powerful as mine. Had I ever considered seeking political office? I assured her that my political days were over. All I really desired was a chance to serve the world in practical ways, by solving scientifically problems of population and social hardship. Her face shone with idealism. She was my disciple. 'And you will, dear Prince! You will!'

With such commitment and support, I knew that my stolen future was about to be restored to me.

When I returned to the port a few hours later I discovered to my astonishment that *Les Bon' Temps* had upped anchor. Ashore I asked what had happened to her. The hotel manager told me that apparently there had been some urgent business. 'The coastguard was involved.' Shura had been unable to contact me but had left my luggage with the baker. I found a note attached to my carpet bag – *'Sorry, old fellow. I know you're among friends. We'll look you up in Rome!'* At first I was depressed, upset at losing my cousin's company, but clearly his urgent business was dangerous and I suspect Stavisky had encouraged Shura in what he had done. I knew I was something of a liability to the political broker and was not greatly disappointed. I was now free to enjoy the company of my American admirer! Da Bazzanno had already invited me to come with him to Venice. Fate had determined my path for me. Once before, with Esmé, I had set out for Venice. Now at last I would arrive in reasonable style with a paramour almost as delightful as my little sweetheart but more of an intellectual equal. I seemed, at that time, to be ascending, slowly but surely, a golden staircase with my dreams about to be realised. I had journeyed into the Land of the Dead and I had been face to face with the Beast; I had braved the oceans and the deserts and learned to live among savage nomads. I had flown where none had flown before, and I had discovered secrets previously forbidden to white men. Journeying through a dozen different versions of Hell, I had survived. Now these hardships and spiritual ordeals were about to be over, and I was to be rewarded.

There could be no more perfect a candidate for Mussolini's service. I had been tempered in the fires of the most extreme experience not once but many times. I had died and been reborn in the birthplace of civilisation. I had first-hand knowledge of politics in many countries. I was thoroughly conversant in American and European literature, music and painting, while sharing an aversion to the neurotic obscenities of certain French and Norwegian 'artists'. Inevitably I would add to Il Duce's greatness as he would add to mine. His was a mighty soul ready to embrace the future and all its brilliant uncertainties, its monumental rewards. I saw myself in a Griffith film, marching up the Appian Way to the Gates of Rome, striding through the wide streets to the Palace of Il Duce, up the steps and through corridors to that vast hall where at last Mussolini himself stepped away from his desk, from which he directed all affairs of state, and came forward to embrace me.

'*Il ragazzo è arrivato!*'

I will admit I came close to weeping as I visualised the scene.

That night, my pleasure was complete. At around eleven, after we had dined at the hotel, Fiorello da Bazzanno made us get into a huge Mercedes he had hired and drove us down the curving, rocky road to Palma where he had arranged for the local cinema to be available, together with a projectionist. We sat in the comfort of the first-class seats, da Bazzanno, Margherita Sarfatti, Miranda Butter and myself, while before us, larger than life as he should be, the Masked Buckaroo rode again! Before a background of prairies and buttes he performed his acts of daring and skill, defending justice wherever it was threatened. We watched as the White Ace's twin Lewis guns raked the skies clear of Hun battle-birds or I embraced Gloria Cornish, the loveliest lady of the screen, with a passion which was electrically conveyed to the fascinated audience. Da Bazzanno flung himself into the adventures, hissing and applauding, clapping me on the back whenever my screen persona performed a particularly spectacular piece of heroism. Even Signora Sarfatti drew amused relish from the proceedings and her manner to me was even warmer when the lights went up. Miranda Butter was ecstatic. She clapped her little pink hands together and cried that I had revived all her most wonderful memories. She had seen several of my movies before as a girl, and had been entranced by them. 'That must be why I was reminded of Valentino!' Later she would apologise and repeat that my looks were far more refined than the ex-gigolo's, that I was so clearly an aristocrat and Valentino merely a coarse peasant of the type who appealed to the commoner sort of girl. Encouraged by her remarks I introduced her to some refined aristocratic pleasures that very night and at last the ghost of Esmé was laid to rest.

Next morning, in the flying boat's miniature saloon, Fiorello spread out my blueprints and sketches, the photographs and news cuttings I had managed to save from a hundred different disasters. My Desert Liner especially impressed him. He became almost exaggeratedly enthusiastic. 'But my dear Max, with just a few of these ideas you could transform the world! Why has no other government put them into production?'

The financial collapses of the past years were not conducive to investment, I said. And, what was more, I had chosen to show my designs only to a few select people. It concerned me that they might fall into the wrong hands. Imagine the Reds equipped with such inventions! Fiorello agreed that the notion was terrifying. 'You carry a terrible secret, my friend. Now it is clear to me why these days you lead such a discreet life. And yet here you have been the most public of figures! You have nerve, Max. I don't think I could stand to be the guardian of such earth-shattering secrets. Or to live such an exhausting double life. How have you been able to sustain it for so long?'

'I have been waiting,' I spoke gravely, 'for the right man to emerge, the kind of man who will mount his own horse and brandish his own sword and lead his own troops into the field to drive back Red Jewry even as she now masses against the West. I have come to the conclusion that Mussolini is that man.'

'A wise conclusion, indeed!' Fiorello promised he would secure me an interview with Il Duce as soon as we arrived in Rome. 'In two years whole fleets of your desert vessels will be crossing Italy's North African Empire from the Atlantic to the Red Sea! And your flying cities will establish our Dominion of the Air. The New Rome will continue her great march towards Destiny, recovering her ancient heritage and establishing the benefits of Roman law across the whole planet. That is our historic destiny. Rome's was the greatest empire, the greatest system of universal justice the world has known. She established civilisation wherever she marched. As we civilised Libya, so we shall civilise the whole of Africa. Then Asia, too, will welcome us. Bolshevism will inevitably fall. What's more, our New Rome shall be cleansed of the corrupting influence of the Pope and all his minions. Her new gods will be her living emperors, as they were in the days of her greatest glory. Mussolini, who bears the blood that founded our patrician dynasties, will be our first Caesar, taking his rightful place at the helm of the world-ship. But in place of Caesar's legions will be Caesar's gigantic bombing aeroplanes, Caesar's mammoth tanks, Caesar's radio-controlled flying centurions. And you shall be Caesar's armourer, the practical interpreter of his great dream. The chief engineer of our new Roman Empire!'

I enjoyed his vision but was also amused by it. 'Old Rome's strength was in her soldier-engineers. While she commissioned them to solve the problems of the empire, she was strong. When their skills were used to make increasingly magnificent spectacles, then she fell.'

'She went soft,' agreed da Bazzanno, his equine face glowing. 'But we have become hard again and we shall stay hard. It is our duty to impose the Rule of Law upon the whole world! For what other reason were we put here?'

'By God?' I asked a little sardonically.

'Yes, yes! By God, if you like, old comrade. You remember the days when we were in the wilderness. When our ideas were regarded as intolerably *outré*? Look at us today? We say which ideas are *outré* and which are not! We are the masters now!'

Such talk was commonplace in those heady times. We were all still stuffed with idealism and ambitions to save the world. The ideals and principles that we stood for seemed on the brink of sweeping the entire planet. But, of course, we reckoned without the manipulative powers of Big Business. We rested too readily on our laurels. That is when the Devil always wins – at the moment when you believe yourself victorious.

Italians in those days were certainly among the few peoples who seemed victorious. All else was doom and chaos, the promise of violence on every street corner, uncertainty about every coming day. Jobs, once considered secure for life, were in jeopardy. The promised future, which had been offered as soon as the War was over, had crumbled like fairy gold. No nation in Europe was free of fear. Most of us fully expected to face the threat of Bolshevism's all-engulfing hordes which, as was generally agreed, must soon begin to press upon our borders as their Mongol ancestors had done a thousand years before; as if the whole of Europe lay awake at night listening for the jingle of harness, the snort of ponies, the guttural whispers, the pervasive smell of death, which signalled the coming of the Oriental outriders.

True Russians were not the enemy. But true Russians were no longer the rulers of their own land. Communism is the name of Attila's fifth column. Asia has conquered Russia but Russia will arise. The Church is not dead. The Grand Patriarch is not gone. There must be a final reconciliation when the Pope shall bow to Greek authority. A final great union symbolised by this historical recognition and reconciliation. The spirituality of the Greek and the practicality of the Roman shall again combine to unite the world and make it whole again. And safe again.

Conversations with da Bazzanno helped give intellectual form to my ideas. With dawning joy, I realised that an outlook I had once believed mine alone was shared by a growing multitude. A few thousand understood – but millions instinctively supported us. We knew a glorious moment. The frustrated dreams of a decade must eventually become reality. The midwife for this momentous change in the history of the world would be a simple schoolmaster from a remote mountain region who had led a march on the capital to demand power in the name of his nation! We could soon be living in truly epic times!

We spent a couple more days in Port d'Andratx while the repairs were completed. I introduced my friend, the retiring young Spanish officer Jaime Pujol, to da Bazzanno and the ladies. They took enthusiastically to Pujol and made him welcome. A small group of us usually dined together. Da Bazzanno rarely joined the *ras* who were on vacation here and privately told me that they represented the necessary end of administrative Fascism but they were not exactly the soul of the movement. His duty was not to upset them or to make them feel that he was condescending to them, and whenever he fell in with one or was forced to pause at a table where several of them sat, he would adopt a slightly vulgar manner and exchange a coarse joke or two.

Margherita Sarfatti hated them, murmuring the opinion that they were all baboons. It didn't matter if they called themselves Bolshevists or Fascists, they were just a bunch of gibbon apes snapping and snarling and struggling for ascendancy. They wanted power for the basest of reasons. 'To fuck,' she said in English, 'to feast and to frighten creatures weaker than themselves. The only three things they can actually feel. Those are the three Fs of their fascism.' Pure fascism, she said, could be understood only by intellectuals and artists.

'But surely,' I insisted, 'there is an ideological struggle? You can't believe that everything reduces to bestialism?'

She shrugged at this and laughed into the air. She gestured with her cigarette. 'I would like to think that it didn't, Prince Max, but I suspect that I see only the truth. Not palatable, I suppose, to you dreamers.'

'Quite right. I am inspired by altruism and idealism. They mean more than meat and drink to me. The brute motives you describe are as far from mine as can possibly be.'

She seemed anxious to change the subject, perhaps because I resisted her cynicism. 'Which I suppose is why I like dreamers. Da Bazzanno is no more practical than you are, for all his talk of

40

machinery and efficient violence and the rest of it. There must be a difference between the likes of you and the likes of those swaggering gangsters over there. But not quite the large difference you would prefer to believe.' And she showed hearty amusement at my chagrin. 'Without them, dear Prince, our Duce and his ministers could not survive a day.'

'They are the salt of the earth,' I said. 'I have every respect for your old fighters.'

'Just as well, for they have no respect whatsoever for you. You should be grateful for their tolerance.'

I found her cynicism a little hard to accept. I caught her watching some of the *ras* with a speculative eye and could only conclude that she felt sexually attracted to those tough pioneers of the March on Rome, Mussolini's most loyal administrators. In spite of her physical stillness, her expression was forever restless, forever bored. She seemed perpetually on the point of creating a crisis, though I never knew her to engineer anything of the kind. She was completely loyal to da Bazzanno, at least while attached to him. Her flirtations were almost always intellectual, in the nature of a specialised and abstract game. Da Bazzanno was proud of this quality in her. He would watch her from a table or two away, remarking to me on her beauty, her cool easiness, her clever manipulations.

'We have not made love in a year,' he told me. 'We do not need to. And we are so happy, Max. Of course, we still see other people.'

I understood perfectly. I, too, had known the joys of purely spiritual love; the case with myself and Mrs Cornelius. Though married, we had never physically consummated our union. The spiritual compact was far more satisfying. One learned to relish the subtler ecstacies of the desert life, I told him. Eventually they became preferable to all others. In the desert, 'love' took on a more important meaning, when it truly was possible to love one's camel more than one's wife. In the desert one must frequently choose between life and death. The desert does not tolerate empty words.

Da Bazzanno blew his nose on a silk Liberty handkerchief and remarked approvingly how much harder I had become since he had last seen me in Rome. He repeated that he meant to introduce me to Mussolini as soon as possible. 'Italy has always honoured such men as yourself, Prince Max.' His enthusiasm rose. 'The editor-writers, the soldier-poets and the philosopher-engineers – those who combine the talents of a man of action and a man of creative intellect. You have read Jünger, of course. It's all in *Storm of Steel*. So much better than Remarque's novel. Every great Renaissance artist was also an expert duellist. We cannot turn our backs on our violent natures. But we can control that violence and direct it. Promise me, Max, that you will come with me to Rome – that you will throw in your destiny with ours – that you will become an Italian! A modern Italian!'

I restrained myself, merely smiling and saying that I was seriously considering the idea.

'We take off for Venice in two days' time.' He refilled my champagne glass for me. 'You will love Venice. And then – to Rome! What do you say?'

When I hesitated, anxious not to seem too eager now that my great dream was so close to realisation, he became apologetic. 'My dear fellow! How insensitive of me. You are afraid that this diversion will interrupt your career as an actor. You must have many contracts and obligations!'

I admitted that I had already given a considerable amount of thought to the prospect of serving Il Duce or resuming my Hollywood career. My agents, I assured him, were instructed to accept no further offers for the time being. Fiorello reached across the table and put his huge hand on mine. 'Your first duty is to yourself, Maxim. To your art. You must not let my enthusiasm, our needs, lead you off your chosen path. But as one artist to another, I must assure you that Mussolini is the true medium of our ambitions!'

This phrase struck an emotional chord in me. I had tried so hard to present a measured manner, but my voice shook a little as I told my friend that my duty was rapidly becoming crystal clear. He had convinced me. I was now prepared to refuse all other temptations, give up previous ambitions and accompany him to Rome, to offer my talents in the service of his master.

'I believe,' I murmured sincerely, 'that I am about to come face to face with my destiny.'

I was close to tears. At last I had found my Tsar.

I was going home.

SEVEN

I had been sleeping and came awake suddenly with no notion of the time. I was alone. For some reason I experienced a rush of terror and then opened my eyes to see that a steward had brought me some tea. He seemed amused. My hand trembled badly as I accepted the glass. He told me that Signorina Butter and Doctor da Bazzanno requested urgently that I join them in the observation cabin.

Still conditioned to crisis, I quickly washed and dressed. I hurried from my quarters, along the vibrating metal passage to the cabin where my friends were already seated staring out of the wide window at the approaching horizon.

'You seemed to need the rest,' said Maddy Butter with a smile. Only then did I realise it was not morning but late evening. We were nearing our destination. That afternoon, while airborne, I had entertained Miss Butter in my quarters and then, evidently, fallen fast asleep.

'I didn't want you to miss this.' Da Bazzanno was alive with warm, proprietorial pride. 'It is, after all, the birthplace of my ancestors!'

I took my seat beside him. The plane suddenly banked, levelling out close to the water, and as the horizon came up again I understood why da Bazzanno had wakened me so insistently.

Most of us see pictures of them from childhood and in some sense know what to expect, yet all the wonders of the world, the Pyramids or Niagara Falls or any of the others, have this in common: we are forever prepared for them and yet never quite ready for their actuality. The actuality is always breathtaking, never disappointing, always better than any representation we have seen. The desert in that Lawrence film was a tawdry backdrop in comparison to the original. The Grand Canyon in *Cinerama* is still merely a cheap illusion. The reality is too vivid ever to become truly familiar.

And so it was, of course, with Venice. Her sky was alive with gold and rose. Her olive cupolas were half immersed in a ruby-coloured aura. Smouldering bronze, silver stone, emerald tiles, a thousand shades of terracotta, canals like mercury, woven into one great carpet of colour whose tones faded or deepened with the setting of the sun. With her vast variety of domes and towers, curves and angles, she surely existed in more than a mere four dimensions.

Da Bazzanno chuckled at my astonishment. Venice's confident beauty contradicted any conventional understanding of space, just as she revealed whole varieties of tints and washes which, I could swear, I have never seen since. As her colours darkened, her lights made little pools of shivering copper and warm saffron refracted in water that diffused and enriched her so that the outlines of her buildings merged with sky and water and made it impossible to know where the reality ended and the mirage began. I could easily believe the whole vast scene to be illusion. I understood how she had resisted her would-be conquerors for so many centuries.

Again *La Farfalla Nera* banked steeply, lending that fabulous city a further crazy unreality. We swept towards the vivid tapestry as if to be absorbed by it. We banked again, making a pass at the water as we prepared to put down. I heard a sudden loud bang, felt a series of sharp shudders, then a sense of bouncing gently forward until at last we settled. Da Bazzanno's next remark was lost under a massive roar from the engines steadying the ship as she came about. She prepared to taxi towards the dark outlines of churches, storehouses, palaces, merchants' mansions, banks and museums built with that same enchanting combination of knowing magnificence and un-rivalled, artless beauty. Even Odessa in her Golden Age could not begin to match the brutal and subtle glamour of that ethereal Queen of Ports whose influence once stretched across the globe, whose style has so frequently been imitated and never successfully equalled, even by Hollywood. Venice's beauty set the standard by which all watery cities, be they Stockholm, Rovaniemi, Amsterdam or Bangkok, measure themselves.

'I'll send my orderly to the harbourmaster with a note,' Fiorello told me. 'They'll come and collect us in a decent boat. We shall be staying at my family home near La Fenice. I apologise in advance for the building's condition. I was only recently able to reclaim it from the people who had occupied it since we lost it in 1797. Their taste was typically bourgeois. I'm having the whole place redecorated.'

I remarked that he had reached quite a height. Ten years ago, as an impoverished artist, he had only dreamed of the world he was now helping to create.

'It's crazy, isn't it?' My observation seemed to sober him. 'Yet isn't there an emptiness about it? Doesn't it feel to you, my dear Max, as if it could fade away tomorrow, like fairy gold? *This* is our time, Max. I doubt we'll have another. We must enjoy it to the full. When we wake up, we could be rotting in some prison or, worse, discover our real selves to be nothing but bank clerks and minor civil servants with cheap ambitions!'

I was a little surprised by his change of mood. Only a day or so earlier he had been describing the triumph of a New Rome which would rule the world for millennia. I said that I thought he was being both too self-deprecating and too pessimistic. He received only what he had honestly earned. 'What you starved for. What you worked for. These are the rewards of the hard, dangerous, hungry years. Your Duce knows what you are worth.'

He leaned forward and kissed me on the cheek. 'Well, let us hope you are right. Meanwhile, I suggest you take my advice anyway. After all, what can you lose if I'm wrong? Life should always be relished by the moment. Death takes everything *but* that moment from us. Everything.'

Miranda Butter was much impressed by this profoundly Latin attitude which to me seemed to carry a certain cargo of self-pity, so unlike our own Slavic soul-searching. Slavic angst contains an intellectual element lacking in the Italian's fiery despair.

'But death,' I said, 'also presents us with that moment.'

My lovely companion gasped and placed her hand on mine. Her eyes were hot with tears. 'That's so true.'

Da Bazzanno shrugged and called for more cognac. His normally droll face was suffused with emotion. He now resembled a pantomime horse playing Ibsen. In silence he grew absorbed in the scene beyond the window.

'What does Venice mean to you, Prince Max?' Maddy still habitually used my formal title in public. 'Do you, too, have family here?'

I shook my head. 'Venice means betrayal. Had she not withdrawn her fleet in 1453, Constantinople would not have fallen to the Turk. Yet now she redeems herself. Now she remains one of the few unfallen bastions of Christendom.' I looked across the black, jewelled waters to where the lights of gondolas and fishing boats came and went against the misty outlines of the quayside buildings, the queerly angled mooring posts. 'She is a marriage of Western and Eastern civilisation. I long to know her better.'

Miss Butter spoke softly. 'We'll explore her together, shall we? But you must remain my spiritual guide and my teacher. I'm so ignorant of European history.'

'Unfortunately for my family,' I told her, 'we are almost nothing but history.' My smile was self-mocking. 'And we are not known for our lack of spirituality, either. We are Russians.'

Da Bazzanno, pulling himself out of his mood, laughed suddenly, displaying his huge, yellow teeth. 'We want as little history in Italy as possible. Until now Italy too has been nothing but history. Picturesque ruins, memories of former glory. We have lived off tourism and tagliatelle for centuries. The new Italy has a place only for the future – the history we are making today!'

We drank to the future in champagne. We drank to the city, to the nation, to the leader. We drank to the fulfilment of our dreams. Our faith was in a fascism as yet untarnished by the actions of its less disciplined adherents. Real, idealistic Fascists, like da Bazzanno, loathed everything that their movement became; a party divided by crude rivalries and guided by orthodoxy which Mussolini himself always sought to discourage.

But then, in our happy innocence, we drank to our Golden Age.

A little later a motor launch, carrying a small blackshirt guard of honour and the deputy mayor, drew alongside. Signora Sarfatti had joined us. She sat across from me. From time to time she offered me a friendly wink. She was completely at ease and exuded authority. We climbed into the launch. I felt uncomfortable, sitting, with my precious luggage, between two stern foot soldiers of the new Italy, but they were eager to oblige us in every way. Within minutes we reached the quay and the blackshirts helped us disembark, carrying our bags to a waiting cart which they proceeded to steer at a trot, with loud whistles of warning, through San Marco's gathering crowds.

To my still befuddled mind we were shadows, insubstantial and colourful, perhaps, but nonetheless still merely actors in some extravagant movie. My sense of unreality was increased by the expressions on various faces around me. The vibrant Venetian air heightened the contrasts. Grotesque, immobile, animated or familiar, every face bore a certain theatrical cast. People's clothes, though frequently of modish design, had the quality of stage costumes. The buildings, canals and

46

alleys continued my impression of an enduring artificiality. Even the voices of organ-grinders, fiddlers, jumping-jack sellers, the hawkers of tin toys, cheap scarves and whole ensembles of masks, felt as if they were orchestrated for the stage. We crossed a couple of small, dramatically arching bridges, passed down a zigzag of twittens, stumbled for a while on a cobbled path running beside a narrow canal over which gaudy washing hung like welcoming flags. At last we entered a small dead-end square smelling strongly of cat urine. Here the cart was brought to an abrupt stop and the *fascisti* saluted. Da Bazzanno returned their salute, took a ring of rattling metal from his pocket and inserted a large brass key into the lock of a rather scruffy-looking door made from ancient, iron-bound wood. Light spilled suddenly into the little square and a shrill voice cackled in happy surprise from within. '*Fiorello! Fiorello! Mio figlio!*'

In the doorway an old man appeared. His back was curved with scoliosis but his huge head beamed up at us, his vast mouth displaying a few brownish teeth. His amiable, short-sighted eyes were bloodshot mahogany, his jowls were covered in white stubble. Dressed in a coarse, brown monk's robe, he appeared to be a priest. His resemblance to Fiorello was striking. If he lived long enough my friend would one day exactly resemble his sire.

Hugging the old man tightly, Fiorello introduced us to his father. Servants appeared, greeting us all with the same nods and grins before carrying our luggage into the house. With warm thanks and ample tips, da Bazzanno dismissed our guard of honour, informed the deputy mayor that he would call at the town hall as soon as he was settled, shook hands and closed the door on the street.

The *palazzo* was like the backstage of a theatre. I half expected to find dressing rooms leading off the main passages of what was, in fact, a typical old Venetian house, built around an interior courtyard completely inaccessible and invisible from outside.

The high-ceilinged passages were lit by candles and oil lamps. They threw long shadows upon walls, staircases and old black beams. Our shadows continued to dance and shudder as we followed the two Bazzannos, deep in happy conversation, through a house smelling strongly of the canals outside and for which, over his shoulder, Fiorello periodically apologised. His whole attention was focused on his father. I have rarely known two male relatives take such tremendous joy in each other's company. I experienced a pang of loss for my own father, whose foolish radicalism had separated us.

I assumed them to have been apart for months, but a fondly indulgent Margherita Sarfatti told me it had been only a couple of weeks since da Bazzanno had departed. 'It is a love affair that has been going on since he was born.' She shrugged and offered me a droll wink. 'How can I compete?'

Not by nature a discourteous soul, da Bazzanno remembered himself soon enough to tell us how he had wanted the house to be ready for guests. 'But we have almost a hundred and fifty years of neglect to cope with. They did nothing. They didn't spend a penny on the place.'

'A Jewish family,' said old da Bazzanno by way of explanation. He shrugged. 'Very pleasant people. Nothing wrong with them. But you know how they hate to part with cash.'

'We're having electricity, gas, water – everything piped in. And new sewers. And walls have to be repointed. Plastering . . .' Fiorello returned his attention to his father.

Old da Bazzanno added: 'They were not real Jews. They went to the same church as my aunt. Everyone liked them. They were generous to the church, she said. But not to themselves. Or the house.' His shrug was a distorted echo of his son's.

'What happened to them?' I asked Margherita, as we continued to penetrate the warren of tiny passages and rooms. She shook her head. She had heard something, she said, but she wasn't sure if it was true. She had an idea they had moved to Austria where they had a son. She sauntered ahead of us to inspect a faded tapestry.

'They weren't Jews at all, then,' interposed Maddy Butter almost aggressively. 'Were they? I mean, they were Christians.'

'Once a Jew always a Jew,' I told her kindly. 'In America you have not had quite our experience of the Children of Abraham.'

I would remember those words some years later and only then understand their full significance. At that time I did not pursue the subject as Margherita had rejoined us with a murmured apology and an enthusiastic diversion on the subject of fourteenth-century Norman tapestry.

Eventually the passages opened out on to a gallery. Here the smell of mould was strongest. We were on the first floor, looking down into a large hall where a table was being laid and a fire made. Clearly the servants had not known when da Bazzanno *fils* would return. We crossed the gallery into another wide corridor. We discovered our bedrooms, our bags already there.

Again I felt I had wandered into some Hollywood historical extravaganza. The rooms had huge four-poster beds. Their iron-hard oak was carved with dark animals and plants tinted with faded gold leafing. The heavy hangings were filthy with age. The furniture was preserved by candle wax and cooking fats, the grease and grime of centuries. Mysterious pictures, so blackened it was impossible to tell the subject, clung to the walls. A small fire had managed to take hold in my grate, and fat copper lamps guttered in iron sticks mottled with oil and verdigris. My evening clothes had been unpacked and laid out for me. My few other clothes were put away in a massive armoire. The rest of my possessions – my films and my plans – had not been touched, but I leafed through my rather dog-eared blueprints and notes to make sure no enterprising trainee spy had removed anything. I also checked that my cache of cocaine was in order. Here I made a happy discovery. With a rush of gratitude I found my cousin Shura, as a parting gift, had left me with ten large packets, sealed neatly in waxed paper like grocer's sugar, of the very finest *sneg*. A year's supply, even if used with irresponsible abandon! To celebrate I called Signora Sarfatti and Maddy Butter to my room, and we indulged a small line or two before dinner, chopped out by Margherita Sarfatti under the gaze of an admiring Miss Butter. She had only with our acquaintance become an enthusiast for the life-enhancing powder. Da Bazzanno had, at least for the moment, renounced cocaine. I had every sympathy for him. From time to time a little fasting is good for the soul as well as the blood. But he did not like to be reminded of what he had given up, so Signora Sarfatti was delighted to join us in this innocent secret.

Later, we enjoyed a simple meal of tripe soup and fried shellfish while da Bazzanno the Younger, in graphic gestures and with wild laughter, retailed the problems they had had with the flying boat. Da Bazzanno the Elder, devoting himself to his dinner in the manner of the aged, occasionally interjected a polite exclamation. I was again reminded of two trick horses from the old *Funabile* enjoying a gossipy manger of hay together. At one moment they might break into the mock-philosophical patter for which Ah-Ee and Ee-Ah were famous when I was a boy in Kiev. The candle flames graced the faces of our female companions with new angles and secrets. The servants all had that prematurely wizened appearance of a people with blood so ancient, so little diluted, that they could be representatives of a different and earlier race altogether.

The Venetians, Signora Sarfatti, a native of the city, would tell me, not only looked different and spoke differently, they also thought differently. They had, she said, antique minds, full of sophistications and experience unknown to the rest of us, full of strange, uncommon assumptions about matters of health, morality, politics and even literature.

'What they value is not always what the rest of us value,' she said. 'The Venetians built their first houses on stilts above the swampy delta islets which in those days were already inhabited by a race whose skills and appearance were not wholly human. The two species interbred. Some believe the Venetians are the only survivors of Atlantis. Their inhuman ancestors escaped the deluge which drowned that extraordinarily advanced civilisation. Venice is full of great cathedrals and churches, yet she is still as profoundly pagan as she is practical. Venice will survive any disaster and adapt herself to any changing conditions. She is a city whose principal trade is in illusion. For her, deception really is an art! And a saleable art, at that!'

Fiorello was familiar with her arguments. He dismissed them with good humour. 'My darling Margherita, the only art Venetians have learned is the art of good living. Everything else is imported. They will trade with anyone. I offer you the real secret of their enduring supremacy. They honestly believe that making money is a moral pursuit, that gold has an ethical and spiritual value, that a man without profit is a man without honour. These aren't the survivors of Atlantis, dear friends, but of Ur! They are the ancestors of all usurers and merchants. And good luck to them.' He signed for her glass to be replenished.

'Fiorello,' she crooned, 'you tolerate everything and everyone.' Her brunette waves tumbled fetchingly across her face.

'That's our great Italian virtue, my dear.'

'The disease for which Fascism is the remedy.' She was sardonic. Her lips pretended sternness she could not feel towards her lover. 'At least, that's what I hear you saying in public.'

'One has to employ stronger, simpler language in public than one favours in private, Margherita. Fascism balances and moderates our natural tolerance. It binds all our qualities of manliness and femininity together in one strong bundle.' I heard an equally obvious note of self-mockery in his voice when he made such pronouncements.

'There does not,' observed Signora Sarfatti drily, 'appear to be a very strong element of femininity bound into our Duce's bundle of faggots.'

'You'd be surprised.' That was all da Bazzanno would give us.

'These things surely are all a matter of interpretation.' Miss Butter's Italian was not as good as her French but it was better than mine. We had agreed to use French as our common tongue. 'What, after all, do the words "masculine" and "feminine" mean?'

Such abstractions were too much for us, so we changed to a different subject. We had Miss Butter inform us of her native Texas, its cowboys and wild Kiowa. She had little direct experience of either, she said, having been educated in Atlanta and raised in Galveston, on the coast. 'Which has rather more to do with commerce and shipping.'

I thought it inappropriate to mention my old political connections in Houston. Miss Butter was at a naive stage in her own political development, full of generalised sentimentality towards lame ducks. Sometimes in private I laughed at her, telling her she could not nurse the whole world's walking wounded. But I had no wish to revive arguments on subjects which still aroused my own passions. I wanted to put all my conflicts behind me and begin my career where the Bolshevists had cut it off some ten years earlier.

I reminded myself that I was not a politician but a scientist. Not an actor, but an inventor. In future my contribution to the human race would be thoroughly practical. I would no longer talk of 'lifting the masses' – I would lift them through my deeds, by example. I understood where my own idealism belonged. I think Miss Butter recognised this. Indeed, it was these qualities in me rather than my political opinions which she found attractive. Aside from my admiration of Mussolini, my fear that civil war must soon break out in France and Germany, a sense of the general causes of our European malaise and a notion of who the chief villains were, I expressed few opinions. What my friends wanted to hear from me was not what they already knew. They wanted my vision of tomorrow where flying cities and vast engineering works brought peace and prosperity to all. I described my notion of a huge airliner which was entirely comprised of wing – a massive flying wing, some thousand yards wide! My steam-car, I told Fiorello, on his enquiring, was now a reality in California. My light aircraft were flying in the air force of Marrakech's Caïd. In France, at a secret hangar near St-Denis, my airship strained to be airborne but was grounded by the squabbling greed of her investors. I had built flying infantry for the Turks and designed a secret weapon for Petlyura in Ukraine. Other ideas of mine, such as the autogyro and ocean-based aeroplane staging platforms, were realities. My intention was never to get rich from these ideas. My first goal was to ease the human burden. Any profit I made was incidental. Again and again Fiorello and Margherita assured me that I was just the type Mussolini wished to recruit for his great army of scholars, scientists, soldiers and engineers. His willingness to give such men as myself a chance was what made him so great.

My earlier sense of urgency, which had enabled me to sustain myself in Morocco and given me a persuasive motive for returning to Europe, had been replaced by a quieter and, I believe, stronger emotion. I wished to take stock of myself as well as the country before I presented myself to Il Duce. What was more, I had fallen in love a little with the delicious Miss Butter. Soon I would be infatuated, head over heels, with the City of St Mark!

Together Miss Butter and I visited Venice's museums and magnificent public buildings, gasping at her astonishing wonders and riches which we came upon often unexpectedly when rounding a corner of an alley and finding, for instance, the white marble church of Santa Maria dei Miracoli. We entered her relatively austere portals to discover a wealth of gold, a feast of murals and pictures and a towering altar which seemed to draw you directly up to heaven. Every square had a character of its own, every bridge opened on to a picture, every garden displayed the orderly beauty of centuries of cultivation, nurtured and shaped to gladden the eye and the heart.

Da Bazzanno had been right. In the daylight, with her bustling business life, her babble of voices, her washing lines and murmuring touts, Venice was nothing but reality. Along the Grand Canal, where building after building spoke of a magnificent history, where Baroque and Gothic and Romanesque, Moorish and Byzantine styles stood shoulder to shoulder against any easy definition, there was a domestic ordinariness to the city. People came and went on a thousand different missions, crossing the bridges, taking the gondolas as others might take buses and taxis, striking bargains, chatting, quarrelling. Few bothered to sit in the little boats which plied constantly between the quays. To stand marked you as a Venetian. In my bones, I knew how at night these people transformed themselves into creatures resembling their inhuman ancestors. These same buildings and canals would be touched by Titania's wand to become scenes from fairy-land where sorcery and magic were concrete realities.

Sometimes I felt I crossed from one version of our world into another. I was discovering myself at the nativity of a modern Renaissance. I was privileged to live in the first years of a Golden Age. Then something went wrong. I could not in those days have predicted how the envious, venal and most banal forces of our century would force the world into a prolonged nightmare, a night-mare from which there now seems no chance of awakening. Perhaps Venice was actually a gateway from one potential reality to another? Perhaps unconsciously I stepped through that gateway and became a prisoner, longing for the just, safe and orderly world I had lost? But in those early weeks I had no such gloomy ideas. My infatua-tion with Miss Butter and with Venice remains among my happiest memories.

A city heavy with such unique history is arrogant but far too well bred to show it. She is narcissistic − infinitely reflected in her own waters − and she is vain. Venice is interested only in herself. She possesses the haughty charm of antique tradition and ancient wealth. Her condescending tolerance is based on the sublime under-standing that she has no natural enemies and that the rest of the world shares an instinctive desire to serve and to please her. Venice owns an elusive heart, a mysterious soul. Even in her silences or in the gay music of her many masques and concerts, in her theatrical performances, you can sometimes hear the beating of a powerful prehistoric organ, the whisper of ancient arteries, the pulsing of forgotten veins. Sometimes a faint drift of unnameable colour undu-lates across a square or passes you on one of the narrow canals. Shadows appear which owe nothing to the position of the sun or the moon.

Her past a mixture of glorious nobility and brutal greed, Venice is the crystallisation of the Mediterranean's fears and needs. She offers all the satisfactions one ever desired and many which one never imagined. With da Bazzanno's own brainchild, the Festival of Fascist Arts, the city had become the Mecca for bohemians, especially Italians who found the new Rome a little too austere for their tastes. Cafés and cabarets had sprung up for their entertainment, attracting performers from Berlin, New York and Athens, from Cairo and Paris.

Despite much of this clientele, I was still attracted to these places. I had spent my youth in them. I received much of my education in them, thanks to Shura and my beloved friend Count Nikolai Feodorovitch Petroff, my Kolya. I was, I admit, addicted to them. Soon Miss Butter was seeing a wholly different side of Italian life from the great public ceremonies of Il Duce and the Vatican. Every kind of sexuality was represented and catered for. Every kind of music, from the sweet, old tunes of Vienna and Prague, to the neurotic modern concoctions of Mahler and his arch-collaborator Schoenberg, from the bitter-sweet accordion to the wailing saxophone, harsh Berlin syncopation and syrupy English vibrato; all of which, I was assured, was untypical of Venice. The city had once been notorious for its lack of public nightlife.

Responding to my curiosity, da Bazzanno informed me with attempted amusement that Venice has attracted another kind of adventurer: the arms trader. All the big people regularly came to the city. No week passed without at least two or three South American governments sending their representatives to shop for guns. The air of the restaurants and cabarets where such transactions took place was very different from the rest of the city and few of the local people welcomed it. The Italian authorities considered Venice a free port and turned a blind eye to these activities.

In the course of a single evening I overheard plans for arming various Balkan factions and part of a negotiation where an Algerian businessman openly bargained for a consignment of Martini rifles to be used against the French.

Miss Butter was writing several stories a day and mailing them back to her paper. She was afraid to wire them. I hinted that secrecy or urgency were not necessary, especially since her editor in Houston was not greatly interested in the intricate corruptions of modern Europe. He wanted more immediate scandals, with personalities and titles he had heard of.

Meanwhile, Maddy continued to interview me and had now decided to write a book about my exploits. 'You are the model of the modern hero.'

One evening, in a cabaret called the Little Gigolo, where many foreign businessmen met but where the show was amusing and not too raucous, I attempted to dissuade her from this perception, but we were both too drunk and she refused to have any of it. She even suspected me of protecting other aristocrats, helping them get out of Russia. 'If only I had the power. I have had no word from my mother in years. I pray for her. It is all I can do.' I changed the

54

subject. I began to speak of my dreams, of my scientific ideas.

She was listening with her usual doting attention when my voice was suddenly drowned by a discordant chorus of some Bavarian folk song shouted vigorously by a group of very drunken Germans who sat together in a corner near the stage. They were ex-military. They had been there all evening, engaged with one of the South Americans, and had been drinking heavily. By their manner and conversation several of them were clearly homosexual. They were openly kissing and cuddling, to the amusement, rather than the disgust, of the other patrons.

I looked up in annoyance as the Germans began the umpteenth verse of their song and saw that a newcomer had joined them. He was large and effeminate in a fur-collared black overcoat and a Homburg hat a size too small for his head. His back was towards me but was very familiar. I was trying to recall the man when I heard his voice raised in angry German which almost at once turned into near-hysterical Russian, then into Spanish, and eventually into broken Italian, all on the same note.

My heart sank. This was not an acquaintance I wished to renew! There was no mistaking Sergei Andreyovitch Tsipliakov or his familiar complaints. His friend of the same sexual persuasion had not turned up. The Germans were far too drunk and careless to help find him.

It was obvious Seryozha, whom I had originally met on the Kiev–Peter Express, was no longer with the ballet, unless as a choreographer. He was running to fat. His ruined face turned away from the Germans. His self-indulgent jowls emphasised his lugubrious dismay. I tried to escape his eye. Then he had seen me. His hand flew to his mouth. His expression changed to one of utter joy. His voice rang through the room. I shrank.

'Dimka! Dimka, darling! Dear heart, they told me you had gone back to Peter and were working for the Okhrana! Are you really a secret policeman now, Dimka, darling? Were you one in Paris? Oh, the stories I've heard! What ever happened to you? Why did you abandon me? Dear heart, I was so good to you!'

My only consolation was that he spoke in Russian, one of the few languages Miss Butter did not understand.

He engulfed me. His wet lips met mine. A small-time Judas.

EIGHT

Naturally I was embarrassed. Yet I could only see this further co-incidence as destined. Events were moving towards some vast and significant conjunction. Everyone was being drawn to Italy and her charismatic leader.

To Miss Butter I introduced Seryozha as an acquaintance from my days in St Petersburg where he had been with the Ballet Foline. To change the subject as quickly as possible I asked him in German if he was appearing at the Arts Festival. This question encouraged a great gust of miserable laughter. 'If only that were true, Dimka sweet-heart. Sadly, I'm on very different business!'

When I asked him what his business was he admitted that he was sworn to silence on the matter, which was of international impor-tance. A little afraid that he might attempt to blackmail me and wishing to insure myself, I told him swiftly in Russian that I too was on secret business, travelling as Prince Maxim Pyatnitski. The American woman was suspected of being a Bolshevik agent. He must be unusually discreet.

Of course, Seryozha's discretion was typical. After offering me a wink and a half-conspiratorial leer, he declared loudly in broken English that he had not seen his old comrade-in-arms 'Prince Pyanisski' since we fought side by side together in the war against the forces of reaction. Happily he was already so drunk that his mistake went unnoticed, and as he breathed gin over Miss Butter's little pink hand he steadied himself by leaning heavily on our table. 'You're the prettiest agent I've seen in years!'

She explained that she was not an agent but a journalist and asked him if he knew Diaghilev. Seryozha, declaring that the famous ballet master was a charlatan, a philistine, a sensationalist, a rogue and a plagiarist, admitted that he had met him twice in Paris. 'You were with me, Dimka, I'm sure. In the Café Pantin? I told him what I thought of his cacophonic eyesores and we were thrown out. That was you, wasn't it, Dimka?'

In an aside I explained to Miss Butter that 'Dimka' was a nickname I'd earned in Petersburg's café society. I could not quite remember how I had come by it. She was showing far more interest in Sergei A. Tsipliakov than he deserved. He had grown even more irritating and foolish. I began to feel that I was embroiled in some primitive and farcical *commedia dell'arte* sketch, the kind of thing on which the Jew Chaplin based so many of his 'original' routines. In Russian Seryozha explained to Miss Butter that I was the greatest engineer he had ever known. In English he added affectionately that we had been special chums in Petersburg. We had met, he said, while sharing a sleeping car together. Did I, he enquired loudly, still use cocaine? He was desperate for some.

In murmured Russian I promised him some superb cocaine, but he must keep quiet. His friends at the other table were frowning and showing signs of impatience, even nervousness. I said that I thought he was wanted back with his comrades.

'They're not comrades! They're gun-runners, Dimka. I came all the way from Manchuria to meet them. Well, more or less. But I did come all the way from Manchuria. And I know it's to do with guns. They won't tell me anything. I'm just a damned dogsbody, really, dear. I *had* to get out of Bolivia. I can't tell you what I had to do to leave La Paz.'

'What were you doing in Manchuria, Mr Tsipliakov?' enquired Miss Butter with that direct, polite innocence only Americans command. I expected Seryozha to become coy, but he answered quickly.

'They have an absolutely huge Russian community. All forced out by the Reds, of course, and wretchedly hungry for *any* kind of art. The old story, ma'mselle. An emissary arrived in Paris. He knew of me and came with an absolutely splendid, unrefusable offer – and the chance to be chief star and choreographer of the Ballet Manchurienne. A *marvellous* opportunity. The Russians were longing to hear Tchaikovsky performed by genuine Slavs and to watch some decent dancing. Of course, I agreed. My heart was touched, you know. I am too soft, as all my friends tell me.' He fixed a large, self-loving eye upon Miss Butter.

'What happened to you there?' I asked.

'Well, darling, I arrived in Harbin, by a most *unseaworthy* Chinese steamer, to discover that I was the entire company and was expected to create an alternative to the Bolshoi out of absolutely *nothing*. Darling, believe me, I did my best. Every silly little Russian girl that had ever had a dance lesson was auditioned, every little boy who had ever yearned for toe-shoes. And I put something together for them. They thought it was wonderful. But then, of course, they didn't want to *pay* for a ballet company. Eventually I found myself in financial trouble. A stupid, pointless scandal. Nobody would give me my salary! Luckily, I became great pals with a successful fur trader, late of Nizhny Novgorod and now of La Paz, who told me that the Bolivians were simply crying out for a good ballet master. He promised to back me, but by the time we arrived in Bolivia we'd quarrelled over a stupid matter and he wasn't speaking to me. I gave private lessons for a while. Then that bastard Salamanca overturned the government and it was all gone. I'd become rather a friend of the president's wife, who was a keen balletomane, and I suppose I was identified with the ruling class. Luckily, I'd made a couple of German chums there and when they got the chance to leave I went with them. It's a familiar tale, isn't it, ma'mselle, for these days? But we soldier on.'

She had not heard my question and had scarcely understood anything Seryozha had said. 'And you're performing at the Arts Festival?'

'I'm here as an observer only.' A dissolute steer, Seryozha widened his huge bloodshot brown eyes and shrugged at me, as if asking whether he had played his part properly.

Miss Butter was in no way confused. 'It's thrilling,' she said, 'to be in the company of people with such experience of the world. I have experienced so little.'

'Then stick with Dimka, sweet mademoiselle,' guffawed the dancer. 'No one has had more varied experience!' He reached to kiss me but this time I avoided him.

'So I gather.' She smiled in a way which suggested she was privy to arcana which would astonish even Seryozha. This further alarmed me since, given the opportunity, I knew what a gossip my old acquaintance could be. I was very surprised that he had successfully kept his purpose in Venice unknown to us. I guessed he must be extremely afraid of his employer. Either that or he had been told nothing at all by someone who knew him as well as I did.

He had money to spend. Producing a handful of large-denomination notes he ordered 'real' champagne. When Miss Butter had retired to

58

the ladies' room, he leaned forward and in a thick whisper, begged me to let him have some *sneg* for old times' sake. I was glad to hand him the rest of a pillbox I was carrying and privately told myself that I had at last settled the account with him I had had since he left his own snuffbox behind all those years ago on the Petersburg train. That box had proven very helpful to me in my first days as an engineering student at the Institute.

By the time Miss Butter returned Seryozha had pocketed my pillbox, muttered something mysterious about putting in a good word with the '*vozhd*' for me, kissed me affectionately on the lips, and informed me to my great relief that he was due to leave in the morning, taking the early train to Vienna and from there to Berlin, where he had been promised his own apartment. 'I'm an official emissary now,' he said before he staggered back to his 'business contacts'. By his gestures, I knew he was dismissing me as an old colleague from the ballet.

Miranda Butter complimented me on my fascinating friends. She had a sparkle to her which contrasted rather sharply with the slightly seedy appearance of those around us. 'This is exactly why I came to Europe. We Americans are all so unsophisticated. You were right to leave when you did, Max. I admire your courage. So few could turn their backs on all you had – Hollywood, fame, wealth . . .'

'We are too old a family to set much store by such things,' I told her. 'We are trained to public service. It is the only kind of work we ever take seriously.'

I saw Seryozha shake hands with everyone at his table and show signs of leaving. He was eager, I was sure, to get back to his hotel and try my gift. He now possessed the contented, almost complacent look of an old cat which has made a successful raid on a well-stocked dustbin.

He waved to us once as he went out, a picture of seedy ebullience. When he had gone, the people he had left leaned back, as if in relief, and were obviously joking about him. One German with the face of an unsuccessful prizefighter made some attempt to imitate him, to loud applause and backslapping.

Seryozha was irritating, but his acquaintances were genuinely sinister. I had never had time for arms dealers. Karl May had given me a clear idea what to think of people who sold guns to Natives. Old Shatterhand would have known how to deal with them and Ace Peters, the Masked Buckaroo, would have rounded them all up and taken them off to jail in an instant. Seryozha's friends continued occasionally to glance across at our table and discuss us in a speculative way. Eventually I called for our bill. We left earlier than we had planned and dropped in at one of the little tent-theatres erected in a quiet piazza where we watched some rather shrill Molière before returning to the Palazzo da Bazzanno where our friend's father awaited us.

As one of the chief architects of the festival, da Bazzanno was constantly busy. Moreover, almost as soon as we had arrived Signora Sarfatti had been forced to leave unexpectedly for Rome. Thus we were left to our own devices. Bazzanno's father complained that he might as well have stayed at their apartment in Rome, but he was a jovial old soul and glad to entertain us in his huge reception room. Da Bazzanno *père* had given up his girlfriend, he said, to move back to Venice. He had to admit, all in all, that he preferred it here. Rome had become so rowdy. 'That man –' he jerked his thumb over his shoulder, referring to Mussolini – 'he loves to hear himself talk. And if he can do it through a loudspeaker or on the radio, so much the better. Honestly, it's like having some garrulous relative staying with you for ever!' He did not share his son's admiration for Il Duce, but had to admit things had improved considerably for them since the March on Rome in which Fiorello had taken part. 'For every one really there, a thousand claim to have been on the march. You would think the whole of Italy followed Mussolini to the royal palace!'

There were always some, I proposed, who would demand legitimacy for themselves by making such claims.

'As you say, signor,' I continued, 'we have a thousand liars for every honest man. With so many lies in the world is it surprising things are as they are? You lie to people enough and they are forced to make up their own ideas about reality. Is that not the secret of Mussolini's success? He thinks and acts with plain common sense, in ways we can all understand. He does the practical thing, just like the man in the street. We need more such leaders.'

But old da Bazzanno, his long face full of bafflement, said he was not sure. 'The secret of power is not action,' he thought, 'but *inaction*. It is what you do *not* do that brings you the greatest rewards. Often the "common sense" of the "ordinary man" leads to unmitigated disaster. I am a dyed-in-the-wool republican, I'll admit. The secret of self-respect is self-rule and noble action – but that brings a politician little power, merely influence, which is only worth so much.'

I was familiar with his old-fashioned fatalistic attitude. An attitude which so weakened Italy and which Mussolini specifically sought to fight. Yet the ancient patriarch was so sweet-natured and so fond of his son, I could not bring myself to argue with him. Unlike modern British children who are without any manners or grace, I was brought up to respect my elders. However, today was not the appropriate time for cynicism. Italy was again making a place for herself in the world. She was the most vibrant force in Europe, an acknowledged leader. While the others sat passively by and let pipsqueaks order them about, Italy expanded and went forward, increasing her territories, bringing enlightenment to her African possessions and fresh pride to her citizens. Was he, too, not proud of his nation?

He told me that he was not sure.

The old house was still in a state of disrepair, with electrical wires emerging from bare brick and piles of plaster scattered here and there. But at night, with the candles and the oil lamps burning, it seemed to come alive, to be its old self.

Da Bazzanno's complaint that the place had hardly been touched since 1797 was legitimate. His house was full of peculiar bits of furniture, oddly woven tapestries and rather mysterious paintings. Maddy and I explored the rooms together, expecting to come upon a secret chamber or a whole suite where a previous tenant still lived, unaware that their relatives had moved away. The place certainly had its ghosts, but they seemed in no way malignant. Had we turned a corner to confront some ethereal nobleman in doublet and hose on his way to the bedroom of a lover dead five hundred years, I doubt if either of us would have been alarmed.

As the festival progressed with vast water-borne processions and almost everyone you met wearing some kind of costume or at least a mask, da Bazzanno's house grew more and more in tune with its surroundings. Venetians, no matter how respectable and conservative, love a disguise. They have made the masque their own, and they are proud of it. By early evening the streets and canals of Venice were crowded with men, women and children in the finery of every previous age. There were cave people and eighteenth-century exquisites. There were ladies from the Second Empire and boys who might have served Lorenzo the Magnificent, soldiers from France and Spain, Huns and Mongols, Japanese samurai, Vikings, *condottieri*, courtesans and harlots, Amazons and Scythians, Chinese mandarins and a thousand varieties of *commedia* characters – Pierrots and Pierrettes, Harlequins and Harlequinas, grotesque old Pantaloons and sweet young Colombines, not to mention all the mooning *inamoratos* who, with guitars and lutes, wailed their passion to the skies or swaggered with a captured mistress on quilted arms.

Soon anyone not in costume or uniform became fair game for these strolling *commedia* actors so skilled at staging impromptu scenarios, usually from the classic repertoire. No one was safe. They would attack young and old alike, involving respectable grandfathers and their dignified dames as cheerfully as self-important youths and their squealing consorts. Willy-nilly all became characters in 'The Comedy of Venice'. For all the victims' threats or cries for mercy, the play would be performed from beginning to end frequently under the good-humoured gaze of local police or blackshirts who joined in the fun as enthusiastically as the rest of us.

Miranda Butter and I took pains to wear at least some sort of costume whenever we went out. I had bought a white papier mâché Trivelino mask, with bulbous nose and staring eyes, over which I wore a velvet cap. My ordinary suit was swathed in a cloak I had borrowed from da Bazzanno's house. The place was full of clothing abandoned by the previous occupants, much of it threadbare or worn, covering a period of a hundred years or more. In this store Miranda discovered a large, cowled cape of tarnished silver brocade and black velvet, which completely engulfed her. She wore a simple 'diamond' mask to match.

So that it would not clash with various traditional carnivals and festivals upon which Venice depended for much of her income, da Bazzanno's was held at this time in high summer. It meant that the disguises were often uncomfortable and could scarcely be worn in daytime. As the festival proceeded, we spent more and more of the sunlit hours at the *palazzo* indulging our pleasures without restraint or caution. Getting dressed only for dinner, we would merge with the masked crowds which flooded through the narrow alleys and tiny squares, a noisy, colourful, good-humoured tide, caught up in the ebb and flow of the city where brilliantly coloured barges and gondolas filled the canals with blazing light and every bridge was festooned with flags, bunting and happy students full of wine and faith and a transcendent belief in a golden future.

We could not fail to be involved in the general sense of celebration. When newspapers reported misery and disaster in all fields of human endeavour, here was the one country in Europe which actually had something to celebrate! That was the miracle of Mussolini's rule. If history, now the private property of Bolshevik Jewry, no longer acknowledges this miracle, why should I be shocked? The interests which presently control us do not wish us to know how much better life was then. The triumphs of democracy were to produce poverty and despair, murder and general bloodshed, a nightmare without foreseeable end. Was it not surprising if Italy was involved in a long love affair with herself?

A year before, the people had handed Il Duce the reins of responsibility and power. By popular assent, he became their *Dictator*, their Speaker. Italian engineering, with its style and dash, had already captured the world's imagination. Aeroplanes like the Macchi 52R, cars like the Lamborghini, locomotives, ships, bridges, dams and public works were all on a magnificent scale. Economically, Mussolini's personal ideas had proven it possible to escape economic disaster not merely by controlling the budget but by investing in public works. Hitler and Roosevelt learned how to do this from Mussolini but sadly Franco, the true reactionary, sold himself to the vested interests of a corrupt Church and Big Business before he ever came to power.

Franco never did free himself from a sentimental attitude towards international Jewry shared by many Latin Catholics. Even Mussolini was forced to accommodate the threat. Neither fascism nor dictatorship in themselves are sufficient remedy. In the end they depend upon the popular will and upon the resources, courage and character of the men who install them. I am the first to admit there have been very few successful fascist regimes. That was not Mussolini's fault. His imitators failed to grasp the most obvious fact – to achieve what Mussolini achieved, one must actually *be* a Mussolini! He inspired lesser men who were never able to match his achievement. To be Mussolini, one also had to be what Schiller called *Selig, welchen die Götter, die gnädigen, vor der Geburt schon liebten!* Or, in Mr Mix's laconic observation, 'born lucky'.

Sometimes in Venice I missed the Negro's dry wit and natural good sense, neither of which were dominant qualities in Maddy Butter's personality. Her eagerness to learn all I could teach her was an attractive trait but she was sometimes indiscriminate. She was a happy puppy, tongue hanging out, eyes bright and utterly trusting of a life that had never given her anything but the most marvellous rewards!

63

This quality is of course repellent in those Americans who display their cultural sophistication as if it were a flag when they are merely signalling their distance from the rest of their countrymen. They receive our sympathy and therefore our tolerance and as a result tend to believe that we are as isolated from our society as they feel from theirs. This, in turn, can prove an embarrassment.

Sometimes Miss Butter's provincial protestations of superiority (in which the name of every great artist of the past thousand years seemed to be <u>underlined</u>) made me a little suspicious. It was difficult to believe her so completely what she seemed.

I even wondered briefly if Seryozha was right and Maddy was a singularly clever Bolshevik agent, maybe even working for Brodmann's section. She shared one thing with most socialists – she discussed art as if it were a moral conviction rather than a source of sublime pleasure. Even the street mummers received her sober respect. While she had the appetites of a Barbary ape, typically she had even come up with some sound ethical reasons for indulging in cocaine and sex. Like the Arabs, Americans are forever coping with their puritanical inner conflicts and have no way merely of enjoying themselves.

When I proposed this, Maddy laughed. No doubt I had made a meaningless joke. Americans are as incapable as anyone of seeing themselves in others' eyes. Only a few of us, self-trained to study our own behaviour with the clinical tolerance of a good anthropologist, have the power to stand back and see the whole picture.

To avoid Maddy's intense conversations about love, life, art and politics, I took to spending as much time as possible in the streets. As soon as the sun began to set I would propose another costumed escapade, so we explored every corner of that relatively small city.

Tiring of the usual splendours of St Mark's Square, the Grand Canal or the Rialto Bridge, with their brilliantly costumed crowds and good-humoured drunks, we wandered further and further into suburbs. Even here the festival was celebrated. We still found it necessary to wear our rough-and-ready costumes to avoid unwanted attention from strolling comedians. We discovered tiny shops presided over by little wizened craftsmen who handled their wares as if they were precious children, and they were content to talk, displaying none of the subtle salesmanship for which Venetians are said to be famous. Indeed, we had been told the city was expensive and its citizens pirates to the last youth, yet we discovered trattorias and restaurants where the food was good and the prices were low, which was as well since I, of course, had no funds immediately available to me. I was forced to accept Miss Butter's generosity. She received an allowance from her father in Galveston as well as the fees paid by the *Houston Chronicle*, but this barely kept us. Da Bazzanno's hospitality was as open-handed as one might expect. Pleasant as it was, we did not wish to spend our entire time in Venice eating with old Signor da Bazzanno. His kindly cynicism scarcely suited our mood. By walking a little way and putting some distance between ourselves and the main thoroughfares and squares, we could eat very inexpensively.

One evening we crossed the Grand Canal at the San Simeone Bridge, discovering ourselves near the railway station. The area was full of cheap rooming houses and cafés, none of which attracted us, so we turned to the right, crossing the first bridge we came to. Here, hardly anyone was in costume and since it was a warm night, I threw back my cloak and removed my mask with some relief, holding it in my hand in case I needed to don it again.

The area was unlike any other I had visited in Venice. Some of the houses leaned as high as six storeys, threatening to sink into the mud beneath their own weight, and the whole place had the atmosphere of some sort of enclave. Troops of merrymakers came and went, but did not seem welcome. I soon realised we had entered the notorious Ghetto, the Jewish area of Venice, which had been here since the twelfth century and which provided us with the legend upon which Shakespeare based his oracular, yet almost philo-Semitic, play *Shylock; or, The Merchant of Venice*, which I had already seen in the excellent silent film version starring John Barrymore.

Only Jews had been allowed to build so high, by special agreement. The alternative would have been to extend the Ghetto area which, of course, nobody wanted. We were intruding and I became anxious to leave. I had no wish to give offence to the Jews. I knew how vengeful they could be. It has been fairly said that Jews have long memories and do not easily forgive a grudge. I already had Brodmann on my tail. I did not need an entire tribe of the Chosen People taking against me! The Ghetto was claustrophic. Narrow streets closed in on us. Brightly lit bakeries, butchers' shops and little coffee houses were everywhere. From their steamy windows dark eyes regarded us; dark hands stroked glistening black beards. The alien smell from the little restaurants was delicious, however, and reminded me of wonderful food I had eaten in Rome's Via Catalana a decade earlier. I was tempted to consider risking the wrath of the Sons of Shem and see if their love of money would conquer any antagonism they might feel towards us. We were hungry and had no idea how long it would take to find our way out of the Ghetto. Maddy Butter, with her usual happy insensitivity to the nuances of our environment, was delighted with everything she saw. We entered a square which seemed to have no exit and I realised to my discomfort that the building immediately ahead of us was a synagogue.

'I'm sure we're not welcome here,' I told her. My instinct said we should turn and go back the way we had come. But La Butter found the whole place wonderfully exotic. She stopped an old woman to ask her the name of the synagogue. The woman responded with a superficial friendliness but could not understand our Italian. When she replied, her accent was equally difficult. It had the strong Spanish sound of most Venetian speech. I asked her in Yiddish how we might get back to St Mark's Square. Either she affected not to understand me or was one of those Jews whose first language was Hebrew. Eventually she shrugged. With a hypocritical smile she continued on her way. Now Maddy saw a dark narrow opening leading out of the square. We headed for this – at the precise moment that a band of elaborately costumed merrymakers spilled from the alley into the gaslight. Urgently I tried to replace my mask and cape, but it was too late.

At once the gorgeously costumed players surrounded us. In raucous Italian they chided us for our 'nakedness,' our 'bad manners'. To be fair they were probably not all Jews. Their banter was good-natured enough. Their blows were delivered with balloons or cloth slapsticks. But even when I replaced my mask they were comically dissatisfied. We had to be 'educated', they announced, in 'appropriate behaviour'. Only then could we become true Venetians and save ourselves from expulsion. There was nothing for it but to go along with their game and put as good a face on it as possible. With a bow and an *avanti* or two, I gave myself up to the comedy.

We were to be the chief players, we learned, in a piece called *Deceiver Deceived*. I was assured I had all the best parts. All of them. I had seen this performed earlier in the Piazza San Sebastiano and had been quite unable to follow it. It involved the flourishing of some score of *commedia* masks, each of which was slightly larger than the previous one, designed to fit upon the other. The chief character was a lover who failed time and time again to cuckold an old man with a young wife. I called on him in the pretence that I was So-and-So the knife-grinder or Such-and-Such the upholsterer, minor characters in the *commedia*, with their own distinctive masks and personalities. All were well known to the local audience. We were forced into enveloping white smocks, and quarter-masks were fitted over our heads. Then we were turned this way and that until we were staggering with dizziness. It is impossible to conduct such an affair with any dignity. I have seen the people on *Sunday Night at the London Palladium* with those abominable compères goading people to speak ludicrous lines and perform ridiculous actions in a sketch even that grand master of communist gibberish Harry Pinta might disown! I have always been baffled as to why people should agree to such humiliation when their lives are not even threatened!

The game began:

First I was the fishmonger calling at the door with a basket of fish. As I was about to embrace my mistress, a creature dressed as a cat seized the papier mâché fish, forcing me to chase after it, to great applause. Happily my actor's instincts came to my rescue. I almost began to enjoy the charade. Maddy Butter, as my *amante*, had very little to do but simper and breathe heavily. I, however, began to play to the crowd. I was used to making the best of a bad stage and an unresponsive audience. Mrs Cornelius and I had toured America's West Coast in just such conditions.

Now I was an old woman selling apples. A third mask was set upon the second. The apple basket turned over and there was much comic chasing of papier mâché fruit. Again I received approving applause.

I found it difficult to see through so many pairs of eyeholes as the next mask was set upon my head. I was a butcher whose sausages were stolen just at the moment when Maddy lifted her rouged cheek to be kissed.

A fourth mask. I began to feel uncomfortable. I was a canary seller, whistling and chirping as best I could within the confines of the mask. Next I was a broadsheet jack. Yet no matter what my disguise, something always went wrong and I was frustrated in my designs.

Every time I donned a new mask, I became less and less able to see. Therefore, to the audience, my actions became funnier and funnier. I stumbled back and forth, bewildered by the shadows and the jumping gas jets, unable to distinguish the other actors or find my lover among them. Jewish hands spun me this way and that. Some directed me to Maddy, others to mincing mummers pretending to be women.

Surrounding us I glimpsed the mocking Hebrew faces, the huge dark eyes and oiled locks, the prominent noses and thick, red lips, who applauded each new caricature I was forced to assume. Was I the focus of their scorn? Had I misinterpreted them entirely? The grotesque papier mâché probosces grew longer until I was supporting a beak some two feet long while the weight of the accumulated masks began to drag my head forward. I found it difficult to hold my neck upright. I stumbled around seeking my 'lost love', locating her now only by her cries. Was Maddy panicking?

By now I was finding it almost impossible to breathe. I gasped, begging for a little relief. But my captors merely jeered and spun me round and round again.

I lost track of the masks. I was the dentist, the soldier, the gypsy and the Jew. I began to struggle for air. My heart was beating rapidly and every inch of clothing was soaked in sweat. The more I begged them to show common sense and mercy, the more they goaded me and added another mask. Baker, musician, prince and demigod. The less easily I supported the weight of the masks, the more grandiose became my roles. I was frightened now. Weeping, I was pushed backwards and forwards, my head pulling me downwards, my body racked with aches and pains, my legs weak and my hands nerveless. I cried for Maddy to help me, but she was joining in the fun. They all thought I was a wonderful actor. I was choking. I was deaf. I was blind. I was dying. Soon I would not be able to draw another breath!

Nothing I said would make them stop. They were utterly pitiless. Another mask was added. And another. I was drowning, I told them. They were killing me. This elicited massive applause from the Jews. I begged them to stop. Their only response was to demand yet another role for me. Was this how all actors ended their careers? Driven to their deaths by public demand?

'Please,' I begged them. 'Please. I can do no more. I am not in good health. I am choking!'

Almost mindless with panic, I wept and begged the Jews for their mercy. They chose to believe my pain a joke, a piece of superior acting, and applauded me further. I was beaten by their sticks. I was abused and humiliated by their fingers. I was tormented by their mockery. I was brutalised by their cruel demands.

I had entered a nightmare I might never escape. This could only grow worse. My Egyptian captivity had declined step by step into a horror my conscious mind hardly dared recall. Was this some dreadful repetition of that experience? I began to think they meant to kidnap me. Miss Butter was, after all, working for Brodmann. Was this perhaps a scheme of Brodmann's? Was he plotting in concert with his Ghetto brethren? They intended to drive me to suicide. For Brodmann this would be a satisfactory conclusion to a case obsessing him since he had relished my terrible shame at the hands of the Cossack, Grishenko. Did Brodmann live to enjoy my mortification over and over again?

'Brodmann!' I shouted. 'I have done nothing to you! For the love of God, Brodmann, let me go!' I reached out blind, pleading hands.

The mummers around me mocked the sound of my voice. They cawed and cackled and clucked. They gibbered and hissed and shrieked. They pinched and they poked and they tweaked at me. They were trying to open my trousers. Brodmann had revealed something about me. But he was lying. My father had lied. Even my mother, poor soul, thinking she was doing her best for me, even she lied. All have lied. Esmé betrayed me. You, too, lied to me.

Salachti. Der Scochet im Goluth. Salachti. Salachti. Jude, mach mores! Jude, mach mores! Kesteneist schrecklich? Nine. Nein. Meyne Engel? Meyne Freiheit? Lieblos, die Fremdeluft is. Sachlichkeit?

The fires danced and threatened. The shadows jeered. Strange little hands slipped under my clothing to fondle me. I felt an urgent need to vomit. But if I threw up, I would drown. The masks would see to that.

They forced me to perform another scenario. I was a matron. A queen seeking her long-lost daughter. From somewhere I heard Maddy's voice. I stumbled towards the sound, lost my footing on the cobbles and fell forward, running to catch up with myself, the weight of the masks dragging me down. I expected at any moment to step off the edge into a canal to fill my lungs with that foul water, the accumulated waste of Venetian Jewry.

At that moment I had crossed some threshold between reality and fantasy. I stood on the brink of the Inferno with no Dante to guide me. I shouted for Maddy to help me, to pull me back into the familiar world. But my voice could not be heard. My mouth was full of swelling paper. Nothing would come out. I could barely draw in air. I struggled with the Jews. I beat at them. And from all sides came their laughter, cruel, rough voices, a prodding and pushing. I was buried in masks. I was drowning in masks. I screamed. My voice filled my body. I began to choke. 'Please! No more!'

Again the masks dragged my head down. I lost my footing in something slippery. Again I fell. Now there was no one to catch me. The great weight of papier mâché dragged me to the cobbles. I was on my knees. I heard water. The Ghetto and its sinister denizens had claimed me. Suddenly I was back in the *shtetl*, with those hands, those clutching fingers, those eyes. There they had wanted to kill me. It was the same. I would die. And no poet to save me. No Jew from Arcadia.

'Why are you afraid?' asked the Jew in the *shtetl*.

They came out of the synagogue and they surrounded me. They put a piece of metal in my womb. You say that this is all my fantasy. But it was reality, then. We knew no other reality. A fantasy only for those of us who were not its victims.

It happened so suddenly. And then we were engulfed.

NINE

I fly no flag, I said. I am my own man. I felt weak. A chill had come to my stomach like a piece of cold metal that can never be warmed, even by blood. Blood alone could quench the fires. We drowned in it, and we were grateful.

The Jew said: 'You idiots, I am a doctor. Quickly! The poor devil's asphyxiating. Get those masks off him before they kill him!'

City of sleeping goats, city of crime, city of crows. The little boys sing untruthful songs. The synagogues are burning. You are alive, said the Jew. You are safe. He had a job on a newspaper in Odessa and lost it. But it was peaceful, he said, in Arcadia.

I find it impossible to understand the motives of such people.

I lay in a little white bed. The sheets were damp.

'What is wrong with him?' asked Maddy Butter in halting Italian.

I had no interest in this. I was sleeping over the stove while my mother ironed. My father had gone. I was glad of it. He brought only tension. I longed for my familiar food, for the honest warmth of home, and it seemed for a little while that I had recaptured everything I had lost. I was in one of the houses off the square, Maddy told me. I was in shock, she said. I had a fever. I had caught something from the water, perhaps.

I thought I noticed Esmé smiling at me from the dark curtains of the room. Everywhere I looked I saw a friend. Captain Brown brought me a drink. Esmé cooled my forehead. My mother prayed for me.

'We must take him back,' said Miss Butter. 'He must be moved. You have been very kind.'

I did not want to leave. I was home. I wept for Kiev and the days of my greatest security. I wept for Odessa and my greatest happiness. I wept for the future that was stolen from us. They all had guns. They were all greedy. They had become nothing but appetite

71

and they fed on destruction. 'Let me stay,' I begged. 'We cannot allow it to begin again. This is our chance. This is our chance to change the story. Let me stay.'

They took me to an ebony barge swaying on scarlet water. It smelled of flour and blood. They laid me down on the sacks. I could not swallow my grief. Little birds flew out of my mouth; tawny rats gnawed at my genitals. They put a piece of metal in my womb. It is a Star of David. 'You will be well soon,' said the doctor. 'You should rest. Your friend, signorina, is of a very highly strung disposition.'

'He is a genius,' she explained. 'An artist.'

A figure rose above my head. He carried a long spear which he plunged again and again into the flowing marble around the barge. I wanted desperately to see his face, but he would not show it to me. Dante, I sought my Virgil.

They said it was Charon and the river was the Styx, but this could not be. I was freed, I said. I have been made whole in the Land of the Dead and Anubis is my friend. They should not force me to make that journey again. It was not fair, I said. I have paid the price. I have answered the questions. I have done the deed. I am clean. I have eaten only clean food. I have put on only clean garments. I have purified my thoughts. I have purified my loins. I am redeemed. Let me stay. It is my home. Let me stay.

The black marble waters were silent. I lifted my head and looked down. A thousand golden eyes stared back at me, the eyes of beasts, unforgiving, ungiving, unkind. I wept for my lost future, for my despoiled past. *Gott herrscht, winkend, leitend, wie Wesen auch, die frei sind, handeln, herrscht für die Gegenwart und für die Zukunft! Spricht durch Tat auch, welche die Sterblichen tun, die Gottheit? Weg zur Freiheit?* I do not think so.

I looked for mercy. I found none. Only sympathy. The little girls lifted their voices. Their skirts were like fresh fallen snow, they were so pure. *Kyrie eleison!* What more must I do? I yearned to kiss his long hands. I cannot deny it – he was a Jew. He showed me a line of poetry. It meant nothing. Love grows from within. There is a coil in my womb. It is copper. It conducts electricity. It is cold. They put it there. It forbids love. Ask me any scientific question. I am afraid of betrayal. There was never enough love. We walked into the twilight. They had pissed on Odessa. You could smell it all the way to Arcadia. From Moldavanka came the stench of old smoke. 'You're a hard one to read,' I said. I could scarcely stop myself from touching him. I wanted his gentleness. I looked for my childhood. Everything was rubble. I decided I must go to the station.

I cry out. My voice is amplified by the bridges and aqueducts. It echoes across the rooftops and comes down the alleys. I must reach the station.

We will get you there soon, they said. Be quiet now. You will wake the city. But my buttocks were alive with ancient pain. Grishenko's whip rose and fell. Brodmann watched in gloating triumph.

I must get to the station. I must get away.

Softly they reassured me but I could not trust those Jews. How could I?

The barge moved through darkness. Too late. We crossed a border. I heard distant laughter. The sky was full of flames and sparks.

They are burning us, I said. They are burning us to death. They have set fire to the *shtetl*.

Just a display, they said. A celebration.

I heard the shrieks and the bangs. I smelled the smoke. Not safe to stay, I said. I cried for my mother and for Esmé. I loved her so much. I wanted her with me. Why did she lie to me? They were all I ever wanted. But how I had longed to fly!

The city of Venus is destroyed. The city of Odysseus rises from the ruins of our common dream. The city of Venus sinks into legend but the city of Odysseus endures, a monument to the Age of Reason. Why could they not leave us alone? What was our crime? We are drowning in our own anger, I said. Nothing is solved. We are making fresh problems. Nothing is reconciled. Blood for blood, they said. Blood for blood. The black barges took the corpses to the coast. Black blood filled the rivers. The streams were viscous and became sewers full of entrails.

The Greeks wept for their stolen souls. They took our future to replace it with an illusion. So many false promises. The black barge carried me through tall canyons. Little birds filled my mouth. I could no longer tell them the truth. The spear thrust at the water. Cruel eyes stared back at me. I discovered no warmth in her breast. I told her that she must escape. She did not understand. It is no longer safe here, I said. Her white arms enclosed me. She tried to make me sleep but I struggled. I could not afford to sleep, I told her.

I asked her to find Mrs Cornelius. Mrs Cornelius can help. My guardian angel. But she could not hear me. We will take you home,

73

she said. You will be safe there. But how could she be telling me the truth? There was no home here any longer that was not dangerous. The dark rivers led only to the Land of Death. They must turn the boat. There was red flame on the horizon. Thick, grey smoke boiled through the canyons and engulfed us. I began to freeze. I am dying, I said. I will die without my past. But the past was dead.

I was lifted in the arms of the boatman. I looked up into his face. Full of distant pity, the face of the Jew in Marrakech stared at me. He had stared until the rats ate his eyes.

They always eat the eyes first, I said. They want no witness to their infamy.

We thought we were cleansing Russia of her sin, cleansing her of the evil within. History is a traitor. Virtue is mocked.

I struggled. But the Jew was too strong for me.

He is the Turnface. That which I execrate is dirt. I eat it not, that I may appease my Genius. Let me not drink lye. Let me not advance blindly into the Netherworld. I am both Man and Woman. I am my own child. I bear my own child. I am the child of myself, which is both Man and Woman. I am created in purity. The Turnface carries my child to the shore. He places me in the Land of Death. When I call to him he is already upon the water, his spear piercing the dark surface below which the Beast swims. By killing myself I can escape the Beast. The Beast has no soul. The Beast cannot follow into the Land of Death.

I am carried through deeper darkness. There are galleries and cloisters which murmur with rage. They are hung with rotting canvases. The fabric disintegrates, falling into rags upon the filthy flagstones. Rusting chains support lamps clogged with the dust of decades; their brass is covered with a patina of betrayal, of ruined dreams and lost causes; all the lies which coagulate here have turned into material filth. No fires burn, yet the shadows slide and twist within the walls. Faces plead from the crumbling plaster.

'You are safe,' she says. 'You are home.' But she does not understand. The Turnface has taken me from my home. Now I am alone in the Land of Death. Must I pay another price? How much must I pay and for how long?

I was carried into the citadel of decay. Nothing is allowed to live. They cared for nothing. They valued nothing. They lived only for power and public glory. Their houses are filled with shame. Their houses fill with excrement. They forget their history and their honour. All they once valued, they now despise. They betray their own souls and for that there is no forgiveness.

Those naked youths drift on a bloody river and the girls scream beneath the starving bodies of their captors. The Turk grins to see his victory. Constantinople has fallen. Tsargrad has fallen. And we, protectors of her ancient virtue, we too have fallen, unwept, unburied.

We too have fallen.

She touched her fingers to my mouth. She stroked my eyes. You are safe. You are home. Sleep and you will be well.

But if I sleep I will die.

Something Americans do not understand.

She is soft against me. As if she can pour her own life into me. She cools me with her tears. But I know her strength. It is almost gone. And then I will be alone. I must get to the station. I must escape. We must find the City.

We will go to Rome, she promises. As soon as you are well. You have a fever. You have caught a chill. We will get you something to make you better.

The old man looks down on me. His face is framed by his cowl. He speaks in a low voice, but I cannot understand his language. He uses a dialect. Perhaps it is Etruscan. His blood has dried in his veins but his mouth is sweet. His eyes contain baffled love.

He sings to me. He sings a song they sang in Ur as the first stones were laid. He sings a song of birth, as if he tries to coax the child from my womb. But my child is the child of Death. My child is dead.

He sings. He places his lips upon mine. He breathes the air of centuries into my withered lungs. He blows dust into my eyes. He blows dust into my nostrils. He blows dust into my ears. But still sleep will not come. To sleep is to die, I explain. Not here, he says. Here you are safe. But I am not safe. How could I be safe in this place where all is decay and the very stones rot, collapsing to atoms before the advance of my enemies? I witness an illusion. I see no substance to this house save the substance of corruption. Worms feast upon the library. Worms feast upon memories. Lice infest the carpets. When you tread on them you sink in the pile of luxury. Only when you lift your feet, hanging with maggots, do you understand how you have left your prints in living matter.

That's the only mark one makes upon Time, he says.

That is all you leave for others to follow.

No, he said. There is more. You must stay. You must go back.

I told him to withdraw. He had made himself my enemy. I could no longer trust him. My only chance is to get to the station. My only chance.

He was sorrowing when he went away. I believe he thought he was helping me.

Then her softness took the last of my strength. But I did not care. She had promised to help me find the station.

I still have no real memory of leaving the Palazzo da Bazzanno. Maddy Butter, in scarcely any better condition than I, accompanied me to the railway terminal. Fiorello da Bazzanno himself came to wave us goodbye. He regretted he could not let us have the keys of his flat. He had already loaned them to another friend. But a call to Signora Sarfatti in Rome had been enough to secure us a lovely little cottage off the Via Nicola Porpora near the Zoological Gardens. He knew it. We would find it a miniature paradise. He would join us in the capital as soon as the festival was over. He was solicitous. 'My dear friend! Your travels have exhausted you, and I was too thoughtless a host to notice. You will rest in Rome, and when I get there we shall relax together. Then, I insist, you must meet Il Duce. He will not want to let you go!'

My experience of the previous night had certainly depleted my nerves. I could hardly lift my head to thank him. I was scarcely aware of my surroundings. Everything had taken on a phantasmagoric quality. The contrasts were stronger, the angles were sharper, the shadows more dramatic. It was as if, dazed, I was watching a Technicolor film in which the brightness had been dramatically heightened.

Our first-class compartment was everything I remembered from the great days of the Russian Imperial Railways. The company had paid considerable attention to the decor. Glowing mahogany was inset with brass and walnut, upholstery was rich black and gold. Deep armchairs had their own tables, electric lamps and service bell. We found magazines and newspapers in all European languages, a small library of books in Italian, French, English and German, a fresh-air system, iced water and a thoroughly stocked bar. For all her experience of Pullmans, Maddy had never been on a train like it. She was delighted with everything. The sensation of luxury began to lift my spirits a little, too.

I had no desire to take a last look at Venice. Instead, I drew the

76

curtains and closed my eyes, glad to sleep. The train drew away from the City of St Mark, slowly gathering speed and turning west towards Padua on the first stage of our journey to Rome.

I hardly noticed the passing of the first few hours until the grey-haired steward arrived to make up our beds. Chatting to us, he laid out the crisp sheets with expert skill. Did we have everything we needed? Did we wish to have a light supper served in our compartment? Clearly the signor was a little unwell. Was there anything he could do for us?

We thanked him and ordered a supper of salmon and salad which we washed down with a little champagne and a glass or two of excellent wine. The meal cleared, I laid out several generous lines of cocaine to speed our recovery. I know of nothing like that life-sustaining drug for replenishing lost energy. In this alone Freud and I were agreed.

When we had savoured *la neve* we opened our curtains to look at the dark hills and occasional lights of the evening landscape. Maddy wept, held me in her arms and told me how concerned she had been for me. 'Those people almost *killed* you! If it hadn't been for that doctor, heaven knows what might have happened.'

I considered what his motive had been. She was surprised. Still the innocent American, she thought the Jew had acted out of nothing but kindness. I agreed that this was possible. I had experienced the phenomenon before, in Russia.

'You spoke much of Russia last night,' said Maddy Butter. 'I could hardly understand a word. But sometimes you used English. Sometimes French. German, I think. I couldn't make much sense of it.'

Anxious in case I had inadvertently betrayed a trust or been indiscreet, I asked her what I had said.

'You spoke of Odessa and Kiev, of your mother. You were going to meet her in London. She is with a Mr Green. Who is Esmé?'

'Esmé is dead,' I told her.

'You cared for her. Was she your sister?'

I nodded. 'Killed by anarchists in Ukraine, 1921.'

'And Kolya?'

'Dead,' I said. 'Lost in the Sahara.'

Her sympathetic fingers touched my hand. 'And Mrs Cornelius? What happened to her?'

'She's a friend. My Hollywood co-star.' If I was uncomfortable

77

with this questioning, at least it gave me the opportunity to explain any mysteries to her and protect whatever secrets had to be protected.

'Your father gave you a bad time, didn't he?' Her voice was balmy with sympathy. 'Was he a monster? What did he do?'

'He took a knife to me,' I said. 'He cut my future out of me. He cut the mark of the Jew on me. I have already explained all this.'

'He was a *mohel*?'

'Of course not! He was a class traitor. A socialist. It was his notion of hygienic science. He believed in rationalism as others believe in Christ. He put the mark of death on me. It is hard to forgive him for that. But he, too, is dead now, I'm sure.'

'He wasn't a Jew?'

I smiled at this. 'There are no Jewish Romanoffs, Maddy. Isn't that something of a contradiction in terms?'

My gentle sarcasm chastened her. She apologised. She knew very little of what she called 'White Russian' politics. I had been reluctant to talk of my more painful past, I said. While I was by no means of a secretive disposition, there were too many others who had not escaped. I had to watch what I said. Again came the memory of Seryozha's suspicion. I could not believe her a Bolshevik agent. But I had heard of more unlikely things. The Bolsheviks had a way of seducing young people and making them do things they would never normally contemplate. A small part of me remained sensibly cautious. What if her own father were somehow under threat?

Still, even as we moved closer to the very heart of the new Roman Empire, I felt the shadow of Brodmann falling over me. Was it possible for him, or one like him, to follow me to paradise? I honestly prayed that my fears were groundless. I must admit it was not difficult to relax and forget any pursuit within the security of Mussolini's great citadel of humane and self-respecting Christendom, that model to the rest of Europe.

In the *Popolo d'Italia*, the newspaper the steward brought us the next morning, we read how Italy was now the envy of the world. From Austin, Texas, to Zagreb, Yugoslavia, Mussolini was emulated everywhere. Foreign politicians were constantly calling on their governments to follow the lead of Il Duce. In Bali, for instance, he was known as *Il Tigre della Roma*. In homes as far apart as Australia and Finland portraits of Mussolini took pride of place.

Everywhere the flags of a reborn and defiant Italy were raised. As we looked from the window, we saw the reality of smartly painted stations, bold posters and well-ordered countryside. We opened the windows and breathed warm air laden with the smell of corn and oil, of poppies and horsebells. Cheerful peasants would pause at their labours in the fields and wave to us; smartly dressed blackshirts would offer us the Fascist salute, and wholesome young girls would smile, full of that spirit of hope which had swept the land.

Miranda remarked how all the colours seemed so much brighter and sharper, how even the blue of the sky was more intense. She said that, though she had already fallen in love with Italy, returning with me made her feel more fully alive than she had ever imagined possible. I was a magician. My example had taught her to listen to her blood, to follow her heart and enjoy the great relish for existence which now suffused her mind and body. She was beginning to understand, she said, how I was one of the world's great teachers. She was privileged to be with me as I journeyed to Rome.

'In Rome,' she said, 'you will be able to fulfil your genius.'

I assured her that such faith sustained me. I would not disappoint her. Da Bazzanno had promised me an audience with Mussolini. All I needed was half an hour with him. Then I could explain all my plans for the scientific wonders I could offer which would continue to enhance Italian prestige.

As a celebration of success to come we enjoyed some more of Shura's first-class cocaine. Locking the door of our compartment and closing the curtains, we made love while the fields and villages of Umbria sped by in all their golden glory, painting our bodies with their almost mystical light. We might have died in Venice and been transported to heaven.

The powerful train made steady progress through the mellow afternoon. At last, exhausted, we slept.

Our steward awoke us, tapping politely on the door to warn us that we were now soon to pull into Rome Central where the train terminated. I drew the curtains. We dressed and packed. I felt the train slow significantly. Looking out of our compartment I saw uniformed porters and police moving slowly by, watching the train's arrival.

Having at last completed our preparations, we descended somewhat belatedly from the train, our baggage carried by a handsome young porter. I paused for a moment to admire the great colonnades, soaring into misty arches and beams. This was merely a taste of the magnificence that was modern Rome.

Under Mussolini's personal guidance old buildings were being torn down. Fine new avenues were created. The enduring monuments of the ancients had been restored and the roads around them cleared. Our taxi took us past all the signs of this enormous project. When it was completed, it would rival anything the classical world had known. It would make New York or Paris seem like mere sketches for cities. Where others erected molehills, Mussolini made plans for great shimmering pyramids!

The whole of Rome was like a huge Hollywood stage, full of busy carpenters, masons and technicians, all working around the clock to create a reality from the fantasy. Sometimes the taxi had to steer around a heap of rubble where some old church had stood or a pit prepared for the foundations of some great modern skyscraper. You could smell the fresh sawdust, the stone chippings, the heat of drills and the drying paint. Sunshine flung great shadows across the broad streets. Everywhere we saw the face of Il Duce, a model to all who followed. These posters encouraged Italians to keep their aspirations high and never settle for the second-rate.

Every other person proudly wore a smart uniform. Women were elegantly dressed. Their children were in the very latest styles. Even the dogs seemed to walk with dignified self-respect, while the cats that, as in Venice, were everywhere, regarded the passing show with a kind of lazy hauteur. Overnight every feline in Rome had been turned into a noble lion.

Nowhere did we see the squalor I had witnessed in Morocco or Egypt. Rome's streets were swept and the buildings clean. Marble and granite gleamed. Silken banners billowed in the breeze. Terraces were brilliant with flowers and shrubs. I was strongly reminded of the beautiful sets which had made Griffith's *Intolerance* such a magnificent spectacle. Griffith had commissioned Italian masons to create those sets. Their same style was everywhere in Rome. The columns and arcades might have been made for De Mille's *Ben-Hur*. As we rode along one of the magnificent avenues I felt almost like a triumphant charioteer responding to the greetings of cheering crowds.

We turned a corner. A troop of cavalry, all scarlet, gold and green, advanced towards us. The taxi stopped to watch them pass. Here were Mussolini's fine young soldiers, stern beneath their heavy helmets, prepared to defend their emperor and empire to the last. I found it impossible not to compare them to praetorians. Another few hundred yards and we encountered a column of smart marching infantry followed by two armoured cars. Their gay awnings and polished brass giving texture to the scene, the cafés bustled with customers, windows reflected brilliant light flooding the whole city, creating a glowing aura. Every child, every animal, every plant took on an added reality.

Of course, Maddy Butter was familiar with all this. For me the change was a revelation. Maddy told me she, too, saw Rome in a wholly new dimension. Her senses had been brought fully to life by me. She spoke of me as her 'mentor'. I, of course, was familiar only with Rome's bohemian quarter in 1920, before Mussolini had saved his country from the tawdriness and failure of hope which had characterised it before. This Rome was scarcely the same city. Now the public monuments and modern buildings were as fine as anything raised in the great years of Rome's ancient glory. She had been transformed. Again she was a city fit for gods.

Amused by my astonishment at this transformation, Maddy pointed out piazzas, avenues and statues erected since the coming of Fascism. 'Signor Mussolini has a theatrical sense,' she said. 'A love of the dramatic. All this was designed personally by him.'

'He clearly understands the purpose of architecture,' I agreed, 'which is to enshrine and encourage the aspirations of the nation. Such monuments give hope and a sense of security, but they also make people proud of themselves. They must appeal to our sense of myth.'

She nodded intelligently. She was a wonderful pupil. She repeated how lucky she was to have a lover so wise in the ways of the world. 'The intelligence of a scientist. The sensitivity of an artist.'

I accepted her praise. 'If, like Mussolini, one has a moral purpose, a duty to one's fellow man, an understanding of the public will, then one informs one's work with these qualities and makes them appeal to the mass of people. This is what one learns in Hollywood. With the talkies, I suspect, the habit of *showing* the public what one means – as opposed to merely discussing it – is disappearing.'

I have always had the ability to predict the future. It is a heavy burden. One I sometimes wish I never had to carry. Now Rome and Hollywood are lost, gone the way of Athens and Constantinople, merely names for things which were once great.

In those days Rome was again the repository of all we most admired and desired, the exemplar of all we most valued. She was a beacon of sanity and decency in a world beginning to fall into acrimonious civil unrest and cruel vendetta. She had become everything so many of us desired. Lesser men would destroy this dream, just as they destroyed Griffith.

Now the wind drifts through empty cloisters and abandoned rooms. Ruined statues, tattered backdrops, rotting costumes are testament to the power and the purpose of our ruined dream. Ash falls on hollow masonry, on spoiled brick and crumbling stone, on the machinery of all our hopes. At least I knew Rome and Hollywood in the blazing years of their power; at least I played my part in their triumph. I resisted for as long as I could resist. The mean-spirited little men dragged greatness into dirty anonymity. I raised my sword against Big Business and International Zionism. I was defeated. They stole our holiest names and made them wretched and worthless.

The taxi drove on through wider streets, between taller trees, through ordered sanity, through that indefinable radiance.

Suddenly La Butter seized my hand and drew it to her lips. I was not surprised by this expression of passion.

Everywhere was purity. Everywhere the white walls and red roofs of the narrow streets into which we now turned radiated warmth and comfort. Not only the great public buildings reflected national dignity and self-respect; that quality was evident in the most ordinary domestic scenes. I could not help but absorb it all with my cinema-trained instincts. Griffith himself might have taken the whole of Rome for his sets, positioned his crowds, his cameos, his long-shots, his pans, his close-ups. I half expected to hear a voice shout 'Camera ready' and another call 'Action!' Thrilled, I looked around me knowing I would soon have the privilege of meeting the producer of this great miracle, the master architect of the New Europe.

Maddy Butter shared my joy. She pressed her soft lips to my cheek.

'Welcome to the Future,' she said.

TEN

Between wakefulness and sleeping we have most of us had the illusion of hearing voices, scraps of conversation, phrases spoken in unfamiliar tones. Sometimes we attempt to attune our minds to hear more, but we are rarely successful. We call these 'hypnagogic hallucinations' – the beginning of the dreams we shall later experience as we sleep.

At first they were no more than nighmares dispersing when I opened my eyes. By the time of my second visit to Rome, I was receiving the most intense and terrible visions. I took them to be a warning.

At first there was just the one dream every night: against the black morning poplars a small woman walks her poodle up the avenue. We seem to be in France. Mist rises from the river, rippling silver, reflected in her eyes and skin. She turns to me. Her hair is white, touched with the dawn's gold. A halo. My mother? Or Esmé? I am not sure. Sometimes they are the same. With agonised sadness in her eyes she murmurs the news. 'Beware,' she says. 'Your good works betray you, for Satan is already triumphant.'

That dream was merely the disturbing prologue.

Later I came to witness all she meant.

They say that I deceive myself. I would suggest we all deceive ourselves. But some fundamental truths cannot be denied. Is a vision any less authentic because it is commonplace?

Those of you who recall D. W. Griffith's magnificent epic *Intolerance*, with its profoundly subtle message, will remember how the gigantic ivory elephants come to life, threatening to crush the tiny figures of the people gathered before them. My second sight of Rome awed me just as those elephants awed the Babylonians. I half expected to be crushed by all that magnificence. As in a Griffith film, one wonderful reality overlaid another, ancient and modern, giving profound meaning to everything I saw. The arrogance and cruelty of the past were contrasted with the positive aspects of the present, assuring us that progress was possible and that the noblest human aspirations would ultimately prevail.

The film tells us that we have come far but have far to go and that, it seemed to me, was the message of the new Roman architecture rising among the magnificence of the old. A contradictory message, perhaps. A complex one, certainly, which required the highest type of mind to read it. Mussolini, in those years of his greatness, had that mind. He could see the broad picture. His genius inspired others to complete the details. Of course, his compromise with the Roman Catholic Church, his passion for women and his fascination with Jews brought him to a humiliating end as Hitler's puppet. He, who had inspired the movement of world fascism, was caught cowering in a borrowed German greatcoat, slaughtered and hung upside down like meat in the Milan marketplace. Yet when I knew Il Duce, he was worshipped with an intensity most Italians reserved only for the Pope.

Like Hitler in his first years, Mussolini made women ecstatic. He would have his aides select from the letters he received and deliver a fresh female to his office every weekday afternoon. The Italian people loved him for it. His virility reflected the virility of their race. This much I already knew from common talk and ordinary observation. Certain individuals carry a kind of magnetism which makes them irresistible to the masses and which Virginia Woolf called 'It'. She, admittedly, was referring to the pornographer and *arabiste* whose films are so fashionable these days.

As far as I am concerned *Lady Chatterton*, *Odysseus*, Hank Janson and *The Well of Loneliness* are all the same. Janson himself agreed with me. He was the only one of that crowd I knew well. I helped him with the details he needed of the Spanish Civil War. He was not present, of course, but had been forced to live in Spain when the courts found him guilty. He had nothing but contempt for the others. They had all done considerably better out of their stuff, he said, than he had from his. He had made the mistake of selling the copyrights of both the books and his identity! Others were now writing new novels using his name!

Janson was a bitter man in his last years, as were Gerhardie and Priestley. Both were deeply jealous of Kingsley Amis and his angry young Turks and hated their crudeness. I met Amis several times.

84

The first time was in the West End when he was posing for a suit commercial (he supplemented his income with endorsements of various products, especially wines and spirits). I knew the photographer. I remember Amis made fun of my accent and would not even listen when I offered him my manuscript and a chance to collaborate. At the time his words hurt me worse than the Cossack Grishenko's whip. From the booze on his breath, the lighting man said they were amazed that he could still stand up. That filth he wrote already weighed on his conscience. There is Welsh blood there. I was unmoved by his insult. After all, I have rubbed shoulders with some of the finest artists in the world and have been on first-name terms with the most powerful men in history. But I was depressed that a national figure should so lower himself. I have since learned that rudeness and self-involvement is characteristic of all but a few writers. They are jealous, petty, envious creatures. Their sense of their own importance is astonishing! I have known dictators with more humility.

Years earlier I had fallen in love with Rome. Now all the pleasure returned, though tinged with a little sadness as I thought of Esmé, who had betrayed me in the end. I found it hard to blame her. She had been a child. She hardly knew what she was doing. For a little while, at least, I had rescued her from the squalid life she had now, doubtless, returned to.

Signora Sarfatti had, we discovered, been wonderfully generous. She had loaned us a magical little half-timbered house in its own walled garden, off the Via Pencioni, bordering the gardens of the Villa Borghese and near the zoo. Reminiscent of the Normandy Apartments in which I'd stayed while in Hollywood, the three-roomed cottage stood in its own tiny courtyard adorned with old masonry and an erratic fountain. Twice a day the dryads and sylphs who adorned it moved into dramatic action, spouting, pouring, gushing, gurgling from almost every orifice. The cottage was decorated in a mixture of rustic and modern taste, which I found pleasing, save for some of the paintings, which were in the latest neurotic styles. The worst of them I turned to the wall before collapsing on the bed.

I had been so eager to leave that I had not given myself enough time to recover in Venice. For the first few days, I lay in the massive bed, which Maddy turned towards the balcony so that I could see into the lovely garden with its fig trees, its orange and white bougainvillea, its profusion of golds and browns in the tawny sunlight. I stared, hour after hour, into a living tapestry. From the nearby zoo came the shriek of a large bird of prey or the yawning roar of a lion. Occasionally the scene would change and become the long, dark avenue of poplars, the winter river, the woman walking her dog turning to warn me. Then began my vision of the ministry of Satan upon Earth and in Heaven and Hell. Clad in the wealth of the Fall, Satan sat upon the throne of all three Spheres. God was overthrown. The arch-fiend triumphed. The Good and the Just were singled out for special punishment. What was our crime?

What was our crime? Perhaps we indulged ourselves in too many sentimental lies. We should have been better prepared. We should have understood our predicament. Now I stand humiliated before our grinning conqueror while the cruellest, the strongest, the greed-iest, the most wicked are rewarded, elevated to the highest command. The rest of us, who tried to make some positive use of our lives, are forced to bow before the will of the Great Lord and are used in any way that pleases him.

I understand such tyranny. I have been its victim more than once. I live in the shadow of eternal fear. Shall I become its victim again? My vision would not leave me, night or day. My vision still comes unexpectedly without warning. I am assured that eternity would be no better. I am doomed to perpetual torment. Such is my reward, for choosing the conquered side. My mistake was to believe in Jesus Christ. The price of idealism is disappointment. The price of idealism is despair.

Unquestionably someone had attempted to poison me in Venice. But I was recovering. The doctors Maddy brought were all baffled. If I had murmured the word 'Cheka', no doubt they would have understood too well and never returned! My old friend Brodmann was rarely far away in those days, gloating over what he had seen in the Cossack camp. No doubt he took particular pleasure in his recollections. At times like these the pain of the whip always returned.

I had not remembered Rome as so Mediterranean a city. Gradually I grew stronger. I took short drives with the fashionably dressed Maddy in the car she had rented. American girls are always resourceful. Their culture demands they be both men and women. I relaxed as she took charge. I delighted in white terraces spilling foliage and bright blossoms down into gardens filled with trees and shrubs. I was comforted by the orderly parks and squares. Mussolini was transforming the city architecturally, and making her the hub of the new Roman Empire. He had filled her with a fresh, inner light. Even the remaining poorer quarters, with their twisting medieval streets, the churches, shops, decaying villas, apartment blocks and public buildings all crowded together, exuded an atmosphere as lively as my own Moldavanka in Odessa.

Mysteriously, although we left messages for them, our two greatest friends were not in Rome to see us. We understood that both Fiorello and Margherita were involved in important affairs of state. At such times Il Duce commanded every moment of their waking lives. As soon as I was well enough, I took Maddy to some of the wonderful haunts I had first discovered with my darling Esmé. The increasingly delicious young American was learning what she called 'Continental ways' with eager alacrity.

We visited the Ristorante Mendoza, where I had spent so many happy hours. Had they seen Laura Faschetti or any of the old gang? They were nervously discreet, though friendly enough. These days it was no longer fashionable to have a left-wing clientele. I did bump into a couple of my old acquaintances but was deeply disappointed. Their only interest was in mocking me or describing with some bitterness how this or that person had 'sold out'. The failure's whine the world over. At least Mendoza's fried artichoke was as wonderful as always. Maddy was amazed at the variety and richness of the food. She had believed until then, she said, that all Jewish food was lox, blintzes and latkes.

What Americans call 'Jewish' food is actually East European. Most of it is familiar to me. But the Jews had to pretend they had invented it, just as the Greeks cannot bear the idea that their entire cuisine is Turkish. They have a saying in Albania: How do you tell the difference between Turkish cuisine and Greek? Answer: One has pork.

Believe me, this is not a palatable notion, but it is the truth. Aggressive Moslemism (and it is by nature aggressive) is something I shall resist to my dying day. My quarrel with that fool across the street is not with his choice of religion. Anyone should have a right to follow his conscience; I have never said anything else. But I hate that grinning fool's cynical wickedness as he passes off his kebabs and shleftikos as authentic. Not only does the public think he's Greek, they think his hideous muck is typical. Maybe I should not blame him. After all, his customers are scarcely gourmets.

Rome in those days was also full of archaeologists. Il Duce had ordered a huge programme of public works designed to resurrect the best of the past and build new monuments which would be their equal. Everywhere you went you found some pit full of babbling foreigners chipping and dusting and studying for all they were worth. Myself, I had little time for them. Their unhealthy obsession with the past showed no respect for the future.

They are all the same, these people. They are suspiciously unwholesome. They grub around in antique filth as if this will give them some insight into the aspirations and inspiration of their ancestors. Is there some profit motive I do not understand? I saw this boy, he could not have been ten. He was selling a stained-glass window in the Blenheim Arms. Only I was outraged. Mrs Cornelius said it would look nice in her front room. Where would you keep it? I asked. What would you tell the vicar? He has no doubt robbed a church. Don't be silly, she said, that's out of one of them big villas up Talbot Road. Drink up and be happy, Ivan. She has a tolerance for thieves. Perhaps she is right. Most of her friends and relatives are rogues of some description. Until these middle-class novelists and TV producers started moving into the area everyone else in Notting Hill lived by and from crime. Fit company, I suppose. I am a fool to notice. Every shopkeeper in Portobello Road says I should 'allow' for some pilfering. They expect even their staff to rob them. It's human nature, they say, pretend you don't notice. I suppose it is cheaper than paying higher wages or having someone keep an eye on the stock every minute of the day. Live and let live? Where would we be today if Mussolini and Hitler had taken that attitude?

Once a week for many years I would meet my old friend Major Nye in the Lyons Corner House across from Victoria Station. He had retired from the army after the war. He ran a market garden somewhere near the Kent coast. He supplemented his pension, he said, by working as a bookkeeper for a firm of solicitors in Palace Street. But he kept in touch with his army chums. Sometimes I met them. They were rather pale, scrawny old men with white moustaches and neatly cut white hair. Embarrassed to be wearing civilian suits like ill-fitting uniforms, they were forever fingering their ties and asking after one another's well-being. Colonels and majors and occasionally captains. All in Civvy Street during the 1950s. All spluttering at the speed with which, under Attlee's Red hit squads, the empire was disintegrating. All their lives they had served an ideal. Now they no longer had a cause. Later, Major Nye worked in

Lincoln's Inn Fields at the Sir John Soane Museum. I spent much of my time there after I first came to London. Mrs Cornelius was not yet back from the Continent. Spain was finished. That was in 1939. Major Nye joined the museum in 1959 or 1960. He was growing a little frail. He had some tummy trouble. An ulcer, he said. I sometimes think stomach ulcers were the bane of that age. Everyone had them. Americans made entire films about those who suffered them. What was it making entire nations clutch their stomachs? I understand the feeling, all too well. In my case it was not an ulcer that caused my pain. Ulcers determined the history of the entire first half of the twentieth century. Drugs will determine the second half. Capital expands all possible markets.

Lincoln's Inn Fields, between Kingsway and Fleet Street, is one of those zones of tranquillity found everywhere in London. Such places were harder to find in Rome in the thirties. Our cottage near the Villa Borghese was a tiny paradise. That December was cool and sunny. We congratulated ourselves on our good fortune. We became reluctant to leave the confines of the little garden. Our planned expeditions were never conducted. Meanwhile our overworked hostess, Sarfatti, sent us hurried, apologetic notes. Fiorello telephoned once, sounding very weary, and said he would arrange dinner as soon as he could. We told him we were not offended.

Eventually, the round of Christmas parties began at the various embassies and press clubs. We were surprised by our popularity. When Maddy was invited she took me as her escort. I recall with nostalgic pleasure the sharp smell of the December air. Yellow light flowed from great houses. Their glowing ballrooms were filled with film stars, politicians and international personalities of all kinds. Sometimes a rumour would go round that Il Duce was planning to attend.

I never saw Il Duce at these gatherings. I got on well with the American Press Corps. They were loud and enthusiastic in their support of Mussolini and the mighty things he was doing. Mussolini had his greatest admirers in the United States and Germany. Negative remarks about him in their press were rare during the 1930s. When he despaired, when he was alone, fighting traitors in his own camp and invaders at his gates, then they turned on him. The American newspapers had celebrated his achievements in 1940. Now they gloried in publishing pictures of his dangling corpse, suspended by its ankles from a beam. They treat their movie stars and sports heroes the same. In my day Thomas P. Morgan, Alice O'Hare McCormick,

Murray Butler, Billy Grisham and Alex Kirk were all 'fans' of Il Duce – 'Musso', as they called him behind his back. The Hearst press paid Margherita Sarfatti enormous prices for her articles. Hearst commissioned Mussolini himself to write for them. These newspapers often supported 'FDR' as the American 'Mussolini'. They would be sorely disappointed by Roosevelt when he made his deadly pact with Red Jewry. His agents still leech the lifeblood from America.

A high point of that Christmas came when I was at last able to have a long, intelligent conversation with Mr Douglas Fairbanks and his talented wife Mary Poppins, who was grace itself, contrary to rumours. He seemed grateful for my enthusiasm. He knew my own work and was generous about it.

Billy C. Grisham, the gigantic dishevelled correspondent of the *Los Angeles Times*, famous for his vivid ties, a close friend of Sarfatti's, told me the secret of her power. The good-natured American knocked back his Scotch and ice, grinning at some naive remark of mine. He mentioned casually that Sarfatti was Mussolini's mistress, and she had been his mistress since before the March on Rome. A Jewess, she was a dedicated Fascist, the uncrowned Queen of Italy, as well as a close friend of the Italian royal family. Her power in the art world was enormous. Now I understand much more.

The house we were staying in, Grisham added, had been left to Signora Sarfatti by a certain Count Raineri Valdeschi. 'He killed himself, old sport, for mysterious reasons. A matter of honour, they said.' He laughed sympathetically at my surprise. He could not resist adding: 'However, the place is much better known as the house where until recently Margherita and the Duce kept their frequent assignations. Now, of course, Mrs Musso is having something to say about that. You know she's insisted on moving in, complete with kids, nannies, maids and mother, to the Villa Torlonia with her husband? He was happy she wanted to stay in Predappio, their home town. But what can he do? He's just made a deal with the Church. They're not priest lovers in Predappio. They had to baptise the First Lady by brute force. Our Duce himself broke in the door of a lavatory to pull her out and hold her down while the priest did the rest. She's still more of your unrepentant old-fashioned freethinking socialist. No chance of a divorce there, now, and I would imagine La Marge is pretty livid. She's running around like a headless chicken at the moment, trying to keep her influence.'

90

I discounted most of this. Journalists are the worst gossips in the world. They love fiction far more than they love truth. But it did explain a little better why we had so easily found entrance into Italian high society. We were receiving such wonderful treatment because everyone knew we were the guests of Italy's uncrowned consort. I was so much closer to my hero than I had guessed! When I told her, Maddy was deeply impressed. 'So she moved out when Rachele Mussolini moved in!'

I had no trouble being accepted, of course. Most journalists recognised me from my work in the cinema and considered me a fellow American. I was plain 'Max Peters' to them. Everyone knew me by that name again. I felt comfortable with it. Italians were in those days exceptionally pro-American. I benefited from their assumptions. Maddy's whispered intelligence to those she trusted let it be known that I was 'by birth a Russian prince'.

I could scarcely have been a more attractive proposition in Rome of the early 1930s! Wherever I went women flirted with me, usually behind Maddy's back but sometimes openly. I was always a gentlemen where the feelings of women are concerned, but I was frequently tempted. I do not believe there were any more beautiful women in the world at that time than in Rome. The city herself instils some special beauty into those who choose to live there. In turn her inhabitants feed something back to her. A love affair flourishes between flesh and stone. Mysterious spirits come awake. New ones are born. All great cities have such periods, when work of unrepeatable genius is created. They return to sleep. Each time they wake, they resurrect the accumulated wealth of ages. This wealth informs the populace and makes its blood sing. Such is the nature of true cities. They are Man's greatest, most complex creation.

To resist the city is to resist life, as Shakespeare's great contemporary put it. We *are* the city. Those who dwelt here before us, those whose spirits still dwell here, we are the city. For time is not a wave or a line, but a field. The sins and achievements of the past are everywhere with us. Even this city, now, this alien London, which so chills my bones, which so armours herself against my embassy, which mocks me, which calls me names, which rejects my ministry, which is so arrogant she believes God alone defended her during the War, even she does not expel me. She knows how it is as natural for me to live here as it is for her to tolerate me. That is the secret of her strength. She judges nobody. She absorbs us all.

That night I went home with much to think about!

We saw a great deal of Billy Grisham and his own family. We 'hit it off', as he liked to say. And from being invisible, we began in the last two weeks leading to Christmas to see our landlady everywhere. Signora Sarfatti attended all the functions to which we were invited and many others besides. Suddenly she appeared in the newspaper talking to foreign dignitaries, communing with soldiers and priests as enthusiastically as she did with painters and writers. Articles by her, chiefly about modern art, appeared in the *Popolo d'Italia*, and she was mostly seen in the company of Americans from the diplomatic corps or with newspaper people. One of those young diplomats became a particular chum of ours and, like the Grishams, sought out our company whenever fate brought us together. His name was Alex Kirk and he had an elegant grace that reminded me of Fred Astaire, only then beginning to emerge as America's greatest ballet maestro. Maddy was enthusiastic about Kirk. She said he looked 'spiffing' in evening dress. All those young Americans abroad had taken to using English public school slang. I found it both confusing and irritating. I sometimes longed for the company of my Albanian princess, the beautiful adventuress Rose von Bek. But she was almost certainly dead. Clearly she had not managed to reach Rome in her aeroplane.

I refused to think of my Rose crashed in some sub-Saharan wilderness or arrested by the forces of the Sultan or any of the other dreadful alternatives which presented themselves. Since I could do nothing for her, nor discover from anyone I met what had happened to her, I forced myself, not without considerable pangs, to put her from my thoughts.

My plane was called *The Bee*, swift in pursuit of sweetness. My love was called *The Rose*, deliciously scented deadly confirmer of life. My city is called *Der Heym*. My city is called *Der Heym*.

I see the silver angels gathering. So few of them. They defend all that is holy. They defend the home. A red tide rises beneath a steel moon. There is no pity in the future. There is no hope in the future. There is no dignity in the future. There is no security in the future. There is nothing to eat in the future. Those liberals promised us a Golden Age and instead took away our future. Mussolini restored that future. For a while, if only in a dream, some vast cinema epic engulfed us and convinced us we had hope. We had something to do. And, for a while, it was true. We did things.

We felt better. We wore uniforms. We embraced our neighbours and united in defence against the common foe which none doubted in those days to be Bolshevism. We were good people, doing good work for a more secure future in which the state would provide. We laboured towards the Golden Age. We climbed into cattle trucks still believing we were on our way to paradise. But it is not fair to blame Mussolini for the failures of his shared dream. We were too content to enjoy the euphoria while it was happening. We should have worked harder to make the dream reality. In this we were diverted, of course, by the usual enemies. In the end both Hitler and Mussolini surrounded themselves by time-serving lapdogs who did nothing but parrot their masters' most banal utterances. I had too much dignity for that. I was diplomatic, but I was never servile.

My only worry in those days was the rate at which we were using up our supply of *sneg*. I needed to make contact with other connoisseurs of the coca-leaf. Discreet enquiries in my old haunts had yielded nothing so far. Cocaine in Italy was now the preserve of the privileged. But once again providence was to come to my rescue in the person of our *patrona*.

Having seen us at several parties where she reassured us that her cottage was ours for as long as we needed it, Signora Sarfatti telephoned us one Saturday morning. She did not wish to impose, but might she call on us that afternoon at about four? We agreed cheerfully, speculating on her reasons for visiting us. Then we wondered suddenly if La Sarfatti did not after all want to evict us. Our idyll could be reaching an end in that little house we had come to think of as our own. We spent the morning putting the pictures and sculptures back in place and generally cleaning but by five o'clock Signora Sarfatti had not turned up. By six, she telephoned to say she was on her way. By nine, bringing a vast wave of scents with her, combining the perfumes of a dozen salons, the smoke of countless saloons, the blended alcohol of several large cocktails, in a colourfully mismatched miscellany of clothing which did nothing to hide her growing corpulence, she entered the living room and sat down at the marble coffee table. Opening her handbag, she drew out a pigskin sack. From this she took a small packet. Brandishing an elegant silver razor, she unfolded the packet and on the edge of the blade removed some white powder. This she spread on the table, chopping it expertly while we looked on in some surprise. 'God, I need this,' she said. 'That's what delayed me. Sorry. Will you sniff?'

The stuff was first rate. When I commented on the quality she beamed as if I had congratulated her on her cooking. 'I'll put you in touch with my little Arab,' she said. 'He won't overcharge you.'

Though we had already sampled the drug together in Majorca, Maddy seemed surprised at Signora Sarfatti's openness. I took it for granted. Our hostess knew we were worldly people like herself. Besides, she was in her own home, doubtless invulnerable to arrest or any other interference in her private pursuits. La Sarfatti was still, after all, 'the Queen of Italy'.

My attitude had changed towards her once I knew her position in Il Duce's court. Now it changed again as I realised she was a regular imbiber. We were all comrades of the beneficent coca-leaf. In those days such ties meant something.

For a while La Sarfatti looked around abstractedly, as if Maddy, myself, even her own sitting room were unfamiliar. Then to recover herself, she settled down comfortably on the sofa with a Campari Orange, suddenly ruler again of her own domain. Soon we were all at ease.

Signora Sarfatti spoke expansively of her work. She had had no time for her usual parties. As soon as her salon began again we should be honoured guests. Did we know the anti-Fascist novelist Moravia? He was a friend of hers, as were so many of Italy's finest painters and novelists. 'Some people are calling Mussolini the New Charlemagne,' she told us, 'but his court is rather more sophisticated, I think.'

In excellent English she asked if we had heard of D'Annunzio's friend, the American poet, Pound. She spoke rapidly, leaving little chance for us to reply. She told anecdotes about people of whom we had never heard. Yet Mrs Sarfatti described a world we both longed to experience. She knew that I was already an internationally popular film actor and set designer and greatly respected my work as an artist, she said. Film was the art form of the future. My work would certainly be remembered. Already, she hinted, Il Duce himself was familiar with my acting and was an enthusiast. Hadn't I originally been trained as an engineer? It is as an engineer, I said, that I would wish the world to see me. Signora Sarfatti recalled I had worked for the French, the Americans and the Moroccans on secret military projects. She assumed I had done work for other governments. Might she look at my designs again? I, of course, was only too happy to oblige her for I knew she had Mussolini's ear and if she were impressed by my plans she might communicate some of this to her lover.

Doing my best to remain casual, curious as to her sudden interest, I was almost trembling as I described what I had built, including my Moroccan aeroplanes now in the service of the Caïd. Listening with polite impatience, she clearly had something specific on her mind. At last, after a few more lines of her first-rate cocaine, she arrived at her point. Fiorello had shown great enthusiasm for one of my designs. Had I seen Fiorello lately? She meant to ask him to ask me for a copy of the plan, it had impressed her so much. A design for a huge war machine capable of crossing large areas of desert? I had spent a long time in North Africa, had I not? Had anyone else considered putting the machine into action? Could she see those plans?

I suppose a lesser soul would have been suspicious of her motives and refused. My copyrights and patents were my only assets since the crash of my California bank. I should protect them. But I sensed she would not betray me. She was genuinely interested in my ideas.

Given my circumstances, I had little real choice. Who could refuse her and in turn risk refusing Il Duce? In any case I found it impossible to resist her charm. Her persuasive powers had helped put Mussolini where he was. I was charmed by her, and only too pleased to get out my plans and explain my massive desert-liner, now redesigned for battle and armed to the teeth with the latest repeating cannon.

She understood I had some idea of the military strength of Morocco and her neighbours. I agreed. For so long in the service of the Caïd and having helped him build his air force, I had become naturally aware of such details. I mentioned that I had worked on several secret projects in America, chiefly in California where my partner had been the well-known entrepreneur 'Mucker' Hever.

With sharp intelligence she asked me about the practicality of building such huge war machines. Would not it be better to build smaller, faster land cruisers which could be more readily manoeuvred? I had the impression she had spoken to an engineer of her acquaintance and was testing me. I knew she was a good friend of the great Marconi.

Still a little puzzled by her interest, I explained how any army using several of my 'Land Leviathans' would not need to manoeuvre. The machines would simply go where the generals wanted to go, crushing entire cities beneath their gigantic treads if necessary.

This was apparently what she wanted to hear. 'Could you make copies of your designs for me by tomorrow?' she asked. I was not sure. I would have to find someone capable of making such large photographs. I would guess there were places in Rome, probably near the newspaper offices. She knew exactly what I needed and gave me the address of a photographic specialist off the Corso d'Italia. She rose suddenly, an explosion of multicoloured fabrics and conflicting scents, took a large envelope from her pigskin sack and laid it on the table. Her knowing green eyes winked at me. She was flirtatious and not entirely dignified for a woman of her years. Yet I was absolutely under her spell. I knew how she had taken control of the Italian art world as thoroughly and with the same will as her lover had taken over the nation's politics. She kissed me on both cheeks. She embraced Maddy. Tapping the envelope with her beringed finger, she said: 'He's bringing me some more tomorrow. That's for you.'

I asked if it was impolitic to know the reason for her interest. She offered me that sudden, charming grin. 'A little!' She was in far better spirits than I had ever seen her.

Before she left, Signora Sarfatti paused at the door. 'You could really build those huge tanks, could you, Mr Peters?'

I told her that I was first and foremost a practical engineer.

'And you'd build them for Italy?'

I assured her it was my one ambition. My whole purpose in being here was to join in the great social experiment revivifying Italy and bringing hope to the world.

She seemed amused, her eyes slitting a little. Maddy moved uneasily, her silk agitated, almost angry.

'If Il Duce called you to work for him could you, as an American, do so with all your being?'

'I am a Fascist first,' I said, 'and an American second.'

—❖ ELEVEN ❖—

My first meeting with Il Duce was on 25 December 1930, Christmas Day. Maddy and I had been invited by the Grishams to join them for 'a real American Christmas'. We arrived on Christmas Eve at their huge apartment off the Via Puccini where they had installed a good-sized fir tree and decorated it in a style I had not seen for years. I was almost in tears as I stared at the copper and silver decorations, the flickering candles, the red and green tinsel.

Ethel Grisham patted my arm in sympathy. 'We miss Christmas most, don't we? Billy got us the decorations in Nuremberg when he was there last month. And,' she dropped her voice, 'you should see what he found for the kids. He says it's like Fort Santa, that town. The capital of Christmas.' A short, pretty woman with strawberry-blonde hair and a matronly manner which made her popular with almost everyone in Rome, Ethel had little interest in her husband's sphere. She worked for the Red Cross and other international charities as a fund-raiser. One of those domesticated women I have often dreamed of marrying. In the end, they do not seem to be my type, though admirable and attractive in every way.

She spoke enthusiastically of Signora Sarfatti as an indefatigable holder of what she called 'The Women's Banner' and never deaf to any American in need. Billy admitted that she was one of the few interesting Italian women in Rome and extremely well educated. Her pleasure in modern art, for instance, was absolutely genuine and extremely sophisticated. She knew every living painter of any importance.

Over drinks the Grishams asked how we had met. We told them. I said how much I had admired da Bazzanno's aeroplane. 'Isn't it a shame about that,' said Ethel Grisham.

I was mystified. Billy explained how the plane had made a forced landing on Lake Lucerne. It still had fuel, needed only minor repairs,

97

but its pilot, da Bazzanno, had disappeared. So that was why we had not seen our friend recently. I said I was surprised I had read nothing about it in the newspapers or heard anything on the radio. Billy pursed his lips at this. He reminded me that not everything which went on in Italy was reported.

I gathered that da Bazzanno had been involved in some business of state and that was the reason for the silence. Maddy Butter was shocked. She continued to ask questions which poor Billy struggled to answer. The massive American was as baffled as anyone. In a characteristic gesture of embarrassment, he pushed his fair hair from his face and fiddled with his sandy moustache. I had learned to read him. When these gestures became frequent, as now, he had something on his mind he would rather not discuss. I did not entirely believe him when he promised to let us know anything he heard. Now I had two missing aviators to consider. Perhaps all of us who have grown up in the age of flight have had such experiences. They no doubt become increasingly commonplace as aviators are replaced by 'flight crew'. But in those days such occurrences were rare. To lose two friends to flight in peacetime was something of a tragedy. My hosts had no particular interest in pursuing the subject. In order not to spoil the occasion I did my best to put da Bazzanno's fate from my mind.

A gourmet cook who had trained in Paris and Boston, Grisham was determined to prepare for us a traditional American meal, and although their cook helped him, he was in complete charge of the kitchen. As our host wielded his spoons and pans, we played games with the boys, admiring their new sets of soldiers, their wooden stallions and glittering tin swords, all of the finest workmanship and impossible to find in Italy. Then at last the Christmas bird was brought out by Grisham wearing a huge red cap and a cotton wool beard, singing some appropriate ditty. The huge, glistening golden turkey, surrounded by *chipolatas* (as a nod to the Italians) and smelling of heaven, came floating into the room like the fatted calf itself.

I was reminded of a scene from one of those magnificent Italian films set in the Renaissance, a mixture of masque and feast then delighting the public. Behind Billy came the cook and the maid with bowls of squash and casseroles and potatoes and beans. Assembling eagerly at the table, we applauded the traditional placing of the bird on the waiting trivet. The whole room was alive with dancing candlelight, rich, exotic smells of the food, the happy sound of children, glittering decorations and the excited talk of adults.

'Merry Christmas!' cries Pa Grisham, his huge hands plucking up the silver carving set with all the delicacy of a matador. 'Merry Christmas! Ho, ho, ho!' And then the first, magnificent slice is carved and laid with easy ceremony upon the waiting plate. Intense, wide-eyed, wide-mouthed, the boys bend eagerly to study the distribution of the meat. Vegetables are passed with a sense of joyous urgency over which Ma Grisham, content in her sense of the rightness of things, presides, directing a little here, helping a little there, so that eventually all plates are heaped and now we are to bow our heads in a simple grace before pouring the gravy and spooning the cranberries, picking up the hot rolls with wincing fingertips and at last addressing the feast with knife and fork in hand.

It was a scene from one of the happiest Hollywood films, when directors were not ashamed to show human beings enjoying themselves in wholesome, simple ways. I only regretted that Esmé was not here with me, and perhaps my mother. How Esmé would have loved it all. True, my mother might have disapproved a little. Our own Christmas fare had rarely been so plentiful or rich. Easter, of course, was our big feast. I still remembered my mother's face looking after me as I took the train to Odessa, never to return. She had died, I was told, in the famines which followed the Civil War. At least she was spared the Bolshevik conquest. As for the Auschwitz story, it was obviously nothing but lies meant to drag me into the Red net. My mother was everything to me. My only reality. Why would I turn my back on her?

Afterwards, when we had all pulled crackers and donned fancy hats and paper masks, we were served with our choice of plum puddings or hot coddlings, mince pies or pumpkin tart. The boys went outside into the courtyard, busy with their new bicycles, their airguns and their Elastolin infantry. Billy wound up the gramophone and played us carols, traditional songs and the latest numbers from Broadway and the talkies. He bought his records at enormous expense, he said, in a shop off the Via Napoleon III. All the Americans and English people went there. One of the new numbers was 'The Singing Buckaroo', from the film of the same name. 'You have your imitators now, Max,' said Ethel. 'You should be flattered.' In a way I was, but it is depressing to see one's best work badly imitated and the imitation come to represent the original. One is subjected to ignorant condescension by the young who know only those who stole from you. We live in a world where thieves are rewarded as a matter of course and honest men are degraded and mocked.

At about eight o'clock, as we danced to the rhythms of the latest orchestras, the telephone rang. Ethel Grisham cried, 'Oh, no! Not the paper!' and Billy went grimly to the hall where he answered the instrument. We heard only a few words, which offered no clue to the conversation, and then Billy was back, grinning in a rather mysterious way and frowning at the same time. 'It's for you, Max,' he said. 'A woman. She preferred not to give me her name. She said it was very urgent. Would you mind speaking to her?' And he led me back to the telephone, leaving directly I had picked it up.

I thought it would be da Bazzanno's mistress. I had been reminded of her by my friend's disappearance and for some reason had expected her to contact me. But it was not Laura. The woman was Margherita Sarfatti. I was sure Billy had recognised her distinctive English. Rapidly and apologetically she asked me if I could be ready to see her in about two hours. I hesitated. She was insistent. 'This is a matter of considerable importance,' she said, 'and I suspect you will find it in your interest.' Enraptured by the glow of this American Christmas, I remained reluctant. 'Mr Peters,' she said at last, 'I have to tell you that I speak on a matter of state. I am permitted to say no more.'

Of course I could only agree to her request. She informed me that a car would call for me at ten o'clock. It might be wise to wear a topcoat and some gloves, since it was cool tonight. She would be obliged if I said as little as I could to my host and hostess. I told her I had no problems with discretion.

In truth I had little to report. My eager friends awaited an announcement. I shrugged as I returned to them. 'I am supposed to wear an overcoat,' I told them. 'It is a cool night. A car's coming at ten. I can tell you nothing else.'

They were all solicitude. I was prepared against the winter night. Outer clothing was made ready for me. The children were sent to bed but we found it rather hard to get back into the Christmas swing. Maddy contented herself with a whispered 'Be careful', and it was clear Billy had already told her the caller's identity. Our small talk was strained and it was a relief when the time came for me to leave. We watched through the curtains. Eventually a midnight-blue Mercedes pulled up in our courtyard below and waited, its engine thumping. I kissed Maddy goodbye, shook hands with my friends

100

and ran downstairs. My borrowed overcoat, too small for Grisham, caught at my heels as I went downstairs. He called it his 'Bavarian Raglan', bought in a fit of enthusiasm without trying it on in Munich, in dark green wool with matching Tyrolean hat. The gloves, too, were a little large but I think I looked dignified enough for whatever it was I was supposed to do, in spite of Maddy's observation. She said the gloves made me look like Mickey Mouse disguised as a human.

When I arrived in the chilly courtyard I knew I had been well advised. Though clear, the night was very cold. His breath boiling, the chauffeur sprang from his cab and opened the door for me, offering me the Fascist salute, to which I replied in kind. A very comforting sensation attends this type of acceptance and respect. I have known it several times in my career. I miss it so much these days.

Major Nye agrees with me that standards are down everywhere. He believes it began when he was a young officer and ladies started smoking in public. He could be right. Small things reflect the larger issues, after all. I found Mrs Cornelius's smoking increasingly distressing, but Major Nye says that most human beings prefer familiarity to anything else. If a custom becomes familiar enough, no matter how disgusting it was once found, people will defend it and preserve it as if it were a cause. I agree. A habit is not a principle, I say. You will not hear that distinction from these fools. They believe that parroting a popular prejudice makes them philosophers.

People vote for the man who offers them what is most familiar. That's why they voted for Hitler. Not for his policies but for his promise to make everything the same as before. Major Nye says: 'This is something we all conspired in. We must all bear a degree of shame.'

'Shame?' I ask. 'Why should I feel ashamed?' I was one of those trying to do something about the situation. Say what you will of Benito Mussolini's later excesses, he saw the world's problems and he came up with a solution. He was not corrupt. He was careless of money. I can vouch for that. He never had any use for it. He understood the responsibilities of power and was able to bear them more stoically and capably than anyone alive!

I had taken the trouble to fortify myself with some of Billy Grisham's fine brandy, some excellent wine and a sniff or two of the first-rate cocaine I had obtained from Margherita Sarfatti.

The car took me through the better class suburbs, through silent, tree-lined prospects and well-lit avenues, concourses deserted save for the ever-vigilant police and the occasional car like our own doubtless speeding on special business in a capital which only appeared to sleep. I knew from the newspaper articles how Il Duce managed to keep an eye on every detail of the state's maintenance. Floodlights picked out ancient monuments and statues, huge billboards of Il Duce looking stern and decisive and bearing the simple slogan 'Mussolini Is Always Right'. Whoever it was designed the sets for that multimillion-pound essay into communist propaganda *1984* stole every one of their ideas for Big Brother from Mussolini, without acknowledgement, of course, as they so frequently steal from me. All the best ideas were decades old! Mrs Cornelius says I should be flattered.

When Mrs Cornelius became ill I tried to get her to the hospital, but she would not go. She said anyone who went into St Charles never came out alive. I found a doctor for her and made her as comfortable as I could, then I telephoned her son. I had the shop to run. He was very good and went round right away. He was with her, at least, when she died. He brought me some papers, some photographs, but I suspect he kept certain things for himself. I know his brother, the antique dealer, has his eye on my pistols but I intend to be buried with those guns rather than let him have them. Should Mrs Cornelius have kept them in trust for so long? They were given to me by a fellow Cossack, and they are my birthright. They are all I have left.

After taking what seemed a circuitous route, the car at last turned into a long, white avenue, lined with carefully groomed poplars and cedars standing dark against the cold, sharp sky. Most of the houses had guards. They seemed to be deserted. Their occupants had gone away for the holidays, but one house, standing back from the road in its own considerable grounds, had a few lights shining. The car entered a driveway. It paused at a pair of elaborately ornamental iron gates. Passing through a cordon of dogs and armed guards we reached another almost identical set of gates. We endured a similar procedure. Hard eyes looked me over carefully before allowing us to go through. I was mystified and not a little nervous. Did this have something to do with da Bazzanno? Was it an elaborate joke? Had Signora Sarfatti tricked me for some horrible purpose of her own? Or had she struck a deal with the Cheka? Was Brodmann involved? Were they deceiving me as El Glaoui had deceived me by making me walk into my own prison?

I had been a fool to go so trustingly into the car. Too late now to reconsider. I looked back at the guards and the gates. It began to dawn on me that this was to be no ordinary meeting with Signora Sarfatti. Perhaps she had not lied. Could I be on a genuine errand of state?

The drive curved, flanked by tall hedges, and for a second, in the yellow lights of the car, I had the impression of water, of mist and of shadowy figures. Then the headlamps were turned off. The chauffeur got down from his wheel and opened the door for me. I stepped out. A moment later, behind me, the car drove away. I was alone, walking down an avenue of poplars. I was walking, though I did not know it then, towards my destiny.

Once or twice, in my overlong coat, I tripped a little. I admit I was flustered. My heart began to pound. My hands sweated. Where was Signora Sarfatti? Who were the figures I could just make out ahead of me? They were obscured by the heavy mist rising from the waters of what I took to be an ornamental lake. There were three of them, perhaps four, their bodies swathed in scarves and heavy coats, their lapels turned up so that it was impossible to distinguish faces. My next thought was that maybe through his mistress da Bazzanno had arranged a secret meeting. Neither outline reminded me of my friend. Another fear: I had offended the Mafia. But the Mafia in Italy was no longer a power. Mussolini had seen to that. Besides, I had no reason to distrust Signora Sarfatti. Wasn't she a supporter of mine?

My feet left the gravel and sank into soft grass. I walked with some difficulty towards the waiting figures. Increasingly, the scene felt dreamlike. Then I realised that some of the figures I saw were not human at all. They were statues, pale ghosts in the pale mist. Though they scarcely moved as I approached, the living figures were darker. One of them was a woman. The other was a burly man a little below average height. Without knowing why I began to tremble.

Now I had almost reached the marble bench beside the lake where they stood waiting. Both were smoking cigarettes. The smell of their Turkish tobacco swamped my senses. I felt nausea. Their faces could not be seen. Of course I already knew who they were. I heard Margherita murmur something to her companion, throw down her cigarette and stamp it out with her high heel. He, too, dropped and extinguished his cigarette, coughing slightly and raising his scarf against the cold air. I think Margherita introduced me. I do not remember. Bile rose in my throat. I heard her utter the name of Italy's dictator. I heard his familiar voice answer. Yet I was close to vomiting. As if I faced an enemy rather than my greatest hero. My legs shook. My mouth was dry. I knew all the symptoms of a familiar terror. But then his warm, strong hand was in mine, and I was safe.

From within his scarf his voice was soft, vibrant. His eyes were intense and respectful. I stammered some admiring banalities. He patted my arm rather as one would try to calm a nervous child.

'Professor Peters! It is Mussolini who should be honoured. I am an enormous fan. The popular cinema is our most powerful instrument for social change. I am also your country's greatest admirer. The kind of wholesome films you make, *Professore*, remind us that there are still some decencies left. Let one man of the New Renaissance greet another as an equal!'

Those deep, reassuring tones soothed me at once. Soon my symptoms were forgotten. He spoke a rather pleasant English, occasionally drawing on French and German for vocabulary, and was perfectly easy to understand. I in turn tried to speak in Italian, which is by no means an easy language for me. I know he appreciated my attempt.

Il Duce went to every effort to put me at my ease. He was amiability itself. He insisted on treating me man to man, the surest sign of greatness, for he needed to prove nothing. I suspected he had only been 'briefed' on my career and knew few of my films, but that résumé gave him an exceptional understanding. He spoke with great admiration of my roles. He assumed I had directed myself. He said the Masked Buckaroo should be a role model to all American youth, rather than the seedy gangsters, the worst scum of Italy, who now filled her press and cinema. America was too tolerant of these people, whom Mussolini's Italy had rejected. In ridding herself of her social poisons, in hardening herself in the fires of radical revolution, the new Italy had no room for such human rubbish. America would be wise to follow Italy's example in cracking down on all the so-called secret societies. I agreed wholeheartedly.

Signora Sarfatti took no part in our talk. She remained near the marble bench, smoking and staring up into the night sky, her breath silver in the harsh air. Il Duce murmured that I was the type of man the state was looking for to head the new Italian Renaissance, the rebirth of a greater Roman Empire. 'Miss Sarfatti tells me you, like many Americans of the first class, are a committed admirer of the Fascist cause. We already have several Americans in our ranks, as you know. I hear rumours of some new leader rising to save your country from her present unhappy crisis. Weren't you in politics over there, for a while? I am a huge admirer of your *Birth of a Nation*. The Knights of the Ku Klux Klan are such romantic heroes. America needs more such heroes, eh? But I understand there was trouble?'

I stammered some reply, explaining the circumstances. I was astonished at Il Duce's intelligence. The newspapers spoke of his remarkable head for detail, the breadth and depth of his understanding. For once they published only the truth.

'And who will be America's new Duce?' he wanted to know.

I was adamant. America could never produce a Mussolini. The country was far too corrupt. He had a quick, alert brain in those days. I was profoundly impressed. He spoke of El Glaoui as if he were an old friend. He asked me what I thought of France's chances of holding Morocco without the Caïd. He asked how many planes I had produced in Marrakech. I said there were about ten types, with perhaps ten of each now in production. Il Duce was impressed. He clapped me on the shoulder.

'Quite a fleet. And these engines which dispense with oil – how practical are they?' I told him that they were extremely practical. In most designs it took time for the steam to reach full pressure. My special designs addressed this problem. I could produce steam engines for planes and airships, speed-planes, fighters and all kinds of land vehicles. The engine was as efficient and as manoeuvrable as anything currently run by gasoline.

Il Duce nodded gravely as we walked, his chin lowered, his hand on my arm, guiding me over the rough ground where my long overcoat trailed. He asked me to describe my Desert Liner. This I now called the 'Land Leviathan'. During my long stay in Tangier I had attempted to adapt my inventions to the needs of the day.

I soon realised that the Land Leviathan was Il Duce's chief interest. Margherita Sarfatti had passed on all I had told her. I did not know then, of course, of Mussolini's plan to reconquer Carthaginian Africa, any more than I knew that Signora Sarfatti, nervous of being displaced in her lover's affections, had found in my ideas a new way to win Il Duce's approval. The more we discussed my machine, the more enthusiastic he became, striding about like a happy schoolboy, barking questions at me and listening intently to my answers. His greatcoat was thrown back, his uniform jacket unbuttoned and his shirt undone, but the great scarf still swathed part of his face. He was afraid of catching cold, he said, and apologised. He had to be careful. All his family were short-lived. He asked me to confirm my landship's enormous capacity, its speed, its efficient firepower. Every inch of her was a revolutionary new design, with parts simplified and systemised so that one spare could do the work of many. I showed where the huge boilers would be and how they would in fact cool the rest of the Land Leviathan, together with powering her electrically operated gas-cannon. Such a machine could penetrate well into enemy territory without need of a long supply chain. 'Imagine the effect of just one of these gigantic raiders entering a modern city,' I said. 'They would think themselves attacked by monsters from Mars!'

Benito Mussolini's eyes kept their expression as he paced in silence beside me. He thought over all I had told him. He tested my engineering and technical knowledge against his own and realised very quickly the special genius of my designs. Il Duce shared ideas with his good friend Signor Marconi. He knew what he was talking about. What were the measurements of my treads? What steam pressure did I propose? He listened to my answers with a deeply furrowed forehead and a forward thrust of his jaw, every inch the ancient Roman Emperor, the widely informed modern statesman. Sometimes, quite unconsciously, he struck a pose already familiar from film and magazines – fist on hip, scratching the back of his head as if in disbelief, his step full of energy, his eyes forever alert. I could not help but compare him to another great hero of mine, the Roman Emperor Marcus Aurelius, whose common sense and wisdom has come down to us.

If I had awakened that moment from a dream I should not have been at all surprised. I could never have asked God for a more perfect reward than this. All my privations, disappointments and struggles seemed worthwhile and all my frustrations were at last at an end, for here was a man who understood genius – *precisely because his own genius was as great if not greater than mine!*

Stoic philosophy was a model for the New Italian man Mussolini wished to create – hard, disciplined, efficient – like the Roman legions of old. The legions which had conquered the world.

One could not help emulating his manner. Like his, my own style became laconic. It was clear he appreciated a companion who was not long-winded. Happily, I have always been a man of action first and words second. It is my nature. It is in my blood. We Slavs are moody and neurotic if we are not busy. We turn to drink and the writing of depressing novels. But we rise nobly to meaningful action, such as the defence of our homeland.

Hitler's greatest mistake was to underestimate the Slav. In the end he came to respect us and see us quite differently, but by then it was too late. The Bolshevik standard was raised above the ruins of the Reichstag. They had consolidated the victory they had begun to win in 1933. Now they rule everywhere and the map of the world drips crimson with their casual infamy. Once I was proud to wear a uniform, but now I sell them as fashion items to young people with no memory. They have not even heard of Mussolini.

As if he had learned all he needed for the moment on the subject of my Land Leviathan, Il Duce suddenly changed tack. He asked was I, as Signora Sarfatti had told him, a convinced Fascist? I hesitated, for I could not lie. At last I answered levelly. I looked him full in the eyes. 'My Duce, I am as convinced of the rightness of your convictions as I am of the heroic destiny which guides you and makes you the inspiration and aspiration of the entire world. I count myself your most loyal follower. But as to the detailed philosophy of Fascism, I must admit myself deficient.'

'Professor Peters,' said Il Duce embracing me, 'you are a perfect Fascist. I believe you are the kind of metal we need in our Fascist Inner Council. This is a group of men whose sense of justice and moral purpose binds them together in a common cause. Although dedicated to the establishment of a glorious new Roman Empire, they are not all Italians. Some, like yourself, are American. Some are French. Still others are Austrian or Albanian. Together we convene to determine the direction and purpose of our empire. We pool our common wisdom for the common good. We are above worldly considerations. We are incorruptible men of great social influence. Those who join the Council must forswear all other loyalties save to myself and, through me, the Italian state. Are you ready to take that oath, Professor Peters, and join our brotherhood?'

Obviously Signora Sarfatti's recommendations were taken seriously by Mussolini. Now I could understand why their relationship had lasted so long. She was not merely Il Duce's sometime lover, she was his eyes and ears where he could not, these days, go. Mussolini's questions had been astute. With her instincts confirmed, he had made up his mind with his usual speed. Naturally I had no option but to accept! I did not experience a moment's reluctance as I took the heavy responsibility he offered. I was enormously elated! I had been granted the prestige, possibly even the power, which I believed my right! The frustrations and humiliations, disappointments and betrayals, faded in my memory. My dream had come true! I can scarcely remember my reply, but of course I agreed. Arrangements would have to be made, said my Duce. He asked if I could be ready to start work the next day. Naturally I would receive an adequate salary and so forth. He waved an expansive hand.

I had enough remaining sense to murmur of commitments – minor business in the US and so on (actually, I needed time to catch my breath) and he was generous. Again the grave nod, the assurance of that gesture, and I was given until 1 January. Who could now deny my destiny?! That date was my birthday, both as a man and as a Fascist.

Once again his firm hand was placed in mine. The interview was over. Mussolini walked with deliberate, thoughtful pace, back towards the great house, a pale shadow in the deepening mist.

Margherita Sarfatti, her usual riot of scents and scarves, clutched excitedly at my arm. 'You made a wonderful impression. He likes you. He normally doesn't give *me* that amount of time these days. He trusts you. He believes in you. You have come at exactly the right moment. You bring him exactly what he needs: a machine which will overawe our enemies and reduce our casualties. We have taken another major step towards the establishment of a truly Fascist world. We shall harness all that is good about our modern age and place it in the service of the ideals and traditions of our noblest ancestors.'

Rather foolishly, I mentioned to Margherita I needed to find a toilet. Apparently my entire system wished to void itself at one burst. She smilingly told me to use the lake. She would keep guard. A little self-consciously, though hidden by mist and bushes, I relieved myself into the freezing waters of the ornamental pond. Before I could pull up my trousers against the near-zero chill, Signora Sarfatti was upon me. Did I feel grateful, she asked, for what she had done for me? I was indeed very grateful. She pressed close to me, her breath smelling of violets and Turkish tobacco, her dyed hair escaping from under her fur.

I was horribly conscious of who she was. Surely Il Duce's mistress would not consider jeopardising everything for a sordid, carnal moment? The place was suddenly silent. I heard a car driving away.

He has gone, she said. She sounded angry, disgusted. He has to get back to his wife and family. He had found an excuse to be free of his peasant brood for a few hours. My private parts in her heated hand, I stood beside the freezing water with my trousers down. Then I found myself turning suddenly to vomit. I heard her crooning behind me. I heard her telling me it was all right. Meanwhile, her hand held tight to my genitals as she stroked and whispered and at last let me raise my trousers and accompany her to her waiting car.

'We'll need a couple of hours,' she said. 'You can tell them whatever you like.' She spoke in a rather detached, casual way, as if to a relative. 'But we'll need at least two hours.' She flung herself back into the cushions of the limousine, scratching her prominent stomach. I was glad that she favoured dim lighting. Yet part of me really did love her at that moment. She was the medium through whom my dream had come true.

However, no matter what I told myself, no matter how I found ways of making Signora Sarfatti attractive, there was one terrible obstacle to my ever achieving a state of lust sufficient to satisfy her. That obstacle would not leave my mind. It informed every action involving my benefactress. Even as she took me back to her extraordinary apartment, which she shared with children and servants, all of whom stared at me from hiding as we arrived, the knowledge kept pounding in my head. I was about to enjoy sexual congress with the 'uncrowned Queen of Italy', whom some called the new Lucretia Borgia, my hero's long-established paramour, the mistress of a superman. A superman, I believed, who would not be entirely sympathetic to my circumstances and would take appropriate Italian action if he ever found out.

It occurred to me, as Margherita settled herself upon me without bothering to take off most of her clothes, that I had become a character in a Greek drama. The irony did not console me.

I became reconciled to my destiny.

My last thought before that extraordinary, fleshy scarecrow began her unusual and somewhat terrifying ministrations was 'What happened to Fiorello?'

I could only hope that Signora Sarfatti's passion would fade with her act of conquest. I was in a state of silent exhaustion when she returned me to my friends' flat at around two in the morning. To my dismay, they were all waiting up for me. The Christmas tree candles had gone out, but the fire was high. Billy, in a dressing gown which could have swaddled Africa, made me a hot toddy. Ethel carried off my street clothes, commenting sympathetically on their condition, while Maddy murmured comfort and enquiry.

My silence was taken for weighty thought. Ethel told her husband to be quiet and suggested we all needed sleep. We could talk, if necessary, in the morning. Billy, with his journalist's nose for news, was, of course, the most eager. But he was a gentleman through and through, the best kind of old-fashioned American, so his courtesy triumphed over his curiosity.

Grateful for this, I allowed Maddy to lead me to bed. Insistently, since Margherita's conflicting scents filled my own nostrils, I stumbled into a bath. From there I remember almost nothing. I awoke in the pink haze of a perfect afternoon with a few soft clouds in the pastel sky and two slender poplars framed in the window whose curtains a smiling Maddy drew back for me. I smelled coffee and croissants. I was filled with an emotion I can only describe as untranquil well-being. My elation at meeting my hero and discovering his respect – indeed his need – for me was almost overwhelming, as was the knowledge of the price I had to pay La Sarfatti for my good fortune.

Bluntly, I felt as if I had been fucked by a demon. None of this can be said, of course. She is still alive, still spending the fortune she has made from selling the degenerate paintings she spirited away when she fled into exile. After she fell out of favour and was revealed as a Jewess, she ran off to America. She now lives, I understand, in

Trieste, where all our histories began. D'Annunzio's noble act of individualism, after all, provided the inspiration for the March on Rome. They now claim the march never took place, that every aspect of Mussolini's career was a circus, an illusion, a further step into grotesque fantasy, but you only have to look at the buildings to know who was fantasising and who was not. Mussolini demanded an architecture which was powerful, brutal and stark – a tough, Fascist architecture. If it did not exist, why is it still being copied around the world, especially in London?

Maddy Butter was grave as she settled her warm little body beside me. Pushing back her pretty curls, she did her best not to seem eager. While I ate from my breakfast tray, she read from the newspaper. She had looked, she said, for some hint of my activities last night, but unless I had been called to help a dog which had somehow climbed a tree in the Via delle Sette Chiese on Christmas Eve and had been stuck for twenty-four hours, howling the whole time until shot by a local *squadristi*, there was no clue. Of course she was quivering with curiosity and, because of my circumstances, I was able to be deliberate, cautious and cryptic in my replies. The philanderer's perfect situation! Unfortunately I was not the perfect philanderer and had no enthusiasm for the role. I swore Maddy to secrecy before telling her that Signora Sarfatti had been the intermediary between me and a very important figure indeed.

'Mussolini!' cried Maddy, eyes shining. I neither confirmed nor denied this. I went on to say how I'd been offered a job doing what I could do best as an engineer. A job which satisfied my ideal for practical altruism. At last my talents were to be put to the public service. I had longed all my life for just such a chance. My eyes filled with sudden tears as I thought of my mother, of Esmé and my loved ones in Kiev. I wished they were with me now to share in my glorious fulfilment. Maddy Butter interpreted my tears as tears of joy. This allowed her to echo the supposed emotion, weeping for my success as I wept for my lost loved ones whom she, no matter how sweet, could never replace.

When I had finished my breakfast, Maddy cut us some lines of cocaine. 'There have been phone calls for you from Tom Morgan of United Press, Signora Sarfatti, who sent her best regards, and Signor Merletti who, I believe, is a tailor. Clearly, things are hopping.' And she paused.

I laughed. 'Maddy, my dear, if I were not discreet I would not have been asked to go where I went last night and last night I would not have been asked what I was asked. Be assured, I have been called to a noble task. One for which God has trained and tempered me over the past decade. All that has happened to me has prepared me for my destiny. I shall be able to rise to the occasion.' I promised that all would soon be revealed.

'Quite,' she said, in an affected English way. 'I'm really not being boring, darling. Do you want me to phone anyone back for you? Billy and Ethel have had to go out – taking their kids to see her aunt, who's French but living in Tivoli. What do you want to do? Go home?'

At that moment I could take no further reminders of Margherita Sarfatti's exotic and bizarre tastes. I elected to remain where I was. 'What did Tom Morgan want?'

'He said to say, "Welcome aboard." Does that mean anything to you?'

I remembered Il Duce speaking of the Fascist Inner Council and its international membership. The gathering of the great and the good dedicated to the task of bringing to reality the Fascist dream. I had already heard it rumoured that Morgan, a great womaniser and spendthrift with a string of mistresses as well as a family to maintain, not to mention a drinking problem and a lifestyle spent with the Italian *haut monde*, earned a good salary advising Il Duce on American and press matters. His critics said he found it expedient to become a card-carrying Fascist. Only then could he, as a foreigner, be completely trusted. A cynical view. Even when it was discovered to be true and his office fired him, nothing was ever made of it. He continues to work in the US, a successful correspondent, to the present day. I saw him a couple of years ago, when he was covering the coronation, and he had no doubts. 'Mussolini was the best thing that ever happened to Italy,' he said, 'and Hitler was the worst.' His argument was that Mussolini was a great man responding to his nation's needs but that Hitler was a fanatic, responsive only to his own appetites and mindless lust for power. We have argued this case many times. 'Mussolini created Hitler,' claims Morgan, 'and Hitler destroyed him.' It is a persuasive point of view.

By late afternoon I was dressed. I called Morgan first. He was not available, so I left a message with his desk. Then I called the tailor, who told me that he understood I needed an urgent appointment.

Mystified, I agreed. I was expected tomorrow at 11 a.m. The tailor gave me a fashionable address near the Ponte Palatina. Not for the first time I began to sense that I was in a carriage being winched rapidly up to the top of a very high roller-coaster. I knew that at any moment I might find myself hurtling forward at a momentum I could not control. Like all men, I am moved by the tides of history. My curse is that I am aware of it. I know what is happening, but I have no means of controlling it. As Margherita Sarfatti herself later said, my curse is to be eternally conscious. She was a ghoul but she was not a fool.

She was, it emerged, a possessive ghoul. When I arrived at the tailor the next morning I was greeted with as much servile enthusiasm as if I had been the Pope himself. A horde of little boys and girls began helping me off with my clothes, measuring me in every conceivable place. And as I stood before the mirror wearing only my undershirt and boxer shorts, feeling secure, I suppose, in what was after all a traditional male preserve, I caught a sound behind me, a fulsome drone of greeting and a vast wave of odours struck me almost physically, announcing the entrance of the woman who was in more ways than one my mistress.

'My darling,' she said in her husky English, 'you are so beautiful in your underwear. Those legs! Ah! Perfection.' And she sat herself down in a chair, attended by almost as many little tailors as I, to light a Turkish cigarette which she inserted in an iron holder, the latest Fascist fashion. I felt like a whore as she watched, in amused relish, the process. Now cloth was brought – a fine, black wool – and laid upon my person in various places. Chalk marks, further measurements, and Margherita Sarfatti, my patroness, smoked and chatted. 'I saw Tom Morgan this morning. He said he telephoned you, my darling. But you weren't up. You cannot be so lazy from now on. Fascists are expected to set a good example. I looked through your cuttings. They were fascinating.'

'Cuttings?' I became a little alarmed.

'Tom got them from the Service. We needed to check up on your credentials and make sure you are who you say you are. After all, sweetheart, you now have responsibilities and we have to know if we can trust you.'

Naively I had not realised that such checks would be made. Not all my press had been positive. I asked, casually, what she had learned from my 'Press Kit'. She smiled, a teasing travesty of coquetry, and said that what they had learned must have been good, because here I was.

She had not understood I had played such an important part in politics. I had been far too circumspect. A Klansman! She and Mussolini had seen *The Birth of a Nation* three times when it first came to Milan. So romantic, so daring. Just the kind of hero for the New Italy.

I decided that the faint note of mockery in her voice was permanent and not especially directed at me. With it she protected herself in a world which, in the intensity of its vendettas and cruelty of its judgements, was far worse than any political world. The world of the international art scene. The budgets of small nations were spent on art, especially by Americans like Hearst and J. P. Morgan, and the power struggle was intense.

She had read some of my speeches. And I had told Mussolini he had no American equivalent! The course of United States history might have taken a very different turn if I had been in power. But she could tell I was a dreamer, a poet-engineer, who had no interest in ordinary political power. There was only one D'Annunzio. My combination of experience and innocence was very touching. She came over to where I stood, draped in black cloth, and made a few murmured suggestions to the tailor, touching my figure with a kind of casual, abstracted intimacy I might have found degrading if I did not have so much inner pride.

By the time the tailoring ordeal was at an end, she took me to lunch in the vast Rolls-Royce which called for us. At least the restaurant was small and there was no one there I knew. She asked why I had given up my political career. I told her that it was chiefly because the Klan had become corrupt. It had lost all its original ideals in its effort to reach accommodation with ordinary bourgeois politics. She was sympathetic. That was the early history of Fascism, she said. But the Klan still survived. I said that I doubted now if it would ever gain real power.

I was first and foremost, I explained, an engineer. In America, because of my connections with well-known producers and directors, I had been induced to act and design film sets. As soon as I had the chance, however, I returned to my first love, my engineering projects.

'Your airships and your steam-cars,' she said. 'Not to mention all your other ideas. I have read the articles.'

114

Clearly Tom Morgan had not turned up the more accusatory pieces. This was very comforting to me. At last I was with people prepared to believe the best of their fellow men rather than the worst. She asked me what was happening with my projects. I explained how the independent inventor and entrepreneur was being squeezed out of America by big corporations and a tax structure which favoured Big Business but did nothing for the small man. I told her how my projects had been bought by these powerful interests and then 'mothballed' or scrapped. The commercial failure of my steam-car, for instance, was a case in point. The car was a victim of the vastly powerful oil companies like British Petroleum and S&O. In offering certain inventions to the US government, I said, I had again been sabotaged. Washington was so thoroughly corrupt you could no longer trust her institutions, even the Patent Office. Besides, I no longer felt that I wished to give the US any more of my inventions, my political wisdom or my theatrical gifts. I was now exclusively at the service of Il Duce.

'Well,' she said, playing with my thigh under the table, 'he is delighted. I have not seen him so happy for a long while. Your war machines, independent of oil, are exactly what we need. Il Duce is concerned in the event of war that any military action should be swift and decisive, over within days or weeks. Any other kind of war is uneconomical and far too wasteful for one's own side. All current strategic thinking says this. Tanks and planes and bombs are what win modern wars. The bigger the plane or the tank or the bomb, the more chance one has of winning. You and Mussolini think on the same scale. That is why you will control the future.'

I was, as ever, surprised at her grasp of the principles. Such understanding was highly unusual in a woman, especially an Italian woman. I could see why, in her youth, she had been so attractive to Mussolini, so helpful to him. She had been married to a businessman, some socialist from her early years. Mussolini, too, had been a socialist, but, for obvious reasons, no mention was made of that these days. Il Duce's journey to political maturity had been swifter than most, but it had been a journey nonetheless.

Margherita was eager for any Hollywood gossip. I explained to her that I had been in Africa on my own particular expedition into the heart of darkness. I had eschewed most things Western and had lost touch with many old friends. I had seen the latest films, of course. Indeed, one of my main preoccupations while forced to stay so long in Tangier, was visiting the cinemas. But I had not seen a talkie until I came to Italy and I must admit I had not been overly impressed. They were full of stilted dialogue uttered by men in spats and women in evening dresses before a static camera. They were all about darkies or people who dressed up as darkies. *The Jazz Singer* was a combination of both. My own preference, so far, was for *Steamboat Willie*. There would come a time when the talking film approached the artistic perfection of its silent predecessor. I had seen no proof as yet.

She was inclined to agree. She was watching an art form turn itself into a sensational novelty to please an increasingly crass public. Was I never depressed that this progress towards tosh seemed endemic in the American arts? She spoke of certain painters and composers I did not know. We were, I told her, dependent on the tastes of the petite bourgeoisie for our livings. We moved towards the common denominator as if it were a cause. I was sure there could be a combination of popular and fine art to meet all the criteria.

'That's what we're producing in Italy,' she said, 'especially in architecture.' She was helping commission some important public buildings but was meeting resistance among certain Fascist ministers. She claimed they hated her simply because she was a woman. 'If a man had done what I have done for Italian prestige around the world,' she said, waving her arm in a panoramic arc, 'he would be weighed down with honours and rewards. Meanwhile I have to make a living as best I can. I have no one but myself.'

A melodramatic statement from someone who had as her protector the greatest man in the history of modern Italy, the natural successor to Garibaldi! I had no clear idea, then, how insecure she felt. Mussolini's wife was no illiterate. Rachele Mussolini became deeply unhappy if she saw Margherita's name in the press. Margherita depended upon the newspapers for her living and her fame. Without them, much of her power was threatened.

Of course, I did not understand this then. I was beginning to slip into that extraordinary sense of security and comfort that comes from finding one's natural place among the powerful. I had never been so thoroughly accepted as I was by Il Duce and his people. I had never felt so safe. Yet that feeling of acceptance and well-being was not complete. I was still keenly aware that Margherita Sarfatti was my chief's long-time paramour. I had a horror of being caught between the two of them. I was still wondering, for instance, what had happened to my friend da Bazzanno, Sarfatti's earlier lover.

In the private dining room, as the uncrowned Queen of Italy took her singular pleasures with me, I guessed it would be some time before she tired of me. I had no choice but to comply. I let my mind drift towards other things. I was astonished that Il Duce could ever have found this rutting harpy attractive. I did not know then, of course, why she should be so repellent to me.

Back at the Grishams' my hosts had returned and were laughing heartily over drinks. Handing my coat to the maid, I asked the reason for their amusement. Billy said they had had at least ten different telephone engineers round that day. 'It shows you're much more important than me, Max!' and he lifted his glass in a toast as Ethel handed me my champagne cocktail. I did not follow his reasoning. Then he told me that a visit from a telephone engineer was considered to be identical to a visit from the secret police. His phone, he said, was thoroughly tapped. He didn't mind, since the office's phone wasn't tapped and he could always use that. This seemed childish stuff to me and I ignored it. It pleased people to pretend they were constantly under Il Duce's personal surveillance. It gave their escapades an added thrill, I suppose. The whole rather cynical tenor of the conversation depressed me. I had had an exhausting day and needed to relax. Billy and Ethel did not 'coke' and I felt a need for some more of the nourishing powder. Politely I wondered if they would mind if Maddy and I returned to the Villa Borghese. Of course they understood. Billy drove us back in his own car. He was in a merry mood and kept beginning sentences which he did not finish. I thanked him warmly for his hospitality and help. I regarded him as my best journalist friend in Rome. I would let him know the story as soon as I could, even if it were the middle of the night. He was grateful for that.

The sun was setting as we let ourselves back in to our little cottage. Orange rays touched the firs and cedars, turning our terracotta to comforting fire. In spite of all the mementoes of Margherita, I was glad to be there. I was sure she would not bother us. Her natural preference for conspiracy would not allow her, I suspected, to bring things out into the open, not when there was an ounce of drama or advantage to be squeezed from the situation.

Maddy was unsurprised that I went to sleep early. She contented herself with writing in her diary. I read most of it later. It was concerned with banal speculation about my new job and a schoolgirlish

117

enthusiasm for my talents and place in history. Clearly Miss Butter planned to marry me and perhaps even take me back to Texas for a while. I would be the living version of the European trophies with which Hearst filled his overblown palace. I knew she would not be happy if thwarted in her intentions. I therefore decided upon the wisest path: caution. I hoped to divert her from her ambitions. I prayed that Margherita Sarfatti would soon be sent off on one of her cultural missions to some faraway country. My only prayer was that she did not take me with her.

Next morning there was a knock on the door. Maddy and I were eating breakfast, discussing the best way to get to Ponte Palatina, whether to walk or take the tram. She answered the door while I stepped into some clothes. Tom Morgan entered, his face a map of all the pleasures a pressman was ever tempted to taste, the little blue, red and yellow veins describing his various routes to hell via paradise. His bluff manner edged with the morning's miseries, he handed me an envelope. He looked forward to seeing me at ten o'clock that evening. The address was on the envelope. He tipped his hat to an enquiring, bright-eyed Maddy, complimented her on her hair and morning robe, and returned to his waiting taxi.

Miranda frowned when he had gone. She clearly did not like the man. Perhaps she already sensed a rival and thought it might be Tom. In some small agitation, she went off to change. To reassure her, I tossed the message unopened on to the table. By the time we were walking together, her arm in mine, she seemed to have forgotten all about Tom Morgan. When we got back, as if suddenly remembering Tom's visit, I picked up the envelope he had given me.

The address was a villa off the Via Aurelia not far from the Vatican City. A salubrious area, where it did not abut the railway lines. The envelope contained two silver buttons, each one the symbol of a bundle of rods surrounding a double-bladed axe – the *fascisti* upon which Mussolini's name and power was based. They were extremely elegant. I had seen something similar worn by the highest members of the Fascist Grand Council, that group of men, largely drawn from the professions of journalism and public relations, who now helped their chief run the country. But I was still not entirely sure of their significance. I did not show them to Maddy, who was almost weeping with curiosity. Smiling, I assured her that as soon as I was relieved of my oath of secrecy, I would explain all.

That night I stumbled somewhat wearily up the long drive of a

118

run-down villa whose back garden went directly down to the railway tracks. Clearly the place had been picked for its position rather than its visual aspects. I even smelled urine near the gates, as they were opened for me by two smartly uniformed members of the Fascist Militia, now an official arm of the Italian Armed Services.

More of the blackshirted militia, with their kepis and brightly polished jackboots, were present in the grounds, some controlling eager dogs spoiling for trouble. On the top steps to the entrance portico, Tom Morgan himself was waiting for me. He was in full uniform. I noted that he wore the same studs he had given me that morning. It was clearly the badge of a high-ranking *fascisti*. I saluted him. He was pleased by my response. 'Oh, you and I are not the only Americans capable of thinking beyond our domestic boundaries, Max. Our brotherhood embraces the world, wherever the white race is dominant.' He shook me busily by the hand. 'I've read about your work in America and I don't blame you for leaving. But you're among good friends here, Max.'

As always, the alcohol on Tom's breath remained my predominant impression of the man. His was not a type I naturally took to, though I have no doubt of his sincerity. He led me through corridors and halls smelling strongly of mould. Although the place had not been lived in for years, there were many signs of activity.

In two rooms I was sure I saw splattered blood on the wall. Blood always makes that pattern when someone has been shot at an angle from below. Again I grew a little nervous. I am not one of those, like so many I knew in the old days, who were excited by the smell of blood and gunpowder. Some even lusted for it. Their disease was caught in the trenches after so many months of warfare when violence became a habit. Women were excited by it, too. Men were taught that violence was good for them, that they flourished and were made hard by it.

Almost every country had such ideas after the World War. Many in the Klan believed a new civil war was coming and that they had to be ready for it. These Kennedys and Humphreys and Carters will be the cause of it. They will drive the Klan to take up their guns, no matter how reluctantly. I was in the Hilton Hotel on Park Lane when the news came of Robert Kennedy's assassination. There was a TV playing in the lobby which was full of American businessmen. They all wear the same kind of three-piece suit and a tie, which is meant to look like something from an English public school. They have soft, self-indulgent, unformed faces. As soon as they heard the news of the assassination, they put down their briefcases and coffee cups and began to applaud. I was there. I heard it. I was waiting to meet a TV producer who was going to make a film about my life. Nothing came of it. My life has been too incredible. I tell the story to illustrate that it was not only 'crazies' and 'extremists' who were driven to distraction by the Kennedy clan and its descendants. Decent American politicians and capitalists shared frustrations with the assassin.

The same with Matteotti. Of course, I have every sympathy for the man. He was murdered. But he brought it on himself. He was an unrepentant socialist and a constant critic of all that was positive in modern Italy. Mussolini had absolutely nothing to do with the crime. Margherita Sarfatti told me herself. When the news was brought to him and he was handed Matteotti's bloodstained documents, Il Duce said nothing until everyone was gone. Then he began vomiting blood. His digestion remained poor from that moment on. That was how strongly he felt about murder. Scarcely the reaction of a man who condoned brutal methods!

We entered a room whose walls and windows had all been lined with black velvet drapes, edged with scarlet and gold. The only decoration in the entire room was above the ornamental fireplace. Over it hung a magnificent portrait of Il Duce holding in his hands the Sword of Islam and the Roman *fascisti* respectively, ready to bring justice, dignity and honour back to his empire. An inspiring portrait. One I had not seen reproduced before. This showed the inner strength of Il Duce glowing from his determined, aggressive head. Every man gathered there around a huge oak table, wore an identical uniform – black jacket, black jodhpurs, black boots and a black cap. The only decorations were the epaulette buttons, the belt buckles and the silver *fascisti* at the collar.

The others greeted me in silence, contenting themselves with bringing their heels together and raising their arms in the Roman salute. I replied in kind. This seemed to meet with their approval. Without any further ceremony, the ritual began. I was made to stand upright before them at the table while each of the men there fired questions at me. For the most part these were telling queries concerning my background and my abilities. Clearly they had been briefed by Tom Morgan. Some of my interrogators, their keen eyes boring into mine, were American. Others were French, Spanish,

German, Swedish, even English. They were from all walks of life. No doubt between them they represented most of the professions. This was the Fascist answer to the Freemasons and the Jews, the Communists and the Moslem Brotherhood, who swore secret oaths and were the enemies of everything we held dear. In a future world, perhaps, we should have no need for such secret gatherings. But for the moment, with the world on the very brink of the final chaos, they were extremely necessary.

My ordeal over, the uniformed men sat down around the table. I was led away to a small anteroom, also smelling strongly of damp. Here, two batmen helped me out of my ordinary clothes and into my uniform including the black silk shirt worn under the jacket. It had been delivered in anticipation of this visit. I looked at myself in the mirror. In those days I was young and vibrant and cut an extremely handsome figure. I had been hardened by my ordeals. My pain had given my already attractive features extra character. I was at the height of my physical beauty as well as my intellect. I had the good looks of the best type of Italian.

Now in the flickering light of great flambeaux which burned on either side of Il Duce's portrait, I was inducted into the Fascist Inner Council. I swore to abjure all other loyalties and oaths and serve only Il Duce, His Excellency the Dictator Benito Mussolini. I would lay down my life, if necessary, in his service. That oath rang around the rafters of the ancient villa, bringing vibrant new energy to the old stones. The very firelight seemed to tremble to its rhythms. Then, to a man, we lifted our arms in that noble salute, which a Roman legionnaire reserved for his peers or his superiors, and roared, 'Hail, Mussolini! Hail, Il Duce!' We were a single, powerful unit. Nothing could hurt us. Nothing could disturb our security. Nothing could stand in our way. We had control of the future. We were going to make it unrecognisable!

The rest of the meeting was highly congenial. I was truly among friends.

I returned home to my Miranda. She did not fail to be impressed by my new uniform, the insignia glittering in place. She fell into my arms, hungry for sexual satisfaction. And in my newly energised state, I pleasured her again and again. She admitted she had been jealous. Now she realised she was foolish. How could she be jealous, she said, of a monument, an inspiration.

A few days later, on 1 January 1931, my thirty-first birthday, I took up my position as Minister of Overseas Development in the Inner Cabinet of Benito Mussolini. My tailor had made me five identical uniforms so that I should have fresh ones at all times. My offices were a vast suite on the second floor of the Villa Valentino, into which light poured, creating long black shadows and pools of blinding whiteness. I was reminded of the best type of movie set.

During the first weeks of my new position I paced in and out of these great shadows, frequently alone. My appointment had been announced in all the newspapers. I had begun to receive invitations from the highest sources. My status was never greater. However, I was without any kind of assistance or practical furniture. The rooms had been empty for years, and the taste of the minister who had occupied it, perhaps when the place was first built, had been fussy and showy and full of ugly little stuffings. I wanted office furniture in keeping with my modern position. Clean Austrian lines. Plenty of light.

I wrote out my suggestions in longhand and gave it to Margherita Sarfatti, my only visitor. She came frequently. I was always glad that I was able to shower at the office and return home to my Maddy in one of my spare uniforms. Apart from that occasion at the Villa Torlonia, I had yet to meet my chief. On one level I was glad, for I was not sure I had enough emotional energy left to cope with Mussolini's raw vitality. But I have to say I was growing impatient.

The first weeks of 1931 were a round of parties at which I met many of the most important heads of state, film stars, actresses and designers. In common with my colleagues, I wore my uniform a great deal of the time. Only Tom Morgan did not wear his. Instead he sported a silver *fascista* behind his lapel. He told me that American public opinion was not quite ready for the news of his elevation.

I grew a little apart from Billy and Ethel Grisham, although Maddy continued to see them. We were so busy with official functions that somehow we were now always announced together as Professor Peters and his fiancée Miss Butter. I had attempted to stop this, but Maddy of course was delighted. I had loved my Esmé. I had loved my Rosie. I loved Mrs Cornelius. But I did not love Maddy with the same profundity. I made it very clear to her that I had no intention of marrying her. She argued with me. I compromised. We should not marry until my work for Mussolini was well under way. She understood completely. I must be sure to get plenty of rest and relaxation, or I would kill myself in Il Duce's service. That would do nobody any good. I reminded her that our new lifestyle was a result of Il Duce's favours. We owed him a great deal. Our social life and our status had improved enormously. She had not come to Italy, she said, to improve her social status. She had plenty of that back home in Texas. What she was interested in was politics, engineering advances, social progress – everything Mussolini was achieving in Italy. As her country wallowed in Depression. What was needed there was the same kind of dynamic leader. I understood her viewpoint very well. I shared it. However, I pointed out, things moved at a different pace in modern Italy. She should not make the mistake of confusing American simplification with efficiency.

I think she was suitably chastened by my little lecture. By then things had begun to move at last. Not much later, after some conference which Il Duce attended, I came to my offices one morning to find them fully furnished and thoroughly staffed, with aides, secretaries, office boys, filing clerks and everything to go with them. Clearly the Supreme Leader of Italy was ready for me to start work.

I had a huge modern desk to sit at and brass fittings to catch the light, deep carpets to pace upon, polished panelling to admire, familiar works of art to ease my soul and great armchairs to lounge in. I found myself nervously awaiting the arrival of Margherita Sarfatti, wondering which piece of furniture she would choose to use first, when suddenly the door opened and Mussolini walked in, his hand outstretched, his eyes full of concern. He was a gravely sympathetic bull. '*Professore*. We have some work to do, eh? I am so sorry you have had this trouble. Everyone involved has been chastised. You must let me know personally if there is anything else you need. Is the furniture to your taste?'

I stammered my approval. I had felt like this only in the presence of Hollywood's greatest producers. I understood how, with so many functions to supervise, so many things to consider, such men steadfastly refuse to give someone they respect merely half their attention. They wait, as I do, until their full attention can be employed.

Again Mussolini stressed his admiration for my film work, his love of America, his admiration for, in particular, her fine engineers. He was shorter than I remembered him, a little below my own height, but very stocky and radiating masculinity. He shared Margherita Sarfatti's taste for colognes and sometimes seemed to wear several at the same time, but nothing could disguise that radiant, animal quality which came off him in the way the stink of power comes off a lion's hide. Il Duce arrived directly at the point. He wanted to see what my Leviathan might look like in action. Italy had some of the greatest modellers in the world. Would it be possible to make a large-scale model, complete perhaps with a desert scene of some kind. As realistic as possible? I said I would be delighted to provide such a model, but I had no idea when it would be completed.

Mussolini was affability itself. He grinned at me in that ugly, comradely way he had and punched me lightly on the arm. In ten days, he said.

I said I was amazed at his powers of prediction. 'If I say ten days,' he told me, 'then it will be ten days. You will see.'

He had inspired and empowered me.

Sure enough, in ten days' time, the entire main boardroom of my ministry had been given up to a vast table on which we had prepared a complete desert scene, down to the smallest detail. The only thing we had not had made were the railway trains which were the best German type, and the model soldiers, which were also German and very lifelike.

Sitting in the middle of this scene was the massive model of my mobile ziggurat, the greatest war machine ever designed. I showed an excited Mussolini how it could be moved by remote control. I ran the trains and I set off the little gun batteries in the forts and towns. As the guns popped, flashed and smoked, Mussolini's massive head split in a great grin. It was that attractive grin only his intimates were ever allowed to see. That grin, I think, made Mussolini human. The charming, uncalculated expression of a happy Romagnan peasant, it spoke of a big, generous, boyish heart. It was our Duce's best-kept secret. His tragedy. He could not afford to let a rapacious world know that he was a man of sensitivity and fun.

We played with our new models the whole day, yelling like children. The massive machine crushed fortresses and towns, its guns fired in all directions, its huge treads turned. I was extremely proud of the realistic effect. Clearly Il Duce could not have been more pleased. He had a photographer and a cinematographer come in to take close-up pictures. 'This will convince them,' he said, sticking out his chest and bringing his fists together as our Land Leviathan rolled over trench positions, crushing whole battalions of tiny clay soldiers.

Towards the end of the afternoon Benito Mussolini turned to me, eyes shining. We were both invigorated, united in a bond of fellowship. Our tunics were off, our shirtsleeves rolled up; we drank glasses of fizzing water and contemplated the scene of our miniature triumph. Both of us at that moment could see the grand reality ahead. He shook my hand. 'Professor,' he said in his vibrant, musical English, 'we are in business. I want you to come home and meet the wife.'

My heart sank.

I prayed Mrs Mussolini did not have her rival's predatory tastes.

THIRTEEN

On the way to the Villa Torlonia Mussolini seemed a little gruff. I wondered if he felt embarrassed by his earlier enthusiasm. But he remained friendly enough. The big limousine took us through the busy streets of lunchtime Rome. We travelled with an almost super-natural smoothness. We stopped at a traffic light and were again surrounded by our motorcycle escort. My chief cleared his throat and moved his mouth in that almost comical way so many found endearing. 'My boys are great lads,' he said. 'I allow them no special privileges. The same demands are made on them as on all Italian children. We are raising them as decent, gentlemanly Fascists. I take no credit at all. My wife is the best in the world. She tells me, "You stay out of my kitchen, and I'll stay out of your politics." She's from a very political family. You heard about my daughter's wedding! Never again! She's in Shanghai now. Very happy. Thank God I needn't go through all that with the boys. We have a cinema in the house. The boys are flying-mad, too. I told you they're great fans of "Ace" Peters? They've watched all your films. *White Aces, The Flying Buckaroo.* They'd be enchanted if you'd tell them a bit about your film days.' He shrugged, almost apologising. 'I told them I knew you. They made me promise they could meet you. I hope you don't mind, Professor Peters. Perhaps an autograph as well? They've been studying very hard. If it would not embarrass you too much . . .'

'On the contrary, Chief.' I was honoured. Almost no one was allowed into the Mussolini family sanctum. This invitation demon-strated how I was truly valued by Il Duce. I was relieved to hear, moreover, that the reason for the privilege was something as whole-some and simple as a papa's promise to his sons!

At last we had negotiated the great press of Roman traffic and arrived at the gates of the Villa Torlonia. It was my second visit, of course. Now I could see the security police everywhere. The wide street was deserted. Ordinary Italians avoided it, together with the nearby cafés, in case they should be arrested as suspected assassins. I understood the identity of the shadows I had seen in the grounds. We went through a couple of anterooms until we entered a pleasant, spacious room with windows looking out on to the garden and the lake beyond. A large table had been set with a white cloth. On it were the usual breads and condiments found on any comfortable Italian board. The linen, cutlery and tableware were of good quality but not at all pretentious. From nearby came the smell of cooking. Mussolini called a greeting and suddenly the place filled.

First came two boys of about eight and eleven in their black-shirt school uniforms, a little dishevelled. Following them was a stocky woman with a wide, cheerful face, her brown hair drawn back in a tight bun, a linen apron covering her cotton print dress. After them entered another pleasant young woman whom I took to be a secretary or governess. She had charge of two younger children. She was followed by a black-clad maid carrying a large tureen and another carrying plates.

When everyone was around the table, having greeted Il Duce affectionately much as they would greet the head of any respectable household, they stood by their places looking expectantly in my direction. After a pregnant pause, for the Chief was incapable of any action without an element of drama, I was introduced.

The servants curtsied. Mrs Mussolini came up to me, grasped me in her powerful, motherly hands and kissed me on both cheeks. I looked as handsome off the screen as on it, she said approvingly, and sat me down between herself and her sons, who eagerly asked me questions about my stunts. Not since Morocco had I found such an adoring audience. I must admit I rose to the flattery, describing all the people I had known in Hollywood, telling them of amazing feats and impossible escapes. Laurel and Hardy (whom they loved almost as much as me)? Laurel remained an Englishman. Hardy was shy. I described the daring of Tom Mix and Hoot Gibson and confirmed the angelic beauty and off-screen generosity of Clara Bow. Meanwhile Rachele Mussolini helped us to the soup, first me, then her husband and then the others. I enjoyed her sturdy minestrone made without wine and served with excellent fresh bread. Signora Mussolini assured me she had baked the loaf that morning.

I might have been visiting a prosperous farmer and his family in the Romagna, the scene was so comfortingly ordinary. Mussolini's instincts were perfect. Here was the reality to which he returned for supper before spending the evening with his family. He did this as often as possible. Only towards the end, I heard, did he forsake these habits. By then he had become enamoured of Hitler and of Clara Petacci. His wife, she would remind me when we met that one time after the War when I went with Mrs Cornelius to Italy on a package holiday, had warned him against both. These enthusiasms were to conspire in his downfall. She was to write a touching memoir of her husband. Rachele was well aware of her value to him. She loved Mussolini with that deliberate lack of criticism her culture had trained her to prize as a virtue. And Rachele had his ear on almost any question. They made, he sometimes said proudly, a perfect fighting unit, like any Romagnan peasant couple used to the hardships of existence and the realities of survival.

She was a good-humoured woman with a happy smile. Far from being the philistine peasant of popular gossip, she was dignified, well educated and, when occasion demanded, grave. She kept her feet firmly on the ground. Hardly anyone from the Romagna region was not a socialist and an anti-cleric. Like parts of modern County Durham and Northumberland. Today whole villages are communist. But she was no more a bigot than if she had come from a particularly devout part of the country. Like her husband, she formed her own opinions and had good reasons for maintaining them.

As if I was a long-lost nephew, she took to me in a matronly way. Perhaps I filled an emotional void for her. The Mussolinis had recently lost Il Duce's brother Arnaldo who had died of a broken heart on the death of his son Sandrino from leukaemia.

Finishing his meal rapidly, my Chief leaned back with a groan, which he tried to suppress. His wife ignored him, as if she was used to him. He winced, then grinned at me. 'Indigestion,' he said.

'He's a slave to it,' she confirmed disapprovingly as the plates were gathered up. In fact, La Sarfatti told me, he had a serious ulcer. It had ruptured on the night he heard Matteotti had been murdered.

Mussolini stood up. 'Meetings with ambassadors this afternoon,' he said. 'Come on, Professor. I'll give you a lift back to the Villa Valentino.'

The boys begged me to stay longer.

Mussolini laughed at this. 'Don't you have school this afternoon?'

They begged me to come back in the evening. Bruno in particular had questions about stunt flying and Vittorio wanted to know how you got to act in films.

Signora Mussolini took charge of her sons. Perhaps I might like to come back some evening? She would make me a decent supper and we could watch some films. Her husband seemed perfectly content with this arrangement and so we left. I had enjoyed the visit. For me it was such a relief to be a guest in an ordinary household. Signora Mussolini had taken me under her wing, just as my old Aunt Genia had done years before in Odessa. I envied Il Duce his security. I was to pay several visits to the Villa Torlonia that year. They remain my happiest memories of Rome, in spite of the success I enjoyed there. I watched movies with Mrs Mussolini and I told her boys stories of my flying exploits. They called me 'Uncle Max' and she was pleased. Since Mussolini's brother had died, she admitted, there had been an aching absence. She knew my work must be exhausting and was so grateful I could find time to spend with them. I would always, she said, be a welcome guest. I found it a great relief to know I had somewhere I could relax.

Many lack the character to carry the burdens of public life. The small pleasures of privacy, those intimate moments in obscure cafés, visits to galleries and entertainments, begin to turn into public appearances. And, of course, one's personal life is subject to all manner of minor and irritating constraints.

We special ministers were not required to wear our uniforms at all times, but Il Duce made it clear how our public image was of paramount importance. As long as that was properly maintained, so was the state. Admittedly the Italian, English and American press was not unkind to us and one's more intimate secrets were never aired – at least while one remained in office.

A case in point was poor, honest Augusto Turati, whom I met once or twice in the days before he was so thoroughly disgraced. He was a notorious pederast and paedophile, though an excellent and honest party secretary. While he continued to perform his public duties properly, such matters were never put before the people. However, when, shortly before my own appointment, Turati rather foolishly criticised the party as corrupt, he was replaced.

Everything came out then, of course. Mussolini, who had turned a blind eye to his friend's escapades, was shocked at the details presented to him by the OVRA, his special police department concerned with internal affairs. He never spoke of Turati again.

129

Il Duce himself was highly tolerant of human foibles, though he had few of his own. His view very properly was that while a man served the public effectively, there was no need to dig up the dirt. 'After all,' he would say, 'there are few of us who haven't something in our past which could be interpreted unfavourably.' If this attitude led to certain party members occasionally taking advantage of their positions, it also meant that public confidence was maintained. Franklin Roosevelt said we had nothing to fear but fear itself. To a nation, said Benito Mussolini, morale was more important than money. Both agreed that image and prestige were far more valuable than gold reserves.

'Gold is a fantasy,' my friend would say, as we played upon our desert battlegrounds. 'It has no more intrinsic value than this.' And his stubby, powerful fingers would claw up a mound of sand from the table, dribbling it back over the ruins we had just made of a well-defended fort.

'We give it power. It has none of its own. What makes gold and diamonds valuable are their artificial scarcity. The British and the Dutch, together with the Americans, control most of that trade, which gives them their power in the world. Alone, these minerals can feed no one, kill no one, help no one. They are a fantasy. Their worth is in their beauty. Yet nations destroy one another for gold. So if mankind is willing to struggle and die for one fantasy, why not another? America's greatest asset is not in her raw materials, but in her exports of fantasy across the globe.

'Without Hollywood, America would be like Canada. Nothing. Fabulation is America's greatest skill. It comes from having so many mad religious visionaries settled there. These people who accuse me of drawing an inaccurate picture of Italy are merely those whose own fantasies are at odds with mine. What is an "inaccurate picture"? Is the Wild West an inaccurate picture? No, it is an idealised vision. Similarly I describe the best we can become as a nation. After all, how much of a line is there between "idealism" and "fantasy"? What we are interested in, Professor, is the power of the human will to *create reality.*'

A common theme in those days. Mussolini expressed it well. I realised how pathetic El Glaoui's provincial dreams had been. Mussolini promised me I would soon have the engineering and material resources of the entire Italian Empire at my disposal. Meanwhile, we needed to shroud our plans in secrecy. Much as I wanted to shout my successes from the rooftops, I understood this. My oath to Il Duce put my life in his service. Here was a leader I could trust, whose intelligence, experience and vision made him my equal.

In common with some of the old *squadristi*, I grew a handsome beard. This gave me a fierce, aquiline appearance, like an engraving of one of my Cossack ancestors. It suited my new aggressive enthusiasm. Maddy said I looked like her pioneer ancestor, 'Black Bob' Butter, who had founded the family fortune. But I think she had an otherwise rather ambiguous reaction to what she called my 'whiskers'. I was in two minds about keeping them until Mussolini himself complimented me on them.

Some three times a week, if he was in Rome, Il Duce came to see me at my offices. Guards would be positioned at the great double doors, with their carvings of warring centaurs and satyrs. Then we would discuss where we had left off, how we had won the last of our battles, what problems we had discovered, and so on. Now two Land Leviathans stood some two feet high on the game table, facing batteries of guns and larger numbers of troops, as we tried out increasingly complicated strategies. Upon arrival, my chief would unbutton his tunic – he called it 'loosening my stays' – and take a small cup of coffee. Then he would give his entire concentration to the matter in hand. I noticed with no great surprise, since Italy had been an ally of Britain in the Great War, he preferred to fill the enemy positions with German soldiers.

The amount of time I spent with Il Duce created a certain jealousy towards me. Some of his people felt overlooked. Notoriously, Il Duce was growing remote from his old friends, those who had been with him from the beginning. I heard this constant, if not very audible, grumble from among the *ras*, *squadristi* and *gerarchia* of the old guard, who had won the revolution but failed to absorb their leader's lessons in statecraft. I heard similar complaints from several members of the Fascist Grand Council of which our Chief was head. If the American Revolution had been the work of a group of lawyers creating a land fit for lawyers to flourish in, then the Italian rebirth was chiefly in the hands of men who, like Mussolini himself, had been writers, publicists and journalists and who wished to create a nation where the writer was paramount. Their interest was not the day-to-day practical running of state affairs. They wished to maintain the morale of the country, in keeping the goals, as well as the achievements, of Fascism to the fore.

'We must all march forward singing,' said Turati, two days before his disgrace.

Mussolini did not want to hear such thoughts. He was forever repeating his view that while Italians thought of themselves as a nation of wine-loving opera singers they would never compete with the austerely successful Teutons, who, of course, had successfully conquered Italy after the Roman Empire withdrew to the East.

I think Turati's reference to song was a mistake. I had attended one or two of his little parties. He was not an evil man. I believe he meant well for Italy. But, as Mussolini put it to me, 'If you shove your fist up a little boy's arse, the next hand you shake will smell of shit.' By which Il Duce meant, I suppose, that inner corruption, which has nothing to do with sexual preferences or the enjoyment of the world's other many pleasures, is more important than outer. He did not object to Turati's symptoms of what Il Duce always called 'the German sickness', but the rule was, as Lord Joyce once said to me in the years when he was a simple commoner rather than a broadcaster, never to upset the ladies or frighten the horses. A rule the British would do well to remember, since they are no better than the others these days with their miserable kowtowing to every dusky ex-colonial who decides to castigate them in print. They were once the most successful Teutons in the world. Now, of course, we have the Americans.

Except when we were experimenting with our models or when on a whim he would occasionally decide to take me for a drive at the wheel of his huge Mercedes-Benz, zooming through the streets of Rome late at night, when little attention needed to be paid to lights or signs, Il Duce remained a very private man. He even checked himself from revealing that infectiously broad and charming smile. He habitually pushed his lower lip forward, firming his jaw against the cares of state, striking a deliberately belligerent pose by drawing his brows together in an almost comical scowl. The Bolshevist cartoonists loved to parody these expressions. Yet it was a conscious mask assumed for public appearances or for when he met a fellow Head of State. He could not afford to appear weak or indecisive. He was, after all, a superman. Our job was to support him in what-ever positive ways we could. Therefore, to present another image of Il Duce was an act of national sabotage.

Turati had been one of the first to realise the importance of what came to be called *ducisimo* in promoting a national identity.

Mussolini's favourite theme, that Italians would only be respected abroad when they lost their image as a nation of *mafiosi* and *gigoli*, made considerable sense. If other people see you as weak and foolish, there is a strong chance you will come to see yourself in this way. I have observed husbands, convinced by their wives that they are of a certain character, begin to behave accordingly. Women, of course, are masters of this sort of thing.

For this reason Mussolini treated Italians to a constant litany of Italian successes – in the Arts, the Sciences, the Humanities. All agreed that Italy led the world in style, for instance. It was imitated everywhere. No longer a nation of opera singers, but of the great *condottieri*, said Mussolini.

'And this, *Professore*,' he added, laying a firm hand upon my massive piece, 'is what in the end impresses the world. Spectacular weaponry! Imagine the astonishment of the world when our futurist arsenal is revealed! The threat of war, Professor, brings many a great power to her senses. With machines like this we shall restore our African and our Eastern Empire without losing a single Italian life!'

The idea of war was still unpopular in Italy. Mussolini knew that if gains could be made with minimum losses his prestige would be even higher. His prestige and Italy's prestige were indistinguishable and interdependent. For this reason we worked in secrecy. A few hints of our project were released to the press. I was not named, save as a famous American inventor advising Il Duce in his great plans. We were designing a homeland defence system which would be second to none. That system would make the Maginot Line seem old-fashioned and hopelessly ineffective. All European countries in those days were prepared for another war. Few had the heart for it. Mussolini argued that war was identified with the bloody folly of the trenches. He reminded me that British tanks first broke that appalling stalemate. The modern equivalent of flying cavalry, the tank, together with the fighting aeroplane, changed the rules of warfare.

The months went by. I enjoyed a status I had never known before. I had won respect, power, approval, the company of international men of affairs. I was party to all the political secrets of Europe. I knew only one small frustration. I should have anticipated it when dealing with a man of so many responsibilities. Il Duce would not let me know when we would be ready to put the prototype into production. Whenever I asked, he would offer me some reason for delaying. Then he would turn the conversation to some other invention of mine and insist that a model be commissioned. Thus the surrounding panelling of the boardroom's walls was soon supporting shelves containing massive models of all my inventions. One of these was my long-range bombing aeroplane, the so-called 'Flying Wing', which contained much more extra fuel than ordinary aircraft. Although we were not yet giving employment to Italy's engineers and steelworkers, we were making her toymakers rich.

Factories were not yet tooled up to produce the Land Leviathan's full-size prototype, but over the next months our people brought to life a whole series of designs. I felt the euphoria I had known when I had worked on films, though ultimately, of course, we aimed to produce reality rather than illusion. I was disappointed Il Duce showed little interest in my more domestic inventions, such as the Radio Oven, but glad he remained enthusiastic about the rest, a product of what he insisted on praising as my 'Fascist sensibility'.

'These machines, Professor, are the expression in steel and cordite of our Fascist ability to crush all opposition in a single efficient action.'

He would walk up and down our long model room studying a multi-engined flying boat here, a dynamite engine there, a jointed aircraft carrier, a superfast mobile gun and so on. Set against suitable backgrounds, the models created an astonishing impression of reality.

To my intense relief even Margherita Sarfatti was banned from this inner sanctum to which only my Chief and myself were privy. Here Il Duce could let his hair down (figuratively, since he was going grey and was forced to shave his head). He could forget the cares of state. I was flattered that he wished to spend so much time with me. I sometimes wondered what my company offered him. I knew nothing then, of course, about his plans for the rapid expansion of Italian influence into Africa and the Balkans.

Although he loved to speak in terms of war – the war for wheat, the war against crime, the war on terror, the war against alcoholism and so on – Mussolini's nature did not lean much towards Mars. He enjoyed the game of it but had very little stomach for actual violence. He was probably never happier than when he stabbed the buttons of his radio-control, making my great War Ziggurat fire this way and that, rolling over infantry divisions, squadrons of cavalry, tanks, anti-aircraft guns, planes, forts and palm groves with mighty dignity. Sometimes Mussolini seemed a rather shy, almost timid person. When his defences were down he would ask quite naive questions with a direct, schoolboy innocence which made me admire and like him all the more.

I have heard it said that Fascism is not an ideology but a conflict of ideologies. If that were true, perhaps Mussolini mirrored that conflict just as much as he resolved it. While he controlled himself, he held Italy, with all her own inner conflicts, together. When his conflicts got the better of him, he was forced to make draconian decisions rather than find compromise. Then his power left him. Then Italy was lost.

Only when Mussolini was thoroughly decisive was Italy badly served. Perhaps this sounds like treachery against a man I still treasure as a friend. Yet it was Mussolini's powers of compromise which enabled him to represent the Italian people and allow Italy to survive, just as my own similar powers have led to my own survival. One is neither a hypocrite nor a liar if one is by nature a diplomat.

In spite of his firm and necessary aggressiveness at the negoti-ating table, the Dictator always left doors open for alternatives. Tom Morgan believes that Hitler closed those doors for Mussolini and so initiated Italy's downfall. Franco, says Tom, had far more sense and kept Spain stable until the present day. Tom bought a house in Spain, which is very pro-American, but he often visits my shop when over here to see his doctor in Harley Street. At least he and I still have our admiration for Il Duce in common. I, of course, understood Mussolini a little better than Morgan. Indeed, one thing Margherita Sarfatti, who perhaps knew her lover better than anyone, said to me was that I brought the man she had admired and respected back to life.

Sarfatti never told me much about her intimate episode with our friend. Yet sometimes, in the middle of making love to Maddy Butter, I would be seized by a chilling thought: could Mussolini and Margherita be discussing me? Might Margherita inadvertently reveal something to alert her protector to the truth? Nothing I could say would be believed by Mussolini. He would see me as her seducer (rather than her whore!). Disgrace would be the least I had to fear! For all his sensitivity, Il Duce was an Italian first. I was well aware how fiercely Italians defended their honour. This caused me to lose a certain spontaneity. Maddy began to complain that I had no time for her. When I explained how I was wearied by cares of state, she seemed satisfied, but some of her old, easy gaiety was lost in those heady first months.

Unfortunately, Margherita still found time for me. I think she was one of those people who feel obliged to keep all lovers, old and new, under their control. When she was in Rome I was often her escort in public, sometimes with Maddy as well, attending an opening of garish modernist art or sharing a box at some screeching contemporary opera. Maddy always complained of the smell. I was tempted to tell her she didn't know the half of it. I was not at that time Margherita's only lover, for her ardour, if not her peculiarity, had cooled a little, which was just as well, since I had developed bad headaches in the days when Il Duce was particularly energetic and demanding of my involvement.

One day in the restaurant where I usually met her, Margherita showed me the French and Swiss newspapers. To my amazement they had published shadowy pictures of my Land Leviathan, claiming they had been taken on secret manoeuvres in Libya. I was shocked. I had no doubt the pictures were of my models. They were so poorly reproduced, however, that they could have been the real thing if one did not know better. When I first looked I assumed for a moment that Mussolini had ordered a Leviathan built in secret. But certain features revealed both machines as the models we had installed in the Villa Valentino. The story, of course, was preposterous. Not a nut or bolt of the real thing had yet been made. Even at a most optimistic estimate, the project would take years to complete.

When I got to my office I immediately began enquiries to find out how a photographer could have sneaked through to a room only my staff was allowed to enter under the toughest security. They knew nothing. I was sceptical. I suspected some sort of Bolshevist plot. Brodmann, or even our own OVRA, kept files on everyone and might have spies in my people's ranks. The photographs had been hastily taken and were not of professional quality. Any Brownie could have been used! I wrote a quick personal note to Il Duce saying I was baffled by this leak.

I waited in some nervousness to hear back from him. He might see this as an indication of disloyalty or un-Fascist laxity on my part. He could strip me of my rank, perhaps even expel me from Italy and consign my inventions to oblivion. Or claim them as his own.

Two days later I heard a familiar sound outside. The Fascist *squadristi* positioned themselves on both sides of doors flung open to admit the Dictator himself. I expected his expression to be stormy. But he was grinning in his familiar way as the doors closed and we were alone. My stomach turning over, I rose and saluted. He waved me back to my seat with an affable hand, unbuttoning his uniform jacket and loosening his belt.

'*Professore*, you are worrying about nothing!'

He picked up one of the newspaper cuttings from my desk. 'Who could tell anything from this? Does it matter how those photos came to be in the foreign press? Enough that they are believed. The newspapers are doing our work for us! Don't you see it? Even before we have built our first machine, the world is alarmed, wondering where, how, what – when? Eh? Meanwhile, the machines will soon be in production and those who believe the pictures to be fakes will be shown to be fools, so we win on every level.'

Il Duce had a knack of calming my worst fears. '*Professore*, you are living in the Dark Ages. This is the world of modern communications when the truth can be tailored according to need. Let's say someone on your staff required a little pocket money and gave the press these pictures. It has done no harm. Of course, you will make sure it doesn't happen again. But as long as the world is mystified, we are strong.'

My relief was considerable. I would keep my job! Mussolini continued. I must think of him as the star of a cinema film, he told me. The whole art of the film is to suspend disbelief, win authority for the director without being obvious. The director does not succeed by drawing attention to himself or his own skills. He draws attention to his star, his script, his sets.

'Now since in this case I am both director and star, I have to make careful distinctions. I have to delegate, of course. I have to rely on experts. You, Professor Peters, are one of my experts. As your admission to the Fascist Inner Council shows, your worth is thoroughly recognised. Once our machines are in full production you will get all credit for your work. We shall put your name on everything. The Peters Land Cruiser. The Peters Long Range Flying Boat. The Peters Jointed Aircraft Carrier. Meanwhile, the state requires that Mussolini's is the only name associated with our projects. Now that there has been a little scandal, we can reveal a few other details, perhaps let another vague photo or two be published. These will serve to keep the world guessing. Of course I understand your concern and appreciate your position, which is why the *Popolo d'Italia*

137

has asked to run a series of interviews with you, concentrating on your many achievements in America. As we speak, the Italian Academy is considering inviting you to join its distinguished company. I learned today, and this is strictly between us, that you are to receive the Fascist Eagle First Class. Your efforts are not going unrewarded. Your salary, I understand, is also to rise in accordance with your new position.'

But none of these honours, none of these rewards meant as much to me as knowing that Il Duce was not displeased with me. I was close to tears.

'My Duce,' I said, 'I live to serve you and the Italian nation.'

That was all he needed to hear. Again his manly lips split into a boyish grin, his massive hands spread wide. If the desk had not been between us, I know he would have embraced me.

'Come,' he said, heading for the door into our 'secret' room. 'Let's have a look at the monsters which are making the French and the Swiss wet their knickers.' And we were again at play.

I speak, of course, with a certain levity. I came to understand how my Chief used these exercises for many purposes. First, they relaxed him. Far more than the women who were brought every afternoon to his office, our machines of the future took his mind off the cares of the present. He could lose himself in his dream. Second, they enabled him to plan. His instincts were perfect at this time. As far as the world was concerned our weapons were so terrible, so effective, the chances of them being used were slim. My Land Leviathan would guard the boundaries of the New Roman Empire. My huge Flying Wings would carry passengers as easily as bombs. My jointed floating Aircraft Battle Stations could be always ready to launch my superfast skyfleet into the skies. Such weapons meant peace, not war – a peaceful, secure Italy, firmly established within her natural imperial borders, threatening no one and unthreatenable. That was all the average Italian longed for. Look at *Things to Come*, which Korda made in 1936, if you want see a vision of the clean, predictable, decent future we hoped to achieve. In that wonderful film, which also owed something to my ideas, men of refined education and of the very best character take charge of the world and put it right. This was all Fascism wished for. Yet I do not believe H. G. Wells ever claimed to be a Fascist.

Only when Mussolini, pressured by other powers, brought his plans forward did things begin to go wrong. Where once whole towns had swarmed to cheer him, soon he was lucky to find the stationmaster still on duty when his train came in. The same happened to Hitler. Their people put them in power because they wanted the secure stability of peace, not the uncertainties and privations of war. If Hitler and Mussolini had not set their feet on that inescapable course – admittedly because they were terrified of Stalin – the world would be a very different place today. There would have been no abolition of National Service, for instance, and therefore no hippies. My cities would rise into the skies. My city would be called *Roma* and she would bring Law, Justice, Order and Probity to the world. My ship is called *Byzantium*, the spiritual heart of our faith and our idealism. My ship is called *Leviathan*. She crushes the cities of the enemy. She swallows them. She shits them. They are called *Carthage*. They are called *Jerusalem*. *Meyn Schiff ist* The Sword. She flies in defence of all that is holy, all that is noble, all our history. *Meyn Schiff ist* Der Heym. *Meyn Schiff ist* Der Heym.

Sometimes when overtired I felt I was involved in a vast Hollywood epic in which the star really was Mussolini and in which the people of Italy played the extras. Much of his work was designed to create the illusion. He believed the reality would follow.

Cynics have said there were resources only for the illusion, none for the reality. I know better. If Mussolini had stuck to his true course and been a little stricter with some of his antagonists, such as the Jews and the Catholics, he or his son would be in power today. He was foolish to be so accommodating to Hitler. I speak as a neutral, judging Hitler neither way, but there was an element of instability in the Führer's make-up I never detected in Il Duce. Hitler was misadvised from the outset. If he had known what was going on in his own higher echelons he would have made a cleansing of the stables much sooner. As it was, he cleansed the wrong stables of the wrong elements. Röhm was a rough diamond, but he was heart and soul for the Nazi cause.

Margherita Sarfatti believed sincerely that if she had been beside him, Il Duce would not have made the mistakes he did. Yet others believe *she* was his worst mistake!

The Albanians have a saying: There are three things you should never trust. A dead viper, a wounded boar and a Jew turned Catholic.

Margherita argued that the worst mistake her lover made was to achieve reconciliation with the Vatican. Once he let the Jesuits back into the corridors of power, Italy was lost. In spite of her opinion,

Margherita, of course, took the expedient of converting while the ink was still wet on the agreement. Signora Mussolini, it was said, never accepted the Church. Her Romagnan relatives must have wept when they learned about the pact. They felt betrayed. The worst crime Mussolini ever committed – again at the instigation of the Roman bishops – was the attempted Catholicisation of conquered territories which had been Orthodox for centuries! That is no way to win friends. Mussolini lost many friends in the Balkans. Those who say he was responsible for the murder of King Alexander of Yugoslavia cannot know history! That territory was a battleground for centuries. Christians fought Moslems, Serbs fought Croats, fascists fought communists. They know nothing else but contention.

Many claim nationalism to be an essential element of fascism and so it is. That is why there are so few international fascist organisations in comparison to the communists. But Italy's form of nationalism and Spain's form of nationalism are very different, say, to the kind of small-minded nationalism one hears so often in the UK. I cannot tell you the number of times I have been insulted. 'Jew' is their favourite, of course, but there are many others. I tell them my blood is pure. It is Slavic blood, Russian blood, the finest blood in the world. The only blood, I point out, which Hitler feared. Save for his own, of course.

To be honest, I was not over-employed as Il Duce's Minister for Overseas Development. I arrived at eleven, knowing the Duce to be a late riser, and lunched nearby from two until four. In case Mussolini should require me, I was never very far away from the office. Similar routines were followed by all the other ministers and officials. The rest of my time was spent occasionally servicing La Sarfatti, taking tea with Maddy, chatting on the telephone with acquaintances and so on. Occasionally I would give an interview to the foreign or domestic press.

Some of Italy's most prestigious magazines ran long articles on me and my exploits. I still have a few of the cuttings. They tended to be vague about my present position, saying that I was in charge of a number of top-secret projects. I knew, of course, that Brodmann and his friends in Moscow were noting all this. I considered asking the Chief for a bodyguard. However, I would have had to make too many explanations, since he believed me to be a Russian-born American. All the leading Fascists were no doubt targets for Bolshevik assassins. I had to hope that our own OVRA were doing their job behind the scenes. Sometimes I thought that I had noted a car following me and hoped it was only a discreet bodyguard.

What if it were Brodmann, armed with a silent gas-gun, stalking me? I am a man of sanguine patience and sanity. I rarely let such fantasies gain the upper hand, but sometimes the effort to sustain common sense can be considerable.

Official functions actually came to be some of the least boring duties. The whole world came to Italy to see how Mussolini's Fascism was performing. Once again I was introduced to Marion Davies when she came to Rome with William Randolph Hearst. She did not recognise me in my uniform or my beard. She was a pretty, agreeable woman, a little inclined to gush. 'When you come to America, Professor,' she said, 'you must give me or Mr Hearst a call. If there's anything you need, just ask. I hope you'll have time to stay with us at San Simeon.'

I had no particular dislike for the woman, but this was the second time she had issued such empty invitations. I think it was a habit with her. She had no real power of her own, of course. She either forgot to relay these invitations to Hearst or demurred when he objected. I don't know. That said, Miss Davies was a far better actress than Anita Loos gave her credit for, but much of that talent was probably reserved for private life. She hid behind her blonde curls and long eyelashes like a panther behind a curtain of foliage.

Hearst himself, almost as elephantine as my old backer, the turncoat Hever, simply breathed and grunted at me and uttered some platitudes about America needing a taste of Fascist discipline and so on. Their goodwill was flattering, of course, but they had no real idea of the weight of responsibility we bore. I met Corinne Sweet again and several stars whom I had known as bit players. All were familiar with my films and rather extravagant in their praise. I think some of them were simply astonished that a professor and member of the Italian Academy, a minister of the state, could also have been a successful film actor.

Much of their response was of what I called the 'talking dog' variety. That is, they they didn't actually listen to my words. They were merely amazed that an actor could talk at all. My experience made me invaluable at receptions where these actors and actresses were entertained. Maddy and I went to them all. And because we went everywhere, we were invited everywhere else. It became second nature to get home from the office at about six, relax a little with

Maddy, change into a fresh uniform, or civilian evening clothes if appropriate, and be off out again to a reception. At one of these I met the poet Pound, a fierce, sickly, unkempt little man with no sense of humour and a tendency to create causes from the most casual material. I also met Marshal Pétain, Zaharoff, the armaments king and Sir Anthony Eden, the dapper dandy and famous lover of Princess Margaret. For all that Hitler was an enormous admirer of Mussolini, there were relatively few German visitors in those first months, though this was to change.

I met Karl Nertz and Isolde von Köln, the dancing team, who were part of a visiting troupe. They knew Seryozha, though not well. He was now in Berlin, but they were not sure what he was doing. They had seen him at the fashionable bohemian Café Schmetterling about two days before they left Germany. Full of admiration for what Mussolini was doing, they feared Germany still faced some form of civil war. 'It is almost inevitable,' he said. 'The fighting between the Nazis and the Sozies has become epidemic.'

Mussolini, although he gave a little help to them and the occasional encouraging nod, did not really take the Nazis seriously. He thought they aped the crudest of his ideas. He had not yet been alerted to the dangers of International Zionism. He believed Hitler and all his people were homosexual and always referred to the future Führer as 'that garrulous little German rouge boy'.

Mussolini was sometimes as susceptible to believing antagonistic propaganda as anyone. The only Nazi he had any time for at all was Göring, whom he described as an officer and a flying hero. They had met briefly, once or twice, I think. Hitler habitually used his friend Göring for diplomatic missions. Göring also knew Margherita. She had helped him buy modern paintings through her various friends in the gallery world. He had also bought a few old masters. She had no great respect for his taste.

Margherita was furious at not being invited to the first big reception attended by Göring and his Nazi entourage. My Chief insisted, with uncharacteristic vehemence, that I come but that Margherita (or Maddy, for that matter) did not. He allowed no excuse. 'It is a man-to-man affair,' he explained soberly.

I had planned to go on to a special 'powder' party with Maddy that night. Now she would have to go without me. I would try to meet her there later. She, too, was unhappy at being excluded. The function was being very carefully orchestrated, I explained. The Nazis were doing well at the polls. They might be a force to be reckoned with. She was unreconciled. It sounded to her as if Mussolini was muzzling the press. The idea was ludicrous. I pointed out that Tom Morgan would be going, as well as other top reporters, including Billy Grisham.

The reception was in fact a rather large affair. I doubt if many more people could have been crammed into the vast halls of the Villa Trajanos, with its countless galleries and staircases. With the significant exception of Margherita, everyone who was anyone in Rome was there. No wonder she understood herself to be out of favour with Il Duce!

I spent the first hour or two being introduced to one ambassador and his wife after another. Eventually I met Captain Göring himself. He seemed a little detached, chuckling a great deal but in response to nothing in particular. Possibly he could not understand me. His Italian was minimal – kitchen Italian, as we used to call it – good enough for instructing the cook. He was even then rather fat and wearing a suit cut in such a way as to hide the worst of his bulk. His vanity was second only to his self-indulgence, though he was an amiable fellow of the old South German type which is nowadays dying out.

Like so many of those early Nazis, Göring worshipped Hitler. Mussolini found his enthusiasm irritating. The German, true to form, did not notice. Ethel Grisham, drifting up in an incongruous ocean of green tulle, eventually saved us and bore Göring off to meet 'this delicious English woman'. 'She's just your type and she's dying to meet you.'

Mussolini muttered something to me about the crassness of the 'German bumboys' and was then forced to do his diplomatic best with the ambassador and his dumpy wife while I talked to Tom Morgan, Billy Grisham and one or two other pals from the press corps. Everyone but Tom was rather mocking about my uniform. I told them that they were lucky to earn such good salaries. They could afford suits. We servants of the state had nothing to wear but black serge.

'And nothing to eat but black bread, I suppose,' said Billy, amiably popping half a gram of caviar into his mouth. They were pleased with my elevation but like good friends saw no harm in ribbing me about it. That and their knowing winks around La Sarfatti, they reserved for me alone. When I was with Maddy they were more respectful. I regretted she was not there. Tom Morgan, a little drunker than the rest of us, told us some leering story and then nodded across the hall. 'That Hun looks like Fatty Arbuckle playing the lead in *The Merry Widow*.'

He spoke of Captain Göring. Like some favoured bull at a cattle show, the German preened himself before a woman he evidently found attractive. 'What a stunner, eh?' said Morgan, nudging me. 'I bet she's an actress.'

I turned to look. As I did so an intense and complex emotion suffused my entire body. The 'stunner' was the woman I knew better than any other still alive. My wife! My eternal! My soulmate!

'She is indeed an actress, Tom,' I confirmed quietly, putting down my drink and adjusting my uniform. 'She is an exceptionally fine one. She is my greatest leading lady. Miss Gloria Cornish.'

Everything else forgotten, I hurried across the room to greet my guardian angel. She was, of course, the wonderfully beautiful and voluptuous Mrs Cornelius.

She sensed my presence. A platinum radiance in pink and silver, a cloud of beaming Guerlain, she turned.

I began to approach. For a heartbeat she paused, then she recognised me. ''Ello, Ivan!' Her genial voice was more lusciously sensual than ever. 'Wot's wiv ther face fungus?' Her enormous blue eyes took in my uniform, my orders. 'Turned out nice again, I see.' The tip of her pink tongue wet her ruby lips. She winked, one old survivor to another.

Mio angelo! Mia amante! Mia sposa! My life!

FOURTEEN

Of course she had not changed. She was still my angel. Only Mussolini gave off that same almost supernatural wave of animal magnetism. My eyes as full as my heart, I kissed her hand. 'My dear Mrs Cornelius.'

'Smarmy as ever, aincher, Ivan?' She was her familiar amiable self. 'Still, I got ter admit it's good ter see a face I know. Found yerself somefink official an' steady, eh? Workin' fer th' corporation. Can't say I blame yer. I'm done for in ther English talkies. It's me accent. So when I got ter Berlin I took up with little Baron 'Uggy Bear over there.' She indicated a short, dapper German with a huge Kaiser Wilhelm moustache and twinkling blue eyes, whose grey haircut looked as if a hard brush had been glued to his head. He wore formal evening dress and chatted to Count Ciardi, whom he seemed to know well. 'Pappy's not reely a baron. That just what a corl 'im 'cause someone said 'e was a Press Baron and I wasn't sure wot that was. I corl 'im "Baron 'Uggy Bear". 'E was good enough ter 'elp me back on me feet, but I'm thinkin' of goin' inter cabaret, maybe in Berlin. Pappy's 'ot ter get me goin' in ther local talkies, but I'm a bit chary o' that world, if yer know wot I mean. Still, it's orl wide open fer English artistes. They love us out there. An' 'e sez some other girl can do me ther German. Wot d'yer fink? Oh, 'ello! 'Ave yer met –' She turned to address the enormous beaming German, an infatuated Zeppelin, who was clearly entranced by her.

''Ermann, is it?'

He bowed, clicked his heels and shook hands again. He did not recollect me. I supposed we all looked the same to him in our black uniforms. Although not quite as tall as he appeared from his photographs, Herman Göring was considerably wider. He spoke now in confident, but inexpert English. 'Delighted to make your acquaintance,

Professor Peters. We have heard much of your achievements in Germany.'

I was surprised. I began to realise how much I had attracted the attention of various foreign governments. The newspaper pictures had done exactly what Mussolini had anticipated; they had whetted the curiosity of the other powers. Slipping easily into German, I made small talk with Captain Göring. Grateful to be speaking his own language, he admired my vocabulary. I told him how I had worked with Germans in the Ukraine during the Civil War when we were all trying to get rid of the Reds. This interested him. He had assumed I was an American. 'Naturalised,' I explained to him. 'Before then I had direct experience of the Bolshevik terror.'

'You must meet a friend of mine,' he said. 'He's here tonight. His company's making this film about the Russian Civil War. They are hiring genuine veterans. Real Russians. You could be of great help. Did you come up against the Red Cavalry, for instance?'

'You're bein' borin', boys,' chided Mrs Cornelius. She smiled up at Hitler's bulky emissary. Göring's job was to attempt an understanding between the Nazis and the Pope. It was as well I did not know this at the time or I would have spoken my mind. One of the most disastrous policies Mussolini and Hitler formulated involved accommodation with Catholics who ultimately did as much as anyone to sabotage their efforts. 'You tol' me, 'Ermann, you woz lookin' fer a party ter go ter afterwards.'

The man was well bred and immediately dropped the subject of politics, saying only to me: 'We must talk again. In Germany we have a great respect for the scientific tradition.'

Jokingly I said that for my taste there were a few too many Jews running the scientific establishments there. He hesitated at this, doubtless because he was here on a diplomatic mission, then laughed heartily. 'Very good!' he said. 'Very good, Professor! I think you and I will get on well. You must come and see us in Germany once we are in power. Great things are happening. Il Duce's inspiration, Adolf Hitler's genius and German practical knowledge will transform the country and in time the entire world.'

Although his expression seemed fixed in a jovial smile, he was evidently not relaxed. Mrs Cornelius nudged him. 'Wot does it take ter make a Kraut let 'is 'air down?' she asked me, winking. Again he was hugely apologetic. He was here on official business. It was so difficult to move from one mode to the other. 'Wot abart this

146

party, then?' She dropped her voice. 'Yo're just the chap, Ivan. 'Ermann wants ter know if there's anywhere they do the 'okey-cokey rahnd 'ere,' and she put a finger to her perfect nose.

I was confused by all these turns of events and pulled my card from my inside pocket. On the blank side I scribbled the address where I hoped to meet Maddy Butter later. 'I might be there myself,' I said. 'Mention my name. Gallibasta.' I winked back. At which point, to my absolute horror, a figure in a uniform which would have seemed garish on the stage of the Vienna Comic Opera, taller than Captain Göring by almost a head but threatening to rival him in corpulence, moving with what I can only describe as a kind of monumental mince, cracked its jackboots together, offered the Fascist salute and regarded me through rheumy, affectionate eyes which failed to hide the signs of a thousand disappointments. He uttered a wide, ghastly grin. 'Good evening, Herr Captain,' he said to Göring, whose expression of distaste was undisguised. 'Maxim, dear. Did I hear somebody talk about a party?'

Mrs Cornelius's natural generosity betrayed us then. She did not know the newcomer. Maybe she did not wish to travel alone in a taxi with Göring. 'I'm sure we're orl welcome,' she said. 'Yo're wiv the German party, too, aren't yer? We'll go tergevver! 'Uggy won't mind.'

In spite of the horrible embarrassment at meeting Seryozha again, and in such unexpected circumstances, I was curious as to how he had managed to come back to Italy after only a few months – in a uniform of his own design and as part of the unofficial German delegation! When Mrs Cornelius led Captain Göring off to meet an old friend from the British Embassy in Rome, I was left with my slobbering ex-dancer. He, of course, wanted to open his heart to me there and then. His boyfriend had sent him here, he said, to keep an eye on things. 'Ernst's a really top-ranking Nazi, you know. A bit of a brute, really, but he has his points. Well, they're all totally rivalrous, darling. It's worse than the ballet! Nobody trusts anybody else and Ernst's afraid what he calls the "eggheads" are going behind his back. They wouldn't let him come now, so he sent me instead. I'm his aide. His eyes and ears, he said. They had to agree to let me do it. It's at his expense, anyway. He even paid for my uniform. I met him in Bolivia. It's all secret, of course. I hear you're doing well in the government now. There are no private jobs worth having any more, are there? It's the Crash.'

At that moment, Ferucci, who had no love for me, but knew that I was a particular protégé of Il Duce, came over to murmur that our Chief would like to see me when I could slip away. I made it my business to drop Seryozha, telling him I would meet him later at the party.

As soon as I could I got to Il Duce's side. He was making ready to leave, shaking hands with Vech, the elegant Spanish military attaché. They seemed on excellent terms. Mussolini still refused to smile in public, but there was a hint of a curve to his firm, ruthless mouth and when he saw me he was clearly pleased. My Chief did not want me to meet the Spaniard, however, and in fact almost pushed Vech away as he came to talk to me. Il Duce was in a particularly good mood. I think the admiration of the German contingent was far greater than anticipated. His old confident, ebullient manner had returned. 'Professor, we have some urgent business to discuss.'

I was mystified. He took me by the arm and began to lead me back towards his private room, divided from the main hall by a velvet curtain. Here all the guards were *squadristi* and sprang to attention when we entered. I was particularly proud to be treated in this way. Many of Il Duce's other ministers there that night would have been envious. I appreciated this public confirmation of my status. In the room was a table laid with exotic food and drink. Il Duce brought his special guests here, either to honour them or to speak with them confidentially. 'That was Colonel Vech. He has been authorised to approach us concerning our secret project.' Il Duce explained that the Spanish had seen the sensational reports of our Land Leviathan in the papers. I think their own secret service had also done some research. My guess was that they had had no luck in stealing our plans so had approached Il Duce directly, to ask if the machines were in production. No doubt they could use a number for their own purposes in North Africa.

'This is good news!' Mussolini's dark eyes twinkled. 'Such a sale will help finance our own production. Of course I told him we could not possibly discuss such things. I did not even admit that we had a "secret weapon". Have you said anything tonight?'

I was somewhat stunned. 'You have sworn me to secrecy, my Duce.'

Mussolini approved of my loyalty. However, he argued, if we could convince them to give 100 per cent financial backing to our project, without their knowing it we should be able to begin production all the sooner. 'We need to show them a couple of small plans, a simple picture or two. Have you got a little something to whet their appetites?'

I was still rather baffled by this change of attitude. I was silent.

'He will have to see something tonight,' my Chief continued. Vech was leaving first thing in the morning.

I was by now breathless with astonishment. Until now only Il Duce and myself had been privy to my inventions. Tonight there was talk of Spanish involvement. Mussolini himself had sworn me to secrecy. For mysterious reasons of his own he was prepared to admit that we were building a war ziggurat. His lightning mind sometimes understood situations and helped him make long-ranging decisions, rather as a first-rate chess player sees a whole range of moves open up for him. So I had learned to trust him. But it was impossible for me to guess the reason for this radical change of policy. I assumed he would eventually illuminate me.

Meanwhile, I stammered something about not having the keys to my document chest. He gestured expansively. He would drive me round to my house in his own car. There I could pick up my keys, he would take me to the ministry, I could find the plans, and his chauffeur could relay them directly to the Spanish Consulate. Typically he was in a hurry to put all this in hand instantly. I suspected he had a further liaison that night. Il Duce liked to get things done immediately or not at all.

I stammered something. He accepted this as acquiescence. Clapping me on the shoulder as if sensing my confusion, he promised we would not sell out Italy for a handful of Spanish doubloons. Certain specifications would, of course, be held back. Only a cruder version of the giant tank would be presented. He had not forgotten about naming it after me. Imagine what this would mean! Hundreds of Peters Leviathans guarding the frontiers of the free world against the combined Red and Yellow threat! My name would become a permanent addition to the military vocabulary.

He again sought to console me with promises of my coming public status. He failed to realise how used I was to my name appearing before the public. I was all for a speedier move towards full production of my machines, but I believed the entire project a secret shared only between myself and Mussolini. I could not readily readjust to this new development.

149

'And, of course, there will be material benefits,' he said. 'Part of the Spanish money should rightfully go to you.'

I did not work for money, I reminded him. I had no more interest in it than did he. We had a common vision.

That was the closest I ever came to rebuking my Chief and he accepted it.

We left the hall by the special exit. Il Duce's car was waiting, its engine running. Passing the main entrance of the villa, I saw a man and a woman leaving. I did not recognise the woman. I was surprised not to have noticed the man while at the reception. Surely it was the mutual friend Mrs Cornelius had mentioned earlier. A tall, slender Englishman, not in uniform on this occasion. He had once been romantically involved with Mrs Cornelius. I knew him as Major Nye, a British agent! Then I realised the importance of that reception. Now I knew that several crucial conversations had taken place that night. Political decisions had been made which would change the face of Europe for ever.

His chauffeur beside him, Mussolini himself had taken the car's wheel. I was by now used to his wild, extravagant driving. Tonight he seemed determined to shake off the fleet of secret service cars which began to follow us. Indeed, he was successful with most of them. He liked to entertain himself in that way sometimes. Particularly as he had almost given up the violin. Like Sherlock Holmes he had once played it every single evening for his own solace.

Il Duce knew exactly where he was going. 'Professor, I was thinking about your house. You need a bigger one. That place is far too cramped for you.'

Although he had never spoken of it before, I remembered that this was where he had once met and made love to the woman who these days preferred to satisfy her lusts on the leather furniture at the Villa Valentino. I was still uneasy about that situation. Obviously my association with La Sarfatti had made me more enemies than friends. She was not liked by the old Fascists and her influence over the Chief was thought to be excessive. She was sensitive to such things. Clearly, from her recent moods, things were not going wholly her way. Voices at court were raised against her. Ferucci was her sworn enemy. Some old affair between them, I guessed. Had someone told Mussolini about us?

In spite of the little house being only a short distance from the

150

reception, it took us over an hour to get there. So obsessed had Mussolini become with outrunning his own guards that he was thoroughly lost. He did not have a native's knowledge of Rome and her maze of streets. Eventually, he told me, most of the old, medieval mess would be torn down. He was tired of these fusty labyrinths. He would show me a model of the city that had been built a year or two before. Because of problems with land ownership, some of the building plans had been put back. The new understanding with the Vatican City was going to help that situation. He would leave behind him a Rome that would make the ancient capital seem only a sketch for the glories to come.

He laughed at his own audacity. Sometimes, as now, it seemed there were at least two Mussolinis – one was the boyish, self-mocking idealist who had come out of poverty in the poorest region of Italy to save his people. The other was the sophisticated, modern politician, forced through historical realities to take hard, painful decisions. Few visionaries make good politicians. Few good politicians have much in the way of original vision. That is the inextinguishable irony of the world. When visionaries are allowed to dominate daily politics, their talents are wasted, their decisions are a disaster. Yet occasionally there springs a man of vision who has the intelligence and will to overcome any discrepancy. Mussolini, of course, was just such a man. Nothing that happened between us subsequently has ever given me cause to change my view.

Unfortunately, such giants also attract pygmies who elevate themselves by association. These pygmies, scarcely noticed by anyone, almost always drag the giants down. Only Franco took the example of his colleagues and, like a good army officer, selected the best men for the work he had to do in Spain, bringing a stability his nation had not known for centuries. Though he lacked Mussolini's towering greatness, he had a much better background. Mussolini and Hitler had both served in the trenches with distinction, but they had never been considered officer material. Blood will out, as they say.

My Chief tugged suddenly on the wheel of the huge car, making the tyres squeal and judder. Arnaldo the chauffeur uttered a kind of gulping scream. The whole vast chassis swung in an arc as Mussolini applied the brake.

With the engine still running he grinned, panting, at me. I was still recovering from the shock. Until the Chief pointed it out, I did not notice that we had arrived at my house. I asked Il Duce if he would care to come in and rest, but he refused. No doubt he had memories he did not wish to revive. He said he would wait in the car and smoke a cigarette. He asked me if I had a match.

The evening had been a confusing one for me. While in the cottage I planned to help myself to a quick sniff of cocaine (of which Il Duce rather prudishly disapproved) and thus be able to continue in better mood. As I walked up the little crazy-paving path past the fountain, I thought I saw two figures through the window. Opening the door I went in quietly. A man stood with his back to me. Slowly he was turning one of the pictures I had placed facing the wall. He adjusted it and stepped away from it. I saw that several other pictures had been turned, all of a similar style. I did not demand to know what he was doing because I recognised the set of his shoulders.

When, however, I coughed and he looked back rather wanly to see who it was, I did not immediately recognise his face. One of his eyes was closed shut, badly bruised. His nose had been broken. His mouth was split and scabbed, and most of his front teeth were missing. I felt sick. The single large brown eye regarded me with the expression of a dying horse. It was Fiorello da Bazzanno.

'The pictures,' he said. 'They're mine. Don't you like them?'

I would not have hurt his feelings for worlds. This was the man who had done most to help me reach my present eminence. 'I love them,' I said, 'I was afraid the sun would get to them. I know nothing of oils. My God, Fiorello, were you in a crash?'

'You might say that.' With a sigh he flung himself into an armchair, wincing. 'A fall from grace, maybe. I'm not the golden boy I was a few short weeks ago, Max, as you probably know.'

All I knew was that his plane had been found. He had been missing. I told him how worried we had been.

I was rather distracted, aware that Il Duce himself was waiting impatiently in the car. I could not find my office keys. As I went towards the bedroom to look for them, Maddy came out. She seemed surprised to see me. 'Oh, Max,' she said. 'I'm not sure you want to get involved in this.'

'Involved?' I was under my original momentum, still searching for my keys. 'I'm delighted that Fiorello is safe. I have something to do. It will take less than an hour. Then I will be back.'

'Fiorello isn't safe,' she said. 'At least, not that safe.'

'I can't find my keys,' I said. 'Have you seen them?'

She suggested I look in the box on my dressing table. Sometimes I put them there.

'What do you mean?' I asked. There they were, in the box! I snatched them up. 'Not safe? He's here, with us!'

'I wasn't sure how you'd take it,' she said.

'Take what? Listen, my darling, I have a car waiting. It is very important that I leave immediately. Take what?'

'Fiorello's on the run,' she said. 'He was caught coming back from Switzerland. He never made it to his plane. They kidnapped him. Beat him up. One of them was de Vecchi, the Education Minister!'

I agreed it was terrible but was glad he was safe now. When I turned to leave, Fiorello was standing in the doorway, his lopsided, hideous face looking like something you would find in a charnel house, scarcely human at all. 'I don't expect you to help,' he said. 'I was trying to get Laura clear of the country. She's all right now. She's in Austria, I'm sure.' He shrugged and glanced away. 'Bloody commy.'

'You helped a *communist?*' I asked disbelievingly. Suddenly the enormity of my situation struck me. My legs lost their power to hold me. I sat down on the couch. Outside with his motor running was the supreme Fascist. Inside, a supreme traitor to Fascism. Should they meet, I would be irredeemably compromised. But there was nothing I could do save dash back out to the car with the plans and hope Maddy had solved the problem by the time I returned. I began to give up any idea of going on to the private party.

'He'll be gone when you get back,' Maddy promised.

I willed strength into my legs, staggered to the door and reached for the handle. As I did so a key turned in the lock and it began to open. My legs threatened to fold at the knees again and I fell back, expecting to see my Duce himself.

Margherita Sarfatti stood there, an affectionate Fury in yellow and black silk. 'Darling, I couldn't wait to see you! I've been longing for you. You must tell me everything that happened tonight.'

I tried to speak, but no words came. I attempted to shove my way past her, but she pushed me back into the room, pausing with a look of almost comic outrage when she saw that we were not alone.

Slowly she absorbed the scene. She looked from me to Maddy to Fiorello. Her breathing seemed to grow more rapid, as if a dragon fired up its venom. And then she screamed.

'There's nothing between us, honestly,' said Maddy. 'I think maybe we all need a drink and a sit-down.'

I, too, was close to screaming. Had Il Duce seen Margherita come in? If so, would he draw any particular conclusions? After all, we were in her house. Mussolini would come to investigate and find me harbouring a traitor while keeping a liaison with his mistress.

'I really do have to leave,' I said.

'How long has all this been going on?' Margherita wished to know. 'Now I realise the depths of treachery you've plumbed! I helped you all! I gave you everything! My own blood I would have given you! And this is my repayment? I am nothing, eh? I don't even get an invitation to the little boys' parties any more. This insult will not be forgotten. Both of you I nurtured as a mother – as a lioness her cubs. I taught you everything. I even made you characters in my book. I protected you. Both of you would be in prison if it were not for me. Yet behind my back, you plot and scheme. Well, Il Duce shall know of this!'

As I tried to frame a reply that would buy me the time I needed, I heard a tap on the door. This was certain to be Mussolini.

Not one of the million explanations which entered my head had the slightest ring of truth. I sighed and prepared myself for the inevitable enquiry. I had perfectly ordinary explanations, though Fiorello's presence would take a little imagination.

I drew back the door, ready to face my Chief in all his rage.

But it was not Mussolini. A jolly gust of laughter announced the arrival of the not insubstantial Hermann Göring, Mrs Cornelius, Baron Huggy Bear (looking a little dazed) and an extremely drunken Seryozha who was scarcely able to stand but staggered between the other two with a look of depraved sentimentality on his face worthy of Kominski or one of the other great clowns of the old Kiev circus. 'Why!' exclaimed the smiling German. 'You're already ahead of us! The taxi driver was right after all. I hope you haven't sniffed up all the "snow", ha, ha, ha!'

I stood there open-mouthed. The vast captain waved my own card under my nose. A taxi driver had read the wrong side.

'Ain't yer goin' ter let us in, Ive?' suggested Mrs Cornelius a little peevishly. 'It's bleedin' freezin' art 'ere.'

I stepped back.

Mrs Cornelius led the way into the house. "Ow *sweet!*'

154

Fiorello's ruined face expressed the dumb comic distress of a *commedia* horse. Disapprovingly, Maddy folded her arms.

Göring flung himself into one of our comfortable armchairs. 'Is all the fun over? Who has the happy-powder?' His thickly accented English was indecipherable to everyone but me. They ignored him. Mrs Cornelius handed her coat to Fiorello, looking over her shoulder for her dapper little protector. "Ave yer met Pappy?' Assured she had not lost him, she turned. 'Gawd! What 'appened ter ya? Somebody beat yer up?'

'Oh, *la vie sportif*, you know . . .' Gracefully Fiorello took her coat, helped the bewildered Baron off with his and handed the clothes to Maddy Butter who had by now recovered at least a patina of conventional hospitality. 'Can I get you all a drink?' she wanted to know. 'Camparis? Manhattans?'

'Fuck your Campari Manhattans,' said Margherita Sarfatti, hurling herself on to the sofa. 'Hello, Hermann, *mein Liebchen*. How was the party?'

Maddy grasped at the only fact which had so far been presented to her. She looked steadily at me and said in a small voice as she poured the drinks, 'Do I understand that you and Margherita have been having an affair?'

'Not at all,' I said.

'Judas,' said La Sarfatti absently. She was smiling at Göring and helping herself to a bar of chocolate lying on the table. 'Did you get that Lautrec I recommended?'

'Oh, Margherita! I am still a poor man, you know!' He asked again after the *neige*. I had begun to realise Hitler's ambassador was something of an addict. I felt sympathy for him, of course. I have always said that if the drug begins to use you, that is when you should stop the drug. I was to learn later that he favoured narcotics, like morphine, which have a debilitating effect on the character as well as creating addiction. I have always warned young people off such drugs. Stimulants have a completely different effect, creating dynamism and positive progress in society – unless a narcotics user decides to use them! Then a very strange result occurs. Hermann Göring, whom I last saw at Nuremberg, was a living example of this. Fifteen years earlier, however, he was not the slave to his addiction that he later became. Ultimately, of course, Hitler had to renounce him.

I was still trying to reach the door. I had decided to say nothing

155

further but to make my escape now, while attempting to redeem myself later. From outside came an impatient toot.

Fiorello came up to me. 'Max, I don't plan to involve you. But you must realise what's going on. They beat me up – *squadristi* thugs. I escaped. They were planning to kill me, take me up in my own plane and dump me out alive. They said so. But nobody could fly. De Vecchi's their boss. He really hates me. I don't think Mussolini understands. Remember Matteotti? That wasn't his fault. Someone has to tell the Chief. You know how much I admire him. If you could put in a word, perhaps, we could clear all this up. He doesn't mind as long as the communists are gone from the country. I was simply getting rid of another one.' His attempt to smile was unfortunate.

I murmured that there was little I could do. I had no power and little real influence. I was a scientist, not one of the political people. I was sure if he threw himself on Mussolini's mercy everything could be sorted out.

The horn sounded for the second time. Impatient to begin with, Il Duce would be furious by now.

I thought of suggesting to Fiorello that he go personally and ask Il Duce for clemency. It seemed a convenient moment. By now Maddy had poured the drinks and was placing tall red glasses into uncomprehending hands. 'Do you mean to say,' she continued firmly, settling herself on the couch between Göring and La Sarfatti, 'that you and Max have been doing something behind my back?'

'And who is Max?' asked Göring agreeably.

Seryozha had found the gramophone and was winding it up. 'What marvellous records,' he said. 'You can't find these in Berlin.' He put on 'The Last Round-up'. I think it was Gene Autry's earliest recording. As the first bars began to play, Seryozha threw up discreetly behind a chair. Göring smiled apologetically to his hostess. 'He is not German,' he explained. He leaned forward and whispered something to her. Maddy got up and went into the bedroom.

The horn sounded for the third time. The beating of my heart suggested I could probably not live much longer.

Maddy came back in to the room with our cocaine and the apparatus for taking it.

It occurred to me to ask Fiorello if he knew the best way of getting into Switzerland. The Baron was moving admiringly around the room gazing up at the paintings and murmuring his praise. He seemed under the impression that he was at an opening.

156

Maddy, stone-faced, began to chop out lines of coke for everyone. As Seryozha fell to the floor, his face striking the carpet with a peculiar soft crunch, she incorporated his line into her own.

Fiorello was still beside me. I had begun to tell him that our leader was outside in the car and might be growing impatient when I felt pressure on the door handle. My first thought was to hang on to it, hold it tight and resist any further intrusions. My second was to begin weeping.

My third, as the door opened to admit a glowering Benito Mussolini, was to fall against the wall with a groan.

'That's awfully good of you,' said Captain Göring, in his best English. 'I can't tell you how much I've been in need.' Bending forward over the marble table, he put the little silver tube to his nose and inhaled his lines in a single bovine snort. He seemed to expand to twice his size, threatening to burst the walls of the room. He sat back on the couch. 'I love my wife,' he said. 'I love her with all my soul. But a man is a man.'

Mussolini regarded the scene in disgusted silence. His smouldering eyes glared from face to face.

'*Caro!*' cried Margherita Sarfatti, rising like a blustering pheasant from cover. '*Caro mio!* Thank God you are here!'

I looked for Fiorello. He had disappeared.

Where Fiorello had been standing a moment ago, there was Mussolini. Hands on hips, a look of irritable disapproval on his features, he turned his back pointedly to the others. He spoke quietly. 'Are you ready?'

I saw my keys on the table next to the line of coke Maddy had cut for me.

'Sorry if I'm breaking anything up,' I said casually. 'I was looking for my keys. Ah, there they are! Sorry I have to go. It was nice to meet your friends, Maddy.'

Save for Göring and the Baron, the others were all staring at Il Duce. Ignoring the uncrowned Queen of Italy, Mussolini turned once to stare thoughtfully at an obliviously happy Captain Göring before leading the way back to the car in silence. I heard Margherita's wounded shriek behind us, but she did not come out.

We got into the car. Il Duce shook his head. 'What's Margherita doing with that Hun? I've been trying to keep them apart all week. Did you invite them?'

'Certainly not,' I said, reflecting privately that Maddy would not take a sanguine, European view of my arrangement. 'Thinking I would be away, she no doubt arranged to see him there. But who knows? She's a strange one. Maybe she can seduce him? To be fair, he seems besotted with his wife. Surely Signora Sarfatti wouldn't attempt —?'

'You don't know the half of it,' said Il Duce. 'You want to be careful of her.' An expression passed across his face which, in a lesser human being, I would have taken for terror.

As we drove towards the ministry, Mussolini began to lecture me on the dangers of having anything to do with Germans. 'They want to gobble us all up. And as for these Nazis — it is a corruption of everything I have ever said or worked for! A mishmash. Family man or not, that Göring is a degenerate. You saw for yourself. They're all vicious boy-buggering dopers and masochists. Hitler goes everywhere with a nancy boy he calls his secretary. They admit it openly. That fudge-packer Röhm makes no secret of it. He's even published his love letters to his catamites. They give Fascism a bad name by associating themselves with us. As Italy rediscovers her manhood, Germany becomes feminised. Because they've won a few seats in the Reichstag they think they can compare themselves with us. It makes me feel sick. They're a gang of psychopaths. Not one of them has done an honest day's work in his life. Believe me, Max, Germany can never be anything but an enemy of Italy.'

If only he had heeded his own judgement. But he was too trusting. In the end, abandoned by all, he swung upside down in a Milanese meat market, one carcass among dozens. It is a tragedy which will be told down the ages, just as *Julius Caesar* and *Caligula* are told. At least those ancient emperors weren't warned by a gypsy they would *not* die by violence. The last assurance Il Duce clung to. The last betrayal.

Mussolini's death was symbolic of the entire twentieth century.

And we wonder why our young people no longer understand their history!

Il Duce came with me as I went to my office. He was still talking. He did not seem especially upset with me but was clearly out of sorts. He spoke of traitors, of people he had elevated to positions of power and responsibility and who even now turned against him. How was it possible? What harm had he ever done them? Indeed, he was their benefactor! I could not tell if this was his subtle way of warning me of his displeasure, or if he remained simply aggravated by Signora

158

Sarfatti's success at finding her old friend Göring. He paced about grumbling while I hunted for the plans we needed – simplified drawings which would give nothing away.

'I'm going to have to be more severe with these bastards,' he said. 'They're taking too many liberties, Max.' He turned his glaring eyes on mine. I blinked. When I looked again he was grinning.

He sucked in his lower lip and stared at the ceiling, the plans in his hand. 'But meanwhile we have finance for our machines!'

He was extremely pleased with the idea of obtaining Spanish capital. I think he had probably been worrying over fiscal matters. While others slept soundly, Il Duce was up, pacing his lonely corridors, taking Andrews Liver Salts for his ulcers and mulling over the affairs of the day. I had the distinct impression that my Land Leviathan was moving a little closer to reality.

We returned downstairs. As the door of his car was opened for him, he turned, rapping my chest with the rolled-up plans. 'By the way, I was supposed to ask you this earlier. Signora Mussolini you know. She thinks you're wonderful. She – well, my son Bruno, who you get on so well with, he's mad on flying as you're aware. Your films probably gave him the bug, eh? We talked this over, and she thinks he's ready for flying lessons. As long as he's taught by someone we both trust.'

'An excellent idea, Duce,' I agreed. 'No better time for a boy to learn. I was younger than Master Bruno when I first flew. Hand-eye coordination is everything in a good airman.'

'We knew you'd agree,' said Mussolini. He tapped the side of his leg as he sometimes did if a weight was lifted from his mind. 'When's the soonest you could take him up?'

What could I say?

'Mm?' asked Il Duce.

'I'm honoured, Chief,' I said. 'I'm at your disposal.'

'Well,' he said, 'we'll discuss the details tomorrow perhaps. Thanks for your time, Professor.'

The door closed.

With mixed feelings I waited for the secret service car to slip out of the shadows and take me home.

Reluctantly I got into the car. I could still not be sure if Il Duce had absorbed the scene at my house or whether he would start to think about it later. I was certain, however, that Maddy Butter was in no doubt about what had been going on.

FIFTEEN

Why do you cry?
  I am hungry.
No, you are merely greedy. A Jew.
  I am in agony.
A complaining old Jew.
  I beg you on my life for help!
A melodramatic Jew.
  My soul is being destroyed.
An exaggerating old Jew.
  I am not a Jew.
That's what they all say.
  I am not a Jew.
Then you are nothing.

160

SIXTEEN

My mother is *Juno*. She is the goddess of the golden ship.
  My mother does not exist.
My sister is *Esméralda*. She is our city's most glorious jewel.
  My sister does not exist.
My brother is *Odysseus*. He is the wanderer between the worlds.
  My brother does not exist.
My brother is *Isaac*. He is the recorder of all our deeds.
  My brother does not exist.

They called him the Jew-Greek and they reviled him.

Their coarse, violent laughter brought bile to my throat. I lost control of my bowels.

Here is another Jew-Greek, they said. What shall we do with him?

Meyn Schiff is called Der Heym.

Meyn Schiff is called Der Heym.

My ship does not exist.

My father is called *The Turnface*. He is mentor to the dead.
My father is called *The Negotiator*. He bargains for the dead.
My father is called *The Trader*. He is the speaker for the dead.
My father is called *The Word*. He is the memory of the dead.
My father does not exist.

My city is called *The Hero*.
　My city does not exist.
My land is called *The Dream*.
　My land does not exist.
My nation is called *The Just*.
　My nation does not exist.
My empire is called *The Soul*.
　My empire does not exist.

—❧ TWENTY ❧—

When I arrived back at the cottage our courtyard lamp was still burning. In the circle of orange light Mrs Cornelius and Captain Göring were leaning heavily against the wall laughing uncontrollably while between them they attempted to lift the groaning Seryozha, who had taken on the colour of a cadaver. Baron 'Huggy Bear' Hugenberg was nowhere in sight. I dismissed my driver and hoped I was not otherwise under surveillance. My Chief would not, I guessed, be pleased to learn I was continuing to hobnob with foreigners. As the car disappeared, da Bazzanno emerged from the shrubbery like the newly risen dead and joined us, wearing one of my best summer suits and a fresh silk shirt. Göring appeared to notice him for the first time. 'My God,' he said sympathetically. 'You look like you were caught by a bunch of Sozis!' But Fiorello didn't understand him. He shrugged and I think he winked. 'Hello, Max. We're looking for a cab.' My friend put his ruined hands in my pockets.

''Ow was the boss?' Mrs Cornelius hiccupped. 'Pissed off, was 'e? I 'ope we're not letting you down socially, Ivan.' She and the fat German shook with a fresh wave of spluttering and giggling. In their state everything was comic and ridiculous. Even Fiorello was infected by their mood. From the beaten pulp of his face he seemed to be grinning.

I would be glad to be rid of them all. I was impatient to see Maddy and try to explain myself. Surely she would understand when I told her how Signora Sarfatti had blackmailed me. The likely hostility of Sarfatti was also imminent. It would lose me the protection of one powerful patroness, but, assuming my flying skills had not deserted me, I had another in Rachele Mussolini. She was even more powerful and effective because she hardly ever used her influence. Unless Mussolini mentioned my liaisons to his wife she would certainly remain my ally. If she did not, Mussolini would inevitably turn against me. My dilemma seemed to become more complex with every passing moment. A Borgia courtier would have sympathised.

I had so much at stake. Within a year one of my most cherished inventions would become reality. At last I was on the brink of world recognition. Already my name was whispered in the higher echelons of the world's foreign services. In scientific circles, too, there was much talk of Mussolini's new engineering genius. Margherita Sarfatti had made no secret of her 'discovery' of me and, of course, the high-ranking Fascists accepted me as an equal. I was on excellent terms with Farinacci and Grandi. I was a member of the *fascisti*'s most exclusive order. I had sworn a personal oath to Il Duce. If I broke that oath I would pay with my life! The fate of poor Turati reminded me that I could lose all I had won as rapidly as I had gained it. Not long before Turati's disgrace, Il Duce had spoken of him with affection and admiration. Now his name was never mentioned. As far as the stern Duce was concerned, Turati had never existed. Yet only months earlier before that able man's dismissal at Rachele's suggestion, Mussolini had praised him in the *Autobiography*. Turati, a courageous veteran of the World War, was a man of clear mind and aristocratic temperament, Il Duce had said, able to give the party the style of the new times, the consciousness of the new needs. 'Hon. Turati' had 'accomplished a great and indispensable work of educational improvement of the Fascist masses.' He was a precious element in the party. Yet Rachele had taken some minor sexual peculiarities as signs of a bad character. She had told me so herself. No doubt she had given me a gentle warning.

Almost weeping with anxiety, I saw everything being snatched away. 'Why didn't you phone for a cab?' I asked Fiorello, growing angry. They threatened to wreck all my dreams!

I walked past them. I put my key in the lock. It turned but the door would not open.

'She's bolted it, I think,' said Captain Göring.

'Madame Sarfatti?' My panic rose.

'Still in there,' said Fiorello. 'They threw me out.'

My heart sank.

I made one or two efforts to call through the door in case Maddy intended to hear my side of things. I instinctively knew there was little hope of cool discussion that night.

Eventually a huge taxi turned up guided by the jubilant Hugenberg. I accepted Mrs Cornelius's offer and returned to their hotel as their guest. 'For a nightcap,' said Mrs Cornelius. 'It'll give 'er a chance to cool down.'

The Excelsior Hotel was all silvery chrome, gold and green marble. Rather than try to enter its subtly guarded portals, Fiorello murmured something about having caused enough embarrassment and slipped away. I hoped he had not attracted the attention of the OVRA, Italy's answer to Stalin's Cheka.

I was not sorry to see him go. His lack of self-discipline astonished me. He was, after all, a leading Fascist. The kind who should be setting an example. He had sworn an oath, as I had sworn an oath, to serve Mussolini and the Italian state above all else, including life and liberty. Then he had allowed the sickliest of sentiments to weaken his Fascist resolve so severely he was prepared to help a communist, an enemy of his nation, evade justice! How could I believe anything he told me? Had he actually been beaten up by his communist friends? Captain Göring had instinctively put his finger on it. An experienced flying ace and soldier, Göring had led his own defensive squadrons in the streets of Munich. He had learned at first hand to recognise the hallmarks of leftist brutality.

The rest of us hesitated in the lobby. I, of course, was still in uniform, as was Captain Göring, so we received the most courteous attention. We planned to have a drink in the bar but the place was still crowded with foreign delegates. Obviously we could not drag Seryozha in with us. Tiring of our discussion, Mrs Cornelius said she was done in. She needed to get to bed. 'Which reminds me,' she said. 'I think this is yours, Ivan.' She put my box of cocaine into my hand. 'I certainly don't need any more o' that nasty stuff.' And with a prim goodnight she took her baffled Baron off.

Looking at his massive wristwatch, Göring, too, declared his intention of retiring. 'Regretfully, I am expecting a visitor in an hour. A matter of politics. We must stay in touch, Professor Peters.' He took my hand in a serious embrace. 'The delegation will be in Rome for a few days more. Give me a ring. We must talk aeroplanes, eh?' He asked me to oblige him by making sure Seryozha was comfortable. Then he, too, entered an elevator, filling it at a single step.

As soon as the lift doors had closed, Seryozha's vast body suddenly shook all over as he became alert. 'Hermann?' He turned to me. 'I think fate has once again thrown us together, Dimka, dear. It's OK.

It's all this rich Italian food. I feel so much better now.' He offered me a vast leer.

Afraid that anyone else should overhear his conversation I gravely told the enquiring manager that I would see Seryozha to his room myself. My main intention was to get both of us out of the public eye as soon as possible. He gave me the key.

Only by promising Seryozha to have a nightcap with him could I get him into the lift and up to the third floor. Further reassurances were needed to make him stumble quietly to his rather cramped room near the service elevator at the back. I had expected something much grander. Even as he fell through the door, he apologised for his quarters. The party hadn't been able to pay his way. The Nazis were spending all their money on the elections. He didn't have rich friends like Göring. He didn't have millionaire mother hens like Hitler or successful actresses like Goebbels. He didn't have contacts with the powerful industrialists like Strasser. He wasn't related to old money like Hess. The list went on in this vein. His own patron, he insisted, was entirely independent, a military man of the strictest integrity. He himself received only a small allowance from his 'Ernst', who was notoriously frugal, disdained most civilian comforts, and insisted on living upon what he called 'an honest soldier's pay'. Unusually the ballet boy would not reveal the name of this paragon. Loyalty was the thing he prized most, he insisted, and disloyalty was severely punished.

As I shut the door behind us he began to undress. Then he tangled himself in his trousers and collapsed again on the carpet. I helped him up. I had no intention of staying. Only as I sat him on his bed and turned to leave did I realise again that I had no money and absolutely nowhere to go. The thought of enduring Seryozha's attentions disgusted me. Moreover I feared he would steal my *sneg*.

Then my problem was solved. Seryozha slid back down to the floor, placed his head on his arm and began to snore. Letting him lie there, I slipped out of my uniform and hung it carefully in his wardrobe. Buttoning my cocaine box into one pocket, I climbed into bed. The day had exhausted me. Probably I took a foolish risk, but I was desperate for sleep.

In spite of my anxieties, I slept deeply for several hours. At about five in the morning Seryozha's cumbersome mass engulfed the bed, and he seized me in his damp, yet muscular, embrace. As I felt his huge tongue slithering into my ear, I resigned myself to the inevitable. I could afford no further scandals.

Seryozha had always been a heavy sleeper. Next morning I was able to leave him sprawled among the stains of his own juices, get into my uniform, and take a little breakfast in the hotel before walking to the office. Descending the hotel steps I saw a taxi pulling away. In it was Margherita Sarfatti. Had she come looking for me and then changed her mind? Or had she been Göring's 'political business' last night? She was rumoured to have been his mistress and to have acted as Mussolini's go-between. It did not suit Il Duce's policies for him to be seen by the other foreign powers as friendly to German radicals, so perhaps that was what had been going on last night. Surely my exhaustion was making my eyes play tricks? Conscious of the gaze of the ordinary people, who were in no way impolite, I took pleasure in my stroll through the sunny dawn streets to my office.

As hoped, I was the first to arrive, going immediately to my dressing room where my uniforms were kept. Washed and changed, as far as my staff knew, I had spent the night like any other night.

Telephoning the cottage, I received no reply. Was this as a sign that I was still unforgiven?

As an instinctive precaution, I went to the files and removed certain copies, making up a short dossier of my designs, together with photographs of the models lining the walls of our 'war room'. All this went into a large envelope labelled 'Manufacturers' Brochures and Specifications'. This I put in an attaché case. I had no intention of betraying Italy, but these were my livelihood, my passport to immortality. Although my faith in Il Duce was in no way diminished, a misunderstanding might attract his disapproval. By now the poison-tongued gossips could have whispered stories and already be amplifying my innocent associations. From the evidence, Mussolini could form a completely erroneous idea of my behaviour. In the unlikely event of my dismissal, it was wise to take out a little insurance. While Mussolini was altogether a greater and more honourable man, my experiences of El Glaoui were still fresh in my mind.

Again I telephoned Maddy Butter. Again there was no answer. I had little money and most of my documents were at home. I remained at my desk for an hour or two. My staff were impressed to find me at work so early. I explained how I had been under special orders from Il Duce. Together we had worked into the night.

My secretary said she had heard that we had been in. I looked worn out. She was sympathetic. I told her I had better go home for an hour or two and get a little sleep. She ordered my car.

I took my attaché case with me when I left. A limousine was waiting for me outside. The driver saluted and opened the door for me. His name was Santucci and he was a sergeant in the political police. Not knowing what the OVRA would make of my behaviour, I behaved normally, pretending to work on documents as he drove me through the lunchtime streets.

After a few miles the car was forced to slow and eventually stop. No amount of official threatening could budge the policemen on duty. They were supervising an increasingly complicated problem. The cause of the traffic jam was a broken-down number 5 tram bound for Piazza San Croce, a Pente Negro-bound number 5a bus, a horse-drawn bakery van, two taxis, several cyclists and a variety of other people and vehicles. The spectacle of Italians in furious debate would have engaged me had I not been otherwise distracted. I grew impatient. The driver could only stick his head out of the window, scream at a few people, make the odd stab at reversing and then sit, tapping his wheel, while the debate between the drivers and others grew more heated.

Over an hour later I reached the cottage. Telling the driver to wait, I entered the courtyard and put my key in the lock. This time it turned.

Everything of Maddy's was gone. Not a stick of make-up or a scrap of clothing remained. All my things were exactly as I had left them. There was no note.

My mind leapt to the obvious conclusion. La Sarfatti had seduced my girl! I knew she was capable of anything. Had Maddy gone with Margherita to her apartment? Or had they gone back to Venice? I imagined them planning all kinds of terrible female vengeances together.

My nerves worsened. After I had made arrangements for the locks to be changed and the keys sent round to the office, my driver headed to Margherita's place on the Via Nomentane. Taking a short cut, we passed the back wall of the Villa Torlonia. I had not realised it was so close. The car pulled in before an ornate entrance. La Sarfatti's flat. Though this was guarded, everything gave way to my rank. I took the stairs to her door and rang her bell.

A maid answered. The signora was not at home. She had gone

to the country or perhaps Capri. She had not been awake when her mistress made the decision. I asked if another woman had been with Signora Sarfatti and the maid shook her head. I showed her my party book and told her it would go badly for her if she was lying to me. She swore that her mistress had been alone.

It grew late. If Il Duce needed me, he would find me gone. It would be another mark against me. I returned to the cottage and was relieved to find no one had tried to contact me.

I now wondered if Maddy Butter was really as innocent as I had assumed.

Maddy telephoned that afternoon. She had found herself a nice little place near the Ponte Tarantino. We should remain apart for a while. She didn't want to hear my explanations but needed time to think things over.

Her actions were a little too cold for someone who had represented herself as an innocent virgin only a few months earlier. I was deeply disappointed in her. I told her as much. She simply wasn't the stuff progressives are made from. Sometimes I was astonished by American conservatism. How had they had been such enthusiasts for Mussolini and, until the Führer let himself down, Hitler? Their own US Nazi Party lasted far longer than the original! Yet most Americans, though supporting Mussolini, did not really have the will to change, as the ballot boxes revealed, and Franklin D. Roosevelt, who would have qualified for euthanasia in some countries, was elected. In those first years many called him 'the American Mussolini'. Their optimism was to be proven utterly unfounded.

I recently spoke to Mrs Cornelius about this. We sat in the window of the East and West last Friday morning in Westbourne Grove. She was having a cup of the sickly Madras coffee she enjoys and I was sipping a lassi. The owner is Mr Hira, a Hindu. He tells me that most of the people from the Indian subcontinent who work for you are the lowest class of Moslems. It is impossible to find a decent South Indian chef. His eldest son is at university, reading mathematics. They share this ambition in common with the Jews, of course.

We watched the people coming and going from the Portobello Market. On Fridays they are mostly dealers. They wear old-fashioned country-style suits, stout tweed skirts and shapeless hats woven by mad Orkneymen or else some variant of the current fashion, all black velvet and dirty lace, like Mrs Cornelius's feckless children. They arrive early. By noon the pubs are crowded with them enjoying

171

the euphoria of dealers everywhere, talking of legendary coups and fabulous profits. I find it impossible to get served.

On Fridays we usually walk up Kensington Park Road to have a drink at Finch's. Then we take lunch at the fish restaurant there. Lately it has become too expensive and attracts the wrong sort of clientele. We content ourselves with the Windmill across from the Odeon. Very few dealers ever use the place, which is run by the better type of Greek family. The restaurant does a very good lamb joint. I always have two helpings of their roast potatoes. They remain well priced and friendly. Mrs Cornelius has a soft spot for them because her daughter was almost born there. She reminds me how the young Jerry rushed into the Alhambra, the nearest pub, to call the ambulance on their phone. He returned half an hour later, just as the ambulance was arriving, and he was almost too drunk to climb in. She was in labour. The Irish clientele of the Alhambra, under the impression that his sister was already born, had insisted Jerry help them toast the baby's good health. Catherine was born, as she put it, in the shadow of Wormwood Scrubs. Actually it was Ducane Road Hospital, one of the best in the kingdom. I have nothing but admiration for the staff there.

The specialist there asked, for the first time, if I had had my operation on medical or religious grounds. Medical! I cried. At least he did not automatically assume me to be Jewish. I almost kissed his hand. Mrs Cornelius insisted the chips at the Windmill had brought Catherine on. 'Not many people get ter be Windmill girls at her age, eh, Ivan?' She was back at home by the next day. She said she never had any trouble conceiving them and hardly any less trouble popping them out. She was an amiable if inattentive mother.

Mrs Cornelius reminded me that almost any political figure who showed any personality was called someone's Mussolini. 'It was amazin',' she said, 'just 'ow many people go through their entire lives lookin' for someone to boss 'em about! Some bastard starts shoutin' orders at 'em an' they brighten up like a brass knocker! Hermann told me Adolf's war record was amazing. 'E loved obeying orders, too. Takes one ter know one.'

Given how widely travelled she was, Mrs Cornelius has a rather simplistic and stereotypical view of foreigners, especially Germans.

She remains convinced 'they'll do it again'. Do what again? I ask her. Defend themselves against their exploiters? All Hitler wanted was a Polish Corridor, and the French and English used it as an excuse to attack him. They were eager for the chance. He was liberating the Poles from Jewish dominance. She must remember Germany during the Weimar days! No honest person could walk the street in safety. Male and female prostitutes were everywhere. The common people were horribly demoralised. Their intellectuals had become cynical, their teachers hopeless. The only stability left was in institutions like the army. Where were they supposed to turn to avoid the civil war everyone predicted? Would the Allies have stepped in, as they did in Spain, if there had been internal war? No. They were waiting only for Germany to tear herself apart. They hoped any winner would turn on the Soviet Union and rid them of the other threat. They were foolish to expect that particular free lunch. The Americans made the same mistake in Vietnam. There are no free lunches in realpolitik. The Germans themselves found that out to their cost. The British learned that lesson from their centuries of colonialism, which was why they were so reluctant to enter the Common Market. Or the New German Empire as Major Nye insists on calling it. I hardly ever see him these days. He is on his smallholding in Kent. His wife is dead and his daughters are married. He says he's never been happier.

I saw him several times in Rome during that uncertain period. I know now that he worked for intelligence, keeping an eye on the Nazis as well as the Fascists. He took the Nazis seriously, though he was not entirely uncritical of them. He admitted to finding Göring, for all his corpulence and vulgarity, charming. 'It was impossible,' he says, 'to believe that a man who looked and dressed like a lovesick baron in a Viennese operetta could be capable of evil.'

'Perhaps he was not capable of evil.' I have always been able to take the broad view.

Sometimes Major Nye is a little too judgemental. After all, look at the British record of genocide. I find it ironic that the survivors of the Irish famines and clearances were the same men who lynched Negroes in New York and joined the American Army to fire into unarmed Indian villages, a rather more direct and efficient act of genocide than any their own families ever suffered.

History and God alone put us in a position to be aggressors or victims. It is not unusual these days for a person to know both roles in a lifetime. I cannot find it in me to judge all those now branded as 'war criminals'. Were all Germans villains? All Jews heroes? Surely it is time to forgive and forget? You who never knew the all-pervading stink of fear filling your guts, eating your bones, taking control of your brain and bowels, should not judge us who have had such experiences. Believe me. I am not excusing anything. The death camps went too far. But remember, there were only four of them built. The rest were concentration camps.

In Rome Major Nye made an appointment to visit my office. I received very few people there and was glad to welcome him. He took my mind off so many other matters. Of course, I had no hint of his real reason for seeing me. He was interested in my inventions. Years later he told me how part of his brief was to check up on my Land Leviathan. By 1931 rumours of my great moving battle tower were rife in Europe.

Since Mussolini's territory bordered their own, the British were chiefly interested in learning his African ambitions. They were inclined to think of him as an ally. Most British politicians admired Mussolini. Chamberlain, Eden and Churchill spoke warmly of his intelligence and acumen. David Lloyd George, who invented the National Health Service, saw him as a fellow 'wizard'. Sir Oswald Mosley, under the influence of his wife and sister-in-law, left the British Labour Party to form the British Union of Fascists. All these people believed Hitler a parvenu, a coarse interpreter of Mussolini's genius. Certainly, without Mussolini a Hitler would probably not have emerged in Germany. And without Hitler, of course, Mussolini might still be keeping a steady hand on Italy's tiller. Like us all, he fell under a madman's spell.

Typical of his caste, Major Nye asked me no direct questions. He was never admitted to my inner sanctum, where my models were displayed. Most of our conversation was casual, about sights seen, art admired, food eaten. He might have been any tourist. Did he seek my company because I might be in contact with Mrs Cornelius? I was glad to patch things up between them. We all had tea together at the English Tea Rooms near the Spanish Steps where the English poets used to catch food poisoning. The English will risk almost any danger for an infusion of Typhoo or Twinings. The place smelled of damp wool and digestive biscuits. It reminded the tourists of home.

I remained shocked by Maddy Butter's extraordinary rudeness. I wanted to confront her, but she avoided me at every turn. She had no proof that I had deceived her, save La Sarfatti's word! Yet she maintained complete silence. Her telephone was never answered. I saw her twice from the window of my official car. Once she was standing outside a large toyshop in the Piazza di Espagna studying rows of model soldiers in the window. I wound down the window of the car, but a newspaper seller thought I was signalling him and shoved a copy of the *Popolo d'Italia* in my face. When the fool was disposed of, suffering a severe telling-off from a policeman on the beat, Maddy had disappeared. The second time I was passing the Palazzo Venezia, where the Head of State traditionally had his offices, and saw her driving through the gates in a brand new red Fiat tourer, saluted by the guards. I guessed she was at last interviewing our Chief. I could only pray he was not also interviewing her. Billy Grisham showed me a cutting from the *Houston Examiner* that discussed the 'charlatans and exploiters' who thronged Mussolini's court. She did not mention me by name, but it was clear who the 'certain Russian-American con artist' was supposed to be. I prayed my leader had not seen this piece, or at least had ignored it as it deserved. Clearly no scandal impressed him. I kept my position.

For the following week there was only silence from my Chief. I did not find this especially significant. He had left Rome for a special tour. The newspapers said Il Duce was inspecting the draining of the Pontine Marshes but Grandi, whom I bumped into at the café where he usually took his lunch, winked at me and said, 'The Chief has a new enthusiasm,' by which he meant a new paramour. 'It's not the marshes he's draining! And not the Italian delta he's exploring.' He whistled a few bars of 'Yankee Doodle Dandy'. He was given to coarse jokes of that kind. Frequently they were as vulgar as they were mysterious. He reassured me, however, that I was probably not out of favour. 'The boss's powers of concentration are genuinely remarkable,' he said, 'but sometimes he focuses on one thing to the exclusion of everything else. Sometimes weighty affairs of state, sometimes Turkish wrestling holds.' One of Mussolini's closest friends and associates, Grandi had been left twiddling his thumbs for months sometimes, waiting for Il Duce to return his attention to whatever pressing matter was at hand.

I spent as little time in the cottage as possible. Seryozha had found my phone number and had called me several times. I told him it was unwise for me in my present position to spend too much time with foreign nationals. The OVRA were suspicious of such liaisons, and I would jeopardise my position. He understood but spoke of passions which had to be released. Could we not meet in secret?

I told him I could see no such possibility. The OVRA knew every movement of every one of the state's officials. Their duty, after all, as representatives of the people, was to ensure that the people's servants were behaving with due responsibility. Bureaucrats could no longer secure little nests for themselves in which they could practise any decadence.

Of course I exaggerated the power of the secret police. True they were everywhere, but this was really to their disadvantage. When I met Gilbert Keith Chesterton, the founder of the British Empire Movement, an author and journalist in his own right, who planned to make Notting Hill a Fascist enclave, he described a story in which every character who seemed to be an anarchist was actually a secret service agent. The joke in Rome was that the secret police were watching even more secret policemen who were watching still more secret policemen and so on! To some degree you could avoid them. Frequently, a small tip would secure their discretion, for they were usually very poorly paid, and they were never the unreasonable bullies propaganda made of them. As it was, I do not believe I was watched excessively. Those police people made themselves very obvious.

Maddy Butter had certainly disappeared from Roman society. I must admit I missed feminine company. I took tea several times with Mrs Cornelius and her Baron. On occasions we were joined not only by Major Nye but by Captain Göring, who now travelled frequently between Rome and Berlin. He seemed very sympathetic to me. He understood my predicament with Seryozha. He often remarked how difficult it was to get rid of old but embarrassing friends. One day, by way of reassurance, he told me how 'Lieutenant Kranz' was currently a guest of the Ministry of Works and was being taken on a special tour of Rome's antiquities. 'It keeps him out of trouble,' said Göring with a hint of a smile. 'You must not judge us by our admirers, any more than we would judge you by your relatives.'

Göring and I were almost friends during those weeks. He spoke often of his wife, who was an invalid. He felt very sentimentally towards her. In fact, he had a softness to his character which people used to call Austrian. Franz Stangl had this same characteristic, but it did not stop them hanging him all those years after the event. The thing he cared most for, even before the Führer, was his wife's approval. He would not make a move before he had that.

Of course Stangl did not tell her everything. The SS were trained in discretion. As they were informed on the first day of their training, their job was to do what ordinary people could not do. Their work was arduous and sometimes difficult, but their sufferings were what made Germany hard and allowed those ordinary, honest citizens to go about their lives in security, comfort and happiness. It took an especially dedicated type to join the SS in the early days. Schnauben himself explained this to me in Dachau. Only later, during the war, did the SS begin to recruit any kind of foreign riff-raff and that, of course, is when their troubles began. I do not defend them. I scarcely have reason to remember them before they received their unfortunate reputation. There are good and bad in every walk of life. I know what the SS was *intended* to be. Heinrich Himmler, a colourless and humourless individual whom nobody could stand, turned it into the bureaucratic monster it became. Röhm said that his troops had to have shoulders broad enough for the public to lean on and backs broad enough to hide the horror which threatened. Civilians, he said, were inclined to panic at the sight of a spot of blood.

Röhm would have made the SS what it was supposed to be – the epitome of the Nazi ideal, not a glorified butchering corps. Schnauben knew this. Major Nye is inclined to agree with me. He says this century has been a great century of idealism, in which millions of human beings at last began to believe that they could alter their destiny and improve the human condition. That idealism was one of the most wonderful things he ever witnessed. But he also believes it was subverted by Big Business and its servants for the most appalling and banal ends. The faith that once sent missionary youth to Africa now sends selfish boys to Coca-Cola for 'the real thing'. The country most able to translate human longing for justice and peace into a good sales pitch and pervert the noblest ideals to commercial exploitation is today the most successful. America is living proof of that. Everyone wants to live in America where money and God are inextricably married.

Only Mrs Cornelius says she has no wish to go there again. 'They got a buckbone where their backbone ought to be.' She doesn't want to waste time with them any more. The British have always been jealous of American wealth. They were jealous of them in the War because they fought with ordnance rather than men. Both nations in their way have dedicated themselves to avoiding experience. They have the superior attitude of a people who have never had to beg for their bread. They think this reflects a natural super-iority. Well, the Germans thought the same thing until 1945.

And perhaps they had better cause.

I contacted my journalist friends in case they had heard from Maddy, but they seemed honest in their ignorance. Nobody knew where she was. Judging from the stories she was filing, said Billy Grisham, she was almost certainly covering exclusives out of town. She seemed suddenly to have carte blanche with the Italian authorities.

The telephone began to assume unusual importance in my life. I waited for Maddy to phone. I waited for my Chief to phone. I even waited for Margherita Sarfatti to phone.

None of them phoned. But suddenly one Monday, completely out of the blue, my secretary took a call from someone on Signora Mussolini's staff. Rachele suggested we meet the next day for lunch. I would be expected at the Villa Torlonia at the usual time. I had almost forgotten my Duce's request for me to teach his boys to fly.

Was that the reason for my invitation? So uncertain had I become that I immediately wondered about Mrs Mussolini's motives. Was she inviting me to give me a dressing down? Or to relay a secret message from Il Duce who wished me to perform some discreet task for him? A thousand possibilities passed through my mind. However, I was not, as I had begun to fear, *persona non grata* at the Italian court!

Then at about eleven o'clock that same day, I received another telephone call, this time from Margherita Sarfatti in Milan on a long-distance line. She had tried to contact me earlier but could not get through. Apologising for her earlier poor temper, she spoke of my patience, my kindness, my intelligence. She knew I would forgive her.

As a gentleman, there was little I could say.

She suggested we meet for lunch the next day. I told her I already had an important appointment. I might, I said cautiously, be able to meet her that evening.

She accepted.

Now there were further intricacies to contemplate! In casual conversation with some of my fellow Fascists I tried to find out if something unusual was happening. They were unaware of any such atmosphere. They advised me to relax, as they relaxed, and enjoy the pleasures of office. They tried to get me to meet attractive women of their acquaintance, but I would have none of it. I was still aware of Rachele Mussolini's bright judgemental eye.

I had dinner that evening with Major Nye at the Excelsior. He was complaining about the French. 'They're behaving like peasants as usual. As if a few miles of land is worth making so much fuss over. The French have never been able to beat the Germans on their own. It's damned unseemly how they insist on their spoils. That sort of attitude puts the whole of British diplomacy in question.' Britain was a good friend to Italy. Nye himself saw the German point of view. The reparations question was one which should have been solved and then forgotten about. The Germans wanted a chance to get back on an even keel. 'Unless they do so soon, there'll be civil war there. The Soviet Union will get involved, and no doubt the rest of us. They have to find some kind of stability.' His main hope rested on the moderate Nazis. He was clearly on good terms with Göring, who passed our table in high spirits. He was surrounded by a group of high-ranking Fascists, most of whom were also out of uniform. They seemed to be congratulating him.

'He's just seen the Pope,' Nye told me. 'Apparently it went very well. Odd, really, since Hermann's a Protestant. Still, that's politics and the Germans have a big Catholic vote to worry about. Thankfully that hasn't been a British problem for some centuries.' He ordered his pudding.

He had heard of Mussolini's meetings with Göring via their mutual friend Margherita Sarfatti. 'You know her, don't you?'

I told him that I knew a lot of people in the Italian art world. I had lived here as a student ten years ago. It was in my interest to remain discreet on such matters. He understood.

'Well, she's still a strong influence on the old boy.' He had heard that the weather in London was wonderful. He told me something about the cricketing club he favoured. I continue to be puzzled by how the English managed to invent most of the sports enjoyed around the world when their weather makes them largely unplayable at home.

'You should visit England soon,' Major Nye insisted as we parted. 'I assure you we know how to put the best resources in the hands of the best men. Especially in science and engineering.'

He gave me the nearest thing I had ever had to an invitation. I would have been wise to pursue the matter.

Unusually for me, I took the step of drugging myself to sleep that night. I felt that I had to be especially alert the next day when I met La Sarfatti.

Altogether I had endured a troubled few weeks, since the night of that party. The arrival of so many foreigners and old friends in Rome had unsettled me. It might have been better, perhaps, had we never met.

TWENTY-ONE

My main concern was that, in her mindless jealousy, Margherita Sarfatti had given Mussolini a distorted version of events, implicating me with Fiorello da Bazzanno, the communists and even the Nazis. I saw no reason why she should attack me, since she had initiated our relationship in full knowledge that Maddy was my mistress. Fiorello was as much her friend as mine and had last been seen in her company. On the other hand Italo Balbo and several members of the Grand Council had mentioned in passing how Sarfatti could be as vengeful an enemy as she was a generous friend. Although Mussolini now knew my worth, it was she who had first helped me to my present position and might in turn topple me from it. Perhaps Maddy had poisoned her mind?

Could I really be in danger? I had done nothing wrong or disloyal to my Chief. Certainly I did not fear for my life, as I had under the savage El Glaoui. Even the prisoners sent by Mussolini to Lipari or Ponzione were self-declared enemies of the state and had received set sentences. If Sarfatti accused me of rape, things would merely be more awkward. Mussolini had an old-fashioned view of such things. He would see it as a sign of my virility. Rape is not easily proven, especially by a woman of her reputation. My main concern was for my work. I could not bear to see success snatched away from me so soon. I was helpless. Because of my Chief's mysterious absence, I was without allies. If he was against me now, I was friendless. Had Sarfatti arranged to see me simply to relish her triumph?

> Jewels like stars on her forehead scattered,
> Making a picture of the beast whose tail
> Strikes hard on men, whose blood is chill . . .

says Dante, taking us through Purgatory. Sarfatti was both beauty *and* the beast. I began to realise the character of the woman Fiorello had painted as a she-leopard in his *Divine Comedy* sequence. I wondered how he would have depicted Mrs Mussolini.

After some consideration I decided to wear civilian clothes to my lunch with Rachele Mussolini. I selected one of my most elegant suits with soft hat, gloves and a cane. Over my patent-leather shoes I wore a pair of the elegant spats Il Duce himself had made fashionable. Then I ordered my car. Rome was unnaturally calm for the time of day, and we arrived a little early. I was driven through three checkpoints and the now familiar gates of the huge villa. The car swung round to the back of the house, past the stables and the menagerie, until we reached the rustic gate to the courtyard where Rosa Casalini, Signora Mussolini's attractive assistant, waited for me. Around her feet swarmed the usual crowd of happy dogs.

Signorina Rosa greeted me warmly. This was a good sign. I relaxed at last. I had allowed my fears to get the better of me. Miss Casalini said she had missed my visits. No doubt I had been very busy with the various foreign delegations now in town. Not to mention this business with the Pope. She hoped all that nonsense was settled. She would be glad to see the back of tourists. They were bad enough in the summer, with their Baedekers and their atrocious Italian. Il Duce, of course, had been especially busy finding time to visit the Pontine Marshes and see how 'the war for dry land' was going. Il Duce, she said, might try to drop in for lunch. He was only just back in town, so it was unlikely we should see him. Obscurely, I felt relieved. She took me up to the dining room on the first floor where the mistress of the house was waiting.

Rachele Mussolini had on a pretty dress of dark green silk. It suited her colouring and showed off the large rose pearls at her throat. Her hair had been marcelled and she wore, I think, a touch of make-up. Yet her body and face were still those of a stocky resilient peasant. That same sturdy dignity would see her through all coming vicissitudes. Now it informed her honest smile of greeting. She had none of the court's hypocrisy. When she came forward to embrace me and kiss me on both cheeks, I felt welcomed by a doting sister. Benito, she said, had told her I had been unwell. A falling-out with my girlfriend, too, she had heard. A handsome fellow like me would easily find another fiancée! I was not to worry. Thousands of girls would break their hearts over me. I must not be weak and allow the first one to come along to claim me. I was both too modest and too good-looking. She laughed easily. A dangerous combination for both parties. But in particular I should watch out for opportunistic 'vampires' who attached themselves to men of power and sometimes even brought them down. She continued in this vein as she seated me beside her while I exchanged affectionate greetings with the Mussolini boys. The younger children were absent. Only rarely were they brought to these lunches. They were looked after by a Romagnan girl, Carla, from Il Duce's own village.

After seeing him almost daily for weeks, I said, I had not been in touch with Il Duce for some time. She was sympathetic. 'He's like an overgrown boy. He pursues passing enthusiasms, then another distraction comes along and the previous craze is forgotten. Yet never forget, dear Max, that my husband is a serious person. He always returns to matters of substance. He telephones me regularly, of course,' she added. 'I know he has been very busy with affairs of state. These German events and so on. And he had to go off for a few days to the country, to see to things there. The French are being their usual contrary selves. He has so much to do. So many weighty matters. I believe he is also reforming the judiciary this week.'

I enjoyed her familiar blend of domestic anecdotes and passing references to her husband's sometimes world-shaking political decisions. She followed his arguments perfectly and could repeat them. Contrary to what many later said, she was completely behind Il Duce's policies, at least up to the late thirties when Hitler began to have a stronger influence. The only reason she did not speak more about politics was her own sense of propriety. She was naturally discreet about Mussolini's business and equally silent about his affairs. She always blamed the women but would block any attempt to speak of such things. She loved him as only a Romagnan woman can and remains intensely loyal to his memory to this day. Margherita Sarfatti painted this retiring and intelligent woman as a savage. Rachele sometimes said little, but she had been known to drive off overenthusiastic lovers with a stick. She had a strong territorial sense. Only two women ever 'defeated' her: Sarfatti and Clara Petacci, who died with Mussolini at the hands of the communist 'partisans'.

The meal was delicious. I said how much I had missed her table and our conversations. She apologised. She had left town herself for a little while. She had also been talking to Grandi about aeroplanes and airfields, she said. He had been a little vague. Did I have any thoughts on the matter?

Of course she wanted to discuss Bruno's flying lessons. It emerged she had dissuaded her husband from giving the lessons himself. 'He is too daring! Too erratic. He flies by instinct, but such instincts are hard to communicate. I wanted someone more experienced. Like you.' For about half an hour, with Bruno present and making enthusiastic suggestions, we talked about the relative merits of Fiats and SVA-4s for training. We discussed basic flying routines. I pointed out my unfamiliarity with modern controls. The planes in my films, for instance, were all from the Great War period, mostly Spads and Albatrosses. Virtually all the machines I had known since then were my own! I would not like to take the young man up without first being thoroughly familiar with the machines in question.

She was pleased with my remarks. 'Flying, I think, is his vocation,' she said, after Bruno had been sent off to school again. 'I must let him follow it. I would be a fool not to. And Il Duce, you know, is very pleased. But a mother fears . . .'

I understood. I reassured her that I had been flying since before the War. I would do nothing to jeopardise her son's life or my own! 'I am inclined to err,' I told her, 'on the side of caution.'

I must admit I was not particularly happy with the responsibility. It would have been unwise of me to broadcast the fact, but I had very little conventional flying experience up to that time. Most of it had been fairly disastrous. I knew that even a minor bruise or a bump to Bruno's head would bring the full fury of the family down upon me.

Eventually it was agreed. A Fiat would be the best plane to train in. I would set about finding one.

'I would like to begin as soon as possible,' she said. 'Perhaps an initial "hop" this coming weekend? And more intense lessons once the school vacation begins?'

I could only agree.

Later Signora Mussolini linked her plump, muscular arm in mine. She asked me if I had much work waiting for me at the office. Before I could answer she said, 'Never mind. I want a handsome young escort for the pictures this afternoon. Would you mind?'

She was my strongest supporter. How could I disagree? We went together to her cinema, a luxurious little theatre designed after those private viewing rooms used by directors. I soon knew why she had invited me. The first film was one of my own, *A Buckaroo's Courtship*, which, she said, was her personal favourite. Side by side in the red

plush seats we watched an Ace Peters who belonged to a more innocent age. Gloria Cornish was my leading lady. Both Rachele and I
enjoyed the scene where, kneeling in my saddle and drawing down
my bandanna, I reached to kiss my love as she leaned over the rail
of the train's caboose. Inwardly I mourned for my lost youth. I had
forgotten how wonderful those days had been. The next film was a
romance, *Her Secret Man*, a locally made confection of the kind that
appealed to women. Il Duce's wife wept lavishly through the final
reel. Then, with Vittorio back from school, we watched several
cartoons, including a Mickey Mouse I had not seen. I think it was
one of the talkers, but the Villa Torlonia was not yet equipped with
sound apparatus. Vittorio was as keen on the cinema as Bruno on
flying. He wanted me to teach him to become an actor. I felt I
would rather be tutoring him at that time than his brother.

Assuring my patroness that I would make every effort to have a
Fiat aeroplane ready and in perfect condition by the following week,
I left. My peace of mind had only partially been restored. At least
I had not fallen from Rachele's or her husband's favour. If anything
she was better disposed to me than ever.

I was relieved to know Mussolini had been unavailable to
everyone, including his wife. And clearly Signora Rachele knew
nothing about any other irregularities. Her view of men was old-
fashioned. She had only certain expectations of us. Rachele believed
all males to be pretty much the same in certain respects. If women
didn't cater to them they were fools. She was thoroughly on my
side. Indeed, I wondered if Rachele had heard something to make
her so sympathetic to me. Perhaps I would get a fuller picture when
I met my ex-mistress for drinks at the Excelsior? I looked at my
watch. There was an hour to prepare for my next encounter. I made
an excuse. The office needed me.

I met Mrs Cornelius in the hotel lobby. My angel was a cloudy
dream of pale blue, gold and pink. Her cloche was a helmet of
spring flowers. She complimented me on my silk summer suit, my
matching hat, gloves and spats, my silver-topped ebony cane.
Catching sight of us both in the huge mirror I admired the beautiful picture we made. She was an exquisite blonde English rose. I
was a dark South Russian nobleman, a high-ranking *fascista* with my
beard trimmed in the imperial style. I wore a fresh flower. The only
sign of my rank was an inconspicuous lapel badge.

I enjoyed one of those moments of rebirth, of self-discovery, which

Proust talks about at such interminable length. I told her how I was a new man. I was celebrating the coming of the season. I had put the past behind me.

'Always for the best, Ivan.' She was approving. 'Don't wait to let ther blood dry, that's my motto.' She would be leaving soon for Vienna, she said. After that they were going on to St Crim 'for the Chemmy'. She wouldn't mind a bit if I wanted to come along. I told her that affairs of state kept me too much in Rome. I would like nothing better than to spend some time with her in the South of France. Unfortunately, I reminded her, I had not had time to return there and clear my name. The thought of a single waltz with her on the floor of the Café Sacher could make me throw all responsibility to the winds. If I had not sworn a blood oath to Il Duce himself, I added.

She chose to hear this last as a fanciful irony. 'Keeps ya busy, does 'e, Ivan? Well, I'm trying to get a party up. Between you an' me, 'Uggy's all right but he's not exactly the liveliest wire most of the time, if ya foller me.'

I promised her I would seize the opportunity if Il Duce released me. She waved over my shoulder. 'Wotcher, 'Ermann!' I turned. ''Ello, love.'

'Heads will roll!' A boom of jovial German, like wind catching a sail. Across the dark blue carpet in his enormous ivory lounge suit which gave him the grace of a great clipper ship, his arm extended like a spar to save the rather dishevelled, slightly agitated Margherita Sarfatti who, oblivious of all but him, bobbed at his side like a bumboat, came the stately bulk of Captain Göring, his smile lighting the smoky lobby like a fog lamp.

Although hardly taller than me, the man had astonishing presence. He was the best bred of the Nazi hierarchy. His original plans for the concentration camps were bastardised as soon as he put petits bourgeois like Himmler and Heydrich in charge. I speak from personal experience. That never came out at Nuremberg. Now we all know how such omissions were typical of those American drumhead post-war courts. The assignment of blame is far more important to the American soul than the discovery of cause. Like most kulak cultures they believe analysis to be forgiveness. From beginning to end, though, I will admit to Göring's increasing greed after his first wife died. But he remained a gentleman and on the whole a loyal friend. Was it his fault if Himmler and the others conspired to block the messages I sent? Certainly he was never implicated in the scandal which was to destroy more careers than mine and claim many lives. He had every expectation of taking over the reins of government after the War and was astonished by the court's attitude. They wanted blood, not justice. Look what happened to poor Joyce, Wodehouse and Pound. The Americans wanted to destroy the Nazi dream for ever. But dreams of such yearning magnitude do not die easily. Göring knew that. He said as much in his final testament.

When the unofficial Nazi ambassador saw us he grew hearty with relief. Clearly he had had enough of La Sarfatti. 'My dear friends! How good to see you.' He tacked expertly towards us, murmuring an apology as Margherita Sarfatti was whisked smartly to starboard, almost losing her clutch on his pale shantung.

Only then she saw me and hurled herself free of his gravity, a motley whirl of tassels and trim.

'*Caro!*' she said, flinging her arms wide so that her extraordinary scent struck my face like a wall. '*Mio!*' She remembered where she was and cooed back over her shoulder. 'The main thing is, darling, that the press got their pictures.' I was kissed and whispered at. We should soon be alone, she promised, as if the episode in the cottage had never occurred. While I remained mystified by her rage, I was relieved to be forgiven. The thought of resuming my sexual duties was not, however, attractive.

Mrs Cornelius made a prim, dismissive greeting of some kind. She turned in search of Hugenberg. 'Don't forget me offer, Ivan,' she said.

Suddenly Göring was also waving farewell, saying something in German to Margherita Sarfatti which I did not catch. She answered a little distractedly and turned to me. 'Any news?' she said.

I had absolutely no idea what she meant.

'Of whom?' I felt inane.

'We'll talk later.' Her smile changed. 'Well, my dear, how have you boys all been?'

I was unsure of her tone. 'Boys?'

'I'm used to it,' she said. 'But you might tell the Chief. I think it's time this particular game was finished.'

I had no reply. Clearly Margherita had less idea of our Duce's whereabouts than I. She fluttered until she had made herself comfortable in the great basket of her chair, settling like a partridge on her eggs. Then she fixed her bright, hard eyes upon me. 'Well, darling!'

'You're out of sorts,' I said as the waiter arrived. 'A drink?'

'After all I've done for him lately!' Viciously she ordered some fashionably complex cocktail in a glass the size of a chamber pot. I had a Campari Fizz. I wished to keep my head as clear as possible. As Major Nye used to say of his own lady wife, La Sarfatti was going off like a fire in an ammunition factory.

'I feel so sorry,' she began. 'Everything is my fault. I should never have gone over. I was convinced she was already keeping her assignation at the hotel with *him* and we'd be safe. I expected to surprise you when you arrived! And then, of course, *he* turns up! He must have been tailing you!'

I assumed at first that she spoke of Fiorello, then of Mrs Cornelius and Herr Hugenberg, perhaps of Seryozha. Then I wondered if she was referring to Göring. I listened carefully in the hope of refining some sense from her outpourings.

'It's that peasant bitch, isn't it?' she said to me. 'Rachele's watching him like an owl.'

I had no notion of her drift.

'Why did she have to come to Rome? She's crazy. She's interfering in matters she can't possibly understand. Il Duce is loyal to her, of course, but she can't give him what I give him. And why is she picking on me? I hardly see him. Why doesn't she pick on that whore of yours? She's the one who takes up all his attention these days!'

Sarfatti seemed to have gone utterly mad. I made an effort to change the subject. 'Have you heard anything more from Fiorello?'

She stared at me. 'What?' It was as if she had never known our mutual friend.

'Did he make it to Switzerland?'

'Oh, of course,' she said. 'They all do. Darling, the reason I needed to see you is for your sake.' She gave a little, self-deprecating snigger. 'I fear I need my little house back.'

She was evicting me! From spite? As a strategy? Was this the only price I was being asked to pay for being rid of her?

'Naturally,' I said. 'That was always our understanding. If you could give me a day or two to find new digs.'

'I need it rather urgently,' she said. 'Rather soon. Tomorrow, my darling. I hate to do this to you, but it's all very sordid and concerned with money, about which I understand absolutely nothing. But those who do follow such things are the masters now, darling, aren't they?'

I was breathless. 'I suppose I can find rooms at a hotel near the office . . .'

'Why not here, darling? They have marvellous drinks and wonderful service. I know the manager. I can get you a special rate.'

I would be content with something a little less elaborate. I would ask my friends for suggestions.

She fluttered across the glass table dividing us and settled on me like a carnivorous moth. 'You are the perfect gentleman,' she said. 'I always have the right instincts. I should learn to trust them more.'

A short while later she would be on a boat to America, never to return. To save her from the political situation, Il Duce exiled her. It was entirely for her own good. To her credit she understood that. She was one of many Italian Jews who found happiness in the New World.

As we sat there, she asked after my friends in the press corps. I had seen only Tom Morgan. I had even lost contact with Billy Grisham and his family. I gathered he had been reassigned to Berlin.

'The press is more fickle than any woman.' She nodded as if in confirmation of her own wisdom. She became contemplative and returned to her chair. We had reached an impasse. I wondered if I had inadvertently given her some more pieces in her jigsaw.

I filled the silence. 'Has Captain Göring bought any pictures?'

'Not really. He's far too busy with politics these days. His attention is on politics rather than art! And his wife is ailing, too, you know.' This last appeared to be entirely irrelevant. 'He carried his message to Il Duce. He carried his message to the Pope.' She inspected her hands, perhaps for stigmata. 'He took a message to Berlin. He brought a message to Rome. He did what he had to do. And soon he will leave.' With a dramatic expression of wounded bitterness she called for another cocktail.

I guessed what had happened. Il Duce did not blame me for my affair with his mistress. He knew her too well for that. He blamed her. He had clearly found another paramour who interested him far more. I was not out of favour. All Sarfatti had left to offer her Chief was her contacts within the new, young Germany. Evidently he had been using them, because neither Göring nor any of his entourage had met Mussolini officially. Her house had been a useful meeting place for the men. In spite of this she was no longer a woman to be seen with. No doubt she had exaggerated her current role to gain a moment's prestige.

I looked at my wristwatch. 'Well, I must make my plans. I shall be busy with my move.' This would be a good time to begin my reconciliation with Maddy Butter. Once I located her, I could promise her I had made a clean break with Madame Sarfatti.

'You mustn't feel rushed,' she said. 'I could perhaps arrange to give you some more time.'

As I rose I became increasingly formal. I told her that I would not think to impose on her any longer than necessary. Did she plan to dine at the hotel or could I call her car for her?

She shrugged. Her drink arrived and I left.

I hoped that I had not been seen. Rachele Mussolini had her own spies. It occurred to me that Il Duce's wife had warmed to me again because I was clearly no longer seeing Sarfatti. I must choose my company carefully for the next few weeks. Meanwhile, I considered taking a refresher course in flying. But how could I do that tactfully? I wondered.

I ran into Major Nye in the lobby. The tall Englishman was talking to Balbo and a couple of other high-ranking *fascisti*. Balbo was supposed to have killed a priest in the early twenties, a story that dogged his career. As well as being Italy's most famous aviator, Balbo, a competent and intelligent man, had the unfortunate appearance of Popeye's enemy Bluto in the cartoons everyone loved. He was known privately, even by Mussolini, as 'Air Minister Bluto'. In his mid-thirties, as were most of the leading *fascisti* Grand Councillors, he would have done well to shave off his beard or cultivate a more refined one, like my own. I think he believed it made his face look thinner. In my view his beard was his downfall. He was eventually sent into exile as Governor of Libya. In the end, they said, the great aviator was glad to go. I had cultivated him at one stage. He had shown every interest in my descriptions of the planes I had built. He even asked me to send him over a few plans, but Mussolini blocked the idea. He said Balbo would only have bogged things down in red tape.

I joined the group for a moment. It would have been impolitic to do anything else. Besides, Balbo was just the man who might help me. Almost embarrassed by the vigour of my salute, they returned it in kind. The other three were the voluble and volatile Farinacci, who agreed with many of my ideas and was still regarded as a sound man by the party rank and file, the dapper, garrulous Grandi, Italy's charming Foreign Minister, and the polished Cardinal Gasparri, with whom I also shared important opinions. A slightly disparate group, it did me no harm to be seen in their company when chatting to the Englishman.

I murmured to Gasparri that I was impressed by the way he extended his diplomatic talents to the international scene. He smiled and drew a perfectly manicured finger to his sensitive lips. In contrast to Balbo, the cardinal was almost ostentatiously well shaven. He advertised his own grooming as others might advertise their rank. His flesh had the blush of fine talc. He was golden pink with an aura of assured authority. Even the richly woven scarlet cloth of his robes had that same quality of invulnerable softness. His smoothness, of course, was his great strength. I have met theatrical agents with a similar manner. It made him the best negotiator between the Palazzo Venezia and the Vatican.

Cheerful and fashionable as always, Grandi the Foreign Minister sported, like me, the pointed beard and half-wax of a pre-war *boulevardier*. He was probably the ablest man in Italy and Il Duce's best friend. Grandi turned against his Chief in the end, became a declared anti-Fascist and fled to Lisbon where, I gather, he is now a tobacconist.

I mentioned to Grandi that I was about to be homeless. This set the little man to laughing heartily. 'Dumped you, has she? Or has he?' It seemed half of Rome was aware of my affair. I shuddered.

'If you like,' I said. 'Anyway, I'm glad it's over.'

Grandi said I would get used to it. 'We all get used to it after a while.' I was not to worry. I would have a house in twenty-four hours. 'It's just a question of telling some impoverished old fart of a nobleman whose family stole it from some other old fart of a nobleman that he has to vacate his seat. His thousand years are up. Now it's our turn. We'll relocate him in the country.'

He was joking, of course. Only later would such jokes be interpreted by the humourless Americans to suggest the Fascists were brutes.

As I left them, Farinacci wished me good luck. He was a far-sighted man, poorly used by his people. He alone saw that the state could not tolerate a separate constituency. We had made our peace with the Pope, he had said, but we would never make our peace with the Grand Rabbi. Those people had international loyalties and

191

simply could not be trusted to be good citizens. Wisely, the Grand Rabbi converted to Christianity, of course, in 1955. What does that tell us?

It was impossible just then to have a private word with Balbo. I told Grandi I would telephone him in the morning. I asked the concierge to have my car brought round. I was just in time. As I stepped through the doors of the hotel and descended to my waiting Mercedes a voice from behind me cried: 'Dimka! Dimka, dear!'

I saw Seryozha reflected in the polished metal. Everything on him was loose and flying. He was a wild pirate schooner to Göring's dignified ship of the line. He swerved erratically in pursuit of me.

I did not turn round. I got into my car and told my chauffeur to drive off quickly. I heard a thump on the car's trunk. When I did risk a glance back, I saw Seryozha angrily shouting at a group of *squadristi*, who had appeared from nowhere.

The streets were still busy. It was not yet twilight and Rome, lively as always, was going out to eat. The lights of the trams were golden and scarlet against the deepening blue of the sky. The creamy stone was vivid with posters. Cafés and restaurants came alive. The energy of the city was visible everywhere. As the car took me through the park, I sat back and enjoyed the beauty of the late-spring flowers, the last of the children trooping back from their play, young courting couples, elderly women with their dogs, the old men sitting in groups, smoking and mocking everyone not of their class and generation. There was a tranquillity and stability about this scene that Rome had not enjoyed since the War. It showed why Mussolini was so revered here and how much he had given his people.

The sun was setting as we reached the quieter suburbs. The soft light washed away most modern buildings. Ancient walls covered in climbing shrubbery might have been the villas of Roman nobles. We came at last to the little gate of the cottage. I got out, said good-night to my driver, glanced around to see if any OVRA people were keeping an eye on things, saw nothing, opened my gate and noticed that there were flies everywhere. Through the half-light I could make out a large creature lying on my doorstep. At first I thought it was a leopard or some other animal escaped from the nearby zoo. Then I realised it appeared to be a sleeping Labrador, an English dog then very fashionable in Italy. I wondered how it had managed to get through the gate. As I drew closer, I noticed that the dog's head lay at an odd angle, its eyes partially open. There was liquid oozing from its muzzle and staining the stone. As I bent to inspect it, a strong smell, half-dog, half-death, hit my nostrils. It had been dead for some hours and was no longer stiff.

I was completely mystified. Had the Labrador made its way here and expired? Why would someone put it here? Perhaps it had been struck by a car and managed to get to my house before dying. Now I saw the creature had been shot in the throat with a small-calibre gun. Was it someone's guard dog?

Rather than inspect the corpse further, and feeling my lungs filling up with the unmistakable and almost indefinable smell of death, against which all normal animals react, I stepped over the beast and opened my door.

As soon as I had put the lights on, I took a little 'snuff' to clear the stink from my nostrils and lit some anti-insect candles in the hope of keeping the flies out. Already some were in the room. Feeling quite ready to leave the place, I began to pack up my personal documents. Then on an impulse I rang the exchange and got a number for the local police. I telephoned the police and told them of the problem. They were sympathetic. They would contact the necessary municipal office who would send a team in the morning to remove the dog. I was tempted to use my authority with them, but I had already been cautioned against this by Tom Morgan. Il Duce hated his 'secret party people' making their status public. It simply wasn't the gentlemanly thing to do. I understood all this, having been trained in old-fashioned American courtesy by that great patriot Major Simmonds. I could try more tactful methods, I decided, if the flies got any worse. I continued with my packing. Someone would come in to remove the majority of my things when I found new quarters.

At that time of the evening the sunset noises from the zoo carried over through the open window. I realised I was going to miss the roars and shrieks. The telephone rang. It was Quinto Navarra, Mussolini's private secretary. He had heard I was thinking of moving. I told him I had been evicted by my landlady and he laughed. He understood completely. Had I found another place yet?

I thought he had telephoned me to help with my accommodation. Instead, he asked if I was in good spirits. I told him that I was in excellent spirits until I had come home to find a dead dog on my doorstep. It was a mystery how it had got there.

Navarra was extremely concerned. He would have some people come and remove it at once. What colour was the dog?

I found this question a little strange. It was a black Labrador, I said. A male.

'Black? A bad joke,' he said. 'We'll have it looked into. I'll call Bocchini's office.'

A joke? What sort of joke? And who would play it?

He was not given to loud laughter but he seemed amused. 'Someone who wanted you to think you were a Mafia target, perhaps? The black dog is their calling card.'

I knew nothing of such people. I had made no enemies among them.

'It isn't the Mafia,' Navarra assured me. 'Il Duce has pretty much eradicated the Mafia. They wouldn't dare. Do you have other enemies in Rome? Or perhaps America? Did something perhaps happen years ago?'

I remembered Annibale Santucci and his people who had helped me in San Francisco. I had never doubted that they were involved with organised crime. But we had parted on the best of terms.

And then, of course, it came to me.

Brodmann!

Quinto Navarra thought little of the whole thing. 'Schoolkids used to do that with dead dogs all the time. It terrified some people! Particularly Jew shopkeepers the kids didn't like. It used to scare them silly, thinking the Mafia had taken against them!' Again he seemed to laugh to himself. He said that he had just left Il Duce. Much as he regretted not being able to come to me at my offices as usual, Mussolini would be glad if I visited him at the Palazzo Venezia in the morning. He would like a quiet a word with me.

Normally I would have been delighted. This was certain proof that I was still *persona grata* with our Chief. But I was deeply confused as I replaced the receiver and continued to pack. I turned on the radio, hoping for some dance music, but the stations were already closing down for the evening.

A little later came a knock at the door. No doubt Navarra had sent someone to remove the dog.

I opened up to find Seryozha standing there. He offered me a knowing leer.

Clutching two bottles of champagne in his hands, his pockets revealed glasses, some bread and what appeared to be the contents of a good-sized larder.

'Are you starving?' he asked. 'I am.' He stepped over the corpse

194

and came in. 'Is that your dog, Dimka? Aren't people brutes? I saw you at the hotel, but you didn't see me. Luckily I still had your address. This is our chance to be alone together with nobody knowing!'

I guessed that any secret service novice could have kept watch on Seryozha while doing the crossword puzzle and listening to a football game, but I could not easily get rid of him. I closed the door. He embraced me. I felt the bottles digging into my back as he kissed me. 'Now, Dimka, dear. Where shall we have our little picnic?'

I told him I was delighted to see him but that we did not have long for our meal. I had an appointment with my Chief.

'Then we shall make the most of our time,' Seryozha promised. 'After all, in lovemaking, quality not quantity counts!'

I had become so alarmed at the threat of Brodmann back on my trail that I hardly cared what Seryozha said or did. Unless he was in the pay of the Cheka, which was a possibility, his company was better than nothing. I felt Brodmann would not strike tonight. He would give me time to think about the implications of my *Fido Negro*.

I hardly listened to Seryozha as he prattled on. I was all too familiar with his kind of gossip: who was friends with whom, who hated whom and so on. He let me know that Göring and 'the Berliners' hated his patron, 'Ernstie', who was, he said, a 'real Nazi'. Göring and company had already gone over to the forces of international capitalism against which the Nazis had been determined to fight as thoroughly as they fought Bolshevism. The corporate state was betrayed! I did not give this stuff much of my attention. I was distracted with more immediate matters.

It occurred to me that I might contact my acquaintance Monelli at the OVRA headquarters and tell him that I was being threatened by a Chekist. But the situation would be impossible to explain and unfortunately would conflict in certain key areas with my official biography. Apart from Mrs Cornelius, who always supported me in whatever role I played, only Seryozha among our mutual acquaintances now knew me to be Russian. Fiorello, with luck, had escaped and would be no danger to me.

When I left that evening, taking a whining but reinvigorated Seryozha with me, I had nowhere else to go. I told him I would drop him off at the Excelsior.

The car arrived. Again we were forced to step over the rapidly decaying corpse of the dog. By now Seryozha was full of sentimental misery for the dog's fate and began speculating on the kind of bastard who would do that kind of thing. I delivered a still emotional Seryozha back and told my chauffeur to take a spin up the Tivoli road for a while. I was anxious to clear my head. Attempting to relax, I somehow could not enjoy that perfect Roman evening to the full.

When I returned to the cottage, the dog was gone. Everything was perfectly clean. Navarra had been as good as his word. I showered, got into my pyjamas, read through some newspapers I had bought on my way home and then, though I was not particularly tired, went to bed early.

Next morning, smart in my best uniform, my morale improved, I forced myself to think of nothing but work and matters in hand. I arrived at the Palazzo Venezia about half an hour early and as usual gave my name to the guard. Positioned everywhere were the tall, handsome young noblemen who formed Mussolini's special 'Death's Head' guard. Each was sworn to defend the life of Il Duce with his own. In their smart black uniforms, with silver skull-and-crossbones insignia on black fezzes, with silver daggers at their belts and the latest rapid-firing carbines on their shoulders, they were Mussolini's own healthy praetorians, the best of the new Italy.

I was taken to a waiting room where several others already sat. I was disconcerted. Having expected to see Il Duce alone, I felt rather like a petitioner in a medieval antechamber. Indeed, I was unpleasantly reminded of El Glaoui's court.

The affable Quinto Navarra soon found me. With apologies and excuses he led me through a private door. Less privileged visitors would be taken through an elaborate series of vast rooms before being presented to Il Duce, but Navarra guided me along the back corridors until at last we passed through a curtain guarded by two *squadristi*. We came out on to the huge landing of dark panelling and sombre murals, which lay before the so-called Hall of the Globe, the *Mappamondo* room, now Mussolini's office. Here Navarra led me straight past the guards, set me on my way and quietly closed the doors behind me.

I had heard of this hall but never previously experienced it. My meetings with Mussolini had always been of a more private nature. About seventy-five feet long and fifty feet tall, its walls, ceiling and panelling were decorated with entire panoramas of Italian history. In the distance, at a huge desk lit by a single lamp, sat Il Duce who gravely signalled me forward.

I felt inflated, rather than reduced, by the sense of occasion. Proud in the uniform of my rank I strode forward to greet the greatest soldier-philosopher since Alexander. His massive shaven head and muscular torso were an impressive silhouette against the light. As I came nearer, Mussolini suddenly stood up and came round his desk towards me. Even as I raised my arm to salute him he put his own out. We shook hands. He was warm. He was abstracted, urgent. He said how good it was to see me. How much he had missed our discussions and especially our strategy meetings. He was even now trying to convince the Finance Ministry of the need to fund all the Peters prototypes. Affairs of state continued to engage him. But I must not despair. The Land Leviathan would soon be an impressive reality. The Peters Supertank might be a good name for it, didn't I think? He had a few details to finalise with the Spanish government. Ten machines were as good as sold. With the money paid by the Spaniards, we would build our own ten first. Then we would build their ten. With the final payment, we could build another ten. And so on. He imagined a fleet of monstrous land ironclads perhaps a hundred or two hundred strong. 'Enough to awe the enemy and dissuade resistance before it begins.'

As always I was inspired by his vision. Even as I stood in his comradely embrace, I could see my armies of flying soldiers, of massive battle-engines and bombing aeroplanes streaming rank upon endless rank into a golden future. I saw myself as Mussolini's foremost lieutenant. I would be his most magnificent marshal, Roland to his Charlemagne. Leading his legions against all Italy's foes, I would establish another great Holy Roman Empire, stretching from the Sahara to the Pyrenees, from Lisbon to Constantinople, a great shield against Islam. My cities would fly. Flying cities would dominate the tranquil skies, keeping order upon the earth in a new Pax Romana. That world would abolish usury and establish the corporate state, would again be given over to natural farming and enlightened animal husbandry, to the skilled artisan, so that none should be without work, none should go hungry.

In spite of all his optimism, however, I sensed that Il Duce was in a rather gloomy and contemplative mood. No doubt the recalcitrant Vatican and legal profession were causing him problems. But he said none of this to me. He changed the subject. 'I gather,' he said thought-fully, 'that you're getting on well with the German delegation. One of them's a friend of yours, eh?'

'An acquaintance I'm trying to avoid, if the truth be told,' I said. 'It's a bit awkward. He's a Russian ballet boy I've helped out a couple of times. I think as a result he's developed a crush on me.' I had no wish to be associated with what Mussolini called 'rouge boys'. 'I find it all rather disgusting.'

'Strange bedfellows, eh?' said Mussolini with a wink. He was in a comradely mood. 'I hear you broke up with that girlfriend of yours.' He offered me a sharp, penetrating look. Did he mean Seryozha? Of course not.

I assumed he meant Maddy Butter. Or could Sarfatti have said something? I was struck by a thought: were they playing a game? Had Mussolini discovered the truth? Had the black dog's corpse been placed on my doorstep at his instructions? Had Maddy's accu-sations been believed? My left leg began to tremble. I knew a moment's terror. I needed to see Maddy, to find out what she had said. Was she back in Rome, her press assignment over?

'You must be feeling a bit fed up.' He strolled over to the huge carved lectern on which was arranged an atlas almost as tall as himself. 'Needing a change. Someone told me you're moving house.'

He had forgotten that he himself had suggested I move. I agreed that a change would do me good.

'Maybe even a vacation?'

I had work to do for Italy. I had no more need of rest than did my leader.

This pleased him. 'You are a true *fascisti*, Professor. A hard-working Renaissance man.'

'You are my model and my ideal,' I said. I spoke only the truth.

He accepted this with his usual almost shy acknowledgement. 'But it seemed to Signora Mussolini today that your nerves were a little bad. She remarked on it. And you know how much she cares about you. You are going to teach Bruno to fly. We need you in the best condition, Professor Peters. I, too, have a special interest in your health.'

I said that I was honoured. I had, indeed, experienced one or two minor personal problems, but these were all now behind me. A dead dog on my doorstep had not improved my mood. But I was ready to put my shoulder to whatever wheel Il Duce presented!

198

He frowned, thrusting his lower lip forward in that characteristic way. 'Perhaps you need a break. A change of scene. Maybe our mutual interest could be served. I desperately need someone I can trust. There are so few. You are one of them.' He turned towards the enormous window, head low on his chest. A long pause. Then: 'Professor, I want to offer you a very special assignment. I wouldn't even talk to the Grand Council about it. It can't go beyond these walls.' His brooding eyes fixed on mine. 'It can only be between you and me. I want you to act for Italy.' He stepped back, as if to study his effect on me.

I could not respond. I stammered. I would do anything for him. Anything for my new nation.

He nodded, taking this for granted. He placed a hand on my arm. 'You are certainly already aware that Captain Göring is Hitler's Special and Secret Emissary. That is the identical role I have in mind for you. Are you prepared to leave Rome for a few weeks?'

'If necessary, Chief.' This was something of a shock. I was a scientist, an inventor, not a secret service agent. But I had sworn an oath to obey my Duce to the death. I could not refuse. Moreover, if I was away from the city, I would have a chance to polish my flying skills before returning.

His expression confirmed his own trust in me. 'It's not a pleasant mission. You'll have to mix with some obnoxious people. You'll be travelling to Munich and Berlin as my secret emissary.' He noticed my reaction. 'The public knows nothing of your affiliations, you see. Only of your fame. Anyone else could not accomplish this. As an American film star you can go anywhere and not be under suspicion. The Nazi boys all know you, of course, and have a pretty good idea what you do. They'll be wanting to find out about our inventions. You will give them a hint and no more. It won't do any harm to exaggerate a little. It will be in your commercial interest as well as Italy's to let them believe we are further ahead with production.'

'But what excuse could I possibly have −?'

He raised a silencing hand. He had thought of this, too. 'Anyone who asks, you can say you're curious about the new political movements in Europe. Meanwhile, you will be Italy's eyes and ears. You speak Geman. You know Göring. In particular, you have the scientific and engineering experience to take a look at some of their own undercover projects.'

'A spy, Chief?'

'A special intelligence officer. Those Krauts plan to rearm if they come to power. They have some good people helping them. Göring confided all this to Margherita Sarfatti. They plan to make bombers disguised as commercial aircraft. They have half a dozen new aerial weapons ready for production. I don't trust them. Before we had our own weapons programmes under way, the Germans could be in Austria, then Italy. You know what they're like. They're promising revenge against us all.'

'Excuse me, Duce,' I asked levelly, 'but are you asking me to find some sort of evidence that Hitler and company plan to attack Italy?'

He became circumspect. He took me by the arm. He insisted: 'I've told you. A foreign ambassador does not spy. But you are a loyal Fascist now. Should you discover information of use to this nation, you are honour-bound to relay it to us. That is all I ask you to do.'

I was confused. 'But what of my work here? We are almost at production stage. We can't afford to have anyone discover what we're doing, surely?' I was genuinely distressed. Did he mean to abandon our engineering projects? 'The flying lessons for your son Bruno. Signora Mussolini might be disappointed . . .'

'I am talking a matter of two months at most. While you are gone I will set the initial factory work in motion. When you come back you will be in a position to supervise an ongoing project.'

Two months would, it was true, give me a breathing space. I could use the time to my advantage. And if Brodmann were really in town, I would be able to leave before he realised it. No doubt the dead dog had been his idea. Seryozha, too, was becoming a serious embarrassment. Sarfatti was threatening to come back into my life. There were other looming complications. I was, of course, still hoping for a reconciliation with Maddy Butter.

'My fiancée . . .' I began.

Mussolini scowled. He did not think this was a serious subject. 'Women are easily come by. Most of them are whores at heart. You need to forget your American and look for someone as loyal as my Rachele. When you find her, marry her at once.'

I paused. I took his point. Moreover, I did not share his dislike of Germans, or indeed, of the individual Nazis I had met. To leave Rome for a couple of months and experience the vibrancy of modern German political life might be exactly what I needed. So much the better if I was performing an important personal service for my Duce. I was sure he would not let such loyalty go unrewarded. In addition, it would throw Brodmann off the scent. The dog, I was convinced, had been only a warning. Classic Chekist psychological warfare.

However, this led to another thought. What if I was captured and tortured for my scientific secrets?

Mussolini put his arm around my shoulders. Together we marched up and down the length of that huge room. He reassured me that such things only happened in fiction. Internationally known actors (and engineers) could not easily be spirited away. The community of nations would have something to say about it! The Nazis were anxious to improve their public image. 'They will court you, but that is all to the good. You can sow the seeds of rumour about our secret weapons and that will be useful to us.'

He took my hand in both of his and stared into my eyes for a moment, as if filling me with some of his own resolve, his own inexhaustible courage. Others have mentioned his hypnotic powers, and I can vouch for them.

The few necessary arrangements had already been made with the Germans, he said. The present German government was viciously anti-Nazi and highly suspicious of Italian Fascists. Thus it would be unwise for me to travel on my Italian passport. Could I use my American passport? Although I would seem to be on my own I need not worry. There would be an OVRA man looking out for my interests at all times. Göring had been put in the picture as much as necessary. He had friends in Berlin. Some were in the Reichstag itself. While it would not be wise to have too close a contact with the affable captain, he would be there if needed. Mussolini had thought this through carefully. I would also receive a regular allowance as a state employee. This would come in the form of payments from a publisher. 'Göring has already spoken warmly of you, in spite of his well-known prejudices. He is, at root, a practical politician like myself. Not a rouge-using lunatic like his boss. They will, of course, suspect you. If you could, perhaps, obscure things a little, it would help. I'm not very worried about the German National Socialists. They won't increase their vote in the next election. But some of the Catholic nationalists will. The army is backing them. Those are the people to get close to, Professor. You're not likely to make many more friends in the National Socialists anyway. Apparently they are already bickering among themselves. Hitler's on his way out. They lack Fascist discipline. One week I hear Strasser's their "Duce" – the next it's Hitler again – or Röhm. They have as many factions as they have members. That's fine. Nobody wants the bastards to get too much power. But I need an idea of how much of their party is likely to listen to us. Are they really pro-Fascist? We don't know. I must admit I haven't heard good reports of any of them except Göring. Possibly the Strasser brothers. My guess is that Göring's the man who will eventually lead the party. Him or Gregor Strasser. Not his brother. He's too unstable. Of course, the whole country's unstable. There could be civil war before Göring, for instance, becomes the next Chancellor. He's their strong man. He's the only one an old fart like Hindenburg would trust. I'd bet Göring is letting the others fight it out. But there again, everything could change by next Tuesday. That's why I need a man like you there for a while. My eyes and ears, eh?'

'I am still a little confused, Chief . . .'

'The Krauts need more money from me, of course. They are always begging for handouts. I want men like you there who'll let me know the best horse to back. And I especially need to know any plans they have for rearmament. I can spare few men of your rank, my dear friend, or I wouldn't ask this of you. I need a loyal Fascist, yet someone who is not evidently pro-Italian.'

I was flattered by the honour. I could not think what merited so much responsibility.

Mussolini told me Navarra had arranged money, documents and so on. I could leave whenever I wished. Perhaps tomorrow would be a good day. There were reservations for me on the Rome–Vienna train which would connect me with the Munich Express.

'So soon?' For a moment I had a suspicion he was getting rid of me. Why? Jealousy? Did he see me as a rival for his wife's affections? For Sarfatti? For whom? But it was not in my nature to refuse this great man. Neither could I easily suspect him of lying. Weakly, I asked whom I should contact when I reached Munich.

He said that would not be a problem. Captain Göring himself would be my host as far as Munich. One of his people would see to my hotel and so on. All I had to do was to have my trunks packed. I should ask Navarra for help.

I had several other rather crucial questions, but now he became impatient, glancing at the floor, looking away from me, tapping his pencil against the table. He was in no mood to give further answers.

He hastened me towards the door. 'And don't contact that journalist friend of yours. That girl. Maddy?'

'Butter?'

'She must know nothing.' His expression once again grave, he wished me God speed. With tears in my eyes I promised he would have no reason not to trust me. Maddy? Was that why I was being asked to take a sabbatical from Rome? Was she suspect?

Navarra was waiting for me when I left. He steered me quickly to the secret exit. As I went out, I thought I glimpsed a woman very much like Maddy Butter coming in. Had she at last managed to get her interview with Il Duce? No doubt it was a trick of my imagination. But it would have been a queer irony.

In spite of Il Duce's advice my curiosity got the better of me. When I returned to my office, to tidy up a few things, I telephoned Miss Butter's apartment. I wanted to leave with her blessing. The telephone was answered by a maid. Miss Butter had a hairdresser's appointment. She would not be back until that afternoon. I left no message. I could not risk seeing her personally. She might even be the one who had betrayed me to Brodmann and was indirectly responsible for the dead dog on my step.

She had still not returned by that evening. Then a uniformed valet and a team of *squadristi* arrived at work to take me back to the cottage. They wanted me to supervise the packing of my trunks.

I tried to telephone Signora Mussolini but could not get through. Just as I was dialling the number again, the phone went dead. The dolts at the phone company had turned off the phone a day too early.

Rather than waste time in useless fuming, I changed and took myself to the fashionable Caffè Florentine for dinner. Once again I was 'back in the dream'. I felt both excited and disturbed. I had been given no time to consider my decision. Admittedly, as one of Mussolini's inner circle, I had sworn my oath and had a duty to abide by it. I must obey Il Duce's orders no matter how mysterious they were. I had to admit I was curious to see Germany as she was now.

My misgivings suppressed, I ate a solitary meal. As I was finishing Balbo came into the restaurant. He saw me and grinned. Marching over, he waved to me, his decorations jingling. 'I hear you've been exiled to Germany, Professor. She must be a bit above average, eh?' He winked and leered. I had no idea what he meant. Repelled by his peasant coarseness, I did my best not to respond. He seemed envious of me. Had I been given an assignment he craved for himself or one of his cronies? I did not even bother to ask him who 'she' was. His suggestion was meaningless. He was jealous of me, I was sure of that. This made me feel a little better about my new duties. I merely smiled and let him think what he liked. He shrugged and went off to join some friends in an alcove.

I took an Armagnac in the bar. The place was now empty of most Fascist delegates. They had returned to their various constituencies. I saw Major Nye come in with Mrs Cornelius. I signalled to them, but they went past without seeing me. I looked for them in the restaurant but could not see them.

At that moment I felt suddenly isolated. A marooned sailor too weary to cry to passing ships. I could not understand why, with a new adventure ahead, I felt so depressed.

Why had I become so obscurely gloomy since discovering that dog? I remained disgusted by the kind of monster capable of such mindless cruelty.

I prayed I was wrong about Brodmann. I concentrated on plans for my new journey. I consoled myself. I was still serving the Fascist cause. I was content to assist my Duce in any way, even by going into exile, as Balbo put it. In no time at all, I thought, I would be back in Italy supervising the building of my Land Leviathan. Once my name was famous as an engineer I could travel wherever I pleased. I need no longer rely on my reputation as an actor.

TWENTY–TWO

Maddy Butter was still not home by the time I left for the Termini Station. No matter what time I phoned she was always out. Only when my luggage had been loaded and the *squadristi* had left could I sit back in my large comfortable seat and forget her. I had not planned to leave Rome. Considering the problems I would have to face if I stayed, however, this short 'fact-finding' vacation would do me good. Thanks to the sterling efforts of the young *fascisti* assigned to me, everything apart from my handbags needed for the trip was stowed securely in the luggage vans. I appeared to have an entire *de luxe* compartment to myself. Though for a couple of months I would be travelling under-cover, I would still be travelling in style. Il Duce knew me better than I knew myself. My spirits were already improving. I became filled with that sense of joyful expectation which usually accompanied a new journey. Only when I was moving did I feel truly secure.

I looked forward to enjoying the company of my travelling companions. Mrs Cornelius and her Baron were on the train, though they planned to go on to St Crim. I sincerely hoped that Seryozha was not. I had no particular anxieties, save that Seryozha would get drunk and start babbling about our days in St Petersburg. I was surprised not to see any of the German delegation boarding.

Soon after the train departed there came a tap on the glass door. In the corridor stood an exceptionally tall, oddly coloured indi-vidual with a nose like a hammer set in irregular features, deep-set eyes beneath bushy brows, a thin upper lip drawn habitually over the lower which gave him a kind of perpetual smile, a jutting lantern jaw and an expression of polite apology. He wore a grey tweed English overcoat, a dark grey Homburg and carried a gold-chased ebony stick with which he signalled politely for me to open the door. When I frowned enquiry, he put the head of his stick to his lips and raised his eyebrows, perhaps a question?

When I slid the door back he entered, clicked his heels together, gave a rather idiosyncratic Fascist salute, lifted his hat, called me 'Herr Doctor Peters' and announced himself as Doctor Ernst Hanfstaengl. In perfect American English he asked if I would prefer to speak my own language. I knew he did not mean Russian. In my role as Max Peters, the American actor, I said English would be fine. Unbuttoning his overcoat, he asked if he might sit down for a moment. He was about ten years my senior, with that youthful air, that unlined, inexperienced sheen on the skin you see on so many modern businessmen. His light blue eyes held a kind of amiable amusement, as if his own existence was absurd to him. His pale, close-shaven face flickered with a dozen half-formed expressions. His mouth was sensitive beneath that Teutonic nose. In spite of his obvious eccentricities, he was evidently what we used to call 'the better type of German'. At my assent, he lowered his assortment of large limbs into the seat and with careful concentration arranged them in a familiar order.

When he was sure everything was where he wanted it to be, he sighed and put his hand towards me. I shook it.

'Hanfstaengl,' he said again, as if to remind himself.

Sitting back in the seat he looked out of the window and addressed the scenery. 'Well, it's a shame. But here we are.'

I did not follow him. I made a small enquiring noise.

'Herr Göring,' he explained, smiling. 'I do apologise. They didn't get the message to you, I take it?'

'Apparently.'

With a peculiar jerk of his shoulder, Doctor Hanfstaengl took out a cigarette case. Smiling like a schoolboy, he offered it to me. When I declined he put the case away. 'I'm the messenger, then. Göring's wife Carin?'

'He has spoken of her with great affection.'

'Oh, he couldn't survive without her. But she has had something of a relapse. So he flew out early this morning for Berlin. I agreed to be his deputy and take care of you. My pleasure, of course. We have friends in common. I think, in Tom Morgan and some of the other press guys.'

'You're a journalist?'

'I do a little writing. Luckily my family's fairly well off, so I don't have to struggle. We have a print business in Munich. I'm Hitler's foreign press attaché. I saw you at the embassy a couple of times.

You were with that English chap. Nice fellow. Major Pye. I was staying at the Ambasciatori. My family always does; we get on well with the staff. I find the Excelsior a little vulgar. What part of the United States are you from, Doctor Peters?'

I said that I had been born in the South but that I now called Hollywood my home.

He detected another accent under my English. I explained how my parents were first-generation immigrants. From Spain, I told him. Their original name was Gallibasta-Pujol, and they came from the Andalucia region. Hanfstaengl was on very good terms with the de Riberas. Did I know them? I told him that I had spent very little time in Spain. In recent years I had travelled chiefly in the Middle East and North Africa.

I answered an unasked question for him. 'That would explain why you haven't made a talker yet. What were you doing out there? Researching a part?'

It had been a journey of personal discovery, and I was not yet ready to talk about it. He seemed to forget his question as soon as he asked it. Taking off his overcoat he drew from an inner pocket a silver flask which he offered to me. I refused. 'You seem equipped for all occasions, Doctor Hanfstaengl.'

'Well,' he said, 'I suppose it's my job.' His bones shifted in an eccentric shrug.

He had studied at Princeton and lived in America for years. Then as he put it, he had answered Hitler's call to come home and fight for the cause. Did I know New England at all? I had only lectured there. Mostly I knew the South and the West. For a time I had been involved in politics and was associated with, among others, the famous aviator Major Simmonds. I knew Washington well. We talked about mutual acquaintances.

'Putzi' Hanfstaengl was excellent company. When he suggested we lunch together, I readily agreed and followed him down the corridor to the dining car. He moved with the massive, oddly co-ordinated grace of a young carthorse, head bent, arms flailing, his expression always cheerful as if he expected everyone to share in the comedy of his own disorganisation. Mrs Cornelius and her Baron were already installed at their table, and we asked if we might join them. The Baron smiled up at us vaguely, as if at an entertainment, while Mrs Cornelius agreed with alacrity. 'Oh, do!' she said.

She leaned towards me as I sat down. 'Good for you, Ive,' she

said. 'I 'ad a feelin's you'd make it!' She winked. 'Those Aye-taye
buggers was usin' you. An' 'oo knows 'oo that Yank gel wos bonkin'.
They 'ad you set up nicely. You're well out of it. Ya comin' with us
to San Cream?'

I ignored her jealous references to Madame Sarfatti. I was on my
way to Munich and Berlin. I needed a break and had always wanted
to see Germany. For one reason or another I had never managed
to get there. This seemed a good time to be going. It would be a
short holiday. A matter of a few weeks at most.

'You must not judge Germany by what you see now,' Doctor
Hanfstaengl insisted, picking up a menu in one hand and a napkin
in the other. 'But wait a couple of years – then there'll be a difference!'

Mrs Cornelius had had enough of all this talk. She was sick and
tired of golden futures, she said. All she wanted at the moment was
an ordinary present.

Doctor Hanfstaengl found this so amusing he almost spilled his
mineral water. 'I must admit I sometimes tire of the coming apocalypse.'

Would Mrs Cornelius be staying long in Vienna? She shook her
head. They were going to some concerts and a couple of operas.
She hoped they were jolly ones. They would be in town for a few
days. Staying at the Bristol, she said. Where was that funny Russian
friend of mine?

Looking about the dining car I was glad Seryozha was not there.
I had not looked forward to fending him off all the way to Munich.
Casually, I asked after him.

'Oh, I don't think Hermann wanted to lose sight of him,' said
Doctor Hanfstaengl with a grin. 'You know how they all spy on
one another. The Russian boy is a special friend of Röhm's. Hermann
hates Röhm.' I wondered if this Röhm, whom I understood to be
in command of the National Socialist *squadristi*, the *Sturmabteilung*,
was Seryozha's 'patron'. If so, I gathered he had his hands full. From
the radio I knew that a month earlier the whole of the Berlin SA,
the so-called 'Storm Troopers', had been in open revolt against Hitler.
They demonstrated none of our Italian discipline.

Unable easily to ask for more illumination, I decided to bide my
time and let Doctor Hanfstaengl talk. He was far less close-mouthed
than most of his compatriots and was genuinely funny in some of
his descriptions of the Nazi 'old fighters', as the core group called

itself. Doctor Hanfstaengl had been in, he said, since the beginning, almost as soon as he had returned from the US. He had been looking around for some cause to which he could nail his colours. Something worth sticking with. He had seen the terrible results of miscegenation all over the States. People still didn't seem to realise how important an issue it was. At least there were laws in place to stop it. In the US neither big business nor the federal government had any notion of popular feeling. I, of course, needed no convincing and agreed with him heartily. I told him of the poor degenerate whites and blacks I had encountered outside of Carthage, Mississippi. They were all but indistinguishable.

We had the same enthusiasm for films and passed much of the journey to Vienna talking about our favourites. Doctor Hanfstaengl loved Griffith as much as I did but thought the Jewish elements of De Mille's work let it down.

I invited him to join me in my compartment. We spent the rest of the long journey in happy conversation. I must admit, I was glad to be away from the world of politics and armaments for a while. Doctor Hanfstaengl was a welcome change. Everything interested him. He loved music and the arts and travelled widely. He had seen G. B. Shaw perform on the London stage. Shaw was not to be missed. Hanfstaengl was also a great fan of the British playwright Ben Traven and had enjoyed all the Whitechapel farces.

After one change we spent an uneventful and pleasant journey, arriving in Vienna at about lunchtime. Doctor Hanfstaengl asked if I knew the city. When I said I did not he eagerly elected to show me the sights. We had a couple of days here, he said. He must perform a few minor chores but was otherwise entirely at my disposal. What did I feel like doing? We had rooms already booked at the Ritz on Kärntnerstrasse. Not, he added, that it was the Ritz any more. He hoped he could remember the new name.

Once my rather large assortment of trunks had been loaded, Hanfstaengl got us a taxi and asked for the Ritz. The driver knew it well. 'It's called the Hotel Krantz now.' He drove with relaxed abandon. Happily, Viennese traffic did not move with the crazed disorder of Rome's. The journey from the station was reasonably sedate. The grand buildings of this old imperial capital had been allowed to mellow gracefully among a wealth of shrubs and flowering trees. The city had an air of dignified, slightly shabby tranquillity. We drove along wide boulevards dreaming in the sunshine of late spring. The cafés were already full, with tables so close together on the pavements it sometimes seemed people sat at one long trestle. Everything was in blossom. I was reminded of my own Kreschchatik in Kiev, when clouds of petals drifted against the pale summer sky. But Vienna's ambience was more like Odessa's. The Viennese possessed a casual, easy quality, which hardly seemed to go with their rather formal and old-fashioned clothes. Doctor Hanfstaengl pointed out various municipal sights, including the Hotel Sacher where I had once dreamed of dancing with Mrs Cornelius. That pleasure would have to be put off for a while. While imposing, the Hotel Krantz, with its red and white decor, was rather comfortable. Doctor Hanfastaengl was enthusiastically welcomed by the manager. We each had a quiet suite overlooking the garden, and if any particular service was required, we had only to ask.

Hanfstaengl apologised to me. He had some urgent business in the Praterstrasse and would be back as soon as he could. Meanwhile, why didn't I take a stroll and enjoy the city. 'She hasn't lost all her magic.'

After a piece of adequate veal and some strange-tasting coffee I bathed and changed into my new lavender suit. Perhaps a little modern for Vienna, it would give them a chance to see what the beau monde was wearing in Rome. I attracted a certain amount of admiring attention from ladies and jealous sneers from their escorts as I strolled along the Falfnerstrasse admiring window displays and marvelling at some of the confections on display. It felt wonderful to be alone for a while. For all the new Italy's vigours and virtues, I had known little time for contemplation or tranquillity there.

Vienna proved a perfect location for a leisurely and solitary promenade. I might almost have been in Paris. The city had a pre-war ambience so endearing it sometimes brought tears to my eyes as I remembered more innocent days.

I reached an intersection and was searching for a reference point to be sure that I could find my way home, when a tram came jangling around a corner and almost knocked me over. I jumped back and suddenly, standing beside me, was Fiorello da Bazzanno in a wide-brimmed hat and a raincoat with an upturned collar. The worst of his bruising had gone, but he still looked as if he had suffered a serious accident. His pain did not stop his amusement at my surprise. He put his hand out. 'It's safe enough to shake it here, Max.'

I had no wish to snub the man, who had been a good friend in the past, so I suggested we sit down at a nearby café. I ordered some elaborate concoction, half-coffee, half-confectionery, for us both and told him I had believed him to be in Switzerland by now.

He smiled a little unhappily. 'They turned me back at the border,' he said. 'I think they were told to. I'm only here on sufferance. If I can't get into Switzerland then Laura will have to meet me somewhere else. Maybe Prague. My German friend Strasser lives there now. He's Gregor's brother, a real socialist. And then, I suppose, Argentina. Where all exiled Italians go. Or America. Though with my political record, I have a feeling they won't be pleased to see me.'

Wasn't it extraordinary, I said, how rapidly things changed! When he met me I was all but penniless. Now the boot was on the other foot. My resentment of him melted. I took some large-denomination notes from my wallet and inconspicuously folded the money into his hand. It was the least I could do for the man who had been instrumental in my new elevation.

'It's a turning world, Max.' He thanked me for the money. 'And I'm not sure I deserve anything less than this. It's all very well to talk about the poetry of violence. It's another thing to experience it. I still believe in Il Duce's ideals, but not many of his people do any more. He's out of touch with us. He's become too involved in power for its own sake.'

I repeated Major Nye's perception that all power corrupts. 'Yet I cannot believe Il Duce himself is corruptible.'

'Not in any ordinary sense, maybe.' Fiorello sipped his coffee. His lips were almost down to their normal size. He still looked like a horse who had escaped a serious encounter with a slaughterhouse. 'But this wasn't done by Reds, Max, whatever you think. Fascists did it. Remember my mentioning Matteotti? A piece of accidental butchery. But now we are dealing with systematic terror. They've been doing a lot of it lately. They've crossed a line. I now believe every word Laura said. I just couldn't lose my faith in Mussolini. He united the country. He has done so much for us. The Blackshirts were the inheritors of Garibaldi's Redshirts – men and women of simple nobility who wanted only to see justice done. We called on that spirit, and the people responded. Today the industrialists are still in place, and the people are worse off. It will be the same with the Brownshirts. Money talks in the end. And there's plenty of it about

211

to defend capitalist interests by any ruthless means. The March on Rome was for common justice. Do we have it? Do we, Max?' In Austria, he had clearly reverted to his old anti-capitalist illusions.

He was close to weeping when I left him outside the café and returned to my hotel. In spite of the great sympathy I felt for him, he had to be suffering from serious paranoia, doubtless brought on by his ordeal. Only many years later would I see that there had been an element of truth in his madness.

Doctor Hanfstaengl himself was in a rather grimmer mood. He had run up against some unexpected difficulties. It would all be sorted out soon. We would have to take the early train to Munich in the morning. He hoped I would not mind cutting the trip short. Things were changing all the time in Germany. The party needed him back. My purpose in leaving Rome was to visit Germany, I said. The sooner we arrived there the happier I would be. Unless you have an excessive liking for waltzes, cream cakes and cater-wauling modern music, Vienna has little to offer the discerning traveller.

Unfortunately I did not have time to visit the famous blue Danube. I saw only the brown one.

I am not a natural early riser, so Putzi Hanfstaengl had to wake me up and virtually put me in the shower before I was able to dress myself and make sure all my bags were taken down. I had hoped to spend some time with Mrs Cornelius, but Hugenberg was not part of the Nazi movement. He had no need to cut his visit short. Through misty streets Hanfstaengl and I took a cab to the station and arrived just in time to gain our compartment before the train left. This time there was another passenger, a rather sallow cleric who did not like our looks and aimed his pointed nose into his little devotional even as we entered. We were to have breakfast on the train, but I excused myself and went to the toilet to take a soupçon of the excellent 'snow' Seryozha had given me. He seemed to possess the stuff in unlimited quantities. At one point I suspected he had smuggled in at least a kilogram. He was always secretive about his suppliers.

Putzi had made himself comfortable when I got back. He knew the priest resented our presence and cheerfully ignored him.

I flung myself into the luxury of the seats, stretched and yawned. We used English, which further irritated our fellow passenger.

Putzi and I were discussing the merits of French and Austrian operettas when I heard a woman exclaim from the corridor. I looked up. She was already passing but I noted something familiar about her broad, tall figure in its conservative black silk costume. She turned, as if to confirm something, and I recognised her at once. My old mistress, Baroness Leda von Ruckstühl, with whom I had escaped from Odessa. I had left her in Constantinople. I must admit, I had hoped never to see her again!

She came back, of course. She was smiling with a kind of bewildered malice. She drew open the door in a single powerful movement, standing over me like some avenging Valkyrie, an armoury of layered cosmetics and floral oils. I took control of myself. With puzzlement in my eyes, I rose. 'Madame?' Happily I still wore my imperial. I was experiencing one of those moments I have described before, when all elements of past, present and future seem to rush together.

'I thought you were dead, Prince Pyatnitski,' she said. 'In America, I heard, after the Paris scandal.'

I felt physically sick but somehow I retained my self-possession. 'Forgive me,' I bowed, 'but I do not believe I have had the pleasure . . .'

'You are Prince Maxim Arturovitch Pyatnitski,' she said in Russian. 'The father of my son.'

'My dear lady,' I replied in English, 'I am unfortunately a mere commoner, a humble American actor, no less. While I am flattered by this elevation, I fear you have me confused for another.'

She frowned. I could see I had not convinced her. It would be extremely embarrassing for me if she revealed our past. She knew far more about me than I liked and evidently still resented me. She was not above making the most fantastic claims. Her interest in me had been more intense than I supposed. She had gone to the trouble of tracking down misleading stories about me in the French press. She probably had a dossier as thorough as Brodmann's!

I had no other choice. I had to continue with my bluff. Putzi Hanfstaengl was amused by the scene. He had not taken very much of it in. He could tell the lady was angry and that I was embarrassed.

She did not move.

'You have mistaken me for some other gentleman,' I said again. I made to open the door for her, but she pushed past me and went up the corridor without a further word.

'Phew!' said Putzi with something which passed for a leer, 'a mighty angry doll, what? You're a bit of a devil on the quiet, eh? What did she call you?'

'Well,' I said, 'it's an odd thing. I played the part of a Russian nobleman more than once. I believe you mentioned enjoying *Red Queen, White Queen.* She seems to think that I am one of my screen characters. Poor creature. It's a familiar delusion. As a public figure one becomes used to such encounters. I must have had a dozen in the past year alone.'

Putzi nodded. 'Something very similar happens to Hitler. Women wet their knickers for him and have the most incredible daydreams about him. Some of them even think the dreams are real. And the ideas they get! It makes you shudder what some of those women want to have done to them! Do you get letters also?'

'They are no longer forwarded to me,' I said. 'At my request.'

Hanfstaengl winked again. It was a grotesque twisting of the face which made him look for a moment as if he were suffering a difficult bowel movement. 'They say Il Duce answers all *his* letters personally.'

I smiled at this but would neither confirm nor deny the story. It suited Mussolini, I know, to have his masculinity vaunted in this way. Not a red-blooded Italian man or woman failed to wish him well in the fulfilment of his healthy animal appetites. Few leading National Socialists possessed this natural virility, one of many fundamental differences between the Italian *fascisti* and their imitators.

Putzi Hanfstaengl said no more about the Baroness. She did not bother me again. I saw her only once more during a minor delay on the line a mile or so from the border. The train stopped. We were told we could disembark and walk about, if we wished. I decided to smoke a cigarette in the open air. As I paced the narrow area of grass between track and fence I saw a stunning young woman look up from picking yellow daisies. She had that rich, pale hair, almost transparent skin and luscious blushing red lips of the typical South Russian beauty. Her slender figure might have belonged to a leading mannequin. Hatless, she wore a dress of grey linen with a matching jacket. Her only jewellery was a string of pearls. Her hair was waved in the latest fashion. From her clothes she was clearly a Berliner. Convinced we had met before, I approached her. Then she looked back at a woman who called to her as she descended from the train – the Baroness von Ruckstühl. I remembered then who the girl must be. She was Kitty, the child I had originally courted when seeking the attentions of her mother. She had grown even more beautiful. I stepped into the train's shadow.

One experiences a particular frisson on seeing a woman one knew as a child, especially if she is as striking as Kitty von Ruckstühl. Running towards her was a dark little boy, perhaps the result of his mother's union with a Turk. After I had gone the Baroness had obviously discovered another protector. A powerful Constantinople businessman no doubt found her title useful. The connection between Germany and Turkey was always strong. How had she turned up on the Munich train? I hoped she was making connections to some other city and that I was seeing the last of her. I was sorry we had parted on less than perfect terms. I would have appreciated an introduction to Kitty again.

We arrived in Munich on the following Friday. I found myself admiring the wonderful architecture with its variety of Baroque flourishes. I had never before experienced such peculiar charm in a city. Munich was all pink and gold. She reminded me not of my real childhood, but of my childhood storybooks, my happiest dreams. Even when there was a delay while they searched for my trunks at the station, the city continued to delight me. Some of my luggage had been sent on but other pieces were not with the train. I was only mildly put out. I had not expected to be so entranced by Munich's ambience. In spite of all I had heard of political instability, near-civil war, military putsches and Bolshevik takeovers, in spite of its reputation as the heart-city of revolution, Munich possessed a wonderful air of unchanging security. The luggage remained absent. The fawning stationmaster was called and duly apologised. He would take my address and have my trunks delivered by the following morning. Could the trunks have been held up at customs, perhaps? The border people were so difficult these days. It was unlikely, I said. Although I feigned impatience, I was not particularly upset. The city was absorbing me already. Some cities feel immediately familiar. I told the stationmaster I would be obliged to him for any assistance he could give. Most of what I needed was in the luggage which accompanied me.

Doctor Hanfstaengl linked his huge arm in mine. He was pleased to have a new American friend. A German would have made a mighty and completely useless fuss about the matter. Americans took so much in their stride. He wished Germans were more like

215

Americans and Americans a little less like Germans. He laughed heartily at this cryptic sally. I did my best to join in. While I liked the man enormously, half of what he said made no sense at all!

We had become so thoroughly involved with the lost luggage that I did not have to time to see if the Baroness and her party had left the station. They were probably getting the Berlin train. I was relieved. I would soon be back in Italy, and the woman would no longer be a danger to me. What a shame, I thought, that she should live while my poor Esmé was no doubt dead on some *shtetl's* dungheap. But I had learned long since that life was neither fair nor very controllable and as often as not the good died in agony while the bad flourished in the lap of luxury. Increasingly, we were seeing the rule of the strong over the weak, the exploitation of the state's liberal laws by a few rich and powerful businessmen with international links. It was no secret with what inefficiency Berlin's federal government dealt with local issues.

No wonder the National Socialists were gathering strength. Anyone with a sense of common justice resented such social and economic inequalities and wished to see them overturned. But some of us knew the Bolshevik alternative was even worse. And that was why I have always believed that it was an act of treachery to our shared ideals and culture, our religion and our traditions, to vote for the Reds.

These children who accuse me of condoning every evil have no idea what they mean. A Red Germany would have meant a Red Europe, and a Red Europe would ultimately have engulfed us in the most appalling world war of all time. The Second World War would have seemed as nothing to that war. Armed men were divided between extremes of left and right, recklessly prepared to risk civil conflict. Parties like the National Socialists sought to find a middle ground between the two. The few rough elements who attached themselves to Hitler were no more typical of the average 'Nazi' than the brutes who pillaged Belgium in the name of the Kaiser.

Our cab soon swung away from a quaint tangle of medieval streets into the great tree-lined prospects of the outer city, where huge private villas and municipal offices sat back among well-kept lawns and trees. I do not think I had ever seen such a pleasantly ordered conurbation, with parks and squares and pleasure gardens all adding to its air of cultivated tranquillity. It had rightly been called 'the most civilised city in Europe'. Only then, I think, did I truly realise I was in Germany. Munich, they said, was the heart of Germany just as Berlin was her brain. And what an unexpectedly beautiful heart it was!

At last the cab pulled up outside an imposing four-storeyed house built on classic eighteenth-century lines which would not have been out of place in Washington, save for its colour. It had been erected in a rich, buttery-brown local stone and the woodwork painted in cream with a chocolate trim. Over the huge ground-floor windows and wide mahogany doors the balcony of the floor above formed a kind of porch, set off with elegant wrought iron. On the roof of the building flew a huge 'Hakenkreuz' flag in the old imperial colours of red, white and black.

Our cab had trouble pulling in. Cars were coming and going from this building all the time. The glittering white steps vibrated to the polished boots of brown-shirted NSDAP members who possessed a slightly rougher, wilder look than the modern Italian *squadristi*. They resembled some of the earlier pictures of the *fascisti* who planned the March on Rome. Clearly our audacious Italian revolutionaries were the model for these men. All wore the same swastika armbands. Many had obviously been sewn on by amateurs. Their kepis strongly resembled ski caps. The NSDAP was still a party of the masses, a huge popular expression of a people's deepest needs and dreams.

Putzi apologised for not inviting me in. He said he would be a few minutes. I watched him disappear through the door. The guards not only recognised him, they showed him considerable respect.

From the window of the cab I watched the Brownshirts busy as bees coming and going from their hive. They had expressions of grim optimism, and there was quick, energetic purpose in their step. I was privileged to witness a movement on the very brink of political success, when the theories and the rhetoric could become realities at last.

One unpleasant moment occurred, however, when a scowling SA armed with a club and a dog whip ordered the cab to move on. I made a gesture to show that I was waiting for someone inside. The SA man came towards me as if I had threatened him. I wound up and locked the window. He grabbed for the cabby who remonstrated with him trying to let him know we were waiting for Doctor Hanfstaengl. Eventually the driver had little choice but to obey. He was about to set his machine in motion when Putzi came bouncing back down the steps shouting at the trooper.

The Brownshirt slunk off grumbling, and Hanfstaengl opened the door. 'I'm going to be longer than I thought,' he told me. 'You'd better come inside. It's a nightmare at the moment.'

I took the catcalls of the Brownshirt lads in good part as I accompanied my new friend up the steps of party HQ. My ivory and lilac summer suit, my wide-brimmed panama and my malacca cane seemed unexceptional in the Roman sunshine but were great entertainment for those simple working-class boys. As fervent a revolutionary as themselves, I was seen by them as a dilettante. They could not quite understand what I had to do with the triumph of the masses.

A couple of cool words from Putzi Hanfstaengl, however, and they turned their grinning attention back to their work. Saluting 'Storm Troopers' sprang to open the massive bronze doors. He showed them his party book, but they knew him, treating him with the utmost respect, lifting their arms in the Mussolini salute, clicking their heels and shouting 'Heil Hitler!' It was quietly obvious that Doctor Hanfstaengl was more than a minor member of the new Nazi hierarchy. I was reminded of a scene in *Ben-Hur* when the great Roman general mounts the steps of the senate, saluted by his adoring men.

Thus, with only restrained ceremony, we entered the nerve centre of the movement, not the few shabby rooms of a revolutionary rabble, but the modern appointments of a party ready for the responsibility of government. Decorated in the very latest fashion, they were the epitome of solid, clean, no-nonsense modernity. The finest materials had been used. With over a hundred party members now in parliament, every Nazi knew he was on the brink of destiny. If high morale and boundless optimism could give the Nazis the majority they needed, they already had it with some to spare.

I had not expected anything so impressive. The teak panelling below and the cream walls gave an impression of old-fashioned solidity and of modern airy space. In years to come this style would be copied all over Europe and America.

'Well,' said Putzi cheerfully, 'it certainly beats Corneliusstrasse.' I gathered he referred to their earlier offices. I was delighted by the coincidence.

At all points the guards recognised Putzi, and and most offered him the formal salute. My civilian clothes drew some disapproving looks and murmurs from the more conservative officers, but as Putzi's guest I was secure. He introduced me as one of Mussolini's men. This brought an apology from a staff member. They had not realised I was Italian. Putzi was in a hurry, so there was little time to study the appointments, though I was able to use the WC. I did pause to admire the vast entrance lobby, festooned with swastika flags on walls and ceiling, a symphony in red, black and white. Although I was struck by the similarities of style, I was polite enough not to make comparisons with the Palazzo Venezia. Clearly Hitler and Strasser, the movement's two main political leaders, aspired to Mussolini's position, but the Brown House could not match the grandeur of Il Duce's surroundings.

In one respect there was a marked difference. Compared to the almost churchlike calm of the Palazzo Venezia, this place was cacophony. The halls and stairs were busy with stamping feet and curt exchanges. Telephones rang perpetually. Mechanical noises shrilled or muttered from mysterious sources. With shouts, curses, and a rather copious use of strong language, the energetic young Brownshirts were everywhere. The place stank of their sweat, their masculinity. I could see how, as a party of youth and vigour, untouched by the corruptions of modern politics, the Nazis were gaining so many votes.

As well as the not unattractive odours of busy people, I deter-mined other, less acceptable scents, of human urine and excrement. I remarked on this in surprise. Putzi apologised. 'Rather too much attention to making an impression and not quite enough to plumbing. An old Austrian failing. But that's the Chief.' I was to hear this affectionate phrase many times from Hitler's closest asso-ciates, who never called him 'Führer' among themselves. The best Nazis never demanded perfection in human beings and were always tolerant of a friend's failings. An efficient organiser of others, Hitler paid little attention to detail. His occasional sloppiness of dress and intellect were put down by the Germans as signs of a typical lazy Viennese style.

Quickened by these fresh sensations, my blood leapt in my veins.

I absorbed the electric atmosphere, the bustle, the sense of purpose. Only in Italy had I experienced such a distinctive frisson. Even there, because Mussolini had long since brought a new order to civic life and restored the rule of law, you did not experience this immediacy of purpose and expectation. While having reservations about their discipline, I could not help feel comradeship with these men. Years of poverty, of imprisonment, of suffering the insults and blows of Jews and communists, of living as social outcasts, of being branded as brutes and slandered in the most aggressive terms, were about to be redeemed. A little more effort and faith – and they would have their hour!

Putzi led me up the wide ceremonial staircase to the second floor. Black, white and dark red were the predominant colours against the lustre of the wood and cream paint. The furnishings were simple, rich and heavy. Everything was designed in that folkish contemporary style which looks to the simplicity of the Middle Ages for its inspiration, adding to an impression of strength, power and clean, healthy modernity. Hitler and most of the top people were nowadays chiefly in Berlin engaged with politics, so in spite of his haste Hanfstaengl was able to slip into the *Senatorensaal*, the senate chamber, almost as if to show off his own house. Some fifty huge chairs in dark red leather and massive brass-bound oak were grouped in a horseshoe to face the raised dais with the leader's own seat. Here the party leaders met for their most important conferences. Modelled on the Fascist Grand Council Hall, it had enough places for the entire NSDAP elite. Outside Doctor Hanfstaengl pointed to a plaque honouring their dead. 'And people say we're hard on the Sozis!' He greeted a couple of young lady secretaries. They responded with a sort of shy leer as if they had not yet quite learned tough modern ways.

'Hitler insisted on only the finest materials. They say he got the idea from a film. It cost Thyssen a fortune.' He spoke of the well-known industrialist who had publicly joined the party a couple of years earlier. 'Though the party membership chipped in about three-quarters of a million.' The opulence seemed a little at odds with the populist rhetoric of the Nazis, but I admired the solidity of the setting. Dramatic scenery against which even more dramatic affairs would soon be played! Putzi could not let me into Hitler's own corner office, of course, but he said it was very impressive with a wonderful view, a life-size portrait of Frederick the Great and a magnificent bronze bust of Benito Mussolini.

'I don't know where we're going to get the money for all this,' he added, almost to himself. 'We're up to our necks in debt!' He pointed through the windows to show me construction work still taking place at the back. The party had been so successful in the last elections that they were already having to build extensions. 'But if we don't consolidate soon we'll be bankrupt.'

I saw offices everywhere. Some of them were occupied by smart SS men, whose black and silver uniforms and death's-head badges were closely modelled on those of Mussolini's Special Guard. And like Mussolini's guard, Putzi told me, they were drawn from their nation's finest families, as were all the girls who worked here. 'It's been a while since we were barred from every respectable *Bierkeller* in Munich!' He let out a sudden, braying laugh. 'Even my mother in America has come round.' He saluted acquaintances as they went by and finally stopped outside one of the office doors. 'Here we are.' He let me in ahead of him.

The place was furnished in the same style as the rest of the Brown House, with heavy maroon leather upholstery, cream ceilings and dark, polished wood. The lamps were in the 'folkic' style popularised in America by Stickley. All brass and copper. On the wall was a picture of Hindenburg, then President of Germany, surrounded by other, more intimate pictures of Doctor Hanfstaengl and various party friends in the Tyrol. They all wore lederhosen. I recognised Hitler from his 'Menjou' moustache and untidy hair. Göring was the only other familiar face. With more important things on my mind, I had not paid as much attention to the German newspapers as I should have done. Putzi Hanfstaengl had obviously been on close personal terms with the Nazi hierarchy for years.

In contrast to the sense of order everywhere in the building, Putzi's office was awash with papers and opened books, files scattered, telephones buried. He was apologetic. 'I won't let anyone come in here to tidy up. It's my own fault. And I'm so horribly disorganised. Almost as bad as Hitler. But I don't have a dozen girls running behind me with dustpans . . .'

At the sound of his voice a door opened and in came a pale, thin young woman with an iron bun and a Nazi armband on her grey cardigan. She spoke in that tight, accusing tone only secretaries can affect. Putzi began to apologise to her, his arms waving wildly, his huge hands running through his untidy hair, his strange features twisting in an agony of remorse to the point where both she and I began to smile.

He subsided and asked me to sit down. If I was hungry I could visit a restaurant in the basement, though they were a bit busy at the moment. The food was good, plain South German food, but excellent. The cook was a man named Kannenberg, Hitler's personal chef. Was I a vegetarian? Did I like sausages? They had several regional varieties. Of course, these days Hitler was a vegan.

His secretary assured him that I would be properly looked after. But it was really very urgent that he see Chief of Staff Röhm, who required a simple answer to his questions but was growing very impatient for it.

'Very impatient indeed . . .' The accent was cultured Bavarian with that slightly brutal intonation many these days affected. The voice was quiet, pleasant, a little sardonic. In the frame of the connecting door, his military cap pushed back on a massive, close-shaven head so scarred and patched that every battle of the twentieth century might have been fought across it, his unbuttoned jacket casually revealing an Iron Cross ribbon, stood a high-ranking officer. He had a powerful presence, though he was by no means handsome. A bullet had taken away part of his nose, shrapnel had scarred his face, yet I detected something indefinably noble in the man. He reminded me of a character I had myself played in *The Prisoner of Zenda*, the devil-may-care Fritz von Talenheim, a soldier who dedicated life, soul and honour to his nation's well-being. In his beautifully cut *Sturmabteilung* uniform, this officer had some of the same quality I had observed among even the most brutal Cossacks – the instinctive grace of a man of action. A true contemporary *condottiere*!

He did not salute but put his hand towards me in an almost balletic gesture, meeting my steady gaze with his own. I wished him *Guten Tag*. In his typical Bavarian style, he answered, '*Grüss Gott*.' A sardonic twist to his smile was belied by the warmth of his eyes. I sensed the coiled, casually checked energy of a man used to taking decisive action, a natural commander. While some of his colleagues might need confirmation of their power and surround themselves with the symbols of their authority, this man was absolutely self-assured, without artifice of any kind, save his good manners. Bringing his heels together with a click, he took my hand, almost as if to kiss it, then shook it firmly. 'Röhm,' he said. His fingers were strong but felt like satin. A spark of pure electricity passed between us. Mutual respect. Doctor Hanfstaengl made some unheard introduction explaining I was in Il Duce's confidence.

Used as I was to the company of great leaders, I was utterly over-awed by this man. His photographs did not do him credit. I knew little of German politics, but even in Italian circles Röhm was discussed. He was the army captain who put down the communist uprisings in Munich. With his *Freikorps* he resisted the Red Flood, stockpiling huge amounts of arms and military equipment all over southern Germany. A close friend of Hitler since those days, he was the only man the Führer still called '*du*' and he responded in kind. A deep, old bond of blood existed between the two men. Röhm had created the SA to defend Hitler against physical threat from his political enemies. Driven from the country after the failure of the Beer Hall Putsch, he sought asylum in the Bolivian Army. Then, with the SA in open revolt, he had been recalled by Hitler. Within months Röhm had turned the SA into a disciplined Spartan army of five hundred thousand men. It would soon become almost five million. They said that Röhm, who still insisted on keeping his old army rank of Captain, held the key to Germany's fate. If he desired civil war, he would have it. And if there was civil war, Röhm would emerge as the victor. They called him 'the kingmaker' – the modern Simon de Montfort. It was lucky for Hitler that Röhm was a loyal friend, content to be his first General, his Stabschef, rather than Chancellor.

I already knew of Röhm as a dedicated visionary. He foresaw a well-ordered state run on army principles and with army discipline, slave neither to labour nor capital. This vision made him join Hitler to found the National Socialist movement. He loved politics. But he loved justice more. He loved justice the way another man loves drink. He was prepared to make any sacrifice and take any action to achieve it.

With the unforced charm of the true German professional soldier, this legendary '*alte Kämpfer*', this 'old fighter', bowed and clicked his heels. He spoke softly, almost shyly, with great charm and courtesy. I was reminded of Erich von Stroheim in his more avuncular moments. He would be delighted, he said, to get together, perhaps some evening? He was a great admirer of Mussolini and a student of Italian history. He felt it a privilege to meet one so close to Il Duce. His searching eyes continued to meet mine. I said that I would be honoured. His fame had reached Rome.

'Oh, dear,' he said, turning away, 'I hope I'll have at least a little mystery left for you! *Grüss Gott*, Mr Peters. I will keep an eye out for one of your films! I am something of a cinema connoisseur.'

Putzi snorted quite suddenly and told Röhm to 'stop that at once!' Chuckling he walked with him back to his office to deal with whatever problem had arisen. Again it was obvious that Hanfstaengl was something more than an occasional journalist of wealthy background. There could be few men who were able to joke on an equal footing with the great Ernst Röhm!

I had been highly impressed by the 'Father of the Storm Troopers'. In Italy they believed he must be a brute. His pictures suggested it. But now that I had met him it was very easy to see how he was able to keep control of such a vast militia and why every single one of his men would have died for him as, I suspect, they would never have died for Hitler.

When Hanfstaengl came back he was smiling. 'You made an enormous impression on our dashing "people's soldier". He wanted to hear all about you.'

'Men of action have a certain affinity,' I said, 'which transcends national boundaries. I had exactly the same experience with Mussolini. I, too, was also favourably impressed.'

'I'll let him know,' said Putzi.

Even then I already had a sense of the historic significance of that brief meeting. At the time I was simply elated to have met another equal. How rare it is to find a peer to whom one has to explain nothing. Our meeting was destined.

And yet, for all my intimations, I could not have imagined the fantastic consequences that would result from my bumping into Röhm at the Brown House on that early-June afternoon. They were consequences whose resolution would do nothing less than decide the future of Germany, change the course of history, determine the nature of the century, and perhaps give us a fresh perspective on the complex nature of Man.

Ernst Röhm was not the only famous personality I met in that first week. A constant coming and going of party people went on, chiefly between Munich and Berlin. Most were too busy to play host to a visitor like myself. I did not blame them. I decided to seek out some female entertainment, a girl who could also show me the city. I was not, however, immediately lucky. I had failed to reckon with the conservative Bavarian's disapproval of my summer suits! Some of the Nazis I met were downright rude. It became impossible to introduce oneself to girls of the better type. But I persevered.

Putzi remained only long enough to take me to his opulent house and introduce me to his slender, pale gold wife. He was engaged on some business with various American and English newspapers wanting interviews in Berlin with the Führer. Frau Hanfstaengl, although very welcoming, was rarely at home but made charity visits, chiefly to wounded SA veterans. I heard that Seryozha ('Captain Hoch') was on 'permanent alert' along with many other SA officers. I was reassured that I would not bump into him unexpectedly. I now realised I had been unduly alarmed about meeting the Baroness. She would not know my new name or where I was staying. She had enough malice in her to scheme my downfall, but I would be back in Italy before she had the slightest chance of tracking me down.

I had hoped to see more of Captain Göring. I now learned he scarcely ever took his place in the Reichstag. He was being required more and more to choose between his Führer and his sick wife. The other Nazi deputies were equally wrapped up in the dynamic concerns of the day. I never met Goebbels, who rarely left Berlin. The 'Dwarf with a Devil's Brain', as his enemies called him, was thoroughly absorbed in the complex strategy of national politics.

While I visited Munich's many fine galleries and churches, such things cannot hold a restless mind like mine for long. The up-to-date kinema houses allowed me to see what the German movie world was doing. The films were mostly affairs of sickening violence or cloying comedy.

Surprisingly, I had not yet heard from Mussolini or any representative of his. The Italian secret service seemed unduly cautious. Was I wasting my time? I am the kind of man who feels uneasy if not tackling some important problem. I would have liked to speak to some of the other Nazi leaders. They were never available. The Italians had made a mistake to send me to Munich first. It was a 'heart' town of the Nazi Party, where much of their history had taken place, but political business was still done in Berlin.

Whenever Hitler or Strasser were in town they were always closeted with their closest colleagues. They had no time for a stranger, albeit a sympathetic one. At first there had been some talk of my being Jewish, although mostly in fun, and I had been very quick to correct that error! Soon everyone took me for Italian. In these days the public was first becoming truly aware of the depths of the 'supranational' conspiracy and were understandably angry with the Jews.

Everyone now knew me as Max Peters, even if the *Völkischer Beobachter* described me as 'Hollywood's new Latin American adventure star' and seemed to think I was from the Argentine. I was, they said, of Spanish, Italian and German origin. An Aryan through and through. A strange thing for a pure-blooded Slav to be living such a lie!

Because of some modish jazz dance, South America was all the rage in films that year. Even as I wrote my first reports back to my Duce, I enjoyed a small renaissance. I became a popular figure locally. I made no secret that I was a keen supporter of Mussolini and a friend of Young Germany. I spoke of a common European destiny, of a Union of States which would one day be as great as the USA. I gave a number of interviews in the press, warning of the perils facing modern society. My films began to be shown again, chiefly in the cinemas not wholly given over to sound, and even the Brownshirts treated me with cheerful familiarity now they recognised me. Of course there continued to be incidents. Clashes between Reds and Browns were fairly common. It was wise to avoid the backstreets.

After a month or so I began to feel like an old Municher and was soon able to talk expertly and heatedly on matters of sausages and beer! I did not follow the extraordinary ups and downs of the Reichstag as reported in the German press but instead heard the opinions of Putzi and his circle. Everyone was extremely excited. Their mood infected me. I began to take an interest in some of the personalities. I was surprised that so much healthy controversy existed between party members. This could only be to the good. Hitler's mistake was to favour only one aspect of National Socialism over so many others. Variety, as Mrs Cornelius insists, is the spice of life.

The party was divided into two basic wings: the left, which still clung to its anti-capitalist socialist programmes, and the right, which favoured a system similar to the corporate state founded by Mussolini where private capital continued to flourish but under the firm control of government. Because of its sudden need for election money, the party had been forced to negotiate with powerful interests. The Army, the Church and Big Business were given certain reassurances. Since the onset of the Great Slump, which they blamed on America, the firm of I. G. Farben had been funding Röhm and Strasser, while Thyssen was openly backing Hitler and Göring. Others in the movement refused to take 'capitalist gold'. They clamoured for an immediate uprising against the bosses and moribund social institutions. Hitler had already split with Gregor Strasser's brother, Otto, over questions of race and aesthetics. Fiorello's friend, Otto had left to form the so-called 'Black Front' and was now in Austria. Yet the party was growing. It had now almost a million members with thousands more 'fellow-travellers'. The economic disasters which the masses and the middle classes had suffered had radicalised many Germans. They were considering voting for the Nazis, but barriers of class and tradition remained. Professional politicians looked down on the rowdy National Socialists as anarchist street fighters and little else. Hindenburg loathed the notion of a civilian commoner taking over his office. With a great deal of work to do and much at stake, most of the Nazis were agreed that everything hinged on the powers of Adolf Hitler to convince Hindenburg.

'The trouble is,' said Ernst Röhm one day at a lunch Putzi had been unable to attend, 'Alf's so fucking unreliable. You never know from one day to the next how he'll go. Sometimes he can hold the whole of Germany in his palm; sometimes he's too nervous to ask a waiter for a glass of milk. That slut has turned his bowels to water. He's too involved with her.' Röhm was one of the few people I had ever heard call the Führer by his family nickname. He had come into the beer cellar looking for one of his 'boys', as he called his adjutants, and seeing me, decided he had time for a cup of coffee. I was sitting with the Sternholders, a pleasant couple of Hitler sympathisers I had met at Putzi's a few days before. They lived not far from the Brown House in the same exclusive district and were a little overwhelmed by the presence of the Stabschef.

Röhm put his hand on my shoulder, fixing me again with that honest, direct stare. 'Why haven't we seen you at Röhmannsvilla?' The Sternholders were embarrassed to hear such direct talk. Röhm, who lived his entire life in rough male company, occasionally forgot himself. He apologised. 'I'm a wicked, uncouth man, and sometimes I lose control of my nature. Forgive me.' Bowing, he made his farewells. I promised to visit him at his new villa in what he called 'the Bavarian heartland'. I could see how he had gained his reputation for brusqueness. He had no time for play-acting, he said, but he still valued good manners. The Sternholders thought he was 'too proud for his own buttons' and found him coarse. They were unconvinced by my defence. The judgement of people like them would prove Röhm's undoing. By characterising him as a brute, something less than human, his enemies would later murder him with impunity and have the German people sigh with relief at their salvation. How many years will it take until they realise Röhm was the Caesar they deserved, not the Triumvirate they were finally awarded? And yet, of course, I must take some blame for it all. It is extraordinary how we all appear to have connived in our own destruction! And from the noblest of motives.

A minor drama was taking place concerning my baggage. Everything the young men had packed had turned up at my hotel, the Königshof, near the cathedral. The only thing missing was a case of spare drawings. These were not the duplicate plans and photographs I had put in the large envelope before I left Italy. They were some miscellaneous pieces I had had lying around. I could not remember the case being loaded on to the train. I was fairly certain it had been stolen or confiscated. Most of the work would be useless to a foreign power, but it was irritating to know that I was receiving unwanted attention. My personal sets of documents were thoroughly hidden in linings and spines. I continued to pursue the lost luggage, however, but with little success. The Germans were inclined to blame the Austrians. The Austrians blamed the Italians. And so on.

The world news was increasingly disturbing. Everyone became rapidly abstracted as the financial situation worsened, and Germany once again seemed about to slide into anarchy. For a few days the whole country was unnaturally still, waiting and listening, as a frightened animal waits and listens.

During those first Munich days, as I continued to explore the city, admiring her wonderfully Baroque architecture and nostalgic for more civilised times, I saw by coincidence quite a lot of Ernst Röhm. He recommended restaurants to me, as well as concerts and parks. I had fallen in with a group of young people, many of them members of the movement, whose idealism was as powerful as mine. Eager to hear my impressions of modern Italy, they had been proud to show me their city.

My new friends had many questions. How was financial stability maintained, for instance. I became a proselytiser for Il Duce. I contrasted the sense of well-being and optimism in my adopted country. At a period when even the United States was descending into communism, the Italian example was the only light burning in Europe. This, of course, inspired them. They knew they must one day come to power in a bloodless revolution as Mussolini had done.

229

The size and strength of the SA inspired other young hotheads, however, to speak of 'bloody revolution', of taking over the state by force: this was another subject of noisy debate between Nazis in those days. Today's youth sees only comic-strip images, stereotypes of swaggering SS officers and a demented Führer lusting to rule the world. They do not realise that most Nazis were people like themselves, just old enough to vote and anxious to throw out the old professional politicians who had led them into disaster through compromise and vacillation. They did not want war. Most of them were not even particularly anti-Jewish. They just wanted a change. They wanted something done. The Nazis promised to do something.

Millions voted for Hitler because he was the young head of a young party which disdained the old-fashioned *Junkers* style, which spoke and acted in modern terms. During elections cinema films of Hitler were made by Goebbels to show in every village and town in Germany. The Nazis used radio effectively for the first time, as well as the press. The politician who controlled the airwaves also ultimately controlled the masses. Other politicians wrote articles or addressed town hall meetings. Hitler flew in a modern aircraft to speak personally to all seventeen states of the federation. This, of course, took money, and it was the source of that money which gave certain Nazi idealists pause. In private they were assured that the industrialists would be used to bring themselves down. But in public Hitler, if not Strasser, reassured the traditional German powers of landed aristocracy, industry, Church and Army, that he worked only to ensure their endurance.

I heard Hitler speak for the first time over the radio in the Pohlnerkeller in Wilhelmstrasse. We were all gathered in silence, yet slowly, as the man spoke, his voice rising and falling, coaxing us to tears as well as to rage, a low roaring noise filled the cellar until, as the speech ended, every man and woman was on their feet, raising their arm in salute and shouting 'Heil Hitler!'

A moment that stirred my soul.

Then I realised fully the oratorical power of the 'German Mussolini' and understood why, with all their reservations, the Nazis had made him their spokesman and their leader.

Meanwhile, I still had met no OVRA officer. Had the German secret police recognised and arrested him? There still existed a strong antipathy to *fascisti* in old leftist Weimar circles. Naturally I could

230

not contact my Chief directly. I had been warned to do nothing that would connect me directly with my adopted nation.

Time dragged on. Every second week I picked up a registered envelope at the central post office. It contained only money, in new German notes. Because I was not 'earning my keep', I felt I was here under false pretences. So far no one, apart from Hanfstaengl and Röhm, had shown the slightest interest in me. Perhaps they knew I was a spy.

A couple of weeks after I arrived Göring sent me an apology via an intermediary. He still wanted to talk aircraft with me, he said, and hoped to see me soon. I had not understood that he wanted to talk about aircraft at all! He had until recently represented a Swedish aircraft company. I made allowances for him. Everyone said how the poor man was utterly distracted and had gone into retreat with his ailing wife, scarcely taking any interest in the outside world.

Aimlessly I wrote some further reports. I still had nowhere to send them. I could not risk telephoning. I decided that if I did not hear anything by the end of the month I would find an excuse for visiting either the Italian Consulate or the papal nuncio. I would leave my reports with them. And if they refused me, I would tear them up and return to Rome. I had the impression that the great machine of state had lost track of me! But I still had money and all other necessities of modern life, so I continued to behave as usual. I must admit I did not have an arduous time. I had become something of a minor celebrity in Munich. I occasionally ate at the Brown House, when Putzi or some other major official could sign me in, but it became increasingly crowded and the food got worse. Only party members were allowed entrance unaccompanied. And I grew tired of being addressed as 'Herr Signor'. So I found a pleasant restaurant in central Munich where I would take my lunch almost every day. It was called simply enough the Bratwurstglockl.

The place was frequented by higher ranking SA and SS officers. There I met several men who would become famous later, including Himmler, who seemed a colourless creature, and Christian Weber, a bluff, hearty fellow of the old school. Generally I found the SA fellows more agreeable. Almost all good-natured Bavarians, they were men with regular army experience. With an honest, down-to-earth quality, they would do anything for you.

I was constantly amused that these Nazis were forever assuring me that I did not look Jewish, that I was evidently Spanish. It could be so hard to identify some Americans as Jews or Aryans, because of our Indian blood. I think they associated my style of dress with Jewish vulgarity rather than Italian chic. I did not blame them. They were unsophisticated lads, forever apologising. Their famous unruliness was entirely to do with bad local leadership. Röhm would often say, 'There are no bad Brownshirts – just bad officers.' We were to discover that in 1933, when any scum jumped on the Nazi bandwagon.

I spent more and more time with Stabschef Ernst Röhm. He enjoyed speaking Spanish with me. He was at heart, he admitted, a monarchist, but he was also a realist. He had picked up many ideas about guerrilla warfare and revolutionary tactics in South America and was delighted to learn I had fought against the Bolsheviks in Russia.

'I envy you that,' he said. 'What wouldn't I give to have a crack at an entire division of the bastards.' He loved war as much as he loved life. He was a man of his time and yet oddly out of his time. A man of ruthless hardness, if necessary, but of extraordinary tenderness, too.

That tenderness of Röhm's is what you find in his writings, especially those scandalous letters which he wrote from Bolivia and whose publication was intended to destroy him. He made no secret that he was the author. Only Hitler, he said, insisted they were lies. 'All that hypocrisy will be swept away when we're in power,' said Röhm. 'We'll proclaim our sexual orientation the way the Greeks did – proudly and aggressively.' He believed in the old Platonic ideal. As far as he was concerned, women had only one function, which was to give birth to healthy soldiers. 'I don't believe in treating them badly. But it's as pointless to place a woman in a position of power as it is to put a soldier in the kitchen.' I did not hold his absolutist views, but my blood was stirred by his vision.

I think we were in the Bratwurstglockl, tucking in to sausages, vast Wiener schnitzels and spaghetti, when we first saw Hitler's mistress. I had heard only the vaguest of rumours about Miss Raubal and was a little embarrassed. I had no interest in the private lives of our great men. Their public world is all that should concern us. Lloyd George, sometimes called the English Mussolini, was a terrible womaniser, yet he brought his country into the twentieth century and prepared it for the twenty-first.

When Geli Raubal came into the restaurant, Röhm noticed her over my shoulder and pointed her out. She seemed a typical, silly Bavarian girl with a broad, pretty face and light brown hair. Surprisingly for the summer, she wore a blouse buttoned at the neck and wrists and carried a shawl. She was escorted by a young SS officer, a man so blond as to be, like my friend Kolya, almost an albino. I forget his name. She was very friendly with everyone, almost flirtatious, but there was a heated, unwholesome quality about her eyes I could not define, though I recognised it well enough. Suffice to say that Hitler was not the only man, or perhaps even woman, she would present with her favours.

Röhm confirmed my impression. 'She's a slut.' Röhm did not drop his voice. She knew him and was aware of his dislike. She pretended she had not seen us. 'She's going to get young Alf into trouble one day. And if you think *I'm* indiscreet – well, he beats everything. Did Hanfstaengl tell you about the sketches and the photos Schwartz had to fork out for? Or that damned letter? The stuff they found of mine and published was in comparison the work of a little old lady writing to the pastor. The drawings alone would have brought him down if anyone had seen them. That's what I mean about him. He needs someone to keep a hand on his tiller.'

Chuckling affectionately in that warm way of his, Röhm leaned back in his chair. 'You wouldn't think it, would you? He's always been the same. I rescued him from a Red firing squad, you know. Just after the War when I was still with the Reichswehr, before we got disbanded by those Berlin wankers.' All the time he spoke he was popping little white sausages into his mouth. 'He thought he was a goner, poor bugger. Scared silly. Literally wet his pants. Great courier during the War. Blind brave, we used to say. He'd go into this trance and trust to his luck. I've seen men do that. They become fearless. He knows what it is to be scared for your life – what you'll do to stay alive. People recognise that in him. They have experience in common. He knows their real grievances, how they think. He's a brave little bastard sometimes. Under orders, anyway. He was like my pet dog after I saved his life, and he started working for me. A great Number Two. Would follow any orders. Faithful as they come. He kept getting caught, too. The communists caught him. Then we caught him, thinking he was a commie. Almost shot him, too! He's always been a lucky bastard.'

I was rather astonished at Röhm's confidences, especially offered in his ordinary voice in a large restaurant, but he was not a close-mouthed man at the best of times. When he took some schnapps or 'coked' he was even less tactful. We had hit it off famously. When he was in Munich, he often sought me out. We had a rapport I had only known previously with my beloved Kolya, similar to that which still existed between myself and Mussolini.

In spite of Mrs Cornelius being my best friend, she has always called me 'a bloke's bloke', by which she means I have a certain affinity with other men of action and intellect. While I have enjoyed wonderful relations with women of all ages and classes, I will admit a particular understanding between manly equals translating to the most extraordinary levels of human feeling. Life is lived on the highest possible plane at an unprecedented level of intensity. Not understanding that herself, Mrs Cornelius is inclined to belittle it. She believes all our idealism, all our visionary yearnings, are to do with sex. She has been infected by one of the very people she claims to despise. I speak of that member of the Unholy Triumverate, the arch-Jew Freud, who set out to undermine the cornerstones of Christian idealism and very nearly succeeded. Yet let them make a few disparaging remarks about the Lutheran Church, and the Nazis are characterised as atheists and devil-worshippers! Most Nazis were in fundamental agreement with Martin Luther. Whatever their other failings, both knew the danger to society of the tribe which calls the world its nation.

Mrs Cornelius sighs for me. She says I was a fool not to marry.

A fool not to marry you again, I say.

The days in Munich dragged on. I became bored, anxious for some action. I considered telegraphing Mrs Cornelius at St Crim and risking a visit there. When my boredom grew uncomfortable, I decided to take myself up to Berlin, but then I received a tele-phone message from the Stabschef's adjutant, which was to alter everything I understood about myself and the world! Röhm would be in town late that afternoon and would be delighted if I would dine with him at the Bratwurstglockl. He named an hour. I said I would be there.

Although this was not the first time I had dined with the Stabschef, it was the first time he had made this kind of formal appointment. It gave me an extremely pleasant sense of anticipation. Evidently I was about to be accepted into the Nazi inner circle.

Believe me vain, but I am a firm believer in destiny. Some events are meant to take place, just as some people are meant to meet. Fate or coincidence does not bring us together, but a special kind of destiny. How often has the average person met someone famous and influential? Very rarely. Yet how often do influential people meet? All the time. One has only to pick up a political biography to understand this. In those dark days after the World War, with civil strife erupting on all sides, a few men had the vision, the character and the ruthless will to justice to take control of events. There exists an instant mutual recognition between great men and women. Röhm was one such man. I was another.

'It is as simple as that,' I tell Mrs Cornelius.

She shrugs. 'Brown shirts or brown 'atters – it all comes down to exercising Mister Willie,' she insists. 'Or rather 'im exercisin' *you*.' Sadly, she has seen too much of the coarser side of men. She was never greatly attracted to romance, only to power.

Röhm was already at the restaurant when I arrived. He was standing beside a table, his feet planted wide, his hands folded behind his back, enjoying a joke with his lieutenants. They sprawled in a comradely heap across the big padded benches and, though a little drunk, continued to treat him with respect. He was one of them and understood them. The essence of all the Nazi leadership's authority was based on protocols which were the antithesis of Bismarck's. These were men of the people. Men of action. Men of practical common sense. Men who looked after their own. Young men with blood in their veins. Men who had known all the terrors of war, who had been baptised in fire.

When Röhm saw me he grinned with pleasure. His men knew me by now. We were all regulars. Some whistled greetings. Some had friendly nicknames for me, which I took in good part. They called me 'the Spanish onion' or 'Cowboy Joe'. I waved and gave the Fascist salute. Röhm strode over to me and caught me by the arm, steering me towards his usual table, a dark, secluded archway set on the far side of the cellar and offering a view of its length.

I ordered us both large steins of the dark, rich bock beer he enjoyed here, and before we decided on our food he suggested that after we had dined we drive out to see his new house. I could stay overnight and be back in Munich by the next day. I might find it enjoyable. There were a few people he wanted me to meet.

I had earlier suspected that I was again being invited to join an inner circle. I had said little of my intimacy with Mussolini or some

235

of the other leaders of world affairs, but his instinct recognised me. Of course I accepted.

We ate a large and leisurely dinner. Then Röhm's handsome young chauffeur arrived to tell us our car was ready. The Stabschef was already a little tipsy. He sang some sentimental Spanish song he had learned in Bolivia. He opened his window so he could breathe in the rich, scented air of the Bavarian capital. 'Ah! One has to acknowledge the pleasures of peace. But they are only won through the hardships of war.'

We stopped at my hotel where I packed a small bag containing a change of clothes, a box of cocaine and some papers I preferred to keep with me. Then we were off, driving through the haze of twilight into what seemed to me at that moment an infinitely rosy future.

I was glad of the chance to see a little of the surrounding countryside. The neat, well-ordered Bavarian fields were a symbol of the best of Germany. The German's natural sense of harmony is only occasionally perverted by experiments in social democracy. It is expressed most finely in his music and his mathematics. They are masterly bookkeepers. They exemplify so many of our Christian virtues. They are the Yankees of Europe. Sometimes, of course, they can exercise those virtues a little too fully, as with their generosity towards the Turks.

Röhm, as usual, was stimulating company. He continued to drink a little more than he should, but the stress of his responsibilities was tremendous. The only expression of his insobriety was a somewhat looser and coarser tongue. He loved to relax in manly company, to forget for a few hours the 'Prussian manners' he was forced to cultivate as an officer, a member of the Reichstag and a senior senator in the Bavarian parliament. He spoke of his frustrations with the bloodless, feeble self-abusers he was forced to keep company with, of the protocol he had to observe so as not to let Hitler down. He would do nothing, he said, to damage Hitler's chances of becoming Chancellor.

Feeling a little abandoned by Il Duce and wondering about my future, I was quietly pleased to have Röhm's friendship. While never wielding power for himself, only for the common people for whom he held it in trust, he was the most powerful man in Germany. Without him, Hitler and Strasser could not move. Without his troops, Hindenburg and the old guard could outlast and, if necessary, outfight

Hitler. It crossed my mind more than once that I was becoming close friends with the future Duce of Germany, but at that time I had no intimation of Röhm's real secret.

I relaxed beside him in the staff car's huge back seat while he discussed the work of German painters he admired and asked if they had their American equivalents. I said that the 'folkish' movement had taken odd forms in America. The favoured art form these days was the cinema. Even great artists worked for Hollywood, designing sets and drawing storyboards. He had visited Los Angeles on his way back from Bolivia and had been impressed by the palm trees and the lovely houses. How surprising things were there! How German! With a touch of North Africa. A friend of his was over there. Did I know Ludecke? He was a good Nazi. I had to tell him that my own political links in America were with the Ku Klux Klan. Sadly, I added, the Klan had been taken over by opportunists, its original ideals forgotten.

Röhm was sympathetic. The National Socialist movement was threatened with the same kind of takeover. He was uneasy with this searching out of businessmen for bedfellows. If the party needed funds, Hitler should send a bunch of Hitler Youth boys out whoring. 'There must be plenty of takers for those beautiful, rounded little arses.' It would be a quicker, more honest and no doubt more lucrative way of raising the money they needed. 'But Hitler hardly cracked a smile at my suggestion. Alf's getting very serious these days. Very straight.'

The Stabschef had a hamper for the journey. As it grew dark and the car rushed on through quaint little villages and rolling fields, he took out a bottle of champagne and popped the cork. His strange, battered face had an almost melancholy quality to it, and I saw a hint of sadness in his eyes which he tried to disguise. I did not know what had happened to put him in this mood. He was doing his best to rid himself of it. I wanted to tell him he did not need to pretend anything, that he was with an equal, one who would respect all his secrets.

When he laid a large line of cocaine upon his beefy wrist and took it like snuff I knew for certain that I had found a kindred soul. I accepted his line, holding his wrist with my fingertips as I bent my nose to some of the purest South American snow I had enjoyed in years. In Bolivia the Stabschef had developed a refined taste.

At my prompting Röhm spoke of his youth, of his exile to Bolivia after the Munich putsch. He laughed. 'Before I arrived in Bolivia, buggery was unknown there!' He had met only one 'schitzy' to his taste, just towards the end of his stay. He had admired those 'dark-eyed Latin beauties' from afar, had groaned for them, far preferring them to blonds. Yet no one understood. He would rather have been in prison. He had exercised great discipline, he confessed. As a lieutenant colonel with considerable responsibilities, he could probably have ordered one of those luscious creatures into his bed. And now, he added almost under his breath, here he was, tête-à-tête with just such a beauty!

He was a little slurred in his speech. I was not entirely following his thickly accented Bavarian. He switched off the interior lamps. We travelled in complete darkness, with no light save the reflection of our own glaring headlamps. I, too, had known the pain of exile and the terrors of captivity. In sympathy I reached towards his arm.

A little to my surprise, he turned on the light to look at me briefly. His eyes filled with tears. I murmured a question. There came a pause, a silence as the car's great engine continued to pound and the wheels carried us deep into the German heartland. Then, suddenly, that noblest of all Nazis doused the light once more and seized my hand in his. His deep, thrilling whisper declared his most profound passion for me.

That love, he said, was the purest he had ever known. It was driving him mad.

TWENTY–FOUR

I take Mrs Cornelius to the canal. The council have now paved parts of the towpath, and it is a little easier to avoid the dog muck. Nothing wholesome grows in that sparse manure. They never clean it up. Once every six months some swarthy municipal playboy minces down and dabs a fastidious broom at the stuff. What a privilege to see you, I say. Sarcasm is wasted on him. He would probably understand Turkish if I was willing to compromise with him.

He whines that they are understaffed. Certainly you are, I sympathise. I often see you hiding in the cemetery pretending to work. Occasionally you lack a fourth for poker. But you carry on. You play with cards so faded and damp you depend on complicity and instinct to identify the suits. Sometimes I hear you disputing a flush.

The rain is a filthy drizzle. The grey grass exudes a kind of phlegm. The canal gives off vapours that hang like poisoned ectoplasm in endless valleys of vandalised warehouses. As the pedestrian underclass we have no alternative but to pass through these desolate canyons. The miasma is particularly bad under the bridges and is no good for my chest. Mrs Cornelius complains that it gets in her muscles and arteries 'like freezin' slush'. The troglodytes living in the nearby storm drains and sewers have painted warning challenges on the walls. I am reminded of Germany in the early thirties. Advertisements for concerts and lectures are sprayed with gibberish. Some letters have been misremembered or are upside down. Their only coherence is in what they symbolise. Which these days could be anything. William Blake, the famous British lunatic, is their most popular hero. Like all their predecessors they proclaim the triumph of blind faith over reason. The written word becomes a formal image and loses all meaning, no more than a growl or a reassuring croon, a badge. Nowadays more and more of these subterraneans write in Arabic or Persian. Carthage never sleeps.

'We witness the end of language,' I say. 'The destruction of memory. The death of culture. This is what your Harold Wilson has done for the country. So much for Labour's golden promises!'

'Nobody misses culture much, Ive, love.' Mrs Cornelius believes she comforts me. 'Or language.' With a slender scarlet nail she dabs delicately at the corner of her crimson mouth. 'Just the people 'oo've got time for it. Which isn't many. If the op'ra went tomorrer most people wouldn't notice. When was you last at Covent Garden anyway?'

'That's scarcely the point.' I am remembering those great pre-war performances. Those wonderful, gay Viennese.

Yesterday as we came out of the tunnel we found a dead dog lying on the towpath almost in the water, twisted so that its hindquarters were open revealing its genitals, a red erection. Its short black fur had dried into symmetrical muddy spikes. Its eyes and muzzle were half open, releasing the tongue. It stared over the canal with a resigned and melancholy grin.

'Someone's fallen out with the Mafia.'

I uttered my first thought. In my circumstances, I am reasonably nervous, never sure if that particular vendetta against me still continues.

She tells me I am loony. 'Barkin',' she says.

But I was once threatened in that way, I insist. In Rome. Nineteen thirty-two, I think. You were there when it happened to me. I told you about it on the train to Vienna.

I now know of course who was actually stalking me. She refuses to believe me. Some people live their whole lives in a permanent state of denial. Half of what I say she dismisses or derides, revealing an unconscious defence mechanism against unpalatable truth. I at least shall not be surprised when Brodmann walks through the door with a gun in one hand and a KGB badge in the other.

I have noticed how a threatened man or woman will unconsciously try to turn into the creature they most fear rather than be destroyed by it. We are so eager to conspire with our masters. We have few alternatives and almost no choices any longer. So it was in Dachau. I have been stripped of my rank, humiliated and abused. Never once have I complained.

Of course, in most circumstances complaint meant an immediate and painful death. Even when you have had the science of the method explained to you (in my case by Himmler and Schnauben

240

themselves) it does not make your response any more rational. You know that any escape plans you make are fantasies. Any hope you entertain is a nonsense. I learned that already in Egypt. Those of you who have never experienced this kind of fear have no business judging us. By denying your own vulnerability, you make yourself further vulnerable to whatever threatens you.

Mrs Cornelius says Brodmann would be eighty at least. She says I live too much in the past. And where else should I live? I ask. How good does the future look to you? And has the future provided you with experience? Why should the present suit you better than the past? Is there something wrong with the past? You can forget. You can. What you must lose is the memory of desire, the sensation of innocence, the inability to tolerate what is disgusting. All these will become virtues enabling you to forget desire, innocence, intolerance, love. You will forget and yet memory will persist as a cold sense of loss, a yearning for something better and sweeter which you have forbidden yourself. For with memory comes loss, with desire comes pain, with hope comes despair. Hell offers an absence of virtue. It offers an eternity when all you yearn for is time.

I am an old man. My only consolations are my memories. I cultivate my past like a favourite garden; I order it like a beloved library. I go back to the years of my youth and my power when my good looks were favourably compared to Rudolph Valentino's and Cesar Romero's and my future was golden. I was à la mode.

Until you think back you do not understand how much your physical appearance determined your destiny. I hardly realised at the time what I had in common with the early Nazis. More than any other people, Germans celebrated youth as healthy, untainted by the poisons of the past, unburdened with the compromises and struggles of the 'Men of War'. The Nazis were young. Most of the men who came to run the Third Reich were in their thirties. Their youth, inexperience and idealism were part of their great appeal. Ordinary Germans accepted the Nazis as the vital force to channel that youthful energy back into constructive action. Their idealism united the nation, forming ranks against the common enemy. If their youthful rhetoric was a little fiery, people tolerated it. Watch *Things to Come* if you want to know how we felt about putting the old ways behind us and building a rational world where technology assured our enduring security. H. G. Wells was not above borrowing the odd idea or two from the despised little corporal!

241

Most Germans had known only war, disintegration and violent struggle. Perpetual uncertainty is anathema to that honest, amiable German soul yearning to translate its experience of comradeship into a greater community to include all Germans, rich or poor, noble and commoner. They had been told so many lies for so long, they refused to listen. They equated education with the manipulations of the ruling class. They had lost faith in conventional politics. They wanted not a state in the old sense, but a national community of equals: a mighty German family practising the old German family virtues. These sentiments were repeated over and over again. Jews wanted it, too. Those idealists were not brutes.

The Reds and liberals were mostly men of the older generation. They had amply demonstrated their ineptitude in government, their inability to keep their promises. Yet people still yearned for that promised breaking down of class tensions which shackled Germany. They wanted stability first and foremost. Hitler promised a just and ordered future. Nationalism and socialism had failed, but perhaps national-socialism would balance the best of both philosophies. Ordinary Germans had seen Russia collapse into a civil war almost touching their borders, engulfing Poland and Finland, Romania and Ukraine. Germany could well be next. Their hatred of extremists led the German people to vote NSDAP.

Only the Brown Tide could resist the Red. Röhm was convinced of that. He was dedicated to the elimination of Communism and Big Business Capitalism. But he was no fanatic. He was just as dedicated to his pleasures. It had been a long time, he said, since he felt so truly in love. There was something, he said, about my skin. And those dark Mediterranean eyes. He used to joke about my looking too Jewish for my own good. He was by his own admission completely besotted with me. 'I am a childish and romantic man of a wicked disposition.' He believed he had his own measure. I, however, found him generous and sensitive, loyal to his friends, faithful to his duty. His modesty would be his undoing. I suppose I loved him, too, a little. I was definitely flattered by his attention. Röhm was even more famous than Hitler in many circles. A light would burn in that oddly vulnerable, horribly scarred face when he tried to explain his feeling for me. 'There is a quality in you, Max, that I recognise and need.'

I was at once charmed and compromised. I had important business to complete in Rome. For me this interlude was no more than a holiday. I said nothing of Mussolini to Röhm but reminded him how I was not entirely a free agent, that I worked for the Italian aircraft industry.

Röhm had no problem with this. He was, however, deeply interested in my South Russian battle experiences, assuming that, as an American flyer, I had longed for action. He himself had considered joining the Air Corps if only to get out of the trenches, but he was already too old. I had to describe for him in detail the period I spent fighting beside the Cossacks during that ruthless war between Red and White. He was trying to guess what might happen to his Germany in the event of a civil war. He listened with deep sympathy to my stories of capture and torture.

Once or twice Röhm was moved to tears. And the Jews, he said, did this to your manhood? I explained how it had been necessary later to become a Mussulman when I rode with the Tuareg. I was terrified in that synagogue. They were going to set fire to us. They put a piece of metal in my womb. They tore off my Christian flesh. I can still feel the thing. It has six sharp points like a star. Röhm makes fun of me. 'Are you *sure* you're not Jewish?'

I have to lean against the tunnel's rotten brick. Overhead there is a constant rumble, like tumbrils. 'Can't you hear it?'

'It's your appendix, Ivan,' says Mrs Cornelius. 'You ought to 'ave it out.'

My appendix is the last thing that should be removed. I have to avoid the doctors at St Charles. They will loot my corpse soon enough. Those *Pakistanische* butchers will dig the gold from my teeth. Who knows how much precious metal is in me? I am weighed down already. 'I beg you, Mrs Cornelius — if I die first do not let them melt me for scrap. They'll try to get me into the crematorium because that is where they steal the metal. Let me be returned to the earth with all my treasures.'

'I'm not buryin' ya with all them old bits and pieces!' She is outraged. 'An indoor junkyard!'

She has always spoken disparagingly of my machine parts. Where else can I keep them but my flat? Has she seen the price of lock-ups?

'I was not referring to my engines but to my bones.'

She deliberately misunderstands me. She stands there grinning. The dog is behind her. Its sad, reflective eye contemplates the threatening surface of the canal. Anubis is dead. The grey warehouses and useless factories form a background whose symmetry recalls Dachau.

'You blokes 'ave such 'igh opinions of yourselves.' She looks back at the dog. 'You'll be lucky if the council drags yer off in a plastic bag. We're just bodies, you an' me, Ivan. We don't get no fuckin' obituaries in ther *Times*. Wot you so worried about? Immortality? It beats me 'ow people take you wankers seriously. It's bad for yer. 'Ermann lost 'is grip in an 'urry. But that 'Itler was creepy. Clammy.'

'You are too cynical, Mrs C. Is it a crime to demand a little recognition? We were trying to save the world. And that makes us wankers?'

She takes me by the arm, and we move towards the next set of arches. Her tone softens. 'I wasn't just talkin' about you.'

'Well,' I admit, 'I can't defend Hitler in that respect.'

Hitler in truth was a walking pharmacy. That was why his skin was so cold. He had pills and injections for everything. After 1931, when political success was at last a real likelihood, his stomach began to bother him. Even before that he was given to long periods of detachment. The more successful he became, the more he withdrew into himself. He was fundamentally shy.

Röhm said Hitler's instinct was to keep all his balls in the air. He was a feckless Austrian at heart and hated reaching decisions. Decisions were usually made for him by events. *Schlamperei*, in Röhm's view. His friend 'Alf' had become addicted to a cycle of longing, of repressed desire, violent fulfilment, then guilty retreat and denial. 'Just like his sex life.'

Röhm knew far more than he could say publicly but was often loose-tongued when drunk. Like so many Germans of his generation, Hitler discovered sex in the trenches and knew only extremes. Röhm was by nature a bluff Bavarian, 'open heart and open mouth', as they say. He hated intrigue as much as he hated secrets. Only on the subject of his friend was he at all reticent. He never revealed the name of the young lieutenant who had opened Hitler's sexual floodgates. The seducer was in civilian life a well-known painter who had taken an interest in Hitler's architectural drawings. In turn one night the lieutenant had shown Hitler some of his special etchings. Confusion. Repulsion. Attraction. Yet it had still been rape in the end. Hitler responded with horror. He retreated into denial fearing he would not be able to control such lusts and emotions. Control, even then, was hugely important to him.

'That's what made him such a good dispatch runner.' Röhm and I were relaxing one evening in his hot pool. Röhm drank Bollinger from the bottle and smiled with affectionate reminiscence. 'He was afraid at any minute he'd again feel Lieutenant Feistfucher's throbbing bongo up his scrawny jacksie. He fairly flew along those trenches. He was more terrified of his own desires than he was of death. And believe me, Max, he's pretty fucking scared of death! Fascinated, too. Always running back and forth from the edge. He knows what makes him afraid and therefore knows what works on other people. You could call it the common touch. They love him for it.'

Röhm massages my shoulders, thighs and buttocks. The action is painful to him. He has hard, expectant fingers. He is terrified they will turn into claws. He plays the piano to exercise them. 'We used to call him "Alfy-run-and-fetch" in the mess. You're never sure of soldiers like that. But now I respect his talents. He's special. We're still a perfect couple, him and me. Sides of the same coin. Yin and yang. Male and female. Talk and action . . .'

Röhm obviously carried, as the Americans say, a torch for Hitler. Almost everything he did was because of those powerful feelings. His obsession with me was strong, but it was of a different quality. 'Alf' and 'Ernstie' had parted a few years earlier, ostensibly for political reasons. Röhm had not desired the separation but had accepted the reasoning. I speak of an age when it still meant something to give up personal desire in favour of a higher principle. Those old fighters were bound together by far more than cooling affection.

'Doctor Diamond finks 'Itler 'ad thyroid trouble.' Mrs Cornelius grows thoughtful. 'It makes yer eyes bulge.'

'He didn't start out looking like that,' I remind her. 'He wound up bulging, I agree. Everything changed after '31.'

That was before I met him, but his colleagues still complained how distant he was to his old friends, how close to Big Business, the men he had always described as vampires. Had they already bought him? Would they now determine his political direction?

'He's a performer, that's his drawback as well as his advantage,' Röhm said. 'Typical actor. Can't resist an audience. And it loves him. It probably doesn't matter about the colour of the politics with him as long as the crowd responds. He says the crowd is like a woman. He flatters it, frightens it, fucks it.' To the end Röhm was inclined to make excuses for Hitler. 'Besides, Strasser can afford to be snotty. He takes his money from Farben. And he has his own thriving business. We can't do what we have to do on a few pfennigs in the hat.

We have to keep the Nazi balloon up. Hitler has to get his "eggs" from somewhere! At least until we're ready to strike.'

Röhm believed in the Nazi slogans. No longer a monarchist, he wanted common ownership and what he called 'a clear battlefield'. He was convinced that Germany's ills could only be corrected by a violent revolution and an absorption of the regular army into his SA. His classless people's militia would uphold all the old Spartan values. Meanwhile, if a few foolish tycoons thought their interest lay with the Nazis, the Stabschef didn't care. He had massive secret stockpiles of weapons and ordnance all over Germany.

I think he rather yearned for the past before he had gone to Bolivia. He spoke warmly of the good times they had all had in the early days. They had been more light-hearted then. 'Hitler was a great comedian. Professionally, Max, you would have appreciated his talents. On those long drives, he used to keep us in stitches.'

'I never saw that side of 'im,' Mrs Cornelius admits. Hitler of course had tried to court her. He was always attracted to actresses, especially English ones. He couldn't get enough of Jessie Matthews.

Putzi Hanfstaengl, himself a keen fan of the cinema and also something of an amateur comedian, agreed that Hitler was a first-class mimic. Putzi's main job in the 1920s was to console Hitler at the piano with selections of favourite musical numbers.

'He could imitate anyone – voices, mannerisms, attitudes, everything. Peasants, politicians, *Junkers*. But nowadays he relies on me to cheer him up. Me and those endless romantic comedies and cartoons he watches.'

He needs to relax, I said. It is the same for me. Mindless, silly entertainment is what you need when you have such heavy responsibilities.

But Putzi was unconvinced. Left to himself, Putzi insisted, Hitler would do nothing but watch his screens and eat cream cakes. 'Some men are by nature voyeurs. It's bad for them to have their dreams come true.'

Putzi was a little anxious about the coming revolution. Röhm condescended to Hanfstaengl in a way he did not to me. 'I think you, too, Putzi, are not ecstatic at the prospect of your prayers being answered.' There was in Röhm a bit of the jovial sadist.

Privately Putzi told me he wanted to be in movies. If not as an actor, then as a director or producer. A musical arranger even. He had always lived in his dreams. He preferred them to reality. He sought me out whenever he had the chance and pumped me on my Hollywood life.

One day Röhm came back with a French-language version of *Buckaroo's Code,* and we watched it together. He was impressed.

'You have a vocation I think, Max, just as do I,' Röhm decided. 'What a pity you gave it up. You remind me a little of Alf.'

His opinion, of course, was coloured by his affection for me.

We mount the steps to the street. Slowly, arm in arm, we turn for home. Friday afternoon in Golborne Road and the lifeless rain falls a little heavier on this decaying tail of the Portobello Market. They sell fake antiques up at the south section now. Tourists shriek with delight at their discoveries of reconstituted scrimshaw and reproduction Brummagen jugs. Here at the north end they find only irreparable fan heaters and profoundly stained kettles. The second-hand tools and yellowing paperbacks are all that's left of dead old men's work and dreams. I used to sort through bombed houses which contained better junk. The perpetual rain rusts everything not protected by that mixture of grease blended with nicotine which forms the local varnish. Nothing gets it off. In fire you watch it melt with the metal.

The assembly of stallholders and their listless consumers has the unhappy permanence of a displaced persons camp. Refugees from bleaker interiors, they huddle under sacks, plastic bags, old coats. Rain soaks the grey burlap and tarpaulins over the stalls. It seeps into the shops, streaking the floors with a kind of mucus. Toothless women gape in the cheerless doorways of chip shops. You cannot tell that they were ever anything but hags.

The people are colourless. Even in the grey light they are like simplified drawings, silhouettes. No matter how close you go to them the details of their faces and costume grow no sharper. They puff a thin roll-up into an ember and cough on yellow smoke. From the corners of bloodless mouths they mumble at one another. Their faces are defined by lines of grime, sketch maps of a thousand small disappointments.

Mrs Cornelius pauses to pick through some miscellaneous domestic objects. She gives an enamel saucepan her disdainful once-over.

'After the War,' I tell her, 'I was still in politics. There were no blacks here then. Just Irish and Poles. Perek Rachman brought the blacks in.' But, of course, I did not blame him. He was good to me.

247

They picked on him during the Keeler business because they thought he was a Jew. It killed him.

'Wos that when you wos wiv Colin Jordan?' Spurning the saucepan she picks up a set of rusting knives tied together with fatty string. 'When you lived in Portland Road?' She squints down their length.

'Of course not.' She listens to nothing. I never lived in Portland Road. She has no interest in politics. Jordan was much later. He took over the League of British Fascists. Leese's old HQ. They called it the Black House, but it was just a terraced shop. There was a mortician's next door. Leese's widow used to live over it. I had tea with her every Tuesday. She hated the BUF. Mosley and her husband had fallen out years ago. Leese thought Mosley was a liberal. I met the Empire Movement people there. G. K. Chesterton was their most famous member, and of course he died. They were pleasant, mostly middle-aged, but they could not muster more than a few hundred supporters even when we went into the Common Market. Hitler's dream of United Europe became reality. He knew he could not coerce the British. 'They always have to volunteer,' he said. 'They like to think they're in control.' But Leese's Information Service for the Jew Wise, as he called his organisation, was not behind Europe.

Later Leese turned his attentions to the blacks. That was an entirely different struggle and one which he also lost, though his ideas are not forgotten. I have not been down to Portland Road lately. It has an unnatural character with its window boxes, brass knockers and dark green paint. The street is no longer a comfort to me. London was once full of sanctuaries. Today there are fewer and fewer of them.

She flourishes a sawtoothed German carving knife. The colour has worn off the wooden handle. 'Ten pee! Look at that, Ivan!' Her outrage swells her. 'It's just like mine. You know my bread knife. And there's a *lot* more effin' rust on this one.' She has found her moral high ground. She replaces the knife and raises her disgusted eyes level with the stallholder's. He murmurs some stock response and glares shiftily at the dark grey tarmac beneath his sodden boots.

Golborne Road is our most wretched street. Its gutters abound with filth swept in from the surrounding boroughs. The locals don't notice or care. Light has no hope of escape from the smeared shopfronts. Mephitic lumps occasionally shift behind the glass. Nothing can lift the fog of desperate nihilism infecting the unwholesome air. I raise my comforter against it. I protect my mouth. Mrs

Cornelius says that it will do no good. The stuff gets in through your skin, she says. Through your eyes. It's like a gas.

Röhm told me he had only a passing acquaintance with Hitler in the trenches. 'He won his Iron Cross fair and square. We used to say he'd "saddled the nightmare". You'd give him an order and he'd go into this kind of trance. Next minute he'd just set off through the shell-storm like he was running up the street to get a loaf of bread for his mother. Flak and bullets everywhere. Screaming, our Alf would run on, faithful to the end. They said he captured a bunch of Froggies single-handed once, but that sounds too much like the Mussolini story to me. Initiative was never really Alf's strong point. Nobody ever promoted him. He was like a lot of soldiers. He preferred taking orders to giving them.'

Röhm runs those hard fingers over his mosaics. We sit on a marble bench beside the wall. The mosaics are still in progress. They are blatantly erotic, reminiscent of Pompeii. He has had experts design them. He knows all the best interior decorators. This is the work, he says, of Sohner, who does the Berliner Film Company's sets and designed Dietrich's costumes for *Der blaue Engel*. 'That's what we should keep Jews on for. I don't mind them as entertainers either. It's the writers you have to watch. But you won't convince Hitler of that. Like me, he's a simple creature. He has an On/Off switch and a Fast/Slow lever.

'When he was working for me, he was like a tin man, an automaton. I broke the ice eventually. During that trouble in Munich after the War when the Bolshies took over and we had to deal with them, he was working for me as an informant. We soon discovered he was a first-class agitator. He'd go into these camps full of commies and just start talking to them. Not much of a regular soldier but a brilliant orator. We valued him. The Bolshies caught him and were going to shoot him. There was a mix-up. My lads got hold of him and were also going to shoot him. If I hadn't spotted him in time, old Gregor Strasser wouldn't be having the problems he's having now. Running the party would be plain sailing for him without Hitler. But Alfy always dithered if there wasn't someone directing him. And then, if forced, he'd make absolutely terrible decisions! He lost his nerve in the putsch and ran like a rabbit. Too many choices. He can't stand it. First whiff of an alternative and he falls apart. Left a lot of comrades for dead, and people were resentful, said he was powder-shy. But I came to understand his virtues. Alf's special.'

Röhm stands naked in front of his huge mirror. His round, scarred face belies his fitness. Stripped he is a Roman gladiator, his feet slightly apart, his arthritic hands in fists. He suffers badly, he says, with his bones. Too many breaks, too many wet trenches. He continues in his mood of reminiscence.

'I had to remain independent of Alf. That's why I resigned the first time in '24. But I came back. Alf's like a wonderful instrument – useless unless regularly played. He gets into a pathetic state before he speaks. He's got no self-confidence. He sulks. You have to push him on. Then he goes out there and just stands for a bit, as if absorbing the crowd's vitality. Apparently Jolson's the same. Works an audience better than he can manage his own life. On top of that Alf knows he's been singled out by Destiny because he didn't die in the War when everyone else was going down like ninepins. They used to call him Lucky Alf even then. I'm convinced that what will get us through all this will be Alf's devilish good fortune. We'll need it when we finally do take things into our own hands.'

I was reminded of my Negro friend, the massive Mr Mix. He had also thought of me as his mascot, his rabbit's foot. But what others saw as luck, I saw as judgement. Röhm might be underestimating Hitler. An excellent military strategist who understood the streets, Röhm left the internal politics to others. He always admitted he was more of a visionary than a day-to-day politician. That idealism would be his downfall.

He and Strasser were the first Nazis to be contacted by Kurt von Schleicher, the army's main political man, who had Hindenburg's ear. Röhm thought von Schleicher too tricky, too Byzantine, but von Schleicher had not been completely deaf to his proposals for a reformation of the army.

'Von Schleicher wants Hindenburg to appoint him Chancellor,' Röhm told me. 'But Hitler has to be Chancellor. We've held out for that all along. We've all told Hitler to stick with it.' The elections for President were due the following year. Hindenburg would run again but was already too old. Hitler would stand and probably wouldn't beat him. However, it would increase his public status enormously. The Nazis had no one else of Alf's potential. They were all working to get him up there. Meanwhile, there was no harm in letting von Schleicher think the Nazis could be persuaded to serve his purposes in the Reichstag.

For all his frankness and understanding, Röhm's loyalty to Hitler was absolute. By force of arms the Stabschef had the power either to make himself Führer or put his friend Strasser on the throne. Röhm was the hand, he told me. Strasser was the brain. But Hitler was the perceptible soul of the movement. An unstable, youthful soul, perhaps, but what the German people responded to.

Röhm thought of Strasser as a more manly equal. They had the same left leanings. But Röhm understood how the common folk responded with religious ecstasy to Hitler. 'That's what the likes of General von Schleicher refuse to think about,' he said. 'They all see Hitler as an instrument they can play their own tunes on. Alf is so pliable he always lets us think that. He even believes it himself. He hates to say "no". But he bides his time, and suddenly you discover to your surprise that you are *his* instrument! It is a kind of psychic ju-jitsu. Uriah Heep, eh?'

Röhm had read Dickens in Bolivia. He shared with Gregor Strasser an intense love of classical literature. One room in his house was utterly different to the others – a soldier's cell, containing only the SA blood-flag, a shelf of books and some military paraphernalia. This was where he often chose to sleep alone. Of a trusting disposition, he was not a complete fool and was unhappy about Goebbels's and Göring's influence on the leader.

Röhm had better things to do with his time than indulge in petty jealousies and refused to get involved in palace intrigue. The Stabschef had his own constituency. He could afford to stand apart. At his chosen moment millions of iron-hard Storm Troopers would spring to his standard. 'Goebbels in particular hates me,' he said, 'because of the old relationship I had with Hitler. He can't poison that. He can't make it not have happened. When all's said and done he knows it's me Hitler will call on if anything goes wrong. The little doctor's scared of me and my ideas. His talk of a "new morality" means getting the chance to fulfil all the grubby little conventional wet dreams he's ever suppressed. And watch that Göring, too. I know you like him but our valiant captain's a sadist at root. The sweeter the outside, the harder the inside, as we say in Bavaria.'

Mrs Cornelius disagrees. She remains derisive. She defends the Reichsmarschall and attacks the Stabschef. ''E was a nasty little boy-buggerer, that Röhm.'

'He was an idealistic boy-buggerer,' I tell her, 'and that's the crucial difference.'

Röhm confided his dreams to me as we wandered through the half-completed rooms.

'I intend to build an army of men who are everything to one another, who have no other loyalties, who are softened neither by the company of women nor the responsibilities of fatherhood. A vast Spartan army ready to defend the nation to the death. It frightens them because we would be what they only talk of being. If Hitler refuses to condemn me, what right have they to do it?'

On reflection he also admitted that Hitler had another good reason for not sounding off about 'degeneracy' in the SA.

Röhm was proud that scarcely a senior SA commander was not of his persuasion. In turn they promoted their own. Few realise how close Röhm's dream was to realisation. The SA must soon take over the training and moral education of the Hitler Youth. Meanwhile, I became an honorary captain in the Foreign Intelligence wing of the SA.

What, I asked, was the Foreign Intelligence wing supposed to do? Who did it consist of? My friend was boisterously amused. 'You, my dear Max! It's your department.'

As a sworn follower of my Duce, thus unable to tell Röhm all the details, I pointed out that my job as designer for the Italian aircraft industry might conflict with my new rank. He reassured me. The SA position was an honorary one. I need swear no special oath which would compromise my allegiance to Mussolini. Indeed, the rank was conferred very casually by Röhm. He sent a note to an adjutant one July evening. We were still in that bizarre, half-built classical villa. The smell of the Bavarian pine forest and heavy, damp mountain soil blended with rosewater and Havana cigars. It was up to me, he said, to find my own uniform if I wanted one. He gave me a spare cap.

Röhm had drawn up the plans for his villa long before he left Bolivia. 'I had little else to do with my spare time. The entire country is repressed by the bloody Roman Church. Apart from the gorgeous Felipe. And his father soon put a stop to that. Hitler's telegram came in the nick of time. I was ready to join the priesthood; I suspected it was the only place I'd find a friend.' He spoke rather tenderly of the Bolivian boy he had known and of another 'chum' with whom he had travelled back to Europe.

Röhm used the roughest of soldier's language in parliament while reserving his cultivated eloquence for his private moments. Probably the best-read of all the Nazis, he shared my enthusiasm for Karl May and *Simplicissimus*. He and Hitler had both once been passionate fans of Jules Verne, but not of Wells, whom they thought too pessimistic and philo-Semitic. The Stabschef could quote from Dante, Machiavelli and many Latin authors, as well as Goethe and Schiller, but he admitted to having no ear for poetry. 'And no nose for wine!' He could not, he said, tell one vintage from another. Which is why he nowadays only drank champagne. 'To be on the safe side.' He was thinking of equipping Röhmannsvilla with a vomitorium.

'I went off champagne,' says Mrs Cornelius. 'It makes me sick.' At one time or another she has identified almost every kind of food and drink as the source of her problem. She will not accept the obvious explanation.

'You have a weak stomach,' I tell her, 'and a hard head, as we used to say in Odessa. The worst combination. My cousin Wanda was the same, although that might have been pregnancy, after all.'

'It's the stuff they put in the food,' she insists. 'We're bein' poisoned.'

'What do you expect?' I ask her. Tesco's, Safeway, Marks and Spencer's, Lyons – all our food comes to us from Jews now! Even the Jolly Green Giant is Jewish. I read it only the other day in the grocery press. Our clothing, our medicines, our finances! The United Nations. Is there nothing the modern Jew does not control?

As in Germany.

The English are content to complain. They never want anything to come to a head. As a consequence they are sliding into historical oblivion. Churchill warned them of it. So did Hitler. They have no Catholics worth worrying about. Cromwell stamped out that particular canker then, as if to compensate for it, he invited the Jews to return to England! There were no Jews for hundreds of years. Cromwell was very much at odds with Martin Luther, who knew his Jew through and through. Consequently the English had no defences against what happened. Within a few generations the aliens had infiltrated everywhere until by the last quarter of the nineteenth century they even controlled Parliament! People turned them into heroes. If that is not a lesson, what must it take? Not that I have any prejudice, especially against Catholics.

Mrs Cornelius comes across a plastic crucifix smothered with some mysterious dirt. 'People don't give nothin' respect, these days,' she says. 'I mean, 'oo they got to look up ta? The Archbishop of Canterbury?'

They say the Pope helped all the 'war criminals' get away. Yet it was impossible at that time to know who were good and who were bad Nazis. Vatican passports got Stangl and Eichmann and the others to South America, but they did not give them automatic absolution!

When in 1930 Röhm returned to Germany in some style, he decided to make up for lost time. He did not know how long he would live or if the revolution would be successful. If it failed, he was sure to be shot. He knew from his reading of history how freebooters, like himself, could become an embarrassment should the war be won. He spoke of himself as Jean Lafitte or Sir Francis Drake, but I think he hoped Fate would make him a Napoleon.

All his experience of life, Röhm asserted, told him that life was a wild hunt. You were lucky if the best you could do was to hang on to your horse. Anything might knock you off at any moment. Luck alone kept you seated when better riders and nobler men fell. 'That's why I live to the full. Knowing any hour could be my last!'

A soldier first and everything else second, Röhm enjoyed his leisure as he enjoyed his work, bringing the same self-punishing intensity to both. Finding love for the first time after the War, he had been happy for a while. He had quarrelled with Hitler over a small political matter and had left the movement. Hitler condemned him as a traitor. 'Alf went into a sulk. Wouldn't talk to me. Well, I failed to earn a living by any other means. Soldiering's all I know. So I accepted a commission as a regular officer in the Bolivian Army, training their troops.' He had learned from them, too. He had picked up much of his understanding of revolutionary warfare from his South American days.

'But most of my time was spent reading and playing the gramophone,' he told me. He wrote long, sensitive letters home to close friends. The newspapers got hold of some and published them in hope of damaging Hitler's standing with the electorate.

Röhm had laughed when telling me the story. 'The electorate preferred to believe Hitler's support of me.' Even when exclusive hotels were turned into public spectacles of unchecked homosexuality, Hitler continued to stand by Röhm. Putzi Hanfstaengl told me that. 'Hitler couldn't afford not to. If Alf condemned Röhm, then Röhm might easily break his own silence, eh? They've all had to stick together over the years. A few words from the Stabschef and that'll be the end of Hitler's career in national politics.' Hanfstaengl knew how vulnerable Hitler was to blackmail. The party had already paid a vast amount of money for some letters and pictures which had fallen into greedy hands. Nobody at that time knew what else was loose. Hitler's letter writing was a lot less discreet than Röhm's, and he tended to embellish his points with detailed anatomical drawings. And photographs. Hitler could deny rumours, but whatever his oldest friend said would have a special authority. They would sink together. And so the alliance held.

'Frightened people,' says Röhm, 'are genuinely eager to obey. They are grateful for orders, no matter what they are. We all found that in the trenches. Men would rather be ordered to their deaths than not be ordered at all. Action consumes some of their adrenalin and makes them feel momentarily better. These studies of mass psychology Hitler's forever reading always come down to the same simple principle: the crowd loves a roller-coaster. It loves to be frightened and it loves to be saved. The crowd is a baby you toss up into the air and catch, a woman you tease with a knife. And that, of course, is what Alf understands in his bones. The common people possess only two controlling emotions – fear and love.'

I remind Mrs Cornelius of this but she is unimpressed. 'They were all such 'orrible ordinary little turds, really. That 'Itler was the worst. Bore the tits off a bull, 'e would. Everyone complained, even poor little Eva Braun, 'is girlfriend. An' she 'ad a lot more influence over 'im than you fink. She tol' me ther fings 'e made 'er do to 'im! Well, to be fair, she said she enjoyed some of it. Like those girls I know up west. You should 'ear what they 'ave to wear! More like industrial overalls than bonkin' gear! An' the blokes who come to *them* are mostly bigwigs in the government an' tycoons. It's ther showbiz boys who like youngsters. Politicians like ther cane. But it was 'ard work, Eva said.'

Though she got on a little better with the women, Mrs Cornelius did not enjoy her intimacy with the Nazis. She said the men always sounded like a bunch of estate agents. 'Total wank artists, Ivan. Ther passengers get it into their 'eads *they're* drivin' the train. So the first thing they do, o' course, is sack the driver. In ther case o' ther Nazis, they went one better. They killed the bleedin' driver.'

So she reduces the heroic struggle of the twentieth century which ended in the death of all its greatest warriors. Our destiny denied us, our memories forbidden, we descended into the grey mud of socialism. Past and future were abolished. Animals live like that. In an eternal present.

But some of us remember. Stiffly Roland and Arthur and El Cid stir in their hidden caverns. Their flexing fingers reach for their swords. Soon the world will enjoy again the glory and nobility of her golden past. My cities will spring from the depths, splitting open the earth as they thrust towards the calm and comforting skies. They will take us to the heights where the air is pure and we can flourish.

The earth has betrayed us. They have soured it for us. Our legends are made into music-hall jokes and bad films. Our heroes become hobgoblins and devils. We are told that our memories are lies, our history is fiction. Our ideals are mocked. Our values are satirised. The old are ourselves. By failing to protect them, we in turn inevitably fall prey to the predators. The logic is obvious. I tell them this. But you only find it out when your body starts to fail you, when you think twice before crossing the street to your usual newsagent because a gang of youths with shaven heads and football colours are standing outside chortling over copies of the *Beano* and the *Dandy*, whose characters they so closely resemble. You have heard their insults for seventy years. You have suffered their threats, and your body can recall every blow they have struck on it. You want no more, so you do without your newspaper. Not that the papers are anything but communist rags.

I am surprised they can read. They wear football caps and scarves like the uniforms I used to see on the Sozis and Nazis. Home-made colours. They enjoy the comforts of collective violence. They slobber after power and fear all responsibility. They lie and they boast and they swagger and they imagine themselves mass murderers and gang bosses. They buy large, vicious dogs. They beat their women. They terrorise their children. And people say the Nazis were bastards.

Franz Stangl led an impeccable private life. Whatever happened at Treblinka and so on was nothing I knew about. His family loved him and were never frightened of him. He was a faithful husband and a responsible father like many of the best Nazis. They were Austrians and South Germans, of course, and disliked the Prussian glorification of war, which was to infect Hitler so badly in his later years. They were solid family men. Whatever they had to do outside, they never inflicted it on their nearest and dearest.

So who suffers most? Or worst? These scalp-heads, these *Mohawkischers*, who bring only noise, filth and violence to society?

256

They are genuinely worthless. They contribute almost nothing in labour or money. They know only to take.

Who suffers worst are the decent men, women and children. Those of us who contribute order and cleanliness to the world. Make those hooligans into pet food, I say to her. Let the kangaroos roam free. Let some faithful family cat feast on their fatty flanks, their beer-fed guts, their coarse meat. Our cities would be quieter. Our dogs content.

We turn into the northern end of the Portobello Road, where the walls of convents and monasteries become an inescapable channel. This is the only stretch where there are no doorways, no depths, nowhere to disappear. The walls of the religious institutions are too tall and too well protected to scale. Yet already the road takes on a different character. Already it is a cut above what we leave behind. The difference is subtle. The stalls still contain the same miscellaneous mixture of false brands, redundant canned goods and hardware looking like loot from some forgotten bombsite. The same hopeless electrics, disintegrating plastic and stained paper, yet here you feel you might just possibly find something you could use. The stallholders are a little more optimistic about their wares. 'Have a look,' they say, 'we can always talk about the price.'

Mrs Cornelius gives this section of the market her considered inspection. You can tell that she feels it worthier of her. She picks up a toy panzer tank bearing a flaking swastika. 'Your big mistake, Ivan, after you got mixed up with them Nazis, was to get mixed up with them 'omos. You never 'ad no common sense, but you 'ad somethin' like good luck! All that changed when you started flirting about with 'Itler.'

'I didn't exactly volunteer,' I point out. Her intolerance is unworthy of her. 'You never used to mind such things.'

'I'm not talkin' about buggery.' She turns suddenly to look at me. 'I'm talking about ther rest of it. You never knew when to scarper. An' it wasn't for want of my warnin' you every five bloody minutes!'

'A Greek chorus,' I say affectionately.

She is amused. 'A bit less of the Greek,' she insists. 'A Greek got me out of England in the first place. I started in the chorus, though.' And she begins her soothing reminiscence of Kilburn Empire triumphs and glory days in Hollywood.

I find it impossible to watch those films any more. There is no equipment for them. For almost twelve years I have been working on a projector I found in the market. But where are the spares? I have tried to make them or take them from other machines. So far I have had no real luck. The old bulbs and valves are impossible to find. What happened to all those projectors? Hitler had one. Mussolini had one. Stalin had one. Franco had one. Hearst had one. Roosevelt had one. Churchill had one.

In the years between the Wars we were all cinema-crazy. Any man with money wanted his own little theatre where he could watch Mickey Mouse, Douglas Fairbanks, Cuddles McTitty and the milkman to his heart's content. Industrialists and potentates bought themselves the convenience and privacy which after the War the BBC would try to imitate with TV for the masses. A chicken in every pot, a car in every garage, a cinema in every home. They bribed the electorate. We got *Sunday Night at the London Palladium* instead of justice. And the masses were content. They are always content until the fantasies on which they feed begin to poison them and then they gaze mindlessly around for some other teat to suck.

'Look,' says Mrs Cornelius, taking my arm. She suddenly leans on me and catches her breath. 'It's brightening up a bit.'

The rain has lifted and the sky has grown paler, but that is all. Not exactly cause for unbridled optimism. But I do not say anything. It would be cruel to dash her hopes.

We are almost at the train bridge and the flyover. We have two bridges now. The stalls underneath represent a halfway point. They make a miscellaneous collection. White Hindoos in hideous orange nylon offer me garish comic books depicting the mysterious battles of their vast pantheon of gods. They hawk untuned bells and stinking joss sticks. They offer handbills.

'No thank you,' I say, 'I have not yet joined the Alternator Society.' The entire area under the bridges stinks of wet fur, some of it from living dogs and some of it from their ancestors, adorning the lice-ridden bodies of the Love Generation. Through this drift the odours of damp rice, of tea and coffee, of fried fat. We pass perfumed candles and bags of spices, all their 'gravey booby' drug materials. Her finger-nails a flight of red bees, Mrs Cornelius runs an appreciative hand over the chrome flanks of a massive toaster which looks as if it had once served a significant mechanical function on a Cunarder. 'They built things to last in them days,' she says.

'They were not affordable to most of us.'

'They're all right second-hand,' she assures me. 'They run for ever.' But I could see that the elements were destroyed. I picked up a birdcage with some of its bars bent, as if in a sudden fit of strength the occupant had forced its way to freedom.

'She had a dead canary with her all day,' said Röhm to me. 'That was the weird thing. Hess remarked on it. So did Father Stempfle. They were called in by the mother.'

He was talking about Geli Raubal. We were in the middle of the most significant event of 1931, though you would never discover that from any of the history books. The facts were there for all to discover, at least for a while. Of course, they could not interview Father Stempfle. He had confessed her. And passed the information on. They did not make the connection. Röhm, of course, knew exactly what had happened. It is hard for a woman to shoot herself through the heart with a Walther PPK 38 of that model. The weakness, said Röhm, of the case. Nobody thought it worth investigating so they didn't put many police on it. That gave everyone time to brush over the tracks. Then Hitler became the property of academic authority obsessed with his 'strategies', 'plans' and war management and his true story faded away. He, however, was never at rest after '31. The beginning of his personal decline came just as his public star was rising. Thereafter his public confidence was almost entirely play-acting and pharmaceutical drugs.

After 1934 only two of us still knew the entire sequence of events. I am the last one at liberty. The other is in prison with amnesia, a vegetable. They say he can't last. I met him during the War, during my internment. British intelligence arranged the meeting. I think they were testing me. He had very little memory left. He knew me and kept trying to warn me, as he had earlier. 'Those Messerschmitts,' he whispered, 'are treacherous.' That, of course, was why he had fled. Unconsciously he had known that he would be his hero's next victim. The journalists and pseudo-historians make some conventional logic of it, but he was as anxious to escape as I was. His action undoubtedly saved his life. His loyalty to Hitler, however, ensured his silence.

In the end he did what he had advised me to do. He escaped by plane. He knew, though his faith was as powerful as ever, that he was a marked man. His beloved, infallible master intended to murder him. In his rejection of conventional religion and his taking up of occultism, his faith in Hitler was his only stability and he could not afford to let it go. But he naturally did not want to die. Hess reconciled the conflict in his typical way. If he was of no further use to his master, then he would leave. And find a way to be of use again. Hess escaped into a kind of limbo. I did not really envy him. I believe I kept my perspective. I have never denied the real issues that lay at the heart of the Nazi cause. My quarrel was with the application of the principles. Many had the same misgivings as time went on. My own experience, of course, might have prejudiced me, but I always prided myself on my openness both to ideas and to fresh experience.

My experience at the Villa Röhm was, I will admit, dreamlike. As if I was in a perpetually running Hollywood epic. Some of Röhm's rivals thought it vulgar, but I was reminded of Hearst's famous Castle of San Simeon and of the Hollywood homes, such as Chaplin's.

Putzi called Röhmannsvilla 'De Mille Bon Marché'. Silks and fine cottons hung everywhere. Marble statuary of boys and young men, fountains, tiled baths and erotic mosaics were all drawn from classical models. A perfect setting for the elaborate parties Röhm liked to throw for his top lieutenants who never failed to bring fresh guests, many of them recruited from the Hitler Youth's finest. The newcomers were always wonderfully impressed. A great morale booster.

I saw something so noble, clean and healthy about those young bodies that only a person with a twisted mind would observe anything perverse in what went on there. True, we tested ourselves and others to certain extremes, but this served to harden us more. Röhm himself explained how we emulated the greatest Greeks and Romans. Whenever heterosexuality was made a faith, he said, civilisations collapsed. Hitler understood that as well as he did. Only homophobes like Himmler and Goebbels feigned disgust. They were addicted to sentimentality and women the way Hitler was addicted to his cream cakes and his dog whips. Their own weakness was why they always railed against him. Göring, with his weight, and Goebbels, with his club foot, had not exactly put the purest sperm into circulation, and as for Hitler, he possessed serious drawbacks, as we said in Kiev, to his stuffing any chicken with his particular pudding.

Röhm had no time for women except as mothers. The rest were sluts and parasites. He found it hard to be polite to most of them. He said they were a distraction, incapable of higher brain functions. They were natural prey to Jews and other vermin. He had loathed Rosa Luxemburg, whom he described as a hermaphrodite and an abomination. He tolerated the army politician von Schleicher precisely because he understood him to have been involved in the execution of Luxemburg and Leibnitz.

Ultimately, Röhm told me, he saw a time when women would hardly be needed at all, and those we had left could be hardened up like Amazons, as auxiliaries and breeders. Hitler's weakness for Geli Raubal was a sure sign things were going wrong. Röhm had nothing against his Chief having a sentimental interlude, but Raubal had become an unhealthy obsession and was getting them both into trouble. She was likely to destroy Hitler's political career. The party couldn't afford much more scandal around him.

Röhm insisted that the light of his old friend's life was nothing but a whore. 'She fucks anything that moves. She'd fuck a turd if it was stiff enough. She's had two of his chauffeurs behind his back and half the damned SS. Everyone knows about her and that SS fellow Zeiss. Yet Alf won't hear a word against the bitch. He's broke because of her. She's getting him to buy her singing lessons and send her to fucking Vienna to become an opera star! No, Mashi, we really don't need young Geli around at the moment. I'm all for her going to Vienna to follow her vocation. I know a nice house on Rosenstrasse. They'll employ her. She can take her pictures with her.'

Röhm, Putzi and Schultz, the Nazi Party treasurer, had been responsible for buying back Hitler's drawings and letters. The go-between was the ubiquitous Hieronymite priest Father Bernhard Stempfle, a sometime contributor to *Völkischer Beobachter* and *Der Stürmer*. The letters, Röhm said, were graphic. The photos were steamy. But the drawings were amazing. Better than his usual doodles. Putzi had wondered what kind of man would make a woman pose like that. And he had come to understand about the dog whips they all carried. He was not grateful for the knowledge, he said. It gave him a rather different idea of the Chief.

'He's completely addicted to the bitch,' Röhm complained. 'And she's blackmailing him, believe me. She could well have corrupted that seedy priest, though I know for a fact he's not interested in grown women. The commies will use her, if they can.'

By coincidence that same evening he presented me with a marvellous costume, a fantasy of lace and silk, and said he would be touched if I would wear it for him. Röhmannsvilla was a kind of Hollywood in itself, and I felt secure there. I was never afraid of make-believe in its place. In this case, of course, I had hardly any choice. I indulged him. I love the sensation of silk. I gave myself up to it and did not really mind the pain at the end. 'Slut,' he said. 'You gorgeous little slut.'

I always believed it pure folly to assume that what a consenting adult does in the privacy of his own apartments has any bearing on his public life. No true historian bothers himself with such questions. A man should be judged by his public actions, not on his taste in suits, sex or soup.

Mrs Cornelius, of course, was involved in the Christine Keeler business, though she never went to Cliveden. Mandy Rice-Davies was her good friend, and they often spent afternoons together. 'The only problem with all o' that,' she says, 'was Chrissy and that loony *Schwarze*, whatever his name was . . .'

'Lucky,' I say.

'They was both barmy and that messed it up for everyone else. Jack Profumo should 'ave known better, but there wasn't much to the rest of 'em.'

We have stopped in the Mountain Grill for a cup of tea and something to eat. George calls a greeting to me from his shrieking, steaming galley at the back. Maria, his wife, calls me a 'dirty old sod' and asks me how I am. All affectionate badinage. The chairs are bent chrome and red plastic. The old Brown House style. Two rows of grey formica-topped tables go from front to back with a central aisle. Maria walks up and down the aisle like a wardress, delivering filled plates, picking up empties. She sees to the condiments. She has her favourites. I am one of them. I never go hungry there. Like her husband she wears a stained white overall. They are almost exactly the same height and weight. They come from Cyprus. We get on well. We have similar ideas about the Turks. They would like to see the liberation of Constantinople. Yet they support Queen's Park and celebrate Christmas. They are not bigots. Everyone comes here, from hippies to police. Black men with impossibly tangled hair openly roll reefers and grin across at the little schoolgirls who have accidentally found this greasy bolthole. Children are in no danger at the Mountain Grill, another of the world's safe places. The café offers greater sanctuary than any church.

Part of George's front door, bolted open now, has been smashed. 'Drunks,' he says, 'crazies. You know.'

'Micks was it?' says Mrs Cornelius. She always blames the Irish. 'They can't hold their booze. It's the same up our way.'

A long time, I tell her, since we had to be afraid of Micks who are all Labour politicians now. She has no base to her prejudice. She merely voices the accepted wisdom of Whitechapel with its deep-rooted secular tradition. Such stereotyping is unworthy of her, I say. I see good and bad among all races. The English are prejudiced against the Irish because they know in their bones Cromwell created many of their ills. Yet the Irish are just as misguided. They blame all their troubles on the English. The plain fact is that the Catholics lost the struggle. What would they have done if Cromwell had not triumphed? Himmler, a Protestant, had no prejudices against Catholics. They were often, he said, the best for special duties. That's why he preferred, whenever possible, to recruit Austrians.

It is a nonsense to say the Christian Churches turned against Hitler. The Lutherans and the Catholics loved him. They fell over themselves to bless the brave SA boys at their rallies. They got up in their pulpits and told their congregations to vote for him. He was a force for stability, they said. Only the Greek Church stood aloof, which was why Hitler wanted to destroy it. He never had any major disagreement with the Pope.

They were talking on the wireless about the Irish famines in the nineteenth century which the English did so little to alleviate. The survivors all went to America and settled there. Where they lynched Negroes and shot redskins. I once looked at the names of troopers who served in the US frontier regiments and who massacred the natives. The names were all Irish. As they were in India. A naturally belligerent people forced from their bogs and slums by English callousness, they went to America to improve their spirits by shooting unarmed people in remote western valleys. Who is the original victim? Who the aggressor? Many of the Indians expected nothing else. They had dedicated themselves rigorously to the total genocide of rival tribes. Yet tell some American, boasting of his Irish and Cherokee blood, that he survives because his ancestors were successful practitioners of genocide, and feel his fist in your face, his boot in your testicles.

History is no longer a study of the past, but a series of legalistic arguments. A public trial in which academics vie with one another to establish who is the victim, who the aggressor. An American habit. Americans never feel at ease until they establish who is to blame for something. They took this from the Germans, who gave them so much more of their culture than the British.

They say Hitler, too, perverted reality, reinvented history. But unsentimental reality moved the Führer. Let us not mention the Israelis, whose rhetoric is identical to the Nazis in almost every respect. They speak of blood, of living space, of ancient rights. With the help of the unwitting Americans, who name themselves Christians but are really Jews, calling on the Old Testament but rejecting the New, they plan a new Carthaginian Empire across the Middle East and the Mediterranean.

'Mind your backs, boys!'

Maria brings my usual. One sausage, chips, a slice and tea. On Saturdays I have an egg. Mrs Cornelius has her own usual. A bowl containing two scoops of mashed potato over which thick tomato soup has been poured. A wartime dish, she tells me. It always comforts her.

Through George's weeping glass I see a sudden ray of sunshine fall on the needlecraft stall across the road. The reels and spools, hanks and balls of bright silks, wools and cottons come to burning life, a magnificent display of jewels. Ornaments sparkle, clothes become more vivid and heads lift almost in surprise. An angel might have paused here.

'I don't know what to watch tonight.' We have finished our meal. It is Mrs Cornelius's whack. She returns from the counter. 'Bye-bye, all!'

For a while the drizzle does not persist. Outside the sun continues to shine on windows and puddles. There is a strong pungent odour, almost of the jungle. I know it to be the soup of half-corrupted fruit and vegetables, paper and animal matter, through which we pick our way, fording the amniotic stream so that Mrs Cornelius can get her fags at her newsagent. This material, pushed into heaps or flushed down sewers, is the breeding ground for new species.

Scientists come from all over the world to study Portobello Road. Yesterday some bespectacled student informed me that the area now has its own separate ecological system. Such things happen only in cities. Rural environments lack the necessary biological complexity. Marijuana grown in that mixture is known to be almost fifty times stronger. No wonder everyone seems to be in a trance. These days when they come stumbling into my shop I know exactly what is going on.

When Mrs Cornelius picks up her Embassy Tipped I buy a copy of the *Daily Mail*, always my favourite British newspaper, as it was Hitler's. Lord Rothermere was a convinced NSDAP supporter and saw a stronger future in his nation's close collaboration with Hitler. If they had followed his advice there is no doubt the British Empire would now be greater than ever. She would control vast areas of the world, including China and Arabia. Instead, she cannot effectively rule the Isle of Wight. No wonder the Americans, who have taken over so many old imperial responsibilities, are contemptuous. Americans have deafened themselves. They shout at one another. They shout at me. They shout banalities, destroying thought.

265

Lately I find it hardly worth buying a paper or turning on the news. Little changes. Who can you trust? That familiar excited babble, confident-sounding analysis, authoritative predicting of trends while everything continues to go round and round in the usual unresolved chaos. Sometimes I come across old newspapers in boxes or as drawer linings. The issues scarcely change. The arguments remain the same. Year in and year out commentators voice the identical views in the same excited tones. Most people are incapable of original thought. They think an original thought is something they haven't read before. It bowls them over. They repeat it in the pub or, if they are middle class, at dinner parties.

Mrs Cornelius refuses to despair. She says you have to laugh.

'What a wonderful actor you are, Max.' Röhm watches the last reel of *Buckaroo's Gold*. I wave to the audience from my mechanical horse. It seems I control a rearing mount. I flourish my hat. My smile is gay. My innocent eyes look back at me from a happier age.

He pours champagne. 'I could swear I'd seen you in something else.'

I can never forget those films taken in Egypt. What if they should turn up some day? The likelihood is not impossible. Röhm, Hitler, Streicher and Rosenberg all have extensive collections of erotica. I cannot remember whether my face was ever visible or not. Röhm, of course, would not need to see my face to recognise me.

Mrs Cornelius and I went to the pictures every Friday afternoon. We had pensioners' passes. But when the Essoldo in Portobello Road changed to the Electric Cinema it became impossible. We had been able to see three features at the Essoldo for 1/6. The Electric charges you a pound for one foreign film whose photography is out of focus, whose plot is indecipherable and whose subject appears to be the director. Progress, indeed. All that has not changed are the seats and the sound system, which remain as bad.

I saw the work of the transvestite adman Warthole there. Naked boys pretending to be cowboys and vampires. What is so original about it? I asked. They were not so long ago, those wonderful parties. Some SA wag called it the 'Kaligulahof'. 'Mr Handy Andy' should make a film about that villa, its luxuries and elaborate fantasies. I could help him. I could write the script. I am not ashamed. Nobody was forced. Those Hitler Youth lads had as much fun as anyone. Besides, I had no choice. Kind-hearted as he was, Captain Röhm was used to being obeyed. He became my only source of income after Mussolini's money stopped arriving. I had enemies in Rome, but I could not investigate, of course.

Mrs Cornelius was quite aware of my circumstances. She never blamed me. She thinks perhaps I should have anticipated the problems. But how could I anticipate what happened? How could anyone? People judge you too readily. They think you deliberately choose your fate. They do not understand how you gradually slide into situations from which escape becomes impossible. What seems a temporary diversion on your life's road looks, in the perspective of history, like a culmination, an example of your inner evil! But I had absolutely nothing to do with any murder. I still could not swear who killed her. Those who knew were shot or fled into exile. Father Stempfle was killed in Dachau, but I never saw him there. Stempfle was one of the keys. Who has heard of him today? The past disappears without record. History becomes a means by which we escape from shame or promote our special interests. We invent whatever we need and forget whatever is inconvenient. Such is life in this sordid Disneyland where wealthy tourists bring in the only money.

Walt Disney was inspired by Mussolini's idealism. He wanted to build a benign corporate state where every American was happy and nothing ever happened to anyone. He died before he could realise this utopia, but they froze his head so that he can return at any time to redeem us. He made so many dreams seem real. I am forced to face the fact that all my dreams came to nothing.

'Up like the rocket and down like the stick,' says Mrs Cornelius, guiding me from the newsagent and back into the crowd. 'That's you all over, Ivan.' A pack of miniature mongrels runs past, under one stall and out of another. A cyclist swerves to avoid them and falls against a display of tomatoes. We move expertly away from the conflict. We have reached the old core of the market, where fruit and veg are still sold, where frustrated locals make every effort to hold their own against the foreign influx. They sell the boojies the rotten tomatoes and the bruised fruit. Friday it is mostly hippies and scalp-heads, dealers of every description. They bring no money in. Whatever they make they take away again.

Here the shops are cleaner and sell recognisable things. We pass both rival fishmongers' slabs, the cheap butcher's, the chain baker's, the white goods shop, the draper's, the hardware shop, the electrician's, the Venicia Café and the baby shop. As we approach the pawnshop, the black bulk of Bishop Beesley, not at first recognisble as

267

human, blocks our way. He is considerably fatter than Göring and, of course, is not a real bishop. His real name is Billy the Mouth and he is again released from prison. Like his daughter he is a confidence trickster. Mitzi is currently in Holloway. They rarely meet. Beesley is wearing his familiar dark suit and pullover, a white shirt just visible. It gives him the ecclesiastical look he feels comfortable with. He wipes his hand on a blue handkerchief. 'My dear Colonel! And the lovely Mrs C!'

He is meeting a mutual friend in the Blenheim Arms, he says. He insists we have a quick one on him. His ship recently came in. 'In a small way, you know.'

Mrs Cornelius accepts, and I cannot be rude. We leave Portobello Road and enter the pub's graveolent interior. Quintessentially English, the smell of fried pies and cigarillos blend with bitter beer and harsh spirits. Dark shoulders press together. Little women, holding their own like defiant fowl, slip in and out with glasses of wine. Shifty boys pass miniature paper envelopes back and forth and argue over money. They glance at well-groomed office girls who sit at the bar grinning and smoking or rummaging through their purses. On the other side of the counter the glowering features of little Mo Collier glare with contempt on all and everything. The world is not up to standard. He smoothes his carefully cut moustache. His neat, dark head sports another idiosyncratic haircut, doubtless the current fashion. 'Near-mutton dressed as almost-lamb,' says Mrs Cornelius spitefully. She was never prepared to like him. He stands with his eyes avoiding his customers, flexing his muscles and catching glimpses of himself in the polished copper. A pocket Hercules in his fashionable sports vest. The Bishop insists on his attention. 'Two halves please, Mo, and a small, dry sherry. Ah, there she is!'

A coiffure that was once pure Pre-Raphaelite flame, but now owes something to Mr Sonya in Elgin Crescent, bobs above the mass. Miss Brunner used to run a local girls' school before the scandal. She is now in private tuition and dresses with the same tempting severity which makes the Bishop her slave. As far as we know, there is no other man in her life. The Cornelius boys tell stories, but neither can ever be trusted to know the truth, let alone tell it. Her uncompromising grey-blue eyes note our presence and are lowered in a brief greeting. She bears herself with a kind of diseased dignity. She is thoroughly groomed but cannot disguise the aura of corruption which surrounds her. She has no power to charm, only to command. She takes a Pernod and makes it clear she has come to meet the Bishop, not chat with us.

A long head hunched in a corduroy donkey jacket turns from the bar. Frank, Mrs Cornelius's youngest boy. His features are inclined to sag. I think he is on morphine, like Göring. They say he works for Hoogstraten, the property tycoon, and tends to ape his new boss. He wears a striped Jaeger shirt and an old school tie. He is better groomed than his brother, at least. He smiles at me, says something to a companion and comes over. Tentatively Frank kisses his mother, apparently unsure what he will pick up. He squeezes my arm in an aggressive and unwanted demonstration of camaraderie. 'How's tricks, Colonel?'

They are always here on Fridays. Even Major Nye comes in on occasions but was offered voluntary retirement and can only rarely afford the fare from Kent. Family business is now his only excuse for visiting the city. We see a few others from time to time. We are the survivors, I suppose. Our means of survival might not always bear much discussion, but I name no names. We have no power. Therefore we cultivate tolerance. The acceptance, I suppose, of the inevitable. We huddle together for comfort. We remind one another of our stories and our great days. Most of us have had a few of those, at least.

I had no plans to spend more than a week with Captain Röhm, but he insisted I stay. Also at his insistence, and with some relief, I shaved off my imperial. He appreciated the action. I was his ideal companion, he said, for this wonderful idyllic place. Then friends turned up. Before I knew it a week had gone and then another. Messengers were sent to the post office, but nothing arrived for me. I had to stay there. Röhm was sometimes absent for a day or two, but there was plenty to do. I spent hours wandering around the vast uncompleted villa. The chief bedrooms and bathrooms were in use and there was a large public room, but most of the rest was only half finished. Röhm never had time to let the builders come back. Somebody was always staying there. But when I was on my own, I might be the last man on Earth.

The spirits of hunters and woodsmen had inhabited the thick, surrounding wooded hills since the beginning of time. I had rarely experienced such peace. I found a beautiful illustrated set of Karl May and absorbed myself in tales of *Old Shatterhand* and *Winnetou the Kiowa*. Röhm also shared Hitler's taste for Edgar Wallace who was, he said, the soundest of British writers in their best traditions. Wallace had been a professional soldier, and like Buchan had a pretty clear idea of the Jew question. On Röhm's recommendation I read *The Fellowship of the Frog* and one or two others. They had none of the appeal of the best Sexton Blake stories and were interesting only when they described some aspect of London criminal life. Through them I grew to know Limehouse, Soho and even Wapping, which was where Wallace was raised, by a bookie, with Jews on all sides.

Forgetting the questions which shadowed my mind, I could read in perfect tranquillity. There was never any threat. One was never taken unawares. Röhm had guards posted at every approach. He feared only the communists. Brodmann could not find me.

According to the rules, Röhm or his aides, but not guests, could make telephone calls. It seemed impolitic to try to contact Mussolini, but I began to wonder what he would think if I had disappeared. Believing me the victim of foreign agents, he might send people to look for me, to rescue me. It would be best if I got in touch with him soon. Why had my money been stopped? I made plans to return to Munich. I neither wished to end my idyll nor offend the great Stabschef, but I have an exaggerated sense of loyalty. I felt it my duty to go, at least for a while. Reluctantly my host agreed, and at the beginning of August on a particularly hot day, I returned to the Königshof.

There was some problem with a room. They had been told of my absence and put my trunks in storage. But they had not been told of my return. I was waiting impatiently for the matter to be settled and crossed the lobby to buy a *Völkischer Beobachter* when suddenly I was on the other side of the revolving newspaper rack staring into the frigid face of the Baroness von Ruckstühl.

I was too surprised and too exhausted to pretend. I lifted my hat.

'My God!' she said. 'Where have you been? You smell like a whore.'

The mistake was a genuine one. Having no time to bathe, I had borrowed some of Röhm's cologne before leaving the house.

'Good afternoon, Leda,' I said. 'You look well. Are you a guest here, too?'

'Why should I be a guest here?' She spoke belligerently, without affection, but I sensed a quiver of the old spark.

I must admit I was reluctant to leave her until I had some idea of what she was doing in Munich. Knowing her hatred of me from the incident on the train, I blew, as best I could, upon older embers.

270

I told her how attractive she was, how she had lost none of her sex appeal, her beauty. Could we perhaps have tea together? A woman of that age is always hungry for such praise. She told me, rather urgently, that she was married. She was now Frau Oberhauser. She did not warm to me. I said it would be good to speak to her alone, to go over old times, to tell her what had happened to me, how I had been trying to contact her. Neither of us referred to the meeting on the train. I was now, of course, clean-shaven.

'But you have nothing to tell me,' she said. 'I already know all there is to know.' Her smile was unfriendly.

'I do not understand,' I said. 'I have been abroad for so long.'

'Indeed,' she said. She was lucky enough to be in possession of an entire dossier on my movements since I had left Constantinople and turned up in Paris in the expatriate community. She had some wonderful news cuttings from America, for instance. As she murmured her triumph, I could barely keep my composure. She spoke quietly and we were not overheard, but I suspect she did not care if there were listeners. It appeared, she said, that I had swindled my way across at least two continents before hiding myself in Cairo.

I told her that I had had no chance of defending myself. I had been protecting others. She knew me. Was I a monster?

I do not believe I have ever been as wounded by laughter. I begged her to take a glass of tea with me. 'And now I know where you are,' she said, and swept into the crowded lobby, leaving through the glass doors to a car. I still did not know where she lived. All I had was a name. I seriously regretted my impatience in leaving Röhmannsvilla.

It took several hours for a room to be found for me. Some sort of crisis was afoot. The political situation in Germany remained highly volatile. Banks were closing down, and ordinary people were panicking. The radio and newspapers appealed for people to keep their heads. But they had nothing else to lose. There were dozens of rumours about seizures of power, tycoons fleeing the country, a peasant army on its way to Berlin. They grew increasingly fantastic. I had too many other things on my mind. I tried to put a telephone call through to Rome, to Margherita Sarfatti. I could contact no one else without arousing suspicion.

I barely understood the news. So much had been going on, I suppose, that it was impossible to explain. New names were everywhere. Old

271

ones had vanished. This situation was critical. That one was calm. In the end I decided to wait until I met a party friend who would explain everything to me.

Luckily the hotel made no fuss about my bill. They had been reassured earlier by Putzi's involvement with me and had seen me arrive in an SA car flying the Stabschef's flag. My room was a little small and at the back of the hotel looking down on the garages, but I was lucky to have it.

I made several more telephone calls. Erna Hanfstaengl, Putzi's sister, told me her brother was in Berlin. 'They're all in Berlin, Max. There's a different crisis every twenty-four hours. I doubt if anyone will be back in Munich until the weekend at least.'

It soon became evident, especially after my encounter with the Baroness, that this was the best time to leave. I would offend no one. They were all too involved with their politics. Yet I still had no money and no credit. In the atmosphere of panic, there would be little I could sell which would raise me what I needed. I decided to try my friends in the Roman press corps. Tom Morgan was in Milan. I left a message with his secretary. I put through another call to Billy Grisham, but again the lines were saturated. Eventually someone from his bureau got through to me. They thought I was their Munich stringer. They told me Grisham was already in Berlin. When I asked for his number they said it was the same as always. I had made them suspicious.

None of the other numbers I tried were of any use. Some had been changed while I was away. I felt totally isolated in the middle of so much urgent activity. I did not, of course, wish to call Röhm, for I knew he would object to my leaving. Göring, my other important acquaintance, was still, I understood, with his dying wife. That newborn Balt Seryozha was as likely to want to borrow from me as lend me the money for my ticket, and I had other reasons for not wishing to resume contact with him. He had clearly been dropped by Röhm.

My inattention to the newspapers for the past couple of weeks meant that everything I overheard was a mystery. The only familiar names were Hindenburg and Hitler. Chiefly the conversation was about money and business and the failure of the banks. The consensus was that America, with considerable troubles of her own, could no longer keep Germany afloat. Once again the Fatherland faced the appalling inflation of earlier years. Already people were becoming suspicious of cash. I felt that I should buy my ticket before I needed millions just to tip the conductor. I tried the Bürgerbräukeller, the Hofbräuhaus, the Eberlbräuhaus, the Löwenbräuhaus and the Löwenbräukeller, all favourite Nazi beer cellars. The young men in the Thorbräukeller, a regular meeting place for the SA, were positively rude. I found no one I recognised.

At length I decided to take a stroll in the tranquillity of Briennerstrasse. The great houses seeemed as tranquil and as inviolable as ever. The Brown House, flanked by trees, had acquired a look of permanence and stability. I waited nearby for a while in the hope of seeing a friend. Instead, I received nothing but insults from the untrained boys, unaware of my standing, who came and went in their battered trucks and delivery vans. At one point I saw a more experienced SA man caution one of these green recruits. I tipped my hat to him as I went by. I bore them no animosity. I recognised in them a vitality which might sometimes express itself crudely but was renewing Germany at last. They did not understand how much we had in common.

Everyone of any importance was in Berlin. I took my supper at the hotel. I had no choice. Because I remained unsure of the Baroness's intentions, I found it difficult to settle down with a book and wait for something to happen. Did she plan to expose me there and then to the Munich press? I was reluctant to walk out on the streets in the evening, since I had already been the object of mockery. I wondered what the same people would say if I put on my Fascist uniform or told them that I was a captain in the SA.

As I passed the concierge's desk one of the under-managers saw me and called politely, handing me a large envelope containing a telegram. I opened it up. Tom Morgan had sent it. I was a little baffled by the message.

REPORTS OF YOUR DEATH CLEARLY EXAGGERATED STOP BUT SHOULDNT YOU BE IN ALBANIA QUERY CALL ME SOONEST STOP TOM

The only Albanian I knew was Rose von Bek, and I was convinced by now that she was dead. Was Tom's query connected with her? And who had reported my own death? It was too late to telephone his office, and he had not left another number. I assumed there had been a simple confusion or that Tom was joking. I would have to

273

be patient and wait until morning to find out. There would be no one at Tom's office before then.

I had not felt quite so desolate and uneasy for some while. I was confident of my overall security, for I knew some of the most powerful men in Europe, yet I was still nervous. However, if civil war broke out in Germany, as some were predicting, Munich was better for me than Berlin. I could get over the Swiss, Czech or Austrian borders fairly easily. My best bet, I decided, was to concentrate on finding a car I could use.

After the War I ran a small repair business until they closed down the arches. I was next door to a man who specialised in pre-war and American automobiles. He made a fortune. Every so often I was able to help him with a difficult job. When the council decided in its wisdom to move us out, I could not afford the expensive shops they offered me in Bassett Road. Besides, I said, the entire row was condemned. I happened to know that. The council is completely corrupt. All Jews and Yorkshiremen. They notoriously look after their own. It was some years before I could open up in Portobello Road, because of the short lease. Mrs Cornelius told me about the place. Her children were small then.

Frank Cornelius is trying to sell Miss Brunner a Ford Fiesta. Miss Brunner points out to him that she was in the garage when the mechanic told him it was a write-off. He apologises. His memory is not what it was. I would imagine there is hardly a neuron in him unsubjected to a bath in some mind-bending acid or other. He no longer describes his body as 'speeded-up circuitry' as he did in the sixties. It seems to me that much of the circuitry is already burned out. His head hangs with superfluous skin as if he wears a larger man's face. His clothes, intended to disguise his origins and display the authority of a higher class, are growing threadbare and stained. I have more fashionable *shmatte* in my shop.

Mrs Cornelius has been in the toilet for twenty minutes. I think she could be throwing up. Her other son comes in, looks around and is about to leave. I have nothing better to do. I raise my hand to him. He comes towards me. He is too thin. His long jacket and tight trousers make him look like some kind of Teddy boy in a woman's black wig. He has on those blue two-tone shoes and a T-shirt with 'Anarchy' written on it. What can he know of Anarchy? Makhno would have gobbled him for breakfast. He resembles an overgrown Munchkin from *The Wizard of Oz*. He is trying to get into the entertainment business, his mother says. He is in touch with that rogue Auchinek. Auchinek is today a rock-and-roll manager. Yesterday he was an immigration specialist. The less said about that the better.

'Afternoon, Colonel,' says Jerry. He at least has never addressed me by anything but my full rank. 'I was looking for Cathy.'

His sister is not here. His mother, I say, is in the toilet. He looks at his watch. 'Bit early, isn't it?'

I must admit I was thinking the same.

I have never liked Jerry. At least Frank works for a living. The only one I ever had time for in that family was Catherine, and now she has become a communist! They were not my children, but I had hopes for them. Mrs Cornelius did not. She expected them to survive, nothing else. How they did it was up to them. She was of the old-fashioned cockney persuasion which felt that if you reached the age of thirteen without major illnesses, you were probably going to live until forty.

She comes out of the toilet. 'It's filthy in there,' she says. 'I had ter clean it up a bit. Someone was caught short before they got their knickers darn. 'Ello, Jerry. I thought you was at Elstree this week.'

'We wound it up early,' he said. 'Drink, Colonel?'

I look at his roll of notes, knowing it will be gone in a day or so, and wonder if I should mention the money I have loaned him over the years. Not once has he paid me back. When he was a boy I used to think he was charging me for his mother's time. Of course, business was booming in those days, and I was always open-handed. But it was the little girl I liked best. A minx, as her mother said. I still had plans then to return to my old pursuits. I got into the antique clothing line by accident, and it was meant to be a stopgap. At first I just sold military memorabilia on a stall. It did very well. Everyone wants that material. Especially the Nazi daggers. There were so many of them made. Enough for everyone, I used to think. It seemed the whole of Germany was in the SS before the war ended. Of course I had no time for the SS nor for Himmler. He perverted our ideals. He was a criminal. I have never quarrelled with that particular Nuremberg verdict. And it was sheer nonsense for him or Schnauben to suggest I had any hand in his ruthless and entirely indiscriminate killing of unwanted social elements. I was asked some questions. I answered them. Nothing more.

275

'A blacksmith makes a shovel,' I used to say. 'This does not make him a gravedigger.' How can what one talks about as a mental exercise have any bearing at all on another's attempt to make that notion an actuality? My involvement with the Nazi Party, such as it was, was entirely idealistic. Gradually, as the years went on, I began to see the weaknesses and perversions of the system, and eventually it became clear to me that the Nazi cause was lost, long before 1945. By then, of course, there was little I could do about it. I was never a fanatical follower of Hitler and, with the exception of Dachau and elsewhere, most of my connections with the party were purely social. In those heady days of 1931 it was impossible *not* to meet Nazis!

Jerry passes some notes to his mother. She makes a kissing motion and tucks them away. I am glad to see someone has benefited for once. He has been working as an extra on the set of some science fiction 'Star Opera'. He becomes the centre of their attention. Mrs Cornelius and I were once genuine stars, with our own series, but we did not talk and we were not in colour. At least in the American pictures. The German ones have disappeared. You never see them. In those days our films concentrated on subtleties of character. The plots had a strong moral content. Now it is all sensation.

Jerry talks about actors and the director as if they are his best friends. He tells anecdotes he could not possibly have witnessed. He inflates the importance of his role. He hints that he has slept with screen temptresses. He throws famous Christian names into the air like baubles. He describes the problems of fame. He blossoms into life on the attention of that seedy crowd. Hitler was the same. Why can no one ever see through these people?

Moorcock, who has already glamourised them in his cheap melodramas, seems as happy to swallow Jerry's tarnished offerings as anyone. He buys him a drink. He is clearly besotted, totally fooled, just as all his kind were in the thirties. Offer these middle-class thrill-seekers a smooth-talking gangster and they fall over themselves to report his lies. Offer them your experience, your certain knowledge of repressed truths, and they laugh at you and turn what you say into a joke. There is a fashionable way of putting these things which I have never learned. Yet if they would listen to me, they would hear so much! They are ridiculously impatient. The young are incapable of reading. They have a diet of tabloid filth and BBC indoctrination. They are so fond of attacking *Mein Kampf* (which I do not say is perfect), yet how many of them have read a paragraph, let alone a chapter?

276

At that time I accidentally met Father Stempfle, who claimed to have written most of *Mein Kampf*. As I wandered rather aimlessly through the hotel, I suddenly saw Gregor Strasser in the hotel lounge. To be precise, I heard him first, for his great, bluff Bavarian boom was famous. He was talking to an odd-looking individual who was seated in a corner, huddled deep in one of the big armchairs, trying to steady a coffee cup as he craned his mad chameleon head upwards and spoke urgently to the Nazi leader. I had never been introduced to Strasser, but I knew Röhm would vouch for me. Strasser wore a good, conservative tweed suit and looked every inch the solid South German businessman that he was. Yet his tightly cropped and shaven head revealed the other side of him. He clearly modelled his appearance on that of Mussolini.

I saw why so many favoured Strasser over Hitler as leader of the Nazi Party. Strasser's hearty manner made everyone around him feel better. Röhm had told me how Strasser was the most popular man in the Reichstag these days. Even the socialists respected him. Once he heard my story, he would be bound to help me. Hastily I tried to force a passage through the tightly packed chairs towards him. However, fate intervened. We were not to meet. Even as I called his name and began to cross the lounge, pushing between a press of people taking tea, he turned away, clapping the seated man on the shoulder. 'Herr Strasser,' I shouted. But there were too many others creating a babble in the place. He turned, calling out to a top-hatted old gentleman to wait; he was on his way. And then he was gone.

'He's avoiding you, too, eh?' said the strange creature to whom Strasser had been talking. I could guess easily who it was. I had heard of him from Röhm and some of the other SA.

I was brief with him. Clearly Strasser regarded him as a nuisance. Very few visitors to the Königshof wore a rough homespun monk's habit or, indeed, had quite such filthy fingernails. Obviously the famous Father Bernhard Stempfle who belonged to the old German hermit order of St Hieronymous. His tastes, Röhm had told me, were not always solitary. A contributor to the anti-Jewish and -Catholic press, Stempfle was also employed by Amann, Hitler's publisher. His work had a similar approach, though was a little narrower. When Amann needed someone to sharpen up Hitler's rather rambling prose, the priest was the ideal candidate. In those days it was not unusual to be both a trained journalist and a man of the cloth.

Father Stempfle had been very influential in the early days of the movement. He was the one who acted as a middleman for Hitler when he was blackmailed. I think his mistake was to get too close to the Führer. He grew unwholesomely fascinated with Hitler's private life. At my silent rebuff, he withdrew like some seedy tortoise first into his habit and then into the shadows of his seat so that it seemed someone had merely thrown an old garment down. I have never seen anyone disappear quite so naturally. The somewhat ostentatious wooden cross around his neck bounced on its rope, then his reptile head appeared above it again glaring at me in the most violent manner!

I had read some of his articles in the *VB*. He was a little fanatical on the question of Jews but basically sound. Like almost every founder member of the Nazi Party (which his vows did not allow him to join openly) he was of below average height, with brown hair and a somewhat unweathered skin. I had heard that he shared a taste for morphine with Göring and Co. His deep-set eyes and shaggy appearance reminded me a little of Lionel Barrymore in his wonderful (if not entirely accurate) rendering of Rasputin the Mad Monk. Father Stempfle had some kind of lair in the woods outside Munich.

His hand reached out to take my sleeve. His eyes betrayed a sort of malicious mirth. 'Do you have some prejudice, young man, against people of my calling?'

'Of course not, Father. I was not sure –'

'That I would have anything to do with the likes of you?'

I shook my head. Rather than draw further attention to myself I let him draw me down to the chair beside him.

As soon as I was seated, he acted as if I were about to attack him, pulling himself back and looking wildly around for help. 'Who are you? Explain yourself!' Only when I introduced myself did he grow calmer, but in spite of initiating our meeting he remained strangely uncomfortable. I did not mind his refusal to shake hands. I think he suspected me of being Jewish. Indeed, I think he probably suspected everyone of being Jewish.

He began muttering to me in a nervous manner, and whenever I tried to lean forward to hear him better, he would flap his hands. His general behaviour was eccentric. I supposed it characteristic of hermits that they should not feel particularly at ease in large crowds, but he was by all accounts not the most reclusive of Hieronymites.

278

He had spent time at Röhmannsvilla. I understood from Röhm that he only occasionally acted as a padre, usually when some sensitive party matter was involved.

Röhm and Stempfle, I recalled, did not get on particularly well. I could see why. I sensed something ungenerous and self-referential about the man. He was very brusque. When he did start to speak, he allowed no interruption. Stempfle, too, it emerged, was on the search for money. He had been to the Brown House and found it empty of anyone he knew. Claiming he didn't have a penny, Strasser had told him to ask Amann. Stempfle had already been to Amann, who was out of town. The monk had been everywhere. They were threatening, he said, to cut off his electricity.

I was trying to think of a way of asking him why he did not move to a cheaper cave when the waiter came over and told me I had a long-distance telephone call. Did I wish to take it in my room? Glad of the opportunity to leave the miserable priest, with a quick apology I wished him luck and went swiftly up the stairs to my room on the first floor.

I picked up my instrument. It was full of static and half-heard conversations in a dozen languages. Somewhere in the background I could hear a woman's voice, then a man speaking Italian, and then the woman again. I had expected Tom Morgan. But perhaps he had passed my number on.

'Maddy?'

'Maddy!' This was a shriek which shredded the static to a barely audible whisper. 'Why would that double-crossing bitch be calling you? To laugh at you? To tell you that her new boyfriend is a better lover? That he wants to kill you?'

Unmistakably La Sarfatti.

I apologised even as she asked me when I had left Albania. The line faded again, and her voice became the distant shriek of a frustrated eagle. I was astonished to hear Albania mentioned again.

'I have never been to Albania,' I told her. I was not sure she could still hear me.

She faded back in. 'We all thought you were dead,' she said. 'Didn't you know? Il Duce has put a price on your head!'

I was unable to take this seriously. 'What am I? An enemy of the state? Or does he think there was something between me and Rachele?'

'Something between you and Rachele? Aha! I always knew the

279

bitch was too good to be true. That might explain it. We were told you'd sold all our military secrets to the Albanians.'

'I have no sexual involvement with Signora Mussolini! The only military secrets I know are my own. My own inventions. I could scarcely renege on myself.' I now remembered the missing case. No doubt the thing, containing miscellaneous spare drawings and photographs, had been stolen by Albanian agents when we transferred in Austria. They might well have been following me. I was a fool to be so naive. Now the pictures, which were of no particular use without explanations, were in enemy hands. They might even think the models were real!

I told her that it could all be easily cleared up. She must talk to Mussolini – or get him to talk to me.

'Why would he talk to you, of all people, darling? He went to such elaborate lengths to get rid of you.'

Her story was becoming increasingly ludicrous. If I had not had the telegram from Tom Morgan I might not have believed a word.

'That's nonsense,' I said. 'Why would Il Duce want to get rid of one of his key men?'

'Because he's taken a fancy to his key man's woman? You idiot, Max. He got you out of the way so that he could have a clear field with that little American bitch.'

'Maddy?'

'It suited her, too. She hates you now. I tried to explain everything, but she wouldn't listen. Darling, I'm your only friend here!'

It seemed to me that Sarfatti had been intriguing far too much in Rome and that she had been poisoning Maddy's mind against me. I felt attacked by an entire Amazon army. But why should I believe La Sarfatti? She must have several ulterior motives for calling me.

'But my projects,' was all I could think to say before the line grew noisy again. I had the impression she was telling me I had served my turn in some elaborate strategy of Il Duce. I did not for a moment think it likely, yet I had been surprised at Mussolini's sudden decision for me to go to Germany and at Maddy's complete refusal to see me.

She began to reply. She spoke of Spain and Greece and Albania, of a way to convince them there was absolutely no point in trying to resist an Italian army. Something about 'psychological warfare'. It was another of her concoctions. She was addicted to intrigue and gossip.

280

'. . . convinced the OVRA had caught up with you . . . Austria . . . the Albanians . . .' Fewer and fewer words came through. Eventually I broke the connection.

I was cutting myself a line of cocaine from my diminishing store when a knock came at my door. I was expecting no one. I slipped my materials into a drawer and got up to answer.

At any other time I might have received my next visitor with considerable enthusiasm. I had dreamed of her ever since I had seen her on the Munich Express. But now I was alarmed, reluctant to admit her. She stood in the corridor frowning. Her wonderful hair caught the light from the window. She was dressed in layered silks of pale blue, yellow and light green. Her grey eyes held a slightly puzzled amusement. Her perfect skin glowed. Her perfect hand reached towards me.

'Good afternoon, Colonel Pyat,' she said.

TWENTY–SIX

I hardly noticed she had used my Russian rank and name. I kissed the tips of those well-shaped fingers. I stepped back to admit her to my room. I had anticipated this moment more than once, but now I was only shocked.

'Good evening, Fräulein von Ruckstühl,' I replied.

'Oh, I'm still Kitty to you, Prince Maxim.' She knew the effect she had and was enjoying my reaction. 'I nursed a crush on you for years. I used to ask Esmé about you. Don't worry. I'm not here to propose a liaison.'

I was not at that moment disappointed.

I apologised for the size of my room as I offered her one of my chairs. She shook her head. With swift, impatient grace she moved to the window and opened it slightly.

'I thought I'd better tip you off,' she said, taking out a silver case from her slim leather purse and lighting a flat Turkish cigarette. 'My mother is nuts.'

'Come,' I said. 'I was unable to get in touch with you. I had no intention of abandoning either of you. Her distress is understandable.'

'That was for the best. She took up with an Armenian fur trader, and he got us both to Leipzig. Then she met Herr Oberhauser, and we moved to Munich. He's stinking rich – or was the last I heard – and gave her everything she wanted. Except one thing, of course.'

'A child?' I thought she had mentioned a son.

'That brat's not yours. It was you she wanted. All her frustration turned to hatred. She's paid detectives, clipping agencies. She's got a full-sized file on your activities since you left Constance. Scrapbooks and everything. You'd be flattered. The French airship swindle. The American airship swindle. You seemed to specialise for a while.'

She put another cigarette into her holder and I lit it for her. Her gorgeous red lips were arched in a bow, an almost admiring smile.

'I assure you, Kitty, I am not a swindler. I have, I will admit, been a little gullible on occasions. But that is my idealism.'

'Believe me, Max, I don't give a crap about your motives. I really am just here to warn you. My mother's close to Herr Hitler. He used to come to our house. She's helped him in all sorts of ways. I think she's got a crush on him. She used to hold his head in her lap and stroke him. Pretty sickening stuff. Apparently he has lots of older women who like to look after him. A creep, of course. But that's beside the point. She knows you're Jewish, and she intends to let everyone else into the secret.'

'You mean she *believes* I am Jewish.' The implications of Kitty's news were almost too much to take in.

'Well, whatever you say. The old cow thinks she has proof. She says you were born in Odessa in the Jewish Quarter. She found that out from some relative of yours. A cousin? A girl?'

'Wanda is dead,' I said. 'And so is Esmé. I was born in Kiev of old Russian stock.'

'Well, she's got it all down there in black and white. You have a little time. She wants to go to the Brown House and hand it over to the Führer personally. But he's not likely to be back from Berlin for a while. You can easily clear up any business you might have in Munich. He's not likely to have time for her just now. That's it. I just came to do you a favour. She says your real name is Crick.'

'I have never heard it before. She thinks it is a Jewish name? My name is the one I gave her. I have since Anglicised it to Peters. There is nothing sinister about that. In modern Europe it's no longer fashionable to be connected with the Russian aristocracy. In fact, it is positively dangerous. I am a Christian of the Greek persuasion. I was born in Kiev and moved to St Petersburg. Certainly I knew people in Odessa. I spent my holidays there as a child! And I would, no doubt, have bumped into some Jews. Indeed, I had a friend –'

'I don't give a shit if you're a wop, a dago, a Yid, a Yank or all four,' she said suddenly. I was alarmed by the coarseness of the language issuing from that perfect mouth. Her manner was the norm among the young in Germany. A cynicism, an aggression, a hardness was cultivated by these girls. You could not, I suppose, blame them, given the world they had grown up in.

Kitty put out her cigarette and stepped rapidly towards me. Her golden face moved close to mine. I smelled something delicate on her breath. She kissed me lightly on the lips.

'You don't want to get in too deep with the Nazis anyway,' she said. 'You might find it's hard to get out again. They have a lot of funny friends.'

She opened the door, paused, shrugged and was gone. Almost immediately I regretted not seizing my opportunity. She was ten times the woman her mother was. She was right. I had made a mistake in returning to Munich. I cursed my own impatience. I had never needed a real friend more.

Mrs Cornelius sits in the corner near the dartboard. Her sons have disappeared. She looks up at the television over the bar and sips a small port and lemon. 'Egypt was your moment, Ive,' she tells me. 'You should 'ave turned rahnd and gone 'ome.' I cannot follow her. They are showing a newsflash. A politician has been shot in Cairo.

Egypt, I will admit, was a watershed. In some ways I still feel as if I am living on borrowed time. I had grown reconciled to death there. I had begun to desire it. If Kolya had not rescued me I would have been blinded, then maimed, then left to die, rotting, in al-Habashiya's garden, mulch for his cruel roses. I have been in a thousand nightmares in the course of my life, most of them before I was forty. Sometimes they merge together. They know only so many ways, after all, of brutalising a human being. But perhaps God was training me for my task. What I learned in Egypt helped me survive in Dachau.

'Time!' cries Collier suddenly, his head below the bar. 'Time, ladies.' The Bishop looks at his watch. 'It's nowhere near Time, Mo.'

Scowling, Collier straightens up. He tells Beesley he was quoting Eliot.

The crowd in the pub thins out now as the nine-to-fivers go back to their jobs. Soon there are only the customers who do not work regular hours. They consist chiefly of Irish drunkards, Caribbean pimps and drug dealers, cockney scroungers, hippie layabouts, complaining old crones, whining pensioners, unemployed criminals and people like ourselves, who were here when the area was more respectable. Not so long ago it seems you never saw a black face in this pub. And everyone drank out of glasses or mugs. Now you are offered the choice of the bottle or a glass. Another blow for progress and against civilisation.

Almost every evening we saw pretty much the same crowd, reading its papers, playing darts and shove-halfpenny, intermittently chatting. The pub made a profit. Everyone was happy. But now jukeboxes, stand-up nights, stripteasers fill the place with noise. We are all consumers and consumed. They tell us we cannot afford to slow down. In the old days the carpets and curtains might have grown a little threadbare with the years, but the quality was unmistakable. Nowadays we see no such thing as quality. They know only cheap, bad ways of making things. We are soon due for extinction at this rate. We are creating a generation that will not read or write but will spend its time picking consumer goods from a TV catalogue. All it needs is a picture to point at. The Americans lead the field in this, which is probably why the Voice of America seems to grow increasingly less intelligent as the years go by. Once they addressed me as an adult. Now I am a ten-year-old. And as they speak less and less of any substance, their voices grow steadily louder. They substitute volume for content. Is it because they have to yell across those wide spaces?

I came to relish solitude in the desert.

I could not go back to the United States. Yet I still long for Hollywood as it was in its Golden Age, in the years of my fame. Perhaps if I had been content with fantasy, I would still be there, an honoured has-been taking cameo parts on *Rawhide* and *I Love Lucy*. But my interest was always in reality. I had vision and skill. I wanted only to put my talents to practical use, for the good of humanity. My cities would fly. The world would be rich with growing things. Disease would be banished. Death would be defeated. There would be no pain. No polluted air. No fear. No hunger. No melancholy. Individuals would all work together for the common good. None among us would be disadvantaged in favour of another. The slavery of interest, of usury, would be abolished.

I think my mistake was to put too much trust in others.

Visionaries like myself and Röhm were inclined in our innocence to believe we should support politicians to fulfil our dreams. But politicians are by nature compromisers. This means that they are forever looking for the middle ground. Therefore they always disappoint us. But what moves societies forward are leaders who disdain the happy mean, who seek the extremes of social experiment. Very rarely are we given a Mussolini or a Hitler, whose ideas match our own, who are not compromisers. Yet even these, as I believe I have shown, are subject to the machinations and petty ambitions of followers who eventually bring them low. Even these fail in the end.

I suppose I am one of the very few people who ever heard Hitler say he was sorry.

Röhmannsvilla became a retreat for me. Nowhere else was I welcome. I got there as soon as I could, taking my luggage. Tom Morgan had been in touch telling me to lie low. He would try to establish my innocence, but I heard nothing. Too many other things were going on. The whole of Europe was growing increasingly agitated. Political assassinations became unremarkable, the order of the day. More and more were out of work. Civil strife increased. First the great Austrian banks went down. Then the German banks were closed. Then the great Allianz insurance company. Every institution that had been rock-solid a few days earlier was now discovered to be a crumbling façade hiding a stinking mountain of unpayable debts. Newspapermen were being moved to new locations. Nazis who had never had their names in the newspaper were giving interviews to the foreign press, which meant that Putzi was kept permanently in Berlin. Only Röhm had any time for me. I was his comfort, he said. His relief.

Röhm was not the swaggering gamecock later journalists made of him when he could no longer defend himself. *Time* magazine might refer to him as a 'plug-ugly pederast', but that was because his enemy Goebbels had taken over the propaganda arm from Strasser, whom he hated. Röhm usually disdained interviews. He was actually a subtle, contemplative human being who had reasons for every position he held. One of the reasons he had never wanted anything to do with women, he said, was because they really did soften a soldier. A man who gives up any of his power to a woman immediately loses a disproportionate amount of his power; useful, directed, positive, aggressive power. The same power in a woman becomes diffused, negative, random, passive.

'They waste every part of a man.' He knew that I was very fond of women. I think he believed he could persuade me to his viewpoint. Of course, his main concern was Hitler. He was not the only one who continued to worry that Hitler's obsession with Angela Raubal was seriously weakening him in every way, just at the moment when triumph could have been his. Even Goebbels, the great womaniser, believed that. Himmler, Röhm told me, hated her for her influence over the Führer. Everyone had asked Hitler to give

Geli up, but he would rather have lost his chance of greatness than break with her.

'The bitch is a drag anchor on the entire movement,' Röhm complained. 'If she loses us the Chancellorship, she goes in the sack and into the river like any other alley cat that becomes a nuisance.'

His words were often blood-curdling but spoken so casually or so softly that they contradicted themselves. His penchant for extravagant language earned him his reputation for braggadocio. I never, of course, saw him speak to the Reichstag.

Several of our visitors that August grumbled about Geli. All loyal Nazis, mostly 'old fighters' who had followed Hitler from the beginning, they did not so much blame the girl as what they called 'the situation'. From the letters and drawings he had seen, Röhm knew what Geli was prepared to give Hitler, and he knew what a powerful effect this had on him.

'He's addicted to her,' said Röhm, not for the first time. 'And I suspect she's addicted to him by now. That's how it works. *Folie à deux.* You shouldn't arouse such huge feelings in a woman. They can't handle it. They either go to pieces or try for their own power. She's got her teeth around his cock, and she's dragging him wherever she wants him to go. God knows what she's telling people. If any of our opponents get through to her and she blabs, it will ruin him. One statement to Hindenburg, show him one picture, and the old fart will turn completely against Hitler. He's none too flattering about him now! Alf might as well concede defeat before ever trying to run for the Chancellorship.

'The public will forgive a lot, Mashi. They'll turn a blind eye to more. But, well, as you know, we're not talking about honest fun between boys here, or putting the odd little chicky up the stick. We're talking piss and shit, to be frank. Whips and shackles! And that goes too far. That stuff's not likely to endear the big industrialists to him, and that's who *he's* going to bed with these days. The bastard's sucked more Big Business dicks in the past six months than most whores see in a lifetime.'

That was the most he ever told me about Hitler's private life at that time. I could easily imagine the rest. At the age of thirty-one I think I can safely say I was familiar with most of life's diversions. Anything I had not learned from al-Habashiya was not worth knowing, according to Röhm. I did not, of course, tell him the whole story. That was impossible for me then, and it remains impossible.

There are some things which no sane human being wishes to relive. My time with Röhm during that unsettling period had more to do with refinement than discovery.

'I am besotted with you,' Röhm admitted happily one evening when just the two of us lay upon the thin mattress placed upon the wide marble slab which was his bed. 'I can't tell you what a comfort you are, Mashi, in these difficult days.'

He would speak to me vaguely about Berlin politics, his conversations with General von Schleicher, I. G. Farben and others. They were all courting him and Strasser now. If he wanted to, he could dine out every night of the week at some aristocrat's or general's house. 'Strasser's always been able to get on with those people. A few months ago they wouldn't have let the rest of us be waiters in their clubs. Now the army's coming round. Half the staff are already on our side. Some are open Nazis. They like the idea of a People's Army.'

Röhm believed that the public's eyes were at last opening to the dangers facing Germany and the solutions that he and his friends presented. 'They're getting nervous, these big boys. Funk, Cuno, Wolf, von Schroeder, Diehn, Thyssen, Bechstein and the rest are falling over themselves to meet Hitler in the Alps, at Berchtesgaden, in railway sidings, abandoned warehouses, old factories. Anywhere the press can't catch them. They don't want to be *seen* with Hitler any more than he wants to be seen with them. The party rank and file wouldn't understand how we're exploiting Big Business, and we couldn't afford to explain. But it makes me uncomfortable. My only consolation is what I'll do to the bastards when the power's in my hands. They fear a threat to their comfortable lives. They're afraid Germany will fall to the Bolsheviks. They can't see she can as easily fall to us and that we are no better friends of Big Business than the Bolshies. They're all beginning to shit their pants. That's why they began courting us, giving us money as a kind of insurance, thinking it will buy them their liberty when the revolution comes! They offer compromises before we even state our terms. It always amazes me, Mashi, how eager most people are to give up an advantage when they have almost nothing to be afraid of. Frequently, fearing no more than some minor social embarrassment, they will kill themselves, rather than face the disapproval of their fellows. Those bastards lust after approval the same way I lust after you! It makes them tame and easy to deal with.' Such thoughts reassured him. He sipped his champagne and smoked his cigar. He stroked my hair, confiding in me as another man might share his thoughts with a wife. 'You'd be surprised how many sheep one good dog can herd. No disease travels faster and infects more thoroughly than fear. Fear's a wonderful instrument which you only have to use for a while. Soon people develop a habit of obedience, which becomes in time self-regulation, if not self-discipline.' This amused him. 'That's when we shall have our German utopia, Mashi. We'll do it in less than one generation.'

'Do you wish to die?' God asked.

'Yes, God,' I said. 'I wish to die.'

'Do you wish to die painfully?' God asked.

'Yes, God,' I said. 'I wish to die painfully.'

Only through obedience that is automatic and absolute can one find a centre. I think of it as a core of calmness which is all but inviolate, perhaps the soul. A rare being, a god indeed, can find its way to the soul to torture and even destroy that. The true artists of their kind. The true geniuses. Had I the disposition, I could myself have been such a genius.

A wonderful dream. I was so relieved to be back within it. Life at the villa somehow redeemed my Egyptian captivity with al-Habashiya. Röhm would have given me anything I wanted. He called me by pet names. He called me *El Vaquero Enmascarado*, and indeed I often wore a mask. He loved the mystery of a mask. He was in love with my eyes. They were reflective pools, he said, in which to drown all his cares. The hardness of his hands, gentle as his touch could often be, made my own skin feel a thousand times softer to me. I became deliriously pliable. I had never willingly succumbed to such a force, even with Kolya, my spiritual partner.

I had been anxious, thinking I could be wasting time with Röhm, but I came to realise this interlude was exactly what we both needed. We were cut off from all modern communication, guarded by the gigantic dark green spears of a Teutonic pine forest, enjoying the gentle music of a broad, mountain river, one warm, glorious day following another. Returning from Munich or Berlin, Röhm brought me gramophone records of all the latest jazz tunes, as well as the French chanteuses he enjoyed. Röhm possessed a large senti-mental streak that he never revealed to any but his closest friends. He also brought me books and magazines. These helped me catch up on all the latest topics. He even found me some issues of the

Sexton Blake Library dealing with matters of the moment, such as striking miners, Arab slavers, the machinations of Big Business and the mysterious death of a man on a London tram. They were in English, so Röhm could not read them. He did not mind. He also brought films back with him. Berlin, he said, was a positive treasure house of erotica. He enthused endlessly over repetitive scenes in which one comely set of buttocks followed another set of massive genitalia into a perpetually pumping, forever ejaculating, future. I could not enjoy them, fearing that the next film he brought home would be one of those I had been lured into making in Egypt. I was always relieved when the scenes began to run, and I was not presented with moving pictures of my own poor sore organs inserted over and over again between Esmé's ever-yearning orifices. I summoned little enthusiasm for even the most artistic of films and rather hoped that my apparent boredom would discourage him. The films also reminded me of my worries concerning the Baroness. Was she still in Munich? Did she still intend to turn me in?

After an absence of almost a week, Röhm came bustling back. He had been in Berlin, he said, then Munich. Hitler was driving him crazy. I asked him if there had been any messages for me at either the Königshof or the Brown House. He admitted that he had forgotten to ask. 'But I did receive a visit from an old friend of yours at the Brown House.'

'Putzi? Captain Göring?'

Like a kindly uncle attending a favourite nephew's birthday party, Röhm grinned at my puzzlement. 'Oh no. A much older friend than that.' He was still wearing his light travelling cape. As he flung it off he threw a large buff envelope on to the sofa beside me. 'She brought me a present. She'd been trying to see Hitler for a week. He's still in Berlin being an arsehole while his girlfriend's screwing the chauffeur. Your friend's going to Vienna, she said, with her husband, so asked me to pass this on to the Führer, who hadn't had time to see her. Naturally I told her it would be in his hands within twenty-four hours. She went to Vienna a happy woman. I think when she gets back next month, she expects me to present her with a wallet made of your delicious skin, Mashi.'

Sipping his champagne cocktail, he watched me as I sat down heavily on the couch. Because of the heat I was virtually naked and felt suddenly vulnerable. He said nothing. He merely went on watching me, loosening his jerkin as I undid the envelope and drew out that dossier of lies and misunderstandings which the former Baroness von Ruckstühl, Frau Oberhauser, claimed was the true story of my life. I felt sick. Here were all the French reports accusing me of deliberately setting out to ruin honest people. Here were stories of my 'swindling' the Turks, stories which claimed I was a member of Stavisky's gang, a Jew from Odessa. The lies were endless, yet all supported by alleged facts and offered in the most authoritative tones.

I began to stammer that I was a victim of a long-standing campaign, that she had manufactured all this material.

'I'm getting used to this sort of thing,' said Röhm comfortably. He came and sat down next to me. 'Let's have a look at it together, Mashi, shall we? What a naughty little type you seem to have been . . .'

It must have cost a fortune to assemble that dossier. I was astonished at its detail, a careful and clever selection of material designed to show me in the worst light. The praise, for instance, that I had received for my political speeches in the USA was mentioned nowhere, nor was my extensive work with the knights of the Ku Klux Klan. My acting career was all but ignored. Mucker Hever's version of events was given where my steam-car was concerned. He was quoted extensively, but with no mention of his jealousy. My misfortunes were presented as if I had planned a series of elaborate swindles. Yet I had always earned my living honestly. My own trusting character, which rarely questioned a contract, or indeed demanded one, was what had let me down, not some venal ambition.

'We couldn't have done better ourselves,' said Röhm. 'This is OGPU quality.' He spoke with some humour. To my enormous relief he understood the dossier to be a fake. 'You've obviously offended some powerful Bolshies, Max.'

I thought at once of Brodmann. Obviously the new Frau Oberhauser could not have put the dossier together herself. Brodmann and his Chekists had compiled the file and passed it on to her. They intended to ruin my status with the Nazis.

I saw Brodmann recently in the pub. I needed to have words with him, but he was always too quick for me to confront. Passing the Soviet Embassy in Bayswater, I pointed him out to Mrs Cornelius. She said it could be any old Russian Jew. It could be me, she said. She knows how to upset me.

Generous as ever, she begins to distribute her son's largesse.

291

'Double vodka, Ivan?' she says, waving a fiver. 'Same again all round.' I take the money and go up to the bar. Mo Collier is glancing at a book while he pretends to wash glasses. It is called *The Anarchist's Guide to Applied Terrorism.* These untried young men think revolutionary politics is a romantic game. One cudgel landing a few times across his narrow little bottom and he would soon discover what kind of game it is. Personality disappears under punishment. The Communists and the National Socialists did not believe in babying their political opponents. It was the nature of the age. Only the flyers had time for chivalry. On the ground and in the streets it was total war. But what the history books will not admit is that we were often defending ourselves. We were forced to fight fire with fire.

Collier ignores me and my proffered note. Suddenly he picks up a brass handbell and begins to ring it. 'Time!' he yells furiously. 'Time!'

I put the money in my pocket.

'There's one thing I am sure of,' said Röhm after we had looked at the file. 'You're not Jewish. I can smell a Jew at a hundred paces, and you don't smell like a Jew. You smell like an Italian-American. Believe me, it's absolutely distinctive. But it would be bad news for you if Hitler, or worse Himmler, saw this. They're like Father Stempfle. Anyone who isn't pale as a corpse and with a shock of blond hair is potentially a Jew. This, I'll admit, makes most of us potential Jews. We're going to have to start offering more precise definitions if we're going to deal seriously with the problem of separating citizens from non-citizens.'

'They would believe me Jewish just because a crazy woman has accused me? Just because I have Mediterranean looks?'

'Some of them will believe you're a Jew if you can walk and talk and count up to ten.' Röhm laughed heartily and gave me a friendly punch. 'And if they thought you'd been inside the Brown House! Oy vey! They'd be looking for a Jerusalem colonel to cashier on the spot.' He made as if to flick a cigarette lighter. That was SA code for a gun. 'No, Mashi, I've no intention of losing you just yet.'

By this I understood that he was not going to pass the file on. 'Oh, I'll do what I've done before in situations like this. Usually, when someone's discovered to their horror that some local SA boss is of the Spartan persuasion, I pass on a page or two of the more innocuous "evidence". Just looking at that makes it clear the person is exaggerating. They seem to be the lunatics and nit-pickers. That way if she asks Hitler about it, he'll say he's seen it and dismissed it. She won't be able to pursue it, and everything will be fine. There's nothing to it.'

I told him I would be for ever in his debt.

He smiled that shy little smile of his. 'Oh,' he said, 'repayment shouldn't be too arduous for you.'

My relief was enormous. Our celebration was extensive. The cocaine consumption alone was staggering! That same night, a couple of hours before dawn, a car called for Röhm. He had to go back to Berlin. I was rather pleased. I would need time to recover from his somewhat excessive demands.

'Time!' cries Collier. The sound of his bell would cut through even the happiest ambience. Here it sounds as if it tolls for the end of salvation. Grey heads rise up. Bottles are lowered or hastily lifted.

'Your glasses, gentlemen, please. Look to your glasses!'

This English 'closing time' is a nuisance. Mrs Cornelius offers Collier some incoherent insult. 'An' they say the Nazis was tyrants!' She takes my arm. 'Come on, Ivan. We'll 'ave a drink at 'ome.'

Outside the sun is still trying to break through. We stand on the concrete pavement near the public toilets while Jerry and Frank reassure their mother they will be visiting her soon. Billy Beesley rolls from the newsagent removing the paper from two Mars bars. He has eaten one before he rejoins us. A little brown stuff, like blood, trickles into his jowls. 'Well,' he says, 'I have some parishioners to visit. I'll say pip-pip for the mo.' Miss Brunner, it seems, has already left. We watch Beesley's stately mince as he disappears into the crowd.

''E looks like 'e's found himself another mark,' says Mrs Cornelius without much relish. ''E's only been out a week. Poor cow 'ooever she is. Anyone deserves better than Billy.'

She and I cross the road and continue down Blenheim Crescent. Half the houses on the other side are boarded up. I hear there is some plan to build a new luxury complex. Who will occupy it? The gypsies? The blacks? The old council houses are no longer good enough for their tenants! It makes me sick. Those people would still be grubbing in the dirt for insects to eat if it were not for the 10 per cent or so of us who are remotely civilised. And they say they have a right to better living conditions! What qualifications have they for these rights? That they were born? In that case the rats and

293

mice have rights. They, too, were born. Let us make sure they are housed in five-star hotels.

'Well, look 'oo it isn't,' says Mrs Cornelius.

The frail, thin figure of Major Nye is making its way up Blenheim Crescent towards us accompanied by another, slightly bulkier figure. Both wear khaki raincoats belted at the waist. They have bowler hats and umbrellas, pinstriped trousers and well-polished black shoes and wear the same regimental tie. It is all they have left of an empire they once defended with all their finest idealism, courage and discipline.

They raise their hats when they see Mrs Cornelius.

'Hello, old boy,' says Major Nye to me. 'We were rather hoping we might bump into you when we didn't find Mrs C at home. We knew we were a bit late for the pub. We've been having fish and chips in Ladbroke Grove.' His skin is so thinly stretched over his almost fleshless head that it seems transparent, marking the veins and bones, tracing the progress of his blood. His pale grey eyes are as amiable and as baffled as they have been since Suez, when his entire understanding of his responsibilities changed. Beside him, a little browner, just a touch plumper, but otherwise almost a twin, is his old regimental colonel, Jim Pym. They have been enjoying their monthly reunion. Both men are so fragile these days that I cannot see them continuing this pleasant ceremony for much longer. They will have to speak by telephone, I suppose. And then one will die and the other will die. Their wives are already dead. Their children, I gather, have mostly emigrated. The best they can look forward to is being accepted by the Chelsea Pensioners. At least it will give them the chance to wear a uniform again.

Like myself, Major Nye has been on the sidelines of some monumental events, but I do not believe he ever played the same kind of crucial role as I played in the rising dominance of the Nazi Party. I personally will be very sorry when I can no longer chat with him. We are of a similar age and have had many similar experiences around the world. Also, of course, we were both in love with the same woman. That is why he still comes to Ladbroke Grove.

We return to her basement for tea.

Major Nye always called Hitler 'that grubby little agitator'. He had no time for Röhm, sadly, or most of the others. 'Göring seemed jolly enough on the surface, but frankly I never had patience for any of them.' He believed that the best in Germany had been wiped out by the War. Only the cripples, the walking wounded, the exiles were left. The business people were almost as bad. 'They possessed a very low standard of intelligence,' he says. 'The brains had either been killed or had enough sense to stay out of the limelight. German government was in the hands of a few survivors. It wasn't fair to punish them the way the French did. France just wanted the rest of the Allies to hold the poor bastard down while she kicked him a few times. She's never recovered from being beaten so often by Bismarck. In French history, Napoleon was a fluke. Not that he and Hitler didn't make precisely the same mistakes. Men of destiny always do, don't they, old boy? At least,' he added, 'Napoleon had had the sense not to let businessmen or the army make political decisions. They were the absolute worst people at that. Any time business or the army dominate politics, that's when you might as well pack your bags and leave. The one thing the British Army understands,' he says, 'is to stay out of the brawl. Getting into it was the German Army's greatest mistake. They should have held aloof. But I suppose they were too afraid of Röhm.'

He and Colonel Pym often discuss matters of strategy.

Mrs Cornelius takes down her best teaset. She balances the teapot on a pile of magazines while she clears a space on her coffee table. 'Sorry about ther smell,' she says. 'I think it's ther cat.'

'Well, it's always been a mystery to me,' says Colonel Pym, 'why any decent army officer should not have taken one look at Herr Hitler and seen at once what a little turd he was.'

''E was vulnerable,' says Mrs Cornelius, searching for her biscuits. 'That's orlways a plus in a politician. It's ther same with them pop stars, innit? Women recognise it. Men c'n sense it, but they never know wot it is. 'Itler could've been knocked art at any time, but they all looked after 'im. Why d'yer fink them rich old ladies loved to mother ther little bugger? They thought 'e was a sensitive artiste. 'E was the Liberace of 'is day.'

We are silent. Not one of us can think of a response.

During the following weeks Röhm had certain rooms in his villa set aside for meetings. He made me stay away from them. People would be driven up to one particular door and admitted. They never saw the rest of the place. Their impression was of an austere military base.

Röhm said the meetings would have bored me. He admitted that most of the time he himself was bored. 'But if we're to defeat the

Antichrist,' he said jokingly, 'we must make friends even with swine. At least for the moment.' He was clear-headed about his political ambitions. I did not agree with all his views, but there was no doubting his integrity.

Röhm shared this with Strasser, whom I met at last. The great-hearted chemist came to dinner with two or three of his people. After the others had left, I joined the two friends for drinks. Strasser was charming. He smelled of the most expensive cologne. His clothes were of excellent English cut. Strasser made me feel very comfortable. He had seen my films. He did not, as some of the SA chiefs did, take me for Röhm's fancy boy. We discussed literature. I told him about the English fiction I read. I mentioned G. H. Teed and Anthony Skene. He himself was a great fan of Schiller. 'He is humane,' he said, 'in a way that Goethe is not.'

Strasser was the greatest gentleman who ever led a political party. His terrible mistake was to remain true to his ideals. That, I fear, could be the sad epitaph for many of us.

I will not forget those evenings of camaraderie during the late summer of 1931 when it was still possible to plan for a golden future, to dream, as they say, the impossible dream. I feel I was privileged. The threat of the Baroness laid to rest, the mystery of Mussolini's behaviour at least partially explained, I felt able to relax.

The talk that evening soon returned to Hitler. Among these people, Hitler's ups and downs were a constant subject of debate.

'He's a bloody Austrian,' said Röhm. 'What do you expect? He's sloppy and easygoing most of the time. He just happens to have this charm, this gift. We can't switch it on and off whenever we feel like it. We can't twist the public round our little fingers. And so we're annoyed! We're jealous.'

'I'm annoyed,' said Strasser, passing a big hand across his head, 'because he's compromising every principle we ever stood for. That's why I'm annoyed, Röhm.'

'He's pretending to compromise.' Röhm poured champagne for us. 'You know him. He'll soon bite the hands that feed him. You worry too much about that. After all, you're prepared to sort out an arrangement with Farben.'

'That's to do with my business. And none of us argued against the strategy of taking money, if offered, and doing precisely what we want to do with it. I just wonder what cattle trading Hitler is doing on *my* behalf!'

'I don't mind him putting his tongue up a few arseholes,' said Röhm. 'It's what's going on in Prinzregentenstrasse that I'm bothered by. Apparently there was another row recently. All the neighbours heard it. Her mother was involved at some stage. She's on Hitler's side. She'd have to be. The scandal would be even worse for her, wouldn't it – Hitler's sister helping him bonk her own daughter, his niece. And what bonking! She wants him to pay for singing lessons in Vienna. He wants to keep her with him, though he's never there. He suspects something – and he's right. He can't let her go. He's terrified she'll tell someone else about their private lives. Geli knows her power all right. She's already threatening to send his letters to his "new friends", people who are on the brink of giving us millions. If they see some of the mildest of the pictures I've seen, they might offer to buy a few for their own collections, but I don't think they'll be the supporters Hitler needs. She's already picked up the phone and rung Thyssen. He didn't know who the hell she was, luckily, and put the receiver down on her. That's what I heard from Hess. Of course, Hess doesn't take any of it very seriously. He sees everything as a kind of play going on in front of his eyes. He's a perpetual audience! He never criticises. That's why Alf loves him so much.'

Strasser found this amusing. 'Adolf's in love, Ernst. Give the man a break. Lovers' tiffs. You're radiating jealousy! You can't stand it because he's taken up with females! You think he's a pervert, don't you?'

Röhm took this in good part. He chuckled. 'I won't be the only one who thinks it, if she's as good as her word. Look, I have a very clear idea of what's going on.'

'You've been hiding under their bed, Ernst!'

'The bed's probably the only safe place in that apartment. Believe me, I know precisely what happens. She's already told half her girlfriends. And I know what she thinks about it. It doesn't even suit her. I also know what she thinks she's going to do about it.'

'You've got hold of some of those Soviet microphones and put them in the flower vases. You've got a two-way mirror and a film camera. God in heaven, Ernst, these are the spy fantasies of people like Himmler! Are you buggering the SS chauffeur? Is that how you're finding all this stuff out?'

Again Röhm could not help grinning broadly. He shook his head. 'Oh, better than that, Strass,' he said. 'I'm buggering her confessor.'

Strasser said something about preferring to see his Schiller onstage, but it was clear Röhm had made an impression.

The mood of the evening became almost sombre. Röhm suggested I retire. He said that there were important party matters he and Strasser had to discuss, and I shouldn't be burdened with them.

Major Nye was in Berlin while I was in retreat at Röhmannsvilla. He said that he had never known a city not at war in quite such a dither; it was as if there was nothing to do and everything to do. Political strategies had grown so complex there wasn't a single individual who could be sure of anything. The best they could hope for was a wiping out of the war debt, a chance to start again. Daily the Communists and Socialists introduced increasingly radical bills into the Reichstag, which Hitler would immediately quash. Strasser, working within the system, consistently attempted, sometimes with Communist connivance, to put his socialistic ideas into law. Röhm was behind him. They were now at constant odds with Frick, Göring and Goebbels. Hitler, as usual, was in the middle, unable to make up his mind whom to support. He seemed incapable of uniting his disparate elements. Nye believed Hitler deliberately fostered this bickering between his lieutenants, but I am inclined to agree with Röhm: Hitler hated making decisions. He asked everyone's advice and then could not reconcile the opposing ideas. So he did nothing. When he was not standing in some remote forest clearing reassuring one of the captains of industry, he was utterly involved with Geli Raubal. Nye had heard this from both Strasser and Himmler. Neither man was happy with the situation.

'Strasser was the only one I could talk to. Radical as he was, he was sane and fundamentally decent. Of course, he was obsessed with the Jewish Question, like all of them. I told him there wouldn't be a Jewish Question if there were not a German Question. That was precisely my view about Ireland and England. I mean, you can't just chuck people out after they've stopped being useful to you, can you? No decent firm would do that, let alone a nation. Well, Strasser saw what I meant, and I think he pretty much agreed with me. He didn't hate anyone, that man. He just wanted to see a bit of decent justice. I think he'd have been perfectly happy with a constitutional monarchy. Chancellor Brüning was trying for that, you know, before General von Schleicher took over.'

Major Nye shakes his head. 'Now there was an army man I simply could not get on with. Wrong sort altogether. Dabbled in civilian

298

issues. It just isn't done. The German Army knew that as well as the British or the Americans. But, like the Americans, the Germans always think a man who can run an army or a corporation can run a country. They are precisely the last people to run a country! Well, almost the last. Most of the Nazis were the sorts of people you find in the Blenheim Arms these days. The dropouts and seedy misfits. Imagine them suddenly put in charge of Britain.'

'Heaven forbid,' says Colonel Pym.

'But not the blacks and Jews,' I say.

'Oi!' calls Mrs Cornelius from her kitchenette. 'Are yer still talkin' abart ther War?'

'Just the causes, Mrs C.' Major Nye is apologetic. He winks at us, but it is her approval he desires most.

'Their allies thought anti-Semitism was an engine they could discard once it had driven them to power,' says Colonel Pym. 'They didn't realise it was the movement's *raison d'être*. What? I think the War was incidental to that.'

I have a soft spot for these old English eccentrics.

Röhm admired the English. They were good soldiers, he said, and about as honourable as you could get in the real world, South Africa aside. The best Englishman, he always said, was what the best German aspired to be. He did not by this intend to denigrate his own people. He was a dedicated patriot. He meant that the English were Germans who had had certain historical and geographical advantages. Needless to say, Cromwell was his great hero. I have noticed how all the Continental radicals admire Cromwell (presumably for his stand against the Catholics) while the British show virtually no interest in him at all. To them the Roundheads and Cavaliers are the stuff of Romance alone. 'The English are self-disciplined in a way which we must educate the Germans to be,' Röhm said. 'But what became second nature to John Bull over the course of centuries must be drummed into our honest Michael in a decade. That's the only way to get real lasting social change. The Russians have made a mess of the whole thing. They are hysterical. It is their weakness.'

He was a little vague as to the precise means of force-marching an entire nation through five hundred years of social change. The joke used to be that the Nazis got rid of the class system by getting rid of the classes. But it was only after 1931 that the killings began in earnest. And after 1934 Stabschef Ernst Röhm, Father of the SA, patriot and friend, had no further interest in the world.

I often reflect on the irony of a people who so consistently punish the best and advance the worst.

Major Nye has to get back to Kent. Colonel Pym needs to catch a bus to Fulham. They rise and put on their identical raincoats, buttoning and belting in precise, familiar ways, as if they only truly come to life when they are adjusting their uniforms.

TWENTY–SEVEN

I was never a prisoner at the Villa Röhm. I had simply become nervous of leaving. When transport was available I would go into Munich, perhaps to see the latest films. Röhm never kept much cash, but he would give me enough for my simple pleasures. I no longer felt vulnerable to Frau Oberhauser's threats. The problem with Mussolini could easily be cleared up once the international situation had settled down. I must admit I had become rather lazy, even euphoric. I had never rested for so long and not had to rely on my own wits. I luxuriated in my situation. I could not return Röhm's affections in the same measure, but one cannot help feeling warm towards a person who calls you his 'Latin angel', his 'dark-eyed ideal' and offers you the world if you will stay just a few more days, a few more weeks.

I had the impression that I was to some extent hiding in the lion's cage. Röhmannsvilla was probably the safest place in Germany at that time. My patron was without question his country's single most powerful man. I considered it a tribute to his modesty and dedication that he hardly realised it. Even when he boasted of the numbers he commanded, I don't think he really believed them. Five million is an almost impossible figure to contemplate. The only problem was the isolation. Röhm's radio did not get good signals because of the surrounding trees.

Unable to find a *Völkischer Beobachter* on any news-stand I finally had to make do with a *Telegramm Zeitung*. There, on an inside page, I read of a tragedy which had taken place at an apartment house in Prinzregentenstrasse. A young woman who lived with her mother had shot herself. She had not left a note. The young woman was the eldest daughter of Frau Angela Raubal, a housekeeper.

I did not, even for a second, believe the story.

Geli Raubal had made her last threat, engineered her last scene, attempted her last blackmail. Someone, either Hitler or a friend, had finished off the 'yowling alley cat' at last. The Führer was free.

I hold no brief for murder. There are few excuses for taking another human life. The Lutherans and the Catholics were wholly agreed on that. In times of war or during certain national crises the taking of life could be condoned, said the pastors and the priests. Well, whoever killed Geli Raubal might claim those precise reasons. My own view was that it would not have mattered had she lived or died. The important thing would have been to find any incriminating papers and get rid of them. Her word was worthless without some kind of proof.

Had someone shot her while trying to find those pictures? I knew Röhm would probably enlighten me to a degree. He might even know whether Hitler himself had done it or not. If Hitler had killed her, it had probably been an accident. I felt rather sorry for her. She had seemed an ordinary, silly Bavarian *Mädchen*. As Mrs Cornelius's youngest son Frank said the other day, she must have felt like Lois Lane being fucked by Superman! The reality was a little bit more than she bargained for. A superhuman, after all, has superhuman needs. This must have seemed very bizarre to a typical little girl from the country! The two of them could never have known anything close to ordinary life. She was, after all, also his niece. The whole thing was perverse, why so many of Hitler's people had begged him to give her up. They saw nothing but disaster in the situation. One way or another she would not have lasted.

I remember hoping that Hitler's political ambitions would not be threatened by any scandal. I did not think it his fault, after all, that the strain of being the mistress of a great politician had told on the weaker type of girl.

Since Röhm had arranged to pick me up there, I went down to the Bratwurstglockl where I expected to find an acquaintance who knew me from the villa. Becker was already installed at a table with some of his Hitler Youth chums. The place was alive with gossip. Everyone had their stories to add. The details were often incredibly gory and related with great relish! Eventually I pieced together the account which Hess gave me later. Hess apparently believed that after one of her canaries had died, Geli had quarrelled with her 'Uncle Alf'. She still wanted Hitler to let her go to Vienna to become an opera singer. Suspecting she intended to keep a liaison, Hitler refused. Geli had threatened to 'talk to the papers', let some of his 'big friends' in on a few of their secrets. With harsh humour he had reminded her of the fate of Mata Hari. He was busy with intense cattle-trading politics in Berlin. They were on the brink of victory, with a real presence in the Reichstag, backed by an SA now larger than the regular army. Later he would discuss the matter reasonably. For now she must be patient. A subsequent screaming match had aroused the entire apartment house. Witnesses were clear from her urgency that she had another agenda. She planned to embarrass him so badly he would give in. Hess believed she had an arrangement with some SS man she knew, the mysterious Zeiss. She, of course, had denied this. A car called for Hitler. Her uncle had meetings of the deepest importance and secrecy. He left. As he got into his car, she appeared on the balcony. 'Won't you let me go to Vienna?' she cried, for all the world to hear. He answered abruptly, and the car drove away.

The next morning the housekeeper found her in her bedroom. She had been shot through the heart with Hitler's Walther PPK 38. The gun was near her hand, suggesting suicide. She had been beaten. Her mother's first thought was that Geli had been murdered by Himmler. She called Hess who had good connections with the Munich police. He arranged for an inconspicuous investigation, a verdict of suicide. Geli had been a good Catholic. No note was found.

'The strange thing was,' said Röhm as we drove back to the villa, 'that all that day she'd been carrying Kutzi around. Like a sort of warning – like fate. Don't you find that a bit spooky, Mashi? A dead canary? The bird was still there when she died.'

Of course, he said, he had not intended to kill her. She was still hysterical when he arrived. He thought she might have been expecting someone else. They both knew Hitler would not be back. He had gone there to warn her off and collect any letters and other material she might be hiding.

'I tried to calm her down. She'd go quiet and then start screaming again, and I'd have to slap her. Oh, you know. She was like a mad animal. She never had much reason to begin with. She wouldn't tell me where the stuff was, so I started looking for myself. I was pissed off with her, I'll admit.'

While he was looking through her purse for her keys, she had threatened him with Hitler's automatic.

'She didn't even know about the thumb safety,' said Röhm. 'You can't pull the trigger without pressing down the safety at the same time. I took it away from her. I told her she was in a game whose stakes were far too high for her. She should go back to Obersalzberg or wherever she's from. She was dragging the Chief down. I don't know. She got hysterical again, and she got shot. She'd made me so jumpy. My own nerves were on edge. I'm not a bastard. I don't go around killing civilians. I only meant to warn her off. But at least it's over now, and Hitler can get on with his work.

'We've got less than a month to go. Schleicher wanted to introduce Strasser to Hindenburg, but we have to be sure it's Hitler. Strasser can't get the votes in the country. He can't talk the way the Chief can. That meeting will get Hitler the Presidency or at very least show how Hindenburg is taking him seriously. That alone is worth millions of votes. This is the big moment, Mashi. With that bitch out of the picture we've a clear run at it. Still, as you know, I never had anything against her.'

He was genuinely shocked by the accident. Murder was not his style and everyone knew it, which was why so few people ever mentioned his name in connection with Geli Raubal's death. Those who believed Hitler had somehow sneaked back and killed her, those who thought Himmler was the murderer or that her mysterious lover Zeiss had done it, or that it actually was suicide, never even brought up Röhm's name casually. He was highly respected in the movement. Only later did Hitler have some suspicion.

'Nobody was a saint in those days,' I remind Mrs Cornelius. We are happy to be alone together. She has her scrapbooks out. We see our own youthful, painted faces meeting in a faded embrace while behind us Fokkers and Camels clash in a stunning dogfight. I hardly remember making it. We did so many in such a short time. I find an advertisement cut from one of her film magazines. 'Ace Peters and Gloria Cornish. *The Air Knights*. A DeLuxe Serial.' Who cares for romance and glamour any longer? Every print that went around the world has crumbled to brown powder. We are a mere step away from Wolfit and Irving, whose theatrical performances are now only hearsay, whose records are so disappointing. People cannot believe it, but in our golden years Mrs Cornelius and myself were people of some substance and influence. Stabschef Röhm was proud to be seen with me. People asked for my autograph. Schoolboys pointed me out to their parents. Of course, all this gradually went away as the fashions changed, but that is not to say that we did not once have position and respect. For a while we knew fame again, but those films I made in Germany, while I have no reason to be ashamed of them, were not of my personal conception!

Röhm was especially demanding of my time and strength in the next few days. I was a comfort to him, he said. He had never dreamed of knowing such comfort. A boon he scarcely deserved. He was always saying such things about himself. He once described himself as a 'cruel and wicked man' no good for civilian life. But that, I know, was his way of simplifying himself. He was far more complex than that. I believe he was uneasy about Geli Raubal's death for quite a while after the event. He insisted on playing nothing but Strauss and Lehár on the gramophone. He became sentimental in unfamiliar ways. Offenbach produced an almost wolfish glee in him. He all but wore out the grooves of 'The Nuns' Chorus' in an orgy that happily did not involve me in very much activity.

Soon, however, Strasser's car was at the gates. The big deputy, no longer jovial, was hurrying through the villa, averting his eyes from the things he didn't want to look at and talking urgently to Röhm. Clearly there was an unusual crisis, since Strasser was making only his second visit to the villa. He didn't want to have to answer his wife's questions, he said. He was one of the few in the Nazi hierarchy who did not have scandal attached to him.

I heard Röhm. 'Well, he was cracking up before it happened.'

Strasser was adamant. Hitler was worse than he had ever known him. 'I've seen that bastard go down on his knees beside his desk and start chewing at the carpet, beating on the floor with his fists and squealing that he is going to kill himself unless we do what he wants, and that was normal compared to the way he is now, Ernst. Believe me, I've been with him for almost a week. I'm going crazy myself out there in Tegernsee. Angela's been there for a bit, but she's had to go back. You know the funeral's in Vienna, and Alf isn't allowed to go to Austria. Too dangerous, anyway, to risk a challenge to his German nationality. We can't trust anyone else. Even his sister's beginning to wonder, since he keeps wailing that it's his fault and that he killed her. He didn't kill her. That's one thing I am sure about. Göring or Himmler had her killed. They had the most to lose. Some SS goon, no doubt.'

From Röhm's troubled expression I understood the problem he was facing. He was a man who hated secrets. Even if the secret protected him, he still hated it. But he controlled himself.

'Well, what does he need to pull him out of it? You know Alf. He's all self-pity and blithering needs one minute. The next he's barking orders and throwing his weight around.'

'It's the second Alf we're going to need for Hindenburg,' said Strasser significantly. 'I don't think the old boy will be much impressed by the first. We need our Führer at his brilliant best.'

'We'll send someone else.'

'Me? You have to go – you have to reassure him about the army. He'll respond well to you. Frick or Göring? He'll see through them immediately. Goebbels? Hindenburg can't stand the little dwarf. Nobody has Hitler's authority. We can't start changing leaders now. It has to be him.'

'Fine. Then it will be him.'

'But he's a gibbering mess.'

'Then we have to straighten him out.'

They began a long argument, referring to many things meaningless to me, so I went to have a bath.

When I next went by the room, I heard Röhm say, 'Well, we'll get him a whore. These girls know what to do.'

'Not that specific. And he'd guess what she was immediately. If we trained her, we'd have to let her in on too much. The story would travel faster than a dose of clap in a dugout. It would be all over Germany in three days.'

I heard Röhm murmur something.

'Oh, certainly!' Strasser was contemptuous. 'And what do we do then? Take her into the woods and shoot her? The Munich police are already watching us. They would love us to make a slip like that. I don't think even Hess or Putzi will be able to keep another dead girl out of the picture.'

Again something from Röhm. Strasser's reply: 'I agree with the cure, but I don't agree on the doctor.'

Soon afterwards Strasser left, cursing the situation and begging his old friend to come up with some ideas. Röhm explained a little to me. Hitler had taken the death of his niece far worse than anyone might have expected. He was utterly devastated and saw his politics as the cause of his loss. His only reason for driving himself as hard as he did was so that eventually he would be able to marry Geli. She was his muse and his inspiration. Without her he was incapable of going on. Let someone else lead the Nazi Party.

'Alf's like his mother. She always responded the same way to a setback. A lot of melodrama and then a total refusal to face the issue. That's why we could never promote him in the army. Strasser's staying with him night and day. He keeps making half-hearted attempts to kill himself. They're out at Tegernsee now. Amann's place. It's remote. Nobody will bother them. Alf always goes there to restore himself.'

'Did Geli live there, too?' I asked.

Röhm said it wasn't far from there. Obersalzberg. It probably wasn't the best place to forget, but Hitler would not agree to go anywhere else and now he was refusing to leave his room. He would not get out of bed except to find Strasser and run endlessly over the events: what he could have done to stop it, what he should have done, how he loved her, how he would do anything for her, how it was all his fault and so on. Then Hitler would start weeping again, swallow some more pills and return to bed. He had pictures of her, notes she had written him. He stank. The Führer had not bathed since he heard the news. He had scarcely eaten and had taken a good many sleeping powders, but they had not worked. Strasser thought they had made him talk all the more volubly and exhausted him even further. He was thin and haggard. His hands shook. He could hardly keep himself from drooling. He wept constantly. He moved like an old man. He was like a drug addict deprived of his morphine. If Hindenburg saw him in that state it would confirm his every prejudice about this 'seedy little Bohemian corporal', as he always called Hitler.

'It's typical of the swine to falter at the last hurdle!' Röhm was ferocious. 'Him and his fucking guilt. He didn't kill the bitch after all!' This was a little insensitive. While I did not know Hitler, the man's affection seemed to have been genuine enough. It was not in Röhm's nature, unfortunately, to go over old ground.

'What Göring told me,' says Mrs Cornelius, who enjoyed a brief liaison with the Reichsmarschall a short while after his wife died, 'was that Geli's lover did it. The SS boy she was going to go to Vienna with. Zeiss? They were terrified of Hitler. When she told the boy Hitler wouldn't let her go, he shot her in a lovers' quarrel. Himmler had Zeiss shot later, but a lot of people still think it was Hitler himself.'

'It was neither,' I insist. 'The killer was Röhm. He told me so.'

'Well,' she says, 'there you go.'

She always says such things when she believes I am lying or exaggerating.

307

'Study the facts,' I say. 'It is all there. You only have to read between the lines – anyone can. The case is so obvious once you know.'

'I don't need to do any studying, Ivan,' she says. 'I got it from the horse's mouth, didn't I?'

'Stupid horse. Big mouth.' But Göring had his good points. I have no wish to confirm the stereotype.

'Oh!' She shakes with affectionate laughter. 'And you was so bloody clever yourself!'

'I think you could at least acknowledge my experience,' I say.

'I believe what you boys got up to,' she says. 'It's just what yer make of it, you know. I 'ave to larf.'

'What I did was not important? Strasser or Göring would have been the new Führer and everything would have gone along exactly the same?'

'Well,' she says, 'there you go.'

But I know every detail. Every detail. If it had not been for me, the party would have self-destructed. The communists would have won. I made a sacrifice I will never admit to. Hitler's guilt kept him in that condition, and his guilt had to be grounded.

In early October with only a few days left before the arranged meeting with Hindenburg, Strasser telephoned Röhm at the villa. Father Stempfle, who had been Geli's confessor, was with him now, trying to convince him that Geli had always had suicidal tendencies while at the same time assuring Hitler his niece had deserved her full Catholic burial. This might be confusing the Chief all the more. Strasser said that both he and Stempfle had tried talking Hitler round, but he would begin to weep silently and refuse to respond. He was turning into a melancholy vegetable.

Röhm repeated what he had said before. They should try the known solution. It had always produced a catharsis in the past and clearly functioned as an act of absolution.

'I told Strasser that it had to be one of us,' said Röhm that night as we prepared for bed. 'Someone who is already in on it. That's Rudolf Hess, you, me, Gregor Strasser, little Bernhard Stempfle.'

'To do what?' I asked.

'To do what you do best,' he said. 'I could make only one choice in the end. You. Will you do this for us, Mashi? For me? For Germany? Believe me, you're the last damned card we can play.' He explained what they wanted me to do.

'That's not a natural role for me,' I said. 'There would be difficulties, also, in the anatomical respects.'

Röhm explained how my costume would overcome those problems.

I was sure that it was possible for someone else to perform the ritual he described, however. While I understood the urgency of the situation, I simply did not have the heart for the role. Indeed, the thought terrified me. I could not play it with any kind of conviction. I did not tell them that the role was in some respects familiar from my Egyptian days when I had been a witness and a participant.

Pausing, with profound pain in his eyes, Röhm mentioned the file he had taken from Frau Oberhauser, the former Baroness von Ruckstühl. Clearly he had deliberated for a long time. He knew he was threatening something rare that we had built between us. 'Then we would have to investigate these claims and discover how you, a suspected Jew, managed to inveigle your way into the holiest shrines of National Socialism.'

I grew a little sad at that moment and was deeply shocked. 'A suspected what? My dear Ernst, whatever else you accuse me of, do not call me that. It is a disgusting slander. You yourself have said how you know for certain I am not a Jew.'

Röhm was silent. He turned away in shame.

I understood him well and was even sympathetic. The struggle he must be having with himself! His whole body was shaking. This was tearing him apart. For the love of his Fatherland and all he held dear, Stabschef Ernst Röhm was prepared to blackmail his 'sweetest love' and destroy almost everything honest and pure between us.

'Only you could pull it off, Mashi. You have the skills, the physique, the actor's gift . . .'

'You want me to pose as some dirty little whore –'

'A game, Mashi. Just a game. We've played it before.'

'I have not played that role for you, Ernst. Never.' My heart was sinking. I knew what this meant. Our idyll was drawing to a close. Yet still I resisted the inevitable. 'Why not get some girl from the street? She needn't know –'

'We can't risk it. Just as we can't risk any more killing. Half the cops in Germany are waiting for a chance like this. That's why you, at least, are guaranteed your life, Mashi.' He turned, red-faced, with tears in his eyes. And then I realised the full horror of what had been contemplated.

'You'll lose nothing, Mashi. And the Fatherland will gain everything!'

I still wasn't sure I could do what he wanted. 'He would realise the deception, Ernst. You know he would.'

'You haven't seen the shape he's in. Believe me, the pills have taken every ounce of judgement.'

'Then how will this work?'

'The way it has always worked. What do you think that little slut used to do for him? She kept him moving forward. I don't know what you call it – but it got rid of any guilt he might be feeling about what he was doing.'

'Guilt?'

'There were things he promised his mother. Other loyalties. He had to give them up. He had to give a lot up, Mashi, to get where he is.'

I could not resist those pleading eyes. My friend was desperate. As a Christian I could only forgive him. I would have to help him. I, of all people, had come to understand how Christian duty must sometimes come before personal feelings. I bowed to his necessity, but an enormous sadness filled me. I knew a great love affair was finished. Love was what we both sacrificed.

That night Hess arrived from Munich driving the massive Mercedes received from an industrialist well-wisher. His old friend Father Stempfle was with him. Röhm had already suggested how I dress and had packed a bag for me. I was wrapped in one of his greatcoats. Perhaps instinctively recognising me from that encounter in the hotel, Stempfle looked at me with the same peculiar, gloating disgust he offered to most of the world. He moved so that he sat across from me with Röhm and began to eat a liver sausage, smacking his lips and glaring at me with happy sadism. The leather of the seat was cold. I felt utterly helpless.

Röhm had brought a case of chilled champagne and huge vacuum jug of coffee that he kept making me drink. He also had a sack of plums. He would check his watch and make me eat five every hour, while Father Stempfle coached me in a litany which added to the queasiness I soon felt from the fruit. The priest must have milked every single lurid detail from the girl and added experiences of his own. Of course, thanks to my sojourn in Arabia, none of this was unfamiliar to me, but I was aware how precision was important.

As we drove I wondered who else Stempfle had told about his

310

discoveries. Hitler himself had recommended Stempfle as Geli's confessor. As a good Catholic she needed someone to whom she could retail her sins, and Hitler needed a priest he could trust. Had Hitler deliberately set Stempfle up as Geli's confessor to learn the last of his niece's pathetic secrets? Was he aware of every infidelity or planned liaison? Whatever the motives, Stempfle had been her most explicit inquisitor and had heard every moment of her private life with Hitler. He had copies of the letters and drawings he had bought back on Hitler's behalf. He showed me Geli in a variety of postures. They were familiar enough but not especially palatable.

'Dirty little slut,' said Röhm, glancing through the pictures. 'You can tell she liked it.'

Mrs Cornelius has fallen asleep in the chair she allows no one else to use. Sometimes I think the thing is organic, a part of her. It sustains her like a life-support system. Every so often she returns to it and replenishes her energies. The very smell of that chair suggests some kind of amniotic concentrate. The noises she makes, deep within herself, resemble the distant yelps of feasting animals. With her head thrown back, her teeth out, her crimson mouth open and her blue mascaraed eyes closed, she seems in a kind of rapture. Her head, gloriously auraed in streaky reds and browns, resembles a primitive sculpture, some pagan Goddess of Death, some Rhiannon of the Portobello Market. To others she might seem ugly, but I see only nobility on that growling mask, the mark of wisdom, long experience and inexhaustible power.

We have both known the heights and the depths. We have ruled hearts and been ruled by them. We have known worldly prestige and fame. We have enjoyed the fruits of our successes and explored the byways of pleasure with tolerance and open minds. We have seen history made and realities changed. We have not lost sight of our dreams. We have seen them fade and sometimes we have had to put them aside. This century has not rewarded faith. We did what we had to do. We made our compromises and we survived.

'He might want to lick your arse and nuzzle your cunt,' said Father Stempfle, his lizard hands shaking as he guided me through the letters. 'Here's what you should do.' He showed me the moulded rubber.

Hess was clearly glad to be driving. He had already been tortured by what he heard of the compromising letters and drawings and had refused to look at anything. Even Putzi Hanfstaengl had leafed through them, to his dismay. But all Hess had between himself and the chaotic infinite was his loyalty to his leader. He clung to that loyalty as others cling to a religion, in spite of all contradictions and rational evidence. His grip on sanity, on life of any kind, depended upon that loyalty. Hess was oddly disassociated from real life, as if he was watching a film which bore no relation to his ordinary existence. He studied the world with a kind of bemused, accepting smile. Nothing in the universe meant more to him than loyalty to Hitler. He appreciated the influence of men with firm ideas about what was valuable and what was not. It made him a worshipping parrot, a useful man, a typical Number Two. Hitler was fond of him and admired his faithfulness. 'His very soul is brown,' he would say.

We raced through dark little medieval villages and quaint hillside towns, past farms which had survived Germany's troubles since the time of Charlemagne, past ancient pastures and rich orchards, all the wealth of old Bavaria. Röhm made me do something to Father Stempfle to make sure I knew exactly what they were talking about. Stempfle kept his eyes shut through the process and made noises through his teeth. Röhm, knowing how much the perverted divine hated it, grinned from start to finish. The relish he was taking in the old man's dismay helped me get through the process, I will admit. I felt a kind of secondary pleasure in Röhm's sadism. Nonetheless, I had to gag out of the window.

'You'd better not do that later,' said Röhm. He stroked my shoulders; he caressed my thighs. 'You know I would never normally ask you for such a sacrifice.'

He looked at his watch. He made me drink some more champagne and eat five more plums. I protested. I did not have the stomach for it. Everything would be over soon, he said.

A huge silver moon hung in the black space between the mountain peaks. The car grumbled and whined up the steep roads. Birch and pine forests fell away below us. There were lights in distant valleys. Tall hills surrounded us. The air was richly scented by the trees and wild flowers. Röhm said this was his favourite time of the year up here. He became strangely melancholic. He knew that something was dying in both of us. The last of the summer wine, he said. He and Hitler had always planned to end their days here when their work was completed. He had a feeling something was stealing his future.

We passed through a dark village. A few more minutes and the car pulled up outside a small lodge decorated with fretwork in the typical local style. It stood on a hill in its own grounds among the trees.

'The view is stunning at dawn,' said Hess. 'We were happiest here, eh, Ernstie?' He and his Führer had spent some of their best times here. Hitler had dictated *Mein Kampf* to his adoring secretary as his fame grew.

'Carefree days,' agreed the Stabschef and sighed.

Gregor Strasser was waiting for us at the top of a flight of wooden steps. He was unshaven and unslept. He looked at me and pursed his lips, as if he shared my own opinion of my inability to play the necessary part. My legs were weak. I could hardly walk. My stomach was churning. I wanted desperately to go to the toilet, but the special clothing I was wearing prevented that.

Strasser led us in. The place was unnaturally hot. It smelled of perfume, boiled sausage and other sourer scents I could not identify. Strasser apologised to Röhm and Hess for the state of the place. He had not thought it a good idea to get a woman in.

I sensed an odd silence about the room, as if we were attendant upon a recent death, a lying-in.

'This is crazy,' murmured Strasser. 'It can't work.'

'Then come up with a better idea.' Röhm, aggressive and impatient, was used to coming to decisions and then moving with them, like any soldier. 'It's worked before.'

'But with a real girl. A particular girl.'

'Believe me, Strasser,' Röhm insisted. 'It's not a real girl he's obsessed with. What have you told Alf about this?'

'He doesn't care. He's spiralling down deeper every day. He'll be completely catatonic at this rate. Like shell-shock. He and Hindenburg will make a perfect pair, each about as gaga as the other. The public will be spoiled for choice.' Strasser spoke with a fierce edge to his voice, as if he himself were on the point of psychological collapse. 'Meanwhile, the bastard's draining the life and soul out of everyone.'

'You didn't tell him?' Röhm indicated me.

'I said there was someone coming to help him . . .' Strasser looked me up and down once and turned away, nodding. 'Well, I'll admit the make-up's convincing. Someone's got a good memory.'

Röhm told me to put on the wig and the mask. He pulled the greatcoat off my shoulders. 'A little masterpiece,' he said.

313

Hess uttered a sudden burst of bovine amusement, as if the Minotaur had at last seen the funny side of things. I don't believe he had any clear idea what was going on.

'A dead ringer for our little canary,' said Röhm.

Mrs Cornelius's red lips curve in a smile of pure delight. She dreams of her happiest moments. Her great bosom lifts and falls; her hands are now as gnarled with arthritis as Röhm's. They lie in her lap like the claws of a venerable bird of prey. We were never really predators, Mrs Cornelius and I. I am remembering my youth. I look down at my threadbare plaid shirt, my old cardigan, my grey flannel trousers, my dirty shoes. How is it that we so rarely see ourselves through our younger eyes? What would I have made of an old man like me? Would I have shown him respect, acknowledged his pride and his history? Or would I have mocked him as the young mock me now? They believe I am like them. That all I have to back my opinions is prejudice and ignorance. Yet I have stood shoulder to shoulder with great men in the face of unvanquishable evil – and have vanquished that evil. How many of these 'bother boys' can say the same?

I do not claim the experience left me unchanged.

Röhm went to get Father Stempfle out of the toilet. The priest had done all he could, he said. He was a hermit and needed privacy. He began to whine something about his fee. For a priest who had taken the vows of poverty and spent every waking hour talking of Jewish greed and rapacity, he had a very clear idea of his own financial worth. At the Bratwurstglockl they all said he was buying children from some slum dealer over in Cologne, but what he did with them, if anything, nobody really knew. Our normally tolerant, easygoing Stabschef had a genuine contempt for the man. Röhm said he'd had enough of Stempfle's 'finer feelings'. Stempfle's future and everyone else's depended upon kicking Hitler into some semblance of rational humanity for when they went to see the Reichspräsident on 10 October. It was up to party members to support any measure which would get the leader back at the helm. Anyone who didn't use their fullest efforts was a traitor and would be treated like a traitor. He made a flicking motion with his thumb, as if to start a cigarette lighter. Stempfle had been at the Brown House often enough to know what that meant. Röhm told Stempfle to stop spluttering and run me through a couple of points again. The old lizard was shaking worse than I was by the time Strasser led us upstairs to the loft bedroom where Hitler slept.

He knocked on the door. A wet, enquiring noise came from the other side. Strasser seemed to think this was a good sign. 'Ernst's brought someone to see you, Alf.'

Strasser opened the door.

Röhm took me through. The place reeked of staleness and oriental perfumes. Joss sticks and scented candles were burning everywhere. In the far shadows was a small double bed with an old-fashioned canopy. Books and papers had been discarded one on top of the other. Ornaments and other objects lay in corners. Some of them were smashed, as if they had been flung against the wall.

'Alf,' says Röhm. 'How's tricks?'

'Cup of tea, Ivan?' Mrs Cornelius has woken up. She yawns and gusts. 'Cor! Wot old age will do ter yer. Wot's ther time? Me watch 'as stopped.'

She rises from her chair to make the tea. I watch her moving like an old steamer, still graceful, still sturdy. She is well over seventy now.

I collect the dirty cups and follow her into the kitchen.

'Look, Ivan.'

She is craning to peer through the basement window above the sink. At eye level it faces the tangle of weeds and overgrown shrubs she calls her garden. She strains until she can see the sky.

'It's brightenin' up.'

Röhm went in first. He made a kind of crooning noise, as if to soothe a troubled dog. The sound was clearly familiar to the creature in the hidden depths of the bed. I heard a muffled response.

Röhm moved swiftly and lightly, like a soldier expertly making his way through no man's land, until he was over there in the semi-darkness with his old friend, stroking his head, rocking it against his lap. The queer pathos of the scene aroused the most profound and unexpected feelings in me. I understood Röhm's instinct to comfort and nurture the drooling, unlovely thing on the bed and was actually disgusted by my own tenderness.

The eyes turned towards me. I saw no change in them, no pain or warmth or desire which might inspire my feelings. Instead, something in the set of the head, the movement of the mouth, the turn of the wrist, a kind of mimicry of real emotions, were as successful at involving me as if they had been real. Instinctively, like a great screen actor, Hitler was able to arouse in me real concern and pity. I do not believe he was at all conscious of what he did. I think I understood him. It scarcely mattered to his artist's soul if the feelings he inspired were inappropriate or even false. To inspire the feelings was sufficient. (An artist with the soul of a gangster, Major Nye thought.) Only incidentally did this bedridden creature exploit its own condition. Of course I had been completely unprepared for this. I felt faint in that airless room. I marshalled my emotions. I had relied on my panic and my terror getting me through the ordeal, but I could see how these unexpected responses might also help. In some amazement I found myself entering into the mood. Röhm looked up and nodded to me. Tentatively and a little unsteadily I moved slowly towards them.

'Here she is, Alfy,' whispered Röhm. 'Here she is.'

Hitler's pale, bloodshot eyes shifted from my mask to my legs to my panties, my crotch. His skin was a mottled silvery white illuminated with the deliquescence of a corpse. The familiar face, so stern and confident in his pictures, was puffed and lined with exhaustion. I noticed gelatinous moisture on his head and arms. The eyes remained a yearning vacuum, the eyes of an unfed incubus. I recoiled and then recovered. I made a sympathetic feminine sound. Once this was over, I reminded myself, I would be free. I was sick of fantasy. I would go to England, collect the money waiting for me, and resume my life.

Hitler spoke. His voice was a reedy vibrato, the voice of a sick child. '*Wer ist es?*'

'Your friend,' murmured Röhm. '*Deine Freundin.*'

I held the dog whip like a sword as I drew a deep breath of the hellish atmosphere.

'*Dein Engel.*'

I composed a smile.

'Your angel.'

I lift my left leg and bring the red spike heel down between Hitler's naked shoulder blades. I push him flat to the dirty carpet. The spike depresses his white flesh and leaves an almost bloodless mark. I press again with the right foot. Another deep impression. The black leather of the dog whip caresses the back of his head. He is blubbering some sentimental nonsense into the pile.

—Shut up, you bad, filthy little louse. Filthy little louse-boy. Naughty louse-boy filth. Shit-eating, piss-drinking disgusting little Yid. Bad, bad, bad doggy. What are you?

—*Bad doggy.*

I balance myself and grind the red heel down into the left shoulder.

—Bad, dirty little Alfy. Bad, stupid little Yid bitch.

Another babble of wet grizzling. —*Mummy. Mummy.*

—Dirty, filthy worthless Yid louse. What are you?

—*Worthless. Yid louse.*

I grind again. —What are you?

—*Worthless Yid louse, mistress.*

—Dirty Yid louse eat shit.

There are now a dozen circles branded into his back. They look like the marks of the plague.

He grovels. His spittle makes my shoes glisten. I draw the whip across his head through his matted hair.

—Bad boy, I say softly. His tongue tastes my ankle. I am surprised at my own tone. —Dirty little Alfy. Dirty little shit. I am almost affectionate.

TWENTY–NINE

I draw back my arm. The heavy black whip is perfectly balanced. I could hold it like a foil, if I wished, between the tips of my fingers. But I grip it firmly, flexing my muscles as I gather my strength for the first blow.

Hitler's narrow bottom is lifted.

I lay a swift series of stripes across his buttocks. They are still very white but the blood is beginning to come up.

I begin another series of blows across the backs of his legs.

—Disgusting little queer. Dirty Yidshit queer. Filthy, stinking little shitheap. Naughty, naughty little pansy slut. What are you?

—*Pansy slut, mistress.*

I hardly hear the sounds he makes. The rhythmic whistling of the whip, the thick smack as it strikes yielding skin, the patterns criss-crossing the flesh, all absorb my interest.

—What are you, Yidshit?

—*Filthy little Yidshit, mistress. Filthy Yidshit whore.*

—You make me sick. You make me want to gag.

THIRTY

I piss in Hitler's mouth.

I spread my legs so that I look directly down on Hitler's white face.

I discharge a forceful stream of pale green-yellow urine. The urine soaks into his dark, matted hair. It glistens in his moustache. It runs down his chin, his ears, his neck and over his narrow chest, darkening the carpet. His breath becomes an eager gasp.

—Open your mouth, Yidslime.

The mouth obeys. An independent entity.

—*Mummy.*

—Bad dirty Yidboy, dirty little slimeyboy. Drink it, queerboy. Drink it, wankerboy. Bad, bad, baddy boy. Drink it all up. Nasty, nasty, dirty boy.

I piss into the black depths. The liquid splashes loudly against his teeth, and makes a hollow sound as it cascades down the black void of his throat and into his skull.

—Yum-yum.

THIRTY–ONE

I shit in Hitler's eyes.

The loose stools fall one after another like wet, stinking eggs breaking on his gargling head. The excrement slides off the skin and slips to the floor, leaving brown streaks across the face.

—Yidshit queerboy. Cowardly, nasty, dirty whore.

—*Ja! Ja!*

—Disgusting, messy, dirty, sloppy, careless little pigyid.

—*Ja! Ja!*

I squat on his face.

—Foul little subhuman scum. Lick my arse clean.

He writhes and rolls. He begs for mercy. The smell is strong. His whole head and upper body are now covered in sticky filth.

—Bad, naughty, dirty Yidshit queerboy. Bad doggy Yidshit queerboy. Lick it up, dirty boy. Lick it all up for Mummy.

THIRTY-TWO

I force the dildo into Hitler's anus. I use my own shit to lubricate it. Hitler groans and shivers. He begins to beg me to stop. I push the dildo in harder. I take his ball and squeeze it. He begins to thrash. I clutch at his penis. It slips out of my hand. I take a tighter hold on it.

—Dirty little Yidqueer bad boy Mummy's bad boy dirty boy dirty dirty boy dirty Yidboy queer.

I dig my nails into the soft flesh. I twist the dildo to give him the maximum pain.

He starts to scream. The noise inspires my efforts. I shout at him. I jump back and kick him. I take the dildo out and shove it into his mouth to stop him blubbering.

—Shut up, queerbaby bumboy dirty queerboy bumbaby, crybaby Yidboy. Bad naughty Yidboy. Dirty Yidqueer bumboy. What are you?

—*Dirty queerboy fuckmemummy.*

He writhes on the floor at my feet, the dildo in his mouth, his cold eyes moving with a disturbing vitality.

—Bad dirty Yidboy queer. Bad boy, bad Alfy, bad, bad, bad Alfy.

—*I didn't mean – I didn't want – I didn't do it – It wasn't my fault. It wasn't my fault.*

—Only your fault.

The whip rises and falls. —Dirty boy. Bad boy.

I kick him to the ground so that he lies spreadeagled on his face. I walk on his back. I shout at him. I take the dildo and push it into him again.

—*No, Mummy. No, Mummy. My angel, my angel . . .*

—No isn't a word we use. Bad word. Naughty word. Punish dirty Alfy.

I take his head and grind it into the shit. I make him roll in the shit. I make him lick it up. I whip his legs. I bugger him with the dildo. I piss in his mouth. I trample his body. I spit on his genitals. I shriek at him. I call him more names. But only the names I have been taught.

Blood pours from his rump. The room is like a slaughterhouse.

—Punish him. Bad Alfy. Bad Uncle Alfy.

—*Please, Geli. Please, Geli.*

His screams blended with my own.

I left him sobbing on the bed armoured in his own juices.

I looked back briefly as I closed his door. Through the filthy crust those pale, unsouled, unblinking eyes were staring at me, as if to remember me. Only for an instant did they meet mine.

They flickered with chilling triumph.

THIRTY-THREE

'He has a beautiful mouth.' Röhm settles himself back in the deep seats of the car. He removes his soft hat, smoothes his military head. His scars are livid in the occasional flashes of artificial light from a streetlamp or window. He is periodically flung into deep, sharp shadows. Out of uniform, he always seems a little plastic and unco-ordinated, as if the belts and stiff flannel help sustain his equilib-rium. In repose he looks like a disappointed child. As I remove the lipstick and mascara, he sighs. The cigar he smoked before leaving is still on his breath.

'Did you notice, Mashi, what a soft, beautiful mouth the Führer has? Like a girl. Of course, he'll want to kill us both after this. He'll savour the wait. Like a cat. He'll hardly know he's doing it, then he'll pick his moment. That's what he's good at. He understands sadism because he understands masochism. It involves patience, passivity. Only a few days ago he and I were reflecting how the world runs on sadism. Do you follow me, Max?'

My friend radiates a strange, euphoric humour. Perhaps sensing our lack of intimacy, he has become unusually loquacious. 'The de Sades run the world. At the top, the cruel but high-minded soldiers, aristo-crats and creative artists. Their orders are translated by honest bureau-crats, esteeming authority above everything, passing on the orders to brute sadists at the bottom. My SA boys, for instance. Scum for the most part, but the middle layer gives a political legitimacy to the whole operation. The decent middle doesn't understand the addictions and joys of sadism. They can even produce civilised rationalisations for everything! They're trained to understand only the notion of just punishment. They can't imagine the calculated use of terror as a refined political instrument. We have to accept these realities, even if we don't discuss them in public. The better we know our system, the better we can use it to effect. If we are to rebuild German civilisation, we have to rid ourselves of the grime of Judaeo-Christian repression. We must learn to be healthy brutes again. Alf and I used to talk a lot about that. The power of cruelty, you know, to achieve high ideals. Channel your desires one way, and you become a criminal psychopath. Channel them another way, and you become a great political leader. We worked it out years ago. In the War. Those Jews in Vienna, imitating real people as ever, took our insights and sentimentalised them for the millions. Their pseudo-philosophers and -psychologists had a stranglehold on popular culture. But we were sustained by our secret knowledge. More romantic days, Mashi, in many ways. You're lucky to have me as your own personal guide!'

His wounded face shakes with humour. 'I am your Virgil. You are my Dante! The conversations one has at the height of one's ecstasy! Every so often you remember them, and a taste of the ecstasy comes back. At least a taste of it, eh? I envy the young. I hate them.' Almost reminiscently he fingers his crotch.

Scarlet, white and gold, the great crucifix swings like a pendulum across my field of vision. How could Christ create Dachau? Scarlet and rich, dark gold through the scented smoke. *Kyrie eleison! Kyrie eleison!* The crucifix sways in the hazy air. What Jew could know such grief, such joy in Christ?

When he said 'kill us both', did he mean himself and Strasser?

Strasser was in front with the driver and heard none of this. He had folded his huge, shaven head down into the collar of his camel-hair coat and appeared to be sleeping.

'Well, he'd hardly bother with me,' I said.

The Stabschef looked at me in surprise. His mind had been elsewhere. He seemed to have forgotten his earlier remarks. Then he smiled. 'Oh, don't be too sure. Alf and me used to play such games. Such bloodthirsty games.' Röhm began to laugh. 'He has a memory for detail, our Alf, even if he's inclined to forget the broader issues.'

'Not in that state.' I had now removed all the make-up. Not at that level of possession. Something else had taken hold of him. I was a symbol. A memory. A substitute. I no longer existed.

'Especially in that state,' said Röhm. 'I know. He can be a mean little pincher and hair-puller, our girlie. Never remembers a favour. Never forgets a slight. Still, I only said he'll want to kill us. I didn't say he could. It's me and Strasser have to worry. You'll be fine, Mashi, while I look after you.' Then he chuckled in that pleasant, easy

Bavarian way he had and slapped me on the knee. 'Alfy can be tricky, but not that tricky. I'm his strength and he knows it. I keep his feet on the ground. Without the SA, the parliamentary party's nothing. We're the muscle and they're the brains. I've never pretended to be anything else.'

He frowned for a moment and dug hard at a thumbnail, trying to clean it. His hands were not entirely knotted with arthritis and were still one of his best features. A sculptor's hands, strong and sensitive. No stranger would guess his daily pain. Scarcely a bone in his body had not been broken during and immediately after the War.

'That's how I function and how I want to function. As a simple soldier. Once Alfy's brought the SA into the Reichswehr, all tension will be over. We'll have a people's army with people's officers. Alf's got to keep the generals sweet, but my men have been promised jobs and are getting impatient. They need proper army discipline. Alf will play the plutocrats at their own game. When the time comes their heads will roll. At heart he's still one of us. It's not him I'm worried about.' And then as if he had said too much, he closed his mouth so tightly that his lips whitened and made the scars over his nose and cheek look like the valleys of the moon. 'He won't kill you, Mashi. I'll see to that.' That was the end to our conversation. He smoothed his moustache like a grooming cat then, drawing on his gloves, fell into a half-sleeping silence.

Was he speaking the truth? Or had he merely succeeded in binding me further to him? Without his patronage, I was in danger. Or so I must believe until I learned otherwise. I did not have the courage to ask Röhm how he knew the extremes of Hitler's behaviour.

The morning was still dark when we stopped at Röhm's favourite roadside café for breakfast. Strasser preferred to wait in the car rather than go into that typical steamy Bavarian working-man's place, stinking of boiled sausages and strong coffee, and full of burly, ruddy fellows in blue overalls and heavy work shirts. I felt a little threatened by their closeness and their curiosity, but Röhm was clearly at home, joking and hand-slapping his way up to the counter to order our food while I sat in the booth nearest the door. I could still smell shit. I had no liking for the place. Its masculine philistinism was tangible. Two or three SA lads sat together at a table, but they had their backs to us. Röhm seemed relieved when they walked out without recognising him.

One of the workers did ask Röhm if he wasn't Captain Röhm of the Nazis and, when he reluctantly admitted it, thumped him on the back and wished him all the best. I wanted only to leave. Of course, that acceptance was exactly what Röhm enjoyed about the place. In the past he'd joked about what they'd say if they found out the 'smear' stories, so vehemently dismissed in the *Völkischer Beobachter*, were only a fraction of the truth.

He relished the weight of their heavy hands on his back and arms. Their congratulations. Their manly approval. Their balls. He blossomed. Good luck! Good luck! *Grüss Gott! Grüss Gott!*

Even I picked up some of their approval by association, especially when I explained my bad German. '*Amerikaner!*' they roared happily. They all had relatives in Texas and Wisconsin. Many people forget that the greatest American settlement after the colonial years was by Germans.

I envied Röhm his sense of place and people. I had lost both in Russia. I longed for the comradeship I had known with Shura in Esau's in Odessa's Moldavanka. We, too, might have formed a corps and gone off to fight together. Shura and I could have driven the Bolshevik from our homeland and put a beneficent new Tsar upon the throne. A Tsar who acknowledged the universal rule of Christ and the eternal grace of Jesu Kristos, Lord of the Greeks. Raboni!

We took Strasser some coffee and sausages and returned to the car. 'You'd better get yourself a girlfriend,' Röhm said thoughtfully, not looking at me. 'You know – something smart or tarty – whatever you prefer, as long as people notice. It's just a precaution, like dragging a false trail and turning signposts. Standard practice. For my own part I intend to spend more time with my mother and sister.' Absently, he again patted at my leg and continued to stare out of the window. He spoke in rapid associative phrases, revealing him as the fine field officer he had been. 'Yes, that'll be useful. Cover all our backs. And we'll have to see what we can do with those engineering ideas of yours. The one thing Alf and I are agreed on is that armour's the secret of winning tomorrow's wars. Musso's going to have to give you up. The bigger, better and faster the armour, the quicker the victory.'

Because of our particular histories, I had never been much of a Germanophile, but I had high respect for Germany's great writers like Goethe and May. And I liked their hard, practical approach to modern problems. The Greeks were their models. That balance of mind and body, that celebration of human ingenuity. These Nazis understood that the future lay in a healthy populace, a rigorous pursuit of excellence and of technological superiority.

My ambition was still to get to England and work for one of her forward-looking engineering firms, to exploit my patents as a recognised inventor. Mussolini had betrayed me. Another mind poisoned against me. I had money waiting for me in Whitechapel. Relatives. Yet I sensed something in the German soul yearning for what I had to offer. Ernst and the others had the courage and the vision to be clear about what they wanted. Nothing less than a renewed Fatherland.

Would it be here, rather than under a Duce whose mind had been poisoned against me, a Duce no longer approachable by the common man, that the revolutionary machines of the future would be embraced? As usual my idealism, my hopes for improving the world, were leading me to become involved in the politics of a race that had never much engaged my attention, while my original plans to reach England were increasingly neglected.

I blame myself as much as Röhm. We had so much in common. Our views on history and politics were almost identical. Only in our solutions to the problems were we in any sort of disagreement, because I had experienced Red Terror at first hand. He was a persuasive, flattering host. His cocaine came from Vienna, from the same source as Freud's. I had not enjoyed this life of luxury so much since Hollywood. But my vocation was forever calling me. I felt an even greater need to get to a drawing board, to found an engineering works and begin one of the projects I had planned. Though Röhm appreciated my worth as an inventor, if I was to stay, I needed to meet someone who envisioned Germany's future in the hands not of a disciplined workers' army but of a scientific elite working in harness with that army.

I began to speak of this to Röhm, but he was not in the mood to listen.

'We'll go to the pictures tomorrow afternoon,' he said. 'There's a film I want to see at the Karlsplatz. A comedy. It'll cheer us up. We'll meet at the *Kino*. Fourteen forty-five sharp. In the foyer. Dress down. We're going to have to take some ordinary precautions.'

As I have said, Röhm was rapidly distancing himself from me emotionally. For once in my life I was too dim to realise it. I should have known a soldier like him could not afford to lose himself in

327

love. Part of his contradictory nature was explained by his masculine duty being constantly at odds with his feminine sensitivity.

The sun had still not risen when we returned to Röhmannsvilla. Yet I had to remain in the car while Röhm went cautiously in to get my things. Strasser said very little. Not once had his eyes met my own. He seemed no friendlier towards Röhm. No doubt he considered himself superior to us. He was a deputy, of course. He had a wife. A business. He had his own car. He would drive it home.

Our chauffeur restarted the Mercedes's engine. Röhm was embarrassed and a little apologetic. He offered Strasser a reassuring gesture and turned to me. 'It's no good your staying at the villa. We'll have to avoid too much friendly association for a bit. Don't want you to be endangered, you know. Don't want anyone putting one and one together and making two, eh?'

I murmured that I appreciated the need for discretion, but what would our driver report? Röhm was amused by this. His driver was a trusted SA man willing to die for his Captain if necessary.

We drove directly to Munich and the Königshof. Noticed only by a frowning night porter, I made my way swiftly to my room. Dawn came at last. The night seemed to have gone on for ever. Another foul dream over. I must admit I was totally exhausted and wished only to forget the entire disgusting episode. Why had I allowed myself to be dragged into Röhm's scheme? And for what? How could that perverted creature in Tegernsee ever hope to be Chancellor of Germany?

A man's life plan takes him down some strange paths, I thought. Then I sniffed one of my powders and, my mood much improved, was soon in a deep and dreamless sleep.

I slept until noon when I was forced awake by the loud banging on my door. Thinking it was a telephone message from Röhm to change the time, I dragged on a dressing gown and stumbled to answer the knocking. Instead of a busboy, I was greeted by a somewhat surly Frau Socking, the head housekeeper, who had until now been rather pleasant. Her speech seemed rehearsed. 'I am sorry, Herr Peters, but you have to vacate your room today.'

'At once? An emergency?'

'Refurbishment works,' she said firmly but without conviction. 'The manager has asked me kindly to ask you to find fresh accommodation.' She softened apologetically but recovered herself. 'By tomorrow.'

I was baffled, suspecting every kind of attack from every possible source. Had Hitler found out about me? Unlikely. Had Röhm turned against me? Equally unlikely. Mussolini's people? My male and female nemeses, the Baroness, Frau Oberhauser, and Comrade Brodmann? Surely neither of these would have influence over such a respectable hotel? I protested. I would speak to the manager.

Realising I would be meeting Röhm in a couple of hours and knowing that he had considerable influence in Munich, I decided to avoid serious confrontation. After bathing, 'coking' and preparing myself elegantly for the day, I strolled down to the lobby and ordered some coffee. At the reception desk I asked to speak to the manager, knowing he was almost certainly at his lunch. Sure enough he was not currently available. I left my card and said I had an important meeting this afternoon. I would return later. Meanwhile I assumed my room would not be disturbed. I would no doubt be ready to leave by that evening or the next morning. I also took it for granted that the presentation of a bill would not add insult to injury. I spoke with some force. I had no intention of being identified as a common bilker. They knew that I was a Hollywood star. To his credit the youth at the reception desk dropped his gaze, blushed and promised to pass on the message. I made it clear that I was extremely displeased.

My own belief at that time was that my association with various high-ranking members of the NSDAP had not improved my standing at the hotel. Röhm and Strasser were associated with the party's left wing and had once even proposed a pact with Soviet Russia. The party was not, after all, the party of the rich and powerful, but the party of the poor and powerless. What was more, hoteliers were infamous snobs. Too many Prussian noblemen had declared themselves socialists for a gentleman's politics to be trusted any longer.

Influential anti-Nazi elements in Munich included top policemen and politicians. The press speculated wildly about the Raubal case. Some hotels, shops and restaurants went so far as to refuse Nazis service. What possessed them to punish only the Nazis, when the Sozis were equally guilty of excesses, I need not tell you. The flow of stolen imperial gold from Russia into Central and Northern Europe at that time was as steady and as unstoppable as the Rhine herself.

I had already experienced the management's animosity, and they had been cavalier in moving my room. Whatever the reason – and

I did not suspect a mistake – it was prudent to look for a hotel that would give me credit. My credit at the Königshof was overextended. No doubt this had not improved their attitude in spite of my assurance that I was due to receive sums from Los Angeles and New York at any moment.

Without credit, however, it would be difficult to find a decent place. I would have to make some rapid arrangements. Taking a discreet pinch of 'snuff' on my wrist, I strolled through the pleasant autumn weather to meet Röhm at the Karlsplatz. No doubt he or one of his powerful friends might be able to help. Yet underlying my pleasure in the day was a shadow of a question. Had I already been betrayed? I pushed the ideas aside. I am not by nature a suspicious man.

In compliance with Röhm's request, I had dressed 'German' in my borrowed Crombie and Tyrolean hat with a big scarlet scarf flung over my shoulder. On the inside of my lapel was my party badge, the fashion among many middle-class Nazis.

Still something of a somnambulist, I managed to get to the big cinema at Karlsplatz. An historical extravaganza was playing as the main feature. I remember being mystified by the title, *Der Kongress tanzt (Congress Dances)*. Would I have to endure some unfathomable expressionist film of which the Germans were so proud? I had already seen *Caligari* and the like, and while I had found *Der Golem* especially involving, I was not a great fan.

I entered the lobby at the same time as my friend in his wide-brimmed beaver hat, a loden overcoat with a tall wolfskin collar, dark glasses, the usual make-up over his scars. Today Röhm, too, wore his badge inside his lapel. Pretending to take an interest in the posters for coming presentations, he indicated I should join him in the men's urinal. As soon as we were alone, he gave me my ticket. We would go in separately, he said. I had not, he was sure, been followed.

This was surely overly cautious? But Röhm was a planner; his success was due to his ability to foresee every possible detail. So we entered the auditorium individually after the lights had dimmed. When it was safe, we joined each other in the dark of the expensive back rows. He had bought one of those boxes of chocolates they sell in foyers. He told me to eat all the dark ones. He preferred milk. He shouldn't have chocolate at all with his arthritis.

Even as we settled in our seats, the interior was slowly transformed to a glorious cathedral of multicoloured neon. There came the wafting scents of spring roses. Pretty blonde girls in traditional costume went up and down the aisles freshening the air with spray guns. Then the whole theatre vibrated to the roar of a single, massive chord. Playing selections from well-known film scores, from the lovely operettas of Strauss and Lehár, the great organ began to rise from the pit.

My Virgil seemed tense, but he was jovial enough in his passing remarks, loosening his clothing and lighting a cigarette. The back of the *Kino* was completely empty. A few couples occupied the front seats together with some solitary men, but nobody was interested in us. Unusually, Röhm smelled of spirits. I heard the swill of a bottle in his pocket.

We began as usual with a newsreel. The excitement of the current political situation, the dominance of the Nazis in the Reichstag. The need for strong government. A rally of Nationalists and their own supporters, the impressive Stahlhelm battalions. Various Nationalist politicians were prominent. There were pictures of Hindenburg and of Hitler, of von Schleicher, von Papen and various other politicians. A general milling about outside parliament. Sozis raising their clenched fists in the air. Storm Troopers giving Nazi salutes, clearly in defiance of a disapproving constabulary. Nazi deputies returning the salutes as they made their way en masse into parliament. Socialists returning the clenched fist signal. All it needed was a deputy or two making scissors with their fingers and we should have had the entire scissors-paper-stone routine. Perhaps that was the origin of Churchill's famous V-sign?

A mixture of Nazi uniforms and conventional pinstripes. Hess and Strasser mounting the steps. Scenes inside the Reichstag. Where is Hitler? Goebbels speaking to the congress. Shots of the corner of Prinzregentenplatz. Policemen interviewed. Considerable space given to the death of the niece of 'prominent young Munich politician' Adolf Hitler. Various other men gesticulating urgently. A general sense of tension and uncertainty. Röhm seemed horrified when, for a few moments, his gigantic uniformed image appeared on the screen. He was, of course, an increasingly well-known figure. No mention of him was made by name, but the marshalled ranks of Storm Troopers were testimony to his power.

I do not remember if there was sound. In those days the newsreels did not always have it, since most regional theatres were not converted. Röhm seemed unhappy with the reporting. He said that it was UfA news and that meant it was slanted towards the ideas of a few reactionary old industrialists who wanted to restore the Wittelbachs and the Kaiser. He relaxed into innocent amusement as we watched a concoction called something like *Nie wieder Liebe*. I found it mildly funny but Röhm was roaring and slapping at himself, his bottle forgotten. He was in excellent spirits when the two-reeler came on, a Western with Buck Jones. Jones was a new star, the best type of All-American boy, righting wrongs and rescuing fair maidens. Full of wild action and wholesome heroics, the film was well above the usual quality. People find it fashionable to mock at morality these days, but I see nothing amusing in showing evil thwarted and virtue triumphant. Röhm loved these tales. He nudged me once and whispered in fun that Mr Jones was an even better rider than I. The film had been given a decent budget. The subtitles were German, of course. Not a talkie, but a musical soundtrack had been attached. Röhm agreed with me that he would rather have a live orchestra.

Next came a pre-war Douglas Fairbanks Keystone comedy in his old style, with organ accompaniment, the titles in Gothic German, giving them all a vaguely Victorian quality, but the sparse audience filled that great cinema with appreciative laughter. Mack Sennett was a hero in Germany. They were fond of saying how much of the technology had been invented by Germans, how many of the American film-makers had German names. I sensed a peculiar feeling of goodwill towards America in those days, because the USA had not fallen into the vengeful trap of the rest of the Allies and made vast, unmeetable reparation demands on the defeated country.

With over a third of her citizens of German origin, America had no great animosity towards Germany. America had not been the cause of inflation. Wall Street, as Germans were fond of saying at that time, was not Wisconsin. When Röhm explained the reality, it made perfect sense. Most of Germany's major national debts were either paid in deliberately inflated currency or written off. Big Business had taken advantage of a disaster which left ordinary families destitute but allowed private companies to make massive profits in foreign currency. Until the government produced the new hard mark those few fat businessmen benefited very well from inflation. Their profits were not poured back into the needy country but sent to Switzerland, England, Liechtenstein and America. Röhm understood this as well as any Bolshevik.

The understanding was beginning to dawn on the victors, too, I think, that an impoverished nation impoverishes the nations it trades with. The French and American Jews in particular had been quick to take advantage of Germany's rock-bottom prices. With his eyes fixed on the screen, Röhm talked through the Keystone comedy in a low monotone which only I could hear. He was clearly a man obsessed. He had come here with the intention of forgetting his problems, but the problems had followed him into the *Kino*.

He only fell completely silent when the main feature, a glossy confection set in Vienna some time early in the nineteenth century, began, a talkie. I must admit, I was astonished by the quality of the sound. It was as if a full orchestra was playing in the theatre and the voices of the performers filled the air like a choir of angels. Slowly I was drawn into the wonderfully complex plot, featuring Metternich's various machinations with wonderful romantic performances from Lilian Harvey, Conrad Veidt and Willy Fritsch. We even saw our great Russian Emperor Tsar Alexander represented. Waltzes were danced and balls were given, peasants sang and the world was merry, full of promise, for together we had defeated the threat from Napoleon. A high moment for Europe.

Both Röhm and I were enraptured by the film. I fell in love with Lilian Harvey. I could almost smell her. She was gorgeous and naturally graceful, a girl of the people very much of the Mrs Cornelius type, with the same helmet of white-blonde hair. The vital young Englishwoman, singing beautifully in German, was a great star here. The scene where she sings on her way to visit Willy Fritsch (as Tsar Alexander) and all the peasants join in with her has been copied a million times since. The background of the charming romance was the founding of the Holy Alliance between Prussia, Austria and Russia after Napoleon had been exiled to Elba. A serious political theme, telling us something of current political attitudes, which also engaged Röhm's attention.

The Germans, of course, had always led the field in kinematography, and there was no faulting this extraordinary operetta, the form in which they were also the unrivalled masters. The extravaganza was produced with so much more flair and taste than those more famous American musicals which came to imitate *Der Kongress tanzt* and its successors.

No wonder the Hollywood studios were all over Berlin, especially at UfA's great Neubabelsberg headquarters where American scouts were courting all the top directors and stars. Germany, as the German papers never stopped telling us, was second only to America in film production and exports. UfA owned film, distributor and the cinema we sat in.

We left just before the lights went up. Röhm said he hadn't seen a more delightful film in years. We were both humming the melodies as he led me into the street and hailed a cab, shoving me through the door and giving an address in the respectable southern suburb. Once in the cab he pulled down the blinds and relaxed. 'Nobody on our tail,' he said.

I began to think he was disturbed. Or did he know more than I did?

I asked him where we were going, and he smiled tenderly, kissing me briefly on the cheek. 'Home,' he said. 'You'll love it. They'll love you. You'll behave yourself. You always do.'

Sure enough, to my enormous astonishment, Röhm was taking me to meet his family!

Röhm's mother and sister lived in a very pleasant house in a tree-lined avenue. The main parlour, where I sat while Röhm had a private word with his sister, was dominated by a mirror-polished ebony grand piano. Otherwise the room was rather sparsely furnished and seemed hardly used. It looked out through long French windows to a balcony and the wide street beyond the trees. Prints of Ney and Wellington hung on the walls, pictures of Cromwell's victories, military engravings of Prussian cavalry on parade. A bust of Beethoven in black marble looked over the piano. Pale green wallpaper. A pretty Meissen urn on the piano's dark reflection. Clearly Röhm, rather than his mother and sister, had furnished this parlour. It had an austere, masculine air to it, was not 'lived in', but more likely 'mused' in. Röhm played the piano less and less because his long, sensitive fingers had begun to feel, he said, as if they were full of shrapnel. I knew the sensation. Sometimes I have it in my stomach.

I could not help being mystified. First Röhm warned that our intimacy must no longer be public. Then he took me to visit his mother! I think, looking back, that he was in emotional turmoil and I must say I cannot blame him. Perhaps he wanted me to see this other side of him because some instinct warned him that he would be ferociously libelled by his enemies within the party and, through them, by the world. Did he understand that somehow I would survive the coming deluge? Is that why he wanted me to know what I already knew, that he was a sophisticated and sensitive human being? Behind that military swagger, that Bavarian bonhomie, that fixed conservatism of his class and calling, there was, I believe, an artist, an intellectual. He could be cruel. At times he could certainly advocate and order brutality, even if he did not take part in it. But these were brutal times. Like the soldier-priests of old, a man had to cultivate the sword as well as the pen to survive in post-war Germany. I was not nervous of him. He loved me. In a way I also loved him. Germany might fear him, but I did not.

Certainly at that moment I was more nervous of meeting Frau Röhm than I was of being the victim of Hitler's vengeance. A servant girl shuffled in wearing a somewhat ill-fitting uniform, as if she had only recently taken the job and inherited the previous incumbent's clothes. With a peasant's heavy-handedness she brought in a coffee tray and a cake stand while an older, rather stooped woman followed her, carefully carrying some plates. Like the maid, the woman was dressed in black, but hers were familiar widow's weeds of the kind worn by so many women in those days. Behind this matron came a woman only a little older than Röhm himself, I guessed. She, too, wore a simple black dress with a black jacket. Her expression was amiable, on a broad, glowing Bavarian face. I detected no close family resemblance. Röhm's features were altogether finer than his relatives' and suggested that his father's had been the dominant genes. Neither woman wore much make-up. Frau Röhm had a healthy, rather scrubbed appearance. These plain women somehow looked out of place in that austere, masculine room. They needed the comforts of their class, their floral prints and chintz and china, to give them any colour at all.

They arrived like strangers and arranged stiff-backed Empire chairs around the coffee and the cakes, smiling and nodding at me vaguely, as if they were not sure I could speak. I clicked my heels and bowed in the Prussian fashion. They seemed impressed by this. We exchanged greetings. As we did so, Röhm came hurrying back into the room. He kissed his mother's hand, patted his sister on the arm, asked after his brother, who was not at home, and announced me as Herr Max Peters, the American film actor. Then I suddenly guessed he was fulfilling a promise to them. His mother and sister already knew who I was and had probably seen some of my films. Like most women, they were curious about celebrity. A hint of Hollywood engaged even the least imaginative *Hausfrau*.

While the clumsy servant handed us our plates and offered elaborate cream pastries, I made conversation in my rather old-fashioned German. I had learned more Yiddish than German when I had worked for the Jew in Odessa, but I think I succeeded in answering their enquiry. I was not planning to go back to Hollywood immediately. I had fallen in love with Bavaria. But, of course, I was still an employee of Il Duce. This was another personality who interested them, so we chatted a little about Mussolini whom, naturally, I was not particularly well disposed towards just then. I told them what a wonderful woman Signora Rachele Mussolini was and what lovely children she had, how Signor Mussolini took a personal interest in his sons and, no matter how busy with affairs of state, was still able to give them the attention and discipline they needed from a father. I mentioned that Signora Mussolini had personally asked me to teach her son Bruno to fly. Like their father they already rode very well. The boys would grow up as true Italian gentlemen.

This news was greeted with considerable approval by the women and caused Röhm to murmur some remark into his coffee cup which had both of us smiling. But I recovered myself. I had no intention of letting Röhm down. He clearly had considerable affection for his mother yet addressed her in that familiar, faintly mocking, slightly hectoring way his generation had with older people. I think that, too, had something to do with the War. You became impatient with their sentimentality. You could not tell them of the horrors you had seen.

Frau Röhm asked me what I thought of the Vatican. Had I been received by the Pope? I told her that the Vatican did something to my soul. I would soon be granted an audience with the Pope. She said that she hoped the Pope would now be able to do something about the political situation. Mussolini had kept his word and restored the Vatican's power. She was a woman of sharp intelligence. She spoke of the crisis in the Reichstag, the threat to Brüning's chancellorship. Rather than correct her misunderstanding of the situation, Röhm chuckled and said there seemed little hope of the Chancellery now, but perhaps next time. We were trying to run before we could walk. 'Alf's temporarily lost his powers. All we can do for the moment is keep him up there in general view. It would be fatal if he lost his position with the public now.'

Frau Röhm had listened without hearing him. When he had finished she turned to me with a pleasant smile. 'You are a famous

336

American cowboy star, I understand, Herr Peters. But all Americans are from somewhere else, I know!'

I told her that my parents were from Madrid. Until recently my great-uncle had been Archbishop of Sta Maria. I did not really lie so much as use a code, letting her know how I was 'one of us'. This stopped any barrier forming between us. She was, as a Catholic, clearly reassured by my response. That I held to the true Eastern Church was unimportant. That we both worshipped Jesus Christ was what bound us. I was telling her that I accepted her value system. It is often a mistake to accuse someone of telling a lie. Often they are telling the truth disguised by a lie.

I brought up the Jewish Question in relation to their domination of Hollywood. Contrary to later distortions, Röhm and his family were not rabidly anti-Semitic.

'I've nothing against an honest Jew making a living,' said Röhm. 'Though usury's the bane of modern economics. My complaint is that he then has to give his fifteen brothers and brothers-in-law a living – which means equally honest Germans are in the soup queues because Jews give jobs to Jews. You can't blame them. We shall have a quota system so that Jewish businesses can only employ so many non-Aryans. At least it will give us a level battlefield.' (A far cry, I think you will agree, from Treblinka!)

'A few heads might have to roll in the present government.' He laughed. He was using conventional phrases. These were the years of strong language, of newspaper hyperbole, where the vocabulary of war had infected all aspects of everyday life, just as military language translated through sport infects modern English. He never meant literally that people's heads should be chopped off. He simply meant that Sozis and Nationalists would have to be replaced with National Socialists so that they had a large enough majority to pass such laws. He did not anticipate the punitive so-called Nuremberg Laws which Röhm had absolutely nothing to do with, of course, and which Hitler borrowed from America.

Fräulein Röhm seemed to wish to change the subject. As Röhm's mother talked to him about a relative who had recently fallen ill, his sister moved to sit comfortably beside me on the lumpy couch and asked if I understood that cats had a religion.

'Do you keep cats, Herr Peters?' she asked rather diffidently.

'No, madam. I fear I am away from home too often. You have cats of your own?'

'Not at present, Herr Peters. Do you know what cats' religion is? They believe that when they die they become humans. They live for seven or ten or fifteen years, as some cats do, and then they die and turn into humans. That is a sweet idea, don't you think?'

'Very, Fräulein. Extremely. Touching. And who are these people who were once cats? Can we recognise them or do they move secretly among us?'

'Babies,' she said. 'They go from kitten, to cat, to baby and eventually to human maturity.'

'What then?'

'They become kittens again, I suppose.' She smiled playfully. It was odd to see such imagination sparkling from such unremarkable features. 'It is not a very complicated religion!' She laughed again with unexpected, girlish spontaneity. She loved cats, she said, but it was impossible at the moment. The significance of her expression escaped me even as I nodded in sympathy.

Röhm had the soldier's ability to relax in any circumstances. He seemed the only one actually comfortable on those chairs. Looking at his short military haircut and the way he held his coffee cup, I was suddenly reminded of a tonsured priest, and for a moment saw my friend, the leader of a great military force, as a monk on a visit home from the monastery. Many of the Nazis had the same puritanical rhetoric which had driven the Normans and helped them hold a conquered England, so I took it sometimes with a pinch of salt. The rhetoric was useful stuff, a kind of sustaining fuel, but it was not realistic. I am always pleasantly surprised by originality in the apparently unexceptional and warmed rather strongly to Fräulein Röhm. I could see that we might have a good, platonic friendship if I stayed longer in Munich. I think I had made a friend I would be able to see again. It occurred to me that while I waited for my opportunity to visit England, I could return temporarily to Vienna, which seemed a good place to be to test the waters, but once again I had no employer, no money and no certainty of being able to keep myself in the necessities of life. At some stage I would have to prevail upon Röhm for funds.

As Fräulein Röhm chatted to me, I must admit these anxieties went through my mind. She asked me if I planned to take any acting roles here in Munich. I told her that I was first and foremost an engineer. It seemed that the sooner I was in contact with some German manufacturer, who would buy my patents and offer me a royalty, the better. I was, I said, at present obliged to her brother, but that situation was, of course, untenable. She seemed disappointed when I remarked that, should I stay in Germany, I might find myself a flat in Berlin. I had privately formed the opinion that Bavaria was something of a backwater, its predominantly peasant culture both narrowly religious and prudent, glad to welcome tourists who, even in the darkest days, supplied many towns with their main trade. Munich, while delightful to look at, and full of the old, good-hearted spirit of those poets and painters attracted by the largesse of the Wittelbachs, themselves great patrons of the arts, was not at the heart of things, only at the heart of the NSDAP, which had started there. Even the party's centre of gravity was shifting to Berlin.

I said nothing of this to Röhm's sister. I had no wish to end my relationship with him. However, as the duties of party and army consumed him, he would be spending more and more time in Berlin. I merely told his sister that Berlin was where one had to be if one wished to get things done. She understood this. She said how hard all the travelling was for Ernst, with his arthritis being so painful. She darted him a sympathetic smile. Laughing, he assured her that these days he travelled first class on the best trains and in the finest cars. He had come quite a way from when he was reduced to selling encyclopaedias door to door like so many ex-servicemen. His mother pooh-poohed this as something he should not talk about, and I was reminded of Röhm's respectable background. This was the man who had called himself a wicked, brutal creature. Yet, of course, that was far from being the whole individual, as he proved when, at his mother's request, he played some Schubert songs for her on the piano.

Frau Röhm made me eat more cake but did not press her son. She said that Ernst had to watch his figure now that he was a great public man. He had always loved stories of the American wilderness, she said. Was I familiar with the work of Karl May? I told her that Old Shatterhand and Winnetou the Apache Prince were my constant companions as a boy. I almost made reference to old Professor Lustgarten, who had lent me the stories in Kiev, before I realised it would contradict her impression of my having been born in America. I found myself hesitating, at a loss for words. Röhm, believing me to be in trouble, made an excuse for us. He sprang up. We had a meeting, he said. Suddenly we were putting on our coats.

339

In the hall the women asked me to sign their friendship books and with simpering grace hoped that I would stay in Germany to make some films for them. They were both delightful. As we left, Frau Röhm gave my friend a large, awkward-looking parcel tied up in newspaper. 'For the dog,' she whispered.

I kissed hands. I hoped I would see the ladies again. Röhm was now in a hurry and bustled me and the parcel down the drive to the ordered taxi which would take us back to central Munich. He was a little embarrassed by the package of bones. 'She loves my Griselda.' He often left his Alsatian bitch with them when he went away. He felt better when she was there to protect them. Griselda was currently guarding Röhmannsvilla. I had rarely seen the animal.

He put the bones on the floor of the cab and instructed the driver to take us to the Königshof. I reminded him that I was being thrown out of that hotel. He nodded at this, but his attention was on our surroundings. He looked right and left, craning his head to peer through the small back window. 'Just a precaution,' he said. 'If the cops are checking on us, they won't get much, and if it's one of Himmler's new overzealous Boy Scouts, they'll tell him I took you home to Mother.'

'Won't that add to his suspicions?' I asked, but he laughed happily at this suggestion.

'Not a bit! That's the beauty of it. Alf knows I never even let my special friends meet her. You're very privileged, Mashi.'

'I appreciate that,' I said. I again reminded him that privileged as I was, I needed a roof over my head.

He nodded, frowning, something else on his mind. He looked at his watch several more times. 'It'll be all right. I'll speak to the manager. No, no. That would be stupid. We'll find you somewhere to hide out for a while, don't worry. Be a good idea for you to move. But I might have to get someone else to help you. I can't even spare an adjutant. I've got to fly up to Berlin tonight. God in heaven, Mashi, have you been whoring up in that room?'

I was offended, and he apologised. I knew of no reason why the management was taking its attitude unless certain enemies I had made in Soviet Russia had succeeded in exerting their influence. He agreed it was a strong possibility. If there was another file, like the one he had received from Frau Oberhauser, it could put me in an awkward position. 'You always think you've covered your angles and then comes the one you haven't anticipated,' he said. 'All the more reason for you to move out of the limelight. Anyone's limelight.' Deep in thought, he began to hum to himself, tapping his fingers on the seat rest.

We were rounding the corner, running into the busy evening traffic of Prinzregentenplatz, when he slapped me on the arm. He had a solution. 'That loony von Schirach's in town, and he's bound to know somewhere. He looks after all the students, the Hitler Youth. He's your man. Great favourite of the Führer's.'

'Then is it wise –?'

'Of course. That's the whole point. The closer to the danger you are, the safer you are. Another thing you learn in the trenches!'

He seemed delighted with himself. He had solved my problem. Unfortunately it did not seem solved to me. Again, I had reason to doubt my friend's grasp on reality. Whenever I tried to raise practical matters he simply shook his head and asked me questions. Had I liked his mother? Did I find his sister attractive?

The taxi drew up outside the hotel. A quick squeeze of my hand, a word of reassurance and he pressed something upon me. Then, rather bewildered, I was in the street watching Röhm speeding away towards his destiny. Thoughtfully I turned and slipped through the revolving doors. I wondered if I would ever see Fräulein Röhm again. In the lobby I looked down at what Röhm had presented me with before I left the cab. Grease was beginning to seep through on to my hands. He had given me the parcel of bones his mother had offered him for his bitch Griselda.

THIRTY–FOUR

At eight the next morning I was again awakened by Frau Socking, but this time her manner was far less severe. She seemed her old self. I smiled at her pleasantly. Perhaps someone had spoken to the manager and I was to be reinstated?

She expressed only relief at my leaving. 'Some boys are in the lobby to help you move,' she announced. '*Grüss Gott*, Herr Peters.' She was already making off.

I called after her that I would be down shortly. A porter could collect my luggage in an hour. Having so little with me, it did not take long to pack. Plans, pistols and my dwindling supply of 'cocoa' were the most important items and these went into my locked case, which I took with me. I left the bones in my room. As soon as my bags were ready, I strolled down to the lobby to meet the emissary Röhm had sent in his place.

I knew both the Stabschef and Hitler thought highly of this young man. In his pictures Baldur von Schirach had seemed the very model of the modern, clean–cut German lad. In the flesh he gave the same impression, though his movements were somewhat awkward. Round–headed, blond, slightly plump, with almost a rosebud mouth, pink-and-white skin, smiling pale blue eyes and an eager, friendly manner, he was a typical Teuton. He offered me that increasingly common *Ben-Hur* salute, a *Heil Hitler* followed by his enthusiastic pumping of my hand. He was dressed in expensive lederhosen, picturesquely decorated with full Bavarian floral flourishes. Over this he had thrown a large leather military coat. I was a little amused. He gave me the impression of a large chorus girl who had left the theatre in too much of a hurry to change.

Von Schirach spoke in the softly articulated educated accent associated with the old North German upper classes. The modern Nazi style was rough and coarse, whether you had started life with it or not. Röhm was a perfect example of this. His motto among his men, who worshipped him, was 'the lewder the better'. He had been well educated and was, of course, from a good Munich family. I have described the Stabschef at home. When he wished, he could revert to his old, civilised way of speaking as he had during that visit.

As I have said, the experience of the trenches was determining the tone of the language. The new style was considered more author-itative, tougher, down-to-earth, practical, showing mocking impa-tience with the old institutions. It reached its dubious zenith in Berlin, where it became the only language you heard in the theatre, unless you attended an operetta. Newspaper journalists adapted the style for their pages. Novelists copied it. Films by Pabst and Lang employed it with relish. It appeared in poetry and fiction by Brecht and operas by Berg. Elsewhere, Schoenberg and Stravinsky were adding their cacophony to the general din. I found it impossible to enjoy a concert without one of these gentlemen introducing the wails and clatters of the synagogue and mosque into the event. If one wished to see a modernist film, the chances were that members of the audience would be hurt in clashes between Commies and Nazis objecting to what they perceived as political bias. Gangster writers spread their harsh, Yiddish-enriched rhetoric among office boys and students. Thus, by aping Berlin street language, the Jews helped proliferate a vocabulary ultimately employed in their own destruction. Everything I had been made to say to Hitler that night was available in some form to those who sought it out. Berlin was awash with aggressive filth.

Röhm argued that the Nazis had brought the language of the NCO to the Reichstag, which was why Hindenburg had been so uncomfortable with it. Röhm added that when people weren't listening, you had to shout to be heard. The Nazis had been shouting for ten years; it had become a habit.

Von Schirach adopted that peculiar half-apologetic stance of his class towards admired members of the lower orders. He spoke with a slight lisp, like Röhm, which I think was considered elegantly Viennese.

Von Schirach introduced himself and his smart boy helpers, Ulrich and Siegfried, who wore the brown shirts and black trousers of the *Hitlerjugend*. As soon as these formalities were over, he switched to perfect English. He apologised for not having a car for me. All available transport was needed because of the situation in Berlin. In a few more days we might discover if justice would out and the Führer was to become the new Chancellor. These were exciting times. As we spoke, the Führer was sitting in his mountain fastness at Tegernsee brooding on the future and coming to a monumental decision.

Adding to all his other troubles, said von Schirach, was Hitler's enormous weight of grief at the death of his poor little niece. Geli had shown signs of instability for some time. Her uncle had done all he could, trying to get her to take a positive interest in the world. He had supported her in every way. Typically, the Führer had cancelled political meetings just to be available to her. He took that sort of interest in all who were close to him. Angela was to have fulfilled her first engagements as a singer, but evidently the anxiety had been too much for her,

I asked him if he had liked the girl. Oh, yes, he said. He and she had got on very well, though she was a little boisterous with him in her country way. She had been a happy little thing. But sometimes she would sink into dark, black moods. He had seen the Führer at his wits' end with her. This was the first time I had heard someone close to Hitler use the Führer title without irony. It meant 'guide' as well as 'leader'. It fell naturally from the young man's lips. I admired his commitment to his Chief, even if my own recent impression of Hitler was somewhat different.

How was he so familiar with Geli's state of mind? Well, of course, it was in all the papers. Even those not vehemently anti-Nazi. She and he had been great pals. A jolly, outgoing person fresh as a mountain flower, she had never lived in a big city before which no doubt put an extra strain on her. She could hardly have known what she was doing. But if you read some of the papers, you'd think Hitler had taken a gun and shot her himself. Wasn't it disgusting what a cynical press did with tragedy! These days no limits were put on the indecencies and uncollaborated scandal they published.

Von Schirach was innocently sincere. I could not help being charmed by one so young for his age but full of zeal and idealism. I saw no mystery in Hitler's liking for him, why Hitler had put him in charge of the movement's idealistic boys. Von Schirach said he would be leaving for the capital fairly soon. Meanwhile, a stiff, old-fashioned Prussian bow and a heel click, given a somewhat burlesque quality by his clothes, and he was at my service. As his boys hefted my luggage, he passed an aristocratic word with the porter and led the way from the hotel. In French I complimented him on his English. He laughed easily. His mother was American, he said. She had been in the theatrical profession and had never bothered to learn German, so he had spoken English until he went to his primary school. His father, though a member of the Prussian Officer Corps, was a great cosmopolitan and famous in Weimar as a theatre director. He had run the Court Theatre, which I presumably knew. 'We have a great deal in common, Herr Peters. I have a background already in show business, you see!'

His laughter was open and refreshing. His attempts to create a bond, assuming acting to be my main occupation, were kindness itself. He became more serious. 'And my family was always very open-minded. They didn't complain much at all when I joined the Nazis. Of course, it wasn't the first patriotic organisation I had been in. Now they and Herr Hitler are great pals. He was so sympathetic over Uncle Karl. And that perhaps is why my heart goes out to him now. My uncle killed himself from shame after the sell-out at Versailles. I hate those bastards who stabbed the German fighting man in the back. I'm determined to devote my life to Germany. My family supported me absolutely. I could have joined the Nationalists or one of the more conventional parties, but they did not object. They have always had bohemian friends even before they knew our Führer.'

He told me all this as we walked rapidly towards the tram stop, his greatcoat flapping around his bare legs, trailed by the Brownshirt boys lugging my bags. The pavements were crowded with busy shoppers and workers beginning to wrap up against the mid-autumn air. The shops were stuffed already with seasonal delights. You would never know the country stood on the brink of economic collapse. I understood the importance of creating a mood of optimism. Every grocery was a riot of red, gold, silver, green and blue. Every carpet shop and furniture store displayed the latest geometric 'jazz' patterns. Every third doorway offered the delights of coffee, chocolate and vanilla strudel, their scents mingling with the sour-sweet smell of beer and sausages. The city was warmed by the acrid stink of cigar smoke and burning oil in the sharpening air. The cafés were full. Music from the latest films poured out of them. Everywhere they were playing Lilian Harvey's wonderful 'Das gibt's nur einmal, das kommt nicht wieder' – 'This Happens Once and Never Again' –

which had been the big moment in *Der Kongress tanzt*. Hinting at a return to the old German values, the song made such a change from the wild, unmusical rhythms of the jungle and the American ghetto which Berliners, at least, had taken to in their millions. I thought about Mr Mix. He would have done well to go to Berlin where to be black was to find instant employment!

In Munich smart uniforms were still in evidence. Policemen, postmen, civil servants, students, Storm Troopers, Stahlhelm, regular soldiers, Salvation Army and others were everywhere, but the War had taken the best of us. An ambulance sang by, scattering horses and cars. Little boys ran in its wake. I watched them until my view was blocked by a great baker's dray full of hot bread, drawn by a team of massive shire horses. With a police constable's help, it turned against the traffic like a great ship taking the wind.

Overhead was a lattice of wires for telephones and electricity. Other cables powered the blue-and-white trams jingling and banging with festive clatter along the broad thoroughfare between tall trees whose golden leaves already clogged the gutters. Horses and motor vehicles jostled, clinked and hooted at pedestrians who dodged in and out of the traffic, much to the disgust of matrons and chauffeurs. Everywhere, in banners and placards, Oktoberfest was anticipated. Already the Bavarian peasant farmers with their equally stolid sons could be seen on the streets. Many of them wore their traditional best. The praises of films were shouted in banner print. *Voruntersuchung!!* (*Storms of Passion*), *Der Mann, der seinen Mörder sucht*. That last was a strange title which struck a chord. How could a man go in search of his own murderer? I never saw the film and so never discovered the answer.

Willy Fritsch and Charlie Chaplin smiled out at us. Betty Annan lifted her skirts to dance. Emil Jannings was sober and stern. Familiar faces. Marlene Dietrich. Joan Crawford. The big success was *Monte Carlo Madness* with the debonair Hans Albers, whom some thought I rather resembled. Louise Brooks. Lilian Harvey. Lon Chaney. Advertisements for beer and political parties added more vivid colour to kiosks, cable standards, postboxes and walls, wherever they would stick. Hindenburg was presented as a vital old knight, his stern eyes staring over his proud Prussian moustachios towards his hinted-at retirement. Many showed pictures of Hitler striking heroic poses as saviour of the Fatherland. Nazi banners boldly confronted the Marxist invaders. The threat from the East was a reality to these people who had lived close to the marches where Christianity came face to face with Islam and her allies. But for a miracle, and the courage of a few fighters, Bavaria would be Communist to this day.

Other posters warned of Jewish power. Still others exhorted us to vote Communist, Nationalist, Christian Socialist, Social Democrat, Anarcho-Syndicalist and for Flag and Country. A dozen millennial visions were pasted across the posts and kiosks and walls of that busy modern town. Perhaps it was too late for us to turn again to the New?

In my view the Nazis were wrong to stop publication of the Bible. They should have let the Old Testament fade into history, remembered only by obscure denominations, revered by a few marginalised sects, like the Apocrypha. The Old Testament and our continued reference to it to this day maintain the Jewish influences all decry but none ever properly address. I cannot understand why such organisations as the White Defence League warn all who will listen about the Bolshevik Jewish threat, yet every Sunday happily tucks its propaganda under their arms and sets off for church! *L'histoire est un perpetuel recommencement.*

Germany was witnessing so much electioneering she had become heartily sick of democracy. Democracy got her no further forward. Ruling chiefly by emergency decree, torn between extremes of left and right, the Reichstag had become a laughing stock. Only the NSDAP offered a genuine alternative to all this uncertainty. Only the NSDAP offered a clear advance. And it was obvious from every poster one saw that the NSDAP was Hitler.

Again, as I passed a particularly dramatic poster of *Der Führer*, I experienced a slight shock as those same eyes which had stared at me in Tegernsee seemed to bore into me again. A disturbing illusion. Later I wondered if Hitler's eyes were not mirrors in which we saw everything we desired or feared. Were such shadows entirely creatures of our imagination, fashioned out of mud and entrails and made reality by a triumph of the will? Strange thoughts for a busy Tuesday in the centre of so much banal human activity.

Munich was vibrant with the sense of coming change. Indeed, she anticipated an apotheosis. A resolution to every dream Germany had nursed from the beginning of the century, when stability and growth would be reflected in the Reichstag's domination by a Bavarian party, nurtured in Bavarian soil, putting an end to the dominance of 'Red' Prussia whose election of so many Socialist deputies in 1914 had precipitated this war. Until now Prussia had been the determining power in Germany's history. But Munich would always remember the first blows of the Nazi revolution struck during 1923, the year of a noble, if unsuccessful, putsch. Now again there was hope, a spring in every citizen's step, an optimism which put smiles on faces and displayed an inner radiance. The soul of Germany was returning to life.

Röhm had the rights of it. Stories of German poverty were dreamed up by the Jewish press, whose owners were only interested in buying cheap stocks in German-owned firms. In spite of all efforts to suppress her, the German economic giant had restored herself to power in less than a decade. We know now how certain alien influences in Germany conspired to produce conditions where only the decent German working people and ex-soldiers, poor mothers and children suffered the results of inflation. Even the *Völkischer Beobachter* had noticed a preponderance of Jews in the shops, stocking up for a season they enjoyed but did not celebrate. Many were not difficult to spot. Others, of course, were better disguised, with Aryan names and looks which could pass a casual glance.

We reached the tram stop. Baldur still talked enthusiastically about Hitler and Röhm. He admired both. He knew that Röhm's bluff foul-mouthed manner hid a sensitive and generous heart. That's what his men sensed, why they loved him so fiercely. Schirach spoke of the people who had benefited from Röhm's open-handedness. He was not a rich man, but was always generous with what he had. A Bavarian of the old, best sort, he knew how to talk to people at all levels. Just as the Führer did. Germany would know true equality under the National Socialist Party. Irrespective of social background, strong men and women would marry and produce the healthiest children in the world, a proud, self-reliant race with room to breathe and grow. Count and carpenter would work side by side to build a finer, cleaner country, whose broad new roads would be laid like wedding ribbons across the nation.

In response to his enthusiasm I asked a little sardonically if the wedding ribbons would be white.

'Oh, white! Of course!' He laughed heartily. 'White, white, white. I love white. So much easier to clean. Ha, ha! White for a virgin Germania, white for her Austrian husband! I wrote a poem on the subject for the Führer. He keeps it in his wallet.' He shook his head as if I had made a great, insightful joke. 'Poetry is another talent which runs in my family. White for the new Germany, black for our swastika, sign of rebirth, red for our blood, our pure German blood. Our Nazi colours are the true German colours. Do you see?'

He was only to a degree describing an idealised self. I said I was not the best person to be asked to evaluate a poetic work. I preferred novels and engineering books. 'Of course you would, of course you would,' he said rather mysteriously, more or less to himself. 'Naturally, we are keeping our eye on the Hamburg elections. That will give us a gauge of our power.' His discussion of strategy and politics was so narrow as to be all but meaningless to me. I was, however, well aware of the urgency of the situation. People scarcely realise these days how the fate of the Nazi Party hung on a knife edge in 1931 and 1932, why Röhm had needed my help so urgently.

At last the number 47 to Viktualienmarkt came along, and we struggled aboard while the driver complained and other passengers suggested we should have hailed a taxi. The thought had also occurred to me, but I did not have money for a taxi and received the impression young von Schirach, for all his expensive clothes, was not rolling in hard marks either. As it was, the two boys bought their own tickets, and von Schirach paid for me. Siegfried was blushing bright red, an unsuitable colour. The boys were far more embarrassed than von Schirach whose insouciance to social nuance was a characteristic of his class. Clinging to the overhead rail as I sat precariously on the edge of the only available wooden seat, with the boys swaying behind him, he spoke enthusiastically about the Jewish Question. The vehicle was a haze of human breath and smoke. The windows were steamed up, making it difficult to see where we were going.

Pausing only to assure me we were almost at our stop, Baldur continued with his cheerful babble. I was in agreement with many of his ideas but was also aware, as he was not, that a member of the tribe was sitting behind him glaring her disapproval. Von Schirach was one of those abstract anti-Semites who had nothing against individuals. He could not really tell the difference between a Jew and a Greek. All Mediterranean types looked the same to him. He spoke with the fire of the convert he was, having been inspired as a teenager by Hitler's oratory. There was definitely something infectious about Baldur's enthusiasm, his sense that something had to be done and done soon.

He was soon to be promoted to Youth Leader of the NSDAP, answering directly to Röhm, and he was very proud. The news would shortly be made public. Hitler and Röhm, he thought, were a perfect partnership – the dreaming philosopher and the realistic man of action. A combination of the German virtues. He laughed loudly again. 'The Führer is a person of rare goodness and sanity, but he needs someone to organise things for him. Like many geniuses, he's both highly strung and sensitive, though he hides it behind a mask of good humour. These Austrians, you know, are naturally easy-going, like most theatre folk. It's their charm, isn't it?'

Naturally I was a little confused and somewhat circumspect. Less than forty-eight hours had passed since the incident at Tegernsee and while it had faded, as all such things fade with the daylight, I found it still difficult to recall that von Schirach's heroic saviour of Germany was the same creature I had left covered with excrement in its darkened lair. Von Schirach was an intimate. Had he any notion of the truth? It seemed not. Some people are so innocent they impose their own purity of vision on everything around them. No doubt young Baldur knew nothing of the darker Hitler. Whatever hints he received he interpreted as the Führer's richness of reference and wisdom.

I was not particularly surprised by this, nor even by Hitler's somewhat extreme means of finding release. Many had discovered such methods, as Röhm had said, in the heightened conditions of the trenches. Hitler was not the first idealistic hero to pursue a private devil. One recalls the great Gilles de Rais, defender of Joan of Arc, remembered by history as Bluebeard, rapist, murderer and torturer of some two hundred children. Possibly the aberrations occurred in direct contrast to altruistic heroism, as if one could not exist without the other. We have all read the Robert Louis Stevenson tale which he originally wrote as *Rabbi Sheckel and Doctor Hide* (altered by the Hollywood sons of Shem to a more innocuous title) in which by day the narrator is an upstanding Aryan doctor, but by night becomes a blood-drinking Jewish monster. The film was very popular in Germany in my day. Perhaps, suggests our story, sides of the same soul are completely unsunderable. If one dies, so does the other. Sometimes I think both forces are needed in balance to make a fully functional human being.

Such people frequently refuse self-analysis, fearing it would only threaten or weaken them, like actors who change parts, from being 'themselves' in the dressing room to being 'themselves' onstage. Like an actor, Hitler needed only to work in short, hard bursts. Between

350

his parts he rested. Perhaps the more important the role, the more he retreated into himself?

The tram stopped suddenly. Most of the passengers began to disembark. The boys waited impatiently to take my luggage off. Evidently they knew where we were going. While showing no insubordination, they clearly thought this job beneath them and were constantly under von Schirach's disapproving glare until suddenly, they darted down a narrow, cobbled side street. For a second I thought they had decided to steal my bags and shouted in alarm. They were carrying everything of importance to my life. We ran to follow them as they disappeared through the gloomy entrance of a low building. Like a tunnel from one world to another, we were all at once in Wonderland, and childhood images came crowding into my head. My soul knew unexpected joy, a kind of memory. In that earlier time the writing had been in Cyrillic. Now it was in Gothic German.

Lit by dancing gas jets throwing fluttering shadows on to the ceiling was a vast covered market. Stalls and cubicles stretched almost endlessly into the half-light. The floor of the great roofed concourse was crowded with brilliantly coloured counters crammed with all kinds of country comestibles. Von Schirach told me this was Munich's famous covered food market, one of the largest in the region. Specialising in delicacies from all over the South, as well as fruit, vegetables, meat and sausages, the place was full of people, in spite of there being so little money about. Folk from the surrounding towns came to buy their annual luxuries and to take advantage of the various beer concessions. Red-faced farmers and their sons strolled around the pitches buying little. Clumps of them exclaimed at the outrageous prices, comparing quality with their own home produce. City dwellers and stallholders regarded them with amiable contempt in the main, but the peasants were by no means unwelcome in this lean year of 1931.

We passed a monstrous pitch the size of a circus tent selling nothing but a huge variety of cheeses on four sides. Medals and ribbons hung from the striped canvas, advertising the owner and his ancestry. Yellow wheels the size of truck tyres, heavy wedges of blue-veined Cambozola, Stilton and Roquefort, slivers of delicate French Brie and Camembert, and all the good, solid pale pinks and browns of the local varieties, together with the Goudas and Edams and Cheddars. Their combined scent hinted at the ultimate cheese. Beef bones and deer carcasses, hares and rabbits, chickens and geese hung in military ranks from the steel hooks. I smelled blood, fur, feathers, fresh-killed. Glittering candies and rich mounds of chocolate; flowers, toys and slabs of shining fish; wooden booths selling hot dumplings and vanilla custard.

Rising into the gloom, steam streaked the roof's dirty glass. We pushed through crowds lining up against a pork butcher's elaborate canvas, decorated with gold medals and shields, proclaiming prizes won as far away as Saxony and the Sudetenland. Electricity and naphtha buzzed. The wealth of smells made you want to stop and begin eating. You felt you could eat the air itself, it was so rich. Massive men and women commanded those stalls, like so many sea captains aboard their ships. Their wiry, darting sons and plump daughters served the customers, shouting responses and exhortations while still others called to us to buy the best of this, the freshest of that. Old men stood arguing at coffee stalls. Old women disdainfully fingered fruit.

And then, from a little cleared space near the far side of the huge, echoing hall, a hurdy-gurdy began to sound. Its cheerful, cheap blasts and whines, amplified by the roof, again reminded me of Odessa and my happiest days. An Italian with a huge Kaiser Wilhelm moustache and a tall felt hat, a tiny, red-jacketed monkey on his shoulder, was operating the handle of his barrel organ while in front of it danced a little ballerina in vivid scarlet and green. Her legs and feet were bare but she moved with extraordianry grace, her dark curls bobbing above her grave, aquiline face as she pirouetted. Her dark eyes met mine, and I was back in Kiev, falling in love with Zoyea, the gypsy girl, all over again . . .

I wanted to pause, to ask her name. To drop a coin in the cup which a boy, by looks her brother, shook at me. But von Schirach was in a hurry, and the youths with my luggage had not stopped. Again I had to trot to catch up. We followed them through another short tunnel before we had left the market and were outside again, marching against the crowd, down a few more streets to a slightly wider thoroughfare with a large carpet store on the corner, selling a rather more conservative selection than in the more fashionable Munich shops.

I was happy to find myself in a lower-class area dominated by a great, Baroque church. St Peter's was like one of our Kiev churches, though somewhat plainer. The invulnerable old bricks seemed to offer a stable centre. I felt thoroughly comfortable in this district and was again reminded of my childhood. While my father had been connected directly by blood to the most aristocratic family in Russia, therefore making me vulnerable to assassination by Reds, his irresponsible pursuit of socialism had led to all our ruin. So I grew up in a similar area, with children playing noisily in the streets, women gossiping, washing lines hanging across courtyards, with dogs, carts and bicycles everywhere. To me it was like home. Even the stone and brick felt warmer. The smells were more familiar. I began at once to relax. Here I could escape the hustle and bustle of political and sexual life! As I had been burning the candle at both ends, I needed to rest. I began to relish the prospect of peace. With the elections coming in several key areas, I was not likely to have much company among the Nazis, at least for a few weeks. I would spend my time rethinking my situation, considering what I could do to improve my circumstances.

A few more doors down the unremarkable street and we stopped at a shopfront whose windows were protected by an iron grille, securely padlocked. The grilles had received a heavy battering at some time. The red, black and white paint of the outside had flaked and the building hardly seemed used any more. Behind the grilles on the windows were older portraits of Adolf Hitler, 'the saviour of Germany, the keeper of our national honour'. Swastika symbols and the initials of the NSDAP made it clear we were at a local Nazi HQ. I suspected here we would pick up a key to some nearby apartment, but no sooner had Schirach unlocked the side door than the boys were dragging my bags through the gloom, which smelled strongly of dusty old paper, and up a flight of stairs. Von Schirach closed the door behind us, following me as I climbed in the boys' wake, my face a little too close to the nearest pair of tight black shorts whose owner was inclined to sweat readily and had that sour, unpleasant smell of most young boys, but I watched with pleasure his healthy little muscles and sinews rippling with the effort of dragging my worldly goods to the top of the building where we stopped at last. Von Schirach was beaming as he unlocked the door, flung it open and ceremoniously handed me the keys. 'Your flat!'

It was, in fact, a very comfortable little place. I suspected a woman's touch, a mistress or perhaps simply a mother, for it was almost feminine in its furnishings, with everything one might need neatly placed. Schirach had lived here himself until fairly recently, when his circumstances had improved, he said. His rent had helped the party through some thin times. Now the place was here for me as long as I needed it. The party required no rent these days. He understood I had accomplished important work for the Italian dictator. He was a great fan of Signor Mussolini, who had done wonders for Italy. He had undertaken the Herculean task of bringing masculine fire to that quintessentially feminine Italian soul. If anyone could do it, he could. Meanwhile, his emissaries were always welcome in Germany, especially among the ranks of Nazis. They had much in common with the Fascist cause. He quoted a favourite saying of the great dictator's: 'It is better to spend one day as a lion than to spend a lifetime as a lamb.'

I was a little taken aback by his apparently rehearsed speech, as if von Schirach suddenly recalled he had not spoken what he had prepared, so spoke it anyway, as a specific duty. Doubtless Röhm had offered some instructions on how to address me. Now young Baldur seemed to think he had become carried away in his excitement. Like many polyglots, he said more than he should when speaking a language other than the local one. He had revealed a romantic crush on an older man.

This generous emotion continued to radiate from him as he flitted about the flat showing me how to work the stove, where the china was kept, how a certain flap worked in the desk. I had a fleeting impression of an angelic visitation. Then he looked at his watch, raised his eyebrows and apologised. He had to go. Berlin and duty called!

I accompanied him and the boys back down the stairs while he tried to tell me the best baker, the best grocer and so on, suggesting that I could also shop in the Viktualienmarkt, which, as I had seen, offered a convenient short cut to the tram stop. The market was a bit crowded with tourists at the moment, because of the festival, and the prices had gone up, but I would still find it worth trying. There were several good cheap restaurants in the vicinity, also a wonderful new cinema nearby. The whole area was much improved since he had lived there. Even St Peter's, the local church, seemed a bit brighter. I assumed it was a Roman church and that therefore I might attend services if I were here for a length of time. At that time, you will recall, I had yet to accept the faith of my ancestors and worship in the Greek tradition.

As I stood in the street doorway bidding my new friend goodbye, the inner door leading into the shop at the side opened suddenly. I had not known the shop was occupied and jumped slightly.

A black beret perched on the side of his head, a sprightly puckish little face regarded us, looking us over with merry, sardonic eyes. Then, stiffening, the dapper newcomer bowed and heel-clicked to von Schirach. Ignoring me, he advanced upon the scowling Hitler Youth leader.

'*Mein lieber* Baldur!' He opened his arms as if to receive a beloved child. But Schirach's eyes narrowed, and he coloured a little. 'Good afternoon, Herr Doctor. We thought you still in Vienna. Or was it Prague you went to? I believe you are not supposed to be on these premises. I think you should let me have your key.'

'Why so?' A jovial Herr Doctor indeed! He twinkled, he was sly, he was warm, sarcastic. His mobile, clever mouth seemed forever smiling, smirking, sneering or grinning. His audacious brown eyes bore a hint of the Mediterranean, reminding me for an instant of my friend Fiorello. The doctor created the same sense in me that I was forever being watched for my reaction, so that he might respond appropriately, or at least know what to think of me, or how to make me think well of him. Yet his words were sardonic enough and showed no lack of courage. 'Has your lord and master Hitler banned me from the building I first helped him rent? I'm not surprised, since he's an habitual turncoat. He'll turn on you one day, my dear Baldur, and then nothing will save your tight little bum. Not even your convulsive poetry.'

Blurting and blushing, the poor boy pressed a large envelope into my hand and made his escape, warning me that the doctor had no business being on the premises. If he gave me any further trouble the police could be called. The number was in the office near the telephone. He was sorry about the dust. His last words were grimmer, addressed to the newcomer. 'I believe you have gone too far again, Doctor Strasser. I doubt it will be quite so leniently tolerated this time.' But because of his lisp, the words had no weight.

The doctor smiled quietly to himself and, with crooked mockery, bowed to von Schirach. Removing his beret, he placed it against his heart and clicked his heels. 'My good Herr Youth Leader! You'll discover soon enough that Herr Hitler's men are not quite as loyal to Big Business as their "Führer". This murder investigation will only help clear their vision . . .'

He lifted his black beret mockingly, a cigarette burning between his fingers, and dropped the hat neatly back on his balding head. 'My regards to your dear fiancée, Miss Hoffman. And to my brother Gregor, if you see him in Berlin. What a shame about Fräulein Raubal. I heard you were on the scene with Hess and my brother in a matter of hours. Clearing up the evidence, were you? Who did it, eh? Hitler hasn't the nerve for it. Himmler? Don't worry, my brother wouldn't tell me. We haven't been on the best of terms since he made his choice. He's almost as happy to lick Uncle Alf's arse as you are. I have plenty of other friends still in the party. Is Germany's great white hope mortified? How inconvenient for him . . .' He laughed without malice after them. The little boys were bewildered, perhaps waiting for Baldur to strike back at the man for uttering so many blasphemies at once, but von Schirach murmured something about the plane for Berlin and herded them ahead of him.

After von Schirach and his lads had rounded the corner, Doctor Strasser turned his cheerful attention on me. Gregor Strasser's brother was a small man, scarcely taller than myself, but very dapper. His humorous, sardonic manner seemed completely natural to him. He looked at one slightly sideways. Neatly dropping his cigarette butt into the street, he took a small case from his pocket and offered me a smoke but I refused. I told him I had eaten no breakfast or lunch and was beginning to feel peckish.

If I gave him five minutes, he told me, he would be glad to take me to an excellent and very cheap restaurant. A little worried that back numbers of the party paper would be destroyed during or after the elections, he had come from Vienna to sort out some of the old copies. He had no spares, and everything was stored here at what had been the party HQ until they'd moved to the Brown House. He remembered this place in the old days before the Great Compromise, but now it wasn't inhabited much. Was I going to live in the flat?

In spite of Baldur von Schirach's animosity towards him, Gregor Strasser's brother Otto was exceptionally charming and far more engaging than his taciturn sibling. He had a mobile, vaguely Jewish, face which could not help but twinkle and smile.

It occurred to me momentarily that perhaps he indeed had Jewish blood, the reason for his volatility, but it was extremely unlikely. Given their policies the Nazis could not afford to be too careful on matters of early ancestry. For some time I had heard and ignored the persistent rumours of Hitler's own Jewish grandparents. The theory was that these part-Jews so hated the blood in their own veins that they strove to tear it from the body of Germany as they would tear it from themselves. A popular theory, but not one I necessarily subscribed to. Ludecke, whom I met later, believed that the most virulent anti-Semites had strong doses of Jewish blood. Rosenberg was certainly Jewish, he argued. He had known several such creatures. All possessed a certain pathos. But even Ludecke, that irredeemable cynic, would agree with me that whatever blood animated the Strasser family it came from the right side of the Mediterranean!

I began to answer but Doctor Strasser silenced me, a finger to his lips. He straightened his beret, put away his case, and began to sink back into the semi-darkness among huge towers of baled newspapers and magazines.

Come to think of it, he said, he was feeling hungry, too. He would be glad to treat me. I in turn must tell him all about England, which he was thinking of visiting soon. I told him I knew little more of England than did he. I had not been born there. I was an American.

'Oh, you're the Hollywood actor Röhm's so taken with? The centre of gossip in Berlin and Vienna. You're not Jewish, are you?'

'Of course not!' I laughed. I could see Strasser was trying to get a rise out of me. 'But it's true Röhm and I have become great chums. We have much in common.'

'He's a good man. I've hardly seen him since he came back from Bolivia to run the SA, but he's doing wonders already. I wish he was with me and not Hitler. His heart is much more with the Black Front than the Hitlerists. But like my brother he believes Hitler will take them to power. My brother already has more power than he ever thought he could get. He'll lose it if he trusts Hitler too much. Gregor is considered by everyone to be the "civilised" Nazi, and it is to him Streicher and Co. turn. But unless they move quickly they will find they have delivered all their influence to Hitler. Why does everyone think they can take power from Hitler once he has it? We all watched him climb and admired him. But now he is climbing over us. My brother should know better. And, indeed, so should Röhm, who has been around the "little corporal" longer than anyone.'

I presumed he spoke chiefly of the internal squabbling besetting most political parties and rarely noticed by the world outside. For a few minutes I stood in the doorway watching him rummage about in the room, then I told him I would return to my flat and see him in a little while. He grunted assent.

I rejoined him about quarter of an hour later feeling considerably more my old self. The envelope von Schirach had given me contained a substantial amount of money. The little flat was quiet, secure and I could use it to concentrate on my own work for a change. Meanwhile, I intended to cultivate the charming doctor, whose tongue was even looser than Röhm's.

Dusting his hands he emerged from behind a pile of newspapers, put down a box he had been filling and apologised. He lit another cigarette. 'I am only looking for my own work. I can't afford to have it printed again.' Glancing around him he shook his head. He patted at a pile of magazines. 'Not that long ago, my young friend, these dreams were mine. But now it's all corrupted.'

Then, shrugging his shoulders, he took me by the arm, pointed me back into the street, closed and locked the door behind us with his key, and led us in a graceful stroll towards the Viktualienmarkt.

'Herr von Schirach didn't seem to like you.' Automatically I looked up and down to make sure we were not being followed.

'Oh, he's all right. But he has to take Hitler's side in everything. I enjoy embarrassing him a bit. He's not a bad lad. Just an idiot. He thinks the sun shines out of Hitler's bottom!'

We walked slowly towards the market while Strasser explained at length and rather obscurely why he had split with Hitler who, in his view, had made the party into the means of getting personal power at any cost. Hitler had abandoned all their published principles. He would betray everyone who had trusted him, as well as those who had not. He was the reason why Strasser had left and was now based in Prague, where he could publish his refutations of Hitler's lies. 'That bastard Göring, the gimpy snake in the grass, set up a rival paper and Hitler backed it. We had no choice but to sell our interests. I got next to nothing. I have still to see the puny sum I eventually settled for. But it's much worse than that.' Hitler had sold out all the Nazi principles and spat in the face of his supporters. His obsession with the pursuit of power for its own sake would be the end of us.

I had heard similar opinions from Röhm, by no means a slavish supporter of the Führer. A couple of years earlier there had been some kind of split in the NSDAP ranks. The Strasser brothers had taken the side of the more revolutionary party members, who wished to tear down the entire structure of the state and start afresh. Goebbels had initially been on their side but later shifted over to Hitler's camp. Money talked and Goebbels clearly had his price. But Hitler's debt to Big Business, Strasser argued, would mean that the industrialists would continue to control Germany. The situation would be worse than in Italy where Mussolini had sold off all the wealth of the country to the Pope and a few of his cronies. These businessmen, like Thyssen, Krupp and the rest, were the very people, according to Strasser, who had already brought the country down.

'I'm not denying there exist interests forever alien to the German nation, but we weren't stabbed in the back. We had bad generals and a bunch of businessmen who were doing very well out of selling munitions and supplies to the army. Believe me, I love Ludendorff, but he was an idiot. Wars are won by the side which makes the least mistakes. Ludendorff made mistake after mistake, and every mistake cost a hundred thousand German lives. Those must never be repeated. These powerful people Hitler's talking to will insist on mistakes being repeated. And they'll probably make a load of new ones as well! Two kinds of people should never be allowed near the politics of a country. One is businessmen, the other is soldiers. Whenever those interests start to climb into bed with each other, death and destruction follow for the common people. The creeps will be the ruin of us!' All of this Otto Strasser offered in a light-hearted tone which seemed at odds with his words. He continued to laugh as he walked beside me, a dapper figure in his bow tie and loose coat. Some years later John Betjeman, the BBC rhymester, would remind me of him.

While I had not been surprised at von Schirach's lack of insight into Hitler's character, I was thoroughly astonished at Strasser's understanding and hoped I did not show it! Strasser had no illusions. Hitler filled a vacuum. But it was a vacuum within a vacuum!

'Time was he knew himself better than he does now. He's started believing the publicity stories. Hitler's a feminine type, with a destructive mission, not a constructive masculine one. When I met him just after the War, he saw himself as a drummer, a showman. I remember his saying how he felt like a sleepwalker. The crowd determines who he is. He says the crowd is his mistress, but in some ways the crowd is all he is. Nothing is real or genuine about him. Even the title Führer was imposed on him. The Nazis are creating a monster. What the Jews call a golem.'

Suddenly Otto Strasser grabbed my sleeve and dragged me down some basement steps into the dark panelled wood of a restaurant with peeling walls and faded floral pictures just visible through a haze of delicious steam. The narrow room was crammed with heavy stained wooden tables and poorly lit by oil lamps. Two grey-haired women were selling cakes from behind a counter display but abandoned their customers when they saw Otto Strasser, greeting him with glad, maternal cries, sitting us down at the best table, getting us a clean menu, telling us not to have the *Rotkraut* but that the dumplings were fresh.

A wild barking, and from the back of the kitchen came a little dachshund which somehow reminded me, in its perky manner, of my new friend. He petted the dog. He giggled at its antics. He gave it a lump of sugar. His soft, elegant hands stroked its happy head. Our meal arrived, working-class food, wholesome and filling. Strasser ate with considerable relish, talking between bites and I, also, found the food very much to my taste, similar to Russian food in many ways. My muscles and bones relaxed for the first time in days. The strain of the previous night had left its mark.

I was very glad to have met Otto Strasser, a man with a good idea of Hitler's duality. He shared the idealism of everyone around the Führer and had no motive for wishing to see the Nazi Party lose the seats it had won. What was more, Strasser was a man of principle, and an eternal optimist!

When we left the restaurant, Strasser wanted to buy some apples. He led me through another doorway into a newer part of the great Viktualienmarkt. The busy bustle of the afternoon had been replaced by an early-evening lull, a sense of waiting. As we walked up to a fruit stall, I heard the barrel organ sounding again. I turned, scarcely aware of my own quickness of movement, and sought the source.

In a dusty ray of late sunshine, the child dancer I had seen earlier stood at rest. Behind her, on his master's shoulder, the red-coated monkey jumped and gibbered, taking his little fez off and on to the cheap tinkling of the instrument's mechanical heart.

I gasped at the familiarity of it. I might have been gazing again on my gypsy love, the young beauty I had so long ago been forbidden to see. For a second her eyes met mine, and I was sure she recognised something in me.

Strasser bought his apples and was grinning at me. 'What is she? A relative? If not, she's probably for sale.'

I grew a little warm. 'She reminds me of someone I knew as a child.'

'They have gypsies in America, too? My God, they've spread everywhere!'

But these were not gypsies. Their kind was found in most big German cities. They were Italians, earning their living as street entertainers.

This time it was Strasser who drew me away from my little Zoyea, but I went less reluctantly than before. She and I were soulmates. Those glances had proved it. I knew it was possible to see her again. As soon as I could I would return to the market to watch her dance. What was her name? Whenever I closed my own eyes I saw hers. They were curious eyes, knowing eyes, not entirely innocent eyes. There was no doubt about it. Zoyea was reincarnated. Restored to me. She had recognised me, as I had recognised her.

Sie bewegte sich schlendernd wie ein Junge. Dennoch glaubte ich, dass sie an mir Gefallen gefunden hatte. Vielleicht zogen mich jene Augen an, mit denen sie in sexueller Berechnung jedes Lebewesen zu taxieren schien . . .

But this was natural to my little earth spirit. We were fated, I knew, to become wonderful friends again.

THIRTY-FIVE

Otto Strasser was a man of complex charm and quick intellect. Very open, he told me much about himself. An academic doctor, a literary writer, a naturally sociable and sardonic companion, he had his degree in anthropology and through the persuasions of his chemist brother had only reluctantly been drawn into politics.

While rejecting the Russian model, Doctor Strasser was a convinced and serious socialist, a German nationalist to the marrow. He was horrified by Hitler's willingness to seek the financiers' aid rather than seize power through revolution. Matters came to a head in 1930, and Strasser left to form the Black Front. The party was relatively small, its leader scarcely a threat to anyone, but Göring, Goebbels, Heydrich and Himmler still pursued Strasser relentlessly, attempting to ruin and intimidate him. Regretfully, Gregor Strasser had failed to help in any serious way.

'I know I should give it all up. Write some popular books about pygmies and peasant attitudes, but I can't. I'm an embarrassment. While I allowed myself to be guided by Hitler, I was a hero, he said. Then I began to see flaws in his arguments. I am regarded as an enemy by Big Business as well as by Bolshevik Jewry. Gregor's instincts are to build bridges between all factions. He's an optimist! He's a more typical, good-natured, easygoing Bavarian than I am. He believes everyone unconsciously wants to get along together. I have warned him not to trust Hitler. Hitler uses people and then discards them. Hitler will ruin him. What else can I say or do?'

I had every respect for Otto Strasser even if I did not share his left-wing views. He knew I believed socialism to be a disease which attacks the soul, an infection carried on the air by word of mouth. He eventually came to accept that when he returned to Germany after the Second War. Finding shelter with the Canadians, Doctor

Strasser was one of the few true National Socialists to survive the Second World War.

He wrote me a letter a few years ago. Posted from Munich. 'They have restored my citizenship,' he told me. Hitler knew the meaning of denying German citizenship to a nationalist like Otto Strasser. But this still did not make me comfortable with his socialism, though we were certainly in complete agreement on the Jewish Question.

He demonstrated the difference between us, say, and Hitler. What so few people now understand. There is a considerable difference between a rational interpretation of a problem and a visceral re-action against an entire people. Both Doctor Strasser and myself agreed on the rational approach. The easiest way to rid oneself of Jewish influence was to make it difficult for Jews to disguise themselves.

By this, of course, we did not mean a return to the ludicrous medieval approach of making Jews wear some kind of yellow badge. We saw no reason to permit Jews or Catholics full nationality while both paid homage to foreign leadership. Attacking their dignity and self-respect was cruel. We simply wanted to change their political status, requiring an oath that they were loyal to Germany first and that their interests were German interests. A tax structure could be introduced which made it more attractive to be a true German and accept the responsibilities as well as the benefits of full citizenship, which should not be denied to any decently qualified person, no matter what their racial origin. Until then you would be treated as a respected guest worker in the country, always welcome while you pulled your weight. After a period of qualification, you would swear loyalty to Germany as new immigrants in America must swear loyalty to the United States, forsaking all others. Indeed, all schoolchildren in America are required to take the oath of loyalty every morning. He suspected other countries would soon see the sense of it.

Doctor Strasser did not, like me, feel a strong call of blood. I had no animosity towards Jews. I simply knew Jews would be happier in a homeland better suited to their natures. Their vibrant, volatile blood yearned for a Mediterranean climate. Those exotic hearts came to full flower in the bazaar and the oasis, where gold has an almost supernatural value. Those abstract, intellectual minds could sit and argue to their hearts' content. Artists could plan their canvases and plays. No action would ever be required of them. They would be home. They would be happy. They could study and talk as all Jews would rather do while the waters of Palestine were theirs to drink

363

and the fruits of Israel theirs to eat. They deserved a homeland.

Isn't it what we all desire most? In the thirties I became a convinced Zionist and remain one to this day. I am deeply philo-Semitic. I do share with many Jews, however, the conviction that intermarriage is a mistake.

Otto Strasser believed Hitler's approach to the problem was psychological rather than political, which Strasser thought made Hitler unfit to lead. Germany had almost been destroyed by its senti-mental liberalism, attempting to eat its cream cake and share it. The opposite side of that coin was conservative bigotry and blustering militarism. We had to look at realities and offer the people a genuine alternative to Soviet tyranny and Big Business manipulation. Strasser's Third Way would steer a prudent course between the two, taking the best from both systems. He spoke bitterly of his Kampfverlag, which once dominated Nazi publishing in Prussia. First Gregor had sold his third to Hitler, for some mysterious favour, then Hinkel, the other partner, had sold his third share to Hitler, lured by the offer of a Reichstag seat. The other third, Otto's, was of course value-less. He was a revolutionary. He had no desire to be elected. He knew the compromises one had to make. As a result Hitler had begun a smear campaign against him, calling him a 'parlour-Bolshevik' and worse.

I didn't take this as seriously as Strasser. Slanging matches were a familiar feature of modern German public life. Those with standards tended to stand back from them. Yet that evening I learned far more from Strasser than I could easily absorb of German politics and internal NSDAP rivalries. He filled in the specifics, although I have never been much interested in minor details. As a Russian visionary the larger issues have been all-important. It is for others, of a more ordinary temperament, to concern themselves with the fine print. Like Hitler, I am a prophet rather than practical politician, and I suspect this was also true of Otto Strasser.

Gregor was instead somewhat narrowly pragmatic. His temperament would be the end of him. He would be shot in a concrete prison room, disbelievingly running from corner to corner as Heydrich's bullets sought him through the cell window. A ricochet finished him. A clumsy death for a compromised soul. How I mourn for those poor creatures! How I wish I could go back in time and alert them. If only they had been warned, they might have fled the country. But they believed they could win their case through argument and reason. They

364

never learned the lessons of the trenches, when a bullet not a ballot decided the fate of an unpopular officer.

Everyone close to the Führer understood he was an inspirational symbol rather than a practical leader. It did not disturb them that he had human traits. Röhm and Gregor Strasser were party to his most disgusting secrets yet remained loyal to Hitler. Their own interest was bound to his. What he represented was more important than what he was. The Crown once represented the spirit of Germany. Now Hitler represented it. He was not merely the head of a political party, he was what the young these days call a 'guru'. None of his intimates ever expected him to take the daily reins of power. If his followers accepted the power, they had to accept the responsibility. 'But they're afraid of the responsibility, most of them.' Otto had shaken his head. He felt the calibre of the Nazis wasn't what it should be. Apart from Göring, Hitler's men were not greatly interested in publicity. Power was what obsessed them. It was what they engaged with inside the party. It suited them to have the public worship Hitler. They knew that public worship could turn to public rage and already had plans in place to take over from him. A few years later Mussolini would learn exactly that lesson. He died as the emperors of old had died when they had fallen out of favour, bloodily and without dignity. In the end neither of these men rose to full potential. Otto could see this better than I. The dictators remain to this day a great disappointment to me. They failed to bear the burden they had sworn to carry. They promised Glory and brought only Shame. To the last they did all they could to put their responsibility on to other shoulders. Only Franco survived, and in many ways he was the least of them. More a reactionary than a progressive visionary.

Hitler, shivering in his bunker, Eva Braun comforting him, her eyes bright with excitement at the prospect of their marriage, heard of Mussolini's horrible end and knew he and she would suffer no better at the hands of the Red Army. Hitler understood only too well what torments and disgusting horrors awaited him. A Catholic, he faced the knowledge that the hell he had made on earth was nothing to the hell he would suffer in death. Yet he was prepared to meet Satan rather than be subject to the punishments of Stalin. He was by no means the only one. That is how seriously he took the Red Menace. But some cursed him for his suicide. They believed he had failed his people in their final hours.

Was this Austrian fecklessness of Hitler's really the nub of the falling-out in 1929–30? Otto demanded Hitler take responsibility, not pass it back or shrug it off. The younger Strasser was not interested in power either. Ultimately I suspect he was also unwilling to accept responsibility. He was someone who blossomed best in opposition.

Political disagreements aside, Doctor Otto Strasser was stimulating company. Indeed, in the absence of Röhm, he became almost my only substantial company. We dined together the next night, as he was staying at a small hotel nearby. After a simple supper in a local bistro, we took the tram back into central Munich to the famous Hofbräuhaus. The city at night was full of festive light. The blaze of the trams in the warm autumn air, the sound of a distant brass band, the happy laughter of the people all took me again to my past in Odessa, to those golden days before a few alien financiers and their stooges determined we were too happy, enjoying too much progress and therefore not making them enough money. Munich was like Odessa at her best, not the city of marching mobs and street violence, wretched poverty and cruelty which the documentaries always show to explain Hitler. I saw a few starving children, a few beggars, some ex-servicemen working as street traders and the occasional whore – only what you expected in any large city.

Munich's atmosphere promised happier more hopeful days. Her people knew how to relish their pleasures. The huge green and brown Hofbräuhaus, with its massive wooden galleries and stairways, was a mighty machine for beer drinking. Tier upon tier, bench upon bench of men in lederhosen and huntsmen's homespun, women with floral embroidered aprons and great plaited bunches of blonde hair, hundreds of red or black swastikas on brawny Brownshirt arms. Oktoberfest being at its height, the beer hall also sheltered the cheerful peasants I had seen in the market, by now a little the worse for drink, taking full advantage of their womenfolk remaining at home for at least a few more days. The hall was noticeably pro-Hitler with Nazi advertising and flags everywhere. Doctor Strasser admired the posters' style. He said that the Nazis and the Commies had tremendous aesthetic sense. Their artwork was created by the best graphic artists in Germany. Some beer halls played both sides or were clearly anti-Nazi, but here Hitler was the local boy made good.

Otto Strasser waved his arms at the surrounding campaign posters. 'Have you noticed how phallic the best Nazi propaganda is now?

I'm sure it's deliberate!' Again he giggled. 'It started with our steel helmets, eh? Do you think it's some sort of compensation? All those stiff arms going up and down? All those stiff legs pumping? Has it ever struck you how Mussolini's pictures do their best to make him look like a gigantic prick? Clearly all that sort of thing works, wouldn't you say? But do we really want to give the world to people who would rather follow a penis than a principle?'

He made me laugh spontaneously for the first time in ages. His irreverence helped me recover my mental stability. Soon I was my old self again, and the whole incident at Tegernsee a fading nightmare. I had, after all, put worse behind me. Though scarcely one of Hitler's closest friends, Strasser knew the man better than most and had little reverence for him. I enjoyed his comments.

'He is amorphous, eh? Whatever we desire or feel? Did you ever see that film about the Jewish monster, *The Golem*? Isn't Hitler a golem? The amalgam of everything a Jew has nightmares about, yes?' As usual, he responded enthusiastically to his own somewhat repetitive humour.

Given that these opinions were offered in one of Hitler's strongholds, the very beer hall from which he had organised the famous 1923 putsch attempt, I thought Doctor Strasser rather brave. But he had forgotten where he was. As a passing hard-faced Brownshirt carrying a tray scowled at him, Strasser paused. His quick tongue had got him into trouble but now it saved him. 'And that is why the Führer is our best shield against the aliens!' he added loudly.

In a murmur, he continued, 'How can you trust anyone now? Aren't they all to some degree corrupted? Even my brother Gregor. He couldn't live on a Reichstag representative's salary. Can you credit that? Don't they all have their Big Business patrons now? Even Röhm?'

I shook my head in thorough disbelief. 'Röhm agrees with everything you say. His money comes entirely from contributions by party members.'

'Then he's the only one, no? Thyssen and Hugenberg back Hitler, Farben backs Gregor and Röhm. The Stabschef isn't building that ludicrous house on his party pay. And if Hugenberg's in, then so, of course, is Krupp. When Krupp joins, surely the Americans, French and British will all start covering their bets and backing the National Socialists, too? Ford, IBM, Hearst already back Hitler, knowing he will bring stability. They don't care about the nature of our leadership as long as it guarantees their investments. So Hitler's already getting promises of American backing! Success breeds success. Soon he'll have Scandinavian, Dutch and Italian money, too. A snowball, my dear Peters. Or a concrete ball, maybe . . . ?'

I wondered if my new acquaintance were not a little jealous of his ex-comrades, so I changed the subject, saying how sorry I felt at Hitler's loss. He seemed to have cared a great deal for his niece. But this was a strategic mistake! I set Strasser off again. He became heated, conspiratorial, and began drinking rather recklessly.

'She told me things.' Doctor Strasser offered me a significant leer. 'She told Goebbels things, when he was still in our office. And Hanfstaengl knows about Father Stempfle, Schwartz and the porno-graphic pictures. Schwartz was working there at Corneliusstrasse when he was asked to get the money together to pay off the blackmailer. Hitler came in one morning. He was desperate. I don't know how they raised the money. The party was broke then. The blackmailer was, I'm convinced, the old hermit Stempfle himself, an Hieronymite by calling but much else besides. He insisted the money was owed to him. He's always hated Hitler. He wrote most of *Mein Kampf*, and Hitler simply took it over. Until Max Amann asked Stempfle to look at it, Hitler's original was unpublishable. It was repetitive and illogical. Hitler copied Stempfle's articles out of the Munich papers and used them as his own speeches! Have you heard that hysterical old priest on the subject? You'd never guess he was a man of the cloth! Though he probably only joined to suffer the little children to come unto him . . .'

'Fräulein Raubal, some say, had an unnatural relationship with her uncle?' Back in that room for a moment, I was already sailing closer to the black wind than was prudent. Without the mitigating balance of cocaine I had not willingly drunk so much alcohol in a long time, and my head was beginning to swim again.

Doctor Strasser was nodding his round head rapidly even before I had finished speaking. 'She told Goebbels things,' he repeated gravely. 'And Goebbels isn't easily shocked, eh? He's seen and done everything. With women, anyway, what? Nasty little dwarf. He thought she had to be lying. Didn't want to believe those things of Hitler, hmm? He guessed that Hitler or someone, maybe his driver Emil, who used to flirt with her, showed her magazines, or she'd come across them for herself. You don't have to be a sicko to find it, that's true. The stuff's everywhere. Half the *Kinos* in Berlin show worse. She could have gone to see anything – animals, golden showers, boys with boys – in one of those clubs. Some of them are live. Women are always trying to get you to take them to that sort of place, aren't they? But Fräulein Raubal talked to me. She told me she was terrified of what was happening. Her words to me. She said he was a monster. But that's all she said. Hitler took firmer control of her after that. She became a prisoner, I think. Don't you?'

He stopped suddenly. Three straight-backed burly Storm Troopers had turned on their bench and, steins in hand, were staring at him.

Strasser had now been recognised. I must admit it did not suit me to be seen with someone identified as a critic of the leadership or, worse, a traitor. When my new friend decided it was prudent to leave, I was only too glad to stand up. Without much incident, we made our way back to Corneliusstrasse and a poorly lit local beer cellar which had sparse custom that night. Only a few old peasant men sat drunk in a corner and sang the same obscure dialect song over and over again.

We found a heavy table under a murky arch, and I drew a sigh of relief, very happy to be clear of that dangerous limelight. Strasser himself was alert again, evidently capable of sudden recovery. His constantly moving eyes now surveyed the place even as he signalled for service.

A big dough-faced girl in a dirty apron, with pigtails that looked as if they had been wiping up *Schmalz*, arrived to take our orders. Strasser demanded I try a particularly strong brand of beer. Again I pointed out that I had no money, but he was insistent. He'd had a windfall, he said. So we drank the beer, and I told him of my child-hood in Kiev and Odessa as the son of an American dentist, of my service with the White Army, my flying experience against the Reds and my invention of the Violet Ray which Petlyura had used to stop the Bolsheviks as they swept upon Kiev, and which would have succeeded if the city's power supply had been more certain. How I had gone to France and made my fortune in airship construction, only to lose it, the victim of typically French political chicanery, then become a political speaker in the US, developed a steam-car and later worked as a film star. He was fascinated by my accounts of flying in the service of the Caïd of Marrakech. I did not tell him about Egypt any more than about Hitler. Some things should never be exposed to the common air or the light of day and should certainly never be passed on to another human being. It is the same as knowingly passing on a disease. Some burdens you can only share with a priest or a psychiatrist.

Doctor Strasser thought at first that I was lying. 'You've had more adventures than Münchhausen, no?'

I explained that my situation was the same as that of many Russian members of the aristocratic intelligentsia driven from their home-land by the Reds. People found it difficult to imagine the fate of the dispossesed intellectual, as he must understand. We were forced to earn our livings as jacks of all trades! The Revolution set Russia back a thousand years. But for Lenin I would even now be pursuing the career of inventor and engineer in Moscow or St Petersburg.

Convinced (for he had himself had a taste of exile), my new acquaintance asked a few more questions and relaxed again. Like Captain Röhm, Doctor Strasser was particularly interested in my Russian experiences, though from a different point of view. He wanted to know how effective Makhno's anarchist communes had been, how efficient the commissar system was, how popular the Red ideologues had been with the common people and so on. I could only tell him of my own adventures, but for these he was avid. I tried to explain the complicated comings and goings of the various forces in the Ukraine during my time there. The Red organisers were primarily Jewish intellectuals, some of them from Germany. Their organisational skills made the Reds successful in the end.

Doctor Strasser had met the great Krassnoff in Berlin. He had read the General's moving multi-volume memoir *From the Two-Headed Eagle to the Red Flag*. The book had convinced him that the Russian model was nothing worth following. Yet an alliance between a united Germany and the Soviet Union would form a solid and natural power block, with Poland under shared dominion.

He was retailing the old German dream, but turned into socialist politics! I said nothing. I valued my new friend too highly to offend him. He had met Skorapadsky, who had settled in Munich. The Hetman claimed now that he would have kept our common Tsar if he had retained his power in Ukraine. None doubted Skorapadsky's Ukrainian patriotism, but this was the first I had heard of his Russian loyalties! It was true he had been driven from the Ukraine by the Reds. Like many Ukrainians, he was a good friend to Germany, but had no other allies.

I put it to Doctor Strasser that we, not the German Army, were the ones who were truly betrayed, for we were betrayed by our own allies. Why did the Americans not step in at the right time and save our Tsar? They had the means. They had agents there, like the British. They knew everything that was going on. In the end, even the British and French let us down, but the Americans, as usual, did enough to make a mess but not enough to clear it up. What was the matter with Americans? Ice had crept into their hearts. Surely they had no reason to hate Germany?

He said that the Americans did not understand altruism. And as with everything else they didn't understand, they rejected, hated or sentimentalised it so that it became something else. I agreed. Germany could never rely on America for long-term help. I had not considered before that the culture actually mitigated against altruism just as it mitigated against intellectualism, in both cases because of the vast numbers of Protestants and Jews in America. Together they were lethal! Nothing in Protestant folk stories and moral tales suggested that virtue was its own reward. As in Victorian England, virtue in America is always thoroughly rewarded. Indeed, the reward is always promised. When it cannot be redeemed, it becomes heaven's responsibility. A sentimentalised culture was actually inimicable to genuine altruism. Their charitable organisations always expected something in return for their help. At the very least they demanded pious thanks. Even the Catholics. The whole culture demanded you act like a character in a melodrama. At the moment, therefore, presented by Weimar with an image of decadence, Americans believed Germany beyond salvation.

Doctor Strasser took a polite interest in what I had to say. So it was with Catholics everywhere, he added vaguely. A question of vested interests, and the oldest vested interest in the world was the Vatican. But he parroted this without any real passion, like most Roman Catholics who had escaped the tyranny of their parents' religion. From me he chiefly wanted to know what California and Hollywood were like. Had I met any of the famous stars?

So somehow the rest of the evening became devoted to trivial reminiscence. Doctor Strasser relayed juicy Nazi gossip, and I relayed equally juicy Hollywood gossip. As my spirits began to improve, I realised I was quite enjoying myself. I offered stories about famous stars now completely out of fashion. Otto Strasser's tales were probably equally out of date since he had been so long from the centres of NSDAP power.

That night Strasser took over my couch. He was too drunk, he said, to return to his little *pension*. Unfortunately Schirach had neglected to leave any bedlinen so I slept on the mattress fully clothed, and Strasser slept similarly on the couch. The beer made sleep easier but waking rather harder.

Next morning we freshened ourselves as best we could and stumbled down the uncarpeted stairs into the cobbled street to get some cheap coffee. On the corner a cheerful Brownshirt boy called out the latest headlines while holding the handlebar of a bin-on-wheels, a kind of converted perambulator or sandwich cart, advertising in vivid scarlet against a black background the *Völkischer Beobachter*. Doctor Strasser reached in, flashed a lapel badge, and pulled a paper from the bin while the lad looked on, not sure what to do.

As we left the speechless vendor behind, Strasser handed me the paper. 'This was always a rag. Now it's a rag telling nothing but lies, what?' He stopped rather ostentatiously at the *Münchener Post* kiosk and bought the paper that had most consistently attacked Hitler and raised questions about Fräulein Raubal's death.

Taking me into the nearest tiny coffee shop, Doctor Strasser ordered us some croissants and buried himself in the newspaper. He relished every word of scandal about Hitler. Meanwhile, I read of Nazi triumph and Hitler's heroism in the face of attacks from every side. The fact that the Führer was able to shrug off all such filthy propaganda was a further sign of his superhuman discipline.

Doctor Strasser ate rapidly. Ordering more coffee, he devoured the croissants and read me the wildest of the allegations.

Admittedly, and rather disturbingly, the paper touched on the truth, at least as I understood it. Its publisher had some vendetta against the Nazi leader and no doubt a left-wing agenda of his own. Though the stories were sensational and unlikely, Strasser seemed happy to believe them, at least for the moment, as one might enjoy a cheap novel. He ate another croissant as he grinned and chuckled, rustling the pages and retailing every fresh detail. Röhm's mythological orgies were not left out of the account. Ever since his touching letters had been intercepted and published, the papers had had a field day with his sexuality. Of course, they did not dare use a word like 'queer', though the inference was clear.

Röhm was described as Hitler's closest intimate. Hitler was described as 'unmarried' and a 'confirmed bachelor' while at the same time being his niece's 'protector', as if to make sure of blackening his name on as many counts as possible. Here was a man who was both rapist, impotent, feminine, masochist, sadist, heterosexual, homosexual, asexual, had boyfriends and kept a mistress, while at the same time rushing from one end of the country to the other giving political speeches. No wonder people hailed him as a superman!

And now Hitler could also be a savage murderer. The police were suggesting Geli had been beaten up (by inference Hitler had done it) because she refused some particularly perverse advance. I really had no interest in this nonsense, particularly since I knew far too much of the truth.

'Surely none of this scandal will do Röhm any good with the Reichswehr,' I said. 'They're notoriously homophobic!'

'That isn't the character Röhm presents to the army, of course. With them he is the efficient, sensible officer, the comrade-in-arms, the war veteran. They find him perfectly charming and are happy to believe him when he tells them that the scandals are simply the invention of his enemies, that his famous love letters are mere forgeries. No doubt he lets them think he's a widower with two children he's raising himself. Captain Röhm's a nice middle-class boy, like me. Well educated. Well brought up. Good at deferring to his betters, or at least appearing to. In Germany you are trained to present the face people want to see. Face is of primary importance. What you do, you do. If you are caught, you suffer. Isn't it like that in America?'

'So Röhm is right and will ultimately have control of the army?'

Doctor Strasser took this seriously, folding his paper and lighting a fresh cigarette, thinking for a moment. 'Not likely. The Reichswehr is still the strongest single force in Germany and has tried to stay out of direct politics, though it has a fair amount of influence. The Reichswehr controls Germany. Röhm doesn't. Hitler could sacrifice Röhm to appease the Reichswehr. Or there could be civil war with the regular army on one side and the various *Freikorps*, especially the Storm Troopers, on the other. It would be horrifying, like the Hundred Years War all over again, with no side staying the same, and more and more foreign interests drawn in and ultimately simply annexing parts of Germany for themselves. The Jews have even fewer local loyalties than the Catholics and will take advantage of such a situation. So everyone knows we should avoid it developing. I think the Reichswehr will find a formula, a way of saving face, to incorporate the SA. The army commands Germany, but the army needs a commander. If Hitler shirks the issue and demands command of the army, Röhm will turn against him.'

'And so there'll be civil war?'

'Röhm can threaten it and sometimes does, but he knows as well as Hitler that it would be a bloody massacre, eh?'

'Of the army?'

'Of the SA. Of us. Röhm has the leadership of at least a hundred thousand soldiers. Doesn't he claim four million? He has stockpiles of machine guns and rifles and plenty of them cached all over Germany to be called upon at any time. But it's much harder to stockpile tanks, planes and heavy artillery, no? Isn't he, after all, the one who says that tanks will determine the wars of the future the way cavalry determined the wars of the past? Surely he has only infantry? The French would come in on Hitler's side, and Röhm would be dogmeat, what?' Doctor Strasser remained a realist. He laughed. 'Röhm will have to go back to Bolivia. Or rejoin the Bolshies!'

I knew this to be unlikely.

Suddenly Otto Strasser put down his newspaper, walked to the glass door of the little café and opening it put his hand out in the Nazi salute. He laughed loudly as a man on the other side of the road, who had been loitering there since we had entered the place, turned on his heel and walked up the street, where he pretended to be interested in a shop's display of surgical appliances.

'Himmler's man, almost certainly,' explained Strasser, smiling and shaking his head. 'Von Schirach must have said something when he got to Berlin. A telephone call and here we are.'

I began to make plans to leave Munich as soon as possible. I had more than enough problems with Bolsheviks like Brodmann on my trail! I had somehow angered Il Duce and compromised Hitler. While Röhm could still be my way through to the important political figures of the day, I could not afford to be seen either in his company or in the company of his disgraced ex-colleague. My only hope was that the plain-clothes SS man had no interest in me. Surely Doctor Strasser was the villain? Von Schirach himself had known the truth of the situation and doubtless complained that Strasser had attached himself to me.

After breakfast we returned to Corneliusstrasse. I had thought of going on up to the market, but Doctor Strasser was by now very sleepy and asked if he could stretch out on the bed for an hour or two. This reminded me that I needed to procure some sheets. He impetuously handed me some new marks and told me of a good 'seconds' linen shop in the area. For a man of such slender means, he was generous with the money he possessed. My own was hidden, and I had no intention of touching it until I really needed it.

Doctor Strasser's instructions proved rather vague, and it took me some time to find the shop. I had a sense that I was being followed but could see nobody. The shop was big and filled to bursting with feather quilts and bedclothes. After some bargaining I was able to buy the sheets together with a heavy quilt and a pillow for a good price. The linen did not cost much to begin with, but I bargained the proprietor into giving me a price for the entire bundle. I was proud of myself. I even had some change left over.

The linen shop was on a busy main street on the far side of the Viktualienmarkt. I could just see over my parcels. The old woman who owned the place came to open the door for me. As I was leaving, I glanced almost instinctively into the street. Some traffic had stopped suddenly as a policeman directed a horse-drawn delivery van which needed to back out of an alley. When an expensive Mercedes tourer paused I admired the sweep of its dark green lines until I heard a faint shriek.

'Ivan!'

In the back of the car, glamour personified, sat Mrs Cornelius, her hair a glittering platinum helm. She was waving animatedly for me to come to the car. Her companion, who sat up front with the driver, seemed agitated by the attention. She was tapping the chauffeur on the shoulder, trying to get him to pull over, but her companion was reluctant. I recognised him as her 'Baron Huggy Bear', Herr Hugenberg, the media magnate, with his hairbrush head and massive grey moustaches. He did not respond to my bow. As the policeman waved the traffic forward, he gave the chauffeur a signal to move on. Mrs Cornelius was left half standing in the Mercedes, calling out something I could not hear. Pursuing the car was impossible since I was carrying so much, and I was furious at my lost opportunity. I could only hope she was in Munich for some time and that our paths would cross again.

My bedlinen in my arms, I watched helplessly as the huge machine sped into the distance. Then I began the plod back to Corneliusstrasse, reflecting on the even deeper irony of the address.

In some depression I returned with my purchases, expecting Strasser to be impressed with what I had managed to get for the money. As I approached the house, however, I was alarmed to see the street door standing ajar. I knew I had drawn it shut behind me, and I had the key in my pocket. Afraid that Himmler's men had taken action, I entered carefully and listened. No sounds came from overhead.

Bit by bit, I advanced up the stairs, my sheets, quilt and pillow in my arms, until I reached the top floor and carefully pushed open the apartment door with my foot. Still silent as the grave.

Nervously I entered the flat.

It was empty.

Doctor Otto Strasser had gone. He had left no note, but everything of his had vanished as if he had never been here.

The Himmler man had scared him off. Strasser had used me to lure him away! My sense of being followed to the linen shop was based on fact. Returning downstairs, I saw he had taken his publications with him. Still no note. His wariness, I would learn, was well placed. Himmler's men had more than likely followed his trail to wherever he had next fled. I could now settle safely into my flat and try to think through my position.

But the truth is I did little thinking that week. I made some attempt to contact Mrs Cornelius. She was not registered in any Munich hotel under her own name. She had probably returned to Berlin with Hugenberg.

I also became a little obsessed with 'Zoyea the Gypsy', for the exotic minx had not appeared again in the market, and there was no sign of the organ-grinder or her brother, not even a distant, mechanical note from the barrel organ. The market traders all told me that 'the Italian', as they called him, was working the more lucrative parts of Oktoberfest. You could make a small fortune during this period if you were prepared to go where the money was. He would, I was assured, be back in late October.

I now had a telephone and could talk to Röhm, who would ring to let me know when he had time to pay me a short visit. They were scarcely ever more than that these days. He was always very careful not to be seen and rarely wore his uniform without covering it with a civilian coat.

These were momentous times, he said. The National Socialists had taken Hamburg – a notorious Red stronghold! The vote had been overwhelming. Hitler's policies promised to unify all sides – and how the German soul yearned for unity!

Röhm was amused when I told him how Otto Strasser had suddenly vanished without warning. 'I'd heard he'd been here. He pinched the petty cash, I gather. They'd been keeping it handy for emergencies. And our dear Otto turned up. Always an emergency!'

Röhm told me later that Strasser had the survival instincts of a rat. The man could slip away at the first sign of danger. A sixth sense Röhm respected. People like that had survived in the trenches. He was frankly admiring. 'As the *Titanic* left Liverpool, Doctor Otto Strasser would have been seen tiptoeing quietly down the last mooring cable back to dry land. If I had any sense at all, I would keep Strasser around and use him as a barometer. If Strasser smells trouble, then you should be ready for trouble.'

One of the saddest ironies of my long life is that my friend Röhm left it too late to take his own advice.

He was gone again soon enough, back to Berlin where the action was, with all kinds of preparations to be arranged before May. Even now they were making a play for power and had to seize every opportunity presented during the next weeks. Our 'therapy', he said, had worked well. Alf, thank God, was more or less functioning again, though his old fire was slow to rekindle. He should be in good enough shape by Christmas to do what he had to do. Only Hitler, croaking, screaming, weeping, imploring and going through a silent-film actor's entire range of emotions, could infuse the party members and the electorate with that same sense of mission, of marching together for the glory of a greater, better Germany. A German Germany, said Röhm, pulling on his boots. A Germany for the Germans, he added, fastening his belt. Strong, masculine, progressive. Something good could still come out of all this.

As he was leaving, I asked him point-blank if there was any truth in the rumour I had heard that he was being backed by I. G. Farben. He was wearing his full dress uniform, on the way to a function. One gloved hand was on the hilt of his sword. He had disguised his scars, and in that half-light he looked as he must have before the War, arrogant and handsome. He paused, frowning to himself, then turned to look me full in the eyes. 'He thinks I'm working for him, but he's working for me. I'm happy to take the money he's offered whenever a meeting has been organised. But his head will roll with the rest when the time comes, little Mashi, never fear.' He spoke with quiet conviction.

With the beginning of October came a soft, light rain. It brought a melancholy air to the city as the memories of the festival faded and Munich returned to normal, already beginning to plan for Christmas. Röhm had lent me some money so I was able to buy an umbrella, under which I made my daily walk to the market. I was by now known to the traders who behaved towards me with good-humoured insolence. They called me 'Professor Popoff' for some reason of their own, but they were not bad people and treated everyone pretty much the same. I loved the powerful smells of fresh vegetables and newly slaughtered meat. I so strongly associate these smells with my little Zoyea that even nowadays, when out in the Portobello Road and passing one of those elaborately stacked stalls with its ornate gold and green lettering, I am instantly reminded of her. I can still see her little bare brown legs and feet twinkling across the asphalt as she dances with her tambourine, innocently striking all the poses of the harlot and drowning me in her eyes. I became totally absorbed in her.

She is an animal. A wonderful cat. Her curiosity is never still, fixing on you for just a moment, long enough for you to yearn for her to look at you again. Her attention is forever on the next thing, the next person, the next scene. She is greedy for everything life offers as if she knows her time on earth will be short.

She is a flirt but she flirts without knowing what it is she promises. I do not let those glances mislead me. It is my heart that longs for her again, not my loins. I have lived with such disgusting allegations for most of my adult life. If a man cannot love the innocence and sweetness of little girls, he has no soul, no feeling. Of course I would have wanted a wife, children of my own. She said she had found my mother. Esmé betrayed me. She took my children. Her companions were the ghosts of the unborn. How their voices fill the high, stone arches, mingling with the roiling smoke, the heavy scents, and I can see something again of the heaven I lost when I was driven from my native land. White, green and gold. Sharp. From within it slices gently into the lining of my stomach. Slices a long scar on the inside of my belly. A piece of metal swings in my stomach like a pendulum, and I wonder if I am not entirely artificial now, kin to the mechanical woman of *Metropolis*.

I saw that film and several others at the same time in a very good cinema not far from the Viktualienmarkt. While it showed new films during the week, the theatre had a bill of older, silent films for Sundays. They offered a single price in the afternoons, so it presented

378

the best bargain. To be honest, I was in a mood for musicals and comedies rather than the gloomy fare I received via Messrs Murnau, Lang and Pabst. I slept through most of the second part of *Doctor Mabuse*, though I had enjoyed the original stories. They lacked the texture of the best Sexton Blake adventures and were far more fantastic, but they passed the time. Blake's exploits are based, of course, on the real life of the famous military spy and counter-espionage agent Sir Seaton Begg, for so long in command of the now disbanded MI7. For a while he was my friend Major Nye's immediate boss, though he never directly admitted it!

Lilian Harvey became a great favourite of mine. The English actress was Germany's biggest popular star. Her performance in the rather whimsical *Three from a Filling Station* was not quite as good as in *Der Kongress tanzt*. But her talkies were a little more expensive. Leni Riefenstahl was an athletic actress who appeared at her best in fur against a background of snow. I saw her in several of these ski and climbing epics, shallow things, depending mostly on the German audience's appetite for endless snow and ice. Perhaps the German race really did long for its distant Teutonic homeland? *Die Weisse Hölle von Piz-Palü* was one of her last. A white hell indeed. These pictures were chiefly interesting when they concentrated on the aeroplane-rescue sequences. While they were hugely popular in countries with Alpine areas, they were virtually unknown elsewhere, a very specific genre, like the English *Carry On* film, where a deep knowledge of the culture is required to understand the nuances which are the true stories underlying apparently superficial nonsense. Having been starved for so long of the popular cinema, I must admit I became something of an addict. I still did not feel very secure on the street. In the darkness of the afternoon *Kino*, I was safe.

I went to the cinema almost every day, making sure I left and returned via the Viktualienmarkt. I longed for a companion, someone delicate and tender, to care for.

They came back as the traders had predicted. The entire little troupe looked rested and alert, as if they had been on holiday somewhere. They had probably been eating rather better than usual. A few coins in the boy's clattering box and I was soon chatting with Signor Frau, who came originally from Genoa and was a great enthusiast for Mussolini. Rather than return to Genoa, Signor Frau had eventually decided it made more sense to rent a little house in one of the older parts of the city, near what he called 'the sheds', where a number of barrel organs were stored, rather like taxis, and rented to individuals who found it irksome or expensive to maintain their own instruments. He had prospered during the festival. That money would be put aside for the lean months. His barrel organ was beginning to fail him, and the old bastard of a mechanic would charge him a fortune for repairing it. Things were going badly for him as just the other day his monkey had caught cold. He feared it might die.

The monkey recovered. A rapport developed between Frau and myself. He cultivated the moustache and rather long hair, the bright shirts, the hat, jacket and knickerbockers of his calling, which, he explained, the Germans expected of him. At home, however, he wore the same clothes as everyone else. As far as I could tell, he had lived in Munich so long his German was without accent. He admitted, laughing, that most of his Italian was now in his singing. He scarcely even spoke it at home. His wife was German but had been killed in an explosion at the fireworks factory where she worked. Flares. Three days before the armistice, he said. Their baby had just been born, and his boy was two. His wife's sister had looked after them. Then she got married and moved back to Hanover. Heckie, the girl, was old enough to look after the house. He patted her shoulder. 'She's been my little wife.'

They were good children, he said, and a great support to him. They were his consolation. He had never remarried. To be honest there was less strain. He didn't think he could marry another German woman. They were kind-hearted and treated you like a king but were a bit too neat and tidy for his taste. Heckie was a proper little woman. She ran the household and a good deal of the business. I can smell her warm skin, her soft brown neck, her curls, her strong little body straining and squirming under the first intimations of her sexuality.

That mixture of fresh vegetables, herbs and spices was for me the smell of wealth and comfort, of certainty. Of romance. And also the smell of dawning lust. I can hear the cheerful staccato of the barrel organ, snatches of song, excited chitter of the monkey jumping on the singer's shoulder, a sour-faced boy moving through the crowd with his box, her delicate brown limbs flashing in shafts of sunlight falling through the dusty glass above. The cheap lace of her costume flaps and bounces on her perfect little body. Those flounces are a vulgar and unnecessary augmentation to her grace and natural elegance. Her lips curve again in a sweet red smile. She promises me so much. She promises me a return to my past, to a time when I was happy.

How she twirled and skipped as her surly older brother moved among the crowd, while her father, his grin apparently as spontaneous as ever, stroked his happy little monkey, turning the handle of the barrel organ, singing along with the machine in a rich baritone. '*Fa la la la! Fa la la la!*' In his tall-crowned felt hat, short green jacket trimmed with gold, brown corduroy knickerbockers, green stockings and bright red shoes, his broad, flashing grin, his earrings, which could be removed at night, he was everything he was supposed to be. The costume was scarcely any different to that worn by peasants in most of this region, from northern Italy through Austria to southern Germany, yet the Italian still found himself called a gypsy when he went out into the smaller provincial towns. Heckie would get touched for luck. She hated it. When not performing, she was a grave child who took her domestic responsibilities as seriously as her professional ones. Her only abiding enthusiasm she kept to herself.

Soon I took to arriving at the market towards the end of the afternoon, so that I could watch Zoyea/Heckie dance, pop a coin into the boy's aggressive box and chat to Signor Frau as he drew the canvas cover over his barrel organ, rewarded his monkey and prepared to push the instrument back through the side streets to the mews where all the organs were stored in common.

By the first week of November Röhm had been almost entirely in Berlin. I remained at a loose end. A few SA men came and went from the Corneliusstrasse premises. They were not sure what I was doing there, and were frankly unfriendly. It was becoming obvious I must discover a new patron or take some sort of job. Common sense said I should have left for Berlin by now, except I felt safer for the moment in Munich. I was definitely safer than I would have been in Rome, unless Il Duce's mood had changed. My enemies probably still had his ear. If I returned I was sure to find myself under arrest, with another false list of crimes added to my name. Yet in Munich I was, to some degree, Röhm's prisoner. He remained very kind and sentimental, but during most of his visits his mind was chiefly on the political struggle. He found it impossible to relax completely. He would 'lend' me whatever money he had in his pocket, yet if I was to become my own man again I must find employment. Naturally my first thought was of my patents. I needed to get the ear of a German industrialist, and the only way to do that was through Mrs Cornelius, who more than likely was not even in the country any longer!

Meanwhile, I was in love and the world was coming alive for me again. Zoyea and I had discovered a common interest.

THIRTY-SIX

And so began what would in retrospect be my epiphany when one dream would begin to be realised and another dashed for ever. Here I again discovered the peaks of joy and an abyss of despair, my 'Alpine' period, a wonderful time of self-expression, personal peril and vocational satisfaction. Ultimately, as always, disappointment would bring not only emotional exhaustion but also physical danger.

For thirty months I came at last to anticipate fulfilment of my original Life Plan. During 1932–34, I found love, artistic expression, serious interest in my political philosophy, respect as a scientist and as an artist. Was the misery that followed the years of my European wanderings worth the pleasures of that time when the world blossomed with glorious hope, before the final betrayals which, I fear, continue to characterise this century? I lay the blame squarely at the door of Herr Adolf Hitler. Once the lie was only common currency in diplomacy and politics. Now it is a familiar instrument of public discourse.

I grew up in a world with firms whose names you could trust. Now those names are turned into manipulative illusions, false promises.

'Alas!' Hitler said at the end. 'My Germans have failed me!' Hitler's interests were neither national nor socialist; they were personal. He was prepared to kill an entire people to fulfil his dream.

The Germans survived and rejoined the family of civilised nations, but now it is too late. Heinz and Nestlé own all the food. These firms are secretly controlled by alien interests. At any time they can decide to kill vast numbers of people. All they have to do is pick up a telephone and give an order. Cyanide will be injected into enough tins of baked beans to kill every British schoolboy overnight.

They already introduce narcotics into our food to make us more easily manipulated by their subliminal advertising, their aggressive attacks on all our old values. I do not totally dismiss the theory that Adolf Hitler, after the death of Angela Raubal, was secretly poisoned, causing all his subsequent decisions. So in the end he fell into the hands of his enemies. He had made enemies of the Jews, when he could have enlisted some at least as willing helpers in his dream to build a new Germany. I speak from experience. There are altruistic Jews. It is a fact. I met one in Odessa. In Germany Strasser had already sketched a perfectly workable plan, which would take no one's dignity or livelihood from them. Typically, too much talk and not enough cash was given to the problem, and so it worsened rather than improved. Julius Streicher must accept much of the responsibility, but overall I do blame Hitler.

The secret little Zoyea and I shared was a mutual enthusiasm which I discovered by chance after she came to accept me. Initially, there was scant intercourse between us. Indeed, she avoided me. The boy was more communicative, but I had no special liking for him. I would occasionally pass on to him an adventure paper and discuss the stories with him, but he had a dull mind, though more amiable than he seemed.

The magazines, some pre-war, were from a huge collection I had found under my bed, together with a whole shelf of Edgar Wallace in French and German. They had belonged to Baldur von Schirach and were fascinating. Most were in English, containing graphic depictions of airships, of rocket-driven space liners, of gigantic vehicles capable of travelling across the American plains without use of rails or roads. My first thought was that the authors had stolen my ideas, but some were clearly unworkable. In the *Aldine Library of Invention, Travel & Adventure*, I found, for instance a tale called 'Across the Frozen Sea', published some time before the world conflict, which proposed a preposterous schooner for sailing on giant skis across the Arctic ice! The power–weight ratio alone would not permit such nonsense! And the presumption that the Arctic plain is as smooth as Streatham Ice Rink is equally unscientific!

The English-speaking von Schirach possessed an interest in engineering and futuristic invention he had not revealed to me. Here were *Frank Reade, Popular Mechanics, Mechanix Illustrated, Science and Invention, Amazing Science Stories, Air Wonder Stories, Scientific American, Dusty Ayres and his Battle Aces* and a dozen others. There were German and French tales from Jules Verne and his followers. Stories featuring Fantomas, *Die Fledermaus* and *Doctor Mabuse* were less imaginative.

384

A rather primitive version of my articulated submarine was anticipated in a tale called 'Into the Maelstrom'. My flying cities drawn
for the American pulp covers in lurid colours were at last part of
the common idea of the future. Here were visionaries much like
myself. Rather than suspect them of stealing my ideas, for indeed I
had anticipated them in almost every sphere, I acknowledged these
writers and artists as equals, confirmation that I was not alone! Here
were men who thought like me, who had the same kind of practical and romantic imagination. Possibly, at some future date, we
could all come together as one scientific family to bring reason and
order to the world. Within a generation we could abolish disease
and hold death itself at bay. We would grow food for the whole
planet and ensure no one was ever hungry. Great aerial ships could
carry goods cheaply and quickly from place to place delivering food
and medicines where they were needed. All that was required was
the political will and the vision of business to back it; then we should
have had not the bleak, mechanistic future of *Metropolis*, but the
clean, aesthetic nobility of *Things to Come*, with white motorways
curving between green hills, twisting alongside glittering lakes and
sparkling rivers beneath blue and sunny skies, on which electrical
cars move silently, directed by robot guides with sensors buried in
roads, cars and lamp-posts to ensure the impossibility of a crash. It
was H. G. Wells's great dream. Out of the ashes of war rises a virgin
world, ruled by wise, well-educated men, eugenically perfect, who
guide us through to the new path which takes us directly to a
bright, wholesome future, without disease, deformity or risk. A well-
regulated but humane future, emphasising education, health, stability
and predictability, the great boons and the continuing goals of a
rational scientific society. This was the vision of von Schirach as well
as Röhm and Strasser, but the shoulders expected to carry the burden
of our plan into the second half of the twentieth century were
simply not strong enough for the task. Germany did not fail Hitler.
Hitler, it must be said, in the end failed Germany.

What a different world it would have been if the Strassers, Röhm
and Hoch, for instance, had controlled the National Socialist Party.
Röhm would have kept his 'pact of steel' with Stalin and become
partners to create an economic miracle to revive Europe with Russia
and Germany at its head. German influence on Russia would have
modified the Bolsheviks, forcing them eventually to restore the Tsar,
while Germany would return some form of monarch to the throne.

In Munich, of course, there was a powerful argument for replacing the Kaiser with one of the Wittelbachs. This might well have happened under Röhm, though he would have limited such a ruler's powers.

An admirer of Cromwell, Röhm was an egalitarian through and through but would have preferred a traditional beneficent monarch to a contemporary dictator. He never intended so much power to be concentrated in one man's hands.

Röhm continued to make rare visits to Corneliusstrasse, now a comfortable apartment for myself and my occasional visitors. I could also now offer them wine and coffee or a snack, though Röhm never ate and rarely drank when he came, usually after dark. I was always glad to see him, if only for a couple of hours to break the monotony of my life. I had little money and little freedom of movement. Röhm still advised me to lie low. Frequently I was at my wits' end for something to do. I complained to him that I felt the loss of music, of ordinary boulevard acquaintances. He told me to be patient. He would take care of things. We both had to be careful. Hitler had not forgotten that evening at Tegernsee. I had best become used to a quiet, uneventful life. An eventful one would not be to my taste. Wasn't that a little vague? I asked.

Röhm apologised. Soon he would be able to relax. At present Hitler was proving a handful. He was back in the running but going up and down emotionally like a whore's drawers. Handling him was very tiring. They were getting new recruits into the SA every day. Quality as well as quantity, he said. First-rate officer material. There could be no objection any longer from the Reichswehr. The sooner his boys were incorporated into the regular army, the better for all. The SA numbers were certainly making Hitler's Big Business friends look up, and the army was equally aware of the troops which could be very quickly fielded.

I read the newspapers only occasionally, usually helping myself to a free copy of the *VB* from the boy on the corner. He knew me now, but never seemed comfortable with my dipping into his barrow. I did not care what he thought. I had tried and failed to make friends with him. The *Völkischer Beobachter* was inclined to go into paroxysms of extravagant praise for the man I had last seen in the flesh in Tegernsee, covered in blood and excrement and gasping for more. It is a tribute to his peculiar magnetism that when I saw him enlarged on the great cinema screen, I was fascinated and convinced!

Many mocked Hitler as an imitator of Charlie Chaplin. They do not realise how much Hitler admired Chaplin, though the feeling was not mutual. Hitler was able to speak to us all because of his common touch, which meant that he enjoyed ordinary pleasures quite as much as the more esoteric escapes of the powerful. He understood the media because he understood what we wanted from it. And he gave us exactly what we wanted. I was not among them, but I have known grown men used to brutal authority moved to tears by their love of the Führer. I suppose I was too well informed and too wise ever to have that kind of response. My heart has always belonged to God rather than Man.

I found von Schirach's collection of scientific magazines far more interesting than speculation about whether the socialists or the nationalists or the communists or the Catholic centrists were going to win this election or that vote. Such things were confusing for the average German, let alone a foreigner like myself.

For the first week or two that she and her family were back in the market Zoyea was quietly self-contained. Her smiles were artificial, entirely for the audience. In repose her face became rather serious and thoughtful.

Platonically I longed for her. Indeed, I longed for any feminine company. I could not feel complete without some sort of woman friend. I do not speak of lust but of my humanity, my need to be a whole man. Moreover, I could not afford to pay a whore. I had just enough for my basic needs. Even if I was careful, my store of *sneg* would be gone by the middle of January. Röhm could not be relied upon. He was still in Berlin more than he was in Munich. If he wasn't in Berlin he was at a rally in Hamburg or a political meeting in Cologne.

Not only was I growing starved of intellectual company, I was sure someone had followed me to Munich, perhaps one of my enemies. Röhm constantly reassured me that Hitler was not on to me. Yet it seemed he would soon see Röhm as the link between himself and the creature who had brought him to catharsis that night. Could Röhm be followed without his knowledge? My only consolation was that Hitler's men would be looking for a girl. Yet might they consider me the link between the girl and Röhm? Twice von Schirach passed on information. Someone had been enquiring for me in the beer cellars and cabarets. I begged him to remain discreet.

Forced to avoid all public places, I longed for music as much as I longed for conversation and eventually found an old radio down in the offices, which I requisitioned. But the set only received a local station, which was provincial and dull and rather too full of Hitler and Co. It would sometimes broadcast operettas. Jazz was forbidden. The music I heard coming from Munich's few basement cabarets was largely made by accordions and can be imagined. I complained to Röhm, but he was too busy to listen with any great attention. Or so I thought.

One morning I was woken up by a loud banging on the door. Alarmed, I dragged on a dressing gown and, keeping my door on its chain, looked to see who it was. A hard-faced brown-uniformed monster wearing a swastika armband stood there. It was Karl Weber, one of Hitler's 'old fighters', an SA lieutenant who sometimes called at Corneliusstrasse on party business, and who had been friendly enough in the past. He stooped, picking up in both hands a large wooden cabinet on top of which was a cardboard box. 'The Stabschef told me to bring this round to you, Prof. Where do you want it?' He put it on my table, an expensive portable phonograph with a box full of black, brittle discs. I had music!

'That's so kind! Where on earth did you find it?'

Weber laughed. 'Not that far from here. One of our lads liberated it from some Bolshy Jewboy they were evicting on behalf of his landlord. They'd been told to keep a lookout for something like this. So here you are. Everyone benefits!' He raised his arm in the familiar *Ben-Hur* salute and was on his way.

As my coffee was brewing I greedily inspected the records, which were mostly familiar German labels like Parlophon, Ultraphon and Homocord. Some were American, Electrola and Victrola. A few of the records had familiar songs and performers. Most seemed to be songs from current Berlin shows. I wound up the machine, took an Al Jolson record from its cardboard sleeve, placed it on the turntable, started the phonograph and carefully lowered the amplifier arm on to the spinning disc.

Not only was the machine excellent, the records had been well kept. Soon my mornings were spent to the tune of 'Sonny Boy' and 'Mammy' or the harsh, catchy cabaret songs of Berlin. 'Die Muschel von Margate' was a biting attack on the oil business. I also enjoyed the haunting 'Surabaya Johnny' or the catchy 'Tango Angele'. Germany was full of such clever, sardonic music in those Weimar years. Most of it disappeared, of course, under the floods of jazz, which Hitler and his Nazis did their absolute best to curb. Not for nothing were the worst juvenile delinquents of the Nazi period called 'jazz-kiddies'.

So powerful an influence was this Negro music that juvenile delinquency actually rose to near epidemic proportions under the Third Reich. No matter how much authority was exerted, the music continued to be played. Eventually, the Nazis gave up and allowed their own jazz bands to broadcast. These wartime songs could often be picked up in England and were often witty, such as *Onward Conscript Army / Marching off to war / To fight for Jewish bosses / And die for Jewish whores / Dressed by Monty Burton / Fed on Lyons' Pies / Fight for Marks and Spencer's / Die for Jewish lies!* All sung to the tune of Sir Arthur Sullivan's rousing 'Onward, Christian Soldiers'! and done as an upbeat jazz number.

Signor Frau's barrel organ, meanwhile, was not as healthy as my new phonograph. While it had earlier shown signs of problems, playing wrong notes, dropping others, wheezing somewhat in certain chords, the machine was what Signor Frau called 'missing'. He would turn the handle but the machinery would not do what it was supposed to do. The notes the organ did play were often wrong, and it was developing a positively ugly sound, as likely to drive away customers as attract them. Some regular passers-by were beginning to laugh or even jeer.

There was nothing that a little intelligence and mechanical skill could not fix. Surely the instrument would not be expensive to repair? I had myself tinkered with a couple of mechanical fairground organs when I worked for the Armenian in Kiev. I mentioned this to Signor Frau. He said any repairs would absorb most of his profit, but with Christmas coming up, he would have to get a specialist to restore it. He was depressed. The thing had already been overhauled once at the beginning of the year.

Familiar with the *Strassenorgel*'s mechanics, I asked if I might have a look. He let down the back on hinges and showed me the interior. The straightforward device consisted of a large bellows, a number of pipes of various gauges, a spiked cylinder rather like a player-piano's, over which passed a series of punched cards, triggering or stopping the appropriate pipes. A bellows supplied the air for the simple system. A borrowed screwdriver, a bicycle repair kit, a can of fine oil, a pair of jeweller's pliers and some wire, and I soon had the

Leierkasten working at full capacity, its voice issuing strong and melodic from the diaphragm at the front. Signor Frau could not thank me enough. He was genuinely delighted. I had made the difference between good times and bad for his little family.

Sitting on a wooden stool one of the traders had lent us, I replaced the casing of the barrel organ feeling that for the first time in months I had done something useful with myself. As I turned to speak to the boy, who had held the tools for me, I saw Zoyea come up to me like a vision. A peck on the cheek, a curtsy and she said very earnestly: 'You are a friend of our family, Herr Peters, and we thank you for your kindness.'

Thereafter, not only did I have a friend, I had employment. My engineering genius, applied to the primitive mechanism of the barrel organ, was in great demand. Those Italians thought me a wonder! And so I began to earn a few marks from other Italians in the same fraternity. Some still spoke habitually in Italian and were delighted that I could converse with them. I was *Il Professore* again, and my meals were also assured. Every evening I was welcome in the homes of families, most of whom were also admirers of Mussolini. I found myself in warm and sympathetic company.

They all lived on the other side of the River Isar in the area of old run-down wooden houses known as Glockenbach-Viertel, built on both sides of a muddy stream running into Munich's chief river. I had grown up in just such a neighbourhood. The buildings had had floors added at random over the past hundred years or so. They had no common design and little sense of order. The houses leaned one against another, forming a kind of organic whole. If one key beam or wall were removed, all the others, so densely packed together and full of humanity, might collapse like cards. Damp rotted much of the woodwork and added to the prevailing smell. Some buildings had been repaired so often with such poor materials they resembled wrecked ships or ramshackle piles of timber. The unmade streets were twisting alleys beneath overhanging balconies and galleries, with blind oiled paper windows and dark, irregular openings running at all angles, and reminded me of the nightmare that was *Doctor Caligari*. Only slowly did it become clear that there were people living within.

I spent happy hours in the district they called the Stables, an old brick mews belonging to a carriage business in the previous century, now housing machinery as well as animals. Here, many of the street sellers stored their stalls, street organs and so on. There was an entire gypsy-style wagon and others in differing stages of repair. There was a show wagon which broke down into a shooting gallery. The game's parts, the rifles and targets, had long since disappeared, but it was still a handsome vehicle. It belonged to the Frau family. He had had some idea about putting it all back together and taking it around the county, but the Reds, of course, had brought in all kinds of petty gambling laws, and he had neither time nor money to obtain the appropriate permits.

I have noticed how the Germans and the Americans get a satisfaction from making laws against human nature. No wonder their prisons are full to bursting. Such laws make you an outlaw simply by being a person.

The Fraus did not use the van because of the cost of re-equipping it. The other vans were more easily adapted for living but were less sturdy. In the crooked building which ran along the whole back wall of the mews was a busy aviary, which I understood to be a secret. Judging by the quality of the ornamental ironwork, the whole thing had been stolen from some Wittelbachian fantasy. Birds from macaws to finches were kept here, and a boy was employed to play a big barrel organ when their screeches became too obvious.

I was never sure if the ranks and ranks of caged birds were for sale, to eat or for company. Neither did I know for certain if it was illegal to keep them. Such age-old practices are usually the first things the Reds outlaw! For instance, in the courtyard one afternoon I witnessed a cockfight. I was privileged to attend as a friend of Heinrich Frau. They were proud of their birds. English fighting cocks, they said, with all the aggression of that tiny island nation. The best blood on earth. Smuggled in from Ireland. The spurs were not elaborate, simply little pieces of leather tied on to the bird's leg through which had been poked a finely sharpened nail, the fighting spur. The sport was a bloody business. Once a bit of glinting feathered flesh struck me in the mouth, but in my excitement, I hardly noticed.

Every night you had to be in the mews by a certain time. A great grille was drawn across the entrance and was not opened again until morning. All was overseen by a horrible old Turkish woman they called the Gatekeeper, which in their argot was also a term for the anal sphincter. She ruled the place while working for an absent owner, Klosterheim, who never appeared and was known only as the Major. Everyone paid their rent to the Gatekeeper, and it was to her they complained. They were convinced she never passed anything but their money on to the Major, rumoured to be a member of the Wittelbach family which had only recently ceased to rule Bavaria.

Sometimes when I worked in the mews repairing the barrel organs and other engines the Italian community used, old Father Bernhardt would pay us a visit. He spoke good Italian and made it his mission to serve the local community, all devout Catholics who worshipped at his church. I took great pleasure in my meetings with a man of refined intellect in that place, and we had some good talks, especially about the Pope and Il Duce. He was a monkey in a cassock, all mouth and no chin, flamboyant gesticulation and brilliant moving eyes, with crimson lips, which in Kiev would have made us call him a 'borscht-fiend' in fun. I think he drank. He certainly gambled, because I saw him slipping his bet to one of the boys who acted as a courier for a famous local gang. 'I long only for the cross and crown,' he used to say, usually after a bad day's gambling. The rumour was he sold church artefacts to pay for his habit, but nobody judged him. He was well liked in the Stables.

Despite its poverty the Glockenbach-Viertel area felt very much like home. What streets were paved at all were cobbled, but some were still nothing but packed earth. Here and there could be seen patches of tarred road, like the hardening scabs of some disease. The gutters were filthy. Some of the houses reeked of sewage. Thin dogs ran everywhere. Ragged, often dirty, children played among the piles of garbage. The river, though useful, was not always pleasant to smell. Yet the people living there were hospitable and generous with what little they had. I found it a considerable relief to join a circle of acquaintances who had nothing to do with the NSDAP or, indeed, the Fascist Party. Politics was meaningless to most of them. They thought in terms of patrons, if they thought of such things at all. They paid a couple of grubby German lawyers when they got into trouble, but mostly they kept their noses out of things. They saw little difference between the Sozis and the Nazis still viciously fighting in nearby streets and wanted none of it. Who could blame them?

While I was nominally a member of both groups, I had never felt at all comfortable in uniform. Now I knew it was not always possible to trust one's party comrades, whereas here, among the *Leierkasten*, the other *Strassenhändler*, their friends and relatives, I

392

enjoyed the easygoing acceptance I had experienced earlier in Odessa, where to be part of one family was to be part of many.

These Italians were, of course, not all street organists! Some sold religious plaster figurines from barrows; others sold ice cream in the summer and hot chestnuts in the winter. Some played the accordion or mandolin and sang. Some even worked at steady jobs in Munich. As in Moldavanka, their lives were neither easy nor lavish, yet they knew the security of their extended family, the knowledge that no one would ever starve. The food was not entirely familiar to me but had much of the quality I knew in Odessa. On those clear autumn evenings, we sat on the banks of the Glockenbach watching distant boats and listening to the sound of a band drifting from the faraway English gardens.

Now to Heckie, my Zoyea, I was no longer Herr Peters, but 'Uncle Mac', and our mutual enthusiasm was for the *Kino*. Only too delighted to discover a young lady with the same relish as myself, I proposed to her father very properly that I take Heckie with me on my next cinema visit. We could go after she had completed her performances in the market. Old Frau was delighted. I was now a brother, he declared, part of the family. His little princess deserved a break. He and the boy could cope. She could go with me at least once a week. When I consulted her, Heckie declared joyfully that she was glad to see whatever films I chose, but her personal taste was for historical epics and adventure films, preferably with cowboys. She shared every German child's fascination for the 'Wild West'. These films were generally cheaper and more plentiful than the serious films and musical comedies I personally favoured.

I had not until then realised how the Masked Buckaroo was still a familiar favourite with the movie-starved Munichers. With considerable surprise and some trepidation I found myself and Heckie watching, at a cinema which had not yet gone over to sound, an episode of *Buckaroo's Bride*, with its outstanding train sequences. By chance the film was one of the few where my face was unmasked in most scenes, largely because of the romance between myself and 'Gloria Cornish' as Mrs Cornelius was known professionally. It was based on the original Warwick Colvin Jr novel, *A Buckaroo's Courtship*.

Thereafter, I became my little Zoyea's absolute hero. Her reserve vanished completely. She became warm, vibrant, full of innocent affection. Who would not have fallen in love with the child! She insisted on our going several times to the same programme until it changed. We had to be sure, she said, to see the remaining two episodes. She spent any spare time looking through old film magazines for pictures of Max Peters, the Masked Buckaroo. Someone gave her a couple of German translations of the Colvin novels, which she read quickly, but said she found disappointing. Zoyea was also a keen fan of Tom Mix and Hoot Gibson, though she assured me kindly that her favourite remained the Masked Buckaroo.

Half an Italian in the house is worse than none, as the Germans say, but those Italians provided my lifeline back to some kind of normality. Much of the time I could forget that terrible night with Hitler, I could forget Brodmann's relentless pursuit of me, I could even forget my relationship with Röhm, as it became increasingly tense.

That Christmas, however, thanks to a chance meeting with Baldur's gracious sister, Rosalind von Schirach, who heard that I had no plans for the holidays, I spent with the Hanfstaengl family. They were determined to forget the cares of Berlin and enjoy the season no matter what. Putzi and his wife had a strong sense of family and valued their private life above politics, a preference which would get them in trouble later when Hitler had absolute power. They took over a hotel in Nuremberg so we could all visit 'the Capital of Christmas' and experience the wonder of the Christkindlmarkt, its lights glistening in the falling snow, as the bells of the city declared Peace on Earth to All and Good Will to the World, while happy citizens carried their cakes and geese and trees and candles home to their firesides where they prayed that tranquillity would come again to Germany and the blight of war would be banished for ever.

Our hotel faced out on to the great square and the market and a city where huge brands in brackets illuminated the ancient walls of castles and churches. Rich shadows moved like ghostly gods against the big old stones. The stalls were heaped with Christmas toys, with boxes of model soldiers for which Nuremberg was famous, with golden angels and musical caskets, tin drums and trumpets, flags and play swords. Everywhere were piles of pastries and candies, treasures of dazzling colour and harmony. A brass band and a small orchestra played carols and other Christmas music. We were distracted by puppet shows and toy theatres, clowns and St Nicholas and a huge nativity scene. Few were not in good humour in spite of the relative poverty. Nuremberg, without doubt, was at her very best, and I could imagine no finer place to spend Christmas. Something about that ancient walled city found echoes in every European soul. The streets wound around the hill like a chord of music creating a magnificent medieval fantasy, maintained and extended by successive generations. The hotel, with its black beams and dark panelling, festooned with glass decorations and greenery, had erected a tall Christmas tree in the ballroom around which were heaped presents for everyone staying there.

All the Hanfstaengls' party thought for themselves, and no unhealthy Führer-worship was found here. Indeed, they often spoke irreverently not only of Hitler but also of colleagues such as Goebbels, Göring, Rosenberg, Himmler and others. Relaxing company indeed! Christmas Eve would be the celebratory feast before, in more contemplative spirit, we recalled the birth of the Saviour on the following day. Hanfstaengl, a Catholic, took us off to the midnight mass, a full service in all its sonorous grandeur, with the organ sending massive vibrations through my legs and groin. The cathedral was a symphony of blazing light, crowded with lifted voices celebrating in one joyous chorus the birth of the Prince of Peace. We prayed that 1932 would bring Germany peace and stability again and shared the sentiments of the presiding priest, who asked that leadership and direction quickly be restored to the nation.

I must admit that most of the spiritual message passed me by because, to my initial astonishment, Katerina von Ruckstühl was one of the Hanfstaengls' other guests. She sought me out. Now she leaned her vibrant little form against me to make it evident that her mind was not entirely engaged with the sublime eternals. I was both pleased and disturbed to see her, though fearing at first that her demon-mother was with her; but Mama, I learned, had decided to visit friends in England. Katerina was quick to tell me that she was on my side in the matter, that her mother could be 'something of a bitch', and that Alfred, her half-brother, was certainly not my child.

Kitty stayed with me after the service. Slender and quick as a cat, narrow-shouldered, long-legged, with an almost triangular little face framed by her short, dark red hair, she had wide-set blue-green eyes, a broad, sensual mouth and a sleepy, mocking manner which was sexually provocative but which I pretended not to notice. She wore near-transparent pastel silk dresses, preferring green and rust, with flesh-coloured silk stockings and patent-leather high heels that shone as brightly as her lacquered head.

Kitty had been abandoned, she told me later as we toasted one another preparatory to retiring. Her mother was in England because she had a new 'flame', someone in the diplomatic corps.

'She still hates you!' Kitty whispered just before we parted. 'I'd love to know exactly why.'

The next day she insisted we take a tour of the old city, which seemed even more of an insane fantasy than Ludwig's famous palace. Everything was of the same red stone tending to a grotesque heaviness when not adulterated by ordinary shops and the market. The Nurembergers had a way of decorating their city to give it a liveable scale. During the Middle Ages their castle meant security and power, but now it was merely grim. The museums, with their many edged weapons and martial paintings, added to this peculiar mixture of attractive romanticism and brute threat.

When we returned to our party that afternoon Putzi was entertaining his guests. The man who came to be known as 'Hitler's clown' was a great pianist and singer of comic songs, as he was pleased to demonstrate. He had always cheered the Führer up during those melancholy days of exile and struggle. At the drop of a hat the gentle 'Smokestack', as Kitty nicknamed him, would sit down at the hotel piano, a cigarette between his smiling lips, and pound out some rather Teutonic Gershwin. He took boyish pride in our pleasure.

Hanfstaengl had also been involved in the Fräulein Raubal business and was very concerned for his Chief. When we were alone later, he confided in me. He was planning a big event for Hitler's birthday, still some months off. While in London, he had fallen in love with Gilbert and Sullivan all over again, and he was seeking volunteers with good operetta-quality voices, planning to surprise Hitler with a performance of *The Mikado*. His other idea was to put on some sort of minstrel show, but he did not think the Führer would be familiar enough with the conventions of the cakewalk and the coon dance.

I agreed he should do something in the European tradition. America's chief contribution to world culture was to cheapen the air with Negro jazz noise and chattering Jews in banal talkies.

Hanfstaengl became defensive. He was proud of his American blood. But in the end his huge head nodded in reluctant agreement, confiding that he had returned to Munich and the family print business because it was impossible to love both art and politics in America. Sales were at last beginning to improve, especially now he had an exclusive contract with the party. I had been to his shop with Röhm. It now sold mostly good-quality posters representing the Nazi hierarchy. Röhm had wanted me to see him larger than life-size, I think! Both Hoffmann, Hitler's exclusive photographer, and Hanfstaengl were making fortunes from their leader's rise to fame. Hitler trusted few Berliners and liked to have Bavarians and Austrians about him whenever possible.

Though the Führer got a royalty, Hanfstaengl was doing so well from his posters that he felt he owed Hitler something. He was having the costumes specially made in London and sent over. They were identical to those worn by the D'Oyly Carte Theatre Company. Like many Americans, Hanfstaengl was more appreciative of the Savoy Balladeers than the English, who tend to dismiss their greatest creative artists and keep them, as a matter of course, from any sort of real advancement.

Hanfstaengl tried to drag me into the scheme as a fellow American. I reminded him I had not been raised in the English tradition. He apologised. He was desperate for volunteers and most of his friends were dashing hither and yon trying to get the Nazis elected to majority power in the Reichstag. These were to be the crucial years, dependent as much upon luck as strategy, like all politics. Hitler never acknowledged his good luck and so aroused the ire of the gods who had first blessed him. The Greeks would have written a play about him! Indeed, Hanfstaengl confided in me that Hitler often saw Pericles as his model. He had read some potted popular history which he was always fond of quoting.

Kitty had not come down from Berlin as I thought. She had old friends in Munich and had arrived at about the time she first visited me. By and large she had not mixed much with the Nazi people. They were altogether too grim and serious for her taste.

Kitty told everyone I had a birthday approaching. The Hanfstaengls loved celebrations and insisted on a party specifically for that occasion. So I celebrated my thirty-second year, quite unexpectedly, in warm company and pleasant surroundings. They held my party all through the day on 1 January, forever finding excuses to toast me and bump me and clap me on the back. The Germans can never resist a chance to enjoy an anniversary. It felt wonderful to be so accepted.

Next morning, the first moment we were alone at breakfast, Kitty asked me urgently if I had any 'coca-een', which was what the drug was called locally. She had a very good source in Munich but had run out. Did I have any spare?

I had not brought enough for two but reasoned to myself that since her contact would be useful to me, I could afford to let her have some now and avail myself of her suppliers later.

'I have a little,' I admitted. 'But I'm short of money to buy more.'

It sent a shock through my yearning system when she stared into my eyes as boldly as any seasoned whore. They called it 'the Berlin look' in Munich. 'You can fuck me for a gram,' she said.

We settled for half a gram.

I began 1932 in a spirit of considerable optimism.

Once the *sneg* had relaxed her, Kitty expanded on her reasons for being in Bavaria. She had followed 'the Mongol' here when he found it convenient to leave Berlin. She told me with a quick, self-conscious grin, that she was part of his 'entourage'. 'I stay there. At his flat.' She had been with him in London but found that not only were prices extravagantly high there (£3 10s for an ounce of raw cocaine), the general climate was puritanical and critical as well. The English were stones. They had no sense of fun. All their most amusing people were already in Berlin. The Mongol had soon shaken the English dust off his perfect pumps.

I had heard of the Mongol. He was notorious. His picture occasionally appeared in a society paper. His name was actually Prince Friedrich ('Freddy') Badehoff-Krasnya, late Protector of Mirenburg, exiled by the Austrian invasion, returned for three weeks by the short-lived nationalist coalition, then deposed by the province's Red Soviet. I knew of him from Röhm, too. The Stabschef had rather admired him. Prince Freddy was a subtle mixture of white and yellow, what some considered the worst possible blend of Prussian and Hungarian blood.

A small, delicate man with immense charm, Badehoff-Krasnya's Mongol ancestry was very evident in his rather devilish features. Röhm found him personable and always willing to help in discreet matters if he could. He had bailed Röhm out once or twice in the old days. I knew also from Major Nye that Prince Freddy was not welcome in many European drawing rooms and received few invitations to receptions. A notorious debauchee, he supported his deplorable habits by putting himself at the service of other rich sensualists. He was the chief means of support of many a degenerate and *demi-mondaine* in the Berlin underworld.

Kitty was enormously attracted to him. 'He can make a slave of me, as he does of so many women.' She told me something of his demands, which she could, she said, only accept under certain conditions and circumstances. He was, however, an easy source of amusement and, of course, of her beloved 'coca', but it was her mother's need for morphine that had first brought her together with Prince Freddy. I was reassured to know Frau Oberhauser had a vice.

Major Nye had told me how Badehoff-Krasnya was famous for supplying English girls to special friends. 'Distasteful as it is to an Englishman's mind, the fact remains that the most sought-after dancers, *demi-mondaines* and entertainers in Berlin are English. So many of our unfortunate little youngsters have fallen into the hands of the Hun traffickers. The procurers know the returns their percentages will bring in Berlin. It's a filthy trade and that man is at the rotten core of it.'

Major Nye had added that if Prince Freddy's talents had been turned in a constructive direction, he would have been one of the leaders of his day. Röhm had thought much the same. That combination of Asian and Teutonic was volatile and at the same time cold. His character contained a particular kind of hunger often only satisfied by opium or some other form of narcissistic hedonism. The Mongol had tenacity, analytical genius, personal magnetism but also a fatal taste for depravity. Outwardly a suave and gentle little man, delicate and old-fashioned in his courtesy, exquisitely neat in his person, he secreted beneath his modest exterior the most refined and excessive sadism. Kitty's mocking cynicism became a kind of fixed grimace when she talked about his vices, but her eyes betrayed her addiction. *La vie sensuelle* would soon devour her. It was not easy to remember that once I had watched her playing gaily in her short skirts and woollen stockings about the deck of HMS *Rio Cruz* as we steamed away from Odessa, exiles together. Now her face was already beginning to show signs of dissolution. I think she was twenty-four. But I cannot deny her attractions.

I soon discovered that the reason Kitty hated her mother was because, in her desperation for morphine, Frau Oberhauser had effectively sold her daughter to Prince Freddy. She could do nothing now, she said, because she was weak. But didn't I think it was wrong for a parent to expose a child to such dangerous company?

Of course, this was, perversely, to my own advantage. In hating her mother, Kitty was inclined to love those her mother hated. No wonder Weimar was a happy hunting ground for Freud's army of Jewish pseudo-scientists preying upon the wealthy in Berlin and Vienna. Release your repressions! they cried. And a black monster with red jaws and glittering fangs, with grasping paws and a huge scarlet prick, was called into being. With him came the ghosts of those ruins yet to be. The ruins of Cologne, Dresden, Hamburg, Frankfurt, Nuremberg, Munich and Berlin. The ruins upon which such monsters thrive. Aggressive carrion willing to seduce when they can or rape if they have to. All innocence is defiled, all belief eroded, all virtue reviled.

The red-and-black monster roars and its saliva is poison dripping upon all that remains of our honour and our wealth. Once there was a power to defend us against the monster. A new Siegfried, we thought, who would drive the dragon of Bolshevism from our midst and establish a bright new order across Europe. Instead, Siegfried took the dragon into himself, or the dragon turned itself into Siegfried. Whatever the result, compromise was the cause. And Hitler's willingness to compromise, his failure to concentrate on the essential issues led him to his monumental, melodramatic self-destruction.

Prince Freddy was related to the Wittelbachs. This meant that certain fawning nationalist interests in the Bavarian capital were willingly blind and deaf to the rumours about him so long as his royal blood graced them with its acquaintance. As a result he was not living in obscurity. According to Kitty, his habit was to make sure that his private life appeared solidly conventional. I would eventually discover that the rooms to which casual visitors were admitted were full of panelling and leather and baize, with hunting trophies and various other masculine badges with which the average wealthy man advertises his vitality and prowess. He also displayed pictures of relatives whose names were associated with the height of breeding and respectability. The bedroom they might see would be sparse and equally redolent of masculine values. He would subscribe to local political parties, charities, business ventures. People would find him a gentleman through and through and roar in angry defence of him if any hint was offered concerning other practices. Indeed, should they find within themselves a desire to taste these forbidden pleasures, Prince Freddy would warn them of what became of people who developed such habits. If they persisted, they were his for ever. Kitty told me this and shrugged weakly. So it was with her.

In some ways the holiday in Nuremberg was my last ordinary

innocent pleasure. When it was over, my descent into several kinds of hell began. I had no intimation of it, of course. After the break, as soon as we were back in Munich, Kitty arranged for us to visit Prince Freddy's extraordinary flat where, she assured me, 'snow' was always in plentiful supply. He could not seduce me, of course. I knew how to control my appetites.

In a note Prince Freddy told Kitty he would be delighted to see her guest. He already knew that the famous American film star, Max Peters, was in town, and he longed to meet me. He had seen many of my films and was immensely flattered that I should want to visit him.

His huge apartment was in a very well-to-do-suburb of the city, not far from where I had met Frau and Fräulein Röhm. The house itself was a rather fanciful one, owing a little to the extravagance of the Wittelbachs, so I was not surprised it had been built by one of that family. It was now owned by a Ruhr industrialist who used it occasionally as a holiday place but rented the upper part to Badehoff-Krasnya. The suburb's broad tree-lined roads were largely unmade at that time and carried little motor traffic but were well kept with sweepers and porters, even through the depths of the Depression.

Only the very wealthy weathered the crisis leading to the establishment of the new gold mark. Few feared a continuation of the poverty experienced in the early 1920s. Germany was a naturally prosperous country, growing more so every day. People feared civil war and were prepared to do almost anything to avoid it. The idea of Nationalist Bavaria marching against Socialist Prussia was anathema to modern Germans. That was why a party whose name included a compromise, which resolved the differences and united the people, was attractive to so many who knew little of the real Nazi policies and therefore did not properly support them when the time came. The fatal flaw was there from the beginning.

We were admitted into the Prince Badehoff-Krasnya's building by a uniformed porter who directed us to an electric lift which took us up a couple of floors. Here on the landing Prince Freddy awaited us. Slender, short and very dark, he reminded me of a Borgia dagger, but he was charming. One could easily see how he had ruined countless lives. His oiled hair was brushed straight back on his head, he had a pencil-thin moustache and rimless pince-nez through which his silver-blue eyes gazed mildly and wonderingly. His lips were thin, tight against his teeth. His hands and feet were tiny but perfectly formed, while his bearing was that of an infinitely cultured, highly bred man of the world, chivalrous, gentle and courteous to a degree. He apologised for his inconvenient living quarters. This floor and the turret were completely cut off from the rest of the house so that privacy was assured.

He escorted us through the conventional apartment then pulled back a curtain disguising a door into a small lobby. From this a staircase rose. He led us up to the top. Soundproofed double doors shut the staircase off from the landing and led into an entrance hall hung with astonishingly vivid futurist tapestries, more extreme than anything of Fiorello's! From the ceiling hung octagonal glass spikes of irregular length, stained dazzling red, green, blue, orange, rose du Barry. Inside the glass glowed electric light bulbs. Beneath them in clashing contrast sat a life-sized bronze of the Naples Hercules, pensive, solid in its colossal power.

As the doors closed behind us dead silence fell. Every door and shutter in that strange flat must have been equally soundproofed. Heavy curtains divided the apartment, hiding doors, windows and walls. The rooms and alcoves were dimly lit with more coloured lamps. It was unsettling to find something so exotic in the middle of Bavaria! Even in Berlin this would have seemed more like a film set than an individual's flat. I could hardly believe these were temporary quarters. The Prince's house in Berlin, said Kitty, was similarly decorated but was much larger and with special rooms.

The apartment's interior gave the appearance of tremendous space and loftiness. Each wall was panelled with floor-to-ceiling mirrors. Between them, a foot in breadth, were wooden columns on which vaguely obscene mural frescos were painted in vibrant reds and yellows and blues. The ceiling was mirror glass; mirrors lined the shutters; the glare was toned down by pastel-coloured curtains, divans, cushions and silk hangings. A great, wide, canopied divan occupied half one wall; a cabinet gramophone, with piles of records, stood beside it. In a corner, inexplicably tangled up with electric wires, cables and green baize shades, was an enormous arc light. The floor was thickly carpeted so our feet were also soundless.

Prince Freddy was self-deprecating. 'I have a taste for the exotic and the modern,' he admitted. 'There is a little Eastern vulgarity in me, I fear. But without the vulgar, we die of good taste, do we not?'

Meanwhile, he made us welcome. He had a Japanese servant he called 'Monsieur Frank'. If we required anything, Monsieur Frank

402

was at our service. Kitty explained how she 'owed' me some coca from Nuremberg. 'You must tell me all about Nuremberg.' He crossed to a lacquered cabinet from which he produced a long yellow Venetian glass bottle. From the bottle he poured into a phial at least an ounce of the life-giving powder. 'I hear it is a children's paradise.'

Refusing money, he assured me that my films had already entertained him so thoroughly he owed me at least that. 'Take it,' he said. 'There is more. There is always more.'

As Kitty and I were leaving, Prince Freddy recommended that we visit the Flashlite Klub, which had opened a few days earlier across the river near Zeppelinstrasse. He had a small investment in the place and could recommend the English girl there. She was unusually talented. He smiled and rested his hand on my arm. I was bound to know her.

For a terrible moment I thought he referred to Esmé, who had so badly let me down in Egypt. Then the Prince produced a hand-bill to show me who he meant. I was astonished. The star chanteuse at the Flashlite Klub was Gloria Cornish! My old friend Mrs Cornelius! I was amused and delighted by the irony. A few days earlier I had yearned for feminine company and worried where I would find my next supply of 'snow'. Now, it seemed, I had an excess of both!

THIRTY–SEVEN

Gloria Cornish was never more glamorous. With the customers' intimate torch-beams playing over her sensuously dressed figure, she stormed on to the little stage of the Flashlite Klub. Radiating *joie de vivre*, energy personified, she blew a kiss to the band, a kiss to the audience. The cellar was thick with cigar smoke and California poppy. It barely disguised the heavy smell of mould. Yet all was transformed, all shabbiness forgotten, when she emerged from behind the velvet curtain. She was sex. She was joy. A golden promise. The nightclub rented out electric torches and encouraged customers to direct the light wherever they pleased. White beams played on the artistes and on other customers who attracted them. Being mostly Bavarian burghers, they were frequently unsubtle in their play with the beams. Yet nothing could cheapen my goddess! Even Kitty, the eternal cynic, was entranced, though she pretended not to be.

These were the days before every chanteuse was expected to look like Lola-Lola in *Der blaue Engel*, a costume which became as formal as an Auguste's face. The real cabaret singers wore stylish gowns, like my Mrs Cornelius.

Clad in clinging apple-green silk with jade trim, her long legs kicking, her arms outstretched, her back bent outwards and her gorgeous figure displayed in all its natural beauty, she danced that sensuous English jazz step in which the whole body swayed in serpentine waves from head to toe. The style derived from the minstrel cakewalks which had a profound effect on British popular entertainment and are running to this day at the New Victoria Theatre.

A four-piece Negro orchestra sat to one side of the stage playing banjo, cornet, tuba and clarinet. Their bowler-hatted silhouettes were flung up against the backdrop by a spotlight. The little orchestra sounded like the wild, beating heart of Africa and Mrs Cornelius's high, fluting voice, full of ironic gaiety, sang Noel Coward's latest

'Twentieth-Century Blues' against their relentless thrumming. Coward was currently a sensation with the Berlin cognoscenti. Then, of course, he was a famous homosexual. Today he is a famous knight. So it turns. It is a well-known fact that the best way of acquiring a knighthood is to be caught in a public toilet with a guardsman.

When she sang in German, 'Fräulein Cornish's' accent was delicious, and the crowd howled with delight. Flowers and money fell on the stage like wedding tributes, and she received them all with laconic grace. *Surabaya Johnny, you have no heart . . .* I had never heard such melancholy sweetness. No wonder she was a sensation in Munich! This was not the first time I had seen her perform. Technically we were actually married, though no intimacy had taken place between us. We had spent many months on tour in America. Naturally, Hollywood gossips had paired us romantically because we featured together in most of the *Masked Buckaroo* and *White Ace* pictures.

With the rest of the audience I was entranced as she sang a gloomy French song called 'Fashionette' and another about an impotent Pierrot.

Her final number, in which she made sensual play with her cigarette holder and those extraordinary blue eyes under huge lashes, was called 'Der Entropietango' and was a typically sardonic piece of Berlin pessimism. The sexual charge in the place was almost asphyxiating. Men and women were equally fascinated by her performance. She had everything the Germans loved, including her English accent. Her show finished with an extraordinary version of a song I knew to be a favourite, but made all the more suggestive by the wailing and throbbing of the little Negro orchestra.

'Don'cher fink my dress is a little bit, jest a little bit, not too much of it –? / And if you fink my dress is a little bit – well, it's ther little bit ther boys admire . . .' Finishing with a rousing chorus or two of *Keep yer 'and on yer 'a'penny.*

She left them on their feet and yelling for more, quite unlike the usual response of the blasé nightclub audiences. As their applause subsided she took her encore. She slunk, she strutted, she strolled and slid from one sinuous step into another. I almost swooned with the pleasure of it. The horns and reeds blared and shrieked, the banjo twanged.

'Oh, the moonlight, the bitter moonlight, oh, the moonlight . . . no heart has the knight . . . Locked in the prison of my dreams, he brings me my

*release . . . Love is a dish he can't refuse. He tastes it once and on he moves
. . . My blood finds harmony in his, true blood mixed with true love is . . .
Must I perish so he can unify our land?'* She sang in English what was
evidently a modern setting for an old folk song with more meaning
in German. There was something in the words which brought the
audience almost to tears, and their emotion filled that tiny cellar,
giving her energy for still another chorus. Swaying, they joined in
as one. *'We will unite, one day soon, / Some day when, we'll united be
again.'*

A yearning for conformity was a stronger pull than sex in those
decent Bavarian hearts. She appealed to the patriot and man of
goodwill, not the pervert. *'And we know we'll be together one day soon!'*

Vera Ellen would pirate this song for crude propaganda during
the War but every German who heard it knew what it really meant.

She left them happy again, with 'A Little of What You Fancy Does
You Good' and 'Please Take Care of My Pussy', then just as she was
giving her final bow, the stage awash with petals and notes, she saw
me and screamed.

'Ivan! Yer little barstard, where yer bin?'

Then she was engulfed.

Eventually she made her way to our table and sat down radiantly,
still acknowledging their homage. She offered Kitty a distant nod.
They were already acquainted, she said. Then she turned her beaming
face on me. 'Ivan. Th' bad penny wot always turns up, eh? I bin
tryin' ter find yer since I saw yer in ther street wiv all yer parcels.
That was ther day I got 'ere with 'Uggy. Did yer get married?' She
cast suspicious eyes on Kitty, who 'frosted' and turned away to smile
at an old brewer leering at her knees. 'I've got a job fer yer. Real
work. We'd almost decided on Jack Trevor, but 'e's landed a contract
anyway. 'E's goin' ter live in Oberammergau, 'e says, where they 'ave
ther play. It would probably suit 'im to play Jesus.' Then she calmed
down, realising how much attention was still on us. She leaned
forward and left a red kiss on my cheek. 'Come rahnd ter the "Exit
Only" door in five minutes and Reinhardt'll let yer in. But I'd rather
yer come on yer own.'

Kitty was more than a trifle disconcerted when I popped her in
a taxi and sent her to spend the night at Prince Freddy's. I had
important business, I said, to be discussed in private. Kitty's laughter,
when I told her this, was crisply disbelieving. At that point I had
no concern for her good opinion. I hurried back to Mrs Cornelius.

I waited a couple of minutes until the bar of the 'Exit Only' door was pushed back, and I was greeted by what appeared to be an elaborately dressed ape. A tiny hermaphroditic creature in a perfect linen suit of pale lilac, calling himself 'Mr Reinhardt', ushered me through the badly ventilated passage behind the toilets and into a scarcely more pleasant dressing room. Poorly lit, save for the glaring mirror, this tiny space was festooned with exotic underwear and coloured silks. Her figure as firm as ever, Mrs C leaned into the mirror, removing her exaggerated stage make-up. I was relieved to see the same vital youth underneath. Roughly my own age, she shared the tendency to unwrinkled skin that had little to do with care and a great deal to do with heritage. Save for facial hair I have remained smooth all my life. Most of my lovers have been fascinated by that quality.

Little Reinhardt scuttled away like an apologetic rat, and I was left to sit in the gold-painted wicker chair she offered me. Some of the paint immediately attached itself to my sleeve, and my attempts to clean it smeared it further. I did my best to relax in the chair's creaking discomfort. What was worse, I was forced to endure the most exquisite pangs of lust while she removed her face, as she put it, and 'slapped the old one back on'. Then she went behind her screen to finish dressing while I relieved myself as best I could in the time permitted.

I was disconcerted by a rapid knock on the door which opened immediately to reveal another familiar face. His knowing smirk was the last thing I wished to experience. I greeted him wearily with a wave of the offending hand. 'Good evening, Seryozha.' Mrs Cornelius was always soft-hearted. How many more of the walking wounded had she adopted? 'When did you slip down to Munich? Where's your uniform?'

'I'm in mufti.' A monstrous wink. 'Special assignment.' His lugubrious eyes leered into mine as those massive lips planted warm kisses on my cheeks. 'Dimka, dearest. I'm a BODYguard!' His giggle was unbecoming in an SS officer. 'On loan from Himmler, who owes a favour to our Gloria's special gent, and my association with the theatre is well known. The Bolshies will go to any lengths to attack us. They hate her because she happens to be friends with a very nice old gentleman who doesn't share their particular views and whom Captain Himmler wants to keep sweet. I was the ideal officer to protect our star. But you have another acquaintance, dear —'

'Keep it darn, Sershi,' called Mrs Cornelius from behind the screen. 'And don't talk so fuckin' much or I won't 'ave nuffink ter tell 'im meself. An' I'm tryin' ter get a free dinner art o' im.'

Seryozha draped his boneless body over two chairs and snorted. Sharing an even more exaggerated wink with me, he leaned forward and hissed, 'It's her favourite darkie, dear. You know! Really sweet – and *so* intelligent!'

The only darkie of her acquaintance I ever knew was, of course, Mr Mix. I remember how disconsolate she had been after my 'Sancho Panza' disappeared off the ship in Casablanca.

'It could not, of course, be Mr Mix –'

'Oh, is it *Mix*?' He tutted with self-disgust. 'I thought it was Dix. The actor, dear, not the cowboy. English is hideous, isn't it, Dimka? Everything sounds the same, like Chinese. All inflection and inference. It's a slippery language, dear. You can't trust it, can you? Not like Russian. You know where you are with Russian.' He took out a snuffbox and cut us all a line of cocaine.

My loyal companion had found his patroness again. Mrs Cornelius had been more than kind to him, willingly devoting hours of her time to helping him. 'Does Mr Mix know I'm here?' I asked.

'I'll tell him, dear.' He raised his eyebrows. 'Sexy, mm?' He took the first snuff. 'Built like a rhino . . . ?'

'My dear Seryozha, Mr Mix was my loyal servant on my travels across America and Africa. Our relationship was always formal. I never expected to see him again.' I accepted his little Lalique mirror, a silver tube.

'Oh, the man's full of fun. So talented and entertaining. You and I, of course, prefer the more slender, East African type –'

'I told yer ter shut it, Sersh.' Mrs Cornelius's voice became a guillotine. 'We'll orl be art o' work if you don't put a clip on them big flapping lips. *Wot a marf, wot a marf, wot a norf an' sarf* . . .'

I began to laugh both at his childish disappointment and at her glaring eyes as she stepped from behind the screen dressed for the street in a pretty black-and-white outfit. She wore a little matching hat on her platinum locks, a red rose in her lapel. With a tiny handbag under her arm, she trotted on slender high heels. I was able to stand up a little shakily and salute her. She said that as usual it looked as if I was rocking the cradle at both ends.

'Yer orl pasty, Ivan.' I was going to need a bit of self-discipline what with the work I had coming to me. 'Yer've got yer big break at last, matey. I've 'ad private detectives looking fer yer, an' everyfing!' She refused to say more until after the fish course.

I took her to dinner at the Restaurant Steiner in Rosenstrasse, an expensive place, all plush and crystal, serving dinner in the old High South German style. The meal would cost me most of my remaining money but would be worth it to celebrate our reunion. She was recognised by several customers who stood up to bow, and she very prettily bowed back. 'Keep in wiv ther sods while yer a'ead, Ivan, eh?'

I agreed enthusiastically.

We finished our fish, but she only really came down to business at the meal's end. Stroking the glass which had taken the last of my month's budget, she offered a huge comradely grin. 'We're quids in, Ivan. I can't see 'ow it can fail. But it was touch an' go until I saw yer tonight. My 'Uggy's got this idea of doing a series o' *cowboy* pictures, 'ere in Germany, and selling 'em ter America!'

She clearly thought the idea mad.

'Which means 'e's got ter 'ave stars *known* in America. Which is where you an' me come in, 'cause them bloody *Masked Buckaroo* serials are orl over ther bloody place 'ere! They get 'em cheap in job lots. Ya know ther sorta fing. Yer can 'ave two Tom Mixes and a 'Oot Gibson but yer got ter take twelve episodes of *Masked Buckaroo at Devil's Jump*. I ain't complainin'. The Krauts fink we're the biggest fing in 'Ollywood! Anyway, we don't 'ave ter go orl the way back ter Arizona. 'Uggy says we can find the right scenery in the East. I fink 'e means Austria. 'E reckons we can crack ther English an' American market wiv somefink closer to its tastes. And there's nuffink the world likes better than a good cowboy picture. I don't know if 'e's right or wrong, Ivan, but there's a bit of money in it for you an' me. Worf a try, eh? Fer as long as it larsts? 'E's gettin' 'is white bloke lined up an' I'm playing the beautiful mysterious princess, o' course, but he needs you for the coloured chap.'

I suppose my inclination was to rise at that point, but politeness made me hear her out. She grinned at my expression. 'It's cowboys and *Indians*, Ive. Yer play this noble defender of 'is wild domain. Child o' nature. Like in *Ther Vanishin' American*, remember? Or *Ther Sheikh*. Very romantic. All big brown eyes an' brooding menace, eh? If only Red Indians did ther tango! A clarsy darkie, Ive. Yer'll 'ave orl ther girlies after ya! An Indian prince, Winnie the Pooh or somefink.'

'Winnetou?' I asked quietly. It began to dawn on me that this
was no ordinary blackface role. 'Of Karl May's immortal tales?'

'That's ther bloke. May. I keep getting' 'im mixed up wiv Karl
Marx. Both 'ad bushy whiskers.' She was delighted at my knowledge. 'I'd never 'eard of 'im. But 'e's big news over 'ere, right?'

'He is Albert Schweitzer's favourite author and what every
German-speaking child has in common. I read and reread those
books as a boy! I could probably quote Winnetou verbatim! They
are what made me the idealist I am today. Professor Lustgarten, my
tutor, had a full set. "Professor Vitzliputzli" inspired my interest in
science, and of course I can vouch personally for May's profound
knowledge of the Sahara. Winnetou, even more than Chingachgook,
was a standard for all natural male virtue. May is a great writer,
whose philosophy and metaphysics are as powerful as his storytelling
gifts.'

'Well, you and 'Uggy'll agree on that anyway. It's ther same sorta
drift. I *told* 'im you were the exact chap. 'E knows yer name 'o
course, and 'e's seen some of yer pictures. 'E fought you wos worf
puttin' down some money for a private 'tec. But Sexton Blake 'imself
couldn't'a found yer! We'd almost given up on yer. Where yer bin?
We fought ya wos wiv that Ernst Röhm, but 'e tol' 'Uggy 'e 'adn't
seen yer fer monfs. Lon Creighton's over in Berlin, and 'e's up for
playin' ther trapper geezer. Thass our Lonny's son. Chip off th' ol'
block. Like old 'ome week, eh?'

'Chaney's son, if he has his father's talent, will be perfect for the
role of Sam Hawkens.' I was growing enthusiastic as I visualised the
kind of film we could make. Creighton was a friend from our
Hollywood days. We had met him with his father. He refused to
exploit his father's name in those days, but it was well known to all
filmgoers who he really was. "E's getting' a contract wiv RKO, but
'e's doing this till 'is first US movie comes up.'

'An all-star picture! Who's playing Old Shatterhand himself?'

Old Shatterhand, a German greenhorn, was May's Texan version
of Natty Bumppo. Every German schoolboy had a clear idea of
what he looked like.

''Uggy really wanted someone local. A German. It's talkin' English,
see. They asked Jack Trevor,' she said, 'but 'e's booked with everyone
at the mo', like I said. 'Ugg's not sure about a real Yank. John
Bentley'd do it, but after that bloody last fiasco in Egypt I wouldn't
trust 'im, frankly. 'Uggy likes ther look o' Cary Cooper but 'e's

under contract and anyway I 'eard wot Clara Bow said about 'im
– biggest cock in Hollywood an' no arse ter push it wiv!' My earth-
spirit exploded with mirth. 'There's some English feller in ther
runnin', too, does 'tec films in Blighty. 'Ugg's goin' over ter see 'im.
They got Lonny's son 'cause 'e wos over 'ere anyway. They're finking
o' some Austrian bloke, Anton Wallbanger or somefink, who can talk
English. You gotta at least be able to fake it in a lot o' diff'rent
languages. That's why 'e wants an English or American actor. That's
ther idea, see? Sell 'em back to America and England and the rest
o' ther empire. Dollars an' pahnds, Ive. Wot they all want ter get
their 'ands on. 'Ard money. Biggest single market, English. Then
German. Then French. Then Spanish. So it'll be plain sailin' fer us,
eh?'

She explained how modern pictures shot each scene over again
in a number of languages. Only later would studios discover the less
expensive method of dubbing. I had just seen Rex Ingram's most
recent film, which was made in Morocco with an international cast,
none of whom could be understood in any of the languages they
spoke! I had known Ingram in Hollywood. The Irishman had studios
in Nice and refused to return to the United States. He said sound
had been the death knell of artistic pictures. He had announced that
henceforth he would paint or write but would never make pictures
again.

The Germans led the world in the production of multiple-
language films. *The Blue Angel* had just been made at UfA's
Neubabelsberg studios, each scene shot first in English, then in
German, then in French. Hollywood, of course, could not make
such films, because it did not have the wealth of actors able casually to speak several languages. It was almost impossible for the
modern European cosmopolitan not to be familiar at least with
English and French if he was German. Italians were often fluent in
all three languages, as well as their own. The only problem German
producers faced was the American and British public's failures to
appreciate the boulevard comedies and military farces, the staple of
the Berlin and Munich cinemas, produced in their dozens. Even the
operettas, though widely imitated, did not pull in the natives of
Bradford and Boston. Horror films and science fiction did reasonably well, largely because they depended on visual effects, and
Germans were recognised as the masters of modern illusion.
Metropolis had been a minor success in the UK. *Die Drei von der*

Tankstelle, with its wonderful contemporary settings and many of the top UfA stars, had done no serious business overseas. Even *Der Kongress tanzt*, immediately imitated by the Americans, did not hit the million-dollar jackpot.

"Uggy's not that 'appy with foreigners comin 'ere an' makin' their pictures,' Mrs Cornelius confided. 'They bring a few dollars in, but that's it. Orl ther real profit goes back ter "Jew York" as 'Uggy calls it. 'E says Germans should be makin' ther movies and *exportin'* them ter America, not the ovver way abart. So that's wot we're gonna do. Quotas on Yank pictures. Cowboy pictures fer cowboys ter watch in Wyomin' an' Texas.' She threw back her head and roared, startling a waiter behind her. 'An' 'is big enfusiasm's Karl wotsit's books. It's like a bloody religion wiv 'im. 'E finks 'e'll convert ther Yanks ter bring back ther poor ol' Kaiser. Yer really reckon 'em, do yer? Them books?'

I told her how May's tales of Turk and Texan were totally engrossing, instilling the love of nature, freedom and individuality which mark the best type of modern man. May compared the Apache to the Turk and said they both represented great races who had fallen on hard times, unable to resist more aggressive enemies. He pointed to Indian architecture to show how the Red Man could attain any level of civilisation he wished.

I began to speak of this. 'Yeah,' she said, yawning. "Uggy's explained orl that more'n once.'

'Exemplifying the finest German virtues while showing due respect for the Red Man's innate nobility and purity of soul.'

'Dead right, Ive. So?'

'This is extraordinary.' I could think of no finer part to play. Yet I had become so used to movies presenting the lowest common denominator. 'You are certain, Mrs Cornelius, that your Baron wants to make a film series based on Karl May's famous philosophical adventure tales? The "Winnetou" books?'

'On the money, Ive.'

'I am honoured.'

I added that I heard the May company was wary of vulgarising the Master's work on film. She assured me Hugenberg had secured rights by demonstrating to the family his sincere reverence, patriotism and belief in promoting Karl May's serious ideas concerning brotherly love and the right of all races to live on their own traditional land, unthreatened by invaders of any kind, whether with guns or with an alien culture. This matched what I had already heard of Alfred Hugenberg. He was a Cabinet minister, leader of a major German political party and German through and through. I had read one of his election addresses while waiting for Kitty to come out of the toilet at the *Kino*. Mutual respect was the secret of civil discourse between nations. While he understood the benefits of democracy, he still supported a monarch on the German throne. A monarch represented the state in a way a president could not. He admired Hindenburg, felt that the old Field Marshal really wished to see a Kaiser restored, and was also obsessed with *der alte Fritz*, Frederick the Great. Germany would only hold her head up in the world once more when she had an emperor. Mrs Cornelius said it was well known in film circles that if you wanted to get a start with UfA, you should suggest an 'Old Fritz' theme to Huggy Bear.

Doctor Hugenberg had been granted the May rights because he was leader of the Nationalist Monarchists and an influential director of Krupp. Since the War he had built up a publishing empire to spread his ideas and had saved the German film industry from extinction or absorption by the Americans. During the hard, hungry years he had turned a bankrupt concern into one of the most powerful and profitable in the world. He could offer the public conscientious and respectable versions of the May books and thus introduce him to Britain and America.

Nowadays, as with everything else, such great men find their names dragged in the mud, and every detail of their past dug up and dissected by the *Daily Mail*, so it is no surprise *Der Spiegel* and its kind, forever attacking their own country and its leaders, published scurrilous tales of Karl May's early life which they claimed had been led as a con man! They also said he had spent some seven years in prison as punishment for his crimes. His 'crime' in fact seemed to be possession of a rich and wide imagination! Sufficient crime in a Prussian Germany to have him jailed.

How hard it is for the unimaginative man to imagine the imaginative man. How hard for the intelligent man to enjoy the simple terrors of the dullard. Does the stationmaster waving his green flag to signal that the train is safe to leave the station ever anticipate the twisted rail, the broken signal up ahead? No, he is satisfied that he has accomplished everything possible. The train arrives safely. The train leaves safely. Whatever takes place on the train or outside the limits of his responsibility is nothing to do with him. He never connects. He never understands the nature of collective responsibility. But I see the whole rail system. I am part of the problem. I take some of the responsibility. I know that it is always my fault when something goes wrong, but it is not very much my fault. Any man's death, says the poet, makes me smaller, because I am everyman. I am everyman. My dreams are what made me exemplary. My experience is what makes me extraordinary. But I am otherwise no different to you. Believe me, Karl May was not the only one to suffer because he was different and above the herd. Today I would be living in luxury on an island in Scotland, tranquil and unassailable, were it not for several bitter twists of fate, any one of which might have sent another mad. But I have my creed . . .

> Gott schütze unseren Zaren!
> Den Bewahrer unseres Ruhms!
> Und zerschmettere unsere Feinde!
> Oh alter, orthodoxer Zar!

They cry out for justice. History mourns. God Himself is chastened before their outrage. I take my hope from the best minds of Europe . . .

> Gott schrieb die Schöpfung nicht als Trauerspiel;
> ein tragisch Ende kann es nirgends geben.
> Zwar jedes Leben ringt nach einem Ziel,
> Doch dieses Ziel liegt stets im nächsten Leben.

How we long for truth and justice to rule, for black and white to regard each other with mutual dignity and cultivate their own cultures, their own proud traditions. Believe me, I am not one of those who say that Karl May laid the sentimental groundwork for German imperial expansion. This is arrant nonsense. Germany had an almost impeccable colonial record. It is the Belgians, with whom she waged war, who committed the atrocities, and Germany punished her for it, yet Germany was depicted as the aggressor in the French and British press.

The Belgian rape of Africa became the German rape of Belgian nuns! Is it any surprise that when the Jews began in the thirties to make their hysterical charges against Germany they were not believed? The air was filled with tales of horror. The screens showed

their pessimistic view of the sacrifices we had made with such monuments of misery as *All Quiet on the Western Front*, *The Four Horsemen
of the Apocalypse* and *Drei Tage Mittelarrest*.

Next day Mr Mix told me that his dream had come true when
he ran into Ingram's crew shooting in Morocco and was able to
secure not only a bit part but a passport to Europe. Ingram, though
disgruntled and unhappy with his film, had been a sympathetic
employer, Mix said. But Ingram had returned to Nice, and Mr Mix
found no more film work. He eventually joined a travelling minstrel
show in Lyons, and learned to play the banjo and the guitar.

'I guess I'm just destined to be in show business all my life, Herr
Max.' He had made his way from Lyons, travelling across the country
as an entertainer, singing mostly Al Jolson songs, working briefly in
Paris with Josephine Baker before coming to Berlin with a show
called *Black Birds*, which was still doing well. There he had gone to
an audition and discovered the songstress he would accompany was
none other than his old benefactress Mrs Cornelius!

We all had a meal together. "Old 'ome week,' said Mrs C. He
had been happy to rejoin her when she, too, transferred from Berlin
to Munich. He had become quite a sophisticate with a taste for
good tailoring. Clearly not all the Munich Fräuleins saw him as a
mere darkie entertainer. Even I admitted there was something
wonderfully masculine about Mr Mix. You felt as if you were in the
presence of a wild leopard, always in some degree of danger when
he was near. And sometimes I think he knew his power.

He told me how they had performed their act in Frankfurt, Hamburg
and Bonn, and had dates already promised for Paris, Amsterdam and
even, perhaps, London. It soon became clear to me that it was in my
interest to maintain close contact with my old friends. Now here he
was, my *compañero* of cattle truck and Caliphate!

I had greeted Mr Mix with a genuine sense of warmth, feelings
he reciprocated when he learned of all my adventures abroad. He
enthusiastically exclaimed: '*Ich liebe Deutschland!*' That is the kind of
emotion Germany inspired at the time, even in those not born there.

So, too, said Adolf Hitler and so said the German people. Goebbels,
who had only recently condemned Hitler as the bourgeois puppet
of the industrialists Strasser still claimed him to be, stood up in the
public squares of all the cities in Germany and reminded the people
how the country had been stabbed in the back by alien financiers
with German politicians in their power, supporting the machinations

415

of Jewish socialism, the Trojan horse of Bolshevik Russia. He pointed out, with surprising eloquence, how their professed pacifism, exhibited in such films as *The Game of Guns*, was no more than an effort further to weaken the German soldier and turn him into a creature without character or meaning, who had fought for nothing, died for nothing and come home to nothing. Who was now nothing, with nothing to value, nothing to defend. Who was only useful as a puppet, a slave to the forces of Big Business, which would gobble him up unless they were stopped. The only countering force strong enough and wise enough to stop them was Adolf Hitler and the NSDAP Party.

I saw Goebbels give this speech in Munich in early 1932. He had a way of getting the crowd's sympathy for his deformity, refusing assistance as he climbed to the podium, his spindly arms akimbo as his skull-face regarded the audience. He could have been a villain in a boys' story, yet within moments he had the audience on his side by joking, appealing to their reason, their sentiments, their love of country.

He had learned from Hitler how to begin quietly and build up, to establish his commonality with the audience, to share its humour and way of seeing the world. But then with a catch in his voice and a tear in his eye, he would remind us what humiliation the great German nation had suffered. 'Look,' he would say, 'I'm just an ordinary chap trying to do his best in the world, trying to understand what's going on. We have the same questions in common. The same problems.' He couldn't help noticing how Germany had been tricked into war and then tricked into defeat. How aliens of every stripe had taken advantage of German hospitality, German goodwill, German honour and who now bled their host nation dry. How only Adolf Hitler, that brave young leader, who had known the same terrors and deprivations as his fellow Germans, could unite the country and make it great again. It was time for dynamic new ideas, fresh will-power, vigorous, healthy Young Germany rising triumphant from the ashes of the Old. A Third Reich, strong and proud, holding dominion over her own lands, the lands the Allies had stripped in their hideous feeding frenzy, rewarding the alien businessmen who had helped them march into Germany and despoil her monuments, her traditions, even her women! Black troops had entered the Rhineland leaving black babies behind. The evidence was there for all to see!

Those troops were the threat the Allies used to control Germany! Whenever they felt like it they could release thousands of Algerians, Somalis, Egyptians and Indians upon the entire country. Germania would then truly know what it was to feel the heel of the black barbarian upon her neck. And, jested Goebbels grimly in a vulgar aside, not only her neck would suffer.

I went to the meeting with Mrs Cornelius, her 'Baron' and Seryozha. Mr Mix had also insisted on attending, though the guards controlling the crowd had not allowed him to come in very close. He grinned at me and waved when from the crowd his eyes met mine.

While I now had my friends back, I was still something of a prisoner in Corneliusstrasse. Mrs Cornelius, Mr Mix and Seryozha were not always available to me, and I wondered if the film contract would ever become reality. I was again beginning to resume my earlier plan of getting to Mr Green, my Uncle Semyon's agent in England, picking up my inheritance and, if possible, settling in the UK for a while.

It crossed my mind that the British Foreign Office would be more than interested in what I had to show them. Von Schirach and Röhm had so far failed to interest anyone in my designs. Röhm said it was because everyone's attention was focused on getting and keeping power. Hitler had promised him the Reichswehr if he played a good hand. He told me not to approach Göring, whom he loathed increasingly, and I was beginning to wonder if Ernstie had any serious intention of helping me.

If it had not been for Baldur von Schirach, I might have despaired of the NSDAP altogether. I had some substantial conversations with the Youth Leader. Von Schirach shared my enthusiasm for the future. Once he saw my designs, he was ecstatic. Instinct told me he would understand them. He was deeply impressed. 'But Herr Peters, you are a genius! I had no idea you possessed such sophisticated engineering skills. Surely you have studied at a great university!' I told him how I had been the youngest Professor of Physics at St Petersburg University.

'Russia?' He was startled, frowning, no doubt working out my age.

Of course not, I told him. Florida. Thus I avoided a too complicated explanation. I had forgotten it was unwise to say anything of my Russian education or even of the important aristocrats with whom I mixed in those days. I had friends to protect. My American passport was worth too much to me. There was, too, always a chance that Mussolini would realise how he had been tricked into turning against me and recall me to Rome, even though I now had work, plentiful sources of *sneg* from the hospitable Prince Freddy, and a pleasant choice of lovers.

Little Zoyea continued to drag me to the cowboy pictures, even as I prepared for my role as the great Lord of the Prairie. I was besotted with her. She, of course, was equally besotted, mostly with my fame, though I think she saw in me some kind of twin spirit. Our 'romance' blossomed. Her father, knowing our relationship to be as harmless as Lewis Carroll with his Alices, continued to smile on us especially since I was able to keep his organ and those of his extended family in spanking condition for a fraction of what it would cost them elsewhere. So I remained a popular fellow in Munich's 'Little Italy'.

One Saturday night, when I had returned home from the Fraus' alone, I found a black Mercedes and its driver outside Corneliusstrasse. I recognised both, and sure enough Röhm was waiting for me when I got upstairs. He was a little distracted. While he had made every attempt to protect me, Frau Oberhauser had grown suspicious of his delays and wanted to know when I would be arrested. She now had the ear of Göring, and possibly of Goebbels, and she was threatening to take her case against me to them! Röhm was doing everything he could, but he wasn't sure how much longer he could keep her away from the others. We would have to make a decision soon. I told my friend and patron he could make whatever decision was necessary, as long as her lies did not become public. I was about to embark on an important new aspect of my career. She could ruin me. She could destroy me. Soon I would have some money. If that would help, he would have my first cheque. He embraced me very tenderly and said that would not be necessary. Indeed, he had brought me an envelope.

There was something profoundly sensitive about his last, almost embarrassed kiss.

In the following weeks my life changed dramatically. In spite of his geniality in Rome, Doctor Hugenberg was at first by no means friendly. He probably saw me as a rival for Mrs Cornelius's affections. He was mollified to some large extent by my enthusiasm for the great Karl May, my contempt for those who had attempted to blacken his name.

418

With his impeccably waxed iron-grey moustache, a sparkling grin and a rather boyish enthusiasm for flags and uniforms, Hugenberg was a man of about my height, of stiff, rather than military bearing with old-world charm. He wore high collars, pre-war finery. He had not served at the front but admired men of action and loved the cinema. During the War he had risen high in the ranks of Krupp. He still had connections to the firm but had realised early how control of the media was of utmost importance in a populist democracy. Bit by bit he had gained majority holdings in almost all the important German studios. He also purchased many publications and was now in a position to publicise his own films and promote his own political ideas in a dozen popular forms. Hugenberg was no socialist and rather suspected Hitler's socialism. He was in fact a convinced monarchist, pointing to British and Scandinavian stability under a constitutional monarch. But he was a realist, prepared to believe what he called 'the brown rabble' to be a useful defence against Bolshevism.

When Doctor Hugenberg learned from Mrs Cornelius that I had fought against the Reds and was an officer in the White Cossack cavalry, his manner warmed all the more. He wanted to know how a young American flyer had wound up in such strange circumstances. I said that I had wanted to take a crack at the Bolshevists. In normal times, of course, I would not have risen to the rank of Colonel. He understood, he said. He knew how rapidly they had wiped out White officers wherever they could. A relative of his was a great friend of Hetman Skorapadsky. He had heard some wonderful tales of Cossack courage. I had a poorer opinion of the Hetman. He had fled back to Berlin leaving us at the mercy of Petlyura, for whom I had been forced to build my Violet Ray and who failed to save Kiev because he lacked the sense to defend the electric power lines feeding my invention.

Petlyura was assassinated in Paris by an angry Jew furious at his alleged pogroms, but his lieutenants were ingratiating themselves with the German authorities as White exiles. The only thing Greens had in common with Whites was that both had been defeated by the Blacks and the Reds in alliance. That the Reds had betrayed the Blacks was almost inevitable, so now we even had Blacks, as well as disaffected Reds and Greens, pretending to be White. Enough, Mrs Cornelius remarked, to turn anyone Blue. Meanwhile, Hitler's Browns made strategic alliances with men offering the bright, multicoloured banners of monarchy! He was convinced, said Doctor Hugenberg at dinner one night, that variety and tolerance were the watchwords of a constitutional monarchy. A republic was always too open to corruption. Look at America with her gangsters and crooked judges! Karl May himself made such points in his romances.

I reminded my new employer how, as Russia collapsed into chaos, I consoled myself with the works of Karl May, absorbing the tales of Arab and Apache, which May had collected on his own adventurings in the Middle East and Far West. Baron Huggy Bear smiled when I assured him that no calumnies levelled against that great German novelist by Red cynicism or right revisionism would ever be received by me with anything but the utmost contempt and disgust. I reminded him that Benito Mussolini, also a keen reader as well as a published novelist, supported King Victor Emmanuel. Hugenberg let me know that Hitler, too, was a fan, though, sadly, scarcely a king. A set of May's books had accompanied Albert Schweitzer into the Congo on his personal mission of honour. A great Christian, said Hugenberg dutifully. He himself was a devout Catholic and was clearly relieved to know of my Spanish connections and my uncle, the cardinal.

Hugenberg had heard good reports of me from the more sophisticated party members such as von Schirach. He knew, of course, that I was a friend of Mussolini's and was glad I had become a co-religionist.

I now regret that for a while I turned away from the faith of my ancestors and embraced Rome. Sometimes it was not always easy to find others of my faith or a place to pray. I have to satisfy that spiritual dimension. I needed to pray and could not always choose where I prayed. I prayed to my mother. I prayed for Esmé. I prayed even in that synagogue. I prayed in the cathedral. For some years my yearning soul sent its messages up to heaven and received no answer.

In Germany I often felt that God had deserted not only me but the whole country. Was He in those elaborate Baroque churches with their pink cherubs and blue-eyed staring angels, their simpering Jesuses? The Greek Church is solid, its artefacts direct reminders of the early Church. These South German churches are infected with sentimental Lutheranism of the worst sort, their relish for the Baroque making them more like the contents of a confectioner's window than a place of worship. Believe me, my flirtation with Rome did not last for long, but while it was necessary, I had to accept the best option.

At least during my time in Italy and Southern Europe I learned to understand the Romish Church. In the end it too betrayed me. There is only one foundation and expression of my inner faith, the true core of my belief, the first Church of the Christians ruled over by the benign Greek whose spiritual centre lies in Byzantium. But when in Rome, as the English always say, speak as the Romans. The Serbian Church in Latimer Road has some of that old spirit.

These churches embrace me. They are stern and take their religion seriously. Even there I do not always find sanctuary. I was in the Moscow Road church when I was arrested and charged with those loathsome crimes. Is there no respect any longer for holy sanctuary? Whoever hated me enough to accuse me, to infect innocent ears with such filth, can have no hope at all for their eternal soul.

Nothing was ever proven, of course. Before God, I am innocent. I know that my looks are against me. The English suspect anyone who is not exactly of their pink-and-pale-grey complexion. If your face has not been hacked by razors and exposed to its daily dose of grimy rain, you are at once suspect. Perhaps you bathe too much? Perhaps you have beliefs? Perhaps you are going to disturb the order of things, befriend their open-minded children, put foreign notions into their heads, infect them with broader ideas than the narrow xenophobic snobbery which the British call an education? Sometimes I yearn for Germany in the old days.

THIRTY–EIGHT

In the intervening weeks I saw nothing of Röhm. I received the occasional word via von Schirach, but the Nazi elite were completely absorbed in politics. I was desperately short of money and forced to borrow what I could. While I could not rely on Mrs Cornelius for 'snow', I was lucky in my acquaintance with Kitty, for she had unlimited supplies. But she was proving an exhausting mistress. She found my little place in Corneliusstrasse insufficiently comfortable, she said. She hated the area, too. Occasionally we would go back to Prince Freddy's bizarre and elegant apartment, but I never felt at home there. Kitty apparently felt no jealousy towards Mrs Cornelius but knew nothing of Heckie. Kitty was familiar with every foible and perversion in the sexual almanac and would have suspected me of all kinds of obscenity. Finally, to placate her, I promised her I would soon have a new, more suitable flat.

As soon as Doctor Hugenberg had personally interviewed him in London, our Old Shatterhand finally arrived to join us. Desmond Reid was in fact an excellent version of just the tight-lipped, arrogant type of Englishman I described. He wore blazers and perfect flannels, an Ascot stock at his neck rather than a tie. His square-jawed good looks and pencil-thin moustache were typical of the contemporary English actor.

Reid had already made several films with Hitchcock in Germany and England. He had featured in a number of 'Sexton Blake' serials as Blake's arch-enemy, the albino Count Zenith. Indeed, I admired him in the movie version of *The Affair of the Runaway Prince* where he had interpreted the role of Blake's most deadly opponent, who played the violin, smoked opium and took to crime to relieve his ennui. He also appeared in *The Mystery of the Silent Death*, *Silken Threads* and *The Great Office Mystery*, all of them two-reelers never quite achieving the same standard and later eclipsed by *Sexton Blake and the Hooded Terror*, with a different actor playing Blake. A rapidly rising star, Desmond Reid had a classic profile and might have been a German of the higher type. Visually, he was a perfect 'Surehand', while his acting was adequate, as was his French and German.

We were introduced at Hugenberg's party celebrating the re-election of President Hindenburg and the defeat of Adolf Hitler which had, by all accounts, sent the Führer into another of his retreats listening to Franz Lehár, reading Edgar Wallace, and no doubt exercising the dog whip he carried to impress Germans with his mastery of men.

Reid had just finished a job in Potsdam, where UfA had a large studio. He had played a cruel commissar in a film set against the background of the Russian Civil War, a historical nonsense, but Reid's screen presence was unquestionable. For the sake of art, I was willing to enjoy a superficial friendship with him. Hugenberg also found him politically sympathetic, for though strongly pro-German, Reid was a great imperialist, a supporter of king and country. He thought the German war would never have been fought if the Kaiser hadn't panicked at the socialist victories of 1914.

Hugenberg and Reid agreed energetically that the wedge driven through their great natural alliance by Edward VII's flirtation with the French had thrown the world into chaos. Red Republicanism was the certain progeny of that bastard union arranged merely so the Prince of Wales should not lose the services of Parisian whores. For that he turned on his own German relatives. His own cousins and siblings. Later, Reid would become a famous correspondent for the *Daily Mail* and would frequently write articles in support of the Fascist cause.

Mussolini was Reid's hero. The actor had known Pound, Fiorello and D'Annunzio. He had been with them in Trieste. They were all great romantics of the old school, he said. 'Worthy to stand side by side with Marat or Browning.' He spoke with warm admiration of those wild idealists whose actions had done so much to improve the morale of the Italian people.

By rights we should have been great friends, but there was some weakness in Reid I could not identify. He tended to avoid me, as if he guessed I could tell there was something fishy about him. I wondered if Reid were his real name. It also occurred to me that, despite his blond good looks, he might carry another secret. As Ludecke points out in his book, the worst kind of anti-Semite is that wretched creature the *Halb-Jude*, or even a full Jew who so hates himself he is more vitriolic in his expressions of disgust than any Rosenberg or Streicher.

My own understanding of the Jewish problem is, like Strasser's, entirely rational. I have nothing against them as a people. I merely believe they thrive best in their own desert fiefdoms or the heightened atmosphere of stage, salon and studio! Just as my blood sings to the winds from the steppe and the roaring of the Dnepr, so must theirs long for souk and sand dune.

Reid was no fan of Goebbels, Göring or Hitler but we had a mutual acquaintance in Otto Strasser. He approved of the Strassers and of Röhm. He understood Röhm's reputation as a swaggering adventurer was merely a persona the Stabschef adopted. At heart Röhm was an honourable member of the Reichswehr and wanted nothing more than to be reunited with the army he regarded as a mother and father. He was the right kind of Nazi, said Reid, basically a gentleman. 'Those others, including Himmler, are gangsters with one solution for all problems.' He drew his fingers across his throat. 'Simple, effective, but bad economics. It would be foolish to deny a country the benefits which Jews can bring. Cromwell understood that. We should profit from the positive side, as in mathematics and music, but they should not be allowed disproportionate political influence.' There should be citizenship requirements. An oath. Even in America, the cradle of liberty, Jews did not stand for Congress.

Reid had bought the English newspapers before he arrived in Munich and allowed me to glance through them. The first story I read in *The Times* caused me to gasp in horror. I had never hoped to read such a thing, but now, under the headline TRAGIC DEATH IN WEST END, I learned of the fall of Frau Oberhauser from a fourth-floor hotel window! My heart went out to her as a human being, but I must admit that the black shadow which had hung over me since Röhm had visited me last at Corneliusstrasse suddenly lifted. The paper spoke of her recent distress at the failure of Hitler to become Chancellor. There was a hint, in the English manner, that she had committed suicide.

I thought of Kitty, now an orphan, and wondered how she would take her mother's death. And what of the boy who had been with her in London? Had his father come for him? The paper said nothing. In other circumstances I would have been at Kitty's side as soon as possible, but I knew Prince Freddy had the means of comforting her.

I showed Reid the piece in the paper. I told him that I had known the lady and had once been of service to her in getting her out of Russia ahead of the Reds. Reid sympathised with me. Had she been depressed? I gathered, I said, that her ambitions had been thwarted lately. It was always the same with those Russians, Reid informed me. They were an emotional lot of buggers. All soul and no sense. Lenin's rhetorical rubbish seduced them into Bolshevism, perhaps the most senseless political system ever devised and one of the cruellest. The whole country was run by Jews. That was what he meant when he talked about disproportionate influence! Control the Jews and there would be a Tsar back on the throne in weeks!

I wished I shared his optimism. He slapped me on the arm. 'Cheer up, old man. Someone should point out to that chap Nietzsche that all his tosh sounds just fine in the abstract, but it doesn't work out at all in real life. Hitler's problem is he has no sense of the practical. How are you going to stop millions of Jews just by snapping your fingers? It can't be done. As long as Jews are identified, we have no problem! It's so much simpler than he makes it out to be.'

Doctor Hugenberg found these views reasonable. Jews should not be allowed disproportionate control of the media, either as producers or contributors. He agreed with me that landscape as well as race memory is in one's blood. The forests and mountains of Germany were as natural to him as were jungles and rivers to an Amazon native.

Mr Mix of course was not with us, so I could not ask his opinion, but I was sure the same held true for the black race. The real abomination of slavery is that it uprooted the Negro from his natural habitat and put him down in a place where he could never feel at ease, never flourish. Place him in the Congo's forests, for instance, and he becomes a different person. The same slouching, mumbling fellow one sees on a St Louis street corner transforms into the healthy, natural man Schweitzer so admired and wrote about. Transported to the Congo, American blacks would bring a level of civilisation which could only raise the region, as Doctor Schweitzer already hoped to do. I knew a number of idealistic young medics in Munich who spoke of joining Schweitzer. While most subsequently joined the SS, one man did go to Africa. His name was König. He died of dysentery within three months of taking up his post with Schweitzer. Doctoring, as Baldur von Schirach said, was a profession any man of sympathy and conscience might choose, just as lawyering was the careerist's first choice.

During lulls in political life, Schirach again began to seek me out. That young man had grown a little estranged from the rest of his family, especially his sister, none of whom were great admirers of Hitler. He loved to talk with someone of genuine scientific imagination. I must say it gave me enormous pleasure to discuss my advanced ideas and the needs of the future with a fellow spirit who similarly brooded on the nature of technological progress.

Zoyea and I, meanwhile, continued our 'romance' with the *Kino*, under her father's benevolent eye. Only when absent from the city itself did I abandon my Italians. Even when there was nothing to repair, they were pleased to see me. I revelled in the ambience and stuffed myself with their cooking. And, of course, I continued to indulge my little princess and became expertly familiar with the film careers of Art Accord, Jack Hoxie, Yakima Canutt, William S. Hart, J. B. Warner, Tom Mix, Ken Maynard and an entire posse of minor cowboy heroes. I saw my own films rather more often than I cared to. We went to triple features with titles like *Branded a Bandit*, *Hell Hounds of the Plains*, *Blue Blazes Rawden*, *Behind Two Guns*, *The Thundering Herd*, *Ace of Cactus Range*, *Jesse James Under the Black Flag*, *Ranchers and Rascals*, *Wild Horse Mesa*, *Fighting Jack* and *Romance of the Wasteland*. I remember those particular titles well. We saw them so many times I could no doubt repeat the captions word for word!

I consoled myself that I would be far more familiar with the genre when I came to play my own part. When making the Masked Buckaroo films, I was unfamiliar with the other cowboy pictures produced in such numbers. I knew many of these heroes to speak to but did not know why they were heroes. Now I saw familiar face upon familiar face, which deeply impressed my Zoyea.

In America the Western was already fading in popularity, not reviving until the singing cowboy created an even stranger version of the myth. But Westerns remained the German favourites.

I loved the boisterous version of *The Taming of the Shrew* with Douglas Fairbanks and Mary Pickford. Their first talker together was a great success. Unfortunately the real-life marriage of the nation's sweetheart and the nation's dashing hero was rumoured to be over, Mary having discovered evidence of Jewish blood in 'Doug's' recent past! Suffice to say Fairbanks was not his original name.

Good as they were in their own engaging way, few American films contained the spirit of Karl May. I knew ours would have a quality even the best of Tom Mix's films lacked – a philosophical depth and moral dimension on a different level entirely.

For a while I lost touch with Kitty. She disappeared from Munich as mysteriously as she had appeared. I heard she and Prince Freddy were back in Berlin. I took two short trips to Berlin by train but made only desultory attempts to contact them. At that stage in my life I was rather glad to have some distance between us. I was fairly sure how Doctor Hugenberg would view our association.

I kept to myself in Berlin. I was unimpressed by a city seeming to embody the most grandiose and vulgar characteristics of Chicago and Communist Moscow. A mélange of beaux-arts classicism and municipal functionalism, it reminded me of a vast Prussian barracks. The studio complex, a short car ride from the city, was bigger than anything I had seen in Hollywood. To demonstrate how deep Jewish culture ran in Berlin, the studio complex was called Neubabelsberg, in honour of the famous Russian low-life writer Isaac Babel who came there once from Paris. I met him casually, and he reminded me of someone. I asked him if he knew Odessa. He had spent some little time there, he said. He had ridden with the Red Cossacks. UfA had some idea of employing him as a scriptwriter.

UfA had made most of the famous German films of the previous fifteen years. Neuebabelsberg film city was UfA's pride and was now equipped with a superb sound system, as I knew from films like *Der Kongress tanzt* and *Walzerparadies*.

Here I first met Doctor Goebbels in Hugenberg's private office. He was courting Alfred Hugenberg. The good opinion of my employer's press and newsreels were crucial to the NSDAP cause. Because Hugenberg was a prominent Catholic he could therefore help them gain the blessing of the Church. In spite of his ugliness, Goebbels had a certain charm. I soon found myself telling him how I had seen him speak in Munich, how impressed I had been by what he had to say.

He had a way of taking you by the elbow and seeming to draw you into his confidence. Certain kinds of women were fascinated by him. Many years later Jack Trevor told me his technique for picking up women. He cultivated an interesting disease or wound. Women were always attracted to medical conditions. Far from being a handicap, Goebbels's twisted foot was a sexual asset! It always struck me as odd that he should be such an enthusiast for euthanasia, a sign, no doubt, of his euphoric retreat from reality. This was a characteristic in almost all the Nazis after 1934. The world began to slip out of their control almost as soon as they thought they had it. That was why they had to demonstrate control more and more, to prove their power to themselves. That mindset simplifies the world in order to understand it, thereby understanding less and less. By use of force they can for a time prove their version of the world. As the world refuses to comply, throwing up more and more surprises, they are forced to grow increasingly violent to sustain their 'truth'.

Such men rarely understand how large a part luck has played in their careers. That failing becomes almost every eminent man's Achilles heel.

I think Hitler realised his luck. He was a natural chancer, as Mr Mix put it, the ultimate opportunist, like a flea who lies dormant until a lucky wind or a useful rat comes by. Then he jumps, hoping for the best. Hitler remained in bed, reading light novels, listening to operetta on the gramophone, until his instincts recognised an opportunity. A chameleon, he would say anything, take any position, certain that the Führer Principle or blind instinct directed his changes of approach. A beautifully simple system needed a beautifully complex man like Hitler to run it. Terrified by his own complexes, Hitler disguised his fear well in company. 'That 'Itler could seduce ther Archbishop o' Canterbury, slimy bugger. Ol' Gobbles is in love wiv 'im,' thought Mrs Cornelius.

Doctor Goebbels had no idea, of course, that I was familiar with his leader's foibles. Like a loyal, half-despairing wife, he retailed much gossip with a kind of mocking admiration of Hitler. This made a fellow conspirator of you, drawing you in until you were involved in supporting Hitler in spite of knowing the reality.

'The Little Doctor' had been talking to Schirach about me. He knew I had invented the famous Violet Ray of Kiev. Some thought that story a myth, he said slyly. I laughed. A few more watts and we should have wiped out the Reds in minutes. The power station was the first thing they hit. We were overwhelmed. While admiring my acting, Goebbels was especially interested in my engineering projects. He and Göring were great champions of air travel. Again I glimpsed a golden future for myself. I was the twentieth-century Leonardo, as familiar with the arts as I was skilled in the sciences. Goebbels clapped me on the shoulder. Men like me were flocking to Berlin because they sensed their bold ideas might at last become reality. 'I'm so glad you're one of us.'

He must have had my background checked out, discovering not only my political stance but my ancestry. I had been circumcised for clinical reasons but had to explain, for simplification's sake, how I had been forced to convert to Islam by the Tuareg in the Sahara. My enforced captivity by the Mussulman and his imposition on me of his religion and its practices was, for some reason, a more acceptable explanation than the simple truth. At least I did not have to mention my dastardly father forcing his scientific notions on me. No wonder I have been suspicious of abstraction and perverse idealism all my life! I prefer actions, not words, to speak for me!

In spite of Goebbels's invitation to his parties, I did not engage with Berlin's infamous *demi-monde*. I had been kept far too busy by Munich's. My Spartan visits to the capital helped demonstrate my conservative values to Doctor Hugenberg, who became less and less suspicious of me and much happier about leaving Mrs Cornelius in my company. I sensed my ambitions coming to fruition, even by such a strange route. The cinema had always been good to me. Ultimately it would lead me back to my true destiny. I remained baffled about who had been responsible for blocking those same ambitions in Italy! Happily, I had never turned over to Il Duce the full details of my inventions.

As a press tycoon, Doctor Hugenberg's friendship also promised to stand me in good stead. As I built up my career again, I intended to renew my acquaintance with Goebbels and Göring. Perhaps after a decent passage of time, I might even show my ideas to Hitler. Hitler, however, was not yet in full control of Germany. Few these days understand how he worked his way through the democratic system, taking full advantage of the German constitution, to gain what he wanted. If the German people had not been encouraged to fear interference from outside, they would never have given him so much power.

The atmosphere of intrigue in Berlin was palpable. I myself again felt I was being followed. At least once in Leipziger Platz I saw Brodmann in a small café drinking a Berliner *Weisse mit Schuss*. Munich had by now become my natural home. I was relieved to learn I would not have to spend too much time in the capital.

Doctor Hugenberg announced that he had decided to produce the 'Shatterhand' series himself, since he had promised May's heirs faithful renditions. I was delighted he decided it was more economical to base production at the Munich studio. I would not have to run the risk of encountering old, unwelcome faces. Of course Frau Oberhauser was no longer a threat, but I could not help wondering about that child of hers. How old was he now? How much might she have told him? Did he, for instance, believe that I was his father? Before I left Berlin I did try to find Kitty again, but she and Prince Freddy were not easy to contact. Many had heard of them. Few had met them. I did not look too hard, fearing the news would get back to Hugenberg. But I longed to know if the boy had gone to other relatives or was now with his half-sister.

Hugenberg explained again how Munich was closer to where he planned to film our outdoor scenes and location shots. The Croatian Alps would stand in for the rocks and rivers of Winnetou's 'Sacred Land'.

Old Shatterhand, exploring the unmapped West, would come upon this Sacred Land, defended by the Red Gentleman, and at first they would clash. Then Shatterhand would begin to understand Winnetou's values and ride side by side with him to evict the alien invaders, sending them back to the East where they came from. The films would have a solid budget, but on no account were they to overrun it. If a film went beyond budget, the extra money needed would be taken from the next film's budget, thus encouraging discipline in actors and directors.

Increasingly, von Schirach visited me there in Corneliusstrasse. Sometimes I stayed overnight with the Fraus but generally I slept in my little apartment. Seryozha was forever offering to put me up in his hotel suite, but I knew what that would lead to. To be honest, I was not really looking forward to travelling with him. He had become part of the film team along with Mr Mix. Mrs Cornelius had insisted on it. She was not one to leave old friends behind.

Our location work would be something of a timely vacation. Mrs Cornelius was less enthusiastic. Croatia was a backward country. She was afraid she would have to 'rough it'.

The day of departure arrived. Doctor Hugenberg's people determined our locations, booked our lodgings in Zagreb and Split and then wished us 'bon voyage'. Taking the train from Nice, our director would join us in a few days.

On that beautiful May morning shortly before I was due to leave Corneliusstrasse, suitcase in hand, I received a note in the mail from

430

Kitty in Berlin. She was coming back to Munich and looked forward to seeing me. I was even gladder to be leaving. Some sense of gathering darkness was now associated with that young lady. I remained uneasy about the circumstances of her mother's death and still wondered how much she had told the boy. At the station I joined the rest of the party. Mrs Cornelius had also had a letter to say Doctor Hugenberg would come as soon as possible. He was dealing with yet another government crisis. Hugenberg's Reichstag duties, the unstable nature of the government together with the Berlin elections, required more of his attention than he had estimated.

Mrs Cornelius was in two minds whether we should board the train, but Reid persuaded her. Hugenberg had had the first three scripts drafted. We had gone through them in a rough rehearsal. With the May company's agreement, one or two modernisations and romantic love elements had been added to give them the wider appeal to the American market. Hugenberg would be with us in a few days. I was inclined to agree with Mrs Cornelius's reservations, especially since the love interest between her and Reid was not in the original books. Hugenberg had reminded me that the films could be pointers to the books whose sales were bound to rise. Nothing a film did would alter the book!

In May 1932 the weather was glorious. Hawthorn blossomed everywhere. Daffodils and wild flowers bloomed as the snow melted on the mountains' lower slopes. Suddenly everything was brilliant green. The train journey from Vienna to the warm, glowing stone of timeless Zagreb was delightful, with sparkling rivers and stately mountains on all sides, the countryside growing steadily more magnificent and wild as we entered a world where the battle between Islam and Christendom was still undecided, though peace of a kind reigned in the new federal kingdom of Yugo-Slavia.

A poor country, Croatia was generally unspoiled. Gypsies in brilliant traditional costumes washed their clothes in the rivers, waving as our train passed. Peasants wore elaborately embroidered blouses, trousers, skirts and boots. Many had a slightly Turkish cast which distressed me until I realised how long this region had been polluted with Ottoman decadence. They would make excellent 'extras' when hordes of Indians were required!

All other considerations aside, the Dinaric Alps, and especially the area known as 'the Devil's Garden', was going to be a perfect location for our films. The snow still lay on the picturesque Croatian

431

peaks. I looked forward to seeing the local beauty spots, the famous lakes and cascades. These were what had first attracted Doctor Hugenberg when he came here as a young man during his 'wandering days', as he called them. In 1932 the area was still mainly known only to hikers and climbers.

While we waited for our director, we were based in Zagreb, a medieval German town in everything but name, with much of the charm of Nuremberg but on a more human scale. The citizens were delighted to entertain international celebrity. They spoke perfect German which made everything easier for us. The old-fashioned town bore only a few signs of twentieth-century improvements. In atmosphere it reminded me of the prosperous country centres of my native Ukraine. I was now in fact closer to Odessa than Berlin!

Croats were often inclined to deny they were Slavs. The middle class all spoke German and disparaged their Slavic peasants. They and the Germans enjoyed a common culture. The Mayor and all his officials turned out to greet us, giving us free meals in admittedly unexceptional restaurants and asking us to sign menus and pose for photographs. Mr Mix was of considerable interest to them, as most had never seen a Negro. They were delighted when, good-heartedly, he entertained them on his banjo. They called him 'Uncle Tom' perfectly innocently, after the character made famous by Louella May Alcott.

With the habits of professionals, we eased ourselves into our work. To look at the glories of the scenery where we would be filming our outdoor shots, we were taken by local trains, carts, bumpy chara-bancs and even, over unmade roads, by sedan chairs, escorted by a variety of Croatian 'characters', every one of whom had a different favourite place they insisted on us viewing. Poor land supported a few goats, but other parts were dramatically beautiful, with water-falls and deep turquoise pools formed by local geological phenomena. Sometimes our explorations required us to travel by horseback or on donkeys. Mrs Cornelius made two such journeys before announcing she would be quite happy to agree with whatever scenery we selected. Filming was going to be hard enough when it started. Only then would she be prepared to sit on a horse all day. She said she hadn't been bounced about so much since she was with that Persian bloke. 'Builds yer calf muscles, Ive, but it's more like physical jerks than a bit o' the ol' wotsit.' All we were waiting for now was our mysterious director Peter Saxon, supposedly on his way from the South of France. He had decided to take the Orient Express as far as Budapest and change there. He sounded like another of that languid English breed to me. I prayed he would do nothing to harm our project.

He did not arrive, in fact, for two weeks, by which time we were all word-perfect and ready for the microphone and the camera. Perhaps Mr Saxon planned his delay?

Mr Mix and I went to meet our director at the train in Zagreb. Any deception 'Mr Saxon' might have hoped to maintain was immediately lost. As the few passengers disembarked, one descending the steps was immediately recognised by Mr Mix. With a huge welcoming grin he sprang forward. 'Howdy, Mister Rex!'

Rex Ingram stood there, elegant in his evidently American camel-hair coat. His wide-brimmed soft hat in one hand, a cigarette in the other, he smiled broadly and shook his head as if telling himself he had been a fool to try anything on! He remembered me when I reminded him where we had met in Beverly Hills. He spoke of Mucker Hever and his recent death in Italy. I had not heard. An aeroplane accident, apparently, with a young woman. His parachute had failed to open, and he had disappeared into the Mediterranean. I was Christian enough not to mention that the man had received his just deserts.

Before we rejoined our party at the hotel, Ingram asked us a favour. 'If it's no skin off your nose, boys, would you mind keeping it buttoned about this? It doesn't suit me for anyone to know who I am. Doctor H is in on it, of course, but I made it a condition he doesn't tell his press people.' Ingram assured me that he had long since forsworn the decadent liberalism of *The Four Horsemen of the Apocalypse* and even wondered if he had not gone too far in the tango scene. Had he, inadvertently, precipitated Valentino's tragically early death? He remarked on my resemblance to 'that poor little wop'.

We were only too pleased to share the great director's secret and spent the ride back to the hotel talking about old times and agreeing what stiff, serious devils the Krauts were. He was rather relieved to hear Hugenberg had been delayed as he would have a chance to work without looking over his shoulder all the time.

Ingram was sick of himself, he said, after his last picture. Nothing had worked out. Mr Mix knew what a lousy movie it had been. The director couldn't believe his own crassness in trying it. As a result he was seriously short of dough and needed some fast, easy work which would give him experience with sound. Otherwise he might have to go back to Los Angeles and earn his living painting movie posters. We assured him he would have our very best performances and we would make sure our fellow actors offered the same! Both of us knew the film was in safe hands with 'Peter Saxon'. (As 'Peter Saxon', of course, Ingram would build another reputation as a novelist. He led a productive life and returned to Los Angeles where he died.)

A personable Irishman, Ingram immediately won our goodwill. He had taken the trouble to read the 'Shatterhand' series in their French translations. Indeed, his pronunciation of the names gave them their own charming sound. I found a little bit of his Franco-Irish lilt creeping into my own major soliloquies.

In *Winnetou: Der Rote Gentleman*, I extolled the virtues of the natural life and the open air while Desmond Reid learned the lore of the West at my side and fell in love with my adopted sister Nosha Tishi, who was actually the only white survivor of a Kiowa raid which killed her parents. She had been rescued by Winnetou's father and raised as his own daughter until she ran away to find herself and become, in the course of time, White Queen of the Kakatanawa Apache. This last was an Ingram touch. He said that an American audience could not accept a love interest between a white man and an Indian, unless she was aristocracy and really white.

Ingram's next act was to change the names of Sam Hawkens, Dick Stone and Will Parker to Davy Crockett, Kit Carson and Calamity Jane, names which would mean more to Americans. We should note that Old Shatterhand's rifle was named Henry, after the famous buffalo gun. Creighton had no problem with his new name, though he was not the Crockett later reinvented by Disney's Fess Porker, a smooth-faced Valley boy who would have looked better advertising hair oil. Carson, too, was more hirsute than he is nowadays depicted, and Calamity Jane was a buxom local character actress who specialised in playing comic parts. Her oddly accented English made her even funnier. Since she had an unpronounceable native name, Ingram rechristened her Bessie Bunter. Plump and content as a pumpkin, Bessie appeared on the screen under that name. She played the comic love interest against the serious romantic story of Mrs Cornelius's unspoken love for Old Shatterhand. Kit and Davy became in Ingram's expert hands a kind of Laurel and Hardy in identical coonskin hats, forever getting into hilarious scrapes, both rivals for the favours of Calamity Jane. He convinced us this was a necessary element in any successful adventure film. For a while he toyed with putting Bessy in blackface to play against Mr Mix, but her make-up somehow clashed with her accent. Mr Mix had to be content with a smaller part as the funny cook.

So that summer, while the NSDAP made wonderful gains across the country and Hitler became a name on everyone's lips, we all moved down to the Dalmatian coast and the fairy-tale town of Split, with its views over the Mediterranean. Dr Hugenberg had still not joined us, but telegrams arrived regularly. The political situation demanded his full attention.

In Split we put up by the station at the Bellevue, a popular five-star hotel only a short walk from Diocletian's Palace. Now a bizarre quarter of its own, its rooms and corridors had been added to over the centuries until the entire complex was a teaming warren of resident families and bawling merchants. Founding the settlement when he had divided the empire into three, Diocletian retired here not far from where he was born. As he sat dreaming in his vast palace, the empire broke into warring factions. In Rome his own daughter was despoiled and destroyed and the true Church exiled to Byzantium. In a fit of conscience, knowing that he had set the scene for centuries of conflict, that his own failure of responsibility would mean Chaos descending like a black fire upon Europe, Diocletian took poison not a quarter of a mile from our hotel. Rex Ingram was intrigued by the story. He started to make notes for a script and planned to talk Hugenberg into financing another film once the Winnetou pictures were in the can.

Split would be the base from which we would shoot our location scenes for *Winnetou: The Red Gentleman* and two planned sequels. Hugenberg saw no point in spending money on a similar trip for every movie. The rest of the films would be made either in the studio or in closer Bavarian locations where the German Alps could substitute for the Dinaric Alps, in turn substituting for the Texas Mountains. Split, while scarcely more convenient than Zagreb, had the advantage of good hotels, decent restaurants and fresh sea breezes. When we were not filming, we found it extremely easy to relax there. Ingram, Reid and myself spent several happy evenings in the company of the youngest of the city's rather attractive whores. But gradually fun turned into obsession as Ingram began to display iron control of his camera, which needed little sound work in these scenes. All the dubbing would be done in the Berlin studios, which had the most advanced sound effects equipment.

The movie we eventually shot starred Desmond Reid as the greenhorn 'Old Shatterhand', Gloria Cornish as Nosha Tishi, Winnetou's adopted sister (and actually the Baroness Henrietta Stark), Lon Creighton as Davy Crockett and Seryozha stained a dark red and in full war paint as Winnetou's Kiowa enemy, Chief Tangua, who also becomes Old Shatterhand's enemy. Thankfully, Seryozha's vanity still gave him a muscular appearance. Stripped and with his hand movements restricted, he was perfect for his part. Even Mr Mix, Ol' Shine, the comical Negro cook, made his role into a substantial one.

In real life Seryozha also doubled as our SS guardian angel, having been given the authority by Himmler. Heaven help us, I thought, if he were called upon to use a real revolver in our defence! With luck he would be the first to be shot!

The second film was to be called *Winnetou: Prince of the Sacred Land*. The same character actors continued their ongoing subplots, but now Winnetou, Old Shatterhand and his beloved Nosha Tishi must face more Eastern invaders, rascally speculators whipping up trouble among the Kiowa and Kakatanawa in the hope of starting an Indian war which would bring the army in and allow them to steal Winnetou's traditional tribal homelands. By the end of the film our band of brothers, standing side by side, had driven out the Eastern invaders, shown them for the scheming crooks they were and reclaimed their whole tribal homeland. Something about this story struck a deep chord in my soul. I gave what were without doubt my greatest performances as the philosophical Apache warrior, whose simple words carry profound wisdom. Here was the epitome of the natural man, the soldier-poet of the plains, a samurai of the rocky deserts. Through all his vicissitudes, you were constantly aware that Winnetou was the superior human being.

At Nuremberg Doctor Hugenberg was later to suffer accusations of racism. Evidence was given in his favour, however, that he had encouraged his company to depict a Red Indian as an example to young German manhood! A strange and complicated form of racism, I think! Similarly there was not a hint of caricature in the depiction of Ol' Shine. The Germans had no tradition of casting darkies in demeaning roles.

What so few people seem to understand is that those who warned of the Jewish threat were not racists. They had nothing against the Turks or the Japanese. Why should they have? The Turks and the Japanese had not taken over their culture and their financial institutions, sending a generation to die in the trenches in order to line its own pockets. Mr Kamitami had not changed his name to Mr Campion, and Mr Atatürk was not demanding that we call him Mr Atkins. I am not an anti-Semite – I am an anti-hypocrite!

By July we had completed most of our location work. The weather was becoming too hot to work. Doctor Hugenberg had failed to join us. We shot some interiors in Split and the villages of the hinterland and then took the train back to Zagreb and from there via Vienna to Munich where we immediately began the sound scenes. Many of these were set against subtle back projections of waterfalls, forests and scrubland, so that while the camera itself had little movement, there was always action in the backgrounds, themselves often reflecting the moods of the characters. Hugenberg, making a dashing visit down to Bavaria, was delighted. Ingram was a master of layered visual narrative and silent meaning. Many of his highly developed skills were now useless to him, yet he did his best and it was wonderful to see him work. I began to entertain thoughts of directing my own film one day. This, of course, led me to consider a new kind of projector and camera, and my brain raced off along another inventive road!

As soon as I was back in Munich I went to the market. I shook hands with a rather gloomy Signor Frau. Zoyea was delighted to see me and pouted that I no longer loved her. To prove it, of course, we must go to see the latest Tim McCoy and Buck Jones as soon as possible!

I found a note in my Corneliusstrasse rooms. Kitty had come and gone from Munich and now returned again, staying at Prince Freddy's apartment. The Hungarian was at the moment, she said, in the Middle East. Some business interest, she thought. So we had the exotic flat and its stores of stimulants to ourselves since Prince Freddy had given her freedom to use whatever was his and do whatever she liked. At that stage in my life, relaxed and no longer feeling dogged by fate and my enemies, I was glad to see her. Since she said nothing of the boy, I asked nothing. Clearly the little chap was in good hands.

Kitty and I enjoyed some extraordinary parties which, after a week or two, I was forced to abandon. Work and duty called. The day's shooting schedule now began at seven in the morning. To keep my concentration I drew more frequently on Prince Freddy's first-quality cocaine.

Our group acted excellently together now, functioning as a near perfect team, save that Seryozha had to be replaced in close-up. He spoke every language with a sibilant Russian accent. Although he was given very little dialogue, he had one or two fairly important speeches, so Hans Greisenbach became his substitute. Greisenbach turned out to be a member of the SA and a colleague of Seryozha's. He told me the SA were not being properly paid. While the men had every faith in Röhm, they were growing impatient, wanting to take with force what Hitler insisted on winning through the ballot box. They were giving Hitler every chance to deliver but, if he couldn't they would transfer their loyalty to new leaders. Strasser and Röhm were a better alternative anyway, declared Greisenbach. The power of the SA was the power of the National Socialist movement. Even at that early stage I foresaw the fault lines which would result in a terrible martyrdom.

THIRTY-NINE

The first Winnetou film was released that September simultaneously in Berlin, Hamburg, Cologne, Frankfurt and Munich at the main UfA luxury *Kinos*, which had superb sound systems in place. Backed by all the publicity Hugenberg's papers could give it, *Winnetou: The Red Gentleman* was an instant success with the German public, who made heroes and heroines of us all. We appeared everywhere in the Hugenberg publications and in other magazines, too. The Elastolin firm did a series of models of our characters. Even Ol' Shine got his own figurine complete with banjo and cooking pots. Elastolin were the very best at producing tiny likenesses. Eventually they would produce figurines of the NSDAP hierarchy and troops.

We were fêted. Kitty was pleased to be seen on my arm wherever we went in fashionable Munich. People mistook her for a film star and indeed I did get her a test. She proved to be a poor candidate. Zoyea also begged me to put her in a film, but her father said she was too young. He did not want her corrupted by such things. I fully understood. Mrs Cornelius became an instant sex symbol, a rival to Lilian Harvey. Unfortunately, the May firm were dismayed at Ingram's minor changes and claimed they worked against the true meaning of the books, which was of course outrageous nonsense. The result was that while the first three films appeared contractually as 'Winnetou' films, by the time we came to plan the next three (Doctor Hugenberg's budgeting cut many unnecessary costs) we had been forced to change our characters to Hawkeye and Cochise of the Fenimore Cooper tales. The two still defended a sacred land, but it was now further to the North-West, allowing us to make better use of local terrain, though in 1933 we were once again filming scenes around Split.

Our team spirit remained high. We had become rather adept at our parts, and only the schedules themselves exhausted us. The work was rather enjoyable. The stories did not vary a great deal from film to film, but the same good values were hammered home.

Mrs Cornelius, separated from her lover, spent a great deal of her time in Mr Mix's undemanding company. She did not wish her name to be linked with mine or Reid's, and I must say I could not blame her. Reid had made himself available to every village maiden between Split and Zagreb, not to mention his many mistresses in Germany. As a matter of pride he never spent more than one night with any girl.

Doctor Hugenberg decided to save money by making a permanent set, so by now Hawkeye and his bride had built a homestead and were thinking of having children. The stories revolved more around the ranch than the Indian village and the wilderness, allowing us to work within the tighter budget Doctor Hugenberg had given us. We found an attractive exotic Jewess, Myra Friedmann, to play the Indian maiden to whom the Apache prince loses his heart.

City slickers from the East were still our enemies, and we defended our territory in a dozen ingenious ways as they became equally inventive in devising ways of stealing our wild paradise. Our philosophy remained faithful to the ideas of Karl May. The public understood who our characters really were. They did not mind what we were called. What was important were the manly virtues of courage, steadfastness, loyalty and honour we represented. No doubt we lit the flame of idealism in many a German boy.

I still have one poster with Reid, Mrs Cornelius and myself dramatically posed against a violent backdrop. 'Greed, violence and savagery lay the land to waste,' runs the banner for *Apache Gold*. We knew all too well what we were defending! With the departure of Chaney, an Austrian character actor played Bowie, and then Seryozha was replaced entirely. He said he was very upset about it, though he was glad to be going. He had grown tired of compromising his artistic principles and would give himself back to the ballet. Sulking, he offered his notice and returned to Berlin.

At last I felt free to move into an apartment of my own in a more fashionable district. The flat in Wurzerstrasse had a good view and was decorated to my own taste. I was photographed in it for publicity articles. The magazines called it 'Winnetou's New Ranch' and other fanciful names.

To my fans I was still 'Winnetou'; that became my nickname when I made public appearances holding my famous silver rifle.

Politicians, of course, now flocked to be photographed in the company of 'Winnetou' Peters. We opened drugstores and groceries, municipal works and cinemas, railway stations and road developments all over Germany, Austria and Bohemia. We were on the covers of every kind of magazine from children's journals to sophisticated picture weeklies. Our appearances were recorded for the newsreels. We were constantly interviewed on the radio. Our off-screen lives were the subjects of ecstatic examination. Doctor Hugenberg was delighted to hint at a relationship between Gloria Cornish and Desmond Reid, since I gathered his wife had discovered some compromising letters. He expressed dismay when Ingram left after the fourth picture claiming that his professionalism had been attacked, but the formula had been thoroughly established, and we had no trouble finding a new and cheaper director in Willi Frisch, though we missed Ingram's genial, sardonic company.

The NSDAP came to full power in February 1933 and almost immediately a sense of peace and purpose settled on the land. Doctor Hugenberg had played a crucial part in the NSDAP success, throwing the weight and authority of his Nationalists behind the 'brown tide'. Mrs Cornelius told me that her Huggy Bear and his friends believed they had control of Hitler. The morning before Hitler took the full reins of power, Hugenberg had held out his fist to her and told her that he had Hitler like that! As a tribute to his authority and integrity he now became Agriculture Minister in the new government and, rather reluctantly, joined the party.

Hugenberg's elevation gave us even more prestige and him far less time to take a direct interest in the films. He had seen the profits of the first two or three and was perfectly content for us to continue in the same successful vein. He knew we were in safe hands, he said.

Though no admirer of the Führer cult, Desmond Reid was also delighted by the NSDAP's peaceful path to power. Soon a new, better German order would restore all the nation's traditional virtues. The Nazis were a no-nonsense party who locked up troublemakers before, not after, they made trouble! We could feel it in the air. All the paradoxes and failures of Weimar were at last being swept away and a firm but fair hand was on the tiller of the ship of state.

Everywhere the new youthful Germany rose like spring sap as the summer approached. We returned from the Bavarian Alps to discover a fresh festive Munich where clean-cut SA youths maintained the

441

role of public militia. They were for and of the people. Counts and carpenters marched side by side, the old order forgotten, as the new one arrived, of egalitarian brotherhood under the guidance of Adolf Hitler, now known only as The Führer.

Strength through joy! From the public billboards young steady eyes regarded the future with confidence and optimism. I was so impressed I decided it might be time to return to my old calling. Having made copies of some of my drawings, I sent them off to Göring at the Air Ministry. Now Germany had a government I could trust, I wanted him to be the first to see what I was capable of. I had a polite note back from a secretary. Göring would be in touch as soon as possible. There was much work to do to save Germany from the quagmire into which she had been allowed to drift. I understood, of course.

When I visited my Italian friends, anxious to see how Zoyea was growing, I found they had mixed feelings about the 'German Mussolini'. Their experience in the markets had sometimes been unpleasant, and the police had been slower to defend them. Perhaps the Storm Troopers mistook them for Jews, they said reasonably, but to make a living had become difficult without some kind of harassment.

I was sympathetic. I understood that laws had been proposed which would force Jews to identify themselves. This would have the positive effect of showing who was not, in fact, Jewish. Meanwhile, it might be wiser to modify their gypsy image and return to a more evidently Italian role. Perhaps they should concentrate on their ice-cream business? They appreciated my advice. To reassure them I revealed I held high rank in the Italian *fascisti* and took orders directly from Il Duce. If there were serious trouble, I would reveal that identity. I also had powerful friends among the Nazi higher ranks, but on that occasion I did not make a great deal of my SA connections, since the Italians saw the SA as their chief enemy.

My attempts to contact journalist friends in Berlin were frustrated. I had even asked Hanfstaengl to see what he could find out about the situation in Rome, but from Mussolini himself I still received no word. It became clear to me that my association with Fiorello and his group had made me permanently *persona non grata*. Signora Sarfatti had no doubt added to the poison, and Mussolini had done what he sometimes did to others he felt had betrayed him: simply cut them out of his life and his memory. That, sadly, is the price a man of integrity pays for staying loyal to his friends. Signor Frau was deeply impressed by my revelation of Fascist contacts, however, even if I doubted their worth myself. He blessed the Virgin and all his saints for the coincidence of our meeting in the food market.

That afternoon for the first time little Zoyea took tea with me in my new flat in Wurzerstrasse. I had hung framed pictures of myself and fellow stars on the walls, all artfully coloured and looking extremely realistic. The furniture was in the latest modern styles, big and solid and reflecting the values of the crafts guilds of olden times with the same simple beautiful lines. The walls were in neutral tones, the pictures carefully lit. The bedroom was a reproduction of Emil Hoffer's famous set for *The Golden Shadow*, and Zoyea instantly recognised the tall posts and heavy draperies. She gasped her delight and hardly dared to enter the room in case she be swallowed whole by the oriental fantasy! It was one of my few indulgences. I had let one of UfA's top designers prepare the place for me while we were filming, and I was pleased with the result.

With her father's permission, Zoyea stayed overnight, sleeping in the big bed all on her own while I was engaged with a number of new lady friends and resumed my adventures with Kitty von Ruckstühl. She found it politic, she said, to leave the capital where there was considerable unrest among the *demi-monde*. Not a few had already been taken into protective custody. Some had been released but would not speak of what had happened to them. They tended to be the ones who now remained silent in any conversation. She said they had done nothing. Many had even been Nazi sympathisers. I could not believe she had the full story. She was speaking from her own subjective perspective with its own special significance. I was not surprised some of Prince Freddy's unsavoury drug-pushing friends might have been given a warning by the authorities. But I pretended a certain sympathy, if only to keep the social peace.

Still I had not asked Kitty about her half-brother. I intended to raise that subject the evening we met in the Caversham Bar of the Hotel Bavaria in the most fashionable part of Munich. I had grown fond of the place and was well known there. But Kitty did not arrive alone. She brought her 'gang' with her. The bar was what Hanfstaengl called his 'favourite watering hole', and he, too, was there that night. Putzi had lost much of his earlier cheer. Events had pushed him into the margins, whereas he had expected by now to be at the centre. He still boasted of his friendships with Hearst and many of the other big American newspaper tycoons, but one had the feeling he pumped up his own ego. He was not aggressive enough to enjoy the public meetings, though he faithfully accompanied Hitler on his flying tours of the country. He hated air travel, he said, but Hitler insisted his 'clown' go with him everywhere to play him to sleep after a hard day with a crowd.

Hanfstaengl came in with a group of visiting Americans, and they sat down together at a distant table. They did not seem to like Kitty's friends, who were a rather bizarre party, mostly theatricals from the Franz Lehár touring company and a couple of Prince Freddy's freaks. At first I thought Major Nye, who entered quietly wearing a soft hat and a raincoat and seated himself in a corner, was there to join Hanfstaengl; but his glance when he recognised me was eloquent, and I said nothing. I was faintly reassured by the English secret agent's presence in Munich. Mrs Cornelius was always safe when Nye was near.

Excusing myself, I went over to greet Hanfstaengl and be introduced to his slightly distant group of acquaintances. He had been made Foreign Press Attaché but was engaged in some passing rivalry with Goebbels over the best approach to the press. We spoke briefly in German, which the Americans did not understand. Why wasn't he in Berlin? I asked. Shrugging, Putzi told me he didn't want any argument. His *Mikado* had been a disaster, sabotaged, he claimed, by the mockery of Göring and the jealousy of Goebbels, who had quite plainly conspired against him. The Führer had not come to see *The Mikado*. Only Hess had arrived, which gave one some idea of Hess's status with the Führer at the moment. Until Hess told him, Hitler had not even realised when it was playing because Himmler and Goebbels had deliberately confused him. When he learned what had happened, it was too late, and Hanfstaengl was chided for being a bad organiser! He had tried to tell Hitler the truth, but the Chief's mind was on other things and he was too busy to intervene, so for the time being Putzi was home in Munich with his wife and children, who were an increasing comfort to him. He was proud of his boy. He wanted a future for him, he said. He was not wholly happy with the direction the party was taking. He was far too loyal to Hitler to say much to me, but he knew I was sympathetic.

The Americans rose after one drink and asked for taxis to their

444

hotels. Putzi apologised and organised this for them. When he came back he seemed pleased to join Kitty and myself. He spoke lugubriously to Kitty, trying to explain how the SA had been overzealous in its wish to 'clean up' Berlin, but those activities were now being curbed by Stabschef Röhm himself. Privately I knew Röhm was concerned with discipline and saw no need to alienate potential friends. Many of the units were almost self-ruling, and he was having difficulty re-exerting control. The men felt, in turn, that he had betrayed them.

Kitty listened to Putzi without much interest. At that moment I realised I was the holder of an appalling secret, one that could easily kill me now Hitler and his men were undisputed controllers of Germany. Certain people, especially Röhm and Strasser, knew what had occurred on that particular night soon after the death of Geli Raubal. Not only did they know who I was, they knew what I had done. And if Hitler began to wonder who in Germany carried his darkest secrets, he would soon begin to make serious enquiries of his friends, and they might be prepared to sacrifice me to save themselves. I don't believe Strasser knew my name. My life lay in the hands of my closest Nazi ally, the only man who had a dossier on me! I was grateful that Röhm's loyalty to his friends was famous. But what if *his* movements and relationships became known to others? Hearing Kitty's litany of complaints, I began to wonder if perhaps I might be in serious danger. After all, some of those arrested had been quite as well known to the public as myself.

Even as Hanfstaengl moved away to speak to the Chinese albino in Kitty's party, I felt a chill. She laid her hand on the back of mine. Her eyes reflected the ice in her glass. Her smile, nonetheless, was rather friendly. We were now alone at that end of the bar. She evidently had something important to say to me. I leaned towards her.

'Max,' she said suddenly, 'did you have my mama murdered?' Pouting, her head to one side, she became alarmingly birdlike.

My stomach turned over at the very thought. A sharp stabbing pain, like edged metal. 'How could you consider such a thing? Your mother and I had our differences, but I certainly didn't hate her enough to kill her!'

'That wasn't really what I asked you.' Her smile slick with misery, she lifted her cocktail in a salute.

'Your mother fell out of a window. Why would you believe I

pushed her?' I was almost reeling with the horror of the thought.
'Why, the presumption was that she – that she was depressed. I read
in the paper that she had died in London. Believe me, Kitty, I have
never been in London. The only acquaintance I have in London is
an actor who appeared briefly in one of my films, and he is no
more a murderer than I am. Why would you believe I pushed her?'

'Because it improves the piquancy, I suppose. You know how easily
bored I get with the stale plot of life. Anything to put a new twist
on it, eh?'

I found it hard to believe she was still so young and had become
so cynical. But the world was a very hard place, as Kitty knew. It
could be as cruel to jazz babies as to war veterans. The whole idea
of death and destruction had become almost modish among certain
young Berliners. She told me Prince Freddy had been asking after
me. He missed my entertaining company, he said. He had to be
content like everyone else with watching me on his screen. Did he
have personal copies of my movies? I was flattered. Were they perhaps
the films Mr Mix and I had saved in Morocco?

'One or two. Well, did you? She was getting afraid of you, you
know. Someone had threatened her. She was sure the threats came
from you. That's one of the reasons she went to London. She left a
box of papers with me in case something happened.'

'My only concern is for the child,' I told her. 'For the little boy.
Is he safe?'

'Oh, yes. Freddie was very kind. Alfred has relatives in Palestine
who took him in. Some of those papers mentioned you . . .'

This, of course, alarmed me. I asked casually what she had done
with the box. She shrugged her narrow little shoulders. She hadn't
had time to look through it much. Just the usual papers. Mementoes.
Memories of former lovers. She had never been that interested in
her mother's private life.

I thought this disingenuous. Since she had shown considerable
curiosity when we first spent time together in Corneliusstrasse! I
reassured her. My opinion was that her mother had become hysterical, perhaps a little paranoid, and had fixed her attention on me,
who intended her no harm at all. If I had wanted her dead, I could
have killed her myself when I was in Berlin or have had one of my
friends hire somebody. I knew it was still a lot easier to find an
assassin in Germany than in England!

Kitty had grown bored with the subject. 'Let's go back to this new flat of yours,' she said. 'It sounds as if you've found somewhere comfortable at last.'

We said goodnight to poor Hanfstaengl and the others and collected our coats. In the taxi Kitty agreed that her mother's hatred of me was probably simply because I had severed my relationship with her, a familiar but nonetheless terrible form of thwarted passion or insane jealousy. I would not have put it past her to have killed herself and then to have let people think I had murdered her!

When we reached my Wurzerstrasse apartment, I opened the heavy oaken door with the odd feeling someone had just left the place. Once again my sixth sense came into play. Had Brodmann found me? Had someone been searching the apartment? Was it Hitler's people? Mussolini's?! Was I growing paranoid, inventing enemies for myself? Probably. After all, I was an internationally celebrated film star. In Berlin they might be common currency, but in Munich people would notice if I came to any harm. I saw no real evidence of intrusion and was quickly distracted by Kitty. She had grown suddenly passionate.

Almost as soon as we had closed my front door, Kitty was unbuttoning her blue silk wisp of a dress and stepping out of it. She wore a matching camisole and pantolettes with flesh-coloured silk stockings and little blue shoes that matched her dress. With a turquoise torque in her hair, she was irresistible as she trotted swiftly with her purse to the kitchen and prepared herself a syringe. Morphine, she said with a slightly apologetic shrug. Her nerves had been bad lately. She thought it was to do with her mother. 'You know,' she said, as she inserted the silver needle into her thigh, 'you always wonder if there was something you could have done. I'm over it now, though. I won't need this much longer.'

I had always loathed narcotics and feared their habit-forming effect. Unlike the benign stimulant, the narcotics are deadly. Opium, morphine and heroin are all of such high toxicity they immediately alter the nature of the body and make it dependent upon what Prince Freddy called 'the bloom of paradise'. Of course, anything she told me about ending her use of morphine was self-deception at best. I have known few to stop the habit voluntarily. To say anything to her would have been useless. She might have agreed with me, might have sworn never to stick another needle into her veins, but within a few hours those promises would have been forgotten.

Once I had thought her Prince Freddy's mistress, then his camouflage. Now I saw that she was his slave. Morphine was never free. All I could do was suggest that she try a little of my 'cocoa'. She was happy to comply, but clearly the cocaine was merely a side dish. The expression and manner which had puzzled me in the hotel bar were the effects of her morphine use.

I made love to young Kitty with some sadness, much to her eventual impatience. The evening was not very successful for either of us, but she fell asleep in my arms, a whisper of flesh and soft hair, so slender that I hardly realised she was there. Early the next afternoon when we both awoke, she found a tin of cocaine in her little bag and offered some to me. She could get plenty later, she said. She retired to the bathroom with her syringe case.

I was due to make a radio broadcast that day, in which I would say how the values of the pagan Red man were those many of us would do well to examine. It was late October 1933, with the festival behind us and that wonderful sense of unity and purpose everywhere. What a shame she could not enjoy it. Could it be true, as Kitty insisted, that life was more dangerous for the nonconformist in Berlin these days? Yet many of the National Socialists were themselves of a bohemian disposition. Surely they would not turn so readily on their own! Unfortunately I was completely misguided. I had not yet realised how these Nietzscheans who boasted of releasing a healthy, unrepressed beast back into the mainstream of German life, were not merely repressing their own earlier urges, but actually repressing those who reminded them of what they had once celebrated. The Spartan's love for Sparta had made that city state stronger than any other. The idea of a pure mind in a pure body, of the love of brother for brother, had bonded Sparta into a single steel-hard weapon enabling her steadfastly to resist all threats to her territory. Those were Hitler's ideals, as well as Röhm's. Röhm had found Hitler an ignorant, frightened corporal and had given him the inspiration, the rhetoric and the focused anger which brought him to his present pinnacle. Röhm remained the true founder of National Socialism. He, along with Strasser, cared more for his ideals than he cared for power. How was I to know in those glorious first weeks of the revolution that this would prove their undoing in the struggle Hitler was already fomenting between his followers as limitless power fell into their wondering hands?

A day or two after the episode with Kitty, Reid and I were on the Munich sound stage, doing some dialogue scenes for *Apache Gold* and *The Legend of Silverlake* which like all the Frisch films were made back to back, thus affording considerable savings. Desmond Reid was no enthusiast for Hitler. A socialist of the nationalist ilk, he was perfectly happy to call himself a Mosleyite. Sir Oswald Mosley, the debonair young star of the Labour Party, disenchanted with that movement's liberal relativism, had formed his own *fascisti*. Modelled on Mussolini's, his party placed stronger emphasis on the Jewish threat, the secret empire of Jewry as he put it. Reid claimed his countryman displayed the usual prudent middle road taken by the United Kingdom since its formation, incorporating the best of the Fascist ideas into their own system.

Reid was critical of Hitler's control. He was hobbling Röhm. Reid argued that if Röhm was allowed to incorporate his men into the Reichswehr, as he had planned, the SA would achieve full military status and allow Röhm to rejoin the army, which I knew, and Reid guessed, was his dearest wish. He could then consolidate not only his power but his comrade Adolf Hitler's power.

Reid was right. Although in many ways unconventional, Röhm loved the status and meaning which the regular army gave a soldier in Germany. Though an accomplished pianist with a fine singing voice and a good turn of phrase as his rather odd autobiography attests, he trusted none of his gifts. History has taken him at his word. Because he neither served in the Second World War nor took part in the extermination of prisoners, his story is not disputed. The Nazi calumny remains and is believed by all sides. Röhm claimed to be a brute and, of course, sometimes behaved like one. But I knew the brute was a frustrated spirit longing for reconciliation.

In spite of both Chaney and Seryozha being absent from them, the 'Western' films continued to be successful in Germany and achieved some distribution in the British Empire, but the response of American theatre operators was largely negative. For them the real Western was dead. The public was only interested in crooning cowboys from Radio City. We attempted to add music to one of our films, where Mr Mix's talents on the banjo were utilised for a barn dance scene in which Gloria Cornish joins Desmond Reid in a duet somewhat spoiled by Reid's inability to remain in key. *Apache Love Song* was not our most successful picture and the attempt was never made again. My own title number was cut completely. In spite of this setback, which meant the film had to be recalled and the musical scenes removed from it, we continued to produce profitable photoplays for the European market and became particularly popular in Italy where I hoped Il Duce was watching and realising what a mistake he had made in believing my enemies. I cannot help remembering when I hear of the success of the so-called 'Spaghetti Westerns' how much the Italians owe to our 'Winnetou' pictures.

I now had my own car, a little Renault tourer in sporty red and cream. I would drive out to the lakes and mountains at weekends, almost always with a different girl. Sometimes Kitty would come with me. Sometimes she would join whomever I was with. The Bavarian resorts were looking prosperous again. I was able to stay at the best lodges and hotels, with magnificent views of crags and water. I was recognised wherever I went, and no comment was made about my friends, who always had separate rooms. I felt something optimistic and positive in the air which even Kitty had to admit was real. Germany had taken a deep breath, got her house in order and settled down again into familiar life. Poverty lay behind her. Prosperity lay ahead. Now we know it was perhaps a fool's paradise, but was it Germany's fault that Hitler broke his promise to her?

While I enjoyed my new lifestyle, I continued to feel uneasy, even guilty, sometimes convinced I was being watched and my apartment being secretly searched while I was away filming. I wrote several notes to Ministerpräsident Göring, mentioning our meetings in Rome, dropping Mrs Cornelius's name until I realised this was probably not sensible. I heard nothing. I even risked a note to Röhm. I knew it was stupid and expected no response. Doubtless for my sake as well as his own, he had stopped seeing me altogether since I moved to Wurzerstrasse. I was still no further forward in fulfilling my life plan. Certainly the career of a film star was a good one, and there were harder ways to earn a living, but I have always been driven by my genius, my need to bring my dreams to life, enriching the world with a thousand solutions to its problems.

The only high-ranking Nazi I saw apart from poor Putzi was Baldur von Schirach. He remained a good friend, though he, too, was constantly whisking around the country these days. He had made photostats of all my plans, which I still kept in my carpet bag at Corneliusstrasse together with my Cossack pistols. Most of my things remained there hidden in a false wall within a cupboard. Although I had a superb new apartment, I realised I felt safer in that ordinary environment near the food market, so familiar from my youth. I was convinced my treasures would be more secure there. Somehow I had hung on to them through all my ups and downs and was even a little superstitious about the pistols.

I now felt foolish for having trusted Mussolini with so many ideas and leaving him with copies of my designs. Was my decision to trust Göring equally misguided? I have grown tired of the sound of my own voice complaining of the inventions Mussolini either claimed for himself or claimed to have inspired. I was stupid to have left them with him.

Von Schirach had been talking to some of General Petlyura's old colleagues. They confirmed, of course, that the Violet Ray had worked and would have driven the Reds back were it not for the power failure. Without my even asking he had offered this information to Göring, who might soon be getting in touch with me, he hoped. Meanwhile, I sped about Bavaria's twisting lanes in my smart roadster with a bevy of neurasthenic jazz babies on my arms and respectful recognition wherever I stopped. Little Zoyea would also accompany us sometimes since she loved riding in motor cars. Occasionally Kitty and I were mistaken for a married couple and Zoyea a daughter by a previous marriage. Often the easiest thing was simply to allow such a harmless deception. When, however, I discovered that Kitty had been tempting Zoyea to try her drugs, I was not amused. Kitty refused to believe that our relationship was innocent. She expressed an attraction for the little Italian dancer and told me she knew what I had planned. After that I did my best to keep them apart.

For some reason *The Legend of Silverlake* was accepted by the American distributors, which meant that I had even more work. UfA told me I might branch out from my make-up roles and get a starring part as an airship commander in a planned movie called *Raid on London*. I longed to play a white man again. Doctor Hugenberg was completely absorbed in political life. Mrs Cornelius guessed there was some sort of power struggle between the former Nationalist Monarchists and the NSDAP. Goebbels was greedy for control of UfA, whose media had so successfully helped the Nazis to power. Hugenberg, of course, was resisting him. Meanwhile, in our own little backwater, we continued to show a profit and were never interfered with.

While Mrs Cornelius had an emotional stake in Doctor Hugenberg's career, the rest of us did not. It scarcely mattered to

451

me who produced our films. They were not politically sensitive and echoed the fundamental idealism of those in power.

In interviews, following the guidelines laid down by the company, I explained how I had been born in Mississippi, attended the University of St Petersburg, Florida, and as a young flyer volunteered for the White cause, fighting Bolsheviks in the air and at the front line, helping significantly in the defence of Kiev until driven back to Odessa where I was forced to take ship in the general exodus. Ever since then I had spent my time fighting Bolshevism. Like so many I found it a relief to know that Germany now had a shield against the East. Like Winnetou's Apache war-shield, the Nazis defended my homeland from invasion wherever it threatened, from within or without!

My truncated biography said that after some time in Paris working on an aviation project, I returned to America where I was involved in various political and engineering projects of national importance until being lured away by Hollywood, originally as a stunt flyer. Feeling that stardom was shallow, I had spent some time in the Middle East, exploring the wisdom of ancient peoples. For a while I had been forcibly inducted into Islam. For several years I had led the life of a modern hermit, roving the desert with nothing but my animals, my notebooks, a few necessary possessions and only God to talk to. Returning to civilisation, I served with Mussolini before answering the call of the new Germany, of Adolf Hitler, to come and work for them. I was, I admitted, a great admirer of the NSDAP and our leader-guide. I applauded the spirit of optimism I detected everywhere I went. I prayed that America's descent into decadence would be halted by the rise of similarly strong leaders and by our public absorbing the ideals and aspirations exemplified by the UfA movies, themselves a continuation of the spirit of the great Karl May.

I was, I knew, a real asset to the studio. Children in particular loved me, and I still received many fan letters from the public. I was therefore astonished when, in March 1934, only a few days after we had completed the sound work on *Apache Territory*, I received a letter at my apartment telling me that my contract as Cochise, the Apache Prince, would not be renewed and that a German national had been picked to play the role in my place! There was no mention of the airship part. Telephone calls to Mrs Cornelius and Desmond Reid informed me that they had not been replaced by German nationals.

Reid seemed cool, and I wondered if he had been involved in my replacement. But Mrs Cornelius was outraged. She would talk to Huggy Bear at the first opportunity. The only other member of the regular cast to receive a similar letter had been Myra Friedmann, who had played my romantic lead. And she, of course, was a German!

I was baffled.

When I contacted the studio I was met with embarrassment and obfuscation. It had something to do with the new Nazi laws, I was told. Doctor Hugenberg had been forced to comply. Everyone felt I had made a wonderful Cochise and nobody could ever really replace me. But the reason for my dismissal remained mysterious. Clearly Mrs Cornelius and Reid, being English, were acceptable. Comic darkies were still in fashion, but Spaniards, Americans, Italians and other riff-raff were no longer needed! Myra called me in tears. She had been dismissed, she told me, because she was Jewish. She wanted to come to my flat and commiserate. I said she was welcome as soon as it was convenient. But really, I did not need her weeping on my shoulder. We had never been close friends.

Happily, I had not spent all my money and was not destitute. On the afternoon of the day I received my letter, I was already leaving messages for Schirach. I needed to meet Göring at once and impress him with what I could do for the new Germany. I was afraid I might be deported. I had no wish to return to Italy or, indeed, to France. Neither could I easily go back to America. I realised that I had been leading a dream life. In some ways I had been lured by the temptations of Satan down the wrong path. I think I knew instinctively that this was God's benign interference as He strove to put me back on my destined road.

I talked this over with Kitty. She was sure the public would soon demand my return. Meanwhile, Prince Freddy had expressed a longing to see me again. I arranged to visit him the following week.

Mrs Cornelius had dinner with me that evening. She was extremely upset. She had not yet discovered the real reason for my dismissal. It was not, she said, as if the part required a Henry Irving. None of the Nazis thought I was Jewish. Many Aryans looked a damned sight more Jewish than I did. The trouble was that she had very little access to Doctor Hugenberg at the moment. ''E feels the Nazis 'ave cheated 'im, gorn back on their promises an' that. Well, I coulda told 'im abart politicians, Ivan. Eh?' She chuckled reminiscently. I think she still carried a torch for Trotsky.

I now know she had a presentiment. She became serious for a moment. 'Too much death, Ive. It's beginnin' ter get a bit niffy 'rahnd 'ere. Maybe this is ther writin' on ther wall. Time ter be movin' on . . .'

I trusted her instinct better than I trusted the voice of my own soul. I remembered how she had tried to warn me of the danger I was in when we got to Egypt, how I had ignored her, how she had stayed as long as she could, but eventually had been forced to get away quickly. Happily, Major Nye had made himself of use to her then. In Cairo I had been deceived into a life of total nightmare, the slave of a sadistic trickster who was on the point of killing me when I was miraculously delivered by fate. I still wondered if my friend Kolya had by now charmed his way into the leadership of some hard-riding tribe. Sometimes I regretted our enforced parting and imagined how we might have lived, heroes of a Karl May novel, princes of a vast Saharan nation, away from all the ills and dirty realities of European and American life. At these times my mind wandered romantically back to those wonderful desert nights.

I occupied my time with writing letters to Doctor Goebbels and Ministerpräsident Göring, outlining my plans for a new Germany in which clean white towers would spring up and curving motorways with graceful lines would merge into a gently undulating horizon below a sky in which my gigantic ships plied their peaceful trade. My great flying cities would rise into the sky, free at last from all earthly follies, free to explore the solar system and beyond. My city is called *The New Dawn*; she cries out like a woman in pleasure. She ascends into a golden sky. She expands in my womb. A star begins to pulse and grow. It is my city. I am free of pain. I am free of despair. I am free of sorrow. Out of Chaos springs Law. My ship is called *The Mother*, and she will bring joy and curiosity to the universe.

I was growing nervous. I tried Röhm at all his numbers without success. I left messages, but it was dangerous to say too much. I heard nothing from him. He was rushing about all over the country disciplining his SA units. There was some fuss with the Reichswehr, pledges made. Threats and rising tempers, spluttered statements, cold demands. Fundamentally an apolitical person, I was not, of course, able to follow much of this. I scarcely glanced at the news pages. Until now my attention had been entirely on the show-business reports. The public would not forget me. Still another of my films was yet to appear. I reassured myself. It would be at least five months before my substitute was seen for the fraud he was. I had more than enough money to wait them out and would use my time profitably by following my conscience and my dream.

Es gibt einen Weg zur Freiheit, as they say. By remaining true to myself, I would survive any setback. This was the hour in which I would be tested.

Putzi Hanfstaengl remained a good friend. When he heard of my plight he laughed rather bitterly. 'We are useful, and then we are no longer useful.' He sometimes wondered if he should take his family to America. He had painted himself into a corner. If only Hitler would come to his senses.

I thought the man seemed buried underneath his followers, no longer able to act for himself. Hanfstaengl agreed sadly. 'He flourishes in the public arena but needs his quiet times, his relaxing times, and is not getting them. He has too much to do. When he's irritable and erratic he turns on his friends, accusing them of every infamy. I am a fool to stay here and not defend myself. Himmler and Goebbels are the only people he listens to. Even Göring is no longer taken seriously.'

Hitler must be listening to Röhm. Hanfstaengl was not sure. He sighed. 'When Hitler changes his mind it means history changes, you know. He claims any new idea is what he *always* thought. How he always planned it to happen. You know the type. One day you're his right-hand man, the next you're a traitor to the whole cause. I can't take it as easily as I once could. I know they believe I'm too soft. They make all the tough decisions, and all I have to do is talk about them. It's true in a way. But I didn't expect . . .' He had not expected power. He had based his life theories on disappointment, as had so many people at that time. When things went his way, he became uneasy, even suspicious, a peculiar syndrome I had witnessed many times in my life. I knew the symptoms well having seen them exhibited in a suddenly successful anarchist or a Bolshevik. It was interesting to see Hanfstaengl, a man so solidly opposed to such people, displaying the same psychology. He apologised, lifting his huge hands as if they were weights, then letting them slump to his sides.

Baldur von Schirach also seemed tired, as if the responsibilities of power were proving too much for him. His sister and mother were hardly speaking to him, he told me. He was being asked on all sides to intercede for friends and could not possibly help them all. He saw me for coffee at a hotel. I had hoped he would have a word with Göring, but after hearing the poor boy's woes, I could not bring myself to add to his burdens.

The day after I saw von Schirach I had an appointment with Prince Freddy and Kitty. I drove to the Mongol's apartment in my little tourer. I was almost relieved not to be working. I rang the bell and ascended into the strange atmosphere. As I stepped into the lobby, I congratulated myself that I could now enjoy my bohemian friend's distractions entirely at my own leisure and not have to worry about my looks the next morning!

Wearing a flimsy affair in salmon pink, as always with matching shoes, Kitty greeted me. Her strange, flirtatious manner, as if she was trying to seduce me for the first time, made me uncomfortable, but when Freddy Badehoff-Krasnya came into the room, he beamed, embraced me and put me at my ease. He was smoking one of his marijuana cigarettes, which I refused. Instead, I accepted a phial of cocaine. Kitty poured cocktails. The strangely jagged door with its metallic glitter shone in even sharper definition than before. From somewhere Prince Freddy's Japanese servant appeared. He drew down a brilliant-white screen, revealing, behind a curtain, a 16mm film projector of superb quality. I admired its 'streamlined' casing and smiled, having some inkling that I was about to watch myself as the Masked Buckaroo.

'Oh, this is going to take you back a bit!' he promised with a wide smile.

Chairs were drawn up, and we settled into them. Prince Freddy said very little but sat close to me and put his tiny hand on my arm. 'This will be a particular pleasure for me,' he said.

I realised at that moment my luck had completely deserted me. All my optimism faded as I watched the images on the screen. Neither the Masked Buckaroo nor the White Ace appeared half focused out of the grey darkness of the past. I had never seen the film before and had no idea where it had been shot. I remember thinking the photography rather poor. Then I recognised the ramshackle scenery. The setting was Egypt.

I rose to go. Prince Freddy's pressure on my arm refused my desire. His gesture had an authority which made my heart sink. And sure enough, the scenes with Esmé flickered to life. I was originally masked, you will recall, with the animal-heads they had made me wear. But in the rape scene I was no longer masked. I watched my poor, tired, reluctant body. All the physical and emotional pain flooded back. Esmé's wide, gasping mouth, the penis endlessly thrusting into her treacherous little orifices. She had drawn me into that trap. She had brought me first to infamy, and now she would ruin me! I was shaking with outrage when the film was eventually turned off. As the lights went on I stared directly into Kitty's crazed and perverted eyes.

Prince Freddy was pealing with cold laughter. 'My dear, dear chap. We aren't prudes here, you should know that by now. We simply hadn't realised you were so talented . . .'

The film was an abomination, I told him. Evidence of the horrible surgery which the Moslems had performed upon me.

'Of course it is!' Prince Freddy turned away as Kitty pressed her little, thin body against me and kissed my cheek. I moved to distance myself from her. She followed. I moved again, sure she had been framing this situation for some time, getting a perverse pleasure from it. The morphine had removed everything human from her. She was entirely Prince Mongol's creature. She let her hand fall and stood there grinning into space like a mechanical doll which had suddenly wound down. Prince Freddy murmured something to her, and she left the room. He relished his complete control of the situation, my knowledge that he could, if he wished, ruin me, even have me put in prison under the new, strict morality laws being issued by the party.

'What are you going to do with the film?' I was furious. Had I been armed I would have killed him.

'Nothing.' He knew exactly what I was thinking. It enhanced his power. 'We are friends, dear Max. Friends do not expose one another to needless publicity. I would not betray you to the authorities any more than you would betray me. You know my discretion already.'

I relaxed a little. True, he had little to gain and might well lose his own reputation if he handed the film over to the police. I began to explain how I had been blackmailed into making the film, how I had been a prisoner in Egypt, close to death. But for a fluke I would never have escaped. There were others in Munich, I said, who could vouch for all of this.

He seemed sympathetic, as usual. 'We are all forced to compromise ourselves at some stage in our lives. We learn humility from such experiences.'

Kitty came back into the room. She was carrying a large, leather-bound scrapbook of the kind used for press cuttings. 'My inheritance,' she said. She handed it to Prince Freddy. She made no attempt to explain the book, nor did Prince Freddy. We all understood what it contained. 'Humility.' Prince Freddy carried the book behind another curtain, leaving me with Kitty. She shrugged. She seemed almost as out of focus as the film we had been watching. I did not need to relearn that particular humiliation, but it appeared I was to have no choice.

At that moment I remember feeling an odd, inner chill, a profound suspicion that Kitty and Prince Freddy had conspired to kill her mother! It is simply not possible for a man of my kind to imagine the levels of infamy such people will go to and what delight they take in trapping others in their webs! For all my experience of the world I remain an innocent. Mrs Cornelius says as much.

I was to pay a price, however, for Prince Freddy's discretion. The new government was blocking many of his old ways of making a living, therefore he must find new ways. He had had some experience with film-making in the past. He had regular customers, many in the party hierarchy here in Munich. He would let me wear a mask – a good one – and Kitty would be my only female partner. It was not much to pay, he said wide-eyed, for his silence. Another man might have asked far more.

I was in an appalling position. If I refused, he would release the film to the press who would be only too glad of the story. It would be big news across the Continent. If I accepted his offer, I compounded my situation and would be drawn in deeper and deeper. Yet I had no choice. How I wished Ernst Röhm were with me. I knew exactly how he would have responded. Prince Freddy would by now be on the carpet with a broken neck. But as it was, he had me in his power.

We filmed the thing at Prince Freddy's place in a day and a night. The camera was locked away, the actors paid and Prince Freddy congratulated me on my performance. He was honoured to work with a pro, he said. With deep dread I knew this would not be the only time he would call on me to perform. My hubris had led me to this, just as it had led to my captivity and torment in Egypt. I could not bear to go through all that again. I considered suicide.

Early in the morning after the filming I returned to my apartment. This time it was immediately obvious my rooms had been searched. The intrusion was less expert than before. Was more than one agency taking an interest in me? At least I had trusted my instincts and kept most of my valuable things in Corneliusstrasse. As soon as possible I would make sure they were safe. Who was following me? Had my association with Prince Freddy been noted by the powers that be? Was he also a spy? My stomach turned over at the thought. I went instantly to my store of cocaine and found it untampered with. I took a massive dose, and slowly my confidence returned. My most sensible plan was to register this break-in with the authorities. That way it would be clear I had no fear of them. Then I must get in touch with Göring and solicit his help. Surely Mrs Cornelius could be prevailed upon to help, considering my potential danger? Putzi still to some degree had the Air Marshal's ear. He would certainly help me. I made myself some coffee, showered and dressed in my best, most conservative clothes, ready to report what I suspected.

Just as I was knotting my tie, I heard a knock at the front door. I hoped it was Mrs Cornelius or even Putzi Hanfstaengl. I had decided to tell them everything, even about Prince Freddy's blackmail. In my circumstances it was just as well to throw oneself wholly on the mercy of one's friends.

I opened the door, a word of greeting on my lips. But instead of a friend I found two uniformed policemen saluting me politely. They seemed a little surprised to see me smiling. One had a typical round Bavarian face, nurtured on good beer. The other was taller, an amiable wolf.

'Thank goodness,' I said. 'Just the chaps I want to see.'

A little baffled by my reaction, they asked if I had noticed any intruders in the building. I was immediately relieved. Obviously I had not been singled out. Other residents had reported the same problems.

Yes, I said, I was pretty sure I had been burgled but had no idea what might be missing. Murmuring politely, the policemen came into the apartment, glanced around, and then asked me if I would mind returning with them to make a short statement at the Ettstrasse police headquarters. They were deference itself. They had already taken this liberty with some of my neighbours. It would only be a matter of minutes. They could talk to me here, but the stenographer at the station could take down the details.

I told them there was little more I could offer. I had not noticed anything missing. Was their suspect some sort of pervert who merely enjoyed entering other people's apartments? They were a trifle insistent. They said how extremely sorry they were. These things had to be reported at the station. Those were the rules. The gesture on my part would simplify their overloaded work schedule. They promised I would be back in time for lunch. Perhaps I could also bring my identification papers, which would be formally needed?

At length I could only acquiesce. I asked for a few moments and went to the bathroom. I splashed some water on my face, took another quick, deep sniff of restorative, put a little extra in my secret pocket, should I need it on the way home, replaced the packet in the usual hole under the sink, found my papers and returned to my living room where the policemen awaited me. I still had no suspicion of what was to come.

─❖ FORTY ❖─

You say there is nothing to fear from the East? I say you are searching in the wrong places. Look to Australia or China or South-East Asia, not to Russia or her empire, who will always be European, for it is Christendom herself that Russia defends, just as her free Cossacks ensured her boundaries for centuries. For it is written that the borders were drawn upon the world by God's own finger tracing them as He traced the mosaics of our history.

For a while I forgot these things. I forgot them in Odessa.

Things I had forgotten in Odessa: I had forgotten so much in Odessa. I gave up the memory of my simple, lustful wanton life, my Golden Age. This was not what I had planned. But in my despair I began to remember again. I have no memory, no memory of that other. Routines are performed, but I forget their origins. My rituals sustain me. I breathed the roses of forgetfulness in that ancient isle, the sweet isle of sanctuary. Believe me, I am not compromising you. Have you ever heard me complain? Nobody wants to know what happened. That's show business, says Brady the child-killer. Is there some primitive sense they have that by killing us they empower themselves? There are more terrible ideas than this, I suppose. But they behave like film stars, these secret service interrogators, these prison guards. *Salachti.* I read what I could in the camps but most of what they gave me was not exactly designed to stimulate the mind but rather to reduce it. There are teachers who take great joy in passing on wisdom. But we must not forget the other kind of teacher, who loves to repress knowledge, to leave us more ignorant and brutal than themselves. Guilty or not, few deserved to be the props for the showmanship of illiterates or sadists.

'Pyat?' He was sarcastic. 'Are you sure your name isn't Finif?'

I understood him all too well. He held up five fingers and then made the old sign for the Devil.

We are our own country, we, the exiles. Our past and present are held in common, as is our pain, but we hold disparate notions of the future. Some of us expect to return, to pick up the threads of our lives exactly as they were the day we were taken away. Others anticipate their old world improved and cleansed. But I know what it would mean for me once I got back. I dream about it but the dreams are not always pleasant. In the most recent dream Esmé sits naked, reading aloud from the Bible in Hebrew while my mother listens. She is not the old fraud I saw that time but my real mother whom I waved goodbye to from the Kiev train. *Finif!* I knew that insult. Five. *Fünf.*

'What'll you give me for half a sawbuck.' He was grinning, this Yankee shyster. He held up a five-dollar bill. 'A fin?'

'A herring for a fin,' I said. 'Don't insult me. Get out of my shop.'

FORTY-ONE

What would make me so lonely, here among friends, where Mrs Cornelius herself sees me almost every day, is always available to me? What makes a man forever alone? What determines his fate? All that is mine, my faith, my memory, my hope, should invigorate me, make me one with the world. Instead, I feel like one who stands in line, shuffling forward every few minutes, to his death. I, who have escaped every transport, every selection, who have escaped death so many times, fear it. As retribution? No, for I shall ascend to heaven, to that divine moment of forgetting when soul and mind take separate turnings and identity dissolves.

What is restored to us in death? It cannot be anything but truth. It can only be the ultimate moment of knowing. Or is it the first moment of not knowing, of the death of self, the end of this witless struggling?

I leave my life and my inventions to anyone who can put them to good use. The rest I leave to Portobello Road and the second-hand trade, for recycling, to comfort strangers and the unborn.

FORTY-TWO

She had just been to see Robert Donut in *The Adventures of Tartu*. Had I seen it? I reminded her of Donut, she said. The film could have been based on my life. Was I ever in the Blitz? Of course, I said, but the film must have come out when I was away from London. What do you remember most? she asked.

The ash in my nostrils, I said. And how it clogged my throat. It made it very hard to see.

I have never been able to get rid of that smell, that sensation of forever being on the brink of taking my last breath. The ash flows over the world. It flows over Dachau and Treblinka and Auschwitz. It flows over Berlin and Dresden. It flows over London and Coventry, over Hiroshima and Nagasaki. It fills the streets of Shanghai and Delhi. It will always be that ash. It is impossible to remove from your skin and hair, no matter what soap you wash with. Soap was always in short supply, naturally. Even the soap seemed made of ashes. We are forever breathing in the remains of our ancestors and of our enemies.

'Tell me, Herr Peters. Are you familiar with the Dachau School?' asks my master. 'With Taschner, Spitzweig and so on?'

'This was a school? I heard it was a munitions factory.'

'No, no.' He is amused. 'They were artists. Very good ones. Your friend Doctor Hanfstaengl's father used to sell the prints in his gallery.'

'Painting is not one of my areas of expertise. I am a scientist.'

'Of course. Just as am I.'

They called it *Vernichtung durch Arbeit*. They wanted to make me *Uneingeteilt*. But there was always too much of me. I was not one of those with *unwertes Leben*. For me there was always

Sonderbehandlung. A disheartening, a disembowelling. They loot me. They take out my organs of creativity. They take out my mind. They brutalise me and in so doing destroy small pieces of me. They sensationalise, making free with my creations. Stealing my images. Stealing my life. Stealing my eyes. Groping my soul. They are greedy for any part of my vitality they can discover. And they call this homage? There are those who pay me back in kind. Who give me stimulus. Who give me respect. Who take a line and tie new knots in it. Who make new stars, new trails, new nations, adding to the seas, refreshing the oceans, making something of themselves, something of myself.

We heard the new Oberführer was Deubel, the Commandant, but we never saw him. Franz Hoffmann was a crook they said. Obersturmführer Ruppert was worse.

What did I do in Tegernsee? What was so wrong?

FORTY-THREE

There was a period, I forget exactly what the date was, when priests kept arriving. There were all kinds, at first from the evangelical religions, but then came many Catholics, after the Pope's encyclical. He doesn't seem to make up his mind, they said. Bishops, cardinals and so on came in on the trains. Many were made to work on the *Plantage*, growing food for the Gestapo and the SS. I learned later they sold it at a profit. They made them wear crowns of barbed wire and carry heavy beams of wood. They got the Jews to spit on them as they went by.

I heard some got away. Some were '*Auf der Flucht erschossen*', killed while trying to escape.

Es gibt einen Weg zur Freiheit. Seine Meilensteine heissen: Gehorsam. Fleiss. Ehrlichkeit. Ordnung. Sauberkeit. Nüchternheit. Wahrheit. Opfersinn und Liebe zum Vaterland.

FORTY–FOUR

Nobody wants to know what happened. They wish to learn how many tanks fought at the Battle of the Bulge but not how many died in Belsen. They want to know the names of every general on the German or British side, but couldn't tell you one name of a concentration camp commandant. Names which were meaningless to us are full of romance and association for them. Names which were of the greatest importance to us are hard for even the historians to recall. What did it matter to Hitler when he knew that at least the war against the Jews had been won? So he thought. What he could not have borne to contemplate is that, like some mad scientist in a movie who passes more and more energy through a monster he is attempting to kill, he only strengthens the monster. Is Hampstead Garden Village full of greater numbers of folkish maypole dancers than it was in 1930? Even the church isn't used today. More residents of that idealised English village use the synagogue just down the road. It is the same with Hollywood. The place is filled with mock-Tudor mansions and granite keeps. For years I remained disappointed in Sherwood Forest and all the other sites I had first seen in Douglas Fairbanks films, because of course Sherwood Forest was in northern California and most of the Merry Men were from Maine. England seemed a mean, grey place after the movies. Instead of Fairbanks, Coleman or Flynn I found myself in a world of cold proprietory and semi-apologetic politesse, those early Hitchcock movies where almost all the action is played out on one set. Usually a pub. Usually in a mean backstreet. Usually in the rain. And too few *Brighton Rock* blondes to help you through the worst of it, though I of course had Mrs Cornelius, at least some of the time. Without that woman, I would not exist.

It was useless for me to protest in that place. He thought all Spaniards were Jews.

FORTY-FIVE

'I gather there have been many burglaries in the area?'

I asked them to sit down, to have some coffee. But they were on duty. They refused. I found my American passport. Most of my other papers were still hidden in Corneliusstrasse. 'And after we have been promised improved law and order!'

'The crimes are mainly directed at individuals,' I was told politely. 'Certain kinds of people are singled out. It's the current climate. Munich will settle down soon.'

'So there is no pattern?'

'Certainly there's a pattern. That's the sad thing. We don't condone it either.' A sigh. 'We believe in protecting all law-abiding citizens of every race and religion. But a formal report must be made. It's the rules.' A small shrug. 'Better wear your overcoat, sir. Chilly this morning.'

I locked my door carefully behind me. The pleasant ruddy-faced policeman tested it to make sure. Satisfied, he gestured for me to precede him.

'We'll have you back here well in time for lunch,' said the lean one.

'I would hope so,' I said. 'I have a meeting with a director. You probably know that I'm a film actor. The "Winnetou" pictures?'

'I was a great Karl May fan as a kid,' said the pleasant policeman.

'Very good of you, sir, to do this.' In spite of his manner, the wolfish policeman seemed a reasonable man. 'These ruffians spoil things for everybody.'

We went downstairs and got into their car. The morning was beautifully cool. The air was unseasonably sharp. A civilian driver sat in the driving seat. He did not greet me. They opened the back door. I climbed in. I sat between them.

'We are going where? To which station did you say?'

'To headquarters. To the old "lions' pit".' The ruddy policeman laughed. Because of its other street entrance, the Ettstrasse *Polizeipräsidium* was popularly known in Munich as the *Löwengrube*, or lions' pit. I was still not alarmed. I was confident the famous German love of formal law would keep me safe, as I had committed no crime.

'I have only the greatest admiration for Munich's police corps, both civil and political,' I said conversationally as we rode along. 'I'm sure you'll soon have the burglars behind bars.' The policemen made no response. The atmosphere became less congenial, and I began to feel a little nervous. They, in turn, seemed embarrassed. I simply could not read their mood. I thought I had best remind them of my connections as subtly as possible. The shadow was rising in me again, the sense of panic so hard to control and almost impossible to recollect. We who have been in its power are despised by those who have never experienced it.

'I'm a good friend of your Chief, Ernst Röhm. I'm sure he'll be glad to know you're looking after me so well.' Perhaps I should not have mentioned my association with the Stabschef. It would have been better to have invoked Baldur von Schirach. I had to take control of myself. I would be home in an hour or so, and all this would be over.

'Not our Chief, as it happens.' The first policeman appeared anxious to make that clear. 'But we all like praise, sir . . .'

'Ten at the most,' said the wolfish one. I think he had misheard me. 'A tick of the clock.' He did not meet my eye but stared gloomily out of the window at a tram we were passing. On the pale blue side of the big, streamlined vehicle was an advertisement for my new Western. I wondered if this visit had anything to do with my recent filming. Could Freddy and Kitty have deliberately given me over to the police? I felt queasy. Other enemies must be considered. Had Kitty's mother's 'dossier' fallen into official hands? Röhm might have been careless. He might even have said something to Hitler. Had the Gestapo themselves searched my apartment?

I was sleepless and shaky. This was how the police always arrested you. Not with shouts and blows and threats, but with polite requests for your cooperation. My emotions were in turmoil. I reminded myself that if I was in serious trouble, they would not have sent two ordinary uniformed chaps. It would have been SA or Gestapo, without doubt. The *Geheime Staatspolizei* dealt with political issues.

They would not be worried about minor burglaries or even porno-graphic movies. I pulled myself together as best I could and returned to my earlier, more formal manner.

The car stopped outside the tall, classical stonework of the Ettstrasse headquarters. The policemen politely helped me from the car. The entrance, imposing and solid, reassured me, and again I was reminded of the well-known German respect for law and order, convinced they would play by the rules. I had done nothing wrong. I was a victim, not a criminal. These chaps were decent upholders of traditional justice.

We went straight past the reception sergeant, who nodded to us and raised his hand in an enthusiastic 'Heil Hitler' salute, so I knew I could not be under arrest. The policemen returned the salute rather less energetically. We walked down Corridor B, heading no doubt for the criminal investigation offices.

But we did not stop at Corridor B. At the end of this passage was a set of doors which the red-faced policeman stooped to unlock with a special key. 'Short cut,' he murmured. Descending a flight of steps we found ourselves in a poorly lit passage with a low roof. The doors on either side had peepholes and little grilled windows. I recognised them as police cells. My heart began to sink. But again we did not stop. We quickly walked the length of the corridor and came to door number 107, on which the vulpine policeman knocked. It was opened, and we went in.

From somewhere behind me I heard a thin, womanish scream, a kind of sob, and then silence. I felt a moment of fatalistic alarm, yet continued to force myself to believe the best. I was a complainant, not a criminal. Because some prisoner had become hysterical did not mean they were being harmed!

The doors were quickly shut behind me and relocked. Suddenly the policemen were at attention on either side of me. The room was full of young men in shirtsleeves, rushing about, picking up telephones, slamming them down, inspecting files, yelling informa-tion at one another. Clearly none of them had been in their jobs long. They seemed to have no idea what they were supposed to be doing.

Removing my hat I extended my hand to the man who greeted us. He seemed one of the few to carry any real authority. He wore an ill-fitting civilian suit. He had a thin, pale face, small, bright blue eyes, prominent ears and thinning hair.

'Good morning, officer,' I said. 'It's kind of you to show such an interest in my case. With so much crime and chaos taking place on our streets, it's reassuring to know the police still care.'

He lifted his arm in a rather languid Nazi salute, offering us a muttered '*Grüss Gott*' and dismissing my escorts. He signalled for me to enter a smaller, much darker room, with barred windows. This, no doubt, was where I would dictate my statement to the stenographer. Yet, instinctively, I hesitated.

'I am of course here to give you details of the suspected violation of my flat,' I said.

He looked at me blankly for a moment then shook his head. 'No,' he said.

'But surely? Your uniformed men . . . ?'

'They were sent to pick you up about some citizenship enquiries. You're not a German national, I understand.'

'No, I'm American.'

He shook his head. He was silent, unhelpful.

'Now look here, officer . . .' I began.

He sighed and indicated the room again. I had no choice.

One chair sat on the other side of a narrow desk. Behind the chair was a filing cabinet on which stood a cup of coffee. The coffee looked as if it had not been touched for days. On the wall was a picture of Hitler riding a white horse and posing as St George setting off to slay the dragon. A rather exaggerated portrait. I had seen it before and remember thinking it was the beginning of the end for Hitler as a serious social force. He had left the world of realpolitik and joined a world of myth and drama. Slowly but surely, and then with ever increasing speed, he would lose his soul's connection to its native planet; it would drift like an asteroid erratically circling the Earth not knowing how or where to land. I did not blame Hitler. He had allowed himself to become weak. His sycophants and advisers deserved the blame, those Byzantine adventurers who specialised in whispering evil: Goebbels, Rosenberg and Himmler. They corrupted everything Hitler's old friends stood for. They had encouraged him to turn his back on the Strasser brothers. I had seen him – can I even now afford to tell? – bewildered eyes glaring from wounded body, as unstrong and as vulnerable in those days as he believed himself to be. That is why he fought so mightily against his inherited Catholicism. His arguments were with his own past, not our common future.

The man in the badly made suit came in, closing the door behind him. Now that we were in private, he shook my hand, rather limply, and glanced around the minuscule room, apologising for the one chair.

'I hope this won't take too long,' I said, reassured by his hand-shake. 'I understand that as well as the inquiry concerning a possible burglary, you wish to check my documents. I was told it would be a matter of minutes. I have a luncheon appointment.'

'Aha,' he said. 'Then let's confirm a few particulars. You have been working in Germany?'

'And paying my taxes,' I said, thinking I understood where this was going.

He nodded. 'You are Mr Max Peters, until recently employed by the UfA company as a film actor? You are an American citizen but until recently were in the service of the Italian Air Ministry?'

'That's correct. I then became an unofficial emissary at large. My main career, however, is as an engineer. I have some important blue-prints, inventions of my own which I had hoped to show to Herr Hitler's people. At present they are with Captain Göring's depart-ment. It was for their safety that I most feared.'

'Indeed. So you have something worth stealing, eh, Herr Peters?'

'Very important documents. But they are still safe. Have you any idea who the burglars might have been?'

'Yes.' His pale eyes closed, and with a small, narrow hand he pinched at the bridge of his nose. 'You are an admirer of Signor Mussolini.'

'Rather more than a simple admirer, sir.'

The hand came down and went into a trouser pocket, re-emerging with a brown handkerchief. He folded it back to make a clean square and blew his nose, folding it again before replacing it. 'So, Herr Peters, you are an unofficial emissary of the Italian government, but prefer to work as an actor?' He turned his back on me and opened the file drawer in the middle of the cabinet from which he took out a slender, dark blue folder.

Surely this was not a file on me! Why should anyone wish to make one? I could read upside down, however, and my name was printed carefully at the top. I became alarmed. I did not know I had been subjected to any official attention. I wished that Röhm was with me to vouch for me, but he was still in Berlin dealing with recalcitrant SA.

'I am proud to have known and to have served Il Duce, but I am a private citizen, an engineer. An inventor. I was fortunate enough to earn my living in the Hollywood cinema for some years, which was how I came to be working here in Munich with the UfA company. Agriculture Minister Hugenberg is a friend of mine. My real qualifications are in science. I originally came to Germany because I saw there was a new, young element here which embraced the future.'

I continued to feel anxious. All this talk of Mussolini seemed irrelevant. Had Il Duce passed on something to the German authorities? Very unlikely. Or had someone revealed my identity to Hitler? Again I thought of Prince Freddy and those films. They formed a link I had not considered before. Could I be recognised from them? I knew Hitler would not tolerate my freedom if I were identified as the person used in his 'therapy'. I could easily suffer the fate of the Man in the Iron Mask and never see the outside world again. I might even die here.

I realised my left knee was beginning to shake a little, so I straightened to attention as the door opened. A police officer wearing the armband of the Bavarian Political Police stepped into the room, removed his cap, put it on the desk, murmured a word to the plain-clothes man and took up the file, a reassuringly slim collection. At least that villain Brodmann was not behind this particular inconvenience. Any file Brodmann supplied would be bulging with his Bolshevik lies. The same was true of the 'dossier' the late Baroness had compiled. My equilibrium returned, and I became determined to answer in my most cultured German so the officer would know he was dealing with an educated man of substance. I should not have allowed the policemen to bring me here. Yet I had done nothing wrong. Perhaps the burglaries had been of a political nature. Perhaps they already knew who committed them.

Dismissing the civilian, my new interrogator smiled pleasantly. He was a round-faced Southerner with pale, pink skin and sharp grey eyes. His manner was regretful. 'My dear Mr Peters. My men no doubt have explained this whole thing. Your life, sir, is in some danger, I fear. There are rogues abroad who are anxious to spill any alien blood they smell. We are, of course, doing everything to crack down on them. A secure homeland is what our Führer has sworn to give the German people, and it is our job to maintain that oath. But this does not mean we tolerate attacks on the property or persons of foreigners. Especially those who have shown us such generous support.'

'I am anxious to offer the Reich every cooperation,' I told him. 'Do you mean that the man who burgled my apartment somehow had plans to take my life? Naturally, in those circumstances, I will answer any question you wish to put!'

He was grateful. 'It's so much easier for us, Herr Peters, when a gentleman is as cooperative as yourself. It saves everyone time and trouble and allows us to process matters more efficiently. Have you applied for residency papers?'

'I am planning to return to Italy in a short while. And I have business in England. My acting jobs were merely a kind of holiday. I was helping out Reichsminister Hugenberg. I was unaware that I required special papers. I came here in order to make a statement to a stenographer.'

'Of course. So much to absorb. Another good reason for keeping you with us in *Schutzhaft*, protective custody. I will set wheels in motion, and when you have the necessary papers, it will be easier for you to move about freely.'

'Custody? My dear Inspector, I have a luncheon meeting. I was told I was only going to be here for a few minutes. To answer a couple of questions. And now you plan to keep me here? For how long? I made no preparations to be here for hours, merely minutes.'

'I do apologise. We are rather overworked these days. Our chaps aren't always properly informed. They do their best, but it's difficult . . .' An apologetic shrug. 'It might be possible for someone to telephone the person you are meeting and let them know you will not be able to make it.'

'Are you telling me I have been arrested?' I had to express my panic somehow. Every instinct told me that I had entered a trap.

'Herr Peters!' He raised his hands to show shock. 'Certainly not. But you have seen what is happening on our streets, at least in the rougher quarters. Roving gangs of young men, many of them probably communists, pretending to support the new Germany by picking on any foreigner they come across. Breaking into their premises. Stealing their papers and property. Attacking them as Jews when they are frequently innocent . . .'

'I am, sir, an American citizen. I served in the War. I fought the Bolsheviks. My family is as old as history. Surely you are not suggesting . . . ?'

'I would not insult you.'

I relaxed to a degree, but my peace of mind was destroyed. Surely Röhm had not betrayed me? What motive would he have? To keep me quiet? Impossible. If he had wished to be rid of me, he would have killed me himself or had one of his SA people do it. We shared too many secrets. More likely one of Röhm's enemies was behind this. Streicher? No. Doubtless one of the new 'Berliners', like Goebbels. Johnny-come-latelys who had jumped on the Nazi bandwagon as soon as it showed signs of success. Well, they would not crack me! I resolved to keep Röhm's secrets, and my own at all costs. I, who had endured the Cossack whip and the exquisite tortures of al-Habashiya, would not easily reveal anything to these people. I have not eaten that which is unclean. Anubis is my friend. I played with the blind children. I became reconciled to my own murder. I who was dead am resurrected. I who have remained pure have endured the torments of death and the land of death and am whole again. I know there is a life to come. I have been promised that life.

I had to give up my documents, my wallet and whatever small change I had in my pockets, but I was not searched. I still had enough *sneg* to last several days, by which time I was sure I would be out. The officer asked, almost as an afterthought, if I was armed. A pistol, perhaps, for self-defence? I was furious. 'My dear sir!'

I was back in the nightmare. I had thought never to be in it again.

Still in my overcoat I was handed over to two brown-shirted SA men, who escorted me up several flights of stairs. They addressed me with gruff lack of respect. The first was a young man with a pale, thin mouth and uncertain green eyes; the second was an older man, who had the manner of a regular army NCO. They were cheerful enough, though they called me a 'rascal' as if I were some sort of criminal, and told me it would do 'my kind' good to see the inside of a jail for a few days. Even then, said the older man, I would never know what it was like to serve in the trenches. It was on the tip of my tongue to reveal to them how I had served with the Don Cossacks, but this would have required further explanation, and besides, I had been fighting against Germans.

Collecting myself, I asked what they meant by 'a few days', and they refused to reply. I said that I fully expected to be free by that afternoon. I was an honest, hard-working professional man. I had paid the German government large amounts of tax. I folded my arms in an attitude of contempt as, at last, we arrived at a dank guardhouse. Here I was handed over to two regular prison warders, who showed none of the uncertainty of the others. They were older men, rough and ready, but not without an air of humanity. Admittedly there was a military atmosphere to the place, but also a sense that if you behaved yourself, 'kept a clean nose', as they say, you would not suffer any particular indignity. The Munich police had a reputation for fairness. I was sure I would be released within hours when they discovered my papers to be all in order. The worst that could happen was that I would be held overnight until Röhm or Göring were contacted.

Their paperwork done, I was escorted along another passage until we reached a door with the enamelled number 47 screwed to it. The guard unlocked this and flung it open. '*Grüss Gott*, gentlemen! You have a new roommate.' His voice was charged with aggressive sarcasm. 'Out you come. At attention, if you please!'

Three men came blinking into the bright, electric light of the corridor.

My first impression was that I was to be thrown in with the worst kind of desperadoes. They were unshaven, pale-looking creatures who wore a motley collection of clothing and had dirty, dishevelled hair. What were they? Thieves? Forgers? Kidnappers?

'Very well. Back in you go!'

I followed them into the dimness, natural light falling through the single, high, barred window of the cell. I regarded them uneasily in case they attacked me. Four bunks were stacked in pairs on either side of us. A WC stood between the bunks. Graffiti on the walls. A stink of urine and sweat.

'You've missed lunch,' said the youngest man with some satisfaction, as the door was swung shut behind me. I heard bolts being rammed home and knew a moment's panic.

'You haven't missed much. Lunch is best avoided.' The tallest of the prisoners came forward, extending his hand. 'Good afternoon, sir, and welcome to purgatory. Are you a transfer?' At my questioning frown, his smile broadened. 'Have you been in the lions' pit before, or are you a new boy?'

I was surprised by his confident, educated tone. I thought at first I had been confined with some kind of crooked salesman but as I grew used to the murky early-afternoon light I saw that all three of my fellow prisoners wore the good-quality clothes of upper-class Germans.

The man who greeted me shook my hand. 'Good afternoon. Count von Zinzendorf und Pottendorf, at your service.' He had the easy grace and refined good looks once associated with the best sort of Austrian nobleman, exactly what he was. The other two prisoners were Doctor Bach, a prominent Munich businessman, and Herr Helander, a Swedish journalist. Doctor Bach soon returned to his bunk, on which were stacked all kinds of foodstuffs, paper parcels and suitcases. In an attitude of despair, he stared around at packets of dates, chocolates, fruit, chicken, several different kinds of sausages, thermos flasks of soup, tea and coffee, bread, cakes and pickles. Many of them still in their commercial wrappers, the foodstuffs made his bunk look like a stall in the covered market. Even the open suit-cases appeared to be full of food. He had been brought here from a single cell yesterday, he said, and was expecting to leave at any time. His wife had brought the provisions that morning. For all his edible wealth, Doctor Bach was the least cheerful of the three. He had expected to be gone from the cell by now. The day before, when being transferred, he had been told he would be leaving that morning. He had mistaken my arrival for the guards coming with his release. Now, his expectations dashed, his tiny black eyes filled with tears.

Helander had no such expectations. He was a photojournalist who had been in Ettstrasse since early March and, like Count von Zinzendorf und Pottendorf, had contributed to the Catholic press, though he had never attacked the Nazis directly. Admittedly his pictures for *Paris Match* had not been entirely flattering. Born in Malmö, he had lived in Munich for years, and his wife was from Munich. He was a little cynical. Without aristocratic connections, he was less likely to be released. He apologised for his present low spirits. Because the arresting officers had found some of his French publi-cations, he believed he might very likely die here, unless he was first transferred to Stadelheim or Dachau. Stadelheim was the Munich prison where Hitler had been incarcerated after his failed putsch before being transferred to Landsberg, where he wrote most of *Mein Kampf*. Dachau was a brand new facility, a modern work camp designed to house hundreds of social outcasts, including communists and anarchists who had acted in some way, either in word or deed, against the interests of the German nation. I had seen an article about it in the *VB*. In rather austere but clean surroundings, men would be expected to serve their time and return, invigorated, to the job of restoring Germany to her place as a power among nations. The camp had been on the newsreels.

I could not imagine I was bound for Stadelheim, let alone Dachau. I told my new companions that I was innocent of any crime. I had left my home early this morning with two policemen to report a burglary. All I could think at the moment was that I was a victim of a bureaucratic accident and would be released after a short hearing. I was not even a German.

At this Count Pottendorf laughed. 'I am an Austrian national, and my arrest was completely illegal. But I have been in Ettstrasse for several weeks and have yet to receive a hearing. We are all innocent of any crime, Professor Peters, I assure you. That is not why we are here!'

He confirmed what my warning instincts had already told me. In the general sweep of the country for those who threatened the well-being of the state, the Nazis had already arrested hundreds, perhaps thousands, many of whom had committed no crime and some of whom simply had the misfortune to bear names similar to those of socialists and others who had set themselves against all decency. We were victims of a huge, mad bureaucracy. The larger the bureaucracy, the bigger the mistakes it made. With the possible exception of Doctor Bach, who might well have run sweatshops, since he was a mass producer of clothing, it appeared we should all rightfully be in our own homes.

Looking as if he might suffer a heart attack at any moment, the portly Doctor Bach put his head in his hands. Herr Helander, a thin, lugubrious young man, whose pale face and hair gave him a washed-out appearance, went to comfort him. 'Cheer up, old chap. You'll be out of here by tomorrow.'

'That's what you keep saying. It's obvious why you are here. You were foolish enough to goad Herr Hitler in print. But I have done nothing. The only reason I am in this place is because I am a Jew. You know what these Nazis have been up to! And all you two did in your articles was to incense them even further! What good have you done for the likes of me?'

Helander and Count von Zinzendorf und Pottendorf were quick to reassure him. There was probably a journalist or socialist called Bach. Several composers, after all, bore that name. Many prisoners had been released when a mix-up between them and others with similar names was discovered. It was just a matter of time before

478

Bach would be back with Frau Bach. Meanwhile, said von Zinzendorf und Pottendorf cheerfully, what point was there in letting all this good food go to rot?

Reminded of his manners, Doctor Bach mopped his head with a large, grubby handkerchief and asked us to help ourselves from his provisions. He and Frau Bach were not Orthodox, indeed they were completely secular, and the food was not kosher. As Helander and Pottendorf tucked in, I ate a little bread and sausage and felt somewhat more human. I was determined to get out of Ettstrasse before I began to degenerate like my companions. How quickly we lost the appearance which commanded the world's respect. At this thought, I removed my overcoat, since it had grown a little warm, and folded it carefully. I placed it on the bottom right-hand bunk, to which I had been assigned. There being no other reading matter, I accepted the offer of Doctor Bach's *Völkischer Beobachter*. The paper was full of triumph. Several threats to the security of the homeland had been narrowly averted in the twenty-four hours before going to press. Jewish communist interests were being attacked and suppressed. 'You see what I mean?' said Doctor Bach with gloomy satisfaction as I read the front page.

Helander and Pottendorf were keen chess players and whiled away their time with mental games. I had always been impressed by this ability to visualise the whole board in play. They entertained me and took my mind off my own troubles as I waited to hear that I was free. The afternoon wore on slowly. Soon the sun began to set and I gave up much hope of being released that day.

When we came to talk, Pottendorf mentioned how his wife had returned to Vienna to work for his release there. At this Helander's brow clouded. His own wife had just been arrested, he said. No doubt she had been asking too many questions of the political police. However, she had been able to contact a lawyer, who assured her that she would see her husband within a few days.

'And, for once, the lawyer was right.' Helander smiled sardonically. 'Last time we were allowed out for twenty minutes in the exercise yard, I glimpsed her waving to me from the women's section. I paid Schwenk, the best of the guards here, and he got a message to her. She's not been badly treated. His guess is that she annoyed them so much and proved such an embarrassment they locked her up. It's just a warning, Schwenk thinks. He doesn't expect her to be in for more than a few days.'

I asked him how long he had been here. A month, he said. He was sure that he and his wife would be released at the same time before Christmas. He knew her parents must be worried sick.

Still slumped on his bunk, surrounded by his array of food parcels, Doctor Bach snuffled and moaned. He doubted very much if his little girl would be seeing her daddy at Christmas. Pottendorf sat beside him and again attempted to comfort him. 'Come along, old chap. We're all in the same boat. It doesn't do to lose hope. Have a chocolate.'

Bach said miserably that while we were doubtless all in the same boat, some of us were first-class passengers and some were not. He had begun to chew inconsolably on a caramel when a warder shouted something at us and swung open the door. We were allowed to fetch water from the communal sink, and I was issued with two rough blankets. When I again tried to ask when I could expect to be released, the warder repeated that he was not party to the decisions of the bigwigs. Supper, brought round by a trusty, was unappealing, so that evening we dined off Doctor Bach's bounty. He could barely bring himself to eat a thing.

The four of us played cards until midnight when the light in the cell was switched off. As soon as he was in bed, Doctor Bach began to sniffle again. We were all as sympathetic as we could be in the circumstances. Again Pottendorf assured him he would soon be free, but Bach grizzled into his pillow for half an hour before his enormous snores filled the cell, finally subsiding into a kind of wet whiffling noise which in turn became a rhythmic sigh.

Distrusting the blankets' cleanliness, I lay down in my clothes praying to the gods of good luck that I would be free by morning. In case my clothes should at some time be taken from me, I hid my cocoa in my mattress. I took only a little as soon as I was convinced everyone else was asleep. I wasn't sure I could take more than one night of this company. Apart from Pottendorf, I had nothing in common with these people. I was far too valuable to the Reich. The Nazis were practical people. They would not waste human resources. A few journalists and businessmen more or less would not be missed. But they needed scientists if their dreams of a revived, purified Germany were to be realised. Göring was bound to respond to my message.

The bells of the nearby cathedral tolled the quarters. I found them more comforting than intrusive. In the early hours of the morning, however, when all the others slept and the only sounds were the distant moans of the disturbed mental deficients in the special block, I had a sudden sink and was forced to draw on my precious store of *sneg* before I again relaxed. My mind sharpened, I tried to go over what I had learned. I concluded a mistake had been made. Röhm would not want me in here. Neither would Hitler. If my involvement in the Tegernsee plot were discovered I would be quietly murdered, I was sure. I also dismissed the involvement of Brodmann, my Bolshevik nemesis, or Prince Freddy. My best bet was to try to contact Hanfstaengl. Although he had claimed to have been inundated with pleas for help, I was sure he would go out of his way for me.

At six o'clock we were awakened by the warders banging on our doors, warning us to ready ourselves for our ablutions and breakfast. The prison servant, a mournful old slattern in a long overall, came in to clean the cell, splashing her bucket of disinfectant about so that we gagged on the smell. We were then forced to assemble outside with our bowls while some kind of awful soup was slopped into them by a shifty trusty whose long moustache bore witness to a score of his own meals. Happily, Doctor Bach's provisions were still edible, and we ate more sausage and bread, washing it down with the remains of his tea and the thin coffee issued to us.

I told Count von Zinzendorf und Pottendorf that he must, like me, feel unhappy about being confined with common criminals but he reassured me. 'The whole damned building is packed with politicals. Every day they take a few away, often to Stadelheim or Dachau, and every day they bring still more in.'

At about nine o'clock a warder flung the door open and ordered us all into the corridor. We were marched in military order and forced to stand to attention while he checked names on a clipboard.

This ritual ended, the warder pointed at our Jewish colleague. 'Heinrich Bach. You are to remain outside. You others will return to the cell.'

With the door closed behind us, we speculated on the reason for Bach being taken away. We could hear his questioning whine in the corridor until his voice faded, and another door clanged behind him.

Count von Zinzendorf und Pottendorf thoughtfully placed the remains of Bach's provisions into his own smart, leather suitcase. He was an old prison hand now, he said, with an apologetic grin. Bach had been using his overcoat as a blanket, and this Pottendorf straightened, plumping the straw pillow and smoothing it. The rest of the food he replaced in Bach's cases, which he settled upon his own bunk. He did not tell us why he was doing this, but since he was the oldest inhabitant of No. 47, we assumed he knew what he was about.

His business finished, he sat down again, crossed his legs and offered us all one of his fat Turkish cigarettes. Helander and I accepted gratefully. As we smoked the richly scented tobacco, Pottendorf explained his actions.

'If Bach returns, then his goods are here for him. If he does not, then we keep the overcoat and the food. Decent food costs a fortune here and sometimes the guards are forbidden to bring it in. I take it none of us has the money to spend on such delicacies?'

'You think Bach is being released?' I asked.

Pottendorf sighed. 'I have a feeling he will not return to our little home,' he said. 'I have noticed that the new authorities have a tendency to place German Jews together in the same group of cells. Maybe they suspect all Jews of being socialists and communists, I don't know. Maybe they plan some sort of mass interrogation. Or a special camp, even. The guards are likely to let us know where he has gone. They're good-natured, if uneducated, fellows, most of them. They know we are gentlemen and not criminals. Helander here served in the trenches with one of them. He was here when war broke out and volunteered on our side. That sort of thing isn't forgotten. They're old soldiers, mostly, and have a common feeling for those who fought in the War.'

'Unfortunately,' I said with a sudden attack of irony, 'I fought in the War on the other side!'

Pottendorf said he had no experience of the Eastern Front. He had heard it was pretty hellish.

'Not so bad from the air,' I said.

The revelation that I was a pilot increased my standing immediately. I could feel their respect. I had forgotten how flyers were regarded as 'knights of the air', chivalrous and courageous no matter which side they were fighting on. Pottendorf, understanding this very well, said he, too, had served in the air force until being shot down and injured. He had been unfortunate enough to be blinded with shrapnel. He removed his darkened glasses to show me his rather bloodshot eyes. 'Happily, my sight was restored. Since then I have devoted myself to peace.' He believed that it was his pacifism

482

which had brought him to this pass since Nazi militarism had first turned him against them.

In spite of having been on opposite sides, our flying days gave us something in common. I told him how my own career had ended when my captured Oertz had crashed into the sea off Odessa. We discussed the difficulties of flying the Oertz. He had never piloted the plane himself, he said, but had heard a great deal about it. Wasn't it difficult to get up and land but performed well once in the air? A somewhat unreliable plane, but a beauty. He was not surprised my machine had let me down. The Oertz was notorious. He asked which squadron I had flown with. I told him that I belonged to the 11th Don Cossacks and had been seconded to the air force.

'So you were cavalry originally!' He was delighted by this coincidence. He, too, had been in the cavalry before joining von Bek's famous '*Staffel*'. He enthused about the Saxon air ace, who had died aged twenty-two, engaged in a dogfight with a squadron of Canadian and American Camels led by the famous US flyer, Billy Batson.

Helander was not particularly interested in our reminiscences, though he expressed every admiration for the men of the flying corps. He had once envied us, in fact. For all our short lives we stood a better chance of a decent death than the poor bastards who filled up no man's land with their wounded bodies, sometimes taking days to die. We admitted that as airmen we had a better war than many. Who wished to face the prospect of lying in mud and filth, holding one's own guts in, perhaps for days, and crying out for help which never came?

Lunchtime arrived and still no sign of Doctor Bach. We asked Link, the guard, who only shook his head, repeating the usual mantra about not being in on the decisions of the prison's commanding officer. About an hour later, however, our cell was unlocked, and two policemen came in, casting a cold eye over our quarters. They wanted to know if Doctor Bach had left any property behind. Pottendorf, holding one of his Turkish cigarettes between his fingers, coolly indicated the overcoat. One of the policemen shouted at him, telling him to stand to attention and to put his cigarette out. In his beautifully modulated Austrian accent, Pottendorf asked which he should do first.

Not sure of his ground, the policeman told him to put the cigarette out and stand to attention. With his fingers, Pottendorf extinguished the burning tip and brought his arms to his sides. The policeman then turned his attention on me, roaring a string of insults, not least of which was that I was a stinking Jewish swine who had published libels against the German people. I would soon get my reward, as 'that scamp' Bach was going to get his. It seemed impolitic to enlighten him.

Meanwhile, Pottendorf learned from the man's companion that Bach had been transferred to Dachau where he would be 'allowed to do an honest day's work' and so earn his freedom. At least it seemed the poor Jew was on the road to liberty. The *Völkischer Beobachter* had been full of praise for the institution, which was to be the model for many other facilities where antisocial elements were sentenced to hard labour until ready to rejoin the ranks of decent Germans. I supposed it would not do the overweight Bach a great deal of harm to get fit and work off some of his extra pounds. I could imagine his tears mingling with his sweat as he lifted his pickaxe, helping to build the bright new nation dreamed of by our Nazi visionaries.

As Pottendorf remarked, at least that night we would not be kept awake by Doctor Bach's symphonic snoring! He looked forward to meeting him on the outside when he would be slender and trim. But we never heard of him again.

Next morning the guard knocked at the door. Six o'clock and dawn had only just broken. I woke from a pleasant dream in which I had returned to my uncle's place in Odessa to enjoy the plump embraces of Wanda, my old love.

'Get up, you lazy sons of bitches. Fold your blankets. Time to wash your filthy selves!'

Half an hour later the square hatch in the door was swung back. Coffee and bread were pushed through. We drank the coffee, bad as it was, but ignored the bread. Again we feasted on the unfortunate Doctor Bach's leftovers.

I fully expected to be notified of a hearing and to be released by that afternoon, but the hours dragged on and no such notification was received. We took turns in pacing the tiny cell. Pottendorf and Helander did their physical jerks. After a while I lost patience and rang the electric bell to attract the warder's attention.

'What is it?' came his voice from the other side.

'I need my case to be heard. Important matters await my decision. I need to know the reasons for being placed in protective custody.'

The warder promised to report my request.

Surreptiously sustaining myself with a little of my coca, I waited for the rest of the day. Pottendorf and Helander said nothing. They seemed strangely non-committal when I asked them what they thought was happening. Of course, they had been in Ettstrasse rather longer than I.

At last, when the afternoon was fading to twilight, the door opened. I arose hopefully only to stare into the face of one of the SA who had earlier come to claim Doctor Bach. His companion stood just behind him. Next to him stood a short, slender creature whose face had the pallor of one living by night rather than by day. He wore a well-cut grey silk suit of a rather exaggerated line, a pale blue shirt and a tie of light turquoise. In his buttonhole was a fading pink carnation. His hair was oiled and parted sharply and was as black as the patent-leather shoes on his feet. His eyes stared peevishly into the cell.

'Do you really expect me to spend the night with this rabble?' he asked the policeman. He turned to say more but was shoved roughly forward.

'He can have Bach's blankets,' said the warder, laughing behind the policemen. 'They're not too dirty. If you don't mind Jew-sweat.'

'My hearing!' I managed to shout before the cell door was closed on us again. 'You told me you would find out about my hearing.'

'No notice, so far,' he said through the bars. We heard him and the police stump off up the corridor. Coarse laughter. We heard the far door slam.

I slumped down on my bunk, oblivious of the newcomer.

Pottendorf, ever-polite, offered the man his hand. 'Greetings, sir. Welcome to our club. I am Count von Zinzendorf und Pottendorf, this is Herr Helander and the gentleman over there is Professor Peters. I take it you are not a German.'

The little man bridled. 'Why should you think that?'

'Because I'm gaining some understanding of the minds of our captors. Our previous cellmate has been removed to be with the other Jews, and we are all foreigners. I am Austrian, Herr Peters is American and Herr Helander is Swedish. You are . . . ?'

Some of the defiance left the newcomer's manner. 'I'm French, but I've lived in Berlin and Munich since the end of the War. You probably know my name. Bernhardt LeBrun?'

485

The others did not recognise him, but I did. 'You're the cabaret comedian! We have colleagues in common. I saw you last at the Simplicissimus here in Munich.'

He turned in some surprise. 'Colleagues in common?' He appeared to find the notion disagreeable.

'I myself have acted in a number of films here,' I told him, 'and I have friends in show business. You no doubt know Miss Gloria Cornish?'

LeBrun snorted with disgust and turned away from me. 'Know that slag! I suppose I do. She got out while the going was good. Went back to Berlin. I wouldn't be surprised if she wasn't the bitch who libelled me and had me arrested by the Gestapo!'

With a shout of rage, I flung myself at him, only to be restrained by my companions. LeBrun seemed taken aback. He preened in front of me, his hands before his face in mock fear.

'What are you,' he asked, his voice squeaking with aggression, 'her pimp?'

I stared fiercely into his nasty little brown eyes, my words forced through clenched teeth.

'Count Pottendorf, Herr Helander,' I said with as much dignity as I could muster, 'I would be obliged if you would release me. This man has just insulted my wife.'

That disgusting little Frenchman believed my beloved had betrayed him to Hermann Göring. Months ago he and she had been on the same bill at the Flashlite – he was the resident comedian – and they had not got on well. LeBrun did not know why he was arrested but was certain it was because 'Gloria Cornish' had said something to Göring. 'I was too outspoken,' he said. But he had always been careful not to attack the Nazis. No doubt 'La Cornish' had convinced her lover otherwise.

I told him that this was complete nonsense. Mrs Cornelius was simply Göring's friend; she was not his mistress. Whatever else they said about him, nobody ever accused Göring of infidelity. But LeBrun claimed Gloria Cornish was an adventuress, ruthless in her jealousy, whom he had first encountered in France, where she had been involved in a famous scandal. 'She slept her way into the movies.' He recognised me, too, he said. He had seen me in Paris. Perhaps with her. He had worked as a waiter at Lipp's, a restaurant I had favoured. I, of course, denied this. I thought it best to say I had never been there at all. I was still worried about Kitty's inherited collection of press cuttings and Röhm's 'dossier'.

LeBrun knew he had alarmed me and pressed his advantage. After some thought he swore he had seen me at Lipp's with Gloria Cornish. This was a complete nonsense. We were never together in Paris. Mrs Cornelius was in the United Kingdom at that time. LeBrun was doubtless terrified, flailing about for any advantage. Anything that might ingratiate him with the authorities. It was disgusting. I refused to be intimidated. I told him he was a madman and a slanderer. He was lucky I did not tear him limb from limb.

LeBrun was in his own nightmare. In his babbling panic he accused all and everyone. He could not understand the reasons for his arrest. His accusations became wilder and wilder. They were so clearly his own transference, as Helander suggested, that my anger eventually dissipated. I came to treat him with disgusted contempt. He was not, it emerged, a French citizen, but was from the Alsatian border. My cellmates disliked him as much as I did. He was a poisonous little homosexual, a natural gossip and troublemaker. We could easily imagine how he had come to be arrested. I could not bear to be in the same cell with him.

In spite of his attempts to engage them in conversation, Pottendorf and Helander did their best to ignore him. At my first opportunity I complained bitterly to the guard. We found LeBrun repellent, I said. When not moaning and groaning about his situation, he was accusing each and every one of us of some imagined crime. None of us wanted to risk going to bed. It was not fair that we should be forced to share quarters with an obvious pervert. The guard was sympathetic. As soon as a single cell was available, LeBrun would go there.

Two days passed and LeBrun was still with us. Worse, I still did not get a hearing for my own case. Obviously I had no need of 'protective custody'. I was an honest American citizen, a taxpayer, a friend of the new Germany. I demanded the Chief of Police be notified. Others might be there for political reasons, but I should not be. I, not LeBrun, was in Ettstrasse as a result of false accusation. It was in Prince Freddy's interest to get rid of me now that he had what he wanted. If Göring were made aware of my presence in the jail he would immediately have me released. I asked for pen, ink and paper and eventually received a few rough sheets, torn from a schoolbook, and a pencil. Doing my best with these materials, I wrote to Mrs Cornelius and to Aviation Minister Göring, but I despaired. Unless they recognised my handwriting, my notes would look like a thousand others they received every day.

Along with writing materials, tobacco and food, the only newspaper we were allowed to buy via the guards was the *Völkischer Beobachter*. Those guards made a handsome profit from us. Even the paper was a few more pfennigs than the published price. On the fourth day of my captivity, I was scanning its pages when I noticed a small news item which referred to foreign Bolshevist elements being rounded up for questioning. Many of these Reds were associated with the arts. Writers and actors were particularly under suspicion. They were responsible for corrupting the minds of Germans through their films and books. I asked Pottendorf if this could refer to us and he said he thought it could. I began to feel less than optimistic.

Sensing my despair, Count Pottendorf reassured me. Even LeBrun was clearly not a Red. If we were suspected of such affiliations we would be with the other musicians and entertainers in Stadelheim and Dachau. I was a victim of bureaucratic thinking, nothing else. Rather than distinguish between us, the Nazis had decided to arrest all foreign artists and writers on the suspicion that they were communists. Slowly, as they investigated us, they would discover who was and who was not guilty and I would be released. My confidence temporarily restored, I determined to make the best of things. I would soon be back in my flat. I prayed that the carefully hidden documents and personal possessions in Corneliusstrasse had not meanwhile been discovered and stolen.

I next began to worry what would happen if, just as I was on the point of being released, LeBrun might bear false witness against me. He was spiteful enough to do so. Did he really remember me from Paris? Certainly I did not remember him from Lipp's. At that time, Mrs Cornelius and myself had moved in different circles. If she had been in Paris at all, she would have been with Trotsky or her mysterious Persian playboy who had brought her to Constantinople. That was before I had driven from Rome to begin my career in Paris. She had been in London. I had received a letter from her, posted from Whitechapel. From there, inspired by my letters, she had gone with an English touring company to the USA. I did not remember the details, but certainly I had not met her again until we were both in the United States where, to our mutual benefit, Mucker Hever had fallen in love with her. We could never have been together in Paris.

So detached from reality had I become that I even thought of killing LeBrun while he slept. He could ruin me. Of course my instincts would not permit it. I value human life. I would not willingly spill his blood, even though he was loathed by all. Moreover, if he was stifled in his sleep, I was sure to be subject to an inquiry.

My fears were groundless, as it happened. Within a day LeBrun had lost his flashy suit and was wearing only a striped prison shirt which went down to his knees. The guards were amused by this. They said he looked better in a dress. They even took his shoes. We found a spare pair in Bach's suitcase that were too big for him, but better than nothing. The guards said he would be issued with some sturdier clothes when he got to Dachau. There he would learn what it was to work like a man.

Happily, LeBrun soon gave up his accusatory mode and spoke to us less and less, snivelling himself to sleep every night. I came close to pitying him. He had bruises all over him where he had been kicked and punched by passing SA. If he had not accused my angel, I would have done more to try to help him. Even when he began to bleed from the nose, I sensed something disgusting about him. Helander, like me, avoided him, but the little pervert became pathetically grateful when Count Pottendorf, a Christian gentleman to the marrow, bathed his face, wiping the dried blood off his nose and lips. Pottendorf spoke in a low tone about Paris, which he had loved, her boulevards, her parks, her quays, calming LeBrun to silence so that we could all sleep.

They say that in monetary terms a barrel of good human gore is worth infinitely more than a barrel of crude oil. Tens of thousands of pounds are needed to buy a few gallons of blood. Plasma is, of course, worth even more. I heard this on the BBC the other day. Not that I believe everything the BBC tells us. Buggers Broadcasting Communism, as Miss Brunner, the schoolteacher I see at the pub, would have it. Blood is literally the most valuable liquid on the planet. Is it because we spill it so liberally, I wonder? The Americans used albumin first at Pearl Harbor. It had astonishing properties. Yet it is also the most easily contaminated substance. Oil, the most contaminating of liquids, kills anything it touches. Our oceans and beaches are forever ruined by it, yet we value oil far higher than blood.

The oil had dried on LeBrun's head and his hair was a spiked mess, giving him an insane, inhuman appearance. Struwwelpeter, indeed! How quickly he had lost his veneer. The rest of us used whatever means we could to keep up our standards, but in a matter of hours the Alsatian went from posturing dandy to slovenly wretch.

The SA began to call for LeBrun regularly. He was gone for hours. He said they were questioning him about French communists he knew. He did not know any communists, he said, whether French or otherwise. He had never had anything to do with politics. He had been beaten up but he would not tell us details. While he was away, we wondered if he was being persuaded to act as a witness against us. Every time he returned he had a fresh bruise and was weeping. Pottendorf said he thought it unlikely they were asking

LeBrun about us. Horrible though it was to contemplate, the SA
men were beating him for their own pleasure, out of disgust for his
kind. He had encouraged them in their prejudice, almost advertised
himself.

One afternoon Helander proposed that LeBrun was being used
by the brutal homosexual element of the SA. After all, Röhm was
notorious.

Naturally I defended my patron. Röhm's enemies had employed
his sensitive letters against him. That Spartan love was a very different
thing from LeBrun's limp-wristed mincing. Helander and Pottendorf
seemed surprised by the intensity of my defence, which made me
realise it was unwise of me to continue. I could do no good for
Röhm or help my own cause.

Nursing his bruises, LeBrun confined himself to his miserable
bunk. The rest of us tried to make conversation. The other two prisoners were interested in my scientific ideas, and it took my mind
off my situation to talk about such things. In America I had invented
a very successful steam-car, but my interest remained mostly in aeronautics. I described my one-man observation airship and asked if
they had ever heard of the giant airship the Americans planned to
build. I was about to tell them a little of my involvement with such
a ship, which, as far as I knew, was still in its shed outside Akron,
when Pottendorf gave a bitter laugh. 'Don't tell me about airships.
Poor LeBrun has already reminded me too much! I lost half my
fortune to that miserable confidence trick that was all over the papers
a few years ago. I was living in Paris at the time. I invested heavily.
I was an idiot. I thought it was the coming thing. Do you remember
that scandal? Some ten years or so ago? They used a Russian
nobleman to front it. He was a convincing rogue. What was his
name? Count something. He married a Parisian banker's daughter,
I think, then ran off with some little whore from Constantinople.
The scheme itself was cooked up by a bunch of Jewish fraudsters.
I haven't a prejudiced bone in my body, but I should have known
better than to trust them. They made millions from it, of course,
but left the rest of us high and dry. Some Russian charlatan claimed
to be the inventor. Another Jew. If you're involved in aeronautics,
you might remember him, Mr Peters. Did that news ever reach
America? I heard the chief villains fled there, but America is a large
country. It is full of defaulting financiers and fleeing criminals. You
must have encountered plenty.'

I was shocked to hear this version of my wholly idealistic Parisian experiment. I longed to enlighten him but, in the circumstances, could not.

'I would not have had to resort to journalism,' Pottendorf continued, 'if it had not been for those rogues. And if I had not become a journalist, I would no doubt not be here at all!'

I was relieved that I had shown forbearance and denied any association with Paris. It seemed impolitic to mention my involvement with the airship company or to try to defend my friend Kolya, for Count Nikolai Feodorovitch Petroff was the man Pottendorf referred to. In reality, of course, I, too, had been a victim of the scheme. Indeed, I had been made the chief scapegoat. My name had not then been Peters, but Pyatnitski. If my friend Kolya had not warned me in time I would even now, no doubt, be in a worse prison on Devil's Island. Yet the real villains remained at large, still free and respected. Only by a whisker had I had been able to get to America, forced to leave my little Esmé behind in Kolya's safekeeping. Doubtless she was the 'little whore from Constantinople' Pottendorf mentioned.

Not times I liked to remember. I found it unbearable to think of the vast consequences arising from French Jewry's betrayal of my best ideals. I, too, had lost much. I wish that I could have told Pottendorf the truth but found myself reminding him I had never been to Paris. I agreed that we lived in terrible times, when Russian charlatans were able to deceive even those of us with considerable common sense. Avoiding the subject of large airships, I spoke instead of my other American ventures, of my great Land Cruiser, my fleet of experimental aircraft built for the Sultan of Marrakech, the various projects I had begun with Signor Mussolini. I had rather expected, I said, to interest the New Germany in my scientific ideas. I had much to offer the Third Reich. But this business had soured me. The sooner I could get back to Italy, the better.

Helander was surprised I had never visited the City of Light. 'Such a sophisticated world traveller,' he said, 'and yet —'

Sadly circumstances had never taken me to the French capital. As a race, the French were unattractive, too volatile and unserious. Bismarck had rightly described France as a feminine nation, as compared to masculine Germany. The whole nation had sunk into decadence. One only had to look at M. LeBrun.

My anxiety was returning. Pottendorf's bitter outburst had again

reminded me of the materials in Röhm's and Prince Freddy's possession. If someone like Pottendorf saw those cuttings he would turn
against me. I might never be released. The Parisian Airship Company
scandal was notorious at the time, especially after my name was
linked to that of my fellow Ukrainian Stavisky. Yet this uncomfortable reference also came as a revelation! Again I wondered if Kitty
von Ruckstühl was actually responsible for my arrest. Did she really
still blame me for her mother's death? Did she believe me to be the
father of her half-brother? In her morphine fever could she have
turned on me, deciding to take up her mother's baton?

I shuddered at how those films might now affect my fate. Masks
could not entirely disguise me. There were the distinctive marks on
my buttocks. These, in turn, reminded me of Grishenko and my
Ukrainian adventures. My thoughts went again to Brodmann, the
only witness of my humiliation. Unless the Bolshevist agent had
deceived them completely, it was unlikely the Nazis would take his
word for anything. Hanfstaengl had no reason to hate me. My association with Otto Strasser could not be known unless someone had
been watching him for a long time. Was that possible? Who else?
Göring, perhaps? Out of jealousy of my relationship with Mrs
Cornelius? Again unlikely. The Fraus had no reason to take against
me. No, the most obvious enemy was Prince Freddy. If I escaped
from this trap, I would ask Röhm to have him killed. I was furious
with him and what he had done.

I was becoming increasingly uncomfortable with the company,
especially, of course, LeBrun. I feared he would remember something
more from when I had been in Paris and reveal my association with
Kolya and his friends. The next time I had the opportunity, I begged
the guard to change my cell. He was especially sympathetic when I
said I feared molestation from LeBrun.

Two days later, while LeBrun was as usual absent, Helander and
Pottendorf were playing chess and I was sitting reading the *VB*.
Suddenly there came a loud shout from outside and the door was
flung back. 'Hurry yourself, Peters. Get your things together. At the
double, man. We're leaving.' It was an SA guard I knew called Fischer.

'Leaving? I'm released?'

'At the double. Quick now.'

Rapidly I gathered up my few possessions, said a hasty goodbye
to my cellmates and stood before Warder Fischer. The massive SA
man had never treated me particularly badly.

'Am I free?'

'You wanted to be free of your nancy boy, didn't you? Come on. Hurry up.'

I was marched along the corridor to cell 40, which the warder unlocked and opened. Bewildered, I stumbled into it. 'What's this?'

'Solitary,' the warder said. Then the door was shut and locked.

The bunk had no mattress, only a straw-filled sack and a pillow. At its foot was a water closet. The cell was freezing. The radiator was not turned on. It allowed me six paces back and forth and was about two paces wide. High above, the window was impossible to reach. Almost immediately I began to feel claustrophobic. By way of self-comfort I lay down on the sack and closed my eyes, determined to enjoy my privacy, if nothing else. Soon, however, the cold made me get to my feet. As rapidly as I could I walked the length of the cell, leaping up and down in order to keep warm. Eventually I wore myself out and stretched out on the pallet again. I had nothing to read, having left the *VB* with the others. I was depressed. My common sense told me I had been foolish to believe I was escaping this place. None of the prisoners had gone out before they had received some sort of hearing. Yet more than one had been released after being put in solitary. Did this mean I could now expect my hearing?

This hope sustained me for at least another week. Occasionally on my way to the washroom, I caught glimpses of my former cell-mates, but had no chance to talk to them. They had another companion now, a bald, emaciated-looking fellow I remembered from my film-star days, which felt extraordinarily remote to me. He had been a cameraman's assistant, I recalled, a Greek or a Turk. The cosmopolitan nature of our cell was being maintained. After a while I saw nothing of LeBrun, the reason for my being put in solitary. He had been replaced by a pallid, squat fellow who seemed to have nothing to wear but a pair of extremely garish pyjamas. I never did discover who he was.

The radiator in my cell remained cold. I became obsessed with keeping warm. I constantly begged the warders to have something done. Shortly after I ran out of *sneg*, whose properties were so useful in protecting against disease, I developed terrible influenza. I began to sweat and tremble badly. Obviously I was catching pneumonia. The guards asked me if I wished to see the doctor. They warned me that anyone taken to the doctor would, these days, usually be passed on to Dachau where they had hospital facilities. I insisted I was not as sick as I seemed.

The best of the guards were genuinely sympathetic. Regulations demanded that prisoners be kept in reasonable comfort, and the original staff of Ettstrasse did their best to stick to the rules. The SA men were less reliable, though some were kindly enough. I could afford a few small luxuries, including the daily paper and a variety of chemist-shop medications, but it took me some time to recover. Still the radiator was not turned on. I longed for something to distract me and begged for a Bible, anything to read. One guard did eventually pass me a book, in English, which I read several times over, relishing the adventures of a slick, American detective who lived in the penthouse of a gleaming white modern apartment building and drove a supercharged roadster. With his barking automatics and sultry lady friends, Dick Dutton helped me escape from my gloom and reminded me of a time when I had also lived the life of a playboy, envied by all. I wished that I could have read some tales by Sexton Blake, Britain's greatest living detective. His courage in adversity was an example which even now I attempted to follow.

My natural vitality got me through my ordeal. I longed for a little 'snow' to put me back on my feet, but even without it I was soon able to stand steadily and feed myself. Was I in a state of shock? How had I descended so suddenly from fame and fortune? One moment I had been a highly paid public figure, the next I was a mere number. Whatever happiness I could achieve was entirely dependent on the mood of my jailers. Every day I asked about my hearing. Every day I begged someone to get word to Röhm or Hanfstaengl, Göring or Mrs Cornelius. I was afraid I would die there.

I had been abandoned. I knew Mrs Cornelius would never have let me rot in Ettstrasse. She was either back in London or on location with no notion of what had happened to me. Göring was horribly overworked. Hugenberg had important Cabinet duties. Röhm was probably still in Berlin struggling to reorganise the army, while Hanfstaengl could already have left for the United States, as he had been threatening. Possibly Putzi was himself a prisoner.

I enjoyed one or two breaks in my confinement. At one stage I was taken downstairs and photographed. I had to fill in forms, giving the details of my arrest. I wrote that I was in 'temporary protective custody' in the hope this would attract the attention of whatever bureaucrat was in charge of the documents. I complained about my cell and was told they were having difficulty finding plumbers. It was on the tip of my tongue to suggest they arrest some plumbers and release some journalists and actors, who were an impractical bunch at best. After a brief medical examination I was interviewed by a young man who warned me this was not a hearing. He had been assigned merely to verify the truth of my written statement. He was almost apologetic. When I complained that my cell had no heat, he immediately tried to sort the matter out, assuring me the police were not attempting to torment me. Ettstrasse, he told me, was never designed for so many people. They were already beyond their capacity.

The prison was becoming more and more crowded. Increasingly, from all parts could be heard the yells, screams and imploring sobs of the prisoners. Fewer regular guards were on the corridors. The SA seemed to be taking over. Some of these were decent enough, especially the older ones who had served in the War. It was the younger, less experienced SA who gave us the most trouble. They were a rougher element, probably ex-communists and worse, who had jumped on the Nazi bandwagon after the election successes of 1933.

I believe the young man who interviewed me meant well, but his intervention scarcely improved matters. After a month I was taken out of my cold single cell and put back with a group. But now I was with well-known Jewish entrepreneurs! Powerful in the outside world, they were in a state of shock. They assumed I was of the same persuasion as themselves. After I politely but firmly told them the truth, they tended to ostracise me. I must admit their action was not entirely disagreeable. However, when I complained to the SA guards about being identified with these people, they laughed and told me that I had better get used to it.

And then one morning in early June the entire cell was ordered into the corridor. There was to be a clear-out. The prison was beyond capacity. Did this mean my release at last? Perhaps they had decided to keep only the prisoners accused of identifiable crimes. With our poor little bundles of possessions, we were marched downstairs and out into the courtyard where lorries were waiting. My anxieties immediately increased. Earlier I had glimpsed from above prisoners being herded aboard these transports. Shouted at, confused and frightened, we climbed into the overburdened vehicles. Where were we bound? Stadelheim? Dachau? My voice joined those of many trying to convince the guards that we had been wrongfully arrested. In the end I realised it was pointless. I was just another scream in the general cacophony.

I decided very quickly that I would rather retain my dignity. I fell silent. I entertained some idea of climbing out from under the lorry's canopy when we stopped and slipping away into the street. Had I any friends left in Munich? An opportunity of escape never presented itself. Having been institutionalised for so long, I had lost all initiative. Eventually I managed to reach a corner of the lorry where I could at least keep my balance and so made the journey in relative comfort. With relief we disembarked. My spirits rose when I saw guards in conventional uniform. From the high, stone walls and the general old-fashioned appearance of the place, I realised I was in Stadelheim. Amid further yelling, we tumbled out on to the cobbles of the castle. I looked around me. The castle's walls were set at regular intervals with the barred windows of dozens of cells. It had been rebuilt and extended since Hitler's time. I had seen it, of course, from the Tegernsee road. For such an old building, it had always seemed a rather agreeable place. From within, however, it had a bleak, hopeless atmosphere.

Blinking in the bright summer light, I must have looked a wretch. My only shirt was worn and torn. My trousers were greasy and my jacket not in much better shape. Over my arm was my winter overcoat. I carried a parcel containing the few possessions I had managed to keep. Yet the warders were not unkind. They spoke to us with that rough good humour I had come to expect from the best of them. One warder even helped me into the building. Nobody shouted at us. We eventually reached the reception office and stood in line before a wide, low desk where officials checked off our names.

'Wankel? Discharge 12th August. Sentence begins at noon today. Jungerer? Release in a year. Sentence began noon yesterday.' When it came to my turn I had to give my own particulars. They had no room in their ledgers for those of us under protective custody and seemed uncomfortable with the idea. I was sent to another desk with a smart SA man, as cordial as the others. He wrote down everything I told him, including my understanding that I had nothing to fear in the outside world, into a brand new leather-bound book, dipping his pen into his inkwell and wiping the nib carefully on a blotter. Then I was marched into the next room.

Here we were told to strip to our shirts. Anything we carried, be it pencils, money, cigarettes, hats and ties, were listed on the outside of a bag which was then sealed. Those with conventional sentences were given prison clothes and told to keep them on, unless they had sentences of only a few weeks, in which case they could keep their clothes. I, too, was allowed to keep my own clothes. This gave me some hope, indicating that I might, after all, only be spending a short time in Stadelheim. Before I moved on to the next stage, I asked the SA man if he knew whether I had received any letters. I had written, I said, to his chief, Ernst Röhm, a friend of mine, and also to Göring and my wife, Mrs Cornelius. He looked at me as if I was touched and shook his head, smiling. If any letters came from Staff Chief Röhm or Air Minister Göring, he would be sure to let me know. Was my wife by any chance also an office holder in the government?

Consoling myself that he would not be smiling quite so widely if my friends in the Nazi hierarchy found out where I was, I allowed myself to be directed into the medical room, decorated with terrifying posters depicting various forms of venereal disease. Here a prison doctor looked me over. Pronouncing me fit, he signalled for my SA escort to lead me away down a long corridor. The wooden floor was evidently maintained by prisoners and was so highly polished it almost dazzled me. I could look down and see my gaunt, sickly features staring back. Moments later a cell door was thrown open.

I found myself in a long, gloomy room lined on both sides with tiers of bunks. A shaft of sunlight pierced through a dusty window above the WC, seeming to increase the depth of surrounding shadows. The cell was occupied only by two young men. One of them was short and fat, the other long and lean. They reminded me of the comic characters from the English magazines of my childhood, Phil May's Weary Willy and Tired Tim. In spite of wearing prison uniform, they were both good-humoured but rather startled by my appearance.

'You're not Jewish, are you?' That was the lean young man's first question. He did not seem dismayed by the idea.

I took no offence. I shook my head wearily. 'No. I am American. My father is of English extraction and my mother's family was originally from Madrid. Papa could trace his ancestry back to the Danes, and Mama's family was in Galicia since before the Arab Conquest. Believe me, I'm used to the question.' I had learned to offer this level of detail. Otherwise, I knew, I would not be believed.

Because of my wounded penis, bequeathed to me by my 'clinical realist' father, many officials in Ettstrasse had also assumed I was a Jew. The truth was too complicated for them. It made no sense to tell them I was actually related to the Russian aristocracy or that I was from South Russia, which in some minds was associated with the Pale of Settlement. As I unpacked my few belongings, I added that I had made it my business, both in my native America and elsewhere, to point out the dangers of the aliens in our midst. Until its takeover by cynical interests, I was a recruiting spokesman for the Ku Klux Klan. If Germany had adopted the same racial laws enacted in Alabama and elsewhere, she would not need to be taking such radical measures now. The American people had a clearer idea what liberalism led to.

This relieved them. They were, they told me, both National Socialists. They shook my hand and introduced themselves. The lean one was Adolf Harben. He was from Karlsfeld. The fat one was an SA sergeant, Christian Weymayer, originally from Pfaffenhofen. Like me, neither had been charged with any specific crime. Unlike me, they were not in protective custody. Harben said he believed he had been accused of some minor treason by his cousin, who disliked him, and Sergeant Weymayer had upset a local official who had had him arrested as a communist. Both expected to be freed soon. They commented on my seedy, hangdog look. Had someone been beating me up? Having arrived in Stadelheim recently, they lacked my experience of the worst prison could deliver.

The rest of their comrades were off on work parties and would be back soon. I looked forward to meeting them, I said. Which was my bunk? I stumbled forward. The two cheerful lads helped me put my parcel and coat on a top bunk at the far end of the cell, but when I attempted to get into it, I was warned that this was forbidden. 'The SA won't allow it during the day. We can sit at this table or walk about. There is no smoking either. They look in on us at random, and if they catch us, we get punished.' Weymayer indicated the peephole in the door. 'On the other hand, if you need a breath of air at night or want to look out into the courtyard, you can stand on the can and get a bit of a view. At least you can sometimes see who's coming and going. It's best to do that in the early morning or evening, before the warders come round. It's about our only entertainment.'

I sat on my stool and read the *VB* for a while. My new friends wanted to know what it had been like in Ettstrasse, so I spent a while telling them until we heard a rap on the door. We stood to attention when the door opened to reveal a trustee in a clean overall, a bucket of soup over one arm, a basket of bread on the other. Compared to what I had grown used to this was Ritz-quality service. The guard doled out soup and bread and moved on down the corridor. The food was surprisingly good, containing a reasonable amount of sausage and fresh vegetables. My life was already improving!

After lunch we played noughts and crosses until our other two companions joined us in the cell. Their faces were bright from their exercise. The pair were as good-humoured as my other cellmates. Pale-haired, grey-eyed, well muscled and bronzed, they were almost identical twins. The Grote brothers. Though on good terms with the others, they were Social Democrats, trade union railwaymen from Vaterstatten who had fallen foul of the Gestapo when they had complained about the closure of their headquarters. Not exactly radicals, they were astonished when they were suddenly thrown into jail. They, too, did not expect to be incarcerated for long. More from boredom than anything, they had joined a work party repairing the walls of the old section and had been promised an early release by the SA man in charge.

The food that evening was barley soup and some tough rye bread. We were also given jugs of fresh drinking water. My comrades told me it was now all right to lie down. We took our bunks. They saw me as someone rather exotic, who had travelled widely, and they wanted to know all about America. I told them stories of my adventures, of my career as a film actor and also as an inventor. They were incredulous, finding my tales almost unbelievable, but enjoying them, they said, whether I told the truth or not. Hearing me was as good as listening to the radio. Now, if I could only produce some music for them . . .

I soon became known as 'the American'. They demanded more stories. They said I should write a book. I laughed. I had known people who wrote books. These days it probably wasn't the safest profession. Even the SA laughed at this. They were as irreverent about Hitler as the socialists. In spite of my situation, I enjoyed that brief period of comradeship. It quickly ended, of course, when the Grote brothers were transferred to Dachau in the middle of June, and shortly afterwards the two SA lads were released.

I was soon the oldest occupant of the cell, which began quickly to fill up with an entirely different class of prisoner, the scum of Jewish Munich, drug addicts, perverts and criminals of the lowest kind. The worst sort of Jew, as we used to say.

I begged the warders to let me go out on work parties, anything to keep me away from the cell as long as possible, and for a while I was employed painting doors and woodwork in the new wing. But this did not last. They were unsatisfied with my work. I said that I was a trained mechanic. What if I worked on the transport? But they were contemptuous. Somehow they seemed to think because I was not a good house painter, I could not possibly make a reasonable engineer. I thought of telling them how their leader was allegedly a good house painter, if not necessarily Germany's best choice of Chancellor, but of course I kept my mouth shut rather than jeopardise my release.

My letters were not being forwarded, but I continued to write to my friends in the outside world. I fell into a deep depression, keeping increasingly to myself. While they did not like me much, the Jewish lowlifes scarcely seemed to mind. Most of them brought the foulest habits with them. They had no manners at all. They talked constantly in corrupted Yiddish. They told disgusting stories and revealed obscene desires. They hated everyone, especially any fellow Jews who had made something of themselves. They hated each other. Eventually I developed a habit of deafness, dumbness and daydreaming, which saved me the worst of their noise. I could not entirely block them out. Their smell was dreadful. They belched and farted and left food scraps everywhere. It was like sharing a room with a pack of rats.

Because I complained, they attempted to put hands on me. But they left me alone when I told them of my powerful connections. The experience was terrifying, nonetheless. Almost the whole corridor was now filled with this riff-raff. As the SA and the regular warders were gradually replaced with the more disciplined but less humane SS, I had no one to whom I could complain. When I did make mild protests to an SA man, I narrowly escaped a beating. He told me that he had nothing against me, but anyone else would have used a club or a whip on me. The SS habitually carried dog whips and long truncheons. According to one guard, they had been trained in their use at Dachau, which had become a centre where all SS prison guards learned their trade. I wondered if the camp were quite the wholesome place the newsreels had described.

Inevitably I sank deeper and deeper into self-pity. Still the worst was to come. I had rarely known such a sense of dread. No point in my asking to see the prison governor or, indeed, the doctor. Any attention from them would prove unwelcome. My fellow prisoners would show their disapproval with violence and curses. That raucous, foul-mouthed riff-raff would know they were the reason for my complaints. Perhaps the worst irony, of course, was that I was branded a Jew by association, suffering not only humiliation from the other prisoners but additional cruelty from the guards.

Only in the dead of night did I know any kind of peace, and even this could be broken by the screams of those who had gone insane or were being punished for some transgression. I lost track of time.

It only dawned on me how much time had passed when I read in the *VB* that the SA leadership was taking its annual leave. It was 29 June 1934. I had been a prisoner for some three months.

It would be misleading to say the events heralded my release, though this was to some degree true. At first I merely thought my luck had changed. Certainly it was a crossroads for Germany and for Adolf Hitler, that night of the 29th/30th, which became known as the Night of Shame for the Nazi Party, the Night of the Long Knives . . .

The summer darkness was warm and rather sticky. The rest of the cell was snoring heartily, grunting, farting, mumbling, a susurration I had come to find almost relaxing, since the noise of sleeping brutes was more reassuring than the noise of wakeful brutes. Our little window was open to let in whatever air there was.

I lay on my bunk enjoying the nearest I could come to solitude, the breeze from the window cooling my skin, when, in the early hours of the morning, I heard a sudden commotion from below.

From past experience I knew the gates to the courtyard were being swung open. Motor vehicles were driven rapidly through. Shouts, screamed orders, as a new batch of prisoners was brought in. I was used to the prison's routine. No inmates were ever transferred at night. The staff went back to their quarters at five o'clock and did not return until seven the next morning. Yet this was clearly a huge shipment of new arrivals!

My curiosity whetted, I got up and stood carefully on the toilet, peering down squarely on to the floodlit cobbles of the courtyard. What I saw astonished me.

Scores of SA men, many of them half clad, as if roused unexpectedly from their beds, were stumbling out of closed, unmarked trucks and cars. They were surrounded by SS officers, evidently prepared for them with truncheons, dog whips and guns, shrieking to confuse them even further. Some prisoners were high-ranking SA officers and they were remonstrating with their captors. Others were drugged or drunk, barely able to stand up. They stood staring stupidly, giving the Hitler salute, some of them grinning as if they believed themselves victims of a comradely practical joke.

And then, from a car, glaring at his guards and murmuring what were evidently threats and oaths, stepped my friend and mentor the great Stabschef Ernst Röhm himself, the Commander General of the SA and, after Hitler, the most powerful man in Germany. He was stripped to the waist, wearing only his uniform trousers and boots. I was tempted to call out to him before I realised this was an inappropriate time. Röhm stood glaring at the SS men, and although I could make out few words I recognised his tone. He approached the SS commander, giving the Hitler salute, demanding to know the meaning of this outrage.

The SS man was not at all cowed. In fact, he began to yell. 'Traitor. Wretch. Assassin. Pervert!' These words were very distinct. My heart sank as I saw my protector shrug his naked shoulders in resignation and stride towards the admission door.

That was the last I saw of him. A number of his men fell in behind and followed him, but others were made to wait outside. I saw them kicked and belaboured as they were arranged in ranks against the far wall while the waiting machine guns were uncovered by the SS. Were mine the only sympathetic eyes observing that scene? I would never know. The guns began to rattle, mowing down brave men who had fought for their nation in the trenches and the streets. They had been prepared to die for their Führer. Now, as they fell, they cried out his name, saluting him, still believing they were sacrificing their lives because of their loyalty to his cause. 'Heil Hitler!' they cried as the bullets tore into their flesh and vitals. 'Heil Hitler!' I felt sick. Clothes were shot to ribbons; blood and entrails smeared the cobbles.

The noise became so great it woke my cellmates. I jumped down and returned to my bunk. I knew in my bones that what I had seen endangered me. The men began to wake, too frightened to look out of the window, yet asking one another questions. I pretended to sleep, but I was very much awake and alert. What on earth was happening?

I would, of course, learn later that Hitler, Himmler and the rest had struck like vipers at their own comrades, taking them as they slept, relaxing at Bad Wiessee, the popular lakeside resort, for their annual vacation.

Röhm and his officers had stood no chance against the vicious SS. Hitler himself had led the attack, wakening Röhm and feigning disgust at what he found. The rest is a matter of record. As my cellmates returned to sleep, I listened to the muffled sounds of gunfire as one brave soul after another fell to the bullets of Himmler's murderers. It went on all night and into the morning. Routines were forgotten. We were neither roused from our bunks nor offered breakfast until around nine o'clock, when we received hunks of bread and nothing else. Not one of us, including myself, had the courage to ask what was going on. But I had seen it.

Later I learned how Röhm held out, refusing to take his own life, refusing to sign a confession. Gregor Strasser did the same, until they shot him through the bars of his cell, not even daring to look him in the eye. Otto Strasser had already escaped into exile. Dozens of others, not even attached to the SA, were murdered in a variety of ways. Father Stempfle, who had written the bulk of *Mein Kampf*, was shot and tortured in the forests outside Munich but would eventually die in Dachau. Von Papen escaped by a whisker, as did a whole variety of patriots whose only crime was to put the well-being of the German nation before that of the Nazi Party. Even UfA's boss Hugenberg lost all significant power. Not one dared resist the Hitler faction.

Thereafter, all their words and deeds became so much play-acting for the benefit of the American press and those ordinary German citizens who had placed their faith in Hitler. They had stepped irrevocably on the road leading to Armageddon, the triumph of communism and the wretched, unheroic death of a leader who had lost his immortal soul on that last day of June 1934.

I had witnessed the death of Nazi chivalry.

FORTY–SEVEN

Ironically, the betrayal of the SA was to bring me temporary good fortune. Stadelheim and Dachau became so overcrowded their staff were refusing more prisoners. Those accused of nothing could at last be released.

The very morning of the anti–Röhm putsch, we were marched down to the discharge room. The place was in total confusion. Some of us received our bundles of clothes and other personal possessions but many did not. I was given the bag belonging to a Jew who I knew for certain had died of a heart attack a few days earlier. Only by demanding my own, when I saw it in the hands of another inmate, could I get what was mine, including my precious American passport. Then I was rushed with a dozen others past blood–spotted walls to one of the trucks which earlier had carried SA men to their deaths.

After an uncomfortable ride back into central Munich, we were deposited outside police headquarters and told to report there. But I did what many others did. I drifted into the side streets and cautiously made my way home. The main roads seemed to be full of speeding cars with darkened windows. I had to assume this was associated with what I had already witnessed in Stadelheim. Some terrible business was afoot. Had Hitler and his people been over-thrown by Goebbels and Himmler? Certainly the SS seemed very much in control.

Instinct told me to avoid my flat. Instead, I huddled in my unsea-sonable overcoat, which at least presented an appearance of respectability, then I headed for Corneliusstrasse, for which I still had the keys. I desperately hoped the SS had not preceded me.

I arrived as the market was waking up, slipped through the gath-ering, incurious shoppers, hearing to my astonishment the sound of Signor Frau's barrel organ, as sweet and clear as I had last left it. Was my Zoyea still dancing for the crowds? I wanted so much to see her. Thoughts of her, as well as of Mrs Cornelius, had sustained me through those terrible nights. But it was dangerous. If my protector was imprisoned, who else might they be rounding up?

Curbing the impulse to reacquaint myself with friends, I at last found myself standing outside the door of my old apartment in Corneliusstrasse. It had, of course, been used by the SA and was a likely target for the SS. There was no need for my key. The door had been bashed in, and I could pass through easily. I saw no SS men here now, only evidence of a hasty search everywhere. I climbed the stairs like a sleepwalker. Still no guards. I had been so happy in that little flat. I had rarely felt safer. Today I was only frightened. The flat's door was broken down, pulled shut but hanging on one hinge. I saw signs of violent struggle. Gunshot holes in the walls. The whole place was in disarray. A brooding stillness hung over it. For a while I had to pause to gather my wits. I suspected the SS had done all they were going to do, but it would still be wise to leave as soon as possible. I went directly to the hiding place under the sink and there, to my relief, was everything I had left. I took a little 'coca' to steady myself, hid the rest in the lining of my over-coat and then packed everything into a Gladstone bag. On the floor of the closet, still on their hangers, were my summer clothes. The pockets had been turned inside out, but the suits were still in good condition.

I was able to bathe and shave in cold water, and soon I was fully restored. A human being again. I looked my old, dapper self, thor-oughly urbane. I turned my wide-brimmed hat at a tilt, put a light overcoat over my shoulders, even twirled a cane. My papers, plans and pistols were in the bag, together with some changes of clothes. I had money in my pocket. And I had one thought paramount in my mind: to get out of Germany while I could. Everything in me shrieked to make that escape.

Driven more by instinct than reason, I slipped from the flat and made my way to the station, taking side streets wherever possible. I had no plan and very little sense of what I was doing except following old impulses. I did not dare take a bus, certainly not a taxi. I was in a kind of trance, not sure I was really free, still 'in the nightmare', that state of refined terror which I had felt in Odessa, in Oregon and later in Cairo. I felt I had a target painted on my back.

I believed I was liable to random attack at any time from blood-thirsty, savage men. Men without reason who would howl after me, throwing stones and bricks at me, hunting me down until they caught me then tearing me to pieces. I had seen them do it in the past, during the Civil War in Russia and to those who would not conform in the United States. I remembered the pogroms in Odessa when I had seen anonymous Jews hunted to their deaths by overzealous Cossacks. I had already been mistaken for a Jew more than once in Stadelheim and could not risk it happening again. The only difference was that my face was well known to hundreds of thousands. I was a famous film star. I was even more vulnerable.

I tried to console myself. My privations had changed my appear-ance considerably. I had lost weight. The shaving mirror had shown me gaunt, hollow-eyed and exhausted. Nobody, I told myself, could possibly know me now. But I certainly did not much look like a confident and prosperous citizen.

Using such a circuitous route, avoiding any street with a policeman or SS man in it, I did not reach the main railway station for some time. Slowly I formed a plan. I was not a wanted man in Italy. I must try to make it back to Rome. There I could either throw myself on the mercy of Signora Sarfatti or hope to explain myself to Il Duce. I was sure he would at least give me his protection if he heard what had happened to me. And if nothing else, I was in a position to let him know what was going on in Germany. Mussolini could be cruel to those he took against, but he could be generous even to his enemies.

On the great concourse I went straight to the foreign desk and purchased a ticket to Rome, via Innsbruck and Milan. The man at the desk seemed surprised but gave me no problem. He seemed nervous, even ill. I tried to chat to him. He would not reply. His eyes were everywhere but on his job. When I turned to find the appropriate platform, I was astonished. The station was teeming with black uniforms. The SS were out in strength, inspecting documents, searching no doubt for those who had escaped them the night before. My SA credentials were less than useless to me. The sooner I got rid of them, I thought, the better it would be.

I looked to see if the Rome Express was in. Then I realised it made no difference. I could not afford to be caught and have my bag searched. Even as I looked, more and more SS troops piled out

507

of trucks and buses into the station. Children and women were as liable to receive their attention as adult men. Feeling strangely invisible, like a ghost, I quietly melted again into the busy backstreets. This was not the right time for me to leave the city, but I no longer knew what to do. I could not seek out Mrs Cornelius. She was already, by many accounts, in Berlin. She would help me. But how could I get to Berlin? There must be more than one SA man out there wearing civilian clothes and wondering how he could escape to his home town or village. Anxious not to attract attention, I walked slowly back the way I had come. Every so often a car might slow down, and I even heard men cursing at me, but they had other prey that day and drove on.

Back at the Viktualienmarkt the sound of the barrel organ grew louder, reminding me that I might find help there. The warm bustle of the shoppers around me was a comfort. I saw no SS people, just the occasional ordinary Bavarian policeman, stolid, friendly and as reassuring as always. Here was the old, familiar Munich. Everything appeared exactly as it had been for centuries. Sure enough my friend Signor Frau was turning the crank of his organ, his son was rattling the box through the audience and little Zoyea was dancing like an angel along the kerb. If anything she was more beautiful. Tears welled in my eyes as I knew a tremendous surge of relief.

My bag at my feet, I stood on the edge of the pavement watching her. For three months she had been a memory, a fantasy. So powerful was the reality of her presence that I did not trust myself to approach her. For half an hour I stood there, hoping she would see me. I was now completely clean-shaven. Every so often her brother would come by with the wooden collecting box, and I would slip a coin in. He frowned at me once or twice but did not recognise me. It was not until Zoyea's eyes met mine that I knew she remembered. She paused in her steps and blinked. Yet almost immediately her expression hardened. No doubt she blamed me for abandoning her without a word. Perhaps she knew I had been in prison and suspected me of being a criminal. I had never found an opportunity to tell anyone what was happening to me. After all, I had left my flat thinking I would be away for an hour at most. She could not have known anything. Wishing to avoid any sort of scene, I ignored Zoyea and her brother and went up instead to her father, raising my hat.

'Signor Frau? Do you remember me?'

The Italian recognised my voice first. His eyes widened in amazement as he recalled my face. 'Herr Peters! We heard you had gone to Hamburg and returned to America! We were rather surprised.' He stopped himself. I think he was going to say that he would have expected me to let him know. Instead he asked, 'Did you enjoy your visit?'

'I was never there. I was abducted. Only today did I manage to get free. It's a long story, my friend. You must know I would have got word to you all if that were possible. I'll be glad to tell you everything, but at present I have nowhere to live. Perhaps you could see your way to letting me sleep in your organ shed for a while? A mattress on the floor is all I would need.'

'You have money?' He felt in his pocket.

I raised my hand. 'I have no money problems. But I do not want to stay in a hotel . . .'

He seemed to understand. Without another word he signalled to his daughter. She came over reluctantly, scowling at me. He told her to take me back to their house and not to ask questions. She was to show me his bed and allow me to rest there. He would be home at the usual time.

She objected. He refused to hear her. 'I know you think Herr Peters has done you a wrong, Heckie, but I know he will explain himself. I want you to be a good Christian girl and do as I ask.'

She obeyed with poor grace. Lips pursed, eyes hard, she jerked her head for me to follow her and stamped off in the direction of their home. As we walked I talked to her. 'I did not desert you, my dear, I promise you that. I had no chance to speak to you before I left.'

'You could have written,' she said. 'We had been due to go to the cinema. We missed a Tom Mix film. And a Ken Maynard.'

'But the police arrested me,' I said.

Her eyes widened. 'The real police? What had you done?'

'Nothing, I promise. You know how confusing it is in Munich these days. Many innocent people are caught up in the troubles. A case of mistaken identity. Just like your family being mistaken for Jews. Do you know about this?'

'You are a communist?'

'I am innocent of everything. But they decided to arrest me, anyway.'

'That's impossible,' she declared. 'Nobody is arrested for doing nothing. Are you an enemy of the state?'

'Of course not.'

She was unconvinced. As we walked, she fell silent, her brows drawn together. 'A swindler?'

'I am not a criminal. The authorities made a mistake.'

'That's what the burglars say in the films,' she declared. 'We used to laugh at them. I am innocent! I did nothing!'

'But you have also seen the films where the man is innocent of murder and everyone declares him guilty,' I said. 'Don't you remember the Masked Buckaroo story where I helped young Jane Gatling's fiancé prove his innocence? That's what happened to me.'

'But you *are* the Masked Buckaroo!'

'They refused to believe me.'

'And they found out you were innocent?'

'I was released this morning. I have been in the Stadelheim fortress!'

With deep concentration, she studied my face. At length she seemed satisfied. Suddenly her little hand had slipped into mine. She asked if I wanted to go to the pictures that evening. I smiled. If possible I would be glad to go. She told me disapprovingly it was almost impossible to see American cowboy films now. The cinemas were showing nothing but historical subjects. I asked if she had seen any Gloria Cornish movies, but she had not. She had seen Fräulein Cornish on the posters outside the cinema, however. She was special-ising in musicals. 'All these English actresses are singing nowadays.' What of my own films? I asked. She said there had been one or two 'Winnetou' talkies, but they had not appeared in the big picture houses. The public didn't care for the new ones. She read the movie magazines. Musicals and historical films were all the rage. That's what were being made now. I should learn to sing, she suggested. Even in America the cowboys were all breaking into song. Gene Autry had thrown Tom Mix and Tim Holt into the shade. She seemed aware how my acting career, at least in Germany, was over. She might even have guessed I was lucky to be alive at all.

I could not tell her the SS were busy with their lists, arresting anyone suspected of being sympathetic to Röhm or Strasser. If I was on a list, I consoled myself, I was probably noted as having been arrested already. I now realise I actually attracted less attention than before the putsch. But prison had made me timid.

At last we reached the mews, arousing the curiosity of the few little children playing there. My Zoyea opened the door of their house. I quickly slipped inside. She took my bag upstairs, came down again and politely offered me a cup of coffee. With some relief I sank into Signor Frau's easy chair. Zoyea busied herself in the kitchen. When she returned with the coffee and a piece of cake, I told her as much as was wise about my wrongful arrest and imprisonment, my sudden release. There was still some danger of my being arrested again. I hoped it would be possible for me to sleep in their organ shed until the authorities stopped showing such a keen interest in the railway station. My plan was to get to Rome as soon as possible.

Zoyea agreed enthusiastically that Germany wasn't the same as it used to be. She herself hoped to go to Italy soon. Her father had talked of leaving. He thought life might be better for them in Spain. His cousin worked there and was full of praise for the new government. Here in Munich, she said, there were far too many gangs wandering the streets, attacking anyone they did not like. She herself had been insulted more than once, as had her father. As I knew, people called them Jews or worse. What had Italians had to do with killing Jesus? Surely Hitler must do something about all this. I agreed. If he did not, he would soon lose the goodwill of the German people. At that moment, however, I did not know if Hitler were imprisoned, alive or dead.

'But those SA were among the worst.' Zoyea doubtless repeated what she had heard in the market. 'With them gone things will be better. Were you an SA, Herr Peters?'

How could I reply, having seen the murder of so many of our most disciplined and responsible SA at the hands of the SS? Was it only last night? I replied that the SS were no better. They merely had smarter uniforms.

Privately, I suspected Himmler would prove a snake in the grass. Even if Hitler survived he would have more to fear from Goebbels and Himmler than he ever had from Röhm. Röhm had put loyalty above everything else. I was sure Himmler planned to replace Hitler as Führer. I recalled the story of Macbeth, reflecting how applicable it was to the present situation. When you spilled your own people's blood in the name of your cause, you inevitably began the destruction of that cause. For every honest soul murdered in Stadelheim and Dachau, a high price would be paid.

Nowadays newspapers find it fashionable to emphasise the Jewish lives lost in the camps, but people seem to forget that thousands of Nazis died in them, too, not to mention millions of innocent Slavs.

Once the camps were established, the path was determined; they had to be fed. In the end, as at the beginning, it scarcely mattered who went to feed the monster. The Jews, Gypsies and Slavs were the most easily available, but we should remember that many Americans also died in Dachau, together with Czechs, Austrians, Hungarians, French and Italians. Were these not equally innocent? The monster is not a gourmet. The monster does not care what blood type he drinks. The stronger the blood, the better. The more blood, the merrier. Blood is worth more by the pint than wine, yet he drinks it as his master's machines drink oil. He is voracious. And just as his master creates more machines to drink more oil, so he creates more machines which will drink blood.

How easily the human monster becomes an addict for money, power, oil or blood or all of those things! When will the day come when neither blood nor oil will be needed to fuel the ambitions of men? My machines would be powered by light. My cities would fly through the cold, pure ether. They would leave all those addictions behind them. They would be inviolable, incorruptible and eternal.

I did not get to the bed. Even as I chatted with Zoyea and sipped her delicious coffee, I fell into a deep sleep and did not wake up until twilight with a smiling Signor Frau and his somewhat unsmiling son standing over me. Signor Frau had food waiting for me, a tender veal cutlet with new potatoes and green beans. He had cooked it for me himself. He was delighted by my praise. Once, he said, he had cooked in his uncle's restaurant. He was curious to learn what had happened to me but remarked that I must always remember he required no explanation from me. I had saved his living, he insisted, and that meant that he was for ever indebted to me.

I disagreed. I had done so little. Yet still he was firm. I would sleep in his bed tonight and then tomorrow. If I still needed shelter, he would see what he could do. I did not resist him. The luxury of clean sheets and a soft bed, together with the prospect of a breakfast as good as my supper, made me weaken. No sooner had I managed to reach his room, strip off my clothes and lie down, than I was asleep again.

I awoke after a bad dream, but I felt well rested. I heard sounds from below, and when I went down I found Signor Frau seated at the table reading a newspaper while his daughter prepared a breakfast of eggs and cheese. The smell of the coffee was enough for me to accept their invitation and join them. The boy had gone off to buy bread, said Signor Frau, and would be back soon.

I looked at the headlines. Hitler had clearly not been a victim. The newspaper was full of the plot against Hitler, foiled by Himmler and the SS. I had never seen so many lies published in such density. Röhm was described as a pervert and a glutton, who had plotted with exiled communists, Strasser and other traitors, both in and out of the Nazi Party, to assassinate Hitler and his closest allies and impose a reign of brute terror on the German people. This had been averted by some loyal SA men joining with the SS to nip the plot in the bud. The Führer had been disbelieving that so many could be disloyal, yet even now was considering clemency for Röhm. This was an obvious lie, of course. I guessed well enough what had happened to Röhm in Stadelheim. I shuddered to think what would have become of me had I remained so close to him. I would realise later how much my friend had protected me. When the lion is abroad, as Röhm often pointed out, the best place to hide is in his cage.

Though I had to be guarded, I told Signor Frau I had reason to believe the SA were involved in no such plot. Any plot was almost certainly from the right of the party. In a whisper, Signor Frau begged me to tell him more, but I could not. I did make it clear that I was not at present a wanted man and was only avoiding the SS in case they associated me with Ernst Röhm. The Stabschef had been a good friend to me. He had been made a scapegoat by Himmler.

Frau had never himself trusted Himmler. 'That little mouth of his looks like an arsehole,' he said. 'And we all know what comes out of an arsehole.'

I had become used to such coarseness in the prison and did not find his language as offensive I might have done.

'With all the commies and Sozis rounded up,' he continued, 'they're now squabbling among themselves. And God help those of us who are caught between them.'

I said 'Amen' to that and together we drank a small cup of very strong coffee.

Frau had decided not to go out to work that day. He would keep me company. I think he felt protective towards me. I feared for him. I asked him if his action was wise. People noticed if you did not keep to routines. He saw the sense in this and reluctantly agreed.

'But you will be careful, my dear friend?' I assured him I would. These days I was nothing but cautious.

When the boy came back with the bread, his father suggested he have his breakfast before readying the barrel organ for the day's work. He begged me to stay in for the day and rest. I should have his bed again. He would be out until the evening, and I would not be inconveniencing him. I could stay here as long as I needed.

I promised I would. Those months in Ettstrasse and Stadelheim had exhausted me. I fell asleep in the chair listening to the wireless. I had not even put on my boots.

The news on the radio was full of Hitler's dismay at SA treachery, which could easily have led to civil war in Germany. It was miserable stuff. The German stations talked of communist perils and of the aliens among us who must be expunged. No wonder poor Signor Frau was worried. He was one of those aliens, as, of course, was I.

How strange, I thought, to consider yourself a loyal German citizen yet be regarded by everyone around you as some sort of interloper.

I was awakened around noon by the wireless, which I had not turned off: more news of Röhm's so-called attempted putsch, reassurances that all the 'criminal elements' were being rounded up and that the threats of civil war or a socialist takeover had been averted. I knew I had best lie low. Signor Frau could continue to give me shelter for a few days, so I would eventually be able to make it back to the railway station and be on my way to Rome. I had been given a timetable with my ticket. If I did not go via Vienna, I would have to change in Innsbruck and Milan since no express ran from Munich, but I had no fears of Innsbruck, even though a nascent Nazi Party had been established there for some time. I wondered what had happened to Otto Strasser and the others who managed to be out of Germany. Had they escaped in large enough numbers to regroup in a friendly country and plan a return? Were they in Prague or Vienna? Possibly they had headed for Innsbruck. Or was there something I didn't know? How big was the Black Front? How many 'secret' friends did Röhm and the others have among the Nazis? What chance did my old mentor have of escaping Stadelheim and getting to safety?

To be truthful I was more than grateful to Signor Frau for his insistence I remain in his house. The organ-grinder's mews was a wonderful sanctuary after my terrible imprisonment. While I still felt the need to flee Germany, until it was safe Frau's was the best I could hope for.

I was left alone in the mornings when the whole family set off for the market, and I ate well in the evenings when they returned. During the day I read whatever newspapers Signor Frau had brought in the previous evening or looked through Zoyea's vast store of film magazines. A number of them had published pictures of myself and Mrs Cornelius. I was surprised how I had altered in those few months. When not playing Winnetou, I had been sleek, urbane, and conventionally handsome. Now I had a gaunt, wolfish look. I was much paler, probably from the poor nutrition. The terror and discomfort I had experienced had caused my cheeks and eyes to sink and even my mouth seemed thinner. Eventually, with a change of circumstances and improved diet, I could be restored to my old self, but it would take some time.

After about a week I agreed to go with Zoyea to a local cinema to watch two very miserable films, one of them American and the other Austrian. *Letty Lynton* featured the depressive Joan Crawford and *Liebelei* starred Magda Schneider, Wolfgang Liebeneiner and Gustaf Gründgens. Directed by Max Ophuls, it lacked much of his familiar gaiety. Zoyea seemed to enjoy both of them far more than I did, and at that moment, certainly, it seemed the magic had gone from our visits to the films. The best part of the programme was an episode of *The Wolf Dog*, starring Rin Tin Tin Jr. I could not help but be reminded of Hitler's own 'Wulf', his Alsatian dog.

The trailers did not promise much better to come. The newsreel was mostly about how the New Germany was restoring herself and consisted chiefly of shots of noble workers with spades and handsome men in uniforms. A smiling Chancellor hosted a party for equally happy foreign diplomats. We watched dutifully before leaving.

As Zoyea had already told me, the cowboys had all but disappeared from the screen. Tom Mix and Buck Jones had been replaced by women's melodramas. *Letty Lynton* was a great success in America when it first appeared there, but in Germany it never had much popularity. The public mood was for more upbeat musical comedies and costume dramas. Glamorous English actresses continued to feature, though Gloria Cornish was clearly not getting the work she deserved. I would have preferred a musical or historical film to the gloomy, suicidal miseries we were forced to endure that evening.

I longed to restore my relationship with my little girl. Her companionship and admiration meant a great deal to me. But I was no longer the glamorous figure she had known while she was becoming a teenager. I was starved for female company. If LeBrun had been right, Mrs Cornelius had returned to Berlin to work for UfA there. By now, with her instinct for trouble, she might have departed from Germany altogether, moving to London or New York.

I was still nervous about leaving the little house and always glad to return to the comparative security of the mews. The SS and Gestapo were everywhere on the streets. Munich had been a stronghold of the SA. I jumped every time I saw a uniform and, having already suffered from prejudice in the prison, I was depressed by the notices in the shops which emphatically said they were German-owned and did not serve Jews. Ironically, I learned to avoid these places, as did the Fraus. Anyone of Mediterranean appearance was in danger of being insulted. Twice I was shoved into the gutter by men who voiced their disgust of me, and once I came under close scrutiny from the police who assumed that the dark-eyed girl with me was my daughter. But after a couple of weeks there were fewer SS about. Their action against the SA was clearly running down.

At the end of a fortnight I told Signor Frau I had better try to leave again and continue on my way to Rome. He was sympathetic. He himself was thinking of going to Madrid where he had relatives. Everyone said how wonderful life was in Spain these days. Was I sure it was entirely sensible of me to try to return to Italy? You never knew when they would turn on you, he said. The Spanish were more easygoing. There was not the same prejudice. Why didn't I wait and see what he and his family decided to do. Then perhaps we could travel as a group? All he was waiting for was a letter from his cousin.

But I was growing anxious. I asked if I could leave the bulk of my papers and so on with him. Was there some place which would be safe? He suggested the old 'show organ' was as good a place as any to stow them. So I left my things, including my pistols, plans and other papers, with him to hide as he thought best. I decided to use my Spanish passport and travel as Señor Gallibasta, a Spanish tradesman. When I had settled again in Rome, I would ask him to send my possessions on to me by registered post. I took only one set of important plans and a couple of notebooks. The bulk of my cocaine I hid among the books. I did not wish to give a potential enemy any suspicion on which to arrest me. I would be able to replenish my supply once I was in Rome.

Though she was affectionate, Zoyea was disappointingly unmoved to hear I was leaving. Clearly I was no longer her glamorous hero, the sharer of her fantasies. I felt a pang, of course, but was not surprised. I, too, felt a lessening of emotional involvement. I had begun to think more and more of my lost Esmé. Why had she betrayed me so? Even now, from that scored and stained celluloid, she threatened me. If I had not tried to protect her, I should never have been compromised by Prince Freddy. I knew such women are always dangerous. I would not miss Zoyea as much once my sex drive subsided. My attention remained focused on potential danger. A threatened animal has little time for romance. Frau's little house was too small for all of us, and the boy remained, if not my enemy, certainly no friend.

What had happened to Kitty? Had she been arrested or had she followed the morphine back to Berlin? I was still in some danger from her. Half tempted to accept Signor Frau's invitation, I knew I had no work in Spain and no one of any influence to help me. Rome remained my only immediate hope. From there I could make my way to London and pick up my money from Mr Green. Major Nye would help me contact someone of authority at the War Department. The English were bound to see the virtues of my designs. I prepared to say goodbye to the Fraus.

It goes without saying how grateful I was to the whole family. I knew I could trust them completely. They had a long history of keeping their mouths shut, of never betraying their friends. In helping me they had put themselves in a certain amount of danger. I did not wish to endanger them any further.

They would not accept direct restitution for their Christian decency, so discreetly I left an envelope of money on the little mantel and, wearing a smart summer suit, raincoat over my arm, carrying a small leather suitcase purchased at my request by the boy, I set off again for the railway station.

Restored in mind and body, if not exactly at ease with my situation, I reached the station to find it returned to normal. A few SS men and regular policemen stood around, but they were bored, not looking for anyone in particular. Approached by members of the public, the SS men would salute courteously and point out civil officers as the correct authority to help them. The boy had found out the times of the Innsbruck train for me. I went directly to the platform, presented my ticket and found a first-class compartment near the middle of the train. The express was already sighing and huffing, preparing to leave. I settled myself in the luxury of a comfortable seat and opened my copy of the *Völkischer Beobachter*, knowing an almost thrilling sense of relief as the train released its air brakes and began slowly to shunt away from the platform.

I was not yet free, of course, not by any means. I still had to fear the railway officials who could cause me trouble if they wished, but it would not be very long before we reached the border. In Innsbruck I would change trains for Rome, via Milan. I relished the coming pleasures of the Eternal City, of seeing my old friends again and hopefully restoring my relationship with Il Duce. I could put all my terrible experience behind me. I had been lured from my original path, which as a young man I had determined to walk. I recalled how I had sketched out my life plan, determined to serve the cause of mankind. My true vocation was calling to me again. After a diversion, for which I had paid dearly, I was now about to return to my vocation as an inventor and engineer.

The newspaper was full of Nazi triumphs. All reference to my old mentor Röhm had disappeared. Hanfstaengl's art publishing firm, which had advertised portraits of the Nazi leadership, no longer mentioned him. The Stabschef had vanished from all official pictures, as if he, Strasser and the others had never existed, as if the world I had known was a false memory. What must rank-and-file Nazis make of this, let alone the German people?

I was not to be alone in my compartment for long. As the train drew away from the station, a well-dressed young man flung his bag on to the seat across from me and plunged in after it, stripping off his grey overcoat and throwing it casually on to the overhead rack. He raised his hat to me before putting that on top of his coat, reached into the side pocket of his bag, took out a book, a spectacles case and a newspaper, placed them on a seat, then lifted his luggage to sit it above him. He was tall, almost femininely good-looking, white-haired, a little on the plump side.

I murmured a 'Good afternoon', to which he responded in an exaggerated Prussian accent, asking me if I minded his smoking. We were in a smoking section. I had no reason to object. I had rather hoped to keep the compartment to myself for a while but was reconciled, merely feeling that faint resentment one has when one had been the first to settle. I agreed with him that the weather was pleasant. He, too, was going the whole way to Innsbruck. He had not bothered to book himself a sleeper, he said. Had I?

I had not. Indeed, I had not thought to do so, since my whole intention when I bought my ticket was simply to get away from Germany as soon as possible. I had not considered my comfort at all. My mind had been set entirely on escape.

So I agreed with my travelling companion that it was an unnecessary expense, since one so rarely slept on these overnight trains, what with the stopping and starting, the shunting and the clank of the couplings being taken on and off. I folded my newspaper. Was he travelling to Innsbruck on business or pleasure?

A little of both, he said. He was a decorative arts importer and had some factories to visit in the Innsbruck area, but he hoped to go to the theatre and enjoy a few restaurants while he was there. And myself?

Milan, I said. I would change at Innsbruck. I saw no reason to offer him any further details.

Was I an enthusiastic train traveller? He lifted an eyebrow in mild enquiry.

I told him that I had a great love of trains, but it had been some while since I had had the opportunity to take one.

He nodded. Had I ever used the Orient Express?

I said I had never made its whole journey but hoped to do so one day.

'I have always had a strong desire to take the Orient all the way from Paris to Constantinople,' he confided. 'I mean to Istanbul, of course!' He added how much he had always been fascinated by luxury trains. He regretted the Bolshevist Revolution, which denied him the famous Trans-Siberian express to China. Did I have any desire to see the East?

I had seen too much of it, especially Cairo and Istanbul. I had no immediate desire to return. He was impressed. What did I think of Istanbul and Kemal Atatürk? Had I ever met the man they called the architect of modern Turkey?

I admitted that I had been in his company more than once. His attempts to bring his nation into line with contemporary Europe were commendable, but he could never hope to achieve his ends while he allowed the Moslem Brotherhood to control politics there. Islamists would be the ruin of the region.

'And why is that, my dear sir?'

'Because your Mussulman is endemically tied to a system of beliefs rooting him thoroughly in the past,' I said. 'In this he has much in common with your religious Jew.'

He was intrigued and wanted me to expand on my theme. It had been so long since I enjoyed the company of intelligent and sophisticated adults I felt almost grateful to him. I explained how Jesus had been a progressive, educated as a Greek and familiar with Greek thought. Mohammed, however, had been a conservative, creating his creed in direct opposition to Christ's teachings. Indeed, his creed had been in reaction to Greek thinking. Christ had preached love and peace while Mohammed had preached war and aggression. Mohammed believed religious faith should be spread by the sword, whereas Christ believed in passive example. Mohammed had taken religion back to the Old Testament, to those same prejudices and dark practices of the Jews. I had no time for Zionism, but if the Jews required a homeland they should be allowed to make one on condition that they give up religion and practise only secular politics.

He found this a novel and amusing idea. 'You are yourself, I take it, of a non-religious disposition.'

I had not yet re-embraced the Greek Church. I said I had a Catholic background with several churchmen in my family. In those years I breathed a different air. Many considered religion to be backward and old-fashioned, and in my love of science I was still inclined to a form of agnosticism.

He, too, had been raised a Catholic, he told me, but had been attracted to Lutheranism before turning to an uneasy form of scientific materialism. 'These days we place all the faith we used to place in God into science and the arts.'

I agreed. I was not sure they were complete replacements, but who could doubt that the Old Testament was responsible for many of the world's troubles.

Yet, he asked, I did not feel that about the New Testament?

'It is the first modern manifesto! It set the tone for the next two millennia. Our present philosophical and political debates all revolve around it. Europeans and Americans are products of it, even if we have no religious faith at all.'

'You believe our purer Christian notions are corrupted when they are brought in contact with Jewish and Moslem ideas?'

'Many of our great philosophers have thought the same.'

520

'Nietzsche would go further. As would young Heidegger. Religion is not, then, a mere crutch, a means of escaping the stark realities of life and death?'

'I understand how we must have some reassurances, some sentimentality.'

'Some hope? You think Messrs Hitler and Mussolini give us that?'

'Indeed I do.' I answered with perhaps exaggerated enthusiasm. I was no longer sure that Hitler's vision had very much to offer me, but Mussolini remained my ideal. He had led the Italians for over a decade and showed every sign of leading them for another two or three at least. I kept the rest of my opinions to myself, not having the measure of my companion. Privately I came to believe Hitler's vitality was neurotic. Mussolini's was masculine, wholesome, natural. At that time I remained convinced he could still rebuild a new Roman Empire whose power would extend across Europe and the Middle East. One day he might even lay claim to the British Isles again, to the kingdoms of the Franks and the Goths. After June 1934 Nazism renounced its place in history. Mussolini had never turned on his own, never poisoned the roots of his cause. No doubt if Mussolini had not allied himself with Hitler, Italy would be again the greatest nation in Europe, perhaps the world. I had not yet completely formalised my ideas at that point. My gut feelings told me what my mind tells me now. Those last glimpses of Röhm as he went to his death, the knowledge of what had been done to Strasser and the others, had all educated my heart, teaching me to trust no one in Germany. Even this personable Prussian with his aristocratic manners could be a Nazi sympathiser. Until I was safely out of the country, I would keep my ideas to myself. Another lesson I had learned in prison.

Herr Stross, as he introduced himself, was himself somewhat circumspect about both the Chancellor and Il Duce. I suspected he was of a liberal, perhaps faintly socialist, persuasion. The present atmosphere in Munich could not be very appealing to him. At length he opened a day-old copy of *Le Figaro* and began to read. After a while, when the steward came to offer refreshments, I asked if I might borrow the paper. He passed it over with an apology for its age. He had received it from a friend in from Strassburg. He had discovered one could no longer buy most foreign papers in Munich. All part, he supposed, of the government's attempt to stimulate German internal trade. 'German goods for German patriots, as they say.' He smiled and ordered a cup of coffee and a piece of caramel cake. As the steward sliced the cake for him, he asked if I thought the new economic policies would save the country.

I had only read the *VB*, which, of course, was wholly behind the German Chancellor. Still cautious, I echoed the editorials I had read, evidently to my companion's boredom. He found it hard to concentrate on my remarks.

Later we took dinner together in the restaurant car. Outside it grew dark. We passed through summer mountains. Some of the trees were already turning gold. Settled among them, little picturesque towns and villages raced past. The steady progress of the train, the wine with the meal and the brandy afterwards, relaxed us both. We became more free in our conversation and had begun to exchange jokes by the time we got back to the compartment where Herr Stross offered me an excellent cigar. As southern Germany went by, a blur of velvet and diamonds, he told me of his family, his married sister who now lived in Wisconsin, his parents who themselves had so longed to emigrate, but were now too old. I spoke of my own childhood, transferring my past to Chicago and Wilmington, describing how I had been schooled privately, by friends of my mother, and had then been fortunate enough to get a scholarship to Johns Hopkins, where I received my masters in science at an early age. Then I volunteered to fight in the War as a flyer, but not through any dislike of Germany. I had known an enthusiasm for airships and planes from youth. I had chiefly joined because I had lost my childhood sweetheart, my greatest support, encouraging me in everything. My inventions had been originally for her, Esmé. I had flown my first makeshift plane only a few years after the Wrights had flown theirs! The machine had been ahead of its time. One used one's body as the airframe. I had another similar design I was currently working on. I told him a little about my one-man airship, describing some of my other inventions to him until, looking at his watch, he remarked we would soon be at the border.

When Herr Stross excused himself and went down the corridor to the WC, I took advantage of his absence to pull down the blinds and sniff a little 'coca'. It had been some time since I had felt so happy in the company of a fellow spirit.

In a while Herr Stross returned and removed his passport from his bag. He had seen the customs and immigration people a few compartments away, he said. I readied my own passport.

A few minutes later the door opened. Two smartly uniformed officials, wearing swastika armbands, appeared at our door and saluted.

I told myself that I was imagining that they were looking suspiciously at me. With a display of confidence, I smiled up at them, presenting my papers.

FORTY-EIGHT

The German officials were not particularly friendly as they gave my papers close inspection, but they were polite enough before passing on up the train, leaving the customs men to check Herr Stross's bag as carefully as they checked mine. As the train moved slowly across the border into Austria, I saw little but a few street lamps, the occasional pulse of a distant headlight; then we had stopped again. The Austrian immigration and customs people were as efficient as the German, and when they saw I was going on to Rome asked fewer questions of me than they asked of Herr Stross.

The train under steam again, I settled back into my seat to sleep. For the first time in many months, my anxiety was melting. As dawn became a golden pink, we reached Innsbruck. Shaking hands, Herr Stross departed to find a taxi while I hurried between platforms to catch the Milan express. We were away shortly after sunrise, and this time I sat in an Italian train. A cheerful, upper-class Italian family made me welcome, offering me newspapers, food and general hospitality, as if I were visiting them in their home. I took a plate of sausage, settled into a seat and read the *Popolo d'Italia*. It was a pleasure to enjoy uncensored news.

For the second time in my life I passed through Austria. This part of the country reminded me of Switzerland, when Esmé and I had hurtled through the mountains, driven by Annibale Santucci in his wonderful Lancia. Lying cheerfully in the busy bosom of the Bertolli family, rarely able to see out of the window, I read every newspaper and magazine they possessed. Oblivious of excited children, complaining well-dressed gentlemen, and elegant, apologetic women, I read about a dynamic, optimistic Italy and her vital, masculine leader and rediscovered my future.

At the Austrian border customs routines went very casually. We were soon on our way into Italy. The sunlight shone on rivers and streams, and the whole landscape was somehow richer and warmer. Cheerfully, I welcomed the Italian officials when they boarded the train. I returned their salutes with a smile and a raised arm. The Italians were far more easygoing than the Germans or Austrians. One officer even returned my salute as he glanced through my Spanish identity papers and was almost apologetic when he asked if I had obtained my entry visa. He could not find it in the passport. I told him I was returning to Italy. I was not aware I needed a visa. I had not needed any special documents for Germany, when I had come in. I had not realised that since Hitler's coming to power the Italians had grown wary. They were taking large numbers of refugees. Dissident Nazis, socialists and communists had flooded into Italy since 1933. Anyone entering the country from Germany was under special scrutiny.

The immigration men were regretful. I would have to disembark while they found out if there was any reason why a Spanish citizen could not at least pass through Italy. They warned me I might not be allowed to stay, but rather be asked to go home via France on the Florence train. In Florence I could catch the Barcelona express along the French coast. Even here, however, they were not entirely sure if the French authorities would allow me passage. These were troubled times. Someone really should have warned me about the visa situation. Had I checked with the Spanish consulate in Munich? Possibly I could apply for a temporary visa while a more permanent one was arranged. I had better come with them to their office. They would help me with my luggage. Someone would make a phone call. Sadly they could not delay the train on behalf of one passenger.

I heard all this with considerable dismay. I had no wish to go through France, where I had unresolved problems with the law. Barcelona was one of the key communist cities of Spain. If Brodmann caught up with me there the Red Spaniards would certainly turn me over to the Russian authorities. I begged the officials to let me go on to Rome, where I had many Italian friends and contacts in the government and where I could easily sort out my papers. They had their rules. They would help me in any way they could, but they had few choices. It was obviously inconvenient for me to go all the way back to Munich. Perhaps someone there could be telephoned.

In another desperate nightmare I was escorted into a police car and driven through shabby streets to the unprepossessing police offices. At least I was not placed in a cell. They were, indeed, very kind to me, bringing cups of coffee, sending out a call for their chief in Brennero asking him to come to the office as soon as possible, looking up the telephone number of the Spanish consulate in Milan. They did everything they could to put a call through to someone from whom we could take advice and perhaps get the number of the Spanish consulate in Munich. Keen supporters of Il Duce, they were flattered by my reiterated enthusiasm for their country but were not very great admirers of the new German government, describing the Nazis as thugs and homosexuals. They knew Hitler had been directly responsible for murdering Röhm and his men. They were the first people I heard calling that savage butchery 'the night of the long knives'. Hitler was a neurotic heading a court of grotesques. An evident feminine homosexual and hysteric, he had turned on his own kind and made an enemy of the Catholic Church, persecuting priests of every persuasion. Hitler had perverted Fascism, produced a travesty of Mussolini's philosophy and politics. One of the Italians, the genial, red-faced, middle-aged Captain Cavori, also mourned what was happening in Spain. Primo de Rivera lacked the character of Mussolini. Now my poor country was likely to become little more than a satellite of the Soviet Union. At least Hitler had averted Bolshevism and civil war. He was not sure that was possible in Spain. Only Italy was truly stable.

I spent all day and all the next night in Brennero. Allowing me to keep myself clean and change clothes, the officials fed me well and worked hard to make my stay comfortable. I resisted drawing on my personal friendship with Mussolini, especially after what I had been told, yet the fact remained that neither the Spanish Embassy nor the Germans could help me get to Rome. I must return to Munich and obtain the appropriate visa or get myself a ticket for Barcelona and try to obtain a visa there. If so, I would have to give them my papers and have them returned to me once I got to Spain. I would not be allowed to disembark from the train en route.

I dared not give up my papers or reveal my US documents. I had little money left. Any further travel must be made in third class. I thought this hardly fair since I had originally purchased a first-class ticket. Once more the officers were courtesy itself. Regulations did not permit me to stay any longer in Italy. They advised me to go back to Vienna where the Spanish Embassy would doubtless accommodate me.

I was in a terrible position. I had good reason for not contacting the Spanish Embassy. I was not even sure how good my documents were, since they had been obtained in North Africa. Gallibasta was by no means a common name. They could easily check on me. My Spanish was imperfect. If I told them I had been living on Majorca, my connection with Stavisky might be revealed. Reluctantly I decided it would be better to take the Vienna train and use my American papers. In Vienna, at least, I would be safe from the German authorities. But where would I find money? Perhaps Otto Strasser could help if he was still there?

After a short, uncomfortable stay in Italy, I found myself in a third-class carriage crowded with peasants and workers who stared curiously at my suitcase and my smart clothes. I was immediately stereotyped as a Jewish travelling salesman. They had seen the police helping me aboard and decided I was some sort of crook forced to leave Brennero in a hurry and returning to Vienna to rejoin my kind. The Austrians among them showed the most appalling prejudice, far worse than anything I had experienced at the hands of the Germans. I attempted to explain how I was a Spanish citizen, an engineer. Those who could understand me at all merely laughed and told me to shut up. Some even made attempts to open my case until I threatened to call the guard and report them to the police when we arrived at the next station. Not for years had I experienced such wretched humiliation. The journey now became a horror. When we eventually pulled into Vienna, I disembarked quickly, my clothes stinking of working-class sweat and worse.

Unless Fiorello was still there, I knew no one in the Austrian capital, but I found some cheap lodgings not far from the station. In the privacy of a room reeking of cheap sausage and sauerkraut, noisy from the street outside and the business of the other lodgers around me, I tried to take stock of my situation. Without the appropriate papers, I was not going to get into Italy unless I could find someone to smuggle me over the border. I would have to forget Rome as an immediate destination. By living frugally, I could survive in Vienna for a while. I wished now that I had stayed with the Fraus and travelled with them. At least in their company I would have made some sort of modest living. Now it was too dangerous for me to go back to Munich. I had burned my bridges. Every instinct told me I would not be safe until Hitler was certain he had rounded up all his enemies. My association with Röhm was enough to damn me. The likes of Baldur von Schirach would perhaps even put two and two together. I had been released almost by accident, because I was not associated with the old Nazis. If I was picked up again, I was not likely to be so lucky.

I became deeply despondent. I had no friends in Vienna. My only acquaintance, Herr Stross, was in Innsbruck and not likely to be staying long, even if he could have helped me. Budapest would be even worse for me, and the only person I knew who had been living in Prague, but might now be in Vienna, was Otto Strasser, himself even more of an SS target than I. Perhaps if I stayed for a while in Vienna I might be able to pick up some information or learn a way of getting into Italy which would not involve me obtaining a visa. Could I somehow contact my cousin Shura with his useful connections with Stavisky? Of course, this association was a two-edged sword. The newspapers said Stavisky was in France. Shura would be with him. But I was still unwilling to risk travelling in a country where I could be arrested at any moment. Perhaps it made sense to go back into Spain, as the immigration people had suggested? I could try to contact Signor Frau's relatives or possibly make my way to Majorca, where I still might find acquaintances.

With my money dwindling, I spent two or three fruitless weeks in Vienna, trying to find work and contacts. I found neither. The country was in another economic crisis. They had no work for locals, let alone for a desperate foreigner. Everywhere I went people assumed I was a Jew. This alone was enough to weaken my morale. While Austria had no official policy towards Jews, decent people did not want to employ them. And no matter how often I assured prospective employers that I was Spanish, they were too blinkered by their prejudices to believe me. They disliked the Spanish almost as much as they hated Jews. Only Jews offered me work, but at such disgusting terms I was bound to refuse.

Eventually, having failed in two attempts to cross the border, I had no choice but to work for a Jewish motor mechanic who put me to repairing the cars of his richer co-religionists. I had never in my life sunk so low, but it paid for food and accommodation over the workshop. I stood this humiliation until the winter, when I could not afford fuel for the stove in my lodgings and was having to wear one of my summer suits over the other. I could not buy winter clothing, and the Jew had no cast-offs to offer me. The cold was the final blow. I could take no more. Deciding it was probably safe now to risk returning to Germany, I determined to throw myself on the hospitable mercy of the Frau family while I decided what to do. Anything was better than having to bite my tongue and suffer under the ignominy of the Jewish heel.

Desperation and circumstance made me rationalise the situation. Perhaps I should have stayed in Vienna or tried to get to Prague, but the only friends I had were the Fraus. So one January morning, not long after my thirty-fifth birthday, I took a bus from the working-class Jewish Quarter and began my journey to Munich.

The bus was packed with returning Germans who had been visiting relatives for Christmas, and I felt I would be anonymous among them. Almost with relief I found myself looking forward to seeing Munich again. Ironically, it proved almost as difficult to get back into Germany as it had been to get into Italy. The authorities were carelessly suspicious and unwelcoming, in spite of my insistence that I was Spanish and not Jewish, that I had a job and a home in Munich. Eventually, I think, they reasoned that no foreign Jew in his right mind would be trying to get into their country and let me in. By early February, no doubt looking considerably older than my years, I arrived back in Munich and went immediately to the little mews where I had left the rest of my belongings. I was anxious to get some winter clothes and the small amount of money I had left there. I arrived late in the evening around the time I knew the Frau family went to bed. No lights were on in the house, and I was hesitant to wake anyone up, but I was too cold to follow my conscience. I rapped loudly on the door, calling out to Signor Frau. Eventually the Fraus' next-door neighbour came out. He told me that they had left a month ago.

I was distraught. Where had they gone?

'I don't know. They had some trouble with the police. He thought it best to visit his cousin. Could that be in Spain somewhere? His boy was beaten up a couple of times. You know how it is. We're thinking we should leave too if things get any worse. It used to be a good living here, but it's drying up.' The Fraus had not left a forwarding address. They had relatives in Madrid, he knew. They had packed everything in a wagon and planned to make a living on the road. He suspected the whole mews was being watched intermittently by plain-clothes men. All Italians, indeed all foreigners, were under suspicion.

'Don't ask me why. We've always been law-abiding. Munich's no

529

longer what she was, my friend.' Everyone was willing to turn against you, to brand you a Jew if it suited them.

Horrified, I thought of my property. Had the Fraus left it behind or had they taken it with them? I had left some of my things in their storerooms. Was there any way of getting in? The neighbour suggested I come back in a couple of days, when the landlord would be there. He was bound to let me have a quick look for any possessions I had left behind. The neighbour's impression, however, was that the place had been cleaned out. Anything the Fraus had not been able to pack into their wagon, they had sold or given away. The organ had been carried in a trailer behind the main wagon.

I reflected that I might have crossed paths with my old friends on their way to Italy. How I wished I had accepted their invitation to journey with them, to take my chances with their little travelling show. In Frau's company, at least, I might have persuaded the Italian authorities to admit me.

Tears came to my eyes as I walked away from the door. I no longer had even my old sanctuary. I did not dare stay on the street for long. That night I slept as best I could in the old organ shed, with rats and other vermin for company. The show organ was there but most of my possessions were gone! They had been stolen. My plans. My passport. My pistols. All I found were a few drawings and some bits and pieces of clothing. I folded the plans and put them in my pocket. I had no choice but to take them with me. In the morning I knew I had no alternative. Humiliating though it was, I would go to Prince Freddy Badehoff-Krasnya's apartment, throw myself on his mercy and beg him for help. My hopes, my dignity, my very identity had been stripped from me. What had seemed impossibly dishonourable to me, even as a prisoner in Stadelheim, now became my only alternative. I would take whatever charity I could from that vicious blackmailer and pornographer.

The next morning I roused myself from the dirty straw I had slept on and tried to clean myself off. I had spent my last money and could not afford a cup of coffee. I had expected to pick up my remaining marks from the envelope stowed with my papers and anticipated being fed by the Fraus for a few days. I could not quite remember where Prince Freddy's house was. I was dishevelled and dirty and twice was stopped by the police as I wandered around Munich trying to get my bearings. My Spanish passport reassured them. Not until the afternoon did I find Prince Freddy's tree-lined suburb. I rested on a bench in the park until I was moved on with threats and curses by a policeman who voiced his disgust at my appearance and what he assumed was my race. I knew that soon I must be picked up for vagrancy, now a serious crime in Germany. I had welcomed the new law when it was introduced. Now, as a vagrant, I might be recognised at police headquarters and find myself back in Stadelheim. I was so tired and hungry, the world began to seem phantasmagoric, unreal, at once deeply dangerous and euphorically safe. Nothing which was to happen to me in the next several hours would seem strange.

Nearing twilight, the air grew cold and the light dim as I approached the house. Not very long ago I had accepted such luxury as Prince Freddy's as normal. Now I received suspicious stares from the few people I passed. I was too tired to care what they thought as I trudged up the avenue rehearsing in my mind how I would approach Badehoff-Krasnya. He owed me something. I hoped the sight of me would at least embarrass him and make him take me in. I was obsessed with the thought of warm clothing. I imagined I could get an overcoat from him, a bowl of hot soup, some socks, a bit of sausage. Some bread. Even more than the food I wanted some kind of recognition, for I was beginning to doubt my own identity.

At last I saw the house and walked up the drive, feeling the sharpness of the gravel under my thin soles. No lights shone anywhere. Had Prince Freddy fled with Kitty, perhaps to Hungary?

Like an automaton I rang the bell. It echoed into silence. I knocked and the house responded with that hollow, dead sound which tells you a building is empty. I knocked again and again, until the last of my strength had gone, and then I sat on the step and wept.

Later, hearing soft footfalls in the drive, I looked up. A tall figure emerged from the twilight. He wore a well-cut leather coat, a heavy fur hat, a scarf. I envied him those clothes. He must be very warm.

Approaching me, the man paused, his voice soft, enquiring, even sympathetic. It took a moment for me to realise he was speaking Russian. My spirits leapt. And then fell. Could it be Brodmann?

'Dimka, is that you?'

Dimka? Few any longer knew me by that name. I must indeed be hallucinating! The last time I had seen this man was in the deep Sahara. By now he must surely be dead. Logically, if he were dead then I too was dead and a friend of the dead. Not only did I no longer care if this were true, I welcomed it. Shaking, I rose to my feet, my arms outstretched.

'Kolya! Oh, Kolya. It is so good to hear you again. I can't believe it's you. Are we dead?'

'Not at all, Dimka dear. Speaking for myself, I am very much alive. Dimka, Dimka. What has become of you?' He was standing over me, his hands reaching out to embrace me, to lift me up. When I saw his smiling face, I began to weep. 'I suspect I feel a little more alive than you at the moment.'

I clung to him. 'Oh, Kolya. You are an angel of providence. I can't believe it. Where have you been? How did you find me?'

His laughter was soft. He was a little older, of course, but just as handsome, just as aristocratic in every movement he made. I had never loved any man as much as Count Nikolai Feodorovitch Petroff.

'Where have you been?' I asked again.

'Oh, Berlin, most recently. Before that I was in Prague for a while. And, of course, Libya.'

'What are you doing in Munich? Are you a friend of Prince Freddy's?'

'Not exactly,' he said. 'My people told me you were here. This place has been under surveillance. I have a new job these days, working for the government.'

'What are you doing? Intelligence work?'

'You've guessed it, Dimka dear.' He reached a black-gloved hand to the lapel of his coat, which he turned back to display a small badge. He seemed at once embarrassed and amused. 'I'm in the special branch of the political police. I was recruited last year. The Russian section.'

I grew dizzy with relief. I had a friend in the police, a new, powerful ally.

I let Kolya guide me back down the drive to the street. It was almost dark. Cars and trams went by on the distant main street. I smelled woodsmoke and pines. As we reached the kerb a car drew up. Kolya bent to open the back door. 'I wonder if you'd be good enough to get in, Dimka dear. We've been wondering if you were still in Munich.'

I obeyed him. The car was comfortable and warm. I saw only the back of the driver's head. 'Where are we going?'

'Gestapo headquarters. There are some questions we need you to answer for us. We'll give you some coffee.'

'Thank you,' I said. 'Would there be any chance of a sandwich, too, perhaps?'

Of course, I had gone mad. Kolya, unlike all the others in whom I had invested my love and trust, save Mrs Cornelius, would never betray me. But he did have an onerous job to do. He had been commissioned to seek out his fellow Russians and compile dossiers on them for his masters. Better than anyone, he knew who the émigrés were and what their politics were. He knew where to find them. He knew the political colour of their groups, the cafés and restaurants they frequented, the magazines and books they published. Earlier he had been sent to interrogate Prince Freddy, after the 'Mongol' had been rearrested for peddling pornography. His predecessors had looked over all the blackmailer's materials, including films, photographs and the Frau Oberhauser scrapbooks. Little of Badehoff-Krasnya's career was unknown to Kolya. His job was to investigate everything and everyone associated with such people. Kitty was in Budapest. She had been released after she betrayed both her master and myself. I had wanted to make her my new Esmé, but she secured her freedom by telling the Gestapo what they wanted. She had accused me of molesting her at an early age, branded me a pederast and a paedophile. Her statements were shown to me. She had told them I was a Jew and informed them of my Russian alias. When Kolya had received my dossier, he had known me immediately. But he had not known how to save me.

He told me all this in the interrogation room at Gestapo headquarters. He treated me kindly. I had drunk the promised coffee, eaten a sandwich, smoked a cigarette. He played no games with me. He let me see my massive Gestapo dossier, mostly taken from Prince Freddy's own records. He explained how it had been compiled and why he could not possibily intercede for me without immediately condemning himself to a concentration camp.

'The evidence is too strong, Dimka dear.'

'But Kolya, I am accused only by a dead woman, her mad daughter and a discredited pervert. What crimes have I committed? What proof is there?'

'Under the old German laws, these accusations would need to be proven beyond a shadow of doubt. Under the new German laws, you have committed several crimes not even listed here. Since the Führer cleansed the stables after the Röhm putsch, the party has become increasingly intolerant of deviance, both moral and racial.'

'Kolya, you know I am not a Jew. You know my origins are purely Russian.'

And in this, I fear, he did betray me. He turned away into the shadows, out of the circle of light created by the overhead lamp. 'I do not know that, Dimka,' he said. 'The evidence is against you. I have explained how, if I were to deny that evidence, I would also be in jeopardy. However aristocratic my blood, I am still, in the eyes of the racialists, an inferior Slav. What I have had to do to convince them of my family's Nordic origins! We are descended from the Russ who came from Scandinavia to establish their leadership over the Slavs.'

'But that is also my blood,' I told him. 'I am from Kiev. My father counted the blood of the Russ in his veins. Our family is as ancient as any on this continent!'

'I believe you, Dimka. But now, if you cannot prove you are not Jewish, you are guilty. Your recent privations have added to that impression. And then there is your circumcision, your connection with Stavisky and his gang, with Odessa.' He sighed and poured me another cup of coffee, offering me a chocolate *Lebkuchen* on a plate. 'My hands are tied, Dimka dear.'

I accepted the cake and ate it greedily. Many months had passed since I enjoyed one as good. I washed it down with more coffee.

'They have evidence that you did not merely interfere with Fräulein Kitty, Dimka. They know about that young Italian girl, Hecate Frau. You were often seen with her. Some of my colleagues suspect the Fraus were part of an Italian spy ring as they have vanished. We were hoping you knew where they were. And then you apparently had some sort of association with Röhm. Baldur von Schirach helped us there. He seems to have exonerated you from the worst suspicions. These investigations, of course, were not mine. I came rather late to your case. They gave it to me because of your Russian origins and that's the only reason we are sitting here together. Otherwise, some unsympathetic stranger might have arrested you.'

'I did nothing with that little girl. She was sweet. She was my friend. We had a common interest in the cinema. The family were supporters of Mussolini. They were not subversive in any sense.'

'Aha. The cinema.' He raised an elegant eyebrow.

'Kolya! Kolya! How can you think such things? We went to cowboy movies together. I was lonely. She loved the cinema. Prince

Freddy blackmailed me into that pornography. I hated it. You know how much I hated such things, Kolya. You yourself saved me from my captivity in Egypt!'

'Well, one or two of my colleagues believe the theory that a victim ultimately becomes a predator. My superiors believe you might have been part of a circle of Jewish pornographers and pimps luring young girls into prostitution and making filthy films. They see you as a rather stereotypical Jew. And I must admit your career, at least superficially, verifies such prejudices –'

'I am not a Jew, Kolya. I am not a pornographer. I am not a seducer of little Christian girls! My God, this is like a comic strip from *Der Stürmer*. You speak of me as if I was invented whole by Streicher!'

'I know, Dimka. But the evidence is so much against you. Frau Oberhauser's accumulation of press cuttings – the airship scandal, from which, you'll recall, I was able to save you. In the Paris newspapers you were already characterised as a Jewish swindler. Much as I would like to speak up for you in that matter, I would not be believed. My bosses have already read the files. Their minds are made up.'

'My letters to Göring offering to help in the rebuilding of the German air force! My one-man airship? What about those? I could still help them build it. The ship would be ideal for spying out enemy territory.'

'I think those letters to Göring might have been a mistake. You know how these people take others' ideas for their own credit. That's the whole game these days in Berlin.'

'Then what can you do for me, Kolya?' I nursed the last inch of coffee in my cup as if I would never taste coffee again. 'Am I to be returned to Stadelheim? What will my sentence be?'

'There isn't much I can do, Dimka. But we are having this conversation in the hope that I can find some way of helping you. You will not go to Stadelheim. And you will not be sentenced, as such. Your chances of release are, I will admit, very slim. If you can tell me anything to mitigate whatever fate they plan for you, you must let me know.'

'What kind of thing?'

'Well, if you have other associates who knew Röhm for instance. You are acquainted with Hanfstaengl, yes? And that traitor, Busch? Perhaps you know where left-wing Jews might be hiding. Any left-wingers, in fact . . .'

'I have no other friends left in Germany. Hanfstaengl would not help me. I did not know Busch was a traitor. What did he do?'

'He was arrested in the early days. When they released him, he tried to go to Vienna, no doubt to broadcast lies about his incarceration. He was arrested again, tried to escape and was shot, it seems. These other friends of yours . . . ?'

'The friends I had were neither Jewish nor left-wingers. They were good Nazis. Even the journalists sympathised with Hitler. I hate socialism and communism, Kolya. You understand that, surely. Look what they have done to our country!'

'Drug dealers, then. Your cocaine habit . . .'

'It wasn't a habit, Kolya. I have had no cocaine for months. The last I got was from Prince Freddy. He lured me into his confidence. I have been able to buy none since.'

'You had no other contacts in Munich? What about the priest, Father Stempfle? Didn't you know an SS man called something like Zeuss?'

'I met Stempfle once or twice. In a beer cellar. I never knew any SS men, I swear.'

'No one at Simplicissimus?'

'Nor at the Flashlite.'

'This Gloria Cornish, your co-star, as I understand it –'

'She abhors all drugs. She was a platonic friend of Herr Göring's. She was forever trying to get me to stop. Do you know where she is now?'

'She might have gone abroad. What can you tell us about her? Her name has been linked with a Major Nye, an English intelligence officer.'

'She hates politics. Nye was infatuated with her, that's all. I can tell you nothing else. I would rather be shot now than compromise that wonderful woman.'

'Don't worry. She is in no danger. There was that other Englishman you worked with. Desmond Reid. Was he not a critic of the government?'

'Well, he was no friend of communism. He might even have thought Hitler soft on Röhm. I have had no contact with him since the last picture we made together. I thought he had left the country.'

'He's in Czechoslovakia. Help yourself, Dimka! Give my superiors something.'

536

'Have I no right to defend myself against Prince Freddy's false accusations? Against Kitty's?'

'Unfortunately Prince Badehoff-Krasnya died in Dachau two weeks ago. He had apparently bribed guards. Sadly he was due to be transferred to better conditions in the Belsen camp. Some relatives had interceded for him. As for Fräulein Kitty, I am told she is no longer in custody. Released from the women's quarters in Stadelheim, she took a train immediately for Budapest. I'm afraid they have left you high and dry, Dimka.'

'Contact Mrs Cornelius. Believe me, she is a good friend of Hermann Göring. She will speak for me.'

'I will get in touch with her personally, I promise, assuming she is still in Germany. I am not sure how much good even a well-connected English actress can do for you, however. Have you any other friends?'

'Hanfstaengl is in Berlin, too, isn't he? Some American journalists.' I named Morgan and Grisham among them. 'And Miranda Butter. I don't know what has happened to her.'

'These are all foreigners and, apart from Miss Butter's, their words are not worth very much, I fear. She was Mussolini's mistress for some years and arranged to have many of his articles published in America. Then something happened and she came to Berlin. She was infatuated with Hitler. But Hitler already had people who were buying his articles. She returned to New York last December. Do you know if any of those journalists had reason to oppose the policies of the present government?'

I could not absorb so much information, if information it was. 'I have not been in touch with them recently. They were not, I will admit, all entirely enthusiastic about Hitler. But this was ages ago, when I first arrived in Germany. Surely they have long since been replaced by their editors?'

'Anything you can think of will be useful and will in turn let me do what I can to help you. Miss Butter, I think, is beyond reproach. Since returning to America she has written the most laudatory pieces about the Führer. Some have appeared in the *New York Times* and the *Washington Post.*'

'Then surely she can speak for me,' I said. 'I had no idea she was linked with Il Duce, but we were good friends. A word from her would make a difference, wouldn't it?'

Kolya lit two cigarettes and handed me one, tapping my dossier with his index finger. 'We have already interviewed her. She did not speak very well of you at all. She seems to think you a liar and a charlatan who deceived Mussolini with some hare-brained nonsense. She considered you a turncoat, perhaps even an Italian spy. Your behaviour towards her in Rome was apparently not the most gentlemanly.'

Were all women by nature so treacherous?! 'It was not I who betrayed her, Kolya. You know how loyal I am to my friends and lovers. I had no choice. That Jewish bitch Sarfatti was forcing me to be her lover. I was being blackmailed.'

'She mentioned your association with that Jewess.' He flicked through the dossier, pausing now and again to read. 'You seem to have made yourself rather vulnerable to blackmail, Dimka.'

'I have trusted too many people. Oh, Maddy! Maddy!' Suddenly I found myself breaking down. My body began to shake. The tears started in my eyes. I could not stop weeping. The tiredness, the humiliation and now this awful shock had taken control of me. How could Maddy, whom I had helped see the political light, who had been my pupil in the ways of the world, betray me? Now I knew she had been Mussolini's lady friend for so long, much was coming clear. At every turn I had been deceived.

'Shoot me here, Kolya,' I sobbed. 'My life is meaningless. All I had hoped to do for the world, all my loyalties, all my loves and friendships, are ashes. I am robbed of any future. My future, too, is ashes.'

'Unfortunately, Dimka dear, I have no orders to shoot you.' Kolya came to put a hand on my shoulder. 'Let us continue. There must be something we can think of between us.'

But there was nothing. My mind was numb. A little later Kolya had me escorted to a comfortable cell and gave orders to let me sleep as long as I needed. He said he would return the next day, and we would put our heads together.

The following afternoon he supplied me with sheets of paper and a pencil. He asked me to write down the names of the journalists I had known and what I thought of their political attitudes, their failings and weaknesses. Then he asked me a little about Mussolini and the work I had been doing with Il Duce. What surprised me was that he did not show a great deal of interest in my association with the Italian leader. Either Maddy had told them everything or Kolya did not wish to compromise me. Even when I mentioned

538

some of my inventions, Kolya did not pursue this avenue. I suspected his masters knew nothing of my real strengths and weaknesses, and he was not going to compromise me any more than I had already compromised myself.

I filled the sheet as best I could.

By the following morning Kolya had finished his interrogation. He had been unable to find anything which would stop the inevitable. I asked what was to become of me. He spread his elegant hands. I would soon be taken to Dachau under indefinite arrest. He would do what he could for me. I would be given a violet armband marking me as a privileged prisoner, an *Ehrenhäftling*, with an individual cell. If he saw any chance of obtaining my early release he would put matters in motion. Meanwhile, he suggested I reconcile myself to my fate. After all, there were worse ones, including that from which he had rescued me several years earlier.

I wept when he eventually left my cell. I feared in my heart that I was forsaken for ever, and I would never see him or any of my beloved friends again.

FORTY-NINE

Surrounded by heretics, I did not become a Mussulman. I know
their object was to make me one: to reduce me from so much to
so little would have been their ultimate triumph. In their hearts they
understood they had sterilised themselves. To ensure a predictable
present, they betrayed their future. Because they were incapable of
creativity, they hated any true visionary. To order a world too complex
for them, they imposed their simplified pattern and then demanded
that the rest of us conform to it. We had to substantiate their infan-
tile certainties. If we refused, we died. Died in the Soviet Union.
Died in the Third German Reich. Died in Italy and Spain and
Hungary. They died because they refused to deny their experience.
They died for justice and the truth. The very men and women who
elected to record the complex variety of the world, whose very
subjectivity provided us with crucial information, were punished
until they conformed or, if they refused, were silenced. I had thought
the powers wanted information. I was misguided. They wanted only
silence. That which refused to confirm and conform to their views
was destroyed. But the evidence for the evidence they could not
destroy.

I do not have my own cell, but I do have the violet armband.
This means that I do not suffer what some suffer, but many of my
fellow prisoners are suspicious of me. They think I might betray
them, I know. The truly privileged live in the *Ehrenbunker*. They are
German politicians, businessmen, aristocrats and high-ranking clergy-
men. You would not be happy in their part of the camp, my anti-
Virgil explains to me. *Alles in Ordnung,* he reassures me. After a while
I become a *Lagerschreiber,* because my German is not so bad. I report
directly to the *Rapportführer,* who is distant but not especially cruel.
What I see others suffering makes me thankful, even though I have
no business being in this camp. When I came in the new *Zugang* I

was taken to the Gestapo in the *Politische Abteilung*, the political department. Their offices were near the main gate (*Arbeit macht Frei* in wrought iron). I was not tortured much, but the screams of the others encouraged me to good behaviour, as one of the Gestapo men, who appeared to be a friend of Kolya's, joked. I explained that I was a personal friend of Göring's and they remarked on how many friends he had in Dachau. You should form a club, they said. But, of course, there can only be two of you in the club at any one time. Three or more and you will be severely whipped. I became used to their mysterious laughter. Now I know to fear it.

1935. Halfway through my alloted span. I pray for ——. I search for ——. How can I communicate with ——? Is —— still with us? Or has —— become senile, still clinging to —— power, refusing —— son his true birthright. The Old Testament is a record of vengeance and cruelty, of unearned authority and unchecked ferocity. Here is the singular God, the only God, the reduced God of Zion. He is not the God I worship. I worship the Trinity. God the Father, Christ the Son and the Holy Ghost. Jesus, Mary and Joseph. Michael, Gabriel and Lucifer. I worship the Trinity. Here, too, there is no complexity. There is only one truth, one answer.

My sinister anti-Virgil instructs me in this singularity, guides me from a dark forest through an inferno into purgatory. Abandoned in my exile, like Dante, punished though I commit no crime, I am alone, longing for my sweet little Beatrice who has been taken from me not once but three times.

For some reason I am put into the émigré hut. There are five huts for 'politicals', two for 'anti-socials' and one, isolated by barbed wire, which is for a *Strafkompanie*, those enduring punishment, usually permanent. Invalids, such as there are, are in the *Revier*, the hospital hut. There are five guard towers, each with a machine gun. The cookhouse is outside our compound, together with the *Revier* and, of course, the SS quarters. Our food is brought in every day in large containers, handled by privileged prisoners like myself. We assemble regularly in the *Appellplatz*, for roll-calls and punishment parades. Fifty thousand of us can be in the *Appellplatz* at one time. From this leads the *Lagerstrasse*, about three hundred metres long, which is lined by poplars planted by the prisoners. On either side of this wide road are the blocks, the huts, and between these runs a *Blockstrasse,* about ten metres wide. There are thirty-four blocks, either lettered B to C and D to E or given odd numbers from 1 to 29, if on the right, 2 to 30, if on the left. All are of wood, originally painted white, standing on cement slabs about ninety metres long and ten metres wide. Then there are the quarantine blocks to which all new arrivals are brought, to be assigned a hut or a work party, or possibly sent on to a subsidiary camp, perhaps to be transported elsewhere. Special treatment is reserved for men in these separate blocks. Every ordinary *Wohnblock* has two sections, of more or less equal size, each with its own entrance. Each part consists of two dormitories, which we call *Schlafräume*, and two day rooms, which we call *Tagesräume*. There is also a latrine and a washroom. We call each dormitory and day room a *Stube*. Each *Stube* contains room for fifty-two prisoners but this will change as more and more are brought in. When I arrived we each had a little cupboard for our personal effects, and even had a stool each in the *Tagesraum*, where we could sit at the table and read or write, if we wished. We had a big stove in the centre of this room and even racks for our shoes. We look back on those days with a kind of nostalgia. Now even some day rooms have bunks in them and new inmates are not given cupboards or stools. These inmates are taken to the north end of the camp to the disinfection buildings, near the angora-rabbit farm which is one of the SS businesses, intended to make us self-funding. Mostly red triangles, the politicals, work there.

Sometimes visitors are brought to the camp. Himmler himself often attends. The huts, both residential and service, have pictures on their walls. They remind us of what we are missing. They are predominantly landscapes and scenes of Bavarian life or framed homilies such as 'Self-conquest is the finest victory'. Some prisoners are cynical about such slogans, but I take them seriously, as I must do if I am ever to be freed. I will not become a Mussulman. I have seen the camp museum. Here, too, visitors are brought. It is an elaborate affair. There are plaster models supposed to represent all types of prisoners. There are also photos. The models and photos show typical communists, Social Democrats, various German statesmen, now in disgrace. They are 'before' and 'after' photographs, especially of former dignitaries who are shown first in their public uniforms, when they were in authority, and then in their striped convict clothes. In the criminal section you see all types, many with hideous tattoos or scars. But of course the largest space is given over to the Jews. Photographs and dioramas show them stealing from their own kind, as well as their German neighbours, bargaining with decent

Bavarian housewives, giving false measure and so on. Often visitors are shown live prisoners, especially those of a grotesque physical disposition. Himmler is anxious to convince foreigners or churchmen that the camp isolates only the worst elements of society. The atmosphere of the camp, they are told, is firm but fair. Many of the prisoners are grateful for the improved food and shelter they receive as inmates of Dachau. If a prisoner dies, he is decently cremated and his ashes returned in an urn to his family. This privilege, of course, is reserved for German nationals, even though many are blackmarketeers or communists.

There are about ninety guards. I must never be *frech*. However disciplined I am some of them will still spit at me and refer to me as a *Drecksjude*, even though I wear my violet armband. They are mistaken. No Jew is given such an armband. *Brillenschlange*, they say, in reference to my mutilated manhood, I suppose, or sometimes *Brillenträger*. I am no snake. My eyesight is as good as anyone's. Yet I must not contradict anyone. *Ja, ja, Herr Lagerälteste Kapp*, I say. *Ja, ja, Herr Rottenführer Rogler*. I must know every rank, as many names as possible. I must take off my cap and stand at respectful attention when addressed. Any lapse can be punished. Most of the prisoners never see our Oberführer Deubel, the camp Commandant, except from a distance. Occasionally, during a special visit from outside, I stand at attention, watching him smiling and joking with his guests. We know which SS men are fair, which are crooks, which are sadists. Oberscharführer Franz Hoffmann, for instance, is a crook. He makes private profits from his job. He is by no means the only one.

(Someone told me that the camp became even more overcrowded. They said that by the end the whole of Dachau was being run at a profit for the SS men, but in my day this was not, I think, the general rule. Perhaps I was naive, but I still believed I would eventually be freed, that there had been a mistake. I soon learned, however, not to voice these expectations to anyone.)

There is also a chapel in the camp, but prisoners are usually too tired or too cynical to attend services, given by a well-meaning Lutheran who comes in from the town. There are already some churchmen in Dachau when I arrive, but even these do not visit the chapel and eventually services are cancelled 'for lack of demand'. Some of the priests are treated almost as badly as the Jews. Most of them are Baptists or worse. *Himmelhund* is a favourite insult.

As a violet armband I am allowed to go to the West Row and

visit the library, next to the canteen. The books are all in German. Kolya has arranged for credit, from my own bank account, so I can also go to the food shop and buy extras, at horribly inflated prices, some of which I distribute among my comrades. This means I am not as unpopular as I might be.

The food shop is housed in the *Wirtschaftsgebäude*, the largest single building in the camp, which contains all our main service departments including the cookhouse and the showers. It is about two hundred metres long. At each end are two wings, each of about sixty metres long. Here, too, is the *Effektenkammer*, the depository for the prisoners' personal effects, also a clothing shop, stores for linen and shoes and the cobbler's and tailor's workshops, which not all prisoners are allowed to use. In fact, most of the customers are the SS and Gestapo. The administrative building is called the *Jourhaus* and there live the *Rapportführer* and the *Blockführer*. On its first floor are the offices of the *Schutzhaftlagerführer*, where I am usually questioned by Sturmführer Schnauben, and the *Vernehmungsführer*. Usually in the morning, I am sometimes pulled from my bunk and brought to the SS offices. Sturmführer Schnauben asks me such stupid questions. At first I wonder where Kolya is. I ask after him. Schnauben seems to have been up all night. His spectacles are a poor fit. As usual, he pinches his nose.

'Captain Petroff is about his business. He has done his job. He is not SS. Why should he be interested in you now? Would you rather be with the Gestapo? It will be nothing for me to contact their office.' He reaches for the telephone. He thinks I fear the police more than I do him.

'I don't understand why the SS is interested in me.'

'You should be flattered.'

Schnauben is younger than me. His grey eyes are grubby stones. His mouth is a thin line. His cheeks are bright, hard spots of red. He is convinced of his own intelligence. He is a philosopher. He is obsessed with me. I am not sure of his instructions. Is his mission to make me into one of the *unhumanische*? Is that why he chooses never to leave me alone?

Perhaps he simply prefers my company to that of the others he interrogates. Countless times he asks the same questions. He sits me on the chair in his little office. The atmosphere is informal. He lets me cross my legs if I want to. He does not demand I stand to attention or respond in a military manner. 'I am not of the old school,' he says. I am suspicious of this. Outside I can hear the camp stirring.

These boys, he says, they were brutalised in the army and even more brutalised in the trenches. Many of them never stopped fighting. Not the best of us, these boys. But maybe the second best. Yes, I fear they couldn't stop fighting. After the War, it was the only way they knew to defend their freedom. You mustn't blame them too much. The main problem of our KZ system now is overcrowding. I cannot tell you how many of us have complained.

He lifts an eyebrow. 'Do you know anything about eugenics? Exterminating a few failures is easy, but how would you kill a million? Electricity? Come along now, Herr Peters. This is a problem for the scientific mind. I shall be reporting on your willingness to cooperate.'

I do my best to engage with the problem. He has called me 'Herr'. I need his approval. 'You would doubtless have to gas them.'

'What kind of gas?'

I find this conversation disquieting. 'Some sort of cyanide. Whatever gas worked best in the trenches. Whatever is most easily mass-produced. This is not my area of speciality. I work for peace. I work for humanity. Why do you ask me such questions?'

'Perhaps you would be good enough to write all this down for me. I will have some materials brought in. And then there are the bodies. How would you dispose of them? There is a hygiene problem, of course. We learned that in 1917.'

'You would have to burn them, as already happens in our crematorium. It would be the only sensible solution. You couldn't plough them under. It wouldn't be decent. Or healthy. Are you discussing some sort of plague?'

'I'll have more paper, pen and ink brought in for you.' He returns to another subject.

They couldn't stop fighting. Like two dogs you try to separate. One turns and digs its teeth into the nearest flesh. That flesh as likely as not belongs to its beloved master. We raise fierce dogs to protect us from the wild. Then, one day, those dogs go mad. The British thought Hitler and Mussolini were the mad dogs who would save them from the Soviet Union. All our attempts to simplify the world result in further complications. *Oy, meyn Foter, meyn Foter! Frugnecht!* Do not ask me these things. I am an engineer, a visionary. Euthanasia is a mystery to me. It would be unjust to mark my papers *Rückkehr nicht erwünscht.* I am not useless. I am not one of those *unwertes Leben,* not *Uneingeteilte*. My cities are planets. They invest with their gravity everything that is beautiful and sane. My cities are free. Leaving all misery behind we can make a new home among the stars. For Jesus was a Greek. He offered a choice between Israel and Greece. They chose Greece. They were Jews but their neighbours called them Greeks as fortunate Palestinians are called Americans. *Quand tu tiens un enfant par la main et que tu lui dis, 'Regarde la cité!'* Leave the lands of the Philistines to those who still covet them.

Schnauben has an unhealthy interest in my penis.

'Because everyone thought it more sanitary. All the British do it.'

'All Britons are Jews?'

'Of course not, Herr Sturmführer. It is an old custom in many civilised countries.'

'This circumcision? It was forced on you in Abyssinia, was it?'

'Perhaps. I don't know. How could I? I have never been to Abyssinia. I am an American citizen. I am well known as a film actor. I am Max Peters. I played Winnetou. Baron Hugenberg will vouch for me.'

'You are certainly very like Mr Peters. I have watched him myself. *The Masked Buckaroo*. Very clever. No doubt you found this likeness useful to you. But Baron Hugenberg claims not to know you. He is a little under suspicion himself, these days. His religion, of course, as well as his politics. We have interviewed him. He never met most of his actors, he says. You must have powerful friends in the USA, Mr Peters. Who would you like us to write to? The President, perhaps? Some great producer? An industrialist? You cannot give me one name?'

'My disappearance was of interest to the film magazines.'

'Not in Germany. Those films have no audience. Max Peters has vanished from our screens. He has vanished from the memories of all his friends.' This causes him amusement.

I will not become a Mussulman. I must keep my *Brotzeit*.

Sturmführer Schnauben enjoys my mind, he says. Perhaps he desires it for himself. He has an interest in preserving it, he says.

I look at the violet banner on my sleeve. 'What crime have I actually committed? I have never been told. Why would they put me in Dachau?'

His eyes catch the glare from the match as he lights another cigarette. As if he burns from within. He leans towards me. He is suddenly inspired.

'I think of Dachau as the palace of truth, Herr Pyatnitski. This is the home of illumination. Here, we are free from secrets. There is no room for lies in Dachau, the very citadel of freedom where all masks are banished. Here, the human soul knows unquestioning rest.' He grins and smoke curls from his lips. 'Not so, the human body. Strange. It is nearly a year since the blood purge.' He relaxes. He turns away.

I am free from fear. Full of calm, I speak directly. 'Why do you torture me?'

He is dismissive. 'You know this is not torture. You know what goes on in the *Politische Abteilung*.'

'Why do you question me?'

Turning, he frowns. 'Because circumstances permit it. Our roles are chosen for us. Our only responsibility is to play them out.'

'You do this for pleasure?'

'I suppose I do. Could it be that I like you, Herr Pyatnitski? Could I have a "soft spot" for you? For hours I take you away from that hut where you are exposed to every kind of wretchedness and horror. I remove you from the company of criminals and lunatic zealots, the bellowing blows of the guards with their dog whips and rifles. I provide you with relative peace. Do you prefer to shuffle along in the work-gangs? Or kneel before the capos? Do you prefer burial duties? Or work at the *Plantage*? Would you like to help the experiments in the medical wing?' He knows the answer. 'Perhaps I feel a kinship with you? Temperamentally we are the same, are we not? Is that how I know you so well? Like you, I am a visionary. Like you, I am a gambler. Like you, I am disposed towards shadows. I take advantage of accidents. Twilight and dawn, the hours of risk, are my favourite times of day.'

Twilight and dawn are when the interrogations always begin. The hours of risk.

'There are no accidents here?'

'Very few. Very few.' Back and forth he walks. 'I wonder if it is not my job to produce more.' He smokes. 'Still, *Dienst ist Dienst und Schnaps ist Schnaps*.' Sometimes he offers me a cigarette but I refuse. These days they give me headaches. But I accept the coffee. Our own is always ersatz. 'As in war, here the world simplifies to a remorseless code. It is why our camp was created. To sanitise the national kitchen. Don't you feel safe here?'

'Safe?'

'And happy, Herr Peters? Your mouth affords me so much pleasure.'

'It is my good fortune, Herr Sturmführer, to have become your duty.'

'Duty? You misunderstand me. What possible duty is involved with you? I have a duty to myself, perhaps. What you observe is my passion for control. A frustrated passion, I should add. Here, because the overall system is so perfect, I can control very little. Too many people arrive here. Those numbers are beyond our authority. Commandant Eicke does his best. He is a conscientious man. He feels his responsibility. We have national programmes to maintain. We have to deal with the numbers. But they are only numbers. I would rather talk to you than talk to my colleagues about numbers. Numbers obsess most of them.'

He drops his head in reflection. The silver skull on his cap grins at me. The runes of his insignia glare. What is it that reminds me of Wagner? Of *Parsifal* in particular? He believes himself to be part of a holy order.

'We are also a training facility. I am a lecturer here. So I work with what I am given. And I have been given you, Herr Pyatnitski, Herr Peters, Herr Gallibasta. Three in one, eh? A bonus. And if occasionally you reveal something of use to the Reich, then everything is justified, at every level. But will that happen? What do we need to know? You are here for your masquerading. For your deceptions. For your folly. For being a Jew. Thanks to you, I have a busy schedule. I am here to instruct and to learn. You must hope I do not become bored with you. All your life you have had value only as an entertainer. Once I do become bored with you, you will join the living dead. You know that Jews don't have a very long life expectancy here? Shorter than ever. One way or another, whether you continue to walk or not, you will join the ranks of the dead.'

He suggests that I am worthless. But I will not become a Mussulman. I will triumph over my captors. I do not believe they exist except in my imagination. I created them, and so they have no power over me.

'I am not a Jew. I am an engineer. An inventor. An actor. I have played many races.'

'You are mixed up, Herr Peters. Mixed-up blood, mind, reality.' He seems almost sympathetic. 'You say you are an American. Then you say you are a Spaniard. Yet Captain Petroff knows you to be Russian. We have such a good dossier, so many witnesses. No secrets here, Herr Peters.'

'You have the word of Reds or Red fellow-travellers. Why can't you hear me? You have only Count Petroff's word? And Brodmann's?' Mentioning this last is a risk. I have already compromised myself too often.

'Brodmann the Jew? The Soviet agent? What can you tell me about him? This would help me in Berlin. And that would let me help you. Where did you last see him?'

'I saw him in Paris. In New York. Perhaps Cairo. Tangier. Rome. He followed me here. I might have seen him in Berlin. In Munich. He is my nemesis. He hates me. He is implacable.'

'He is Cheka?'

'He reports directly to Stalin.'

'About you?'

'No doubt.'

It is clear to me he thinks Brodmann is my invention. But Schnauben is himself my invention. Through him I survive. He is the phantasm I create to facilitate my journey into the future.

'And he followed you to Tangier?'

'He is a bloodhound. I told you.'

Holding a small, leather-bound notebook, Sturmführer Schnauben jots a memorandum with a slender silver pencil. I disguise my triumph. My trick is to make my file so huge it will become impossible to organise.

'Brodmann tells me you are a cocaine addict. Is that how you came by these delusions?'

He frequently makes this suggestion. Before Brodmann, he credited Prince Freddy with the calumny. Then it was Kitty. Then Kolya. Even Mrs Cornelius has been summoned to support his tricks. I reply as I have always replied.

'I am addicted to nothing but the truth. To science.'

'You were naturally suspicious, eh? Naturally given to sweating day and night, raving in your sleep?'

'You know nothing of this. Given my conditions, Sturmführer Schnauben, it is not surprising. I have been here for – for how long?'

'You have been here for almost five months. I would guess that you have a powerful patron, Herr Peters. Oh, yes. Some old fan of yours in Berlin is looking after you. Someone with the Führer's ear, I'd say.'

Mrs Cornelius! 'I'll be released?'

'No, but you will not be shot. I have had no instructions. Not yet, at any rate. Who is it? Some old lover? We are a sentimental people. You should be grateful. Such a thing would not save you in Russia.'

It occurs to me that Brodmann and Schnauben are negotiating an exchange. Am I to be sent back to Moscow? In return for a captured German spy? I have no means of escaping such a fate. Yet what can be worse than this? When I first arrived the stink gagged me. Only I appeared to notice it. I am too refined for this life. The striped prison uniform and cap were not clean. I had to stand before the SS, holding my cap before me, at attention. Yes, sir. I understand, sir. I had to march at a run. Into the barracks. The straw of the palliasse was becoming rancid, even then. There was a brute with a badge on his uniform. He was the hut capo. To prove himself, he behaved worse than the SS. For the first few days I had a blue and yellow star on my sleeve. It was supposed to be violet. I was shocked. This branded me a Jew. When I was taken in to Schnauben, I begged to have this removed. He made a joke. 'Blue and yellow make violet, don't they?' But he saw the justice of this. The yellow star was replaced with a blue triangle, which meant 'emigrant'. My crimes were still numinous, but my status was improved. Only weeks later, after I had suffered the most vicious and humiliating treatment, did I eventually get my violet armband.

'*White Aces*? Is that what you told me one of your films was called.' He looks back through his notebook. 'I understood that was Prince Badehoff-Krasnya's favourite. You told us you were an officer in the White Army.'

'The Germans were our allies.'

'An American in the Russian Imperial Army?'

'A volunteer flyer. I joined in 1916.'

'At the age of sixteen?'

'Exactly. My father was a dentist. He married a Russian woman. Then we all went home to America in 1910. My father took us to Odessa in 1914. By 1924 we were back in New York. Driven out by the Reds.'

'Yes. And then you went to Hollywood. Your films speak for themselves, of course. Would you be prepared to fly for the Reich?'

'Of course. I sent my plans to Reichspräsident Göring. I am an expert pilot, especially of my own craft. Mussolini himself asked me to teach his son Bruno to fly.'

One moment he pretends to disbelieve me. The next, he will

550

accept everything. 'And when you went into film-making with Prince "Mongol", what were your arrangements? A percentage of the profits, perhaps?'

'We had no arrangements. He was blackmailing me. I hardly knew the man. He threatened me with exposure. Originally I didn't know he made pornography. But he concocted a story.'

'Fiction upon fiction.' Schnauben walks to the window. He smokes another cigarette. 'What about these financial dealings of yours in Paris?'

'I had nothing to do with the financial side of that scheme. I merely designed the airship. I had innovative ideas. I wanted to see them made concrete.'

'Oh, yes, you are an inventor.'

'I have invented everything.' My secret. I have invented him.

'Stavisky? He is your cousin?'

'We were never related.'

'You heard he had shot himself?'

'Inevitable, I suspect, in such an introspective man. A private man. No doubt a manic-depressive.'

And Shura? Was he, too, dead? Really dead, this time? My past is reinvented for me by liars. I met a Jew in Odessa. He put a piece of metal in my stomach. I can feel it there to this day. It is in the shape of a star. The points prick at my innards.

'You are a man of many identities. The doctors will be interested in you.'

Taking a deep pull on his cigarette, he strolls to the window and tugs a cord at the bottom of the blind. The blind shoots up with a bang, silhouetting his unreadable face. The grey eyes stare from hollow darkness. The smoke pours from his mouth and nostrils. The sun is up. A voice shrieks an order. Bodies begin to convulse. The Dachau day has begun.

—✣ FIFTY ✣—

Originally thirty-two of us occupied the long block. The majority were red or green triangles or violets, like myself. We were regarded as the aristocrats among the prisoners. Social misfits, such as Jews, gypsies and homosexuals, were the least favoured. Jehovah's Witnesses were also hated, for some reason. They had their own triangle, which was purple. From our ranks were drawn the capos and camp servants. Having, on my arrival, been mislabelled a Jew, some of that mud still stuck to me, so I could not hope for promotion to capo. But by and large my hut-mates were no more prejudiced than I was, and we got along reasonably well. They were almost all red triangles, Sozis, commies or dissident Nazis, like Röhm's SA rounded up in the putsch. Some were genuine criminals. The hut's senior man, an ex-burglar and anarchist called Hoch, was not overly strict.

For the most part I was able to avoid the daily brutalities of the camp. While I continued to amuse him, Sturmführer Schnauben offered me a certain protection from the worst excesses of the guards. They laughed at me. Their nickname for me was 'the ex-Jew'. I was lucky. I was in a wretched position, but I was actually leading a charmed life. They respected my armband. Luckily, nobody associated me with the SA.

I trembled often, convinced that Röhm had died because of what he knew. Strasser had died for the same reason. Almost everyone associated with the Raubal affair was either dead or in danger. Only Hanfstaengl and Hess were still alive, as far as I knew.

By some miracle I had so far not been closely connected with Röhm. Such a large dossier on me existed from other sources; no one had thought to compile one on my association with the party. Physically, too, I had changed. When Baldur von Schirach visited Dachau, he did not recognise me. I saw him sharing a joke with Himmler but it would have been death to have raised my voice. I knew if any one of those high-ranking Nazis should ever recall having been introduced to me in Röhm's company and put two and two together, or if Himmler took a special interest in my file and its details, my end would be certain.

I had no way of identifying my 'protector' in Berlin. Schnauben had mentioned a 'guardian angel' more than once, though never by name. I owed my violet armband to Kolya, I knew. But who else saw to my safety? I was baffled. Suppose Göring, planning to claim my inventions as his own, did not understand them enough to have me done away with but could not afford to release me? I devoted considerable time to the problem. Certainly it could not be Hitler himself. Nor was it likely to be Himmler. Goebbels, too, was not an obvious candidate. It could only be Göring, possibly interceding on behalf of Mrs Cornelius.

With Himmler's help, Hitler had killed everyone who knew even the smallest details of his sexual history. Poor Father Stempfle had been finished off in this very camp. Shot, one of the politicals told me, in the usual spot behind the *Kommandanturarrest*, where he, too, had at first been a privileged prisoner. Dozens of known members of the Black Front had been killed there, behind the *Bunker*. The politicals often spoke of them. Many were left-wing Nazis themselves. Hitler had lost thousands of supporters because of his so-called purge.

Thanks to the circumstances of my second arrest, I was not even regarded by the SS as a political prisoner now, and this, with my violet armband, offered certain privileges. I had greater freedom to move about the camp. I could keep my eyes and ears open. Guards trusted me to run errands for them, rewarding me with extra food and occasional luxuries, such as a piece of soap. As well as *the ex-Jew*, I was *der Spanier* or sometimes *Spanner*. A pun I never quite understood.

While the communist propaganda machine has been blamed for its exaggerations, it is true that in Dachau the Jews were not well treated. They were given the dirtiest and most humiliating jobs, and frequently beaten, even killed, before our eyes for the smallest infringements of camp discipline. Reds and others, many of them pure-bred Aryans, suffered the same fate. I agree with those scholars who say the figure of six million is exaggerated, but nobody can deny the suffering of individuals I saw daily, especially after an old, but unwelcome, acquaintance came to share my quarters. I had hoped never to see him again, that extremely lucky man. I needed no more of the type of luck he brought with him.

He had been on holiday in Rome during the blood purge. Much to his surprise he had returned to find himself under arrest. He remained in a state of shocked dismay, yet more than fortunate to be alive. If he had been at the Hotel Deesen, Bad Godesberg, on the night Röhm and his colleagues were there, he would certainly have died. He understood I would not betray him if he was careful not to accuse me of being Jewish. To Seryozha's good fortune, he had been designated a political, with a red triangle, and not a homosexual with a pink.

Sergei Andreyovitch Tsipliakov had been running to fat the last I had seen him. After so many months, first as a prisoner in Stadelheim, and later in another section of Dachau, he had lost weight but was still bulky and unhealthy when he arrived at our hut. Hoch, our hut commander, had rather let us down. He had abused his privileges. During an attempt to escape, he had been shot. His replacement was Seryozha, already popular with the Dachau authorities as a good, strict leader.

Seryozha's old, confiding manner had disappeared. To the other inmates he presented only a scowling swagger. Gone were his exaggerated, effeminate mannerisms. In the whole of the camp, only I ever knew he had been a ballet dancer. If he thought I was Jewish, he kept the idea to himself. Indeed, he confirmed to the others that I was of Spanish extraction. He understood I had some relationship with Schnauben and could always betray him. He was wary of my violet armband. Needless to say I cultivated him as a friend, though it was not always within my power or inclination, especially when he went on one of his rampages or 'pogromettes', as he described them with a new tone of camp whimsicality.

That so many of these inmates had brought their suffering on themselves hardly excused Seryozha's brutality towards them. He had to demonstrate his skills to our masters. I suppose I sympathised, but some of his actions sickened me.

Even in Stadelheim during my first incarceration, I had witnessed some moving scenes. Certain Jews had been picked on by SA. I had heard them weeping and begging not to be beaten as they were dragged out of their cells. Even the most anti-Jewish inmates among us had been shocked by what was done to them. Some guards and trustees were positively sadistic. A good few of the arrested Jews, who had committed no crime, had died as a result of their privations. In Dachau, however, things were a little different.

To show his zealotry and his keenness, and in the hope of early release, Seryozha made it his daily habit to pick on Jews. For the entertainment of our masters he would force them out of their hut, where they lived in worse conditions than we did, and assemble them there or in the *Appellplatz*. These were usually the Jews who were *schanung*, or off work for some reason. Though I had known him for many years, I would never have guessed this side to his character. He clearly derived real pleasure from hurting the *Strafkompanie*.

On the parade ground Seryozha would sometimes be allowed to use the *Pfahl*, a pole on which a man with his hands tied behind his back could be suspended and sometimes whipped. But usually he made them stand before him in the wide *Lagerstrasse*. There he would kick and beat any 'son of Shem' who so much as raised his eyes to him. He would attack them with his whip or anything else he had to hand. He would revile them, torment them, make them beg for mercy even as he opened his flies and pissed on them. He was a great source of entertainment to the SS guards, who cheered him on. They were almost in awe of him in the early days, before such brutality became the norm. Scarcely anyone there was as vicious as Seryozha when he chose to take against a Jew. Within the first two weeks of our being reunited he had beaten half a dozen 'Jerusalem colonels' so badly that they died of their injuries. He killed two by splitting their heads open with the heavy stick he sometimes used. The Jews knew him well, and their fear of him could often be comical. Those who lived would do anything he told them. He was the one who, for the entertainment of the SS men at Easter, re-enacted the Crucifixion, using a young Christian priest as Jesus and a crowd of Jews as his tormentors. Nailed rather haphazardly to his cross, the man died of strangulation before his three days were up.

Yet to me Seryozha remained the same rather sentimental friend of former days, sharing a nostalgia for our mutual past. Perhaps even Satan himself needs a confidant. He liked to discuss St Petersburg before the Revolution. He blamed the Jewish Reds for destroying his career. Even though he confided in me, he never mentioned what that career had been. In some ways he knew he had turned into a monster and could be remorseful. 'As bad as any Cossack.'

His melancholy made him cruel. No doubt he lived in terror of replacing his red triangle with a pink one. I had no choice but to express sympathy, and he was grateful for that, though he never touched me sexually. I was grateful in turn.

'It's the *sneg* I miss most, Dimka dear. I miss it so badly, you know. The way another man might miss a woman. Sometimes I feel so ashamed of myself when I've hurt some of these people. I am not proud of myself. I do filthy things. Yet I understand how God has chosen me to be their nemesis. If it were not me, it would be someone worse. Jews refused God's revelation. Perhaps I can help bring the survivors to Him. I am His instrument. I know it sometimes upsets you, and I am deeply sorry.'

Not for a moment did he allow himself his former lacrymosity, though he could show a certain kindness. 'I'd never do anything to you, my best and oldest friend. You have always been a good Christian. But unredeemed Jews attack the very substance of our civilisation. By rejecting Christ, they themselves are effectively Christ's murderers, every one of them. Their writings sent hundreds of honest Germans to destruction. They squeak for mercy now, but they did not demand mercy for all those Russians and Poles they killed. You know as well as I do that their Red co-religionists have been responsible for the deaths of millions of our countrymen. And who benefited?'

I could only agree. Moreover, if I challenged his ideas, I might turn him against me. He needed me to support his arguments. I had learned the virtues of silence with both my captors and my comrades. The Jews feared him as much as he feared the pink triangle. He displayed his brute manliness at every opportunity. In the way he strutted and swung his whip, he was determined to present the most aggressive masculinity possible. His friendship was of considerable advantage to me, since we now shared a home in which he was the undisputed master.

Seryozha was especially cruel to Jewish artists. After he had been in our hut for a month or so, he proposed he prepare an entertainment for the camp. With our *Lagerälteste*'s permission, who in turn received it from his *Untersturmführer*, Seryozha formed a number of the Jewish prisoners into a ballet troupe to put on a burlesque of *Swan Lake*, in which Jewish elders were supposed to represent swans, with goose feathers stuck up their backsides. He, of course, did not take part. He was Diaghilev, these days, never Nijinsky.

The burlesque was a massive success, popular with everyone, inmates included. Seryozha became a camp favourite for a while. His 'performing Jews' were even part of a general SS entertainment that Christmas. Seryozha was promised his freedom. Then suddenly, supposedly at the suggestion of Commandant Eicke and to my own personal relief, Seryozha and his performing Jews were taken away in a 'trainload', apparently 'on tour', and I never saw any of them again. Years later I heard a rumour that he had been promoted to the SS and helped set up one of the Polish camps. He had always believed his skills to be underappreciated. Possibly he even left the SS and at last fulfilled his ambition to command a ballet company entertaining the troops at the front.

Not only the Jews were glad to see the back of Sergei Andreyovitch, though he said farewell to me with the most touching tenderness, even risking a comradely squeeze of the hand just before he climbed into the transport.

In retrospect Seryozha's period as hut commandant was almost like a holiday. My new interviews with Sturmführer Schnauben began again soon after the officer's return from leave. He used the Gestapo building near the main gate, which he said was quieter. We were less likely to be interrupted. He was in a somewhat different mood. He told me how much he had missed our conversations.

'I find you an inspiration, Pyatnitski. Your guardian angel still protects you.' He had been in Berlin. I had the impression he had spoken to someone there about my case. Perhaps after all Kolya, not Mrs Cornelius, was that 'guardian angel'.

For all that, I lived in perpetual fear of Schnauben turning against me or being replaced by some other SS officer who would reclassify me as a Jew.

Schnauben had brought some new gramophone records back with him. Bach remained his favourite composer. He was particularly fond of a recording of the *St John Passion*. This was miserable for me. Bach has always seemed irredeemably insane. Yet I had to pretend to appreciate his taste. I do not believe I really deceived him.

'Neither the Jew nor the Spaniard ever had any true affinity for the Baroque,' he said. 'Perhaps you are, after all, a Russian.'

Sometimes I found it impossible to follow his logic, hard as I tried. I did not know if he was joking. Later he claimed he was sure I was American, after all. I lacked any sense of irony. That made him certain I could not be either Jewish or Russian.

Russian blood meant nothing to these people. They despised it. Anyone who was not German was a subhuman whose chief function was to work and die for the Reich. They took their lead from the teachings of the Americans and the British, who for so long had been obsessed with racial definitions. The Reich based their blood laws firmly on those of Mississippi and Alabama. They produced a hodge-podge of poorly conceived legislation which they never really refined.

In recent years I have given much thought to creating a world in which the different races could live in harmony. I have drawn maps showing where the Arabs would live, where we would place the Negroes, what lands should be granted to the Slavs and so on. But as usual no one has listened to me, and we continue to have chaos. The stupidest British mistake was to listen to the Zionists who demanded Palestine as a homeland. The government should have given them Hampstead Garden Suburb where they would have been welcomed and allowed to set up their kibbutzes and their socialist welfare state and not have had so far to travel. They could have built Jerusalem in England's green and pleasant land a mere bus ride away. The Arabs would have been content. There would have been only peace in the region.

Sturmführer Schnauben was interested in my plans for the re-organisation of the British Empire after the war. He would listen with fascination while I explained what was to be done. I honestly believe his respect for my intellect helped keep me alive during those terrible years. He did what he had to do to survive. I have never blamed him.

Ich unterwerfe mich! Ich unterwerfe mich! Ich unterwerfe mich dem Tod. Wiedergeburt des Ego. Oh, Jerusalem. Oh, Schönheit! Verwaiste Knochen. Liebling. Glück und Elend. So ja mit kleinen Vögeln. Vögel füllen die Brust. Vögel picken innen, singen für die Freiheit. Mein Imperium, eine Seele. Vögel sterben in mir. Einer nach dem anderen.

My flying cities transport us to new worlds, where strong, healthy people give birth to a wholesome race living by Christ's laws.

For I am the way and the truth, said Our Saviour. Follow me, He said. Follow me.

My ship is called *The One True Path*.

My ship is called *The Guiding Light*.

My ship is called *The Paradise Found*.

A silence had fallen over Germany.

FIFTY–ONE

German materialism, French eroticism, Roman superstition, English and American greed. What can counter these influences? Only Russian spirituality. And of all Slavs, the Cossacks are the truest Russians. We worshipped our *tsar-batiushka*. Just as the Jews have done in Palestine, my ancestors established their *khutora* whenever it was possible to reclaim land from the Tatars. Some true Cossacks rode with the German forces but most of those were merely Great Russians claiming Cossack blood in order to get out of the POW camps. I am sure there were few true Cossacks fought for the Germans, though this did not stop Stalin from killing so many. Not that I hated all Germans, even during my years in Dachau. I had the library, at least until it became distasteful to me. I began to forget my Russian roots and believe, because I only had Goethe and his compatriots to comfort me, that German was the finest language for expressing human metaphysics and spirituality.

I think the Sturmführer got the idea for our orchestra and choir from me. He would play me Bach and Beethoven on his gramophone. Beethoven I did not mind, though I preferred, of course, Tchaikovsky. The orchestra soon broke up and we were again reduced to gramophone records. Yet I do not think I could have survived in those early months without music. Today everything is drowned out by the thump-thump of Negro drums, the angry repetitions of the jungle we hoped to conquer but which somehow is conquering us. I had seen that schloss as a place of God, a fortress of civilisation, whose family represented all that was admirable and exemplary in German civilisation, yet Mussolini had known better. Today I understand they sell pizza from a kiosk in the grounds and in summer rock-and-roll bands offer concerts to the crowds of soft-faced children whose only knowledge of German culture is the frankfurter and the hamburger.

The Cornelius girl is proud of her new BMW motorcycle. One ride on the pillion was enough for me. German ideas were the ruin of Russia but Russia, through the Holy Church, can still be the salvation of Europe. Rome has failed her. The proof is everywhere. The proof is manifest. *Les donneurs de sérénades. Je respire enfin. Les petites femmes. Il est très joli, très sublime. Moi? Je suis un monstre. Appréhendez vous? Non. Non. Non. La sexualité. C'est fini. C'est dangereux pour les enfants? Ah oui, mais je suis un celebrant.* I do not lack intellect, only education. And for that I am forced to blame Germany. Another year or two and my schooling would have been complete. Simplicissimus himself was never as unfortunate. May I touch her? It is all I wish to do. Either she is real or I am. *C'est impossible pour les deux.* All I wished to do was purchase some furniture. Violento, those colorados. *Wie spät ist es? Hören Sie sie singen? Sie will nach Wien fahren. Wir fahren zusammen ins Gebirge. Ein Flugzeug? Die Sonne geht spät unter. Dunkle Wolken. Stürmisch.* That weather! Yet it is the summers I remember best. If you have never heard marching in a city you could not imagine it. It begins as a kind of rustling sound, like a breeze in autumn trees, then it develops into a rhythmic banging, as sticks pop in a fire, then as if boys beat on dustbins until it takes on a mechanical, deafening quality, not like any human sound at all, but overwhelming your senses. A voice sounds like a loud fault in an engine. When it stops, you want to vomit. I heard that sound in London when the Boys Brigade practised for Armistice Day, reminding me that the British and Germans were not so different. For a while I had an inferior copy of Grimmelshausen, actually in my locker, but that was either confiscated or stolen, I forget.

I am not one of those. *Jenseits von Gut und Böse? Hier liegt Dynamit* indeed. For me there was no *Erlösung.* Schnauben made that clear. He insisted I hear and absorb this message. And was he wrong? I still do not know. Spengler said he understood all too well. If we continued on the road to materialism and relied increasingly on technology, China must inevitably come to rule the world. 'That is the reason for the difference between the Chinese and our friends the Japs,' he told me.

Quelling my panic, I continued to stand at attention.

'There is nothing more effective than the Japanese war machine,' he insisted. 'It will conquer Asia.' Of course, he was wrong. Their machines have conquered Europe and America. *Von Morgen bis*

Mitternacht we must struggle against this, he said. But he wronged me. I could never join his *Maschinenstürmer* no matter what the inducement. I gave the Sphinx the correct answer. Some of us prefer to answer the questions anyway. Some of us would remain silent until death. I do not have this English habit of talking about everything. They have no dignity. They will never have even a glimpse of paradise. *Furcht und Elend* is their only future. No one has ever accused me of lacking *Innigkeit*. The rain on those old cobbled Munich streets smelled sweet as a wheatfield with the dawn dew still upon it and I breathed in the distant air, remembering those cobbles in Kiev, yellow Kiev, gold and full of raw gems. Then came the *Stahlgewitter*. I fled down the long tunnel which ultimately took me to America, then to Africa, Europe and finally to England. How was this *Verwandlung* accomplished? *Das Urteil ist* yours. I was fated to become the organ-grinder's monkey. They say it is nonsense that the Jews controlled everything, but while they did not own every newspaper (the *Jew Pork Times*) or every film studio (*Jew Knighted Artistes*) consider the books they did publish, the movie-plays they did write. Yet I still do not say I agreed with Hitler. The trouble is, of course, that the propaganda against him was inaccurate and absurd so that all his critics were discredited. These Americans are no different. They all believe in flying saucers. As a result nobody wished to build *mein Flügelhotel*, which would make its way round the world landing at exotic cities and picturesque landscapes then fly my visitors home again. *Das einfache Leben!* But they said I was mad. I had nothing to do with flying saucers or for that matter cups or plates.

But even in the depths of the ancient forests where sunlight slants between tall trunks, there is a waterfall and a pool where a dragon drinks. That dragon guards a treasure which can only be won by a hero with a magic sword. Bathe in the dragon's blood, sang the bird, and you will be for ever invincible, only beware the linden leaves. And, of course, it was a falling leaf which was to be my ruin. Seryozha had changed for the worse. I did not like him any better. He had shown me a cartoon by Bakst. He said it was of himself. Those beautiful leaves, all mellow. Autumn is my favourite time of year. It was surprising to find him there. He had read Proust in prison, he said. 'From my hundred and first week,' he said. 'It was relatively civilised. Then they sent me here. But you? Why would you be in Dachau? Now, I mean.' It was my lot to be for ever 'Category C'.

It gave me no real status. Mosley looked down on me, I know, even on the Isle of Man, where I was for a short time. To be 'Category C' was to be a nonentity. At the time I was upset. Later, I came again to appreciate the anonymity. I wrote an article for the *News Chronicle* concerning the virtues of Cossack arranged marriages but I heard nothing from them. They, too, were clearly prejudiced against class C internees.

They have no idea what it means to be a refugee, beginning one life after another, constantly settling, constantly forced to move on, unable to speak one's own language, save to other refugees. It was even worse for me since I despised so many Russians – Trotskyists and left-wingers of every stripe who had wheedled their way into the confidence of the BBC and the Foreign Service. Reduced to a number. They do not realise it. I had no number in Dachau. Or rather the number often changed. No imprinted number. Five. A *finif*. A fin. Quarter of a pound. And even at full stretch all I am is an obscure dinosaur. If only I had been permitted by history to retain my own, noble name. But they would not have been realistic. Not in this day and age.

They keep looking back. Their happiest memories are mixed up with sunken munitions ships, blazing buildings, fragmented planes and grey balloons. The crash of bombs reminds them of their former glory days.

Germany is the custodian of human culture, Seryozha says. We are the bastion against the degenerate Red, the corrupted democrat, the aggressive conservative. We are the only genuine radicals and guardians of culture and German culture is the highest of all.

They formed us into a team and made us pull the great water-filled roller around the streets of the camp, levelling them, making all tidy, so that the stretch between the poplars looked like a French avenue. I heard the *Dachaulied* on the wireless when I was living in Paddington; some youth choir, I thought they said, or possibly émigrés. They were singing a song about Dachau some priest had written.

I cannot forget that Christian priest and the barbed-wire crown they forced him to make and wear, the big beam he carried, the Jews they made spit at him. I never worked on the plantation which the SS said was for our food, but they sold it in the town. Yet it brought, if the wind was right, a smell of growing green, of some small memory of rural paradise. I met a prisoner who had once counted butterflies for a living. He was some sort of scholar and came in for especially cruel treatment from the guards which was why I took pains to disguise my origins. I told them I had been a mechanic and that got me privileges working on the SS and Gestapo cars.

Schnauben asked my opinion.

'I have never been interested in abstraction,' I said. 'I am a practical engineer.'

He made a mouth. '*Hier liegt Dynamit.*'

'What?' I was afraid he would accuse me of some kind of sabotage, of being an arsonist. 'I'm no fire-starter. Fire is far too volatile. You never know what it's going to do. As for explosives . . .'

He seemed amused and bored at the same time. 'Just a sort of joke,' he said.

I laughed appropriately.

'You had better go to the library,' he said. 'I'll give you another pass. Get something out for me, too.'

During that period, before I developed a loathing for literature, I read a good deal, almost all in German. There were a few political books but mostly poetry, non-fiction and novels. I reported the political books, although it had not been my intention to expose the librarian, a Catholic, who was dismissed and replaced by a monarchist. I read *Der Totenwolf* and other books by Ernst Wiechert which were there in several different editions, and that is where I found Grimmelshausen, but I longed for something in English, to remind me of my boyhood. Sexton Blake, needless to say, was not a favourite of the Nazis. Otto Wenninger was another author I found interesting. I admired him for his philosophy and read *Geschlecht und Charakter* more than once. Of the classics, I suppose Tieck was my favourite. *Mein Kampf*, which I pretended to like, was boring; either too obvious or too obscure, and thoroughly long-winded. I found that it revived unwanted memories. They terrified me. I lived in fear of a day when, by unlucky chance, Hitler put two and two together. Karl May and Charles Sealsfield, whose *Nathan, der Squatter-Regulator* struck an especially familiar note with me, continued to be great favourites. I was astonished to learn later that this Austrian Augustinian monk had travelled under several aliases in America and elsewhere. Another man of the cloth I enjoyed was Johan Klepper, who brought me a certain amount of solace, also. Many of the others I forget and my reading was suddenly terminated when an SS guard

563

found me with a copy of a play called *Sladek, der Schwarze Reichswehrmann*. I do not remember the author's name, but apparently he was proscribed. Even when my privileges were given back to me, I found I had not only lost my taste for reading, I despised the activity.

FIFTY-TWO

Abraham, Premier Grand immolateur de ta propre humanité: où ton couteau a-t-il touché ton fils plein de confiance? Antique Sumer, Sumer adorée, ruisselante de peur. Renie le Juif et tu renieras ton passé. Dans quel coin mésopotamien de l'univers Dieu naquit-Il pour avoir abandonné jusqu' à Sa divinité, Sa pureté, en laissant mourir Son propre fils? Illustre Abraham: procréateur fanatique du Mythe sacrificateur. Le fanatique renie l'univers, n'y voit que cruauté, et singe misérablement cette prétendue cruauté qui, en fait, n'est que sublime équilibre. Ich habe keine Wahl gehabt. Ich wurde gezwungen, ihren Richtlinien zuzustimmen. Ich beharrte darauf, ich war nicht jüdisch. Ich erklärte alles. Sie lehnten, mich zu sehr ab. Schliesslich hatte ich keine Wahl ausser mit ihnen übereinzustimmen. Sie hätten mich getötet. Sie töten mich schon.

It is winter again. With nostalgia we look back to the earlier days of the camp. Those who have boots are aristocrats. Those who do not have boots develop gangrene in the snow. Their feet grow black and swell and rot. They limp and hobble through the slush. They will die of poisoned blood if not of the cold itself, but few wish to be taken to the *Revier*. It is gaining an unsavoury reputation. The *Lagerarzt* is not known for his kindness.

The guards make jokes about us. When a transport comes in, they throw boots out into the assembly yard. This is against camp rules, but camp rules are increasingly ignored. The guards are as mad as the inmates. They watch the prisoners scramble and squabble for the boots like ducks over bread.

Few of us now see the horror on the faces of the fresh arrivals. Why should their approval concern us? We are *Lagerfliegen*. They will soon become like us. We crave the approval of the guards, of our captains. Once I longed for books and took every chance to visit the library. Now I loathe them. A reading man is not an invisible man.

I do not become a Mussulman. I have a piece of metal in my womb. Once it poisoned me. Now it is my strength. The metal is myself. I wear no star on my uniform. I have the star which was forged in Odessa. Those others have no core. I carry the star that guided the Wise Men to Bethlehem. Few know how to survive as I survive. At any moment a random action can destroy you. The secret is in routine. Everyone loves routine. Every animal in the world feels secure while it experiences repetition.

My boots fit. They were expensive. I have warm socks. Though filthy, I still have a violet armband. I have a guide, a master. I am always predictable. I have become the SS man's pet Jew. I am his heart's desire. My death will be harder for it, but my life is easier.

Sometimes Kolya visits the camp, interfering with my routine. He appears to have some seniority, though he wears civilian clothes. I am taken to his office in the Gestapo building. He always notes how well I look. I admire his office. It has fresh white walls, dark blue paint and looks out on high evergreen hedges. The only sign of the camp is the watchtower, the machine gun, the guard, the top level of barbed wire. I tell him of Schnauben, my faux-Virgil, and he asks me what lesson I am learning on my journey through Hell.

'That God is either senile or insane,' I tell him.

'Well, Dimka,' Kolya unbuttons his jacket. 'At least you still have your imagination.'

'Can't you get me out of here, Kolya?' Addressing him like this is the one risk I shall take. 'I could serve the Reich.'

'The Reich does not believe it needs you, dear.'

Is Kolya responsible for my captivity?

'Not yet.'

I return to my routine.

FIFTY–THREE

Sturmbannführer Schnauben is promoted rapidly while at Dachau. Therefore I, too, am promoted. He is impressed by my relationship with Kolya. When he refers to Kolya I can hear a note of sardonic respect. Schnauben calls Kolya 'your aristocratic pal from Berlin'. He will not tell me any more about my friend or the outside world. Schnauben only rarely discusses the news of the day, but through him I learn of the Nationalist overthrow of the Red government in Spain. He speaks happily of my suffering country and what Germany avoided through Hitler's vision.

'It could have been so much worse for us. That is why the public loves the Führer.'

The predicted Civil War has come. Heavy fighting around Madrid. Will it spread across Europe? Or will Hitler form an axis with Franco, Mussolini and other like-minded men to throw up a steel firewall against Red incursion?

Yuzmekligim yazim mu? Dicono che quell'uomo, Messer Zid, sia sceso all'Inferno e sia anche tornato indietro. Poco ci manco che morisse. Il hamdu lilla! Je voyage indépendamment à cavernes imaginaires découvertes près de la Seine. Méditations et Révélations. Zna arciblaz en Kartago? Eine zid? Israel zerstört in einem Tag. Karthago zerstört in einem Tag. Peru zerstört in einem Tag. Die Reiche der Sioux und der Zulu zerstört in einem Tag. Mandschurisches Reich zerstört in einem Tag. Russland zerstört in einem Tag. Was bleibt übrig ausser Stolz? Stolz vernichtete sie . . .

'This place has been a rest cure for you,' my master jokes. 'In America you would pay thousands of dollars to be here. You must thank a benevolent state. Public health has improved considerably in Germany. Why, when I first knew you, you were a cocaine addict.'

I nod my agreement. To disagree would be to die. I was never addicted. I have not lost my love of 'snow', but I have ceased to regard it as part of my life. In many ways I am less reliant on human pleasures. Even sex no longer plays a central part in my thoughts. The last film I made with Prince Freddy also destroyed the chains of desire. I was relieved to learn that in the Third Reich all such material was automatically incinerated. However, the record of my shame might exist elsewhere.

'The Führer is a great man,' says Schnauben. 'He has scoured Germany from top to bottom. These days even his old detractors admire him. The Americans send experts to study his methods.'

I piss in Hitler's mouth.

I shit in Hitler's face.

I push the dildo into his arse.

Dein Engel.

In the night, when everyone else sleeps, those triumphant eyes still mock me.

Therefore you are nothing.

'For this,' says Schnauben, 'everyone is willing to forgive us. You, Peters, are a small sacrifice.'

I am a small sacrifice. I understand.

'Thank you.'

Poor Röhm. He gave up everything in the end for his Führer. Can I do less?

Sometimes I think of Röhm in Stadelheim, stripped to the waist in that cell, the gun with its single bullet upon the table. He refused to take his own life, knowing 'Alf' lacked the hardness of heart to kill him.

Schnauben is playing Brahms's *Ein Deutsches Requiem* on his new gramophone. Does the music inspire me? he asks. 'It must be a consolation to you. It is to me.'

I say it is a great consolation. I thank him for letting me hear it. I return to my barracks.

The music meant nothing. I wonder, abstractedly, if Sturmbannführer Schnauben will be able to harden his heart to kill me when the time comes.

Trauriger und alter Gott, sollte ins Altersheim. Sollte ins Altersheim mit allen anderen schmutzigen alten Göttern.

FIFTY–FOUR

I am ordered out of the crowded bunk and into the cold air of the compound. I am to be transferred to Sachsenhausen. I am not told why. I am afraid to leave. I am familiar with that note: *Rückkehr nicht erwünscht*. Not wanted back. If I leave I will die. I think they mean to kill me. They say that Sachsenhausen is worse than Dachau. That is where I could be killed. Sturmbannführer Schnauben congratulates me. He seems almost light-hearted. Is this how he evades the responsibility of slaughtering me?

We are marched at a run to the railway yards. We are formed into groups. A label is placed round my neck. Other prisoners are going to Belsen. Belsen is a show camp. Belsen has restaurants. A choice of menu.

Even in the cattle car the Belsen-bound prisoners act arrogantly. As soon as I say where I am going they treat me as if I have somehow failed a test.

'They'll kill you there for certain,' says one obnoxious young Jew. A lawyer, I understand. I do not find it mysterious why he was sent to prison.

The train is filthy and stinks in a way that Dachau does not stink. We move off. Through the slats I look out at the distant camp. I half expect Sturmbannführer Schnauben to be standing outside, waving me goodbye.

The journey to the north-east takes days. We receive almost no food or water. Some of us die. Our corpses start to rot. Near Berlin, when we are shunted into into a siding, the guards climb on to our roof and grin down at us through the openings. They unbutton their trousers and piss into the truck just as we start to eat our bread.

I change trains in some remote, unpeopled place. I am forced into a truck far more crowded than the last. This truck is full of crazed-looking criminals. I have no idea who they are. Most of them do not speak German. Perhaps they are gypsies.

When next we disembark it is early morning. A mist rises. I am immediately singled out. Shouted orders are indistinguishable from the shrieking barks of the dogs. Steel-helmeted soldiers with guns aimed at our heads. At the double I am marched to a wooden hut and pushed into an office with filing cabinets and desks. There stands Kolya, smiling, as if he welcomes me into paradise. He wears his big leather coat. Even inside his breath turns to clouds.

'Good news, Dimka. The authorities have at last reviewed your case. Those letters and designs you sent to Reichspräsident Göring? You have convinced them of your usefulness. Your efforts have not been wasted.'

Only dimly can I make sense of what he says. 'Convinced?'

'Your design for flying infantry, I believe. They don't tell me much. Now war has broken out in Spain we have a practical theatre in which to test your idea. You are to go to Berlin, to a special camp. You will be given the chance to build your prototype.'

Uncertain whether or not this is some SS joke, I give no re-action. If I knew what was expected of me I would display the appropriate behaviour.

'I'd have thought you'd be delighted, Dimka!'

I understand then that I must smile. I do my heroic best.

'Excellent.' Kolya puts his beautiful hand on my shoulder blade. 'I am to take you to the Institute myself.'

Had my friend rescued me at last?

August 1937. After I had showered and been equipped with a civilian suit, Kolya took charge of me. We entered a large Mercedes with a chauffeur. At once the car began moving.

The landscape, so lush and golden with harvest, was too rich for me. I felt almost nauseated by the sight of it. The food we ate on the way was difficult to hold down. I had to close my eyes to keep the images in. If I opened them for too long I began to cry. Sometimes Kolya would pat my arm and offer me a little distant comfort. Sometimes he would croon to me. 'There, there. It's over. You've paid your debt. It's over.' But I could no longer really believe that. I did not know there had been a debt to pay.

Once I ventured to ask him who had issued the instructions for me to be taken from Dachau. He would not tell me.

'Circles far above my head, dear.'

Kolya could not be responsible for my imprisonment. Maybe Mrs Cornelius was responsible for my release. Perhaps she had spoken to our old friend Göring. He was a well-known humanitarian. But what if this were an SS charade? I did not allow myself to hope too much.

At night we reached a group of buildings protected by a high concrete wall. As the car's great lamps threw the compound into shadowy perspective I thought at first they were film studios.

Kolya seemed relieved we had arrived. When we got out of the car, we were greeted by a man in SS uniform to whom Kolya gave my papers. 'You'll have to sign for him,' he said.

'Are you leaving me, Kolya?'

'For the moment,' he said. 'By the way. Your friend Mrs Cornelius is in custody. She will be well treated if only you cooperate fully with us.'

In a state of some shock I was taken directly to the SS cells. Was I to meet Mrs Cornelius here? The cells were clean, well ordered and smelled strongly of pine disinfectant. I answered basic questions: my name, nationality and political affiliations. The interrogator's sallow face was shadowed by the peak of his cap. Satisfied with my answers, he made some rapid marks on the papers in front of him and grunted. I had learned never to speak until spoken to. He got up and left me standing at attention. Tired as I was I did not move until another SS man returned and told me to follow him.

I went with him across a courtyard into a taller building, along several identical lime-washed corridors until we arrived at a door painted pale green. 'These will be your quarters.' He pushed the door open and made me go in ahead of him. He showed me the sink with running water, a glass, a chamber pot. He then left, closing the door behind him. I did not hear it lock.

Standing in the little cell of my own, with its pristine bed, its sheets and blankets, its radio set and its copy of *Mein Kampf*, I hardly dared to move, let alone undress and get into bed. Everything was antiseptically clean. Opening the top drawer of the little chest at the end of the bed, I found a pair of blue pyjamas, some slippers, not quite my size, some soap, a toothbrush, some toothpaste and other toiletries, all held in a little cotton bag which had my name and a number stencilled on the side: *Prof. M. Gallibasta*. At last they had recognised my qualifications and accepted me as Spanish!

But I was not free of the nightmare. I still trembled with terror as I put the pyjamas on, expecting the door to fly open and guards to be standing there. Even when I had settled between the sheets and switched off the light I listened for boots in the corridor. But it was quiet. There were no screams, no shouts, no barking dogs. Through the unbarred window I heard the ordinary sounds of a late-summer night.

In the morning came a knock on the door. Though I had slept very little I was in better spirits. Already up, I called for the person to come in. A tall, stooping white-haired man greeted me. He wore a loose, blue serge suit, a white shirt and a bow tie. Shaking hands, he introduced himself as Professor Mueller. I accompanied him to breakfast in a big, well-lit canteen full of other men and women clearly of our class, yet all carrying something of the familiar air of *Lagerfliegen*. They did not speak except to say 'good morning'. Few smiled. I imitated them. Mueller offered me a little approving nod. 'We are a monastic order here. We have taken a vow of silence. If we did not, we should be returned to our former condition. That is the first rule.'

I understood. I accompanied him to the counter to collect my breakfast of good-quality bread, a kind of roasted muesli, butter and jam, a slice of luncheon meat, a small piece of cheese.

For the first time in months I wondered about the things I had hidden in Signor Frau's barrel organ. Where, I wondered, was the family now? And were my papers and keepsakes still safe? With SS help, I thought, I might find them again.

As I left the dining hall I was met by an SS man and told to go with him to an unmarked door. He knocked and stood back to let me pass. In a neat office was a large, tidy desk and behind the desk a plump, pale man in pince-nez, his black uniform jacket opened and his tie loosened. He stood up, buttoning his tunic, giving the raised-arm salute. Obersturmbannführer Ludwig Wolfowitz was our SS commandant. He welcomed me to the camp, which he called the Institute. Ordering me to sit down he presented me with the list of questions I had already answered. By now I was a little bolder.

'You understand, Herr Obersturmbannführer, that I am first a scientist?' I told him humbly. 'You know, of course, that I am among other things an engineer. Before my arrest I submitted certain plans to Reichsmarshall Göring.'

'Those ideas are what brought you here, Professor Gallibasta.' Wolfowitz frowned. 'You wish to serve the Reich. We are here to be served! We are interested in your designs, especially your one-man airship, what you rather fancifully call your flying infantryman. We would develop the idea for observational purposes, equipping the flyer with a radio. We will help you in any way you need. You now have a special rank, a new number. You are an F prefix, which means you are the Führer's prisoner. Only our leader can have you moved from here. You will take your orders directly from his office. You will be further rewarded if your work significantly helps the Reich.'

'I am honoured,' I said. He dismissed me.

Everyone at the Institute was equally well treated. We had an opportunity to redeem ourselves, some chance of eventually regaining our former lives. If we did well we could look forward to status, honour and freedom in the community. I had the use of a fully equipped drawing office staffed by highly skilled men and women. Anything I needed was requisitioned for me. My old drawings, the ones I had sent to Göring, were brought in to remind me of my original ideas so that I could prepare a practical design for my one-man airship.

My men and women would rise into the air like spiralling smoke. They would fly like birds between golden cities travelling the skies in orbit above our abandoned globe.

The Institute was a dream, not a positive experience of the real world but at least a temporary release from the nightmare. It offered hope. It returned a future. I laboured hard and swiftly, knowing if one idea were successful I would be allowed to work on others. Always uniformed SS came and went, reminding me that I was F2106 and could be returned to Dachau or worse at any moment. This meant that I kept obsessively to the rules. The facility had many workrooms and sheds I was never allowed to see, just as other inmates were not permitted access to me or my designs. I saw them in the canteen, but only the minimum communication was permitted us. I had a closer relationship with my radio, which broadcast the German programme, chiefly consisting of light classical music and some news broadcasts which kept me apprised of the nationalist struggle against the republicans in Spain and the achievements of Hitler and the Nazi Party in rebuilding a modern homeland.

The only people I talked to at length were the SS and technicians who came to learn how to build the first prototype of what we were calling my LWIX, the hydrogen-filled wing-shaped one-man airship which within months sat tethered in her hangar waiting to be tested. The ship's construction had gone rapidly, for it was a fundamentally simple design. I was very proud of her. The harness below the wing held a small but powerful engine, the aerofoils and the airscrew. Suspended from the wing in a mixture of canvas and plywood, the pilot would be buckled in, using various instruments together with his own arms, legs and feet to steer the little vessel through the air. We called her the *Luftgeist*. She could glide silently through the clouds undetected once her engine was switched off. Then, when necessary, she could become a darting hawk, attaining a height of over five thousand feet. Hovering above a desired location, the pilot, by means of a radio apparatus attached to his flying suit and helmet, also integral parts of the machine's design, could send messages back to base. I had originally planned for her to be armed, but for the moment the Führer wished only to see a non-combative version.

In the hangar I was able to demonstrate the machine to visiting groups of air staff. Surprisingly respectful, they often called me 'Herr Professor' and asked insightful questions. Some were particularly interested in the power/weight ratio, wondering how she would behave in high winds. I believed her light motor, the latest Heinkel could produce for us, was more than capable of propelling her against anything but the most powerful hurricane. Clearly my ship would be better able to perform in conditions where high winds rarely prevailed, such as the European theatre.

I began at last to emerge from the nightmare. Even the SS, impressed by what the air generals had to say, subtly changed their attitude towards me. The *Luftgeist* was certainly a good-looking machine. Her silver wing-shaped airbag was shaped like an aerofoil suspending an empty atmosphere suit capable of protecting the pilot against the worst weather conditions. Swinging from the ceiling of the hangar my *Luftgeist* resembled nothing so much as a gigantic moth.

She was ready for her tests.

The morning of 5 May 1937 I was disturbed at my shaving by a knock on my cell door. Behind his sallow adjutant stood Obersturmbannführer Wolfowitz. He was almost cheerful, waving a piece of paper. 'Good news, F2106. We have been given clearance. The Air Ministry is ready to try our *Luftgeist* out!'

My soul, repressed for so long, began to come to life again. 'Where are we going, sir?' I expected him to name a nearby airfield.

'I must stay here with my duties. But you, F2106, are privileged to be going at once to Burgos by special train. The Führer wishes the *Luftgeist*, which does not officially exist, to have immediate trials in the Spanish arena. A matter of secrecy. We do not want the world to know too much about Germany's business. Your great moment is almost here. I envy you. You will have a chance to meet those filthy Reds at first hand!'

My ship is called *The Death of Hope*.

My ship is called *Das Ende*.

FIFTY–FIVE

I think we first met Moorcock in 1965. We had been to see Mrs Cornelius's children in their pantomime for Holland Park Comprehensive. Mr Auchinek the impresario convinced the school to revive a harlequinade from the turn of the century. The show was very colourful: faded golds, scarlets, deep blues and greens, with plenty of stage tricks and people in big heads. I supplied the old costumes. I bought them in Hastings as bankrupt stock. Auchinek was in love with Mrs Cornelius and so he put all three of her offspring into starring roles. Jerry played Pierrot, Frank was Harlequin and Catherine was Colombine. We expected them to go on to successful stage careers in those days. Even Miss Brunner thought Jerry would be the next Dick Bogarde.

Everyone enjoyed themselves, though I found it all a little vulgar and chaotic. They received write-ups in the *Kilburn Advertiser* and the *Kensington Post*, and Moorcock came to interview them at Blenheim Crescent. He lived round the corner in Colville Terrace and worked for the magazines as a freelance. His piece appeared in *Plays and Players*, but it was too short, made fun of the whole thing and got half its facts wrong. He thought it heralded a rebirth of the old-fashioned panto. Personally I would have sued him. Mrs Cornelius was pleased with it. Frank and Jerry hated it. Catherine said she thought Moorcock meant well.

The pantomime, *The Crock of Oil; or, Harlequin Imperator*, was put on at the old Kilburn Empire. We walked there from Ladbroke Grove, across Harrow Road up to Kilburn High Road. The traffic is terrible on the Harrow Road. We had attempted to find a taxi, but it was impossible. You can spend hours trying to cross against that noisy traffic. It comes in from the west and north, all lorries, buses and vans. It is filthy there. We were late for the performance but were allowed to stand at the back until the first interval when we found our seats. People were very kind. We still enjoyed that atmosphere of camaraderie which has since vanished from the neighbourhood. Nobody has any manners these days since Labour came to power. Once they used to die in church in that good old-fashioned way, celebrating mass. These days they clutch at their hearts as they leave the pub or get on a bus. They die in the street, like animals.

'You take one day at a time, Ive,' Mrs Cornelius tells me. She smiles in reminiscence. 'There's somefink abart your Aye-taye airmen, say what you like. They're sexy.'

She is talking about her time on Majorca after she left Berlin. She stayed with Desmond Reid after she went there with Major Nye, who was acting as an observer for the British government, but all the Italians thought he was a military spy. They treated him with cheerful goodwill. They were euphoric, he told me. They had tremendous morale. Later I was to experience a little of this myself.

We stop on the bridge to watch Concorde go over. What a beautiful plane she is, I say. I never received credit for her, but I am so glad to have seen her fly before I die.

'Wot d'yer mean, yer morbid old bugger?' she says.

That ship is the future, I tell her. One day the airways will be full of such beautiful craft.

'One day,' she says, 'we'll be able to afford a ticket on 'em.'

Sometimes I think she has no poetry. I sigh. 'You are a cynic.'

'If yer say so, Ive.'

'Think what that plane symbolises, dear Mrs C. What her name promises. Unified Europe. A balance of power against communism and rank American materialism. One day all planes will fly beyond the speed of sound. They will be graceful and beautiful again.' We hear the distant bang as she reaches her cruising speed and disappears. 'They bring harmony back to the world.'

She puts her arm through mine. She is affectionate. 'Yer silly ol' sod,' she says.

Mrs Cornelius is modesty personified. She continues to insist she was neither my guardian angel nor my saviour in those pre-war days. She was never in prison, and they lied to me to stop me escaping. But I do not believe her. She was arrested by the Gestapo, I know, for helping me. Pure coincidence, she says, that she left Berlin for Spain. She knew there was a war on, but she'd thought the Balearics would be all right. She'd had such a nice time there before. She had already left Berlin before I was taken to the Institute. Then when Reid went back, she was stuck in Majorca with, as she puts it, that rather jolly bunch of Italian airmen. She didn't see much of Major Nye. He was busy in Palma, and she did most of her entertaining in Andratx, well away from any politics. I think she protests too much. Her influence saved me. My love for her never falters. My faith is always refreshed. My gratitude never fades. She is my muse and my ideal. Technically we are still married, but I will not formalise the matter until I can bestow my true name and title upon her. I have explained this to her, and she accepts the problem with her usual generosity.

Some years ago when I had sold the icon I discovered and had some decent money, I wrote away to one of those genealogy people who make you your family arms and trace your ancestors. I gave them what information I could. They sent me back an heraldic shield. In one quarter were the arms of the Romanoffs, in another the arms of the Pyatnitskis, but the other two quarters they left blank. They said the Soviets had made it hard to trace my relatives. So many had died. So many were in exile. If I could give them more information they would be happy to continue the search. And continue taking my money! I said. To tell me what I already know. Mrs Cornelius agreed. She read their letter. 'It's a racket, Ivan.'

Most people round here call me Peters, a name they can easily remember. Peters is on my bills. Only formally will I give my name as Pyatnitski or Pyat, and even this is not my actual identity. She knows I am a colonel. Sometimes she still introduces me as Colonel Pyat. Her little Cossack. I would be so proud if, before I died, I could make her a princess. I would take her on a honeymoon around the world aboard the *Queen Elizabeth 2*. We would fly home on Concorde. One can still enjoy life in a civilised way, if one has money. There remains a chance that someone will take up one of my patents.

Mrs Cornelius never speaks of her own ordeal as a prisoner of the SS when she was used to ensure my own cooperation. I had no choice but to obey them, or she would have suffered.

After I left the Institute, I was put on a train, together with a crate containing my machine, to Burgos, which Generalissimo Franco had made his capital. The old town was teeming with military people, including many Italians and Germans. I even found a German graveyard beside one of the churches. I was introduced to Herr von

Stohler, a gaunt, introspective civilian in charge of my project, and he explained how he wanted to test the *Luftgeist*. The machine would have only Spanish markings, he said. He wanted no hint of its being German, and since I was also a Spanish citizen, I would be able to pilot her without arousing suspicion. 'We are very grateful to you, Professor Gallibasta.' He was rather relieved to see me, he said. He was courtesy personified. I almost wept with gratitude to be treated as an equal again. At the moment most of the German squadrons were deployed further south. In the north the Italians were far too undisciplined as flyers and they possessed no useful observation aircraft themselves. They were as likely to frighten the enemy off before the Reds could be engaged. My machine was just what the doctor ordered.

Von Stohler was a civilised, worldly fellow with fine features and elegant manners. He was highly respected by the Spaniards. I dined with him in his private apartments while he sketched in the back-ground of the war situation. Tomorrow, he said, I would be sent on to Zaragoza. Franco was about to make a big push against the Republicans, and my machine would be needed to fly silently over-head relaying back the enemy positions. Reassured that I could remain aloft for several hours in this way while coming and going at will, von Stohler sketched out the kind of territory I would be scouting.

'We have tanks and aircraft at our disposal,' he told me. 'But the Spanish generals are of the old school. They scarcely know how to use such ordnance to advantage. If you can give us Republican posi-tions, let us know roughly what kind of armaments they possess, how well defended they are and so on, we can then deploy our fighters, heavy arms and mobile forces. Do you foresee any kind of problem with this?'

I did not. I was eager to demonstrate my one-man airship. If I did well in this theatre, I would almost certainly be allowed to expand my activities and build some of my larger machines. I could further develop my idea of flying infantry. I became very cheerful at the prospect of taking to the air again.

Shortly before I returned to my hotel von Stohler had a visitor. There came a sharp knock on his door, and two high-ranking Falange soldiers stood there saluting. Passing between these men came a short, rather stout individual in full uniform. He, too, saluted in the conventional way and held out his hand first to von Stohler and then to me. I was astonished. The soldier was Franco himself. His eyes were cautious, rather distant, above a well-trimmed Hitler moustache. In his courteous Spanish he thanked me for volunteering in the Nationalist cause. He understood that I was of Spanish extraction. I was a patriot and a hero, he said. My nation honoured me. Heroism such as mine would be rewarded. Had we not met somewhere before? The Balearics, perhaps?

I had not met him as far as I remembered. He was insistent. I agreed I had spent a little time in Minorca with some Italian friends before the War, but I did not elaborate. When politely Stohler let me know that he and the Generalissimo had important matters to discuss, I raised my hat and left.

For some reason I felt a certain chill in my bones as I walked back to the hotel. I could not rid myself of fears for Mrs Cornelius, imprisoned on Hitler's orders. Why I associated that meeting with Franco, which had been perfectly civil, with my last moments with Hitler, when I had seen him glaring at me, I do not know. I piss in Hitler's mouth. I shit in Hitler's eyes. My whip rises and falls. Blood and excrement splatter against the sheets. Mrs Cornelius weeps behind bars. Hitler lusts for her. I shake my head to rid it of these bizarre images. Franco and Hitler had nothing in common, least of all their sexual tendencies. Even Mussolini had more in common with the Spanish dictator.

Two days later I was in Zaragoza. A cool, golden morning on a tranquil airfield. I watched my *Luftgeist* swell and strain as she was filled with hydrogen from a mobile tanker. While I would have preferred them to use helium gas, none was available to us. That rare element was a by-product of the US oil industry, and America needed it all for her own military projects. I was in no real danger, however, from the gas. Only a tracer bullet could ignite it, and nobody would use such ammunition against a machine the size of mine. I tested my harness and the controls, keeping the machine tethered for safety. Everything responded very well. We were ready for our first real flight! Even concerns for Mrs Cornelius were forgotten as I anticipated the pleasure to come.

On 16 March we heard that Barcelona had again been bombed by the Italians based in Majorca. The squadron was led by the dashing young air ace Bruno Mussolini. Evidently his father had found time to give him lessons or commissioned another airman to train him! I must admit I felt a pang of jealousy, a sense of betrayal. That honour should have been mine. The Germans, however, were critical of these raids. They saw Bruno as a typical Italian romantic, a young glory-seeker. Mussolini had achieved very little, they insisted, save to harden Republican resistance. Not long after this Bruno was removed from his squadron and recalled to Rome, some said after Hitler had tele-phoned Mussolini.

The next day, feeling a certain nervousness as well as excitement, I stood with a pair of Spanish aviators on a small airfield near the recently liberated town of Alcañiz watching as Nationalist soldiers steadied the guy ropes of my little airship so that I could be buckled into the combined airsuit and airframe and check that I had clear access to my instruments, my radio and my supply of water. The small fuel tank limited my range. I was unarmed. The engine was controlled from handlebars rather like those on a motorbike. The ailerons were adjusted from the stirrups in which I placed my feet.

My colleagues wished me good luck. I would be up for some six hours or more and had eaten a very hearty breakfast to maintain my energy. We had another beautiful, fresh morning with clear skies in all directions. For my safety I would have preferred a rather cloudier sky, since I would easily be visible from the ground. From the ground few artillerymen would be able to get my range so I had little to fear. The Spanish flyers reassured me. Even if they spotted me and recognised my ship for what it was, the Republicans had very little in the way of fighting aircraft left and few anti-aircraft guns.

Would I have attempted that flight just for the sake of it if I had no fears for Mrs Cornelius's safety? I think I would.

A few minutes later, settled comfortably into my apparatus, I squeezed the handlebar forward, gunning my engine to life. I heard the satisfying whine of the airscrew turning behind me. By moving my legs and feet I controlled my height; with my hands I could angle the machine from side to side. The radio operator's voice came clearly through my headphones. I replied in the affirmative and, as the soldiers let go of the anchor lines, ascended a little erratically into the sky. At first the gas-filled wing responded sluggishly. Then I had the sense of weightlessness one gets from ascending in a hot-air balloon. I felt a little sick with excitement. The ground fell steadily away. Soon I had reached a height of five hundred feet and could look down at the Spanish and German soldiers waving to me as I turned in a graceful sweep to the east, following the railway line

which would take me towards my destination, marked on a map-
board strapped to my left forearm.

I had never in my life felt such freedom or such personal triumph!
My sufferings and humiliations were forgotten. At last I was rising
above all the conflicts and pain of the world, experiencing the
epiphany I had longed for ever since, as a child, I had soared over
the rooftops of Kiev to the amazed delight of little Esmé Loukianoff,
my only sweetheart. This was my first true escape, the escape of
flight!

FIFTY–SIX

Checking the compass strapped to my wrist just below the map-board, I kept a steady course, gradually climbing until I was safe from anything but the most precise long-range anti-aircraft fire. The plains of Aragon rolled away before me, rising towards a line of low hills. Already on the roads I saw columns of trucks and infantry, some cavalry even. I observed no other aircraft in this area but understood that German pilots had been briefed to look out for me and not shoot me down! My markings were clearly Nationalist. Following the railway line I found several trains, some waiting in sidings to move men and munitions up to the front, and used my radio to report that all was well. I was extremely impressed by Franco's war effort. I had been told the Spanish of both sides were poorly armed, but I saw no sign of this. I was involved in a sophisticated modern war, not the confused conflict I had witnessed in Ukraine so many years before.

When I was convinced I had sufficient momentum and the prevailing wind was on my side, I switched off my engine to save precious fuel and let myself drift towards the enemy lines. I tested my radio again and was pleased to hear my own operator responding from the home base. I reported that I had seen no enemy yet.

Ahead were the hills and a series of shallow valleys. As I descended to get my bearings, a whole squadron of Heinkels roared past above me, dropping down upon a long earthworks behind which I now saw the Republican troops sheltering. Machine guns rattled. The ground spurted into life as bullets hit it and light artillery returned the aircrafts' fire. This skirmish between lightly armed Spaniards and German aircraft had its inevitable result. The Republicans had no chance. They were being wiped out and, as tanks appeared, began to fall back, heading for the low hills behind them.

I hovered, knowing I would be unwise to follow, watching as the

Reds were chased all the way up the shallow valley. I was witnessing a rout, and I felt almost sorry for the Republicans who were dropping in dozens. Eventually the survivors broke and fled in all directions. The planes turned and headed back towards their aerodrome, leaving me alone in the sudden silence of that cool, blue sky. I made radio contact and reported the incident. Now tanks and trucks were advancing, followed by the infantry. Aragon must soon fall to the Nationalists. Surely it would only be a matter of time before Barcelona was under siege.

Suddenly a voice broke into my headphones. In Spanish, I was being asked to investigate a low line of hills a little to my left where intelligence thought a division of the International Brigade was holding out. Obediently I gunned my engine. Turning my beautiful ship in a long slow dive, I felt like a huge shark making my predatory way through clear water. The little airscrew roaring behind me, my feet operating the stirrups which gave me extra lift, my hands directing me over the hills. I did not even hear the shots which struck my controls, puncturing the gasbag. How on earth had a few men with rifles managed to hit me? I cast around and saw some battlements. An old castle. A marksman hidden behind the stone walls?

The semi-rigid hull was compartmentalised. Only one section was leaking gas. I could easily get back to the aerodrome. I turned on my radio but failed to make contact. I was being jammed.

A real fear began to overcome me when I made to cut my engine off again and drift away from the enemy positions. The bar controlling the motor refused to respond. I tried everything I could to switch it off, but it still failed to answer my commands. The engine continued to roar, pushing me dangerously close to the line of hills. I was using far too much of my fuel. If I did not cut the engine quickly, I would be unable to make it back to my base under power. The best I could do was to try to gain height. Cautiously I crept up a few thousand feet where it was bitterly cold. The gas continued to escape from the hole the bullet had made, making the machine practically impossible to control.

I tried again to cut power, but the engine pounded on relentlessly. The airscrew at full throttle, I had soon overshot the hills, seeing no troops, but heading rapidly towards the coast. I was now far too deep into Republican territory, heading roughly in the direction of Tarragona and the sea, though I would run out of fuel long before I reached the Mediterranean. Any hope I might have of finding Majorca, say, and her friendly Italian-dominated skies, was baseless.

For an hour, keeping my height to avoid being shot at from below, I tried to stop the engine, but the whole thing remained jammed. Eventually the motor began to sputter and groan. My petrol was almost gone. Another few minutes and the propeller stopped. I was still airborne, but without any means of steering what had effectively become a small lopsided balloon. I was losing height as the left-hand wing, leaking hydrogen, continued to collapse.

I had no parachute, no means of unbuckling my harness without sending myself pitching straight towards the distant ground. Towns and villages sailed by below me. From my map and my compass I saw how prevailing winds would take me eventually to the sea. If I crashed into the Mediterranean at night I would have little chance of surviving but would sink with the remains of my ship. I could only hope that the wind changed again and took me back towards Zaragoza, but there seemed little chance of that.

Evening came. As it grew cooler, I began to drop slowly towards the ground. The sea was closer. The possibility of drowning was increasingly likely. I struggled in my suit, trying to discover a safe way of unhooking and unbuckling myself from the frame, but I could do nothing.

I remember a sense not so much of despair as of fatalism. I hardly saw any point in praying for survival. With my death Mrs Cornelius was free to marry again. My career as an airman was once again cut short by unfriendly Fate. God had no use for me as a flyer. I had cultivated the hubris of Icarus. I promised God that if He should save me now I would never try this experiment again. How many times now had I attempted solo flight only to be sent hurtling groundwards? Now there was even more chance of my dying. God had the common good in mind, not my personal glory! My cities would carry our children to a new security. My cities would fly. As I reconciled myself to my destiny, the fluttering wing collapsed, and I began rapidly to descend.

I was lucky. I came down at night unseen in a rocky field only a short distance from the water. Anticipating my descent, I grabbed tree limbs to slow my progress, using my flailing legs to fling my body backwards, employing the partially deflated gasbag to cushion my fall. I was badly bruised and scratched, but no bones were broken.

I began hastily to unstrap myself until I was clear of the apparatus. Exhausted and demoralised, I had no idea of my bearings but knew I had to get away from the little airship as soon as possible. Its Nationalist markings identified me as one of Franco's men. Aragon was notoriously communistic. The local peasants would tear me to pieces if they knew I had been involved in the attack on their defeated forces.

Luckily I still wore a civilian shirt and trousers, stout boots and a scarf around my neck. The rest of my suit had been built into the harness. I had no money, of course. No papers. I was cold and hungry. My water was used up. I could salvage nothing.

In spite of the pain I walked all that night, following country lanes, seeing no one, making out the occasional lights of a village or farmhouse but avoiding them. Judging myself to be safe, I finally risked sleeping in a ramshackle old stone barn.

I awoke to find myself being shaken by a small grinning boy asking me if I was separated from my brigade. The Twentieth had passed through in the night. He took me for a Republican soldier. Like me, others had lost their weapons fleeing before the Nationalists. Since he seemed sympathetic, I told him I was an American volunteer trying to rejoin my unit. Before I quite realised it, he had taken me by the hand and I was suddenly in a farmhouse full of desperate Reds. I knew panic only briefly before I had control of myself. This was, after all, familiar company. Not for the first time did I find myself in a civil war having to pretend to be a communist in order to survive.

That was how I came under the command of Major Johnny Banks, the Yorkshire trade unionist, and joined the march to Barcelona. For an enemy Banks had considerable wit and charm. His chief boast was that he brewed the best cup of tea on the entire Iberian Peninsula. He infused his men with exceptionally high morale, considering the fact that the brigade had only a few rounds of ammunition left and had been persistently strafed by Italian or German planes pushing home the advantages of the past few days. These battles had left the defenders in a pretty hopeless position. Luckily for me they had no notion of my politics. Major Banks assumed I was a Polish-American separated from his company who would rejoin it as soon as we made it back to Barcelona. The Bolshevist vocabulary was familiar to me, and I fell back into its use with an ease based on necessity.

Thus I had no trouble convincing these Reds of my credentials. I was dressed pretty much as they were. Having left all my German documents in Zaragoza and the others having been confiscated in Dachau, I had no papers, incriminating or otherwise, and I told them I had lost my rifle when I ran out of ammunition. To them I was a comrade and a hero. Indeed, I have rarely felt so thoroughly accepted in my life. Were it not for their politics, I would have had no ambiguity about joining them. My main concern was the same as theirs, to stay out of sight of the screaming German fighters and roaring German tanks.

Barcelona showed few signs of the recent Italian bombardments. The Germans were right to believe they had been quixotic and ineffectual. Billeted at various homes, I elected to remain with the Twentieth Kropotkin Brigade, originally an anarchist unit now commanded by a communist, with numbers made up from members of the International Labour Party and several Americans who belonged to the International Workers of the World, all English speakers. None of the other Americans were from California. I told them it was my home state. We would rest and rearm in Barcelona before returning to the front. Meanwhile we had some leave. At least I had time to think of some way to escape. My only hope was that Mrs Cornelius was not paying for my freedom. The Germans no doubt believed me killed when the plane went down.

Not entirely sure what to do, I found myself in Barcelona's Ramblas district, where the food was cheap and the people very pleasant. This became my favourite place to spend time. I had to try to make friends who were not Reds and get out of Barcelona as soon as possible. My idea was to board a neutral ship calling at Palma de Majorca. There I was sure I would be able to join up with my Italian colleagues. But I dare not arouse suspicion. I had no way of knowing how Mrs Cornelius fared.

As I strolled down a wide avenue one morning, looking at second-hand books on the stalls set in the middle of the streets, I was surprised to hear the familiar wheezing out-of-tune melody of a barrel organ and, to my astonishment, within a few moments was reunited once again with my old friend, the delighted Signor Frau, and his lovely daughter Heckie, my own sweet Zoyea. Though glad to see me, Zoyea had a rather gloomy, self-contained air, as she danced for the Catalan crowd. Signor Frau's attitude, however, was celebratory.

'My dear friend. I have not seen you since –'

Hastily I cautioned him to silence on that subject. I knew he had left Munich, but how had he come here from Madrid? He grew sad. He had been caught up in the fighting there when travelling outside the city. They had started from Munich with three horses. Two had pulled the family wagon. The other drew the barrel organ. This horse was ridden by his son. A Falangist commander in a small village they had passed through decided to requisition the riding horse. Against his father's wishes the boy resisted, lost his temper with the soldier and was shot. The horse was taken.

After giving his son a Christian burial, Frau had determined to get to Republican territory where he assumed he would be safer. He now feared for his daughter's virtue. Things were hardly any better here. When I told him that I was homeless he demanded I come back with him to their wagon. Certain we would meet again, he had kept my plans and my pistols for me. They had a spare bed in the wagon. He did not have to say that the bed had belonged to his dead son. Frau longed to hear my story. I was forced to modify a little, to spare his feelings. I informed him I had been flying for the Republicans when my plane had been shot down. Everything else I told him was as it happened.

But now, I said, I had no wish to go on fighting. I wondered if I could get home from Majorca, but I simply had no idea how to make the ten-hour voyage to Palma. At this Frau began to laugh disbelievingly. He himself had plans to try to join the Italians in Majorca and from there hoped to get a ship to Genoa. Italy was officially neutral and ordinary freighters still plied back and forth. He was in the process of selling his barrel organ but, as I had heard, it had developed a wheeze again. If I could help him repair it so that he could get a better price for it, I was assured a place in the boat he intended to buy. A little sailing vessel was his at very low cost. It would take us to the island in about a day.

FIFTY–SEVEN

'I've never known a luckier bastard than you, Ivan.'

I am not sure Mrs Cornelius knows what she is saying. How is it luck to be brought down out of the skies not once but four times?

She indicates her empty Guinness glass. 'Not only did yer meet up wiv your Aye-taye mate in Barcelona, but when his boat started sinkin' ya got picked up not by a bloody Russian or Frenchman, but by an Aye-taye submarine with another mate o' yours on board!'

'Major Pujol, the liaison officer, was scarcely a mate,' I point out, 'and let's face it, our boat was rotten. Frau had been cheated. It was already sinking when the Italian RS-14 started strafing it. Frau was killed. Zoyea herself was nearly drowned.'

'Put it this way,' she hands me the glass, 'ther boat would've sunk and th' lot of ya'd 'ave gorn ter th' bottom. This way ther sub started lookin' fer survivors an' at least picked th' two of yer up. An' yer'd never 'ave found Major Nye an' me, would ya?'

Sometimes I cannot always follow her reasoning.

She thinks the traffic fumes have gone to my brain. I could accuse her of a similar condition. Or perhaps we are inhaling the new orange paint in the pub? It contains lead, after all. Our accounts of events are not always the same, to say the least. How can a man recollect anything in tranquillity when he lives in such miserable times? Things were not this bad when I first got to England, even though the War was soon to begin.

When I arrived here North Kensington was a decent place to live. In Notting Hill and Notting Dale you knew who your neighbours were, and they knew you. Nobody talked to the police or the NHS. Nobody told debt collectors where you lived. Admittedly there was a certain amount of tension after closing time, but at least you had a good idea who was who, and by staying on good terms with the O'Days, Connors and other important local families, you rarely had any difficulties. You made sure your nose was clean, as Mrs Cornelius said, and, when the occasion demanded, your head stayed down.

That was the same lesson I had learned in Kiev and Odessa's Moldavanka. You kept trouble within boundaries. Local family rivalries were between each other or with the police. The police knew not to start trouble. If the press people called us 'denizens' rather than 'inhabitants' and thought it too dangerous to come down to Blenheim Crescent, we didn't care. Other Londoners had the idea we were criminals and prostitutes. You could not get a taxi to take you all the way home. Cabbies had a line they drew. If you lived below the junction of Westbourne Grove and Portobello Road, they would drop you off at the corner of Ladbroke Grove on top of the hill, making you walk the rest. During the so-called race riots they would only take you as far as the top of Kensington Park Road. And what were those riots? Reading the *Manchester Guardian* you had the impression of hordes of blacks and whites with knives and razors. Go outside your own door and you saw a couple of Teddy boys jeering at a West Indian or three Jamaicans going nose to nose with three cockneys.

Needless to say, most people living in the Gate or the Grove were honest, decent and hard-working, as respectable as any in London. Mrs Cornelius knew everyone. She was related to most of them on both sides of her family. We weren't space aliens. We all talked English, even if the accents differed. TV violence had not yet taken over from *Dick Barton* and *ITMA* on the wireless and the whole family listened to *Variety Bandbox, Family Favourites* and *Workers' Playtime*. The same as everyone, we ate our Marmite on crumpets and our jam on bread and butter. We drank Typhoo tea or Brooke Bond Dividend Tips. On Sundays those who could afford it cooked some sort of joint. The men went to the pub and read the *News of the World* until it was ready. I soon learned to enjoy these customs. Those were my happiest days.

I loved the films, the Ealing comedies, the American musicals, the Westerns. We shared the same radio and cinema stars, read the same daily papers; once a week the men bought *Tit-Bits* and *Reveille* and the women bought *Woman's Weekly* or *Red Letter*, boys had *Dandy, Beano, Hotspur, Adventure* and *Knockout*, girls had *Schoolgirl's Own* and *Girl's Crystal*. If you were more demanding in your fiction you ordered, as I did, the *Sexton Blake Library*, which published four books a month. By the 1940s the stories had become pure fiction and not up to the old standard, but I still found them entertaining. On the wireless we heard the same music. Every week I looked forward to *Big Bill Campbell's Rocky Mountain Round-Up*, a show reminding me of our happiest times in the USA during the 1920s. For more intellectual stimulus we tuned in *In Town Tonight*. All popular programmes with millions of listeners. We talked about them in the pub. The BBC brought us together. Only later, after the death of Lord Reith and the debacle of the Festival of Britain, did things change, taken over by Buggers Broadcasting Communism, as we used to say. Even then not everyone at the BBC was a bugger or a communist.

England began to go wrong after the old King died. I remember how hopeful everyone was at the coronation of Queen Elizabeth. Mrs Cornelius bought a television to watch it. She didn't pay cash. She got it on the 'never-never' when you could buy whatever you wanted on credit. You did not have to be a Bertrand Russell to see the result. Almost instantly we witnessed a falling away of morals, people's failure to accept responsibility for their own actions. You stopped saving and started speculating. This phenomenon was reflected in the large issues as well as the domestic. Even as the English let the old empire slip into the hands of godless black dictators, they anticipated a forthcoming New Elizabethan Age. Presumably we were going to buy that on hire-purchase instalments, too. We were entering an era of prosperity and choice, they said. We had more technicolour films, certainly, and they ended rationing so that you could buy more sweets or cardigans, but they cultivated, in my opinion, a false hope. Princess Elizabeth's marriage to a Greek was significant to those of us attending the Bayswater Orthodox Church, but then Philip was inducted into the Anglican faith and nothing came of that. Once the Greeks had counted on the British to save Christendom. Now the British looked aside and could not fill their own churches.

I sometimes wish I had not witnessed this decline, that I had arrived later, when the worst was over. But by that reasoning, I suppose, I would have been in a camp again somewhere in Europe. English social coherence lasted untouched to 1950 but was disappearing by 1958 when national service ended. Then came commercial television, the Egg Marketing Board, immigration and the notion of individual rights over the common good.

591

'Of course,' I tell Mrs Cornelius, 'I blame Adolf Hitler.' She does not disagree. To fight Hitler, the British Empire had to bankrupt herself. Britain mortgaged her heritage to the United States who pretended to help her fight the War but actually squeezed her dry. She had to sacrifice her workforce and watch her cities, already weakened by Hitler's bombs and rockets, collapse into rubble. Thereafter she was in permanent debt to the American banks. The Jews decided her foreign policy. When the War was over, the best of Britain's young people who survived went to Australia, Canada and South Africa, leaving only the riff-raff, the spivs, the Teddy boys and skiffle-kids. Instead of exporting ships, we exported pop music. Many German and Italian POWs chose to stay here, but Britain could not ask her former Allies for manpower because their own numbers were also depleted. So to replace the men she had lost, she called on the very people she had defended herself against, her 'lesser half-breeds without law or order', as Mr Kipling called them. Darkies and Orientals flooded into the vacuum Hitler had created of Notting Hill, Notting Dale and Brixton.

By 1955 our entire neighbourhood was a festering slum occupied by drug dealers, calypso singers and pimps. Ask poor Perek Rachman! He was destroyed by them and their degenerate allies, the Negrophilic decadent Cliveden set, Jewish aristocrats like John Profumo and whores like Christine Keeler. Her lovers made up half the House of Lords on one side, and an entire steel band on the other. Sports people and film stars like Freddy Fowler and Diana Dors enjoyed nothing better than being seen with Soho gang bosses and their powerful police friends from West End Central.

I knew all this at first hand from Mrs Cornelius. She was still doing film and TV work in 1950, though her roles became smaller due to American movies attracting a larger public. These, too, contributed to the rot. Richard Widemark and Robert Mitcham had a great deal to answer for. I told Mr Widemark this to his face on the bombsite where they were filming *Knights of the City*, in which Mrs Cornelius played a barmaid.

'Mr Widemark, do you know that you are held up as a model for our young people?' I asked him. We stood together in the ruins beside the Thames. Six o'clock in the morning. Widemark seemed unmoved. He asked me politely if I knew where you could buy American cigarettes. I was able to get him a couple of cartons of Pall Malls from contacts I had in the USAF PX.

After 1946 there was not a Hollywood sofa unsoaked with blood or a lake which did not contain a dozen corpses wearing concrete overshoes. For every *Singin' in the Rain* there were fifty *Pickups on South Street*. Meanwhile, the US scriptwriters rewrote our history to make Americans the heroes of every wartime encounter. Errol Flynn (admittedly Tasmanian originally) and John Wayne (who had had a secret sex change operation) personally saved Burma and China from the Japanese. Robert Ryan single-handedly defeated the Germans on D-Day. Those of us who suffered through the dark years of the War, who saw the British flyers going up day and night against the superior might of the Luftwaffe, still felt America might have stepped in a little earlier and, instead of supporting Hitler and Mussolini and Franco, before Hitler declared war on her in 1941, saved us all the trouble of the War and its consequences. No wonder the British public, who suffered so much, became confused by this imported American communist culture. For a while I was quite bitter about it. I watched Hollywood rewriting my history before my eyes.

'You've lost th' knack of enjoyin' life as it comes, Ivan.' Mrs Cornelius cannot help loving pleasure. Like my Esmé, she is an *Erdgeist*. She will never lose her joy in existence. She cheers me up in my most gloomy moments. She will not accept thanks. She still denies she got me transferred to the Institute and from there to freedom, even though she met me in Majorca, after I had been saved by Major Pujol. A coincidence? Extremely unlikely!

When the submarine picked us up I was able to hang on to my pistols, but my papers were lost, as was the last of my near useless 'snow'. I told Major Pujol how I had succeeded in escaping Red Barcelona in the boat, only to be attacked by the Fiat floatplane. He and the Italians were full of apologies, especially once they realised that my dead friend had been an Italian. Zoyea was not so forgiving of them, however, and refused to have anything to do with them or any of the other Italians in Palma even after we reached the city. I was the only one who could comfort her, but she became increasingly melancholic. We remained in Palma for the summer. One afternoon I borrowed Major Pujol's car and motored down the winding roads until we arrived at the pretty port of Andratx. The fishing village had lost none of its charm. We stopped for lunch at the Restaurant Fleming, and there by the big window I saw Mrs Cornelius. She had just finished singing and stood by the big, dark

Broadwood piano looking out to sea. She was a Vermeer. I spoke her name and she turned.

'Ivan!' She came over to our table, chortling and winking at me about my delightful little 'catch', for Zoyea had now become a very pretty young lady.

Leaving Germany, originally she thought for a holiday, Mrs Cornelius had first arrived in the village with Desmond Reid who owned a flat here. Reid, too, found it politic to leave the rather oppressive atmosphere of Hitler's Berlin. Did I know Major Nye was in Palma? I did not, of course.

'I'm orlways 'ere of an evenin'.' Before we left, Mrs Cornelius gave me Nye's card. She was planning to go back to England, she said. 'Dezzie' had long since been persuaded to rejoin UfA and continue to act in German films, but that didn't suit her. 'Too many of me pals keep disappearin'.' Her new passport had finally come through.

I no longer had a passport, as I explained to Major Nye when I finally saw him. He asked if I had any objection to going to England. They needed someone with my skills and brains over there. He could not procure for me a British passport, but he had taken charge of a group of English prisoners who had been fighting Franco and had survived being machine-gunned on the beach as they came ashore near Palma after the fall of Barcelona. If I didn't mind mucking in with them, he thought he could get me to London and see about sorting out papers for me once there.

That was how I was reunited with Major Johnny Banks who vouched for me as a member of the International Brigade. I was 'repatriated' to England in the autumn of 1939, shortly before the outbreak of the Hitler war. Zoyea, I heard, worked in Palma and married after the War. But we were never again to be lovers.

'I have so much to thank you for,' I tell Mrs Cornelius. 'I might have died in Dachau.'

'Y've got yer mate ter fank fer that,' she insists. 'The bloke who joined the Gestapo and then was in the SS. Wot's his name? Prince Nicky Wotsit, wot got yer inter trouble in France. Killed at Stalingrad.' Irrationally she still believes Kolya framed me for the Paris Airship fraud rather than saved me from the worst of the consequences. But I no longer argue. I am not even sure he died as she thinks. I will mourn him only when I have certain news. As usual my reply is logical.

'But why should Kolya have arrested me and then freed me?'

'Maybe 'cause yer dumped 'im in the desert that time? Tort yer a lesson, didn't 'e? Well, 'e could see yer'd be useful in Spain, wot wiv talkin' the language an' that, so 'e orlways knew 'e could get yer art. Didn't they make yer some sort o' spy?'

'I was supposed to gather intelligence. We were testing my ship. They mentioned your name. They said you were in Belsen. I've told you all this. Kolya was explicit. If I didn't do what they wanted, you wouldn't be freed. I didn't know you had escaped until I got to Majorca.'

She laughs. 'An' found I'd been livin' the life o' fuckin' Riley in th' ol' port at Dez Reid's. Croonin' in ther local dance band! I woz earnin' a tidy littel livin' for a few months, while the Aye-tayes an' the soldiers woz still comin'. An' everyfink was so cheap, Ive. Bloody paradise. Still, ol' Major Nye got yer ter England, eh, when they demobbed ther International Brigade. Better than going back ter Odessa like some o' them poor buggers, or France, or Germany, yer gotta admit.'

She minimises her part in all that. Even in prison she was my guardian angel. Kolya was powerless to help me. He told me so. And if Kolya was able to get me released in 1937, why couldn't he get me out earlier? Why, as Mrs C suggests, was it up to the SS? After all, the Spanish conflict began in 1936. By the time I arrived in Barcelona, the war was as good as won. Germany and Italy had thrown their weight behind Franco. True, Major Nye was the intelligence officer attached to the government authorities, but he could not have helped me if she hadn't told me where to find him.

When it was clear Franco had overwhelmed the government forces, Major Nye sent me and a dozen others who had served under Johnny Banks on to Lisbon and from Lisbon home to London. By then the others knew I wasn't American but believed me to be a German anti-Nazi and covered for me. I had actually seen Santucci and his Italians machine-gunning Republicans as they waded ashore in Majorca, thinking they had found at least some brief relief from their demoralising defeats. Whatever my sympathies, this massacre of defeated, tired soldiers disgusted and horrified me. At various times in Palma I had been threatened with hanging, both as a Spanish traitor and as a Russian spy, but I could easily prove the accusations false. Major Pujol had vouched for me all he could without getting court-martialled himself. He even colluded with Major Nye when the time came to get me to England. He took many risks and died, I learned recently, impoverished in Madrid, a minor civil servant.

I know nothing much worse than civil war, which is usually conducted with the worst ferocity. Yet for all the Spanish bloodshed and cruelty, I never witnessed anything as bad as the horrors of Ukraine, nor was Franco, in victory, as vengeful as Lenin, Trotsky or Stalin. Say what you will about the General, he remained a devout supporter of the Opus Dei all his life and was in turn thoroughly supported by that godly society, whose part in the Spanish revolution has never been properly acknowledged.

I hold no brief for Catholics or their leaders, but while Mussolini and Hitler sought rapprochement with the Pope to further their own political ends, Franco received genuine blessing for his efforts. America, too, remained a great friend to Spain throughout the War and long afterwards. The Generalissimo was permanently grateful for that. He believed it stupid to persecute Jews just for being Jews. He felt the same about Negroes. The last letter I ever received from Mr Mix, after he wrote from Washington many years later, made it clear how he owed his life to Franco's pro-Americanism. Only when the Nationalists discovered Mix was an American, and not a Moroccan, did they spare his life. He, of course, continued to work in Europe until the early fifties, when he was recalled to the home bureau and became some kind of civil rights expert at CIA head-quarters. I heard this from Major Nye. I never did understand why Mr Mix stopped writing to me. I am not, I hope, one to exploit a relationship, but that man owed me something. Americans have short attention spans. No doubt he forgot. US intelligence people are inclined to abstractions at the best of times. They are not people to remember favours.

⁂ FIFTY–EIGHT ⁂

Soon after I reached London in 1939 I made for Mr Green's Whitechapel office. I quickly found 22 Leman Street. A worn brass plate announced the name of his firm, Green, Green & Collins (Import/Export) Ltd. Mounting the stone steps to the door, I hesitated before it just as I imagined an old Knight of Chivalry might have paused outside the Temple of the Grail. For many years I had dreamed of climbing those steps, knocking on the door and being received by the kindly old man. Mr Green would usher me into a mahogany and oak office lit by yellow gas casting warmth through the shadows. My Uncle Semyon's old partner would sit me in a big leather armchair and send for a brass-bound box in which my financial papers and scientific patents were stored. My money would have made me considerable interest. Mr Green would congratulate me on my wealth. He would give me avuncular advice on how to invest it. Perhaps I would be offered a position with the company. He might suggest the firm back my scientific inventions. None of this pipe dream was unrealistic but based on promises Uncle Semyon and his people had made.

Yet when I was admitted into a shabby, unpainted reception room, I was told by a girl telephonist that the Greens had, in her words, gone down the drain after the old man's death. The 'old man' was presumably the Mr Green my uncle had originally dealt with. She was the only person I was allowed to see. She was thoroughly ignorant. I was convinced her employers knew more, but even when I lost my temper, they refused to come out and meet me. The place was now a shipping office. Only the name had been retained, she said. She knew of no other connection. Eventually, when she offered to call the police from the nearby station, I left.

Later I tracked down Mr Green's great-nephew, Lionel Shapiro, in Temple Fortune, beyond Hampstead, and put the question to him.

Where is my inheritance? Shapiro claimed to know little of his uncle's affairs. 'He was persuaded to back Lenin's New Economic Policy. Then Lenin died and Stalin cancelled all deals. Between them, Stalin and the General Strike ruined him.'

As you might expect, Lionel Shapiro denied any knowledge of me or my money. He took me into his little house and introduced me to his grandmother, Mr Green's sister-in-law, a wizened old thing, wearing black. When she heard where I was from and what I had escaped, she was kind enough. Her English was thickly accented, but she spoke good German. She made her grandson go up into the attic and bring down some old ledgers, which recorded details of transactions between my Uncle Semyon's firm in Odessa and Mr Green's in London. But they only listed details of goods and money. I was mentioned nowhere. The pathetic pair apologised. They wished they could help, they said, but so many needed help these days. I was convinced they were innocent. Clearly they were not living in salubrious surroundings. I put the sorry story together: out of desperation Mr Green had probably defrauded me of my inheritance and his family of their birthright. But what was the point of pursuing a dead man?

I refused to let Mr Green's death be the end of my dreams. When the Ministry of War refused even to grant me an interview, when they sent back my plans unopened, I accepted that God had abandoned me. He did not want me to fly. And He did not want me to have money.

He knows I have done my best for my fellow creatures. I have shown prejudice to no man. I never attacked those Jews. Why should I? I am not an ingrate. A Jew saved my life in Arcadia. *Stadt der schlafenden Ziegen; Stadt des Verbrechens; Stadt der meckernden Krähen; die kleinen Vögel singen trügerische Lieder. Die Synagogen brennen!* He said he was a journalist. He was a poet. He made me tea. He gave me bread. I have no proof that he put the metal in my stomach. If he did he might have meant it kindly. Perhaps it was a charm. Perhaps it kept me alive. Those *shtetls* were no worse than the camps. I received only kindness there. I almost died in that burning synagogue. Who did I betray? What else have I done? What have I said?

I have given half my adult life to this city. Four times I had the chance to save it from the worst its enemies could fling at it. Four times I was rejected. The first time was before the authorities sent me to the Isle of Man when war broke out. I gave them copies of my plans, excluding certain details. Some, I know, they passed on to the likes of Wallace Barnes, the lunatic self-publicising brother of the would-be Queen of England, who modified them and called them his own. The second time was just after Dunkirk, when they were again desperate for ideas. I spent a week in the country near Oxford talking to various government scientists who were particularly interested in my Violet Ray and my gigantic war submarine, but told me they were too expensive to put into production.

The third time was when the V-2 rockets were raining down. They were curious about my Electronic Dome, a kind of shield over the entire city. Again they lacked the vision to realise the possibilities of the idea. The last time was in 1950 when they became briefly interested in my Russian background. They admitted they found corroborative evidence that I had defended Kiev with the Violet Ray. They had received some hint, I think, that Stalin planned to revive the idea. And Hess had told them something. But little came of that either.

In spite of all the disappointments and frustrations I remain in constant contact with politicians and journalists to this day, offering them my intellectual blood. My miracles. All for the good of the Free World, to help sustain the security of our homeland, to bring into existence a new world order. Even after I became naturalised, they treated me little better! I blame the communists, both in the Kremlin and in Whitehall. At one time more dedicated communists were working for the British than worked for Stalin.

Brodmann's hand was everywhere in those early years. In April 1943 I saw him in Westminster coming out of Downing Street. I am sure he noticed me. Before I could challenge him he got on a southbound number 12 bus. Was he going to Croydon? I doubt it. He was Stalin's personal messenger. Most likely he had been arranging dinner with 'Dandy Kim' or Sir Stanley Blunt. They would have asked him about me, and he would have told them how dangerous I was to Stalin. I suppose I must count my blessings. I was lucky not to be arrested or killed. I was returning from a trip to Westminster Cathedral with Arnold Noyes, who had been a cavalryman in the 10th Hussars. Arnold was a Chelsea Pensioner, another beneficiary of Johnny Banks. Noyes's regiment had served in Afghanistan, the Soudan and South Africa. He had been wounded in a famous battle with the Boers, but I forget its name. Lord Winston Churchill had ridden with them, he said. Noyes was a great admirer of the Old

Bulldog, though he had a great deal of time for the man he called 'Major Attlee', who in his own way had also done his best to defend the empire. Their politics aside, the Labour Cabinet ministers, with a couple of miserable exceptions, were convinced imperialists. Their debts were so considerable they could no longer afford to defend the empire as the US squeezed Britain for repayments of loans.

After he was re-elected I wrote several times to Lord Churchill, pointing out how I had been libelled and schemed against by communists. I thought he must surely understand. Attlee could not help but be bedazzled by the Reds. He had fought on the Republican side in Johnny Banks's own brigade. Churchill possessed only contempt for communists. He understood the realities behind their protestations of friendship. He was aware of their greedy cunning. If I had not kept my plans safely hidden, who knows what Stalin would have done with them? But by the time he was able to hear me out Churchill was already finished, his brain little better than a brandy-soaked sponge. The one letter I received from him was brief and incoherent. A great tragedy. I think he lacked the discipline of Mussolini, yet I am convinced the two men might have become great friends if Il Duce had allied himself with his natural comrades, the British and Americans, and stood his ground, as was his natural inclination, the way Churchill stood his. In the end Mussolini allowed himself to be influenced by the 'rouge boys' he despised and met a fate he did not deserve.

Meanwhile, Maddy Butter and Margherita Sarfatti, who had done nothing to help him in the end, lived out their days in comfort abroad. I saw La Butter on TV quite recently. She has become an expert anti-Fascist and has moved back to Texas where she works for the arch-liberal Lyndon Johnson.

FIFTY–NINE

After the British authorities released me from the Isle of Man I worked for a while at St Mary's Hospital, Paddington. Many US soldiers were treated there. Some had been wounded at the Battle of the Bulge. They had known the German troops and tanks were all around them and had reported this to their intelligence, but intelligence, part of their centralised command structure, had responded that the soldiers were wrong. Tanks or troops could not be there because the German Army was in retreat. I knew how those GIs felt. All my life I tried to warn the world of the real threats. All my life I have been mocked for my pains. Those of us who experienced the German concentration camps knew a similar experience. No one was interested. Even in Palestine and America nobody wanted to know. One denial follows another. Who listens?

While on the Isle of Man I lost touch with Mrs Cornelius and only met her again through St Mary's in 1945 when the bombing was over. The V-weapons had stopped. I for one was grateful. Those bombs got on your nerves. Two big buildings near St Mary's were totally destroyed by them while I was in the shelter.

The first I knew of Mrs Cornelius's presence at St Mary's was the distinctive sound of her voice coming from the American wing, her familiar rendering of 'A Little of What Yer Fancy Does Yer Good'. I thought at first I had gone mad or that I heard a record. She had been employed to entertain the GIs.

Slightly heavier than when last I had seen her but still able to fit into one of her wonderful sequinned evening gowns, she was as lively as always. When she saw me standing there her face flared with pleasure! The wounded men applauded heartily as she brought her number to a conclusion and ran towards me. I knew exactly what she would say:

'Blimey, Ivan! It's ther bad penny again! 'Ow d'yer do it?' She was delighted. She represented so much for me, but I think I, too, represented something to her. She thought my ability to survive all vicissitudes was miraculous. I, in turn, knew that, for all her humanity and my God-appointed good fortune, she remained my guardian angel.

We embraced to further enthusiastic applause. Those soldiers were a generous audience. She insisted I not leave the hospital until she finished her engagement. When she was ready I took her across the road to my lodgings, apologising for them. She told me her own digs were not much better since she had lost her 'soldier' to a German bomb when they blitzed the old Café de Paris. The West End apartment had been in his name, and she had been given notice. 'Which woz just as effin' well. That caught a bomb too abart a month later!' She laughed heartily at her good luck.

I was living across the road in Paddington Street at that time. Major Nye had helped me find my flat when I was returned to London. Classified as a friendly alien, I still had to go to the Isle of Man for a year where I met the charming Lord and Lady Mosley. Major Nye also obtained my release and found me a job at St Mary's Hospital as a maintenance engineer.

Johnny Banks became an MP after the war. He, too, had helped me in 1939. For a while I lived with only temporary papers, working for the big Ford garage on the Harrow Road. I never lost my touch for an engine. After hostilities broke out I presented myself at the War Office to offer my services there. My Land Leviathan and Giant Mole, as well as my superairship, had still to be built, and then was the perfect moment to develop them. But they seemed more interested in my nationality than my plans. Again I found myself embarrassed. Because agreeing with them was the easiest way to go, as Johnny Banks explained, I let the British determine that I was a Polish refugee. A 'free Pole' as we used to say. I was still officially married to Mrs Cornelius. After we were united she had no objection to my using that advantage, now that I was at last in her country. 'After all, Ivan, ya did me ther same favour, and one good turn deserves anover.' Thus we were able to get a council flat, the first we had in Blenheim Crescent. We needed it. I had been badly disappointed.

In 1947 Johnny Banks and Major Nye's friend in social services at Westminster Council were instrumental in helping us soon after Labour came to power. Nye agreed the British public had turned

602

its back on Churchill. I was still not then naturalised, so I could not vote. I did, however, understand why things went the way they did. Americans still ask me, 'How could the British set themselves against the man and the party who got them through the war? Who had defeated Hitler? What on earth was the cause of the Labour landslide?' I find it hard to explain, myself. We trusted Churchill in war, I say, but not in peace. Even the King and Queen were not so popular in those days. Many knew they had planned to flee to Canada during our 'darkest hour'. Certainly the royal couple had tried to make peace with Hitler through Lord Halifax, whom Roosevelt favoured as prime minister over Churchill. Halifax was a well-known and committed appeaser. The puritanical Americans liked him because he didn't drink. Nobody except the public thought Churchill could lead us to victory in 1940, and nobody except the public thought Attlee could make the best of the peace. Attlee gave us the National Health Service, rationalised transportation, school meals and the Old Age Pension. When he did not bring the Golden Age, Churchill was voted back, but by then he was too old. I had the pleasure of meeting him once at the Polish Club. Even when I addressed him in the friendliest of words he was too drunk to speak.

I eventually moved across the road in Blenheim Crescent when Mrs Cornelius's children were returned to her. After her marriage was annulled she got the larger flat at number 77. Then I lost my place and had to take the present one. Jerry, Frank and Catherine all believed I only married her to be eligible for accommodation. When Catherine decided I was actually their father, I think they understood. Rackman was my landlord for a while in Ladbroke Grove. He was Polish, but a genuine gentleman. Rackman never raised my rent, which was cheap enough, so by 1960 it made no sense to move anywhere else. Chelsea became impossible, as did Paddington and Pimlico. All those places have been gentrified now. I refuse to pay thirty shillings a week for a tiny furnished room and kitchenette!

I tell these young people how it used to be, but they have no desire to learn. They hate the past. It conflicts with their identities. They want everything to be romantic, even the worst of it. The past's only function is as escape, to comfort them, to confirm their ambitions, their greed. Anything or anyone who contradicts their invented fictions is rejected, through anger, through mockery, through contempt. I try to help them see how it was; how a situation was complicated or hard to define or hard to foresee, and they insist on educating me in their versions of events. Even the camps. They watch TV or go to the pictures and know exactly how it was. They ask me why we did not resist, why we did not notice, why we 'denied' the truth.

'And you are so different?' I say.

But the past, like minorities, exists only so that they might feel superior.

'Don't listen to the effing Pole,' I hear them say in the pub. 'There he goes, sounding off again, the old fart.' You bring them urgent messages. You try to help them. And they laugh at you, or worse.

SIXTY

Some people will exploit the few who possess a genuine desire to connect with their own history. As clairvoyants prey on the bereaved, these cynics prey on lonely men and women. They assume the authority of the dead. Even I have been deceived, and I am the least gullible of people. I am always sympathetic to those who suffer. My life has been one experience of betrayal after another. Yet perhaps the worst occasion was only a few years ago. Not something of which I speak often, just as we do not speak of the camps. Nobody wants to know. Mrs Cornelius herself has never been told the whole story. 'Not now, Ivan,' she tells me with a shudder. 'It puts yer off yer tea.' Or else it spoils her mood or comes at a wrong moment.

I can give you the perfect example of this kind of self-delusion. Rather shocking, it made me see myself in a thoroughly different light. One should always review one's own responses and ideas from time to time, for the sake of intellectual clarity as well as one's moral well-being. One should constantly challenge one's own presumptions. *Die Götter der Finsternis haben ihre Streitmacht gesammelt. Sie reiten auf dem Wind, der nach Western jagt. Die Briten sind schuld. Sie lassen alles Böse herein. Sie dulden den Osten im eigenen Land. Man betrachte die Portobello Road. Eine Kultur kann Licht und Dunkel nicht ewig im Gleichgewicht halten. Persien wusste das. Was haben die Briten aus ihrem Weltreich gemacht? Einen leeren Namen. Und Karthago bleibt bestehen. Der Moloch wird seinen Feuerschlund öffnen: und die Briten werden hineinmarschieren, einen ihrer Songs auf den Lippen. Weg mit ihnen, sie haben es verdient! Es waren schwarz gekleidete Männer und Frauen; wahrscheinlich hatten wir Samstag. 'Sind sie Jude?' fragte ein junger Mann auf Russisch. Nennt mich Judas. Oder Petrus. Ich wollte es nicht bestätigen.*

A few years ago a letter was sent to me at my shop. This event was in itself a rarity! Usually any correspondence comes to Portobello Road in buff-coloured envelopes and fails to spell my name correctly.

But this was addressed in an educated Continental hand on a pale blue, square envelope of the best quality. Basildon Bond or something better.

The real surprise, however, lay within the envelope, for the majority of the letter was in Cyrillic, a fine, feminine Russian script so shockingly familiar that I raced through the closely written pages to the signature. The hand was that of Esmé Vallir, née Loukianoff, my childhood sweetheart, my ideal. She spoke nostalgically of Kiev and South Russia, referring to events only she could know about. She had good news. My mother had also survived both Stalin and Hitler and was here in London staying in a hotel near the house of a family friend in Princelet Street, Spitalfields.

I am not sure if anyone could imagine the intensity of my response. Because of events in Kiev since I'd left, I had been forced to conclude that my mother was probably dead. Naturally I had made considerable efforts to contact her from time to time, especially through my cousin Shura. Eventually I despaired of restoring those links and privately mourned her. Indeed, I mourned her every day.

By 1969 when I received Esmé's letter, I had become a successful businessman. No longer did I get oil under my fingernails. No longer was I reduced to repairing motorbikes and lawnmowers for Carpenters', the big hardware store in Portobello Road. Some years earlier, with the help of Mrs Cornelius, I had opened my own premises just a few doors down from Carpenters' themselves. In those days you had no trouble getting a lease. The rent was reasonable, and my goods were popular. Tourists came from all over the world. I was selling fine-quality furs and second-hand evening wear, also Guards' and Marines' dress uniforms which I bought very cheaply through the War Ministry. The collapse of the old empire, I must admit, put many fine costumes my way. Frank Cornelius's idea was to call the place 'The Spirit of St Petersburg'. That romantic and misleading epic *Doctor Zhivago* was soon to make Russian nostalgia very commercial.

From the beginning I specialised in furs. Foxes, stoles, bolero jackets, winter coats, hats. Thanks to television serials the girls were rediscovering the elegance of the previous century. I expanded as the fashion demanded. I sold not used clothes, but historic apparel. Heaven forbid I should end my days as an old-clothes man! This was a business requiring taste and a keen sense of the past. Film and TV companies came to rent from me. I did not buy every piece of tat which came my way. I attended auctions. I went to theatres which were closing down. To film studios. In my shop I was soon able to offer costumes from *The Wicked Lady* and *Beau Brummell*, from *The Four Feathers*, *The Drum* and *Great Expectations*. I continue to do good business with the music community.

Reading Esmé's letter surrounded by so much history was a powerful sensation. At that time I even had some Cossack and Hussar uniforms, though they too were theatrical, part of a consignment from a touring production of *The Merry Widow* which ran out of money in Swindon. The manager had appealed for help to Mrs Cornelius, then playing one of the matrons, and I had stepped in with an unrefusable offer that paid for the cast's bus back to London. The uniforms and gowns were of very good quality and needed only a little modification to give them a thoroughly authentic appearance. The majority of them sold within a week. They provided the holiday I took with Mrs Cornelius to Hastings that year.

We stayed in some style at the Grand Hotel. By sheer luck I was able to make yet another 'killing' with some costumes from an ambitious pantomime which had not done as well as expected the previous Christmas. The 'big heads' were genuine Victorian, great vividly painted grinning things. I sold many of the Pierrot, Colombine and Harlequin costumes on to the Rambert Company who were still active in Notting Hill Gate. Several found their way into the Victoria and Albert Museum. Those were very good years for business and the arts, if not for science. But all that changed with decimalisation of the currency, a confidence trick on us all.

Esmé spent several pages explaining what had happened to her since we had last met in Makhno's camp during the Civil War. (*I was fucked so much I had calluses on my cunt.*) Reading her beautiful writing, I began to experience genuine shame for judging her so harshly. What a puritanical fellow I had been! I had been young, deeply in love with her and highly idealistic. But in my disgust, I had been insensitive. She had seemed so hard and cynical. Of course, she had been trying to disguise her shame and outrage. What I had mistaken for aggression was nothing but a protective shell. The letter made all that so clear. Esmé spent only a few sentences explaining how she had escaped the anarchists and returned eventually to Kiev where she had become a schoolteacher. She had seen several of our old friends regularly. Her father had died during the first siege of Kiev, and poor Herr and Frau Lustgarten had been shot as alleged

German collaborators during Hrihorieff's brief occupation of the city. My mother continued to work as a laundress and a seamstress, Esmé said. They met about once a week. I, of course, was always their preferred subject of conversation. They were convinced I had escaped to England or America and made a great success as a scientist. '*Never once did your mama believe you to be anything but alive and flourishing.*'

I had written to my mother a number of times since leaving Odessa, but the letters had never been answered. Eventually I came to accept that she was dead, no doubt a victim of Stalin's planned famines. Esmé herself had lost touch with my mother when she became the representative for a Georgian wine company in Odessa during the period of the New Economic Policy. Soon after Lenin's death she realised things were not going to improve in Russia and while in the Middle East met and married a Palestinian Christian, Edouard Vallir, himself a successful wine merchant. Esmé had never gone home. She and her husband established themselves in Haifa and were very successful. Only after the State of Israel was declared did they find it necessary to move, first to Tunisia and later to Marseilles. Monsieur Vallir died a year after they received their French citizenship.

In 1955 Esmé Vallir sold the business and retired, but she continued to travel. During a visit to Jaffa she spilled some coffee on her blouse and ran into my mother working at a nearby dry-cleaner's! '*I knew her at once. She has hardly changed. Her face is as sweet and noble as it always was and she is still strong as an ox. She, of course, didn't like to tell me her age, but I knew you had been born when she was seventeen, when that wicked father of yours ran off.*' Understandably, this was more than my mother had ever told me! In those days one did not speak of such things in front of one's own children. My mother always sought to protect me from the cruelties of the world. Though she had hinted at it, my father's relationship to a famous noble family would still have constituted a death warrant in those days.

My mother worked at the cleaner's part-time. '*You know how she always preferred to occupy herself . . . She had some terrible experiences, Maxim. She almost died in the famine. Then the Germans sent her to Babi Yar. She escaped with two other women. They caught her again in Poland. They sent her to Auschwitz in 1944, and she would have been killed except she spoke several languages and was useful as an interpreter in one of the offices. She had been selected to die just before the Allies came. Luckier*

608

than most, eh? After over two years in a DP camp, she immigrated to Jaffa in 1948. She was extraordinarily fit, all things considered; you would think her ten or twenty years younger. No doubt her good health also saved her from the "selections".'

The thought of my poor, brave mother, who had sacrificed everything for me, being humiliated and terrorised in one of those camps disgusted and infuriated me. The experience was bad enough when it happened to me, but I was young and male. Everything was so much worse for women, especially dignified older women of her breeding. If she had not escaped from Babi Yar, she would no doubt have died there. The Nazis had a chance to wipe out most traces of that camp. The Russians filled it in then forgot about it. Babi Yar was the same gorge I flew over when, to impress Esmé, I took my first aircraft into the sky. By the time the Allies arrived in Poland and Germany, it was too late to do much. In Auschwitz my mother spent four days hiding under a hut, with nothing to eat, waiting for liberation. When it came, said Esmé, my mother's first thought was to ask after her son. She had always imagined me leading an army unit to her rescue! As I read I was moved to tears. Why did I feel I had let her down by not being there?

Knowing the name I had used in Russia, Esmé developed a habit of searching for it through the phone books of every city she visited. She usually found more than one Pyatnitski or Piatniski, but she doggedly asked the same questions. Only she, of course, knew certain things about us. Esmé particularly remembered that incident of the aeroplane. *You flew down into the Babi Gorge and almost killed yourself!* None of the others had been able to answer her on that issue.

In London years earlier Esmé came across my name in an old book, but I had moved. Not until she was on holiday in London again last year did she pick up a tourist magazine which published details of the Spirit of St Petersburg along with a photograph with my name, describing me as an 'old Cossack aviator who fought against Stalin'. I remember the piece. It was fanciful, written by one of Mrs Cornelius's sons. At the time I had been a little nervous at the amount of detail. Moorcock was involved in the magazine (*London Spirit*) during its brief existence. The 1960s threw up dozens of such publications.

Esmé had tried to contact me then. She was due to catch her flight back to St Malo, where she now lived. The magazine had not published my full address, but she dropped me a postcard anyway, she said. Though she had written in English, it might not have reached me. As soon as she was able, she got in touch with my mother suggesting the two of them visit London the following year and try to contact me again. They had planned to surprise me in the shop. Then they realised it might be too much of a shock. Esmé joked how she didn't know how strong my heart was. My mother had an old friend from Kiev living at Princelet Street, Spitalfields, a private house. It might be a good idea for us to meet there. We would have time to settle, to talk, and, if things became too emotional, we could be left alone for a while. If, however, I preferred them to come to Portobello Road, or somewhere else, she would be happy to bring my mother.

Esmé's delicacy of understanding impressed me. Merely knowing that my mother was alive and in England was enough to strike me dumb. I could hardly breathe as I sat reading behind my till, fanning myself with the pages, so distracted that I almost let one of those Czech hussies steal a green feather boa from the rack. Those girls are whores. They are skilled thieves. This is what communism has taught them.

Few can imagine how Esmé's news affected me. Both the beloved women from my past, whom I had worshipped above life, whom I had given up for dead, were only miles away on the other side of the city.

Spitalfields was an unfamiliar and not altogether savoury part of London. I had been there once or twice to buy stock in Petticoat Lane when first starting my shop, but now auctions, theatres and armies supplied me with what I needed. It seemed another minor miracle that a friend of my mother's had been over there without my knowledge.

I felt, I will admit, somewhat guilty. Perhaps over the years I really had not made sufficient effort to find my mother. God knew I had done a great deal. Even when convinced she was dead I had sent enquiries to the Soviet government and received no reply. I had not known what name she was living under. I could not tell the Reds too much. Brodmann's shadow continually cast itself over my fate. One slip and I would be the victim of an assassin's poison bullet. Anyone close to me was in equal danger. The thought of my mother being targeted for assassination terrified me. Esmé had foreseen this. She had lost none of her intelligence. She had been right to send a letter first. It occurred to me that I did not know if my mother was using an alias. Pyatnitski, while it had become familiar to everyone who knew me, was not our original name. That would be instantly recognisable to anyone familiar with the history of the Romanoffs! Another reason why I had been so cautious about communicating with her.

Esmé had included the number of the hotel where they were staying. As soon as I felt strong enough, I went round the corner to the phone boxes. To use my own phone would be foolish. I dialled the number and asked for Esmé's room. After some time, the telephone was picked up. A tentative voice said, 'Yes?'

I asked if that were Mrs Vallir.

A pause. 'No.'

I risked a few words in Russian. 'Will she be back soon?'

The woman answered more confidently. 'Oh, yes. She has gone to pick up some theatre tickets. Another half-hour at most.'

My heart was beating horribly. Instead of replacing the receiver, I asked breathlessly, 'I am sorry, I am not sure of your name. Would you tell her that Maxim phoned?'

'Maxim?'

I was almost in tears. 'Mother?'

'Oh, Maxim, my boy. So it is you.'

I tried to make a joke, but I knew my lips were trembling. 'No one else, Mother. I'm sorry I could not get back to Kiev as I promised. You had to travel all the way to London to see me.'

She was weeping and even less capable of speech than I. Her words ran together, becoming hard to understand. She had missed me so much. Knowing that we would one day be reunited had kept her alive. Everything was now worth it. Esmé was a saint. Was I married? Did I have any children?

Knowing the phone might still be tapped, I paused to collect myself. I said I would ring the hotel in an hour. If it was convenient, I would meet her at her friend's house in Spitalfields. It would save her another journey and would probably be more convenient for everyone. She began to give me the address, but I told her I already had it. 'Even in London, it is best to assume the walls have ears.'

We were still both weeping when I put the phone down. I had to take control of my emotions before I left the phone booth. I could not afford to let those little ruffians see me in a weakened condition. An hour later I returned to the row of boxes. During the time I was gone someone had used the vacant one as a urinal. I tried the box next to it. Vandalised. Some child had attempted to get the money out of it. Another short walk brought me to Westbourne Grove and a phone good enough to use. By then I was in better control of myself thanks to the exercise.

This time I spoke to a younger woman. Her faintly accented English was excellent. This was, of course, Esmé. We arranged to meet that afternoon at Princelet Street. Then, if it seemed a good idea, we would go on to Liberty. According to Esmé, my mother had long dreamed of taking tea with me at the Ritz, but the Ritz was already full up. I said I preferred Liberty. Liberty was cheaper, better and never overbooked.

At my flat I dressed carefully and conservatively. I did not even tell Mrs Cornelius where I was going. I still had a faint suspicion I might be falling into one of Brodmann's traps. I had not survived for so long without anticipating such things, the legacy of all those years.

A taxi for so great a distance was out of the question. Instead, I walked up to Notting Hill Gate and got the Central Line to Liverpool Street where I easily found a taxi to take me to Brick Lane.

We drove down the mean, narrow road, full of bagel bakeries, rag shops and kosher butchers. To be honest, Brick Lane was never an area which attracted me. The denizens had reproduced their original slums and *shtetls*. The cab turned into Princelet Street. Number 19 was about halfway along an old run-down row of eighteenth-century houses, typical of the time, with an arched doorway and two matching arched windows beside it. Above this were two rows of three windows and above them some sort of attic. Even compared to the nearby buildings the place had a distinctly neglected look. No doubt the home of an impoverished refugee, like so many in Notting Hill these days. The door was poorly painted, the knocker filthy with rust and dirt. I lifted it and let it fall; the interior sent back a hollow echo. Something seemed wrong. Was this indeed a trick? I was poised to turn and flee. Perhaps after all I should have brought one of Mrs Cornelius's sons with me. Too late to change my mind. The door was opened by a smart, stocky woman of about my own age. Her hair and costume were clearly that of a person of substance. She smiled and swung the black door back, admitting me into a narrow hall. On both walls were arranged groups of fly-spotted photographs. The place smelled strongly of onions and cabbage. More of old Kiev came back to me. I hesitated. I removed my hat.

'Maxim!' Her smile was sweet as always. Awkwardly we hovered, unsure whether or not to embrace. At last I did my best to smile in return. I shook hands with her. Her poise and manner were distinctly French. She wore a deliciously floral perfume. Guerlain, I thought. I know these things from the women who come into the shop. I was not a bit surprised at feeling a strong attraction for Esmé.

Needless to say, she was not the bright little girl or the sober young woman I had known long ago, but she wore excellent make-up. Her well-cut clothes were flattering. She spoke good, educated Russian in a beautifully modulated accent such as I had scarcely heard in years. Again tears came to my eyes.

'Good afternoon, Maxim Arturovitch.' She was sweetly sardonic. 'It seems the prodigal son has, if not returned, at least arranged to meet for tea. How are you, my dear?'

'Well, thank you.' Keeping control of myself, I kissed her on both cheeks in the Parisian manner. 'Did you have a good journey, Esmé Alexandrova?'

'We took a plane,' she said. 'So much quicker! The first time your mother has flown. Unlike you, Maxim!' Her grin was mischievously attractive. She had been the first person ever to witness me harness the power of flight, to soar over the towers and steeples of old Kiev. Oh, how she had loved me then! How often I had missed that love!

The house smelled of antiquity and grief, its rooms unlived in and musty. Yet in contrast to the prevailing atmosphere the front parlour was almost opulently furnished, with big armchairs, a solid table, a floral carpet, some heavy, blue velvet curtains. The wooden blinds were half shut to admit two bright bars of sunlight, one of which shone on fresh flowers in a large green vase, the centrepiece of the table. Around the walls were arranged an old-fashioned radio set, a bureau and a bookcase with dark, matching volumes. Over to the right in the shadows stood two stocky old women in black, neither of whom I recognised. One of them stepped forward holding out her arms. And we embraced. I began to shake. Esmé suggested we sit down. The other old lady murmured in what sounded like German. I heard a few words. She went to get us some tea. My mother sat down across from me on the sofa.

'We can go on to Liberty as soon as you feel like it.' Esmé stepped back. 'I can order a taxi.' I remained intensely aware of her floral scent. I noticed how the shafts of light caught her hair. She had good cheekbones, soft skin. She had aged well. 'But if you'd rather stay here don't worry. You aren't disturbing anyone. Mrs Stein's only here part of the week. She's the caretaker. The house hasn't been used for several years. Are you familiar with its history?'

Why should I be? I thought. I told her that I hardly ever came to this neighbourhood. 'In London East and West are two separate worlds.' I did my best to laugh. 'You go through an invisible gate at Holborn.'

'Mrs Stein tells us the place was once well known. They are trying to get a grant, she says, to preserve it. The house was the last of its kind in London, according to Mrs Stein, originally built to accommodate Huguenot weavers, but around 1870 they added on behind. It remained an ordinary house in the front. Perhaps a rabbi lived here. The addition was a tiny synagogue! You can still see all its decorations, prayer books and so on. The last members of the congregation either died or moved away. Mrs Stein has been telling us about it.'

This news confused me. Had Esmé converted to Judaism while in Palestine? This ordinary working-class front room was a synagogue? I saw no sign of such a building. Was this after all an elaborate hoax? Yet Esmé spoke in a matter-of-fact voice. Did she seem over-controlled?

'A synagogue?'

She was awkwardly respectful. She gave a small, uncertain shrug. 'Such places were common, apparently, in this part of London. Poor immigrants could not afford very large ones. The whole thing fills the little backyard! Incredible, eh? Do you want to look at it later? The rest of the house, of course, is just a normal dwelling. You can still see where the Protestants had their looms.'

The woman who I supposed was my mother shook her head, speaking in Russian. She smiled uncertainly. 'No doubt they had to keep it secret. For fear, I would guess, of pogroms.'

'Pogroms?' I was completely at sea. 'In London? The Jews were never threatened. You're thinking of Mosley in the 1930s. But that came to nothing. The Jews were always tolerated in London.'

As I spoke Mrs Stein re-entered the room. She shrugged. 'Pray to God it's true. I heard things were all right in Leeds, but here —? Even today you are never surprised.' She shared a complicit glance with the other two women.

614

I felt extremely uncomfortable. 'So it is now a museum?' I asked.

'Not even that,' said Esmé. 'This room Mrs Stein keeps up. But the rest of the place has fallen into disuse. The Rodinsky family lived here until recently. Then they died or moved away. One, I gather, was mentally disturbed. This is Mrs Rodinsky's furniture. A shame.'

I was allergic to the dust. I coughed, wiping my eyes. Though the house had recently been cleaned, I felt a strong need to get back into the street. Such rooms always made me claustrophic. 'Perhaps we should go straight on to Liberty?'

The old lady – my mother – brightened. 'You find this place a bit depressing. So do I. We'll go have our tea at the restaurant you mentioned. Mrs Stein won't mind.' Then she frowned. 'But it would not be good manners . . .' She began to weep again. 'It is so wonderful to see you, my darling.' She opened her arms, and I was again in her embrace, delighting in the maternal softness of her body, the warmth, her smell. My caution was leaving me. I hugged her as tightly as she hugged me. I had not known such affection since I was last in Kiev, promising to return as soon as possible. I could not control my sobs. 'Oh, Mother!' Only now did I understand what I had been suppressing for so long.

After a while she fell back into her chair, opening her patent-leather handbag and searching through the contents. 'I brought a few things I have kept. I finally got a copy of your birth certificate through the agency in Tel Aviv. I thought it might be useful to you. There was, of course, nothing else saved. The Huns destroyed most of our district, and then the KGB and the partisans finished it off. They dynamited half the city, Maxim. How could Ukrainians do that? I couldn't bear to go back. There's nothing left of the Kurenvskaya. Podol is gone, as I said. And they blew up the Kreshchatik. That beautiful avenue!'

I knew of Kiev's destruction. She was right. The Red Army had done as much damage as the Nazis. Between them they left only ruins. Like Nuremberg and Dresden, local people had reconstructed everything from old plans and photographs. Full-size replicas of themselves. I had often wondered if they then sent out for repro-duction bakers, grocers and shoemakers to staff the rebuilt shops.

'You wouldn't recognise anything.' The old lady dabbed at her face with a handkerchief she found in her bag. She handed me a folded piece of paper. 'Here it is.'

'Thank you,' I said absently. 'This will be useful.' I had something I could send the genealogy people at last. I opened it. I was puzzled. What was wrong?

Frowning, I studied the certificate. I laughed then. 'But what is this, Mother?' I had no idea to whom the thing referred. 'This is for someone called Moishe Aaronovitch Peskonechnya.' The only resemblance to my own name were the initials. The similarity of sound had no doubt confused the authorities. She had not looked at the document properly. Her eyesight was failing. Slowly I folded it back up. I looked from the beaming Esmé to the weeping, smiling old woman. She nodded. 'That was your father. Peskonechnya. A kosher butcher by trade. His father was a rabbi in Kersen.'

I was in a terrible position. Somehow Esmé had been deceived. This poor Jewish matron had honestly convinced herself that I was her son. Whatever the circumstances, I could not in conscience maintain the charade. It would be too cruel.

'For a Moishe.' I handed it back to her. 'Not a Maxim!'

'But that is what we called you.' She was insistent, almost aggressive. 'That's your name, Moishe.'

'I am afraid —' Unwittingly, I was taking part in some ghastly charade. I was more than embarrassed. This old woman, no doubt out of desperate need, had imposed her son's identity on me. Esmé had probably persuaded her that they had been acquainted in Kiev. Perhaps Esmé, too, widowed and lonely, followed a similar psychological imperative?

I could not speak. How could I disappoint the poor, old creature? How could I tell her that I was not Jewish, that the very atmosphere of that wretched little synagogue was rather distasteful to me? How could I show Esmé she had been deceived, was deceiving herself? Before worse happened and the emotional disaster was compounded something had to be done and done rapidly, to bring this sad affair to an end. I summoned my courage.

With gentleness and courtesy I was at length able to address the poor old Jewess. 'Madam, with all respect, I regret that I am not related to you. I only wish I did have a mother like yourself. I long for my family. Much as I would like to be the one you seek, I cannot pretend I am he. I am not, you see, Jewish. I was born Russian Orthodox and remain in that faith to this day.'

Esmé's eyes widened. How I hated to shock her. But the truth had to be faced. I reached towards her. 'Esmé, you have through no fault of your own brought two strangers together. You have been betrayed by your need to make your desires real. I understand that yearning all too well. Believe me, I wish it were otherwise. After these miserable decades . . .'

'Maxim,' she began steadily, 'this really is your mother. You must remember her. And no matter how you and your circumstances have changed, you cannot deny your heritage!'

'Heritage,' I said. 'I have never once denied my heritage. I am a Russian Cossack, descended from Russian Cossacks. I am not a fool. I know my own Slavic blood. My real mother told me everything. My father was related to the Romanoffs and served them as a captain of cavalry. I myself have served in that same cavalry! Believe me, if I could tell you differently, I would. Madam, I wish you nothing but good. I hope you will indeed one day be reunited with your son.'

At that moment Mrs Stein came uncertainly back into the room, the tea things shaking on the tray. 'Is there something wrong?'

The old woman Esmé had mistaken for my mother was sitting down again. She was gasping, as if drowning. 'Moishe,' she said. 'We always called you Maxim, I know. It was better. But you *are* Moishe, believe me.'

All my life I have been threatened in this way. And now here it was happening again with this old woman claiming to be my own mother, trying to achieve what Cossacks and Nazis had so often tried to do and failed.

I owed it to everyone to tell her the truth. 'I am a member in good standing of the Bayswater Greek Orthodox congregation,' I told her as calmly as I could. 'That has been the case for years. I sympathise with your need to find your son, madam, just as I can understand how you persuaded my friend Esmé that you were a woman from her past in Kiev. Believe me, I cannot blame you. We have lived through dreadful times, and we would change them for the better if we could. All of us yearn to restore the past. But I have my own problems. I find this very hard to say. Like you I have borne a great deal. I, too, have been through the camps. Emotionally, I can take very little more.'

'Maxim,' Esmé was trying to be calm and rational, 'you can't deny your own mother. No man would do such a thing. Certainly when there is no longer a need. You don't have to be afraid now. All that is over.'

'Need?' I replied. 'When was there ever a need? I speak of truth. And I speak of falsehood. What is over? For years I have longed to see my mother, just as I longed to see you. You cannot know how many years I spent praying that we could be reunited. My mother did so much for me as a boy. She sacrificed herself. She had such wonderful ambitions for me. She saw to it that I was educated. She encouraged me in all my dreams. Do you think I would not recognise my own flesh and blood? But this lady is neither my flesh nor my blood. She is a poor, deluded old creature whom you met in Jaffa by chance in a dry-cleaner's. You both knew Kiev, I'm sure. She no doubt lost a son years ago, this Moishe. But whatever else she told you, one thing is certain. She did not tell you the truth. If she thinks she sees a resemblance in me to her son, she is deluded.'

The woman was muttering in Yiddish. Still sobbing she rose and came towards me, trembling arms outstretched. I could stand no more. Apologising to Esmé, I fled that nightmare. Something in the woman's eyes reminded me of Hitler.

I walked most of the way home. I believe Esmé took the woman back to Jaffa the next day. She wrote me a note. It had a baffled, accusatory tone. I hardly read it. I had disappointed her. Esmé's taste for sensational self-deception probably came from reading too many Victorian novels. I blamed her experiences in the Civil War. What decent girl could emerge from that ordeal with her mind intact? I would have been so happy in my old age to enjoy friends and relatives from those days, but surely it is better to be alone and sane than complete one's final years in the comfort of lies?

Sadly, I made a choice many of us are forced to make when age threatens memory, when death is no longer our enemy but our only friend.

I said as much last night in the pub to Mrs Cornelius.

She shook her head and winked.

'I've got ter 'and it to yer, Ivan.' She smiled admiringly into her port and lemon. 'Yo're one in a million, an' no mistake. Bloody amazin'! I sometimes wonder if yo're real!'

Only she truly understands me.

She is my muse. My inspiration.

Mein Engel.